First Love
FOREVER
ROMANCE COLLECTION

9 Historical Romances Where First Loves are Rekindled

First Love
FOREVER
ROMANCE COLLECTION

Erica Vetsch,
Susanne Dietze, Cynthia Hickey, Marcia Gruver,
Carrie Fancett Pagels, Martha Rogers, Lorna Seilstad,
Connie Stevens, Jennifer Uhlarik

BARBOUR BOOKS
An Imprint of Barbour Publishing, Inc.

Published by Barbour Books, an imprint of Barbour Publishing, Inc., 1810 Barbour Drive, Uhrichsville, Ohio 44683, www.barbourbooks.com

Our mission is to inspire the world with the life-changing message of the Bible.

 Member of the
Evangelical Christian
Publishers Association

Printed in Canada.

Contents

First Things First

by Susanne Dietze

Dedication

For the One who loved me first.

Acknowledgments

Many thanks to Deb Marvin, whose generous brainstorming sessions bless and encourage me. I also give thanks for the other authors in this collection. You gals are fabulous! Group hug!

But many that are first shall be last; and the last shall be first.
MATTHEW 19:30

Chapter 1

Wildrye, South Texas
Spring 1877

For the first time in her twenty-three years of life, Georgia Bridge was rendered speechless.

"Georgie?" Pa removed his Stetson now that they'd moved inside the courthouse vestibule. He smoothed his gray-streaked brown curls and peered down at her. "The ledgers show missing cattle?"

She blinked in case her vision was somehow affected by the change in light or because of the headache she'd had since studying Pa's ledgers earlier—

Oh. Yes. The ledgers. Missing cattle.

The matter lost its urgency at the sight of a man across the whitewashed vestibule. She blinked again. It was really *him*, all grown up, carrying a worn satchel and wearing a dark gray suit. Looking quite handsome in it too.

Pa's gentle touch on her shoulder drew her gaze back and jostled her tongue loose. "Ward."

"What?"

"Ward. Harper." Her childhood friend. One of her favorite school companions who, when she was fifteen or so, became her favorite companion, ever. He was at the house all the time until that day five years past. A day full of expectations and hope, until he walked out the door.

Ward Harper had broken her heart, and while her heart had healed, she wasn't sure it worked properly anymore. Even now, it thumped in her throat instead of her chest, pumping jitters through her veins and making it hard to breathe.

A low whistle escaped Pa's lips. "I'll be. He's changed a fair piece."

He had and he hadn't. His sandy-blond hair was shorter now, neater than it had ever been when he was younger. His shoulders had broadened and stubble darkened his cheeks more than when he was nineteen, last time she saw him.

But those blue eyes were the same. And they widened when they met her stare across the crowded vestibule.

Ward's gaze fixed on her longer than it should have, considering he spoke with two gentlemen. She might have kept on staring at him too, had the mayor not blocked her view to greet Pa.

After offering a brief hello to the mayor, she shifted position, the better to view Ward while he talked to the fellows she didn't recognize.

He was back in Wildrye. For how long? When had he arrived?

Regardless, it was no wonder he found himself at the courthouse today. He'd probably viewed hundreds of trials since he went to study law at Baylor and then found an apprenticeship position in Fort Worth. He'd enjoy today's events, and not just because he studied law. No, he'd get a good laugh out of this ludicrous, so-called trial.

To think, someone was suing Pa.

Sure to be dropped immediately, this frivolous lawsuit was brought by a neighbor who hadn't fared as well as Pa in the financial panic of '73. Pa's cattle ranch was thriving and his horse-breeding business was ever growing, so more than one person thought he could try to squeeze something out of Pa, while assuming Pa wouldn't even feel the pinch.

Well, Pa did. Every loss hurt, not just her family, but the families who relied on Pa for employment. When Georgie found that discrepancy in the ledgers today, it looked as if the loss of stock would cost Bridge Ranch a few hundred dollars.

But folks like their neighbor Mr. Odell Norwood, who thought to make money off Pa today by quibbling over well-established water rights, clearly didn't care about honesty or integrity.

As the mayor moved off, Georgie bit back a harrumph. Pa's business had grown the right way: legitimately, over time, with a great deal of hard work, patience, and care. He and Ma had been a team, building their home, family, and business together. They did not cheat their neighbors out of water, land, stock, or anything else.

Ward should know that as well as anyone.

Her heart plummeted from her throat to her stomach when he pulled away from his conversation and strode toward her.

"Georgie. Mr. Bridge." Ward offered Pa a hearty handshake, but his gaze returned to Georgie before it was finished.

Of their own accord, her hands smoothed the front of her apricot-and-tan floral jacket. What did he think when he looked at her? Had he thought of her at all? Maybe even missed her?

Enough foolish thinking. He'd made his choice when he left, and she'd lived just fine since then. Her chin lifted and she gave him a full smile to prove the point. "It's wonderful to see you again."

And it really was, even if he'd hurt her.

"It's been too long." Was his expression sheepish? "I haven't been home in two years."

Not since his father's funeral. Georgie had been at a finishing school in New Orleans then and couldn't get home in time for the service.

"I'm sure your mother's delighted you're home." Pa smiled.

"She is. It was hard for me to get back and visit, but I brought her out to see me a few times, hoping she'd live with me. She likes it here, though."

His eyes clouded, and Georgie could guess why. Ward didn't cotton to Elspeth Harper's penchant for drink. Georgie had heard he dumped out his mother's jugs of who knew what behind his barn when he was here for his father's funeral, but Mrs. Harper had acquired more liquor soon after he left again.

Georgie scrambled to change the topic. "How long are you visiting?"

"I'm not visiting. I'm a licensed lawyer now. I'm opening a law firm."

She couldn't contain a grin. Maybe they could be friends again, easing the ache in her chest that usually cleaved her in two when Ward came to mind. His being here would also help the people of Wildrye, who had few choices when it came to help with their legal needs. "How wonderful."

"I'm glad too." He smiled.

"Observing the trial today will be of great interest to you, I'm sure."

"I'm not here to observe." Ward's smile died. "Today's my first case in town. I'm representing Mr. Odell Norwood. Your opposition."

"What?" The way she asked, it was clear nothing was wrong with Georgie's hearing or comprehension. Her dark eyes narrowed, blazing like hot coals in a brazier. "You're representing Odell Norwood?"

Ward nodded.

"Against Pa?"

What could Ward say? That he was sorry?

Truth be told, he wasn't. Not that he liked going up against Georgie, of course. But he had his reasons.

Georgie didn't seem to care. Her jaw set, giving a sharp edge to the soft curve of her cheeks. "You're suing my father."

"It's all right." Mr. Bridge clapped Georgie on the shoulder. "Let's sort it out in the courtroom."

The way she was glaring at him with equal parts shock and indignation, it was obvious this wasn't all right with her at all.

Georgie had never been good at hiding her feelings. He'd always liked that about her, but this time the full weight of her wrath was turned on him. It didn't feel good.

Perhaps it was best if she was angry with him and didn't want to resume their old friendship. When he'd left Wildrye five years ago, he'd had to accept some hard truths. Like no matter what he said or did, his parents were the town drunks, so he'd never stood a chance with Georgie Bridge.

Another truth was he needed to make a living, not just for himself, but to care for Mother. Odell Norwood was a paying customer entitled to proper counsel.

Besides, Norwood was justified. Jackson Bridge might own one of the largest ranches in Texas, but it didn't mean he could break the law and get away with it.

"Come on in and sit down, ever'body." The booming voice of Wildrye's oldest deputy, round-bellied, gray-stubbled Grover McPhee, echoed through the vestibule. "The circuit judge is on a tight schedule."

Ward nodded at Georgie and her father. She turned away in a huff of pinkish-orange and marched into the courtroom, her boots rapping against the hardwood floor. Ward turned to escort Odell Norwood inside the high-ceilinged chamber, and they took their seats behind a polished oak table.

Odell squinted at him. "I saw you jaw-jackin' with Bridge. You weren't giving away anything, were you?"

"Absolutely not. That would be unethical." He pulled a file from his satchel. "I represent you and your interests in this matter."

"Those cowpokes at Bridge Ranch think they own ever'thing." Odell snorted. "But

I got proof they don't."

"Rest assured, we'll present all the necessary documents."

Deputy McPhee ambled past to stand near the jury box. "All rise. Court is now in session. Honorable Judge Kemp presiding."

The circuit judge, a balding fellow with a broad build, entered through the chamber door behind the bench. He sat down and peered at a paper. "Take your seats, folks. Looks like we have a disagreement between Odell Norwood and Jackson Bridge. Are we ready to start?"

"Ready, Your Honor," Ward replied.

"Yes, Your Honor." Dudley Flack, Jackson Bridge's beady-eyed lawyer, bore a smug smile. Beyond him, Jackson nodded. In the first row of the gallery benches, Georgie glared at Ward.

He could feel her burning gaze when he turned back to face the judge. After the jury was sworn in, Judge Kemp cleared his throat. "Let's hear it, Mr. Harper."

This was it. Ward had litigated several court cases with his mentor to advise him, but this was his first as an independent lawyer. Silently, he lifted the same prayer he uttered before the start of every trial he'd ever participated in. *Lord, help me not to stumble, expose the darkness to light, and let Your will be done.*

He stood. "Your Honor, members of the jury, we are here today to seek restitution for damages. Mr. Norwood's property borders Bridge Ranch. I have the deed here—"

"No one's disputing the fact, sonny," Judge Kemp interrupted.

Dudley Flack snickered. Georgie still glared.

"But what seems to be under dispute is the matter of Whistle Creek, the boundary line between their properties." Ward held up a document. "According to this agreement, Bridge's animals may drink from the creek but not cross it. Which they do, often, causing damage to Mr. Norwood's property—"

"What sort of damage?" The judge interrupted again. So much for proper courtroom procedure.

"Trampling Mr. Norwood's vegetable garden. Distressing his milk cow so she's unable to produce. And disturbing local wildlife."

"I beg your pardon?" Judge Kemp bent forward.

"Yellow warblers," Odell interjected. "Those dogs of Bridge's cause more ruckus than a stampede. Scare them warblers away so they don't rest in my oaks and sing."

Georgie's mouth formed an *O*. Jackson Bridge blinked. Dudley Flack chuckled. And Judge Kemp peered at Odell. "This is about dogs, not cattle?"

"And birds." Odell sat up straighter. "The warblers migrate through this time of year. They were my Letty's favorite. Maybe you've heard 'em singing. Sounds like *sweet sweet sweet I'm so sweet*. Prettiest whistle to pass through Texas, and a pretty little bird, too."

Ward took a step toward the jury box. "Mr. Norwood delights in bird-watching, a hobby he enjoyed with his late wife, but his pleasure has been thwarted on multiple occasions by disturbances caused by dogs let loose on Bridge Ranch property. They roam beyond the ranch's borders, barking, digging, and trampling gardens, as I've mentioned."

"I won't get no more lettuce this year," Odell insisted.

Ward nodded. "Despite several attempts by Mr. Norwood to come to an amicable solution with Mr. Bridge's attorney, nothing has been done to remedy the situation."

Dudley Flack sighed. "We offered to build a fence, Your Honor."

Ward eyed Flack. "On Mr. Norwood's side of the creek. It would have cut off his water supply."

Flack threw up his hands. "What are we to do, Your Honor? Build a fence down the middle of the creek?"

"Restrain the dogs." A feminine voice Ward knew well came from the first row on the opposite side of the courtroom. Georgie had popped to her feet. "They're supposed to help the ranch hands herd cattle, not destroy our neighbors' gardens. They don't belong off the property."

Jackson Bridge nodded, but Judge Kemp shook his finger at Georgie. "No more outbursts from the gallery, missy."

"But my daughter's right, Your Honor." Jackson stood as she resumed her seat. "I was led to believe this was about water rights. I had no idea any of this was going on. If I had, rest assured, I'd have spoken to my employees at once about the dogs. I take responsibility for the damage they've caused."

"But, Mr. Bridge!" Flack gaped. "It's a ridiculous suit!"

"That never should have gotten to this point." Jackson looked to Odell. "I'm happy to offer restitution for your damaged garden, and I'll fix the problem so the dogs don't interfere with your property or bird-watching."

Georgie nodded, her lips mashed—following the judge's instructions while still making her opinions known.

Flack's skin paled. "Mr. Bridge, I implore you to give no concessions to this man until we've discussed the implications—"

Jackson held up his hand. "I'll handle the matter from here on out, to Mr. Norwood's satisfaction."

Judge Kemp shrugged. "Is this acceptable to counsel?"

Ward glanced at a satisfied Odell. "Yes, Your Honor."

"It certainly is not." Flack blinked. "My client—"

"Seems your client doesn't need you anymore, Mr. Flack." Judge Kemp nodded at the jury. "Y'all are free to go. Case dismissed."

Ward shook hands with Odell. "Congratulations, sir."

Before Odell could respond, Jackson was at his elbow, his hand extended. "Mr. Norwood, sir, I ask your forgiveness for the mishandling of the situation. I'd sure like to sit down with you and determine what I can do to make things right."

When Odell agreed, Ward grinned.

Something soft touched his sleeve and he spun. Georgie looked up at him. The angriness in her eyes had fled, replaced by shyness. Georgie, shy? "I'm sorry for making assumptions, Ward. I was downright rude."

"You were protective of your pa, Georgie. Not rude."

Her head shook, making the dark curls at her nape bounce. "I've always been too quick to judge. I heard it a thousand times."

"From your ma?"

"From you."

He chuckled. "Sounds right."

She glanced around the courtroom. "An interesting outcome to your first case as a real lawyer, isn't it?"

"This was all we wanted in the first place—a chance to handle the problem like neighbors. But Flack told us your father wasn't interested in talking."

"Well, they're talking now."

"So they are." Behind them, Jackson and Odell spoke about the half-dozen dogs kept by the ranch hands. Flack bustled past, his lips mashed, his gaze downcast.

Ward took Odell's elbow. "Everything to your satisfaction, sir?"

"Aye-up." Odell rubbed the white stubble on his jaw. "Bridge is gonna insist the dogs stay in the proper areas from here on out and speak to the ranch hands who ain't livin' up to their responsibilities. They're gonna replant new vegetables and help me fence the garden too. It'll be much quieter around the yard now. Should see a yellow warbler or two before they move on."

Georgie smiled. "I'd like to see a yellow warbler, Mr. Norwood. I don't think I've ever heard one sing. Might I pay a call one afternoon?"

"Sure thing, missy. Just don't bring any dogs or horses with you." Odell nodded then shook Ward's hand once again. "Thanks, Ward."

"My pleasure, Odell."

His first case in Wildrye, over. Maybe not an official win, but it sure felt like one.

And Georgie wasn't mad at him anymore. The hint of a smile curved her lips as she looked up at him. "How long have you been back?"

"Almost a week."

The smile vanished. "You didn't come by to say hello."

Why should he have? They hadn't seen one another in five years, and Mother never mentioned Georgie in her letters. For all he'd known, Georgie was married by now to some businessman who was her equal in wealth and social standing.

But he couldn't say that. "I've been busy setting up the new office. And spending time with Mother."

"Speaking of mothers, I need to get home. Ma wasn't up to coming to court today." A concerned line furrowed Georgie's brow.

"She's not ill, I hope."

"Not exactly. I just need to hurry home."

Jackson glanced at his daughter before turning back to Odell. "Would you like to come with us, Odell? A celebration supper. Georgie left stew on the stove."

Odell shook his head. "Thanks, Bridge, but I'm obliged to visit my Letty at the cemetery whenever I'm in town."

"Another time, then. How about you, Ward?"

Him? Invited to the ranch as a guest, after what Jackson said about the Harpers? A hot knot tied up his insides. "Thanks, but I'd best check in on my mother. Please say howdy to your family for me, though."

Georgie wasn't the only Bridge he'd cared about. Loved, even, from the time he was a boy. When he left Wildrye, he'd cut ties with Georgie. And he'd lost her family too.

He'd never had brothers of his own. Maybe that was why he'd latched on to Georgie's.

Chapter 2

Oh, those boys.

When she was four years old, Georgie announced to the world at large she wanted a new mama, since hers had gone to heaven, and a baby brother.

God sent a new mama when Pa married fiery-haired singer Lily Kimball, but He hadn't sent a baby brother.

In His generosity, He'd sent *four*.

All redheaded, energetic boys: Kimball, Evan, Josh, and Moses, whom they'd dubbed Little Mo. Georgie didn't much resemble them, since she had her mother Paloma's dark hair, but she'd never felt odd or out of place among them. Their home was a place of love, song, and noise, a busy hive of activity.

Except for the past few months.

After finishing errands in town, Georgie and Pa rode home in the carriage, discussing the discrepancy she'd discovered in the ledgers. Soon, they passed beneath the arch with the Lazy B brand stamped on it, announcing they'd arrived at Bridge Ranch. Within moments, they reached the large white house Pa built ten years ago to accommodate their growing family. The sun was starting its descent into the gold-green horizon, casting a rosy glow on the Spanish-style arches on the veranda and the budding roses in Ma's garden. It would be a pleasant evening to sit outside and enjoy the view and aromas of sage and honey mesquite in the air, but neither she nor Pa wanted to linger.

One of Pa's most trusted hands, Lard Jones, took charge of the carriage and horses. Once Pa informed him about the trial, he and Georgie sneaked into the house on tiptoes, pausing to scratch their white-and-black house cat, Cat. Following the lamplight to the dining room, they found her two youngest brothers, Josh and Moses, setting the table. All wrong.

"Forks on the left, Little Mo." Fourteen-year-old Josh's voice was hushed, but it cracked all the same.

"Who cares?" Little Mo, eight, dropped the fork to the right of the plate.

"I do." Ma appeared in the door connecting the dining room to the kitchen.

Pa rushed toward her, wrapping a supportive arm around her shoulders. "Lily, what are you doing out of bed?"

"I heard you two come in. I couldn't wait another minute to hear what happened in court."

Georgie could understand Ma's determination because Georgie never liked being left out of anything either. Still, Ma shouldn't be on her feet. Georgie pulled out the dining room chair closest to Ma. "Sit down. Doctor's orders."

Ma looked about to protest, but she obediently lowered her eight-months-pregnant frame into the chair. "I'm so big I can scarcely fit."

"It won't be much longer." Pa tucked a tendril of Ma's fading red hair behind her ear.

Little Mo plopped the final fork down. "Then I won't have to set the table anymore."

"Oh yes you will. And you'll put the forks on the left." Georgie pointed.

"Aw." Little Mo pulled a face but moved the forks.

"So?" Wide-eyed, Ma stared up at Pa. "How'd the case go? Did you win?"

"Sort of." Pa smiled. "Why don't we tell you about it during supper?"

"I'm hungry. Or at least, the baby is." Ma patted her protruding tummy.

"Supper's ready." Georgie had planned a simple meal due to the trial, just beef stew to serve with last night's leftover rolls, butter, and two jars of preserved peaches alongside. Nothing fancy, but nourishing all the same. She strode to the kitchen, looking at her brothers over her shoulder. "Call your big brothers and wash up."

While she ladled stew into the tureen, the screen door to the back porch squawked open and clanked shut. "Kim, Evan, suppertime." Josh's voice carried into the house, cracking on the last word from his boy-voice to his deeper man-voice.

Georgie filled a pitcher of milk and dumped the peaches into a serving bowl. By the time she finished, all four boys had entered the dining room, smelling of soap and filling the space with their tall, lanky bodies and boisterous conversation, all the louder because Ma was up and joining them at the table. Her presence was something to celebrate, even more than the court case getting settled.

She slipped into her seat between Evan, sixteen, and Kimball, eighteen. Evan was talking a mile a minute to Ma about his attempt to break a horse this afternoon, but Kim glanced at the door, like he'd rather be somewhere else.

The past few months, Kim had developed what Ma called *moods*. Part of growing up, she'd said. True, Kim had filled out a lot this past year, now boasting Pa's broad shoulders. He also had Pa's skill with breaking horses, and he thought himself quite a man now. Georgie had caught him casting surreptitious glances at their seventeen-year-old neighbor girl, Marceline LaRue, though Georgie was inclined to believe Marceline hadn't noticed Kim was alive.

Not *that* way. Something akin to how Ward never noticed Georgie *that* way.

Georgie glanced at her frowning brother again. He might be eighteen, but he'd always be the baby brother she'd yearned for. She loved him madly and pestered him as much as he pestered her—or at least, used to, before his moods. Even now, it was difficult not to tease him by ruffling his hair.

So she gave in and mussed it up.

"Hey." Kim grimaced and slicked his hair back into the style he'd adopted the past few months. His frown didn't soften after a moment like it usually did, though. This was some mood. Maybe he was worried about Ma.

"Let's pray," Pa said, bringing them all to attention.

After they bowed their heads and gave thanks, the boys filled their plates and Ma eyed Pa. "So? What happened in court?"

Pa's mouth was already full with his first bite of stew, so Georgie leaned toward Ma. "Mr. Flack didn't tell Pa what was really happening. This wasn't about water rights at all.

Some of the hands' dogs have been making a mess of Mr. Norwood's garden and scaring away his birds."

"Yellow warblers," Pa said between bites.

"What?" Little Mo's mouth was full. Ma shook her head at him and mouthed *swallow first*.

"He's a bird-watcher." Georgie passed the rolls to Kim. "He says the migrating yellow warblers sing *sweet sweet sweet, I'm so sweet*. He and his wife loved listening to them, and hearing them each year when they pass through is important to him. I'm sad we're somehow responsible for him losing a connection to her."

Little Mo speared a peach slice. "The bird says *sweet*? It talks?"

"No, son. The song sounds like it, though." Pa's smile returned to Ma. "I told Mr. Norwood we'd replant his garden, and I already spoke to Lard about the dogs. Now we just have to find the missing livestock."

The moment Pa spoke it, his face pinked in regret. Like Georgie, he didn't like concerning Ma these days. She needed rest and calm.

She didn't look calm now, with her brows lowered and her eyes narrowed. "Missing? How many?"

Pa's smile didn't reach his eyes. "Just a few dozen longhorns. We'll find them. In any case," he said, changing the subject, "I've got another piece of news. Ward Harper is back."

Ma's eyes widened, and her gaze held more than curiosity about a neighbor returning home. She'd been the one to hold Georgie when she cried over Ward leaving—a five-minute sob was all Georgie had allowed herself before insisting she was finer than a frog hair. But Ma had never looked convinced.

Georgie forced a smile. "He said to tell you hello."

"I remember him. Is he as bad as his mother?" Scowling, Kim reached for the bowl of peaches.

"Kim," Georgie snapped. What was in Kim's craw tonight?

"Well, it's a fair question." Evan nudged Georgie's shoulder.

"No." Georgie tasted bile. "He's never been like his parents. He's a licensed lawyer, starting his own firm. He looked respectable and. . .just the same as he used to when he ran around with me."

Only handsomer, if such a thing was possible.

But she knew what Kim and Evan meant. And yes, Ward was sober. Unlike his mother, more often than not.

"I was impressed by him today," Pa said. "Competent, respectful, knowledgeable—"

The clank of the brass door knocker against the solid oak of the front door carried through the house.

"Are we expecting anyone?" Ma pushed away her bowl of half-eaten stew. She never did finish her meals anymore. *No room*, she'd say, patting her swollen stomach.

"No." Pa rose.

Their usual guests, Uncle Fred and Aunt Delia, were in Kansas with their boys on an extended trip. If they'd come back earlier than expected, well. . .Georgie calculated the volume of remaining stew. Her cousins Cy and Aaron ate as much as her brothers did, and it looked as if Evan and Josh were already on their second bowls.

At least they had more peaches in the larder.

Pa returned to the dining room, his mouth set. "Son?"

The question could have been for any of the four boys, but his gaze fixed on Kim.

"What's wrong?" The question tumbled out of Georgie's mouth.

Behind Pa, two figures lurked in the hall. Deputy Grover McPhee and Sheriff Sylvester Bly, Pa's friend, but he didn't look friendly now.

The sheriff leveled his gaze at Kim. "Kimball, step outside with us, please."

Georgie rose to her feet. "What is the meaning of this?"

"Kim?" Ma's face blanched, even paler than it had been these past eight difficult months.

Sheriff Bly cast an apologetic look at Ma. "I'm sorry, ma'am, but your son needs to come to town with us."

"I thought you said *step outside*." Kim rose, his napkin dropping to his seat.

"I was trying to avoid doing this in front of your ma." Sheriff Bly withdrew a pair of handcuffs. "Kimball Bridge, you're under arrest."

Lord, have mercy. Georgie tugged Kim's arm, pulling him behind her in a protective pose. "On what ludicrous, trumped-up charge?"

Sheriff Bly sighed, and to his credit, he didn't look happy about what he was doing when he reached past Georgie for Kim's hands.

"For horse thieving. Robbery. And the attempted kidnapping of Marceline LaRue."

Smack smack smack.

The pounding against the front door of the simple wood-frame house on the edge of town drew Ward to his feet. Supper was long past over, darkness had set in, and no one ever called at the Harpers' house. Unless it was another bill collector.

He thought he'd paid the last of them, but if Mother had used the money he'd given to her for something other than the mortgage. . .

"Who is it?" Mother looked up from her knitting.

"I'm not sure." Ward set down his law journal and strode to the front door, just off the parlor. His hand was on the bolt when whoever it was banged the door again.

Persistent, for sure. Probably a bill collector, then. Ward's stomach sank as he pulled open the door, revealing a wide-eyed, dark-haired beauty who robbed his breath. And ability to move or speak, because he left her standing on the porch without a greeting.

"May I come in?" Georgie's voice was soft, tentative.

"Who is it?" Mother called, patting the gray hair pinned into a bun at her nape.

"Georgie." He stepped back and gestured for her to enter the parlor.

She hurried past him, crossing to Mother and taking her hand. "So nice to see you again, Mrs. Harper."

"It's been awhile. You here for your soup pot?"

"Soup pot?" Ward lowered his brows.

"Georgia made me soup about two weeks ago. I was supposed to return her pot, but I forgot." Mother gave Georgie a gap-toothed grin.

Georgie had been visiting Mother while he was gone? Mother had never said so in her letters. Ward assumed the Bridges avoided his mother, after what Jackson Bridge had said about his family five years ago, but clearly he'd been wrong.

Georgie's head shook. "I don't need it yet, ma'am. I'm here for another reason."

Curiosity ate through Ward's insides as he gestured to the chair closest to the fire. "Would you care for coffee or anything?"

"I can't stay. But I need you, Ward. Terribly."

His Adam's apple stuck somewhere in his throat. "What?"

"As our lawyer. I'd like to retain you." She reached out and gripped his hand. Her fingers might be icy, but a jolt of fire shot up his arm. "Kimball's been arrested."

Questions tumbled one over the other in Ward's brain, which wasn't working right with Georgie holding his hand like this. But he knew one thing, despite his addlepated state. "Before you say another word, we must establish something for your own protection. Lawyers have confidentiality with their clients, but you have a lawyer. Dudley Flack."

"He handles business things for the ranch, not personal matters. Besides, I don't like how he treated Mr. Norwood."

Neither did Ward. "But if he's on retainer, your pa might not like you stepping around him."

"Pa was in perfect agreement with me. He doesn't want Dudley Flack. He was impressed by how you handled things today."

Jackson Bridge, willing to hire a Harper? Ward shoved the sarcastic thought away. "Are you sure?"

"Yes." Georgie's dark eyes pleaded, almost cleaving his heart in two. "Will you help me? Help Kim, I mean?"

Helping Kim *was* helping Georgie. And he'd do anything for her. She loved her brothers more than flowers loved sunshine.

"I will." He tipped his head toward the front door. "Do you want to step outside? It's private on the porch, and you can tell me why Kimball was arrested."

"Your mother can hear this. It'll be all over town, anyway." Her arms folded. "Sheriff Bly says he stole Silas LaRue's horse."

"That makes no sense. Your family breeds horses. If Kim needed one, he wouldn't have to take one of LaRue's."

"They've got him on robbery, too, and worse. They say he tried to kidnap Silas's daughter Marceline this afternoon, while Pa and I were at the trial. Silas caught them, and Kim ran off—back home for supper, in fact."

"These are serious charges." Deadly ones, even. But he wouldn't distress Georgie with that now. "What does Kim say?"

"I don't know. They haven't let us talk to him. All we know is what I told you. Apparently, LaRue threatened to take matters into his own hands if they didn't arrest him tonight. But none of this makes sense. Kim's no criminal. Why would he steal a horse when he has access to dozens? Why would he come home and eat supper, if he'd just tried to kidnap someone?"

For the first time, her gaze left his to drift around the room. A coil of shame snaked through Ward's stomach. He'd mailed Mother almost all the money he'd made over the past five years, to live on and to pay off her debts, but there hadn't been enough to refurbish the worn furniture. The house was as shabby as it had been when he and Georgie were young.

She'd never been to his house when they were children. The Harpers were the town drunks, after all. Besides, he'd been mortified to have her in his house because he'd been in hers—both the farmhouse she first lived in and then the larger, grander place Jackson Bridge built ten years back for his growing family. Mrs. Bridge had always welcomed him. Fed him too. Allowed him to spend time with Georgie and her little brothers.

And then Jackson had revealed how he really felt about the Harpers, and everything changed.

Except for his feelings for Georgie. And his God-ingrained desire for fairness and justice, for the innocent to be protected and the darkness exposed to light. If he could do good through his legal efforts, well, he'd consider himself blessed.

First, he'd need to talk to his client. "We'd best get to the jail."

Mother let out a small squawk. "Right now? It's after dark."

"Right now. It can't be helped." He stood and bent to kiss Mother's wrinkled cheek. "I'll be home when I can."

Mother looked past him to Georgie. "I'll pray for you."

She said things like that sometimes, even though she never went to church. Nevertheless, he felt she meant it tonight. "We all appreciate it."

Georgie had moved to the front door. "Can we fix this, Ward?"

He didn't know, but he nodded. "I'll certainly try." He reached for his satchel, hat, and coat. "Let's go."

Chapter 3

Pulling her dappled gray mare, Fly, to a steady stop on Front Street, Georgie tugged her habit skirt to one side of the horse and turned to dismount.

Ward appeared at her knees, arms extended to help her down. He'd climbed down from his own horse with incredible haste in order to be at her side this fast—well, it wasn't his horse, but Oro, a steady buckskin she'd brought along for him in the hope that he'd agree to represent Kim.

Ward's proximity made her stomach flip over, and even though anxiety for her brother rushed through her veins, she couldn't forget the last time she'd been this close to Ward, dancing around the floor at the Founder's Day dance five years ago.

"I know you don't need my help," he said, misunderstanding her hesitation.

"Not to get down." But for other things, yes. Like freeing Kim, and here she was, worried about being in his arms for a half second. Ridiculous. "But I appreciate it."

She placed her hands on his shoulders, allowing him to bear some of her weight, and slid down.

Not even a half second, and it was over, her feet planted on solid ground. They tethered their horses' reins to the rail outside the jail. "Can we get him out tonight?"

"I'm not sure." In the dark, with the flickering yellow lamps dimly illuminating the street, Ward's eyes sparked a deep blue-gray. "I'll do my best."

"I know you will." She joined him, mounting the uneven steps to the jail.

Georgie had never been inside, and it didn't take more than a second for her to decide she never wanted to be here again. The dark, cramped office smelled like kerosene, the odor emanating from lamps that cast a strange glow from underneath greasy shades. Men's voices competed to be heard—the deputies'. Evan's and Josh's. And Pa's.

She rushed to Pa, but Ward hurried to the sheriff. "I'm Kimball Bridge's counsel. I'd like to speak to my client, please."

Sheriff Bly's bushy brows rose in surprise, but then he pointed to a door off the main room. "By all means, then. He's in my office."

"What?" Pa balked as Ward bustled to the office, opening his satchel while he went. "Why wouldn't you let me talk to him, Bly?"

"Because you ain't his attorney, and he's a grown feller who don't need his pa with him."

"At least Kim's not in a cell," Georgie patted Pa's arm. "He's not in with anyone... dangerous."

Evan smacked his hand against the wall. "This is stupid."

"We all agree." Georgie's tone was sharp. "But we must be patient."

Pa let out a long sigh. "Why don't you all go on home? Ma and Little Mo must be worried. I'll stay here."

Georgie didn't want to go, but Pa had a point. It could be a long night. The tension couldn't be good for Ma's condition. Besides, Evan and Josh were riled as wild mustangs, and nothing but trouble would come from it. "Come on, boys. Let's go—"

"Georgie?" Ward's voice drew her around. His head poked out the sheriff's office, blocking any view of Kim behind him. "Your brother's invited you to join us."

Pa's face echoed her shock. "Not me?"

"Sorry, sir. Not just yet."

Though his features were stricken, Pa nodded. "Go on, then, Georgie. Take care of our boy."

"You go on home too, Jackson." Sheriff Bly's words were tinged with compassion. "No more visitors tonight."

Pa's head shook. "I'll wait for Georgie."

Ward eyed him squarely. "This could take awhile. I'll see her home, sir, and give you a report."

"But—" Pa's shoulders slumped. "All right, then."

Patting his shoulder as she passed, Georgie rushed to the door.

Kim sat in a straight-backed chair by the sheriff's desk, crying.

"Oh, Kimball." She enfolded him in her arms.

"I didn't want Pa to see me like this." He swiped his eyes with the heel of his hand.

Ward offered a crisp handkerchief. "We won't say a word. Like I just explained, everything you tell me is confidential. But Georgie doesn't have the same protection. The prosecution can call her as a hostile witness, so if you're sure you want her here. . ."

"I do." Kim took a jagged, calming breath. "I didn't do anything wrong."

"Then tell us." Georgie stood straight. Ward provided a second straight-backed chair for her, placing it behind her knees like a gentleman seating a lady for a fancy supper, and she sat down. "What happened?"

"Well, I guess I did do something wrong. I ran away."

"From home? When?"

"This afternoon. But I wasn't really running from home. I mean, I planned to come back. Later." He swiped his nose. "I ran from Silas LaRue."

Ward sat beside Georgie, resting a pad of paper on his knee. "Why, Kim?"

Kim glared at a page of paper on the sheriff's desk. "You saw the charges."

Georgie grabbed the sheet. "Ward may have seen them, but I haven't." Her eyes crossed at the words. "Robbery, horse thieving, and kidnapping. Ridiculous. I'm sure there's an explanation for the money, but you were riding one of LaRue's horses? With Marceline astride Fuego? Why?"

"Because the one she was on got spooked and scared her."

Ward shifted. "Start at the beginning, Kim, and don't leave anything out."

After a long minute, Kim mumbled something.

Georgie bent forward. "You were going roping?"

"We were eloping," Kim enunciated.

No wonder he hadn't wanted Pa in here. "That's the stupidest thing I ever heard."

"I love her." Kim's jaw set like a belligerent bulldog's.

Georgie started to throw up her hands, but Ward stayed her with a touch. Brief, light, but it quieted her a fraction. Enough to remember to pray.

God, I should've asked You first thing, but I didn't think about anything but trying to get Kim out of here. Will You please forgive me and help us now, and show us how to get out of this mess? Thanks for Ward being here to help.

Ward had to have been sent by God. He was calm, asking concise questions in an even tone that yielded far better results than Georgie's frustrated badgering.

"She'd agreed to elope?" Ward was scribbling notes.

"She did—she'd packed a change of clothes and everything. Which is why I don't understand why she told her pa I took her against her will. Except, well, she's afraid of her pa. He's a bully, and it's worse when he's been drinking."

"Any chance she'll tell the truth?"

"Not unless her pa is willing to hear it. And I'm not so sure he'd believe it. He hates us Bridges."

Ward's eyes flickered with something she didn't understand, but the expression was gone when he glanced up again. "LaRue says he chased you to the border between his and Bridge land and Marceline was begging you to stop."

"We weren't going to my house. We were cutting through Mr. Norwood's property to go to the justice of the peace in the next county—it's faster, and I knew he wasn't home because of the trial. Once Marceline saw her pa after us, she did ask me to stop, but I thought she was scared he'd catch us and she'd calm down once we hit the county line."

"But she didn't." Georgie spouted, but at least her voice was calm.

"She was crying. And when it was clear she didn't want to go on, I left her there."

"And you kept going on LaRue's horse." Ward managed to sound so matter-of-fact, Georgie envied him.

"I took him back. Tied him to a honey mesquite on the edge of their property. I told the sheriff. And Marceline still has Fuego."

"As evidence, according to LaRue." Ward stood, gripping the pad of paper. "This seems pretty straightforward, though. Poor judgment, maybe, but nothing criminal here. Let me talk to the sheriff."

Georgie grabbed his hand, forestalling his exit. "Thank you, Ward. I'm so glad you came home."

The grateful smile Georgie cast on Ward was worth all the time he'd spent studying law, away from her.

But after speaking to the sheriff for five minutes, he wasn't sure he'd see a smile from Georgie again for a while. He shook his head when he returned to the office.

"Kim, the sheriff can't release you tonight unless the LaRues drop the charges."

Georgie's shoulders stiffened. "But they're lying."

"Nevertheless, Silas LaRue's eyewitness account and Marceline's statement can't be dismissed. There must be an investigation, and this may well go to trial unless Marceline changes her story."

Kim's jaw dropped. "I'd never hurt her. Or steal her pa's money. She took it herself so we'd have some money to start with. And we were going to come home in a few days, honest. I'd never leave Bridge Ranch. Or my family. I just knew our folks wouldn't approve of us marrying."

That was an understatement if Ward had ever heard one. "I believe you, but the charges are pretty serious. We'll launch our own investigation, and I'm hopeful in a day or two, this will all get cleared up."

Georgie's eyes dampened, but she nodded. "I'll be back, Kim."

Kim's head hung. "Go ahead and tell Ma and Pa everything. They'll find out anyway."

Poor Kim. Looking like a man mature enough to wed, with stubble on his chin and cheeks, but still so young he ran away when his bride's pa came chasing.

Ward gripped Kim's shoulder in a comforting squeeze. "Don't lose hope. I'll be praying for you, and we'll get you out."

Kim nodded but didn't look up. Georgie hugged him tight and kissed his temple, whispering something in his ear before she left.

After exchanging a few words with the sheriff and lighting the small lantern Georgie had packed in a saddlebag, Ward escorted Georgie outside to their waiting horses. The spring night air was crisp against his cheeks. Was she cold? The night would only grow chillier. Ward held out his hands in an offer to boost her into the saddle. It was the proper thing to do, even if the thought of touching her made his mouth go dry. *Lord, don't let my heart be on my sleeve—or in my touch.*

Placing one foot in a stirrup, she nodded at his hands. Ignoring the shiver of cowardice in his bones at the thought of touching her, he gently took hold, hoisting her up before quickly letting go.

"I'll escort you home." Ward climbed astride Oro, gripping the lantern.

"I don't need protecting."

Ward begged to differ, but he wouldn't argue the merits of having an escort through open land in the dark of night. Not when other tactics worked better. "I promised your pa I'd give him a report."

He'd return Oro too. Walk home. He'd be out half the night, but he'd take Georgie home even if he hadn't promised to speak to her parents. He'd never leave her alone in the dark.

They rode to the end of Front Street, out into the darkness beyond town toward Bridge Ranch. Ward glanced at her, unsurprised by her frown. "You all right?"

"I'm half scared for Kim and half furious with him. What was he thinking?"

"He wasn't." Not about consequences, anyway.

Georgie sighed. "He's been moody lately, so I should have paid more attention to him. I've just been too focused on other things. I help with bookkeeping at the ranch, and things haven't added up lately. Yesterday I realized a few dozen head of cattle are missing. But that's nothing compared to Ma. I can't believe Kim was going to elope when Ma is down like this."

"What's wrong?" Lily Bridge had always been a strong woman with an even stronger voice. Ward had loved hearing her sing in church. Even better, he liked sitting beside Georgie on the pew.

"She's expecting."

Oh. Wasn't that reason to celebrate? Not according to the drawn set of Georgie's mouth. "Is she ill?"

"No, but things have been rough since the beginning. Bad pains. The doctor never expected the baby to live this long, and I'm not so sure Ma and Pa thought it would either. But now the baby is really big, and Ma's lost a lot of weight. It was hard to keep food down at first, but now she says there's no room for food in her stomach. Ma's weak and we're all worried she might not make it." She waved a hand. "Listen to me, speaking on such an indelicate subject with a gentleman."

"I don't mind. We used to talk about everything."

"We shouldn't have, according to propriety." She rolled her eyes. "I was always a hoyden, of course."

"And I went right along with you."

"Remember when we wanted honey sticks, but we didn't have enough pennies for the dry goods store, so we thought we'd make our own?"

They'd been ten. "I remember, all right. The hive hanging from the tree in your aunt Delia's yard wasn't a beehive. It belonged to a few hundred bald-faced wasps."

"Good thing Pa pulled us free and Ma and Aunt Delia knew what to do with the stings." She shuddered. "Oh, did those hurt."

So had Ward's backside, once he'd gotten home. Father had whupped him good. Georgie's pa had been furious, too, but Ward had never forgotten the look of fear in Jackson's eyes that seemed to be the true source of his angry tone. Nor had Ward forgotten the embrace Jackson drew Ward and Georgie into once they were free of the wasps.

That might have been why Ward had always had a soft spot for Jackson. At least, until the night of the Founder's Day dance five years ago, when he overheard Jackson denigrate the Harpers.

It didn't matter now. What mattered was Georgie pulling Fly to a halt at a fork in the road, staring at the path that didn't lead to Bridge Ranch.

Ward drew alongside. "LaRue's ranch."

"One of our *neighbors*." The way she said the word, it was clear she didn't find the LaRues to be neighborly. "I want to talk to them."

"I'll try tomorrow—"

"No, now."

"No, not now, and not you." Ward nudged Oro along the correct road, hoping Georgie would get the hint and follow. "It's inappropriate for you to go now for so many reasons, I can't even list them all."

"I don't care. I want to fix this."

"You could hurt Kim more than help him if you confront Silas LaRue, not to mention it's who knows what hour. They're asleep."

"I hope not, after what they've done to Kim. Leaving him to rot in a jail cell. They should be stewing in their juices with remorse for their false claims."

She'd never been vindictive, but it was clear, even as she joined him on the road away from the LaRues, that she was furious. He understood she wanted to protect and defend her brother, and her rage came from a place of love. But they must tread lightly. "I know it's hard, but Kim's situation is best handled through the legal system."

"It'll take too long. You said there'd be a trial unless Marceline fesses up." Her jaw set. "And with Ma unwell, and the boys scared and confused, and Pa bearing so many burdens including missing cattle, there's a lot to handle."

"And you can handle it better than God can?"

Even in the dark, he could see the flash of frustration in her eyes. "I know what the right answer is, but I can't sit on my hands."

Ward smiled. "Your family is precious to you."

"Family is the most important thing in the world to me."

"After God," he said gently. "We need to trust Him with our loved ones. That doesn't mean it's easy to do." For too long he'd put Georgie ahead of God, clinging to the possibility that he could make a way to be with her while he lived in Wildrye. He'd also trusted in his own abilities to "save" his parents, thinking he could stop them from drinking so much they ruined every opportunity to cross their paths.

That changed five years ago, the night of the Founder's Day dance, when he realized he needed to leave Wildrye. Once he did, and he'd finally given his parents and Georgie over to God's care, something had shifted in Ward. Something significant. In a sense, his leaving Wildrye was one of the best things to ever happen to him.

He touched her arm. "God has Kim in His care."

Her sigh echoed with heartbreak. "I know God is trustworthy. In my head, at least, but I guess I don't know it in my heart as well as I thought, because all I want to do is bust him out of jail."

He chuckled. "Don't. I'd represent you in court, but I'm not that good of a lawyer."

She laughed but sobered as they neared the house. The welcoming golden light of the lamps in the yard cast a warm glow on her stricken features. "This is hard."

Didn't he know it? "First things first. Take it a step at a time, and choose to trust God rather than fight Him."

"I'll try. It might take awhile."

He slid from Oro and reached to help her down from Fly. "In my case, trusting Him with hard things might take years. Maybe a lifetime. But it's still what's best."

Like letting her go. He'd hoped it would be easier to be around her after five years apart, but with her in the circle of his arms right now, so close he breathed in the soapy smell of her and would only need to dip his head a fraction to kiss her rosebud mouth, his hopes dashed.

God, I trust You with my feelings for Georgie. If You won't take them away, please help me to live with them and love her the right way—as a friend.

She stared up at him, her lips parted in—expectation?

Irritation was a more likely reason. His hands fell and he stepped away. "Let's go in and talk to your folks."

Hadn't he just told her, first things first? Well, in this case, Kim, the client, had a higher priority than Ward's years-long, unrequited affections for Georgie.

His feelings needed to come dead last, just like they always had.

Chapter 4

Georgie woke before the sun the next morning, even though she'd only slept a few hours. The previous night had stretched long, Georgie sitting with her parents, Evan, Josh, and Ward in the parlor while Little Mo slept upstairs. Ward had explained Kim's predicament in simple terms. He hadn't minimized the potential difficulties ahead, but when he promised to do all in his power to prove Kim's innocence, Georgie believed him.

Ma didn't cry, but the sadness in her eyes went deep. After a while, Ward rose to leave, intending to walk home, and Pa insisted he ride Oro back to town. Then her family had all trudged upstairs to their beds, but Georgie hadn't fallen asleep for what seemed like hours, mulling over Ward's gentle admonition to her. Even now, in the dark before dawn, she recalled his words, praying about them.

God, do I fight You by not trusting You?

At once she knew it was true, but it was far easier to fight Him than to trust Him because in fighting she felt she had some control.

An illusion, fragile as glass. What would happen when the delusion shattered? When she realized she'd never had control at all, but now she was surrounded by jagged shards?

She'd be broken. Which, truth be told, she was anyway.

I need Your help, God. We all do. Ma and Kim. And the baby, and Little Mo and Josh and Evan and Pa. Her list went on until the the first fingers of sunlight crept through the bedroom window.

She dressed and got to work in the kitchen, brewing coffee and slicing ham. Pa and the boys waved as they filed past the kitchen door, heading out for chores, and by the time they returned and washed up, she'd finished preparing the entire meal. Leaving her father and brothers to the platters of food, she ladled a bowl of oatmeal for Ma and carried it upstairs on a tray, tailed by Cat.

Ma's song reached her before she finished climbing the stairs, a Scottish lullaby Ma had sung to Georgie and the boys, and Ma's rich, strong soprano made the song all the sweeter. When Georgie reached the room, she found Ma in bed, cradling her stomach.

Cat ran past Georgie, leaped onto the bed, and curled at Ma's side. Georgie settled the tray over Ma's knees. "Does the baby like the song?"

"It seems to have quieted him down." Ma stroked Cat's sleek back.

"It's good to hear you singing." Georgie hugged her. "How are you feeling today?"

"Uncomfortable. I'm over forty years old now. This pregnancy business isn't the same as it was nineteen years ago. Or even eight years ago, with Little Mo." Ma chuckled. "I didn't sleep much, though."

Georgie sat on the edge of the bed. "I was up fretting too."

Ma toyed with the spoon, not tasting the oatmeal. "I'm trying to trust God to take care of all of my babies, especially Kim and this little one, however He sees fit, but it's hard. It doesn't matter how old any of you get, I struggle. But He loves you all even more than I do, and I'm your mother."

Her words were similar to what Ward had said last night. Cold conviction settled in Georgie's stomach.

All right. I'll trust You with Kim. I choose to trust You, God—

But what if this goes to trial and Your will for Kim is to go to jail for some reason I don't understand? I don't like that idea at all.

Ma was watching her, a half smile on her face. "I don't know what's going on in your pretty head, but you've been through a lot. Take some time today for yourself."

"We'll see." Georgie had responsibilities. Taking care of Ma and her brothers. Trying to get Kim out of jail. Figuring out what happened to the missing cattle so Pa wouldn't have to worry about it. Not her average Thursday.

"What are you wearing to the Founder's Day dance tomorrow night?" Ma sipped her tea.

"I'm not going." She nudged Cat's nose away from Ma's tray.

"I thought you'd planned to go with the Ramirezes." Diego and Alejandra lived on the ranch, where Diego worked as a blacksmith. Alejandra had grown up on the ranch, since her father worked as a hand, and she'd always been Georgie's closest friend—after Ward. Ma's brow furrowed. "You always go."

"Things are different this year. Kim's in jail."

"Kim's innocent, isn't he? So why should you hole up and hide?" Ma reached for her hand. "Does this have anything to do with Ward coming home?"

Of course it did. Five years ago on the day before the dance, she'd taught him to waltz in the parlor downstairs. Then he'd nervously asked if he could escort her—and her little brothers, confusing her as to his intent. But she hadn't cared. She was so excited for Ward to take her to the dance, she'd agreed. It turned out to be the most marvelous evening of her life, and on the ride home, he'd been so quiet she imagined he was working up the nerve to ask her to court.

But when he'd called the next day, there were no lingering looks like those he'd given her when they danced the reels and waltzes the previous night. Nothing to tell her he felt about her the same way she'd always felt about him.

Instead, he told her he was leaving town and didn't know when he would be back. If ever.

But he'd come home now, and while the thought of him still sent her heart beating fast, aching all those cracks he'd caused when he left, she wasn't sure she wanted to be at the Founder's Day dance if there was a chance *he'd* be there.

"I'm not sure," she told Ma. "But today I have other work to do."

And she couldn't do it alone.

God, I'm sorry I keep pulling my problems back from You. I know You can work them out without me. Please give me patience to trust You for direction.

Right now, that direction seemed to be pointing downstairs, to the breakfast dishes. She scooped up the cat and left Ma to her breakfast.

Ward dismounted Oro and tethered him to the porch of a yellow two-story house in need of a fresh coat of paint and a new window to replace the cracked one by the door. Clearly, Silas LaRue's ranch was not doing well financially.

At once, a pretty young lady with a curly coif of chestnut hair emerged from the front door. "Hello." Her voice was high and clear as a little bell.

Ward doffed his Stetson. "Good morning. Miss LaRue?"

"Yes." Her lashes fanned her rosy cheeks. "I'm Marceline."

Splendid. "I'm Ward Harper. Forgive my boldness, coming to your homestead like this, but I hoped to ask you a few questions about Kimball Bridge."

Her cheeks blanched. "Isn't he in jail?"

Ward nodded. "I'm his attorney."

"Is he. . .faring all right?"

"As well as can be expected." Just as he'd hoped, the news didn't seem to make her feel any better. "I wondered if you could help me. Tell me your side of things."

Her dainty fingers fidgeted with the lace at her throat. "I'm not sure."

"Those charges are serious, Miss LaRue. Kim could be in real trouble."

"Ho!"

Ward turned. A thickset fellow with a bow-legged stride hurried toward them, shaking his head indulgently. "Princess, who's your friend?"

"Um." Her cheeks regained their color.

Silas LaRue thrust out his hand for shaking. "Here to ask my Marcy to the dance tomorrow? Because she's already accepted someone else's invitation."

Ward shook his head. "I'm not—"

"No, Daddy." Marceline stepped off the porch. "He's here asking about—you know."

Ward's head tipped. "I'm Ward Harper. Kimball Bridge's legal counsel."

Silas's features hardened. "One of them no-good drunk Harpers? And if you're a lawyer for them Bridges, you shouldn't be talkin' to my daughter."

Ward didn't bother addressing LaRue's comment about his parents. "I only want her account of the events."

"You have them. That Bridge boy's been followin' her, and when he thought ever'one was busy, he tried to take her."

"Is this true, Miss LaRue?"

She looked at her father. Then at the ground.

"O' course it's true," Silas answered. "Now you got what you came for. Git off my land."

Ward had no choice but to mount Oro and be on his way. He wished he could take whatever path Kim and Marceline had traveled to look for evidence, but he'd be trespassing if he didn't stick to the roads.

Nevertheless, the path to the Bridge homestead wasn't long, and within a few minutes, he arrived at Bridge Ranch. Before he could dismount, Georgie and Jackson were on the porch to meet him, their faces etched in worry. Georgie shaded her eyes from the late morning sun with her hand. "How's Kim?"

"I was with him first thing this morning. He's well enough. No change on his charges, but I've given our strategy some thought and wanted to share with you right away." Ward tethered Oro to the hitching post. "While I'm here, I'll return Oro."

Jackson shook his head. "You got a horse of your own?"

"Not yet." But he planned on it once he started finding clients—

"Keep Oro until this mess with Kim is settled."

A protest formed on his tongue, but it was rooted in pride. Besides, riding Oro while he worked for Kim meant Ward would get everywhere far faster than if he walked, and he could potentially solve the case faster.

"Generous of you, sir." Oro was a fine horse, worth more than Ward could afford. Then again, when it came to the Bridge family, Ward had always been like a boy looking in the window of a candy shop at goodies he'd never have enough money to buy.

Shaking off the thought, he followed them into the parlor. Jackson urged him to sit on a green velvet chair near the east window.

"Coffee?" Georgie hesitated by her chair.

Ward shook his head, and as he'd hoped, she sat beside him. He tore his gaze from her to meet Jackson's expectant stare. "On my way here, I stopped by LaRue's place. I thought if Marceline was willing to elope with Kim, she'd care enough about him to tell the truth, but she seems intimidated by her father."

"He's a gruff one, especially since he's had money troubles." Jackson rubbed the stubble at his jaw. "The Panic of '73 hit a lot of folks hard, but then he lost a lot of cows to disease. I don't think his stock is healthy yet."

Ward better understood the raggedy look of LaRue's homestead. "What do you think of Marceline?"

"She's pretty to look at," Georgie blurted. "I suspected Kim liked her, but I didn't think it was reciprocated."

"So it surprised you to learn she wanted to elope with him?"

Wide-eyed, Jackson nodded. Georgie did the same. "She'd flirt with him, but I also saw her turn her back on him in public to chat with other fellows."

Uh-oh. "So if she snubbed him publicly, it could be argued she wasn't interested in him. Kim was angered by her insulting him and he—"

"That's not what happened." Georgie stood. "I think they hid their relationship from her pa."

"I agree." Ward's voice was soothing. "But the other side will be looking for motives. Witnesses. I need to know what they're thinking so I can be ready to counter any argument they come up with."

"I appreciate you taking such initiative," Jackson said, his gaze captured by something outside the window. "Lard is looking for me. He's acting foreman while Fred is gone. If you'll excuse me a moment, I'll tell him I'll be with him when we're done here."

Ward turned to peer behind him out the window. Sure enough, the lanky foreman in a worn Stetson searched the edge of the house, paper in hand, a concerned expression on his weathered features.

Ward tipped his head toward the window. "Go on, Mr. Bridge. I'll tell Georgie the rest."

Jackson nodded. "All right, then. Be sure to tell her your fee, and I'll have a bank draft sent to you."

Silence hung in the air like dust motes at Jackson's exit. Ward didn't want to talk about money. The Bridges had hired him, but taking money from them didn't sit right.

Georgie cracked a smile. "Payment isn't something you're comfortable discussing with me, is it?"

"Nope. But there is something I want to ask you."

She resumed her seat. "About Kim?"

"About the dance tomorrow night."

"What?" She went still, like a bird becoming aware it was watched by a cat—which she was. A white cat with black splotches appeared out of nowhere, silent as fog, pausing between them.

Ward leaned forward, extending his fingers and making a welcoming *tt–tt* sound with his tongue. "Hello, Cat."

"You know her name?"

"Your cats are always named Cat." Nicknamed, at least. Since Georgie had named her first kitten Cat, the ones to follow were named words starting with *C-a-t*. Catfish. Catsup.

"We might have changed the tradition, you know."

"Did you?"

"No." She laughed. "This one is Catastrophe."

"What'd you do to deserve that?" Ward lifted the cat onto his lap.

"She was Catnap, for about a week. Then she unraveled the shawl I was knitting."

"Not kind of you, Cat." Ward stroked her silky ears. "So, the Founder's Day dance. Are you going?"

A spark lit in her eye that Ward couldn't quite attribute to the morning light shining through the window. "I'm supposed to go with Alejandra and Diego. I don't think it's appropriate, though, with Kim in jail. Are you going?"

"As of this morning, I am. Silas LaRue let slip Marceline's attending with an escort."

Her lip curled. "Really? One day after trying to elope with Kim? Was she stringing him along all this time?"

"I don't know. All I know is she's going."

"If somebody had just tried to kidnap me, I wouldn't want to go." Georgie reconsidered. "Well, maybe I would, to show the world I was fine."

A chuckle escaped Ward's throat. "You're a rare breed, Georgia Bridge. But I think Marceline will go because she wasn't really kidnapped. In any case, it'll be a good opportunity to watch her, see who her friends are. Gauge her behavior. If she tells one person she lied about being kidnapped, says she brought her own horse and nicked her father's money, we've got a witness to corroborate Kim's story. But I don't know her or her friends, so I could use your perspective. Come with me."

31

She didn't smile. "For investigative purposes, of course."

"Sure. Investigative purposes."

"Then I'll go with you."

"I'll come for you at six tomorrow evening." He lowered Cat to the floor and took his leave, his stomach churning with nerves, just like it had five years ago when she'd agreed to go to the dance with him.

A lot had changed since then, but Ward was still a Harper. Still the son of the town drunks, as Silas LaRue had reminded him. Still unworthy of a woman from a good family like Georgie Bridge.

He'd been an idiot to love her when he was a boy, and he was still an idiot to be excited at the prospect of dancing with her tomorrow, even though the evening would not be the least bit romantic. Investigative purposes, she'd called it.

He couldn't extinguish his feelings for her with the ease of dousing a lamp, but he'd be sure to keep his feelings to himself.

Chapter 5

Light spilled from the three-story town hall onto Front Street Friday evening as Georgie and Ward arrived at the dance, and the upbeat strains of banjo, bass, guitar, and fiddle carried from the hall's open doors. Any other time, Georgie's foot would already be tapping, but this was not an ordinary occasion.

It was a repetition of an evening that had caused her great pain. Music beckoned them to dance, just as it had then. Chatter carried over the street. The hint of cool in the breeze whispered against her cheeks. And Ward, freshly shaven and handsome in a dark coat and red tie, helped her down from the carriage he'd rented. Just like five years ago.

But this time, you are not here as friends with the chance of something more. You're here to investigate Marceline.

Nevertheless, his touch sent her heart to her throat, blocking her breath.

Think of something else. Like Alejandra and Diego—were they here yet? Earlier today, Georgie had strolled to Alejandra's cottage and told her all about Kim, his case, and her plans to attend the dance with Ward instead of with Alejandra and Diego. Once Alejandra managed to close her gaping jaw, she'd insisted on helping Georgie prepare, even though Georgie explained that she and Ward weren't going together like last time—this was all about Kim's case, not anything personal. Alejandra rolled her eyes and said she'd be at the house at four.

She came ready for the dance herself, pretty in a pale green dress and with her dark braids intricately coiled at her nape, and she took hot tongs to Georgie's already wavy hair, creating large, smooth coils. Ma then pinned them into an elegant half-up, half-down coiffure. Both Alejandra and Ma forced her to wear her best dress, a beribboned, robin's-egg blue silk confection with a subtle bustle.

Ward glanced at her dress now, out of the corner of his eye.

"You look pretty." Ward's words came out half-strangled, like his collar was on too tight.

"So do you." Ugh. She'd thought to deflect attention from herself by returning the compliment. Instead she'd told him he looked pretty? "I mean fine. Dressed up."

She would not call him handsome.

His chuckle broke the tension. "Thanks."

They stepped inside the hall through the crowded foyer, passing the mayor, sheriff, and several cowpokes from Bridge Ranch. "I don't see Marceline."

"Maybe she's dancing." Ward reached for her hand, guiding her through the people edging the dance floor.

His touch did strange things to her pulse and dredged up feelings she did not want to revisit tonight. *Lord, this is hard. I want to run away, but I also want to trust You far more than I do. Help me.*

A flash of pink sailed past, reminding her why she was here. "There she is."

Marceline skipped down a line of dancers in a reel, holding hands with a tall, broad-shouldered fellow with a blond mustache. Ward's eyes narrowed. "Who's her escort?"

"Abner Hock." She had to pop to her tiptoes so Ward could hear her over the conversations and music. This close, his bay rum aftershave smelled enchanting. *Stop it.* "He's a hand on her father's ranch, one of the few left. I don't know much about him, other than he's been in a few fights outside the saloon."

The song ended, and Ward tugged her hand. "Let's dance."

"I thought we were observing. Not dancing."

"It'll get us closer to them. Come on."

They took places in a forming square, across from Marceline and Abner and next to a couple Georgie didn't know. Everyone smiled at one another except Marceline, who looked as if she might lose her dinner. Then a final couple completed the square—Alejandra and Diego Ramirez, who greeted everyone warmly. Diego and Ward seemed especially pleased to encounter one another again. They were still grinning and talking when the first strains of a sprightly tune began.

Georgie curtsied to Ward, then Diego at her corner, before they started do-si-doing and weaving around the square. When they returned to their partners, Ward spun Georgie in a neat circle, but she clung on an extra moment. "How is this helping us investigate?"

"Don't fret. Try to have fun."

"But—"

Diego locked elbows with her and spun her around. Then Abner did the same.

This was ridiculous. She couldn't exchange a word with Abner, much less ask anything about Marceline. Ward didn't seem to mind their inability to investigate, though. He grinned down at Marceline while he spun her.

He'd better not be swayed by her pretty face.

"Pay attention," Alejandra warned in a teasing tone. Georgie had fallen behind.

"I'm paying attention, all right," Georgie said, speeding up, her gaze fixed on Marceline.

But then she and Ward do-si-do'd and he caught her close for a half second. "Trust me." His whisper sent a shiver from her ear to her neck.

Her skin was still covered in goose pimples when the song ended and a waltz started. She nodded at the couples in her group as they all paired up for the waltz.

"We can't eavesdrop on them now," she noted when Ward took her hand. "Should we speak to their friends?"

"You don't want to waltz?" His lips quirked into a teasing grin. "Is it me? I'm better now than I used to be."

"You've been practicing?" Georgie didn't like the vision in her head of him dancing with strange girls in Fort Worth.

"Maybe." His eyes twinkled. "But you're right. Let's separate and see if we can learn anything."

The room seemed colder when he left her. Georgie rubbed her arms and searched the room for Marceline's gaggle of friends. She'd taken two steps toward a cluster of girls she recognized as Marceline's cronies when Alejandra intercepted her. "Georgie?"

"Aren't you waltzing with Diego?"

"I told him I wanted to talk to you, and he was eager to speak to his old friend Ward." She grinned. "So?"

"So what?"

"Did he say you looked lovely?"

"No." At Alejandra's shocked expression, Georgie rolled her eyes. "He said *pretty*."

"You're in a cross mood."

"I'm not cross. I'm anxious to clear Kim, so I'm going to ask Marceline's friends about her relationship with Kim."

Alejandra's brow arched. "What if she didn't tell any of them about her plans to elope?"

"There's only one way to find out." Georgie squeezed Alejandra's arm and marched over. The young ladies eyed her with scorn, so she forced a smile. "Good evening, ladies. Having fun?"

"What do you want?" The town wheelwright's daughter glared.

"There was a big misunderstanding with my brother and Marceline. I wondered if Marceline has said anything about it."

"She hasn't said a word, to our astonishment," one young lady said, only to be whacked in the arm by her friend.

"Marceline wouldn't want us gossiping about this. Come on."

So much for one of them being a witness on Kim's behalf. Maybe this would be a good time for some punch.

Before she reached the refreshment table, the barber asked her to dance, and she couldn't very well say no. He was more interested in gossip about her *kidnapper brother* than her, though. Then she was obliged to square dances with some of Pa's ranch hands and then a reel with the mayor. Ward clearly didn't mind. He was busy chatting, never once looking her way.

Her gaze flitted in turn between Ward and Marceline. All in all, she had achieved nothing so far this evening but sore toes.

A disappointing evening all around.

After forty-five minutes of watching and waiting, Ward caught the moment he'd long awaited and made his way to the refreshment table. He was the only one by the punch bowl except for Abner Hock.

He took a sip of the sugary drink, trying to look inconspicuous. "Looks like our partners are dancing with other fellas."

"More men at these things than gals, every time." Abner gestured with his elbow at the line of cowpokes holding up the far wall. "Poor fools didn't ask to escort anyone quick enough, I guess."

This was too easy. "You must have asked Marceline to the dance awhile ago, then?"

"More 'n a month ago." Abner took a long pull of punch. "Asked her pa first, actually. He approved heartily."

"So you're courting, then?" At Abner's strange expression, Ward shook his head. "I'm not asking for myself. Just curious."

"Why?"

Ward couldn't very well tell him he wondered if Marceline was courting Abner while planning to elope with Kim Bridge. Excuses clogged his throat. "I—um, I could—"

"Use advice?" Abner's eyes narrowed. "You ain't courtin' your gal yet?"

"Nope." *Thanks, Lord.*

Abner elbowed him in the ribs. "Just ask her, I guess. She came to the dance with you. That says something."

Had it said something five years ago? He'd wanted it to, but with Georgie's brothers along, the evening was hardly romantic. And then he'd overheard Jackson and he'd decided then and there it was high time to leave Wildrye.

But had his escort to the dance five years ago meant anything to Georgie? Had she expected something from him, like a request to court?

Cold pain like ice chips speared his insides. If she'd felt a fraction of what he'd felt for her, he'd hurt her terribly by leaving. He'd been so absorbed by his own pain, he hadn't considered hers.

"Excuse me." He set down his punch and made his way to the edge of the dance floor. The moment the song trailed off, Ward hurried to Georgie's side.

She wasn't even out of the baker's arms before Ward captured her gaze. "May I have this dance?"

Her nod was all the answer he needed.

He'd expected a polka or square dance, but the familiar one-two-three sent his heart to his boots and back up again. A waltz.

Good thing he'd had occasion to improve his skills in Fort Worth at his law mentor's Christmas parties, because dancing with Georgie again, he'd need all the confidence he could muster. He settled his hand on her back, above her waist, and took her hand. Her other hand settled lightly on his shoulder.

His gulp ached his throat. She was the prettiest thing he'd ever seen. *God, help me not to fall for her again.*

If he'd ever climbed out of that hole in the first place. Stepping to the first strains of the tune with her in his arms, he wasn't sure he'd ever really stopped being in love with her. Maybe he'd been fooling himself all this time.

Her eyes sparkled, and he couldn't look anywhere else. He forgot to silently count the time of the music, or to rotate, or anything except stare down into her rich brown eyes and let himself be in the moment.

Something smacked his shoulder, jolting him forward and breaking their held gazes. "Sorry." A skinny cowboy with a shock of yellow hair smiled and pulled his blushing partner away.

The moment was lost. Probably a good thing, too, so Ward didn't make a bigger fool of himself than he already had. But regardless of how he felt for her once—or again—they'd always had fun together.

They could again, couldn't they?

Ward released his hold on Georgie's waist, pushing her into a spin.

"Ward!" It came out like a gasp between her laughs.

There she was, his Georgie, pink cheeked and laughing. He danced her in a circle. Spun her again so her blue dress swirled around her legs. He'd spin her all night just to hear the music of her laughter.

Ward turned her fast for the song's end, and Georgie was laughing so hard she clung to his hand and shoulder. Her sweet giggles were so close to his ear he almost didn't hear the crash.

Georgie spun to look. "What happened?"

Ward's laugh died somewhere around his diaphragm. "Mother."

She stood by the overturned punch bowl, fingers pressed to her face, apologizing to anyone who would listen. Ward hurried toward her, taking her by the arm. "What's happened?"

"I didn't think I hit it. I'm sorry." Whiskey was thick on Mother's breath.

"What's wrong?" Georgie peered around him.

"Hello, Georgie." Mother's voice was too loud.

"Hello, Mrs. Harper." She clearly could tell Mother was inebriated, but she didn't look horrified or judgmental. Just kind.

Ward turned. "I'm sorry."

"It's all right."

It wasn't all right. Mother was drinking again and made a spectacle of herself. People were watching, whispering, even pointing. More than a few muttered *Harper* and some of the words Ward had heard murmured along with it for years.

Embarrassing. Shameful. Good-for-nothing drunk.

He had to leave. Now.

"Georgie, I'll be back to escort you home. I'm sorry to leave you for a few minutes."

She shook her head. "I'll go with Alejandra and Diego. They live on the ranch, and it'll be no trouble, I'm sure."

"But I'm your escort."

"Don't worry. I'll keep investigating after you leave."

That wasn't the point. He had brought her; it was his responsibility to see her home.

Then again, she'd reminded him quite clearly that they'd come for a purpose, to watch Marceline. This was not a romantic evening. He'd let himself get carried away after working for years to quench his feelings for her. And as he gathered Mother and apologized to the mayor for the mess of the spilled punch, he was reminded why he was a fool to love Georgia Bridge.

He was the son of Bill and Elspeth Harper, unworthy in her father's eyes.

How quickly he'd forgotten.

Chapter 6

The next afternoon, Georgie toed the rough wood planks of Odell Norwood's porch, pushing herself back and forth on the swing. And listening.

After a while, she shook her head. "I don't hear it, Mr. Norwood. I'm sorry."

Her neighbor leaned against the porch rail, cupping his ear to the yard. "I saw a flash o' yellow this morning."

"Maybe I scared them off, like the dogs did."

"You're a chatty gal, but you ain't that loud."

Georgie laughed, trying to keep the sound low. "Thanks, Mr. Norwood."

"Well, here comes more noise." Mr. Norwood stood straight. "Howdy-do, Mr. Harper."

Ward? Georgie sat straight too.

Riding Oro, Ward appeared through the scrub and trees from the road, doffing his Stetson. "Good afternoon." His voice was friendly, but his expression tentative when his gaze met Georgie's.

Did he feel embarrassed to see her, after what happened with his mother last night?

Mr. Norwood shifted on the porch. "What can I do you for? Here to visit the yellow warblers like Miss Bridge?"

Ward dismounted and climbed the porch steps. He looked handsome as usual, donned in his gray suit and a blue tie that brought out the hue of his eyes. Up close, though, the fatigue lining those eyes was impossible to miss. "No, sir, but I'd sure like to hear them."

"They ain't singing. Too much noise." He looked with suspicion at Oro, whose broad black lips quietly teased the grass underfoot for a nibble.

Ward smiled. "I won't stay long, sir. Just wanted to see how you're faring."

"No more dogs. I had a good talk with Bridge about things, and look—his men planted new vegetables and fenced the garden. Miss Bridge is here to ask if I'm satisfied, and I am. So you did good, representing me."

Georgie grinned. "Ward's a good lawyer."

Ward shrugged off the compliment. "I was just at the Bridge homestead. They said I could find you here, Georgie, so I thought I'd check on Mr. Norwood and collect you."

He'd come looking for her? She stood from the swing, but her insides swayed as if she were still on it. "Oh?"

"Shh!" Mr. Norwood held up a gnarled hand.

Silence. Wind fluttering leaves.

Tweet tweet tweet too too tweet.

"*Sweet sweet sweet I'm so sweet,*" Georgie whispered, earning a scowl of disapproval from Mr. Norwood. She met Ward's silently laughing gaze.

The little song repeated, lilting and lovely. Try as she might, though, Georgie couldn't see a flash of the warbler's yellow feathers anywhere.

"Hiding," Mr. Norwood said. "Too many folks around."

"We'll take our leave, then, so as not to disturb the warblers anymore." Georgie kept her voice low and tiptoed to clasp Mr. Norwood's calloused hand. "Thanks for allowing me to hear them."

"Come back anytime. Just quieter."

"Sure thing," Ward said after his handshake. Then he untethered Oro and walked alongside him as he and Georgie ambled off Mr. Norwood's property, holding their tongues by unspoken agreement.

When they reached the main road, Georgie let out a loud, long breath. "Do you think the warblers can hear us from here?"

"I hope not." He chuckled. "If they can, Odell will sing a different tune, like *you two aren't sweet.*"

She nudged him with her shoulder. "Very funny."

"I'm done being funny today. Time to be serious."

Uh-oh. "Is it Kim?"

"No—he's fine. I was with him this morning. Sheriff Bly is allowing visitors, so I rode out to the homestead to let you all know. Your whole family's on their way to see him."

"Even Ma?"

At his nod, Georgie's gut clenched. All the jostling in the carriage wouldn't be good for Ma, but she wouldn't pass up the chance to see her boy. "So are we going to the jail too?"

"We can if you want. In fact, you take Oro." He held out the reins. "I've borrowed him long enough—"

"Oh no. Pa says you get him for the duration of the case."

"Then let's go back to your place and get you a horse—"

"Not when we're halfway to town from here. I'll ride back with my folks in the carriage."

"Then we'll have to walk." Ward's brow quirked.

"Or I could ride up with you."

It hadn't sounded forward in her brain, but at the startled look on Ward's face, Georgie flushed hot. "I mean—"

"Sure." Lickety-split, Ward boosted her up into a strange, sidesaddle position with one leg flung over the horn, her blue calico skirt draping just so. He climbed behind her, reached around her to hold the reins, and nudged Oro on. It probably looked odd, but it worked, with her in the circle of his strong, stable arms.

Georgie's heart thumped in her throat.

"I'm so sorry about last night." Ward's breath fanned her cheek. "Leaving you at the dance—I know you were safe with Alejandra and Diego, but I hated abandoning you."

It wasn't as if he'd escorted her because he *liked* her. "You had to take care of your mother. I understood. Besides, I tried to continue our investigation into Marceline."

"Did you learn more?"

"No. She didn't seem to be having a good time, and they left soon after you did." She'd wanted to follow them but remembered her determination to trust God for another opportunity. "So how's your mother today?"

"Sobered up." Ward shifted. "She hasn't been drinking since I've been back. I thought her sobriety was permanent, but I guess she was waiting for me to leave her for an evening."

"How difficult for you, thinking she'd chosen to change."

"She's a Harper. I guess there's no changing that."

She twisted her head to look back at him. "What does that mean?"

"You know what people have always said about my parents. They're drunks. No-accounts. Unreliable."

"Who says that?"

"Everyone." He looked at the dusty road, not her. "Even your father."

No. "When?"

"The night of the Founder's Day dance, five years ago. I didn't know it, but my father had gone to Bridge Ranch that day, asking for a job. I overheard your pa telling some men about it at the dance, how the Harpers were—untrustworthy. No way was he ever going to hire a Harper."

Georgie's eyes shut. "Oh, Ward."

"Kind of ironic now, him hiring me?"

"He didn't mean *you*. You're not your father. You're trustworthy." At once, she knew it was the wrong thing to say. She turned her whole body to better see Ward's face, even though it meant she was almost twisted in half on the saddle. "What I mean is, your parents drank a lot and your pa couldn't hold down a job. I also know your pa used to beat you."

He didn't answer for a few seconds too long. "It's over now."

"The pain may never be over, this side of glory." She touched his cheek. "Same with what Pa said. I'm sorry. It must've hurt something fierce."

"I can't say it didn't."

"People shouldn't judge you for your parents' actions."

"I think that's why I'm a lawyer. I don't much care for injustice." He glanced around her to the road ahead.

"We all knew you dreamed of attending Baylor for law school, but you weren't going to apply for another year. Then, without warning, you said goodbye, without submitting an application, without having a plan. Because of what Pa said?"

He nodded once, but after a moment it became clear that he wasn't saying yes. Rather, he was directing her to turn around. "We're here."

They'd arrived at the outskirts of town, all right, with the jail in full view a half block down the way. And right out in front of it was a ruckus of a fight involving Abner Hock and three redheaded males.

Her brothers.

Ward pulled Oro to a stop out of harm's way, three storefronts down from the jail, and leaped from the saddle. He caught Georgie as she swung her leg around the horn and slid from Oro's back.

Much as he liked any excuse to touch her, this wasn't the time to linger. Still, he gripped her hand and tugged her along the boardwalk. "I know better than to ask you to stay back where it's safe, but I wish you would."

Georgie snorted.

"Fair enough." Ward scanned the chaotic scene—Evan Bridge plugged a bloody nose with one hand but managed to shove Abner Hock into Josh, who ducked as Abner swung at him. Little Mo stood cheering on the fringes of the gathered crowd. Alejandra struggled to keep hold of a basket of produce while tugging Little Mo away from the fight, almost knocking into wide-eyed Marceline.

Georgie's hand slipped from Ward's. "What's going on here?"

"They're fighting. Over me," Marceline marveled.

"It's not something to be proud of, Marceline," Alejandra said.

Ward shoved through the crowd and gripped the back of Evan's shirt, yanking him away from Abner. "Enough. You want to go to jail with your brother?"

"I don't care."

But he did, because the hot pink color faded from his cheeks and he shrugged off Ward's hands.

He hadn't realized Georgie had followed him, but she plunged her index finger against Evan's chest. "What sort of cockamamy nonsense is this, Evan?"

"He said Kim deserves to hang for what he did to Marceline."

"And she's a liar." Josh pointed at Marceline, whose wide eyes filled with moisture.

Abner shoved forward, fists flexed. "Watch what you say about my fiancé. She ain't a liar, and she'd never run off with the likes of a carrot-headed whelp like Kimball Bridge."

Good thing Ward hadn't let go of Evan, or the lad would've thrown another punch at Abner. Josh's hands fisted, and even Georgie, who gripped Josh's arm, looked as if she'd like to wipe the smug grin off Abner's face.

Ward turned Evan away from Abner. "Come on. You too, Josh."

Evan grunted. "But—"

"The truth will out. Nothing good'll come from violence." Ward urged Evan up to the jail porch. Georgie marched Josh, and Alejandra brought Little Mo around the crowd to meet them.

"Cowards," Abner called after them.

"Ignore him," Ward warned the Bridge boys, but his gaze was drawn by a waving woman. Mother picked her way across the street toward them. First things first, though. He released Evan's arm. "Will you fellas go inside, no trouble?"

"Yes," Georgie answered for them. "You too, Little Mo. Go see Kim."

"Wait till I tell him we were in a fight." Little Mo grinned.

"No you don't." Georgie's brows met in a fierce line. "Don't say a word about it in front of Ma, you hear?"

"Aw." Little Mo's shoulders slumped when he followed his brothers into the jailhouse.

Georgie gave Alejandra a quick hug. "Thank you for keeping him safe."

"I'm glad I happened to be shopping this morning. Ay, those *hermanos* of yours." She waved farewell and slipped away a moment before Mother joined them atop the jailhouse steps.

Georgie smiled, even though she was probably anxious to go inside with her family. "Hello, Mrs. Harper."

Mother pressed a kiss on Georgie's cheek. "What are you doing here? Oh, how silly of me. Your brother kidnapped the LaRue girl."

Ward's ears warmed. "He didn't do it, Mother."

"Maybe it was for ransom," Mother went on as if he hadn't spoken. "Now that Silas LaRue has money again, he's ripe for the picking."

Georgie's head tipped forward. "What do you mean?"

Mother reddened. "I shouldn't say. You'll disapprove, Ward."

Ward prayed for calm. "I'm not angry, Mother. I just want the truth."

Mother's gap-toothed smile looked contrite. "Well, last night I went to the saloon. The back. Not inside—I'm a lady, after all."

Ward cringed. "Mother, this sort of conversation isn't fit for Georgie—"

"It's fine." Georgie cut him off. "I'm not a child anymore."

He'd noticed. But she didn't need to hear what went on in a saloon. Or behind it, where the barkeep sold women like his mother jugs of liquor. Georgie didn't budge, though.

Mother licked her lips. "About six months ago, Frank—he's the barkeep—kicked Silas out for failing to pay his debt. His tab was enormous. But last night, Silas was at Frank's with a fistful of cash. Enough to pay off his old bill and buy the saloon a round of drinks. He said he sold some cows."

"Aren't his cows unhealthy?" Georgie blinked. "Who'd buy sick cows?"

"He said they were hale. Two dozen sold, if I recall."

A few dozen healthy cattle? Ward's eyes narrowed. "Georgie, how many of your pa's cattle are missing?"

"Thirty-six. Give or take a few." She shook her head. "Silas LaRue is the cattle thief."

"Let's not jump to conclusions. I'll look into it. You've got plenty of other things needing your care." Namely, her ma and Kim. "First things first."

After a moment she sighed and nodded. "First things first. Pray and trust."

Ward grinned.

"I'll be with my family. Good day, Mrs. Harper. Ward, send word as soon as you can."

"Toodle-doo, dear." Mother waved her fingers.

Ward hated telling Georgie goodbye like this, with her upset and their conversation about him overhearing her father unfinished. Now Georgie had more of the story, but not all of it. Did she guess he left because he loved her but could never be worthy in her family's eyes?

Things would never go back to the way they were five years ago, though, no matter how much Georgie knew about Ward's past feelings. Maybe it was best they didn't finish the conversation. And frankly, he had other matters to handle of greater priority. Kim's case. His mother's drinking. Now searching for evidence that Silas LaRue might be a cattle thief—a serious charge, indeed.

First things first.

He silently prayed while he escorted Mother the few blocks home. *Lord, help me to do all the tasks You've given me to do. May my hands help grant justice and peace.*

But he didn't have much peace in his heart.

Chapter 7

After church Sunday afternoon and into the evening, Georgie watched out the windows for a glimpse of a man on a golden horse riding into the yard, but Ward never came. She'd expected news about Silas LaRue or Kim, or least for Ward to come with no official reason at all, hoping to continue the discussion they'd had on Oro's back about why he left Wildrye five years ago. But he never came.

After drying the last of the breakfast dishes Monday morning, she followed the sounds of conversation to the parlor. Ma paced a path in the rug, and Pa scowled, arms folded.

Georgie folded her arms too. "You shouldn't be on your feet, Ma."

"I can't lie down any longer. I feel like I'm crawling out of my skin."

Georgie exchanged looks with Pa. "The doctor says—"

"I know." Ma waved her hand. "But I need to walk some jitters out." She looked over her shoulder at Georgie. "Frankly, you look like you could use a walk yourself. You've been watching out the window for two days."

There would be no ducking out of this conversation. "I've been watching for Ward."

"With news of Kim?" Ma paused to rub the small of her back. When Pa hurried to help her, she waved him off and resumed pacing.

"Him, or. . .Silas LaRue. Saturday, Mrs. Harper mentioned Silas recently came into some cash selling cows, but everyone knows his stock has been sick. I think he's the one who stole your cattle, Pa, but Ward wants evidence. I'm sorry I didn't tell you, but I decided he was right. We need proof before we all get too excited, and I didn't want to upset you both. Are you angry with me?"

Pa shook his head, but his gaze hadn't left Ma. "I don't like being robbed, but God will sort it out. I sure appreciate Ward checking into things for us. He's done such a fine job helping our family. I have every confidence he'll uncover the truth with the cattle and in Kim's case too. I'm glad we hired him."

"About that." Georgie gripped the back of a chair. "Did Bill Harper ever come to you for a job?"

Pa's gaze left Ma. "Why?"

"Five years ago at the Founder's Day dance, Ward overheard you tell some men about it. You said you'd never hire a Harper." She took a deep breath. "Ward wasn't tattling—he was explaining to me why he left Wildrye."

"I hardly remember, but yes, I did send Bill Harper away. He was inebriated, and much as my heart ached for Ward, I couldn't hire a man I couldn't trust around my family, much less my animals—"

"Oh," Ma groaned. She dropped into one of the green chairs.

"What's wrong?" Pa was at her feet.

"The baby's kicking like a bronco." Ma rolled her eyes.

"We're going to have to teach him how to bust broncs, not imitate them." Pa's tone was light, but the levity didn't reach his eyes.

It was clear all was well for now, but Pa wouldn't be leaving Ma's side for a while. Georgie stepped back. "You're right, Ma. I could use some fresh air. A ride sounds nice."

She strode to the stable and was about to mount Fly when Little Mo called her name. "Can I come?"

Poor Little Mo. He was only eight, and everything with Ma and Kim was surely unsettling him. "Sure."

Once his gentle gray mare, Smoky, was readied, they rode toward the trees lining Whistle Creek. It wasn't the gallop Georgie had wanted when she'd set out, but this slower pace was probably better, since it allowed her to chat with her brother. Following the creek past Mr. Norwood's property, they talked about a host of subjects, from Cat to the fight outside the jail. Then he twisted to look at her.

"Why does everyone call me Little Mo instead of Moses?"

"Because you're the littlest."

"I ain't gonna be the littlest when the baby comes."

"True, you *aren't*. Should we call you Moses from now on?"

His freckled face screwed up. "Naw. I ain't—I *am not*—a big brother yet. Say, we just passed Mr. Norwood's. You really heard a yellow bird sing at his house, and it says *I'm sweet?*"

She had to chuckle at how abruptly he could change subjects. "Sort of. You have to use your imagination. Maybe we'll hear one right now." Pushing her calico bonnet back, she cupped her ear in an exaggerated display. Little Mo copied her.

"All I hear is the creek trickling," he said after two seconds.

"Let's listen a little longer."

Even the horses were still. Georgie shut her eyes. A southbound breeze rustled oak leaves above. The horses' breaths came in soft snorts. Little Mo's saddle creaked—he must be fidgeting. Cows lowed. No, bellowed, across the creek.

Her eyes flew open. Hearing cows wasn't a strange thing in these parts, but Mr. Norwood didn't own any besides his milking cow, and his closest neighbor to the north, Silas LaRue, supposedly had a depleted stock of sickly cows. Georgie knew enough about cattle to differentiate between the *moos* of well cows and sick ones, and these weren't sick. They were in pain.

"I'm going to sneak across the creek."

"But it ain't our land." Little Mo gaped.

"I know. Which is why I want you to stay here."

"You're gonna get in trouble."

Probably. Or maybe she could solve the mystery of the missing cattle once and for all. She nudged Fly through the creek and hopped down on dry LaRue land. Old hoof prints mottled the soft earth—were they from Kim and Marceline's horses, when they tried to elope? Georgie followed the sounds of the cattle.

She didn't need to go far. Nor could she go farther, because just beyond some mesquite trees, Mr. LaRue was at work with a hot brand, burning over the existing brands on cows' hips.

Retracing her steps, she took care to keep low and quiet. Little Mo was where she left him, off Smoky and brandishing two weeds like twin swords. She mounted Fly and crossed the creek again.

"Little Mo, how fast do you think Smoky can run?"

After church yesterday, Ward spent the afternoon researching law books at his small, new office on Front Street, and this morning he'd scrutinized documents at the courthouse, but there was nothing of record about Silas LaRue's financial circumstances. He might as well stop for lunch.

When he returned to the little house off Front Street at noon, Mother looked up from slicing bread. "I was just fixing up sandwiches for us. Did you find anything?"

He shook his head and sidled past her to the sink so he could wash up. "There've been a lot of buyers through here the past week. Only a few remain in town, and after lunch I'll visit the hotel to see if any of them have a mind to buy from LaRue. Maybe someone will know something."

"I wish I could remember if he said anything more." Ma forked ham onto a platter beside the bread. "But I forget a lot when I'm drinking."

Is this the opportunity I've waited for, Lord? Ward leaned against the sink. "I thought you'd stopped drinking."

"I tried, but it was too hard. I'm sorry I embarrassed you at the dance. Did I ruin your evening with Georgie?"

He didn't answer, but she must've read the disappointment on his face. She swiped her watery eyes. "I never thought of how my drinking affected you. Not when you were a boy, and not now. I don't know how you got to be a fancy lawyer with his head on straight."

"You loved me. But God helped me be who He wants me to be. He can help you, too, if you want."

"I want it." A tear snaked down her cheek. "I don't like who I am when I drink, but I can't give it up on my own. And I want to be right with God."

He pulled her into his arms, praying for help and guidance. "The road ahead won't be easy, but I'll be here. May we pray together?"

She nodded against his chest, and there in the kitchen, he led them in prayer. For her salvation, for her healing, for her strength to turn away from liquor.

After adding an *amen*, Ward released her. "Should we eat? We can talk more about where we go next."

A frantic-sounding knock drew Ward around. He opened the door to Georgie, hand poised to knock again, the desperate look on her face knotting his stomach.

"What's wrong?" He reached for her hand. She was frightened, and all he wanted was to keep her safe.

"Little Mo and I went riding. I heard cattle on LaRue's side of the creek. I shouldn't have trespassed, but I saw him branding cows, the LaRue brand atop the Lazy B." She squeezed his hand so hard his knuckles cracked. "He stole Pa's cows."

Ward kept her hand in his while he reached for his hat. "Let's get the sheriff."

"You can. I need to catch up to Little Mo. I sent him back home to tell Pa—"

"I'll tell the sheriff," Mother announced. "You two hurry. And. . .God bless you."

He'd never heard the words out of her mouth before. "I love you, Mother."

"Love you too, son. Now go."

Fortunately, he'd left Oro saddled when he took his lunch break. Within moments, he and Georgie were riding out of town. At the fork in the road to LaRue's place, Ward pulled Oro's reins. "Maybe we should wait for the sheriff."

The last word wasn't out of his mouth before the crack of a gunshot pierced the air, followed by the high-pitched scream of a child.

In tandem, Ward and Georgie dug their heels into their horses' flanks and rushed down the road to LaRue's. There would be no waiting for the sheriff now.

Chapter 8

Little Mo.

She'd meant to protect him by sending him off to inform Pa, a way he knew well, but he'd clearly wandered back to LaRue's property.

Now LaRue was shooting at him. If anything happened—

No. Pray before you panic.

She'd just begun asking God's help when Little Mo, on his own two feet instead of on Smoky, ran around the bend, his features stricken. She pulled up Fly and was on the ground in a moment, pulling Little Mo into her arms. "Are you hurt?"

Panting, he shook his head. Ward joined them, wrapping his arms around both of them.

"What are you doing here?" Georgie checked her brother for wounds. "I told you to go home."

"I saw Josh and told him to tell Pa so I could watch the cows, but Mr. LaRue saw me and shot at me for trespassin'."

Ward's hands fell away. "I think we'd better get out of here."

Too late. Silas LaRue jogged around the bend, shotgun in hand, hatred curdling his features. "You spyin' Bridges! Get off of my land."

Ward lifted Little Mo onto Oro's back and climbed up behind him. "We're going."

But the sheriff would be here in their stead, and Georgie would be waiting for him at the edge of LaRue's property. Or maybe not—hooves pounded around the bend. The sheriff already? But it was Pa, with Evan and Josh, their jaws and shoulders set.

LaRue aimed his shotgun. "I'm within my rights to shoot you. You're all trespassers in the eyes of the law."

Ward snorted. "Not quite, but we're leaving."

"I'm not." Pa's gaze landed on the tears streaking Little Mo's cheeks. "I heard a shot. You aim at my boy, LaRue?"

Any other man would have cowered at the tone in Pa's voice, but LaRue took a step forward. "A warning. I could've hit 'im if'n I'd wanted to."

Georgie gasped. "He's a child."

"Who's spyin' on me and my business."

"My animals are my business." Pa's gaze fixed on LaRue, but one of his hands discreetly urged the others behind him. Ward stared at Georgie with an expression of fierce protection. Once she moved, he scuttled Oro backward, placing himself between her and LaRue, shielding Little Mo with his body all the while.

"They're my cows, but if I sold some o' your animals out from under you, Bridge, it'd serve you right. It ain't fair, you earning a big profit while some of us flounder." LaRue kept shouting while she, Ward, and her brothers moved away. Pa inched back, too, but the way LaRue was yelling about fairness sent a scuttle of icy fear down her spine. Would his finger slip on the trigger?

What had Pa always said about a cornered animal? That's when they're the most dangerous.

Lord, I don't want anyone hurt. Only You can diffuse this situation. I trust You, Lord. With this, and with Kim and Ma and the baby. And with Ward too. Seeing him now, protecting Mo with his body, I'm afraid I'll lose him. Lord, this is so hard, but Thy will be done.

"It ain't fair!" LaRue pulled the trigger. The sound of the blast made her jump and the horses hobble. For one heart-stopping moment, Georgie couldn't breathe, couldn't move anything but her eyes. Her gaze scanned Ward, then her brothers and Pa, for signs of injury.

"Daddy, stop it!" Marceline rushed around the bend and tugged his arm.

More hooves pounded behind them, and then Sheriff Bly and Deputy McPhee joined them. "Who's shootin' who?" Bly bellowed.

Marceline tugged her father's arms down so the gun was aimed at the earth. "I have to tell the truth, Daddy."

"The truth is that boy kidnapped you."

"I lied because I didn't want you whupping me over it."

LaRue's face purpled and he let loose a string of foul language. Ward covered Little Mo's ears.

"I know you don't approve, but I want to marry Kim. He's the only one for me."

"What about Abner Hock?" Georgie couldn't resist. Ward eyed her, his brow quirked as if she was pushing things, asking such a question. But his lips twitched.

Marceline groaned. "He's Daddy's choice. Not mine. Daddy told Abner I'd go to the Founder's Day dance with him. I knew Daddy wouldn't let me marry Kim, but I don't care anymore. I will be Mrs. Kimball Bridge, no matter what anybody says."

Georgie wasn't sure it would happen anytime soon, considering Marceline's testimony put Kim in jail.

"Seems to me we should set Kimball free." Sheriff Bly dismounted.

Georgie's heart cheered. Pa exhaled. Little Mo pumped his fist in the air, almost knocking Ward's hat off.

Ward settled his Stetson back on squarely and held up his hand. "Did you receive my message, Sheriff?"

"Your ma was most insistent, Harper. Said something about LaRue stealing Bridge's stock, but I wasn't sure she was, er, sober." He rubbed the back of his neck.

"She is, and she told you true." Ward slowly dismounted and moved toward the sheriff. "Moses and Georgia saw LaRue rebranding Bridge stock. We allege additional animals were taken, but they've already been sold."

He looked to Georgie, who nodded. "They're on the southern edge of his property, right by the creek."

"And he moved them so they're mingled with other cows," Little Mo shouted, his chest puffing out. "I was watchin'."

LaRue blanched. Then lifted the shotgun and aimed at Pa. Ward leaped toward him and shoved it out of his hand, knocking it to the ground. "Enough."

Sheriff Bly gripped LaRue's wrists. "Good thing Harper stopped you, or we'd be adding attempted murder to the thievin' charges against you. Come on."

Georgie was off her horse and hugging her family before Sheriff Bly could fix the metal cuffs around LaRue's wrists. Her brothers hurried off to find the cows, accompanied by Deputy McPhee and Marceline. Then Ward was before her, smiling, his arms opening to embrace her.

Pa's hand thrust between them, poised to shake Ward's. "Thank you. From the bottom of my heart. We owe you more than just the fee."

"Thank you, but I don't want a dime." His gaze fixed on Georgie, his warm expression unleashing a swarm of butterflies in her belly.

"I insist. You're keeping Oro too." Pa clapped Ward's shoulder. "I saw how you shielded Little Mo and Georgie, and you protected me, knocking the gun away from LaRue—we owe you our lives. And of course I can't forget how you've helped with Kim. I never would've guessed the case would be solved this fast. By you, of all people."

Georgie's stomach clenched hard as a stone, and Ward's smile fell. "Because I'm a Harper?"

Understanding dawned then, leaching Pa's face of color. "Because I've known you since you were a boy. A little boy who played marbles on my porch—that's what I meant." He gulped. "Georgie told me you overheard my foolish comments five years ago. It was the drinking I objected to more than your pa as a person, but I failed to say so, and I shouldn't have gossiped about it. I hate that I didn't keep the matter private, and I hate that you heard it. I'm sorry."

Georgie's chest ached. Grateful as she was for Pa's apology, would it help now? The hurt Ward had harbored all these years etched his face.

But Ward's hand extended for another shake. "Thank you, sir."

"Forgive me?"

"I do. And I hope you can forgive me for holding it against you all this time."

Pa pulled Ward into a hearty embrace. "You were part of our family then. I hope you'll be as close again."

At Pa's release, Ward's eyes went wide. "Sir?"

"I need an attorney on retainer, and you're the finest in the county, if I may say so."

"I say so." Georgie's hands clasped under her chin.

"You've got quite a supporter in my daughter," Pa said as Evan and Deputy McPhee jogged toward them.

Evan whipped off his hat and waved it in a beckoning gesture. "We found 'em, Pa. Fresh brands over the Lazy B. Come on."

Pa stepped away to join them but glanced back at Ward. "Come for supper tonight. Bring your mother."

Georgie heard what Pa didn't say with words—he wanted to care for those Ward cared about, and to help Mrs. Harper, if he could. She didn't think her heart could swell any larger in her chest than it was right now.

But it did, when Ward reached for her hand.

"These past five years, I never thought I was worthy of working for your family, much less being a part of it."

Georgie couldn't hide her feelings any longer. She reached to cup Ward's cheek. "Now I know why you left. You thought we couldn't stay. . .friends."

He squeezed her hand. "Come for a walk with me."

Georgie's pulse beat hard and fast in her throat as she and Ward strolled into the shade of the oaks lining the road. The air was scented with mesquite and sage, and Georgie took long, deep breaths of it to calm her. If her heart kept beating like this, she'd never be able to tell Ward what she'd wanted to tell him for so long.

He drew them to a stop under a large, leafy branch.

Sweet sweet I'm so sweet.

He looked up. "One of Mr. Norwood's warblers?"

It was. A splotch of buttery yellow flashed through the leaves of a neighboring tree. Georgie pointed, hoping her voice would work. "I like how they sing."

It worked well enough. If only she'd thought of something better to say—

"I like how they say *you're sweet*." His smile for her curled her toes. "You're sweet."

"No, they say *they're* sweet. Not *we're* sweet. And I'm not sweet."

"I say you are. I always thought so." He swallowed so hard his Adam's apple jerked against his starched collar. "Remember when you were thirteen and we saw those javelina piglets, and you thought it would be a good idea for us to tame them?"

The surprising topic made her laugh. "They're adorable."

"Maybe, but wild pig teeth are long and sharp." He stared at her hand. "I would've done anything for you. Except, maybe, adopting javelinas. But you were as adorable as the babies, and I knew I loved you then."

There went her heart again. "Oh."

"I was afraid to lose you, but I garnered up the courage to ask you to the Founder's Day dance five years ago. I hoped to kiss you when I dropped you home."

Her lips burned. "But then you overheard my pa."

He nodded. "And I left town, hoping I could get into Baylor without applying by the due date, because I knew then I could never have you."

"But I loved you too. When you left, it broke my heart. I thought it had healed up enough, but you came back to Wildrye and my heart started beating in my throat again, all crazy-like."

"In your throat?" His gorgeous eyes widened.

"Long story."

"I hope you'll tell me sometime." His finger traced her neck, as if feeling for her pulse. Finding it, he smiled—a little smugly, too, like he was pleased by his effect on her. "I love you still."

Oh. "I love you too."

His eyes darkened. "I could sing like a yellow warbler about your sweetness."

Her lips twitched. "All right then, go ahead."

He laughed. "Or maybe I can find some other way to tell you how I feel. Put my lips to different use."

Then he wasn't laughing anymore. His gaze fixed on her mouth again.

"Like what?" she managed to whisper as he lowered his head.

His tender kiss answered far better than words.

When he eventually pulled away, Georgie couldn't focus for a full ten seconds. "Well, that was worth waiting for."

"So is this." Taking her hands, Ward stared into her eyes. "I've been gone five years and back a few days, so I'd like to court you, proper-like, but you should know my intentions. I want you to marry me, Georgie. You're my best friend, my first love, and my last love. Would that be all right?"

She didn't even have to think. "Oh, Ward! Yes!"

Then he was kissing her again, with far more fervor than she could ever have imagined.

"There," Little Mo's voice intruded in her ear. "She said yes. Can we go get Kim now?"

"Yes, son, now. And surprise your ma."

Ward flushed. "Uh, sir, I'd like to speak to you—"

Pa laughed. "Welcome to the family, son. See you at supper."

"Welcome to the family," Georgie whispered. And she sealed it with a kiss.

Epilogue

Three months later

Once upon a time, Georgie asked for a new mama and a baby brother. God gave her the mama and four brothers, and late on the night of her and Ward's first kiss, God gave her two baby sisters. Ma's pacing that day had been more than anxiety; it had been the early stages of labor.

Georgie's baby sisters now snuggled together in their basket, wearing identical white, lacy gowns.

Standing in the church vestibule with her family and Alejandra, Georgie chucked both of the twins' chubby cheeks. "You'll be the prettiest girls at the wedding."

"Not quite." Pa wrapped his arm around her. "You're a beautiful bride, Georgie."

"Oh, Pa."

Ma adjusted the old Spanish lace of Georgie's veil, last worn by Georgie's mother, Paloma. "He's right."

"Thanks, Ma."

"We're so happy for you, sweetheart." Ma kissed her cheek before eyeing her four boys. "It's time. Kim, carry Martha and Elaine into the church, please."

Kim hoisted the basket carrying his baby sisters, named for Pa's precious great-aunt and Ma's mother. They were his "best girls," as he called them, and he didn't seem interested in any other females at the moment. Marceline had left town to live with an aunt, and while Kim had forgiven her, he had no desire whatsoever to marry her anymore.

He winked at Georgie. "You look good, sis."

"Yeah," agreed Evan.

"Nicer than usual," Josh said with a shrug.

"Thanks, fellas." Georgie rolled her eyes.

"I think you look beautiful." Little Mo hugged her waist.

She dropped a kiss atop his slick-backed hair. "You do too. I like your tie."

"I don't." Little Mo tugged the offending blue silk at his throat and then took Ma's hand. "Come on."

Alejandra handed Georgie her bouquet of pink flowers before the familiar bridal tune sounded from the organ at the front of the church. Pa took her arm. "Ready?"

She'd been ready for years. They followed Alejandra into the church.

Uncle Fred and Aunt Delia smiled at her. So did Mr. Norwood. Mrs. Harper beamed from her perch in the front row, her favorite spot since choosing to turn her life over to God. The road to sobriety had been difficult, but she was relying on God for strength. Ward had been an incredible support.

Georgie returned her smile but couldn't hold back any longer from looking fully at her groom. Handsome in a new blue suit, Ward stood between Diego and the preacher, watching with eyes that told her without words how much she meant to him. How much she'd always meant to him.

A quick kiss on Pa's cheek, and then she took Ward's warm hands in hers. There was no hesitation when she spoke the old, beautiful vows. They prayed, they listened to a homily about placing God first in their marriage, and at last Ward slid a slender golden band on her finger. The preacher pronounced them husband and wife.

She couldn't hold back a smile. "Ready to start our lives together, Mr. Harper?"

His lips twitched. "First things first, Mrs. Harper."

What had she missed? They'd exchanged vows. She wore his ring. They'd prayed. His gaze fixed on her lips—

Oh.

He lowered his lips to hers in a kiss.

First things first, indeed.

Author's Note

I hope you enjoyed reading about Georgie and Ward's second chance at romance! It was a treat for me to return to Wildrye, Texas, the fictional home of the Bridge family, first introduced in *For a Song* in *The Cowboy's Bride Collection*. Georgie was four years old in that story, and it's been a delight to spend time with her again.

Susanne Dietze began writing love stories in high school, casting her friends in the starring roles. Today, she's the award-winning author of a dozen new and upcoming historical romances who's seen her work on the ECPA and Publisher's Weekly Bestseller Lists for Inspirational Fiction. Married to a pastor and the mom of two, Susanne lives in California and enjoys fancy-schmancy tea parties, the beach, and curling up on the couch with a costume drama and a plate of nachos. You can visit her online at www.susannedietze.com and subscribe to her newsletters at http://eepurl.com/bieza5.

A Most Reluctant Bride

By Cynthia Hickey

Woe unto them that are wise in their own eyes,
and prudent in their own sight!
<small>ISAIAH 5:21</small>

Chapter 1

Ozark Mountains, Arkansas
1880

O h, Cricket." Margaret Spoonmore, or Maggie, as she insisted everyone call her, leaned her forehead against the white patch on her horse's head. "Mama has yet another pompous, stuffed shirt coming to supper tonight. What do you say we run away together, you and I?" She'd much rather live alone with her horse than marry a man she didn't love.

Cricket nickered and turned to her feed. Obviously, Maggie's only true friend in the world had other things to do than listen to her whining. Sighing, Maggie pushed away from the stall and headed for the house, nestled among the cottonwoods.

She remembered the day Pa moved her and Mama in. He'd been so proud. Ten years of building up his ranch of quarter horses in a rich, Ozark mountain valley, then like a whiff of wind, heaven called him home, and Mama wanted Maggie married off. Life wasn't fair.

"Margaret!" Mama stood on the front porch, hands cupped around her mouth, and yelled.

"I'm here. No reason to holler."

"Mr. Mason will be here soon and you're still in your riding clothes." Mama scowled then pointed inside. "Go get dressed. You know I'm dying. I've got to get you married before the Good Lord has me join your Pa."

Maggie rolled her eyes. A bit of indigestion last month and Mama had thought herself on death's door ever since. The doctor plainly said she was as healthy as a horse. She giggled. As a woman who constantly had to watch her weight, Mama had taken offense at the comparison and pouted for days.

"Zacharius is coming by later to look at Bullet. I've asked him to wait until after our guest leaves." Mama followed her up the stairs. "I do hope you can escort him to the barn."

"Unchaperoned? Mercy, Mama." Maggie grinned. "How scandalous."

"Hush. The man was clear when he stated he had no notions regarding you."

"That was five years ago, Mama. I was a child." Still, her face heated every time she remembered the humiliation of *her* trying to steal a kiss from the mountain's most handsome young man. Since then, she'd avoided Zach like the black plague. Now, her mother wanted her alone with him? Could the day get any worse?

Yep. Mama laid out her pink ruffled dress. "It makes me look like a child."

"Men like women in frilly things, dear. Stuff the bodice if you want more curves." With those embarrassing words, she strolled out of the room.

Well, Maggie refused to wear such an atrocity. She marched to her wardrobe and pulled out a dress of deepest green. One with a simple bodice and full skirt. A dress complimenting her dark hair and fair skin, one that made her feel pretty. Yes, she was petite, more thin than not, but she wasn't going to put on false airs for anyone.

She donned the dress and put her hair up in a fashion her mother would approve of and headed downstairs. A knock sounded on the door. Squaring her shoulders, she greeted their guest for the evening.

The banker's nephew. She hadn't known his name, only his face, as someone pointed him out at church last Sunday. The man was barely taller than Maggie's five foot two and almost as round. Shifty eyes like a weasel's ran over her.

"Miss Spoonmore. You do look a vision." He removed his felt hat and bowed.

"Thank you. Please come in."

"Thank you." He glanced around the foyer. "Nice home. *I* can make it better."

"Excuse me?" Maggie froze.

"Why, didn't your mother tell you?" His eyes widened. "My uncle will remove the loan on this house. . .paid in full. . .on the day we say our vows."

Mama was selling Maggie like a prize colt? She wouldn't get away with it. Maggie was taking Cricket and making good on her promise to run away. "I, uh, fear I have a terrible headache. Please accept my apologies." She hiked her skirt above her ankles and thundered to her room.

She'd just thrown herself across her bed when her mother barged in. "You are embarrassing me."

"Don't you think you should have let me in on your little secret?" Maggie rolled over and glared. "I wasn't aware we had a loan on the ranch, much less that I was a bargaining chip!"

"Don't be so melodramatic. We all have to do things we don't want to do to make it in a man's world."

"I won't." She kicked her legs, very aware she was behaving like a child. "You're selling Pa's legacy."

"Seriously. Get up. Zacharius arrived early. In the meantime, I'll pacify Mr. Mason. But. . ." She tapped Maggie on the head. "You will go through with this marriage. I'm tired of your silly games, and I want *off* this mountain."

Tears rolled down Maggie's cheeks. Pa hadn't been dead a full year, and Mama was already giving up. Sure, it was tough running the ranch themselves, but they had good help and had placed an advertisement in the paper for a new foreman. It was only a matter of time before things got easier. Mr. Mason didn't look the ranching type. He'd most likely sell off the stock and the land to pad his bank account.

"Margaret!"

Maggie sighed and pushed off the bed, quickly redressing in her riding clothes. A barn was not the place for a nice dress. Especially since Maggie intended to leave at the first opportunity. She tossed a few things into a small fabric bag and rushed outside before Mama could ask questions.

She tried to skid to a halt to avoid a collision with the man on the porch. Instead, her feet slipped. She slammed into his broad back. They both fell to the packed clay ground, her on top of him, as they rolled.

Zach Colton grinned up at her. "Well, hello to you too. It's been a long time, Maggie. I can't imagine a better greeting."

Mercy. She scrambled to her feet, trying unsuccessfully to pat her hair into place. "My apologies." Nose in the air, face flaming, she headed for the barn.

Maggie Spoonmore sure had grown up pretty. When she'd try to kiss him when she was no more than fourteen, he'd been flattered. . .and too old at twenty. But now, they were both adults. Maybe he could rethink things a bit. He always did have feelings for her.

He followed behind her, trying not to notice the gentle sway of her split skirt as she marched, head up, to the barn. He definitely couldn't think of her as a little girl anymore.

"Bullet is in here." Maggie opened a stall door, then tossed a bag into the neighboring one.

"What's in the bag?"

"My business." Avoiding his gaze, she pulled a harness from a nearby hook, then placed it on the horse. "She should've foaled two days ago."

Zach's steps faltered as he followed her. "I'm not an animal doctor."

"Then why did Mama send for you?" She glanced over her shoulder.

He shrugged. "I thought you'd know."

Her dark eyes flashed. "All I know is Mama is trying to marry me off." Her gaze roamed over him. "Unless you've money I don't know about, she wouldn't have sent for you as a possible suitor." She tilted her head. "Perhaps you should go ask her why you're here, while I put the mare back."

"I can at least look at her." He ran his hands over the horse. Definitely ready to have her little one. "My guess is you'll have another to add to your herd by the week's end. She seems healthy enough. I wouldn't worry." He straightened. "I'll go see what your mother needed. Will you be here when I return?"

"Probably not." She led the mare back to her stall. "It was nice seeing you again, Zach."

Confused, and a bit hurt by her cold shoulder, he tipped his hat and headed for the house. What put the pained look in Maggie's eyes? She resembled a dog, kicked and unwanted, left next to the road. If it wasn't improper, he'd have gathered her in his arms, just for a moment, and reassured her that whatever her problem was, God was capable of handling things.

He knocked on the front door as hoofbeats pounded the ground behind him. He turned in time to see Maggie on a red horse, her dark hair flying loose behind her, racing across the pasture.

"Where is my daughter going?" Mrs. Spoonmore joined him on the porch.

"I have no idea." He removed his hat. "Ma'am. I'm a mite confused as to why you asked me here. If it's in regard to the pregnant—"

"Pregnant? No. I've a litter of kittens I need disposed of before Maggie wants to keep them all. I thought perhaps that big place you work for might want some to keep away rats."

"Maybe one or two, but not a whole litter. Why send for me? Why not have one of your hired men take care of them? I'm sure, if they were taken to town, a good home could be found."

"Fine, it was an excuse to get you here." She put her hands on her hips. "My daughter is headstrong and stubborn. The two of you used to be friends. You looked out for her. I know you made a promise to my late husband, and I need your help finding her a spouse. I want to go back East. I'm sorry for the lie, Zacharius, but I really don't know what else to do."

"Have you told Maggie you want to leave?" She'd asked him to come so he could help her find a husband for Maggie? The woman was minus a peg or two.

She shook her head. "She wouldn't listen if I did. She's set on this place, but we're in financial straits. If we don't come up with several months' payment, we'll lose everything."

Zach stared at the porch floor under his feet. He had enough funds set aside now to purchase a bit of land for himself. It should be enough to help the Spoonmore's, but it would set him back a few years, and at the age of twenty-five, it was time for him to settle down. He could loan them the money, but if they weren't able to repay the bank. . .

Mrs. Spoonmore stared across the darkened land. "It's not safe for a willful girl to be out alone this late. Will you fetch her back? We can talk more when you return."

"Yes, ma'am." He set his hat back on his head, grateful for the opportunity to have time to think over how he could help his neighbors.

He unlooped his horse's reins from the porch railing and jumped into the saddle. Maggie couldn't have gotten too far ahead of him. He set off in the direction she'd gone, as thunder rumbled overhead.

He glanced at the thickening clouds and rode faster. Getting drenched wasn't on his list of favorite things, nor was chasing after a wayward girl.

Squinting, he made out a riderless horse ahead. He stopped and slid from his horse. As the clouds released their burden, his heart stuttered. "Maggie!"

"I'm here." She hobbled from behind a bush. "Cricket never did like thunder. She shied, and I fell off, turning my ankle." She shoved soaking strands of hair from her face. "There's a hunter's shack, just past the tree line, if you want to fetch the horses."

"Are you all right? Do you need me to carry you?" Zach tried to assess her injuries through the dark.

"I'm fine. Come on, before we both catch a chill."

"We should really head back."

"You can. I'm not going back."

He sighed and followed her, knowing he was going to regret coming after her. "Why not?" he asked, the moment they stepped into the shack, leaving the poor horses tethered outside in the storm.

"Mama is trying to find me a husband. I won't have it." She plopped onto the dirty floor, organizing her wet skirt around her.

"Where will you go?" He squatted next to her and stared into a face so pretty, it took his breath away.

"I don't know." She pushed her wet hair from her face. "I'll find work somewhere."

He turned her chin with his forefinger until her gaze met his. "I'll marry you." At the fire flashing in her eyes, he immediately regretted his impulsive proposal.

Chapter 2

Her eyes widened then narrowed. "Why would you marry me?" He couldn't be serious. Unless Mama had gotten to him too. "We hardly know each other, anymore." Pulling free, she got to her feet and tested her ankle. Good enough.

Why would the very same person, who'd laughed at her proposal of marriage five years before, now think getting hitched was the answer? She shoved open the door that barely hung by a worn leather hinge.

"Stop, Maggie." His soft request halted her progress to the door.

She turned, her gaze searching his face. "What?"

"Don't you see? We've spent the night together, alone, here."

"So?" She swished her skirts and headed to climb on Cricket.

"Your reputation is going to be ruined." He jogged after her. "There is no way your mother is going to let us off the hook. Besides, I made a promise to your father, a promise your mother reminded me of last night."

Her hands stilled as she grasped the saddle horn. She pressed her forehead into the saddle and closed her eyes, dreading what she was about to hear. "What sort of promise?"

"I told your father I would make sure you and your mother were cared for." He stepped close enough behind her, she felt his body heat. "She told me of your troubles with the bank. I have enough money to keep you from losing your ranch."

"And gain a ranch for yourself in the process—as my husband?" It would save them from losing everything. But why hadn't Mama told her they were in trouble?

Could Maggie marry a man who didn't love her? The very same man who broke her young girl's heart? If it would save what her father worked so hard to build, then. . . "Yes, I'll marry you."

Without glancing back, she climbed into the saddle and headed Cricket toward home. She no longer had a need to run. She'd trapped herself in the very act of trying to be free from her mother's plans.

They rode back to the ranch in silence. When Maggie slide from her horse's back, Zach told her he would take care of the animals and meet her inside when he'd finished.

She nodded, glancing up to see her mother, high spots of color on her cheeks, standing in the doorway. "Explain yourself, young lady."

"I needed to get away and sort out my thoughts." Maggie stormed past her.

"That's the most childish thing I've ever heard, and me knocking on death's door. Why, my nerves alone could kill me. You know how fragile I am."

"Mama, please. I need to get out of these clothes." Maggie closed her bedroom door and leaned against it. She was acting childish. Her life felt as if it were spinning out of control, and she was powerless to do anything to stop it. And now Zach had come to her with a proposal like nothing she'd ever dreamed of.

She threw herself across her bed and sobbed. *Oh, Pa, why did you have to die?* Anger toward God for taking away the one person who loved her unconditionally tugged at her.

"Margaret." Her mother knocked on the door. "I need to speak to you about your behavior."

"I'll be out in a few minutes." She wiped her face on her sleeve, then disrobed and wiped the grime from the night away in the washbowl. She dressed in a simple, everyday dress in a dark rose color. She knew Mama hadn't quite gotten over Pa's death and wanted only the best for Maggie, but sometimes her wanting Maggie constantly at her side was a bit stifling. She pinned her hair into a bun and shuffled downstairs. The only person who will be happy after the announcement Zach and she were about to give would be Mama.

"Ready?" Zach met her at the foot of the stairs.

"I suppose." Her gaze flicked to his fresh-washed face and slicked-back hair. He was dreadfully handsome. She wasn't sure her heart could take a loveless marriage to a man like Zach.

"Are you sure you want to accept my offer?" he asked.

Her gaze studied his blue one. Oh, how she loved his eyes. For five years, she'd managed to avoid being nearby when he visited her father. Now, she was marrying the young man she'd fallen in love with, in what seemed a lifetime ago. Was she sure? No. Nor did she see any other recourse. "I'm sure. Let's go make Mama deliriously happy."

"What about you, Maggie? I feel as if you're the one along for the ride. Will marrying me take away your dreams?"

"My dream is to have a successful horse ranch. Marrying you helps me accomplish that." She turned away, her heart breaking at the tenderness in his eyes. He shouldn't worry about her feelings. He was the one marrying a woman he didn't love. Oh, these mountains were full of beautiful women who would give their right foot for Zach to love them. And here Maggie was. . .keeping him from true love because the silly man felt an obligation.

She wasn't only childish, she was selfish, and needed to put a stop to this right now. "Zach, I don't—"

"It's about time." Mama met them in the foyer. "There's coffee and biscuits in the parlor. Come." She waved them in.

Zach put his hand on the small of Maggie's back, burning his imprint into her skin, and guided her into the parlor, Mama's favorite room, full of frilly doilies and knick-knacks. Maggie always felt like a runaway horse threatening to shatter everything each time she entered. This time was no different.

Maggie perched on the edge of an upholstered wingback chair and waited for Zach to inform Mama of their upcoming marriage.

Zach regretted his impulsive proposal the instant hurt reflected in the depths of Maggie's dark eyes. He'd almost retracted it, but marriage to her benefited them both. He could save her ranch and gain ownership of one well past the beginning stages. He could think of worse things than being married to a strong, capable, beautiful woman like Margaret Spoonmore.

He sat in the chair nearest Maggie, noticing she'd avoided the couch big enough for two. He leaned forward, his hands dangling between his knees, and glanced at Mrs. Spoonmore, as she began speaking.

"I'm not sure I know exactly how to act to the two of you being gone all night." She wrung a handkerchief in her hand. "I know it was storming, but for the sake of my daughter's reputation, I would've thought a gentleman, such as yourself, would have braved the weather to bring her home."

"Ma'am, if I may." Zach straightened. He wasn't going to waste time explaining away such ridiculous thoughts, nor would he have risked either of the horses breaking a leg in the storm to prevent what people might believe. "I proposed to Maggie this morning, and she accepted. Now—" He held up a hand when she opened her mouth to speak. "Not because anything improper happened between us, but because I have the means to help you."

She stiffened. "How so? I'm quite aware that my husband thought the world of you, Zacharius, but what the Spoonmores need now is money."

"Which I have. I had planned to purchase land of my own, but it should be enough to catch you up on your payments. I'll transfer my attentions to the Lazy S, rather than start a ranch from the bottom."

"That's wonderful news, isn't it, Margaret? Our problem is solved. And you don't need to marry a stranger." She dabbed her hankie at the corner of her eye. "You are an answer to a prayer, Zacharius. I'll begin wedding plans, this instant." She stood and hurried from the room.

Maggie's eyes widened. "I guess I don't get a say in that either. Coffee?" She reached for the pot.

"Thank you, but I'm capable." He didn't want her to think she had to wait on him, hand and foot, just because they were to wed. He knew she'd prefer to continue working with the horses, rather than stay in the house as her mother did. "Nothing will change, Maggie."

Her hand shook as she poured the coffee, spilling some onto the tray. "Everything will change. I will no longer be Margaret Spoonmore. I'll be Margaret Colton. I'll no longer have majority say in the running of this ranch. You will. Then, there's the, uh, sleeping arrangements."

Heat rose up his neck. "That isn't necessary. I'm aware you're marrying me out of necessity."

"Well, that's something." She ducked her head, but not before he saw the sheen of tears in her eyes. What had he said to hurt her feelings? He never had known how to act around her, not even when she was younger. Even then, she'd had a beauty and confidence that left him flustered and tongue tied.

She handed him a mug. "Sugar?"

He shook his head and grabbed a biscuit. "I'll leave any ground rules for our marriage to you."

"Rules?" She frowned. "There aren't any. You say nothing will change, so that's it. You'll live here, rather than there. My name changes, and little else. We'll settle into a routine of sorts, I imagine, as we figure out who does what better than the other."

"You make it sound like a business proposition."

"Isn't it?" She quirked a brow. "We both want something, and you found a solution."

He sighed and raised his mug to his mouth, immediately regretting the effort to hide as the hot liquid scorched his tongue. He set the mug on the table in front of them. "When do you want to have the wedding?"

"A week from this Sunday," Mrs. Spoonmore said, breezing into the room. "We'll have a simple ceremony after church. Then, we'll have a reception here. The next day, I'll be on my way to Boston."

"Boston?" Maggie's head jerked toward her mother.

"I want to go home. These mountains have never been my home, and now that your father is gone, they definitely won't be. I want to spend the rest of my days in relative peace and comfort."

How much more peaceful could it get than in the mountains, where a person's nearest neighbor was more than a mile away? Zach shook his head as he glanced around the room. As to comfort? Every chair was stuffed, every flat surface covered with some silly thing. Mr. Spoonmore had made sure his wife lacked for nothing. Zach sincerely hoped she took most of the frivolous possessions with her. A man needed room to breathe.

He prayed Maggie didn't love those things as much as her mother did. While he would do everything in his power to make sure his. . .*wife*. . .was happy, he wouldn't toss money out the window either.

He stood. "A week from this Sunday sounds right fine with me. Maggie, may I speak with you on the porch, please?" He held out his hand.

With a surprised look on her lovely face, she nodded and stood, placing her soft hand in his. Once they stepped outside, away from her mother's prying eyes and ears, he said, "I'd like to ask a favor of you."

"Of course." She stared up into his eyes.

"I don't want anyone to know that we aren't marrying for. . .love. No one needs to know it's a marriage of convenience, something that benefits us both."

She took her bottom lip between her teeth and stared across the pasture. After several seconds, she nodded. "I agree. It's best that Mama leave feeling as if she's done her best toward me, and that there are no ugly rumors floating around this mountain. Thank you, for considering my feelings." She moved back into the house.

Zach stood on the porch thinking he should have said, or done, something more. He turned and saw a man duck around the corner of the house.

Chapter 3

Maggie peered over her glass of water at breakfast, amazed at how quickly Zach had settled into life on the Lazy S Ranch. Two days after proposing, he'd shown up on his horse with nothing but a couple of saddlebags and a determination to get to work.

He caught her looking and winked, wiping his mouth on a napkin. "Do you have time today to give me a tour? We could sit down and divvy up chores."

"Margaret's place is keeping up the house." Mama shook her head. "It's up to you to get the needed work out of the hired help. She's been raised to be a lady."

"Well, ma'am, I pray you don't take offense or get too upset, but Maggie and I are going to turn this ranch upside down. Some of the so-called hired help are going to be let go. If we find we actually need them, we'll rehire. But, for now, we'll do with as few as possible. This means Maggie will have to work by my side."

"I had hoped the man my daughter married would expand the ranch, not run it into the ground." Mama stood, her back as straight as an Arkansas pine tree.

"Sit down, Mama." Maggie set her glass on the table. "Zach is getting a feel for the place. After all, it will soon be his ranch. I agree that we need to be financially secure. Which means no unnecessary spending."

"Is my train ticket back East unnecessary spending?" If her nose got any higher, she'd drown if it rained. Maggie didn't know anyone that would say no to her leaving at that moment.

"Not if that is what you really desire." Her mother had made it very clear the mountains were not the place she wanted to spend the rest of her life. She wasn't dying anytime soon, and might actually realize the fact, once she was back where her heart lived.

It pained Maggie to know she wasn't enough for her mother's happiness. Nor would she be enough for Zach. It seemed Maggie was destined to be merely tolerated for someone else's gain. She sighed and stood. "I'm ready."

Zach motioned for her to go first. "I've done a bit of figuring, if you'd like to sit on the porch a moment."

"Away from Mama's ears?" Maggie smiled.

"No offense, but her decision to purchase a train ticket removed her from the work here." He pulled a wrinkled piece of paper from his pocket. "There is, was, a five-hundred-dollar loan on the ranch. If you go through with the wedding, the loan will be paid off. If not, it will stay in my account."

Her gaze clashed with his. "You think I'm the type of woman to make a promise and then break it?"

"No, I'm stating things as the bank explained them." His mouth twitched. "There was one pompous little fella, by the name of Mason, who couldn't form two words into a sentence, when he found out we were getting married."

"That would be the suitor Mama picked out before our scandalous ride through the rain." She peered at the column of numbers on the paper. "We definitely cannot afford to keep this many men. Who can we let go?"

He sat back, propping his feet on the porch railing. "You don't need a foreman anymore. He's the highest paid. If your chef is willing to cook for the men, then you don't need a bunkhouse cook. I'll have to take a closer look at the other hands and use my best judgment. Do you trust me?"

"Yes, but as the face of the ranch, I'd like to be present when you dismiss the men."

"Understandable. Once this unpleasant business is taken care of, we'll see what else needs doing." He stood and offered her his hand.

Her face warmed under his gaze. Perhaps their marriage could be based on a friendship and partnership. Life could still be quite pleasant for them both. Who needed romance, anyway?

After checking with the house chef as to cooking for a few more, Maggie and Zach approached the bunkhouse. The two men they needed to see sat out front, nursing cups of coffee.

Maggie had never had much to do with the men, leaving them to their own devices when her pa died. She'd kept busy with the breeding stock, something that scandalized Mama to no end. Now, she stood in front of virtual strangers, about to fire two of them.

She wiped her sweaty palms down her dress and squared her shoulders. "Gentlemen, I'm sure you've met my future husband, Zacharius Colton. He is now helping me handle the affairs of this ranch. I regret to inform you that we must release the two of you from your duties, effective immediately."

"I was here when your pa was." The foreman, Frank Stanley, shot to his feet. "I've kept this ranch from folding."

Zach stepped in front of Maggie. "It is my decision, sir. We need to put the ranch first, and I'm capable of being the foreman."

"He's after your money, missy."

"There is no money, Mr. Stanley. That's the problem." Maggie tilted her head. "I'm sorry."

The other man, the chef, known only as Brown because of his thick, dark beard, nodded. "I've been bored anyway. Not much to do when the men are out working. It is best I try to hook on with a cattle drive and get West, where a man can make a new life. No offense here, little lady."

"None taken."

"Well, I take great offense." Stanley removed his hat and slapped it against his thigh.

Maggie shrank closer to Zach, as the other man pulled his gun.

---❦---

"Stand back, Maggie." Zach shoved her away from him, then faced the armed man as he reached for his own gun. "There is no need for this, sir."

"I want this whole month's pay. If I don't get it, I'll shoot one of them horses."

Maggie gasped behind Zach.

Mentally calculating how much money he had in his possession, Zach agreed. "I'll pay you the money, then I don't want to see anything but the back of your head."

"I can live with that."

"Maggie, meet me in the barn, please. Let me settle up with Mr. Stanley." He met her wide-eyed gaze, then led the other man to the tool room off one end of the barn. "Wait here."

He slammed the door in the man's face, headed to his room at the opposite end of the structure, and then pried up the board under his cot. He counted out how much he needed, then replaced the board. He sure prayed things worked out here. Funds were getting mighty short, real fast.

Back outside, by the tool room, Zach shoved the money at the man. "Take this and get out of here. Don't you ever pull a gun on Maggie Spoonmore again. If you do, you'll be the one with a bullet in your gut."

The man smirked. "I was going to shoot *you*." He turned and headed for the paddock.

Once he left the ranch on his horse, Zach joined Maggie. She was petting Cricket's neck, her dark head bent next to the horse's red one, whispering something he couldn't hear. Day and night, he thought. Fire and ash.

She stepped back and wiped her eyes.

"Maggie?" Was she crying? His heart lurched. Something he'd done? Or was it from fear over Stanley's threat?

She turned her head away from him, then straightened and faced him. "You handled that admirably."

"Thank you." He frowned. "You weren't in any real danger. It was me he was mad at."

"I wasn't afraid for myself." She hung a bridle on a hook. "Word will get around that we fired them. You'll need to address the others when they return from their work."

"Then we'd best go over these numbers." He spread the financial paper on an over-turned barrel. "We only need two men to ride the fence. I can take up any slack and train the horses to saddle. If we hire a younger man, a boy, perhaps, we could pay less, until he's older and takes on more responsibility. He can work at cleaning the barn."

She paled. "Get rid of everyone else? Times are hard for most folks around here. I'm not sure I can. The cook was idle most of the time, and Mr. Stanley as lazy as a coon, but these other men work hard. Isn't there another way? I'm capable of keeping the barn clean."

"I'll have to think on it some." He ran a hand through his hair and plucked a twig of straw from a nearby bale. Idly chewing on it, he stared at the ceiling. If they had a way of bringing in immediate funds, they could make do. He'd seen several mares about to foal, and noticed the one Maggie had been worried about the other night had birthed a fine colt.

"Have you considered selling any of the horses?"

She narrowed her eyes. "To whom? The people around here would use them to work their farms and can't afford to spend much. The only buyers would come from back East."

"We could put an advertisement in the papers. Your ranch has some of the finest quarter horses I've ever seen. That white stallion could be used for stud. If you want to keep your workers, we need funds."

"I've used Smoke plenty of times. He's fathered many horses around these parts." She sighed. "But, you're right. Let's go see who I can bare to part with."

They marched, without talking, to the paddock, but Zach's mind twirled like a twister. Once there, Maggie leaned on the top railing, folded her arms, and rested her chin on them. "Who do you think will want one?"

"I was thinking."

She cut him a sideways glance. "I'm starting to believe that every time you think something, I'm not going to like it."

He chuckled, bumping her playfully with his shoulder. "Keep the white stallion, and the five mares who have just given birth, or are about to. We drive the rest to Little Rock to auction. We can get a good enough price to keep us going until we can build the herd back up."

She remained silent for a moment, her attention focused on the horses. "Cricket is mine."

"She isn't part of this." He'd never consider selling her horse.

"Good. Then, we can sell the rest. We'll have the herd back up to ten with the foals. We'll keep any mares, and sell the males. Smoke has several years left in him."

Zach grinned. "Once those people in the city see your horses, you'll have a waiting list for any you're willing to sell from here on out."

"*We'll* have a waiting list." Her eyes lit up for the first time since he'd chased her into the storm. "I haven't been to the city in years. When can we go?"

"How about for our honeymoon?"

Chapter 4

Maggie pinned up the last strand of her hair and leaned forward to peer into the speckled mirror. The new rose-colored dress Mama had sewn complemented the sheen of her dark hair and the softness of her skin. Mama had wanted the dress to be white, but Maggie had put her foot down. A dress needed to be worn more than once, especially with the state of the ranch's finances. White was a frivolous waste of a dress.

It was bad enough they'd be spending precious funds on a so-called honeymoon. She'd almost swallowed her tongue when those words came from Zach's mouth. As if the day hadn't been stressful enough with a gun-wielding fired foreman.

"Don't frown, dear." Mama rubbed between Maggie's eyes. "Mustn't mar the beautiful vision you are."

"Thank you, Mama." Maggie's heart warmed. She wasn't the only one leaving in the morning. Mama would catch a stagecoach, then a train to Boston. Zach said they could drop her off on their way to the city.

"Let's not keep the guests waiting." With Pa's absence, Mama was giving Maggie away. "Pastor said wagons have been arriving since early this morning. You should see the spread of food on the tables in front of the church. I think the idea of changing the reception to the church was a better idea than my first one. Why have everyone troop all the way up here? I think the whole mountain turned out for your wedding."

Maggie's hands started to shake. She'd be nervous enough if she was getting married after a period of courtship, but to marry a man she barely knew anymore? Mercy. She plopped onto a chair. "I'm scared."

"No need. You know all about what goes on between a man and a woman. I've taught you how to run a household. Your father taught you about the horses. What you can't do, Zacharius can."

Maggie glanced up. "That's the first time you've admitted to my knowing how to run this ranch."

Mama shrugged. "I'm quite aware of your skills, daughter, but it isn't something you can do alone. I knew you would never leave this land, so you needed a husband. You could do a lot worse than the man waiting for you outside."

There was no one better than Zach in the entire state. Perhaps, over time, he could learn to love Maggie. When he'd stepped in front of her, putting himself between her and a bullet, she realized she'd never stopped loving him. It broke her heart to know he was only marrying her to own the ranch. Cricket was the only living being she'd confessed her feelings to. Maggie sighed and pushed to her feet.

She and Zach had made a deal. She wouldn't back out now.

Side by side with Mama, clutching a bouquet of wildflowers, Maggie stepped out of the back door of the church and walked a path around to enter through the front door. As a harmonica played from the side of the sanctuary, the doors opened, and she began her journey down the aisle to become Mrs. Colton.

Maggie Colton. She did like the sound. Her lips curled into a smile, which widened at Zach's answering one. Maybe life wouldn't be too bad after all. They were already well on their way to becoming good friends.

Mama stopped a few feet from the end of the aisle and let Maggie move ahead on her own. She kept her gaze glued to Zach's blue eyes. His smile didn't fade, and the twinkle in his eyes remained as they turned to face the pastor.

She was so deep in wishful thinking, she barely heard the vows, responding only as needed. Zach looked happy to be marrying her. Was it possible she'd been wrong about his feelings?

"If any man thinks this man and this woman should not be joined in matrimony," the pastor said, "speak up or forever hold your peace."

Frank Stanley stood in the back pew and cleared his voice. "He's only marrying her for the ranch. I guarantee this is no more than a business deal. Miss Spoonmore is selling herself, same as a prostitute would for a gold coin."

The church filled with gasps.

Zach's smile faded, replaced by fury. "Hold your tongue. There's nothing wrong with a man and woman marrying for mutual gain."

Her hopes of him loving her faded, and tears pricked her eyes. Embarrassment flooded through her, weighing down her shoulders.

"Lift up your head," Zach whispered. "He's only angry because we relieved him of his duties. Never cow before a man like him."

She blinked away the tears and took a deep breath. Zach was right. Mutual gain or not, they were to be wed, and she would show them united.

She stared across the sea of guests. Most looked aghast at Mr. Stanley's announcement, very few seemed to disapprove of Maggie and Zach marrying. "Pastor, please proceed."

Zach's smile returned and they once again faced the preacher.

By the time they were pronounced man and wife, Maggie's nerves had subsided until the words, "You may kiss your bride."

Her eyes widened.

"Relax," Zach said softly. "This won't hurt a bit." He pulled her close and placed a kiss on her lips so tender the tears threatened to start anew. "See?"

She licked her lips and nodded.

"I'm proud to be the first to introduce Mr. and Mrs. Zacharius Colton." The pastor beamed.

The guests stood and clapped. Whistles followed the bride and groom down the aisle. Maggie giggled at the sight of Mr. Stanley standing alone on the edge of the church's lawn. The poor man. Filled with so much anger, he thought he could ruin a girl's wedding.

"Don't you think about it," an elderly woman from farther up the mountain said, patting Maggie's arm. "Don't think on it one bit. Why, I was a girl of thirteen when my daddy married me off to my dear Buford because he needed some hogs. We were married for thirty years before the Good Lord took him home. Oh, how I grew to love that man."

"Thank you." Maggie beamed at her. She glanced to where men surrounded her husband. How strange that sounded.

One by one the women told of tales of marriage before love came into being. Maggie hadn't realized before how many marriages started with nothing more than mutual respect. Hope again leaped in her chest.

"There's the bloom a bride should wear." Mrs. Nelson, the pastor's wife, smiled as she made her way to Maggie's side. "That's one fine husband you have."

"That he is." Maggie stood straighter. "May I ask you a personal question?"

"Of course."

"Did you and the pastor marry for love?"

"Yes." She smiled. "But we were lucky. Don't let Mr. Stanley's words ruin your day."

"What if Zach never comes to love me?"

"Does he treat you well?"

Maggie nodded.

"Does he work hard? Want to provide you with a good life?"

"Yes."

"Then, let God work on both of you." She laid her hand on Maggie's arm. "Things will work out just fine. You'll see."

Tension knotted Zach's shoulders. When Stanley had spoken up, trying to cast a pall over Maggie's reputation, it had taken all of Zach's willpower not to punch the man. The only thing holding him back was the devastated look on Maggie's face.

He was well aware she was only marrying him to save her ranch. He was fine with the idea. Regardless of their reason for getting hitched, he intended to be a kind and courteous husband, putting her needs above his own.

As she'd walked down the aisle toward him, dark eyes wide in a perfect face, hair piled high to reveal a lovely neck, he'd thought himself the luckiest man in Arkansas. Maggie Spoon—uh, Colton, was the prettiest thing he'd ever seen. He would never allow anyone to cause her pain again.

He excused himself from the group of well-wishers and went to fetch his bride. "Are you hungry?"

"Yes, thank you." She slipped her arm through his. "And my face hurts from smiling."

He laughed. "You sure are pretty."

"Oh. Well, thank you, again." She averted her gaze as he settled her at a table, set aside for the two of them.

"Let me serve you, Maggie. Will you?"

Surprise flitted across her face. "But, I'm the wife. I should be serving you."

"Let me do this." He flashed her a grin and went to fill a plate with a little of everything, then made another one for himself with larger portions. When was the last time anyone did something for Maggie?

He wasn't blind. He saw how much she did around the ranch, even refusing for the house help to clear her dishes from the table, and doubted she accepted the help in dressing they offered. There was nothing superficial about Maggie Colton.

Plates full, he carried them back to the table and took his seat next to her. "Are you excited about our trip tomorrow?"

"Actually, yes. It's been a long time since I've been that far from home. But who will watch over things while we're gone?" She picked up a fried chicken leg.

"Horace. He's quite capable. I'm thinking of making him my right-hand man. Rupert is also knowledgeable about the ranch. It's in good hands."

She nodded. "I'd hoped I could do more. I'm not the type of woman to be confined to the house."

"I've no intentions of doing that to you. We're partners, you and I."

She flinched and looked across the crowd. "Right. Partners."

He'd said the wrong thing again. "Would you like me to teach you to break a colt to harness?"

Her eyes lit up. "Yes, please. Pa had promised to before he died, but there wasn't time."

"Then, I will, as soon as we return."

How he hated that word, *partners*. At least in regard to him and Maggie. Once, she'd tagged along behind him every moment she wasn't in school. He'd missed that over the years. Now they were married, he found himself taking back words and finding ways to smooth over the wrong things he said.

Women sure were strange creatures.

"How are you feeling about your mother leaving?" He'd never been one to talk much, but he found himself wanting to know everything Maggie was thinking.

"Sad, really." She set down the cleaned chicken bone. "But, she's never been happy here. She'd stayed because of Pa, not me. Mama isn't the type of woman to put a child above herself. I always thought I'd be different when I became a mother."

Zach almost asked her why she couldn't be a mother, but remembered their agreement. "I think you'd make a wonderful mother."

She shrugged. "Who is coming with us to drive the horses?"

Ah, a change of subject. Good. The other one was dangerous. "Dan. I don't think we need more than three of us."

She nodded, putting a hand to her throat. "It's hard to let them go."

"That's ranching. You can't keep them all."

"I know. It's foolish of me to think so. Pa told me I needed to think like a businessman if the ranch was to succeed. I'm trying."

A fiddle started to play across the way. Zach stood and held out his hand. "Dance with me."

She blinked up at him, her cheeks darkening a pretty shade of pink. She slipped her hand in his and allowed him to lead her onto the dance floor.

Zach had touched her hand before, but putting his hand on her thin waist, feeling the bones and muscles move under his hand, he wanted to rethink their marriage arrangement. A whiff of something floral teased his senses. A breeze blew a strand of hair free from its bun and tickled his face. He risked pulling her a little closer. When she didn't protest, he grinned, and rested his cheek on the top of her head. *Zach, you are one lucky man.*

Soon, the makeshift dance floor filled with others and the fiddle played a faster tune. Zach bit back a groan and spun Maggie into the arms of another. It seemed like an eternity before she was back with him. Then. . .gone again. Stupid dance.

He marched to a table laden with pitchers of lemonade and cider, and scowled at Maggie laughing at something her recent dance partner said. Zach shouldn't care. They were married, but he didn't have the same rights most married men did. While he knew Maggie would respect their wedding vows, he wouldn't begrudge her dancing with someone else. She laughed again. He couldn't bear the torture anymore.

He cut in and pulled her close, glaring at the other man, daring him to protest.

The next song was slow. He swayed in tune with his wife, tilting her face to his, locking gazes. Her dark eyes were like mirrors. What did she see when she looked at him? Did she see a man who loved God? A man who wanted to keep her in the fashion she was accustomed to? Or did she see a man who married her for her ranch?

He suddenly wanted her to see him as her husband. He lowered his head and claimed her lips in a kiss.

Maggie's lips tingled from Zach's kiss. She could think of little else as they rode the wagon home. As often as she could, without getting caught, she cut him sideways glances admiring his strong profile.

She almost regretted her impulsive decision to keep their marriage on a business level. How wanton. Her face heated. If only Mama were easier to talk to. For the first time since she was a child, loneliness assailed Maggie. She'd never been very social, but a dear friend to tell her thoughts and feelings to would be a true blessing right about now.

When they returned to the ranch, while Zach turned over the reins to a hired hand, Maggie avoided his gaze as he guided her up the steps and into the house. His hand on her back warmed through the cotton fabric of her dress.

She glanced up at him. "Good night," she said softly.

"Good night, darlin'." He placed a tender kiss on her lips and headed to his room at the end of the house, leaving Maggie feeling more alone than ever.

Chapter 5

Mama, we have to go now!" Maggie sighed at seeing Zach pacing impatiently next to the horses.

"I just don't understand why I have to ride astride." Mama tugged on a pair of gloves. "I've never gotten used to the idea."

"We don't have side saddles, and all hands are needed keeping the horses in line" Maggie opened the front door. What a way to start a honeymoon. An impatient husband, a complaining mother, and a most reluctant bride.

Maggie stepped onto the porch and held the door open for her mother. "We're ready."

Zach breathed deeply through his nose but didn't say anything. Instead, he took the satchel from Mama's hand and tied it onto the back of his horse.

"It's a good thing you wanted to leave early," Maggie said. "Mama might just catch the stage on time."

Zach mumbled something and turned to help Mama onto her horse, then assisted Maggie. "We're getting a very late start," he said.

He leaped into his saddle, motioned for the hired hand to move forward, and they finally began their trip as the sun signaled ten in the morning. Two hours after Zach had wanted to leave. Displeasure showed in the stiff lines of his back.

By midday, they pulled into the small town of Oak Ridge, where Mama would catch a stage for the first part of her journey. Zach and Maggie went with her mother to the station, leaving the hand to watch the stock.

Maggie's stomach sank as the coach emptied of those not going farther. "I'll miss you, Mama."

"My dear. Times are changing. With the trains, Boston isn't that far anymore. You can come and visit with my first grandchild." She planted a kiss on Maggie's cheek and held out her hand to Zach. "Thank you for making this possible. Take care of our girl."

Maggie's mouth dried as her eyes filled with tears. Mama was leaving her alone. It would be her and Zach, rattling around with no one to talk to but the hired help and the horses. Lord, help her.

Once Mama was on the stage and it rumbled down the road, Zach took Maggie's hand. "You look sad. Let me buy you lunch."

Her gaze locked on his. "Do we have time?"

"We'll make time. It isn't every day a gal puts her mother on the stagecoach." He grinned, flashing dimples.

What would he do if she were to press her lips against one? Would he recoil or pull her close as he had at the dance? She wasn't brave enough to find out. "I'd love a restaurant meal."

They strolled down the wooden sidewalk. A sense of pride washed over Maggie as folks sent them approving glances. She ran her hands down the front of her brown split skirt, then straightened the dark blue blouse. Next to her, Zach wore the same colors, except his shirt was the same marvelous shade of blue as his eyes.

Her foot slipped off the edge of the walk, landing her flat on her stomach in dirt and horse manure. She wanted to bury her face and never get up. This is what happened when a girl thought too much about a man and didn't watch where she was walking—she landed in a pile of poo.

"Are you all right?" Zach helped her to her feet.

"Are you laughing?" She narrowed her eyes.

He shook his head, but the glint in his eyes told her it took tremendous willpower not to guffaw. "You, uh, smell."

"Forget lunch." She stormed past him, trying to hold her soiled blouse away from her. How could she have thought him kind? What sort of man laughs at a woman in her predicament? She shoved open the door to the mercantile and headed for the rack holding a few ready-made articles of clothing. The only blouse was one in the ugliest shade of green she'd ever laid eyes on. A large collar with lace around the edge completed the look.

"I'll take this." She dug a few coins from her pocket. "Is there a place I can change?"

The clerk wrinkled her nose and pointed to a curtained alcove. "Back there. I'll make sure you aren't disturbed."

"Thank you." Battling tears and embarrassment, Maggie stepped behind the curtain and changed her blouse. Thankfully, there was a washbasin handy and she cleaned up the best she could. When she'd finished, she stepped out, not surprised to see a grinning Zach waiting.

She shoved the dirty blouse in his hands. "Dispose of that." Nose in the air, she returned to the sidewalk.

"I'd still like to eat." Zach had rolled her blouse into a ball. "Let me drop this off at the laundry. We can pick it up after we eat."

"I thought you were in a hurry."

"I am, but we have to eat."

She sighed. "Very well." Her stomach growled in agreement.

Zach still seemed to be fighting laughter as he escorted her to the restaurant down the street. Maggie chose decorum and ignored him.

He opened the door for her. "That is an ugly shirt." He grinned.

She growled and entered the restaurant, hiding a grin of her own. Now that her embarrassment had faded, she saw the humor in her situation. Nothing had been injured but her pride. She took a deep breath of baked bread and beef stew.

<hr>

Zach shouldn't have laughed, but once he knew Maggie was unharmed, he couldn't help himself. The sight of her lying in manure, face red, indignation written in every line of her lovely little frame, well. . .the laugh felt mighty good.

The waitress, a plump woman with graying hair, approached the table. "What can I get you?"

"I'll have the stew over biscuits, please." Maggie spread her napkin in her lap.

"The same." Zach sat back in his chair. "Your mother had a lot riding on you getting hitched, didn't she?"

"Apparently so." Maggie shrugged. "I had no idea of our financial straits or that she so desperately wanted to return to the land of her roots. She'd loved Pa, I have no doubt of that, but she isn't a mountain woman."

"You are, though." She seemed as comfortable on the back of a horse as she did in her mother's fancy parlor. A room that seemed out of place among the more simple people of the area. Maggie could wear her hair down like a young girl, which he preferred, or up like a woman of refinement. There were a lot of sides to his wife, and he looked forward to getting to know them all.

"The auction is the day after tomorrow," he told her. "I'd like to have the horses out where they can be seen a few hours before. This is late notice, but would you be willing to ride the black mare around the ring a few times? Let the potential buyers see her in action?"

"She is the best of the bunch." Maggie nodded. "Thank you for letting me be an active part of this. The thought of sitting in the parlor doing needlepoint is enough to make me die of dread." She shuddered.

"That was part of the bargain." He raised his water glass in a toast.

Something flickered across her eyes. An emotion he couldn't decipher. Had he said something wrong again?

The waitress arrived and saved him from having to ask. Instead, he focused on the food in front of him like a starving man. He couldn't hurt the beef's feelings.

When they'd finished, they retrieved Maggie's now clean shirt and headed for the horses. It wasn't until they were riding out of town that Zach realized he'd be sleeping in close proximity with his wife that night. Not only for her protection, but to provide warmth.

This so-called business deal was more trouble than it was worth. He should have married her and taken his rightful role in all things. Then there wouldn't be any of this tiptoeing around delicate subjects.

He watched her as she rode ahead of him, the graceful way she moved as one with her horse. Maggie was no longer a long-legged, freckle-faced little girl. She was now a woman, grown with skin as soft as a rabbit's foot and as blemish free as a newborn babe. He was a lucky man to call her his bride.

When the shadows deepened, he called a halt to the day's ride. "Pull off into those bushes. We'll camp here."

The hired hand, Dan, which he said was his only name, led the string of horses into the brush. "Want me to bunk down with them in case of a cougar? They're prevalent around these parts."

"That's a great idea." Zach dismounted then helped Maggie off her horse. "Can you cook over a fire?"

She tilted her head. "Of course, I can. I'm not helpless." She marched away, dragging a saddlebag with her.

"Boss lady is a bit prickly at times," Dan said.

"Yes, she is. I reckon I'll get her moods figured out, same as I would a horse's."

"I am not a horse!" Maggie's voice carried clearly in the night air.

And, he'd done it again. He'd never get her figured out. She was as sweet as strawberries one minute and like a cactus the next. He should have taken the time to talk to his ma about girls when he had the chance. With her dead ten years now, Zach would have to learn on his own.

By the time the horses were tethered, the aroma of frying bacon and brewing coffee teased his senses and drew him like a bear to honey. He didn't mind breakfast for supper, so long as he had something to fill his belly.

"It's all I know how to cook over a fire." Maggie plopped eggs and bacon onto his and Dan's plates.

Zach would not say a word. Not a single. . . "That's fine. Smells mighty good."

She stared at him for a minute. "Will you say that tomorrow, when you eat the same thing?"

He glanced at Dan then back at her. "Yep." He shoved a spoonful of eggs into his mouth to keep from saying anything else.

Things went from uncomfortable to downright dastardly when it was time for bed. Zach stared down at Maggie rolled in the first blanket and lying on the second. She peered up at him. "What?"

"Those are the only two blankets. It gets cold at night." Surely, she could take a hint.

"We had an agreement."

"I know, but. . .never mind." He curled up next to a saddle, pulled his hat over his eyes, and tried to go to sleep.

Several minutes later, a warm, soft body lay next to him. She rolled up in one blanket after laying the other one over him. It might not be as good as sharing, but it was delightful to have her as close as she was.

With a smile on his face, Zach put his back to hers and fell asleep to the sound of a crackling fire, the soft whinny of one of the horses, and some very unladylike snores from his wife.

Chapter 6

The Little Rock stockyards were a din of activity. Maggie couldn't take in all the sights at once and felt very much like a small child at her first Christmas. Cattle mooed, cowboys shouted, horses whinnied...it was the most exciting thing she'd ever seen. Despite her resolve to not act like a greenhorn, a big grin spread across her face.

Zach whistled, attracting her attention. He motioned for her and Dan to lead the string of horses to a paddock near the center of the auction grounds. "We got here early enough to get a prime spot."

Oh, to think the day would get busier, nosier, smellier. If Maggie's hands weren't occupied holding the reins of her horse and two others, she'd have clapped. She slid from her horse and led the string into the paddock.

"I don't want you going anywhere without me," Zach told her. "I mean it, Maggie. This isn't a safe place for a woman to be alone."

As long as she got to stay around the excitement, she'd promise him anything. "All right." She peered around him as a stallion reared, unseating its rider. Before she could think about not helping, she rushed forward and grabbed the bridle. "Easy, boy. I've got you." She crooned nonsense to him until the animal stopped rolling its eyes and stomping. Its owner rolled free of its hooves.

"Thank you, ma'am." The man dusted off his pants by slapping his hat against them. "Hooey, this horse is too skittish for the auction, I reckon. He about knocked my head in."

Zach reached around her and took over. "You're welcome, sir." He gripped Maggie by the arm and pulled her to the side. "Do you realize how dangerous that was? Did you not hear a word I said mere seconds ago?"

She turned up her nose. "You said not to wander off. You didn't say anything about saving a man's life." She peeled her gloves from her hands.

"You know darn well what I mean." He clenched his jaw. After several seconds of them having a staring contest, he shook his head. "You'll be the death of me, Maggie Colton."

She put her hands on her hips. "Are you going to be one of those husbands that lord it over their wives?"

"No, but I do expect you to be submissive when it's for your own good." His face darkened.

"I think I'm old enough to know what's good for me!" She stomped her foot then marched over to Cricket. Her horse was the only thing on this earth that understood her.

In her mind, she heard her father telling her the only one she could count on every second of every day was God. She didn't want to hear about God. If God cared, he wouldn't have left her alone.

She knew Zach stood close behind her without having to turn around. Ever since she was young, she'd known the moment he entered a room or stepped in sight.

"I'm sorry I yelled at you." He put his hands on her shoulders and turned her to face him. "You scared me. When I saw you approach those flailing hooves—"

"I'm good with horses, Zach."

"I know. It's different now that we're married. I'm responsible for you."

"You are the most infuriating man!"

"You're the most exasperating woman!"

She opened her mouth to rebuke him but noticed the corner of his lips twitch. "Oh, how silly we're being." She glanced around at the gathering crowd and lowered her voice. "We're being watched."

"Then, let's give them something to see." He grabbed her around the waist and pulled her close for a kiss. Once she was breathless, he told the crowd they were on their honeymoon and having their first fight.

"If she was my wife," someone called out, "I'd whoop her for talking back."

"I'd take her off somewhere and make up," another yelled.

Maggie's face grew hot. "May we please go somewhere else?"

Zach kept one arm around her waist and guided her to a nearby hotel above a large mercantile. "I'm sorry about that."

"The kiss was an improper thing to do in public." *Please, don't cry, please, don't cry.* Oh, why did she always cry when mad or embarrassed?

"Darlin', I'll take any excuse I can get to kiss you." He winked and opened the door for her.

Her eyes widened, all thoughts of tears forgotten. Mercy, the man could render her speechless. She stood next to a display of bolted fabric while Zach took care of their rooms. That deep green was rather pretty. But, no, they weren't here to spend money but to make enough to carry the ranch until they had more foals to sell.

Zach's idea was a grand one. Soon, she could hire someone else to make her gowns. If things went as planned, which often didn't happen, they'd live quite well indeed.

"They only had one room," Zach said, standing next to her. "With the auction going on, we were lucky to get it."

"One?" Her throat clogged. She tugged at her collar.

"Don't worry. I'll sleep on the floor." He motioned toward a set of stairs at the back of the store. "I've ordered extra blankets."

She nodded numbly and walked stiffly up the stairs. It would be a repeat of the night before. How would she get any sleep with him lying so close?

Zach rolled his shoulders from his spot on the bench and waited for Maggie to ride the black mare into the ring. Sleeping on the floor, even with two quilts folded under him, had not been kind to his back. He smiled. He wasn't going to complain about spending two nights in a row in close proximity to his wife, though.

He craned his neck as Maggie and the horse appeared. His wife was lovely in a dark blue riding suit. Old-fashioned like he'd seen an Englishwoman wear in a magazine, but it suited her dark hair and light skin.

A hush settled over the spectators as the mare danced into the ring, Maggie sitting proud on her back. She led the horse through a walk, a trot, then a gallop. When she'd finished, the crowd erupted in applause.

Zach grinned. There would be a bidding war for the beautiful horse. He made his way down the stairs to where Dan waited with the other animals. He chose a burnished, red-colored colt and led it into the ring as Maggie exited. He tipped his hat to her and winked, pleased to see a pretty blush on her cheeks.

When they'd taken turns leading each horse into the ring, Zach joined Maggie next to the bleachers. Bidding time. The black mare would be sold first in order to catch the buyers with full pockets.

"Let's start the bidding at fifty dollars."

Dan led the mare into the ring.

"Sixty!"

"Seventy!"

Bids rang through the tent. The crowd erupted when the mare was sold for one hundred and fifty dollars.

"Oh, my." Maggie leaned on the split-rail fence surrounding the ring. "That's unheard of for these parts."

"We'll get fifty or more for each of the foals. Probably seventy each for the other mares." Zach rested a booted foot on the lowest rail. "Not to mention you'll have a waiting list for the stallion."

She faced him. "You had a good idea, Zach."

"Ranching has always been a dream of mine." His fingers itched to caress her cheek. Instead, he folded them on top of the railing and watched as the next foal's bidding started at thirty dollars and sold for sixty. They'd be going home with a hefty bank account. And, he'd purchase that green fabric he saw Maggie admiring.

First thing in the morning, he'd go to a bank and have them take care of transporting the cash to Oak Ridge. Possum Hollow, the poor attempt at a town just a mile from the ranch, didn't have anything more than a mercantile and a rundown saloon. If Zach was a betting man, he'd bet the area would grow once word got around about the Lazy S horses. People would flock there with dreams of striking it rich.

Maggie jumped up and down as the last colt, a dappled gray, was sold. "We're rich."

"Not hardly, but we won't starve, and we have enough to purchase a mare I've got my eyes on."

"If you want to buy a horse, why did we sell ours?"

"Because they sold for far more than this mare will. While this is a fine horse, she has good lines and paired with the stallion will produce fine animals for future sales; she isn't the same caliber of the horses we sold. Right now, money in hand is the most important thing. Come." He took her hand and led her to a line of stalls behind the tent. "There she is."

"Hello, pretty girl." Maggie ran her gloved hand down the dark brown horse's white blaze. "You will make pretty babies." She opened the stall door and ran her hands over the horse's body and down her legs.

Zach couldn't take his eyes off Maggie. He'd give all the money in the coffers to have her touch him like that. He shook off his fantasy. "She's up next. Let's take our seats."

She glanced up in surprise at his gruff voice. "She's a fine horse, Zach."

"Glad you approve." He took her hand again and walked fast enough to cause her to almost run to keep up.

"Zach, please slow down." She yanked free. "What has gotten into you?"

"I don't want to miss the bidding." He was an idiot. Maggie had made her thoughts very clear when they'd agreed to marry. He'd known what he was getting into. It wasn't her fault his ego was shattered. "I'm sorry." He held out his hand for her to take.

She did, her gaze on his. "Let's sit at the top. I want to see everything. Can I do the bidding?"

He'd do anything she asked. "Sure." He handed her the stick with their number painted on it.

"Sixty!" She yelled as soon as the horse entered the ring.

The crowd laughed. A man called out sixty-five.

Zach sighed. "You don't start the bidding, darlin'."

"Oh, my apologies. Seventy-five!" She jumped to her feet.

Thankfully, no one wanted to offer more. "We could have gotten her for ten dollars less if you hadn't been so anxious."

"This is fun. Can we buy another? That stallion we saw yesterday. He would make good breeding stock."

"Storm wouldn't be very happy." Zach mentally calculated what the stallion might go for and decided against it. "No, he'll cost as much as the black mare we sold. We'll let one of Storm's offspring replace him when the time is right."

She shrugged. "Where to now?"

"We pay and collect the mare, get her settled at the livery, and make a deposit at the bank. Then, I'm taking you to supper."

"Mercy, I'm getting spoiled. Two restaurant meals in as many days." Her eyes twinkled.

He tweaked her nose. "We are on our honeymoon, after all." He laughed as she gulped then slowly nodded.

"We aren't heading home until the morning?"

"Nope. You have to sleep in the same room as me for another night." He inwardly groaned, not looking forward to the hard floor.

After a meal of meat loaf, mashed potatoes and gravy, and fresh-baked bread, they took a stroll down the main street of town. Maggie glanced around like a child seeing things for the first time.

Right then, Zach vowed to make sure he always had the means to introduce her to new things. Someday, he'd take her to Europe.

She slipped her arm through his and rested her cheek on his shoulder. "It was a wonderful day. Thank you."

He glanced down. "We'll make it a regular trip whether we have horses to sell or not, if it makes you happy."

"Let's go to Hot Springs next time. I've always wanted to dip my feet in the water, but Mama thought it strange."

"Then Hot Springs it is." He'd make plans for their anniversary.

Chapter 7

Two weeks after their trip to Little Rock, Maggie felt pushed aside and useless. The only times she saw Zach was at breakfast where he focused on a month-old newspaper, and at supper where she was forced to make idle small talk.

It had rained the night they slept in the open on their way home, and ever since they'd shared the blankets to keep warm, Zach had avoided her. Was he rethinking his decision to marry her? He seemed happy enough when working the horses or shoveling hay in the barn. The moment she joined him, his mouth clamped shut like a vise.

She grabbed a broom from next to the door and attacked the dust on the front porch as if it were her mission in life to have a pristine entrance. After all, what else was there for a dutiful wife to do but clean and work in the garden? So much for him keeping his part of the bargain. What fun was it to work outside the house if Zach was going to be surly?

"Ma'am?" Daisy, the chef, came around the side of the house. "A fox has been at the chickens. We lost two egg layers this morning."

"I'll get my gun." Maggie dropped the broom and grabbed her rifle from above the fireplace mantel. Tracking a varmint was something she could do.

With her rifle over her shoulder, she told Daisy to let Zach know where she was when he returned, then jumped off the back stoop and headed for the thick woods. She was happier than she'd been the last two weeks. Finally, a job she enjoyed.

She followed a trail of blood until she found a pile of feathers. The scamp had sat right here and eaten the hen. Maggie glanced around. Tiny paw prints in the thick red clay pointed the way the culprit had gone. She followed them until she reached a creek. At one end a waterfall cascaded over a rock ledge, into a small pool. A trail up the mountain curved around, toward the top.

"Well, that's that," she said. The prints stopped at the water's edge. The rascal had swum across.

Removing her boots, she tied the laces together so she could hang them around her neck and stuffed her stockings inside them. Pulling her skirt between her legs, she tucked the hem into her waistband. She might still get wet, but hopefully not too much.

She hopped nimbly from one rock to the other, only slipping once, and reached the other side with one wet foot. She grinned and put her stockings and boots back on before picking up the fox's trail. Thank goodness for several nights' rain. Still, she lost the trail several feet on the other side of the creek.

She could still set a trap at home. She'd have to be wilier than Mr. Fox, but it wasn't the first time a bushy-tailed critter had come stealing.

A twig snapped to her right. She whirled, bringing her gun around. "No bear!" Her pa had always told her to make noise when traipsing through the woods, but hunting noisily would definitely not result in success if she were trying to shoot supper. "Bear!"

When the sound didn't come again, and feeling very foolish, Maggie headed back toward the creek. A bird shot up from a nearby tree. She froze in her tracks, every hair on her arms stood upright.

Maggie was not alone. She also didn't think her predator was of the four-legged variety.

She splashed across the creek, not taking the time to remove her boots or glance behind her. She could look back when she reached safety on the other side of the creek.

Once there, she hunkered behind some bushes. No one stood on the other bank. Really? Had she ruined a pair of boots for nothing more than skittish nerves? Shaking her head, she stood and untucked her skirt. What a waste of an afternoon.

Maybe she could save what was left of the day by catching a rabbit for a stew. It had been too long since she'd hunted. Mama thought it scandalous for a woman to roam the woods alone. But she wasn't here, and Maggie hadn't even received a single letter. It was as if Mama had forgotten all about her daughter.

As woman of the house, she could pretty much do what she wanted. She wanted to hunt for their supper. Maybe Zach would actually toss a smile her way if she came home with something.

She took extra care with the placement of her feet and skirted the edge of the woods, her eyes peeled for a rabbit in the clearing ahead. A rustling in the brush to her left caused her to hunker down. Eyes and ears peeled, she waited.

There! A rabbit's ears stuck up above the grass.

Maggie aimed to where the animal's body would be, held her breath, and pulled the trigger. Her shot rang across the clearing. The rabbit's ears fell. She'd gotten it. She dashed through the grass and picked up her supper by the ears. "Hello, my friend. Thank you."

With a spring in her step, she headed home, happier than she'd been since returning from the auction. From now on, she'd do at least one thing that brought her joy each and every day.

"Hold it right there, missy. Drop the gun."

Maggie stiffened then dropped the gun. She could see the roofs of the house and barn just over the rise. Maybe, if she yelled—"

"Back up, real slow-like, and turn around."

She closed her eyes, took a deep breath, opened them again and turned to face Frank Stanley.

———⊲⊳———

Zach tossed grain into the last horse feeder, then planted his hands on the back of his hips and stretched, popping the kinks out. His stomach rumbled, reminding him he hadn't eaten since breakfast and now the sun was setting.

He closed the barn doors and headed for the water spigot to clean up. He'd doused his head for the third time when Daisy tapped his shoulder.

"Mr. Colton?"

"Yep." He flung his hair out of his eyes.

"Mrs. Colton left to hunt down a fox, hours ago, and hasn't returned." The woman wrung her apron in her hands. "Supper has long since grown cold."

"Why didn't you fetch me? Which way did she go?" Zach was already moving to the house for his gun. His heart set like a boulder in his stomach. Why hadn't Maggie come to him to hunt the fox?

Because he treated her like a leper, that's why. He couldn't trust himself not to kiss her when she was close. Now, what if she was injured or dying in the woods? He'd never get another chance for a kiss. Any harm that came to her was his fault.

He yanked open the backdoor to the house and raced to his room, where his gun waited on a peg in the wall. He put on the belt and holster and grabbed bullets. "If she shows up while I'm gone, tell her to fire three shots into the air," he said, rushing past Daisy. "Keep the coffee hot."

He saddled his horse and galloped across the meadow, not stopping until he reached the edge of the tree line. "This is where I leave you." He patted the horse's neck, knowing it would still be there when he returned. Traipsing through the forest would be faster on foot, and something told him time was running out for Maggie.

Her tracks were easy enough to follow and led him to the creek, across it, and back and through the forest to a meadow. There they led him to the edge of the trees and stopped. He could see the rooftops of the ranch. Whatever happened to Maggie had happened here.

He studied the ground closely, moving aside leaves with a stick. There. A man's booted footprint. Who would take her? He straightened and glanced around.

The man was good in the woods. He knew how to cover his tracks. Hopefully, Maggie was smarter and would leave a trail for Zach.

Despair filled him as the sun set and cast the woods in inky darkness. There was no way he'd find their tracks in the dark. He raised his face to heaven. "Lord, I need Your help. I know You're with Maggie and You're here with me. Guide the way, Lord."

While Zach started and ended each day with a conversation with God, he suspected Maggie harbored some resentment toward her heavenly Father. How much more hurt would she be if something horrible happened to her?

He couldn't return to the house. He needed to keep looking. Being as still and quiet as possible, he listened in the darkness. After a few minutes, the night sounds resumed. He moved on a ways and silenced again. If someone was around other than himself, the animals wouldn't feel safe enough to resume their rustlings. At least that's what he was counting on.

Zach didn't know how many times he stopped to listen. All he knew, feared rather, was that he might be getting farther and farther away from Maggie. He sat with his back against a maple tree and tried to formulate a better plan.

Think, man! He should have brought food and water. A blanket even. What if Maggie was thirsty or hungry or cold? Once he'd discovered her missing, all reason had fled from his head. Now, he was in the woods, without a lantern, in the dark.

He wouldn't find her sitting down. Pushing to his feet, he decided to follow the creek. If he had abducted someone and didn't want to be discovered, he would hide his tracks in the water. He still couldn't think of a single soul who would want to harm Mag— *Frank Stanley.* The only person in the world who could possibly have a grudge against Maggie, and more likely, Zach.

Which made traveling inside the creek bed less likely. Stanley would want Zach to find them. Only. . .he would want Zach to find them at a time and place planned by Stanley. The question was where?

He needed to wait until the sun came up. No longer terrified that Maggie was in immediate danger, Zach found a patch of moss, leaned against a tree, and closed his eyes. Stanley probably wanted to kill them both, but Zach's guess was the man wouldn't hurt Maggie unless Zach was there to see. She was relatively safe for now.

When he woke, the sky was just turning shades of orange and magenta. Zach stood and stretched, easing the aches from his bones. After scooping some water from the nearby creek, he surveyed the area. Where would Stanley stage an ambush?

The mountain rose to the east, the trees thinning toward the top. Craggy rocks provided more than enough hiding places. Stanley and Maggie would have had to walk most of the night to make it that far because if Zach knew his wife, she would have dragged her feet the entire time.

Running and staying in the thick of the trees, Zach headed for a dark spot on the mountain which he hoped was a cave. It would be the perfect place for Stanley to hole up and Zach could approach from the rear.

By the time he climbed halfway up the summit, the sun was high and hot in the sky and Zach had left any source of water behind. He mopped his brow with his arm.

A rock clattered nearby.

Maggie yelled, "Let go of me. I'm tired of being dragged like a sack of feed."

Zach grinned. Yep, his Maggie wasn't making her captor's job easy.

"Shut up and get in there."

"Not until you check for a bear."

Stanley growled. "We'll go together. I'm not stupid enough to leave you here alone so you can run off."

Zach peered down from his vantage point. He'd climbed too high. He'd have to find a way of getting closer without alerting Stanley. He picked up a small pebble and pelted Maggie in the head.

"Ow!" She scowled and glanced up, the frown replaced with a smile when she caught sight of him. "All right, Frank. I'll go first." With a swish of her skirt, she ducked into the cave.

Zach took aim at the other man, but he followed Maggie too quickly for him to get off a shot. Getting to Stanley now would be a challenge unless the cave had another way in.

Chapter 8

"Here. Eat." Stanley tossed Maggie a leftover piece of rabbit.

It didn't look appetizing after being in his pack for hours, then landing on the floor of the cave, but she was starving and needed to keep up her strength. Zach was there to rescue her! But, he might need help. Stanley was a wily one.

She eyed her rifle propped against the cave wall. So close and yet very far away. Stanley would have her on the ground before she could grasp the weapon. The man had already proven he wasn't averse to striking a woman. She touched the tender spot on her left cheek where he had punched her after she'd refused to go along with him.

He shook the canteen then cursed. "Looks like we're going to be thirsty for a while."

Water trickled down the limestone wall behind Maggie and disappeared somewhere behind her. She almost told him so, but if the man was that ignorant he could discover things out for himself. She put her hand behind her, got it wet, then licked her fingers. While not fully satiated, after a few tries her throat was no longer parched and she ate the last of the rabbit.

"You sure don't talk much for a female." Stanley sat against the far wall, close to her gun. "Most women rattle on like a bird. I bet your husband likes you being close mouthed."

Ignoring him, Maggie crawled to the cave opening and peered out. They'd climbed up a fairly steep side of the mountain. Very little foliage provided cover for anyone trying to get close. A small pebble fell to the ground near her hand. She glanced up and caught sight of the toe of Zach's boot. She smiled. Zach was letting her know he was close.

"What was that?" Stanley called out.

"Squirrel." She scooted back inside so as not to give Zach's position away.

"Too bad I can't trust you to stay put. If I could, I'd go hunting for supper. I'd come back with more than a measly rabbit too."

Really, the man was too absurd for words. Stay put? As a hostage, and one he planned on shooting as soon as he killed Zach, of course she wouldn't stay put.

"Yeah, my ma wasn't like you. She talked a mile a minute. The only time she shut up was when Pa came home. She knew she'd get his fist if she spoke before he said she could." He picked up a stick from the ground and started whittling. "That's how it should be. See how pleasant it is with me talking and you listening? Maybe, once you're a widow, we can get hitched. I know how to run your ranch."

Heaven forbid. Maggie shuddered.

"No? Too bad. You'd make me a good wife. It'll be a waste of a good woman when I kill you." He rummaged in his pack, grabbed a plug of tobacco, and stuck it between his teeth and lower lip. "A real shame."

How much more of his rambling could she take? If he kept it up, she might very well shoot herself. Instead, she moved back to the trickle of water and cupped her hands.

"You lying snake of a woman." Stanley yanked her back. "Why didn't you tell me there was water? I'm dying over here."

The moment he filled his hands with water, she scrambled to the opposite side of the wall for her gun.

He lunged after her. His hand tangled in her hair.

She cried out as he yanked her back.

"Now you've done it. I've got to tie you up." He dragged her back to her side of the cave and used a length of rope from his pack to tie her hands and ankles together. "Try getting a drink now, missy."

"I'm going to shoot you myself," Maggie said, glaring up into his face. "You wait and see."

He laughed, the sound booming in the cave. "Going to be hard to do hog-tied."

Maybe so, but she'd find a way. "Get away from me."

He chuckled and returned to his side and his whittling. "You sure are feisty. I can't help but wonder whether your marriage is still business only. A pretty gal like you would drive a man mad."

He truly was a cad. She turned her head to the cave entrance and watched the shadows deepen as the sun started to set on the second day of her captivity. *Oh, hurry, Zach.* She couldn't bear Stanley for another minute.

After what seemed like an eternity, the man started snoring. That was all Maggie needed to start sawing the ropes around her wrists against the cave wall.

Zach stilled when Maggie's cry echoed through the cave. He'd found another entrance, tight and small. But now he faced a fork and had no idea which way to go.

Since one way seemed to grow smaller as it went, he chose the other, darker passage. Within minutes darkness engulfed him and he had to rely on touch to guide him. He didn't know how long he crawled before he realized he wouldn't reach her that way. He'd lost valuable time and now had to scoot out backward. There wasn't another entrance. Not one big enough for a man anyway.

Back outside, he got to his feet. At least the full moon was in his favor. One way or the other, he was going to rescue Maggie that night and make Stanley pay for harming her. Her cry of pain had almost made Zach barge to the cave's entrance with no thought of safety. Only the fear of Stanley killing Maggie once Zach was in his sights had stopped him. The man wouldn't let her go just because he killed Zach. Neither he nor Maggie would make it out alive, unless Stanley was taken care of.

He crept as quietly as possible, careful where he placed each step, and moved closer to the cave's entrance. He peered inside and couldn't see a thing. Only the sound of someone moving let him know the cave was occupied. He had no way of knowing whether that someone was Maggie or Stanley. He pulled back, not wanting his silhouette to stand out against the moon's glow.

Eventually, Stanley would sleep and Zach would make his move.

"Zach?" Maggie's soft whisper beckoned. "He's asleep. I'm on the right of the cave."

That was all Zach needed. He stepped into the cave and rushed to Maggie's side. "Are you hurt? Can you walk?"

"Yes, but I can't get the ropes off my ankles. My hands are free."

"Okay. No more talking. We don't want him to wake."

He pulled his knife from his belt and cut the ropes. Then, grasping her hand, he led her from the cave.

"Wait." She tiptoed close to Stanley and grabbed her gun, then rejoined Zach.

Outside, she stopped. "I promised I would shoot him. Does that make me a bad person? Because I really want to shoot him."

Zach bit back a laugh. "Now isn't the time, darlin'. We've got to go."

"You aren't going anywhere." A shot rang out with Stanley's boast.

Zach grabbed Maggie and shoved her down the mountainside. Pain ripped through his side as they fell, him tumbling after his wife.

When they stopped rolling, it took him several seconds to catch his breath. Only the sight of Stanley coming fast in their direction gave Zach the strength he needed to get to his feet. "Maggie!"

"I'm here." She stood from where she'd rolled into a bush. "You're bleeding."

"We'll worry about that later." He grabbed her hand and led her at a run through the trees. If they could find a place to hole up, they could ambush the man chasing them and stop him before he did some real damage.

"I have to stop." Maggie pulled against his grasp.

"If we stop, we die." His strength was fading as fast as the blood poured down his side. They both needed to stop. The waterfall. *Please, God, let there be room behind it.* "Come on. We're almost there."

He coaxed her to continue their mad dash until they reached the creek. "We've got to cross and retrace our steps. We have to move quickly."

She nodded.

He led her through the creek, then backed up across it, stepping into the same tracks he'd made. "Come on, Maggie. Just a bit more." He put his arm around her waist and half dragged her to the waterfall. Keeping his arm tightly around her, he ducked his head and stepped behind the curtain of water.

The pounding of the water would mask any sound they made and allow them a chance to catch their breath. "I need you to take a look at my wound." He lifted up his shirt. His skin rippled at her touch.

"Just a graze. A deep one, though. I can stitch you when we get home." She bent and ripped a length of fabric from her petticoat. "Not the cleanest bandage, but it's all I've got." She wrapped it around him and tied it tight enough he gasped. "I'm sorry, but that's the only way to stop the bleeding. Now, sit." She plopped onto a damp rock behind them.

Zach did the same and rested his head against the wall formed by the mountain. They couldn't stay where they were. He'd have to face Stanley and eliminate the threat to him and Maggie.

Maggie clutched his arm and pointed out from the waterfall.

Highlighted against the moonlit sky, on the other side of the falls, stood Stanley. He held a gun at the ready and didn't move. He waited, listening for a sign of his prey. Eventually, he moved on.

Zach stood. "Stay here. I'm going after him."

"I can come too. I'm a good shot."

She had a point. She could shoot as well, if not better than him, and she wasn't wounded. "Okay, but you have to do exactly as I say. Can you do that?"

"Yes."

"That's my girl." He slid his back along the rock wall and, shoving branches of a juniper bush aside for Maggie, they exited to the side of the waterfall. He caught a glimpse of Stanley before the woods swallowed him.

The hunter had become the prey. Zach gave a wry grin. This hunter wouldn't stop until his prey was captured. . .or dead.

They followed Stanley's tracks through the woods and into the pasture behind their ranch house. The man had returned to the ranch he'd once poorly managed for the Spoonmores. Zach shook his head and darted toward the barn, Maggie right behind him.

He stopped and listened through one of the windows. The horses didn't seem bothered, but they knew Stanley. It was quite possible that, if he was inside, they thought he was supposed to be there.

"What is it?" Maggie asked.

"Wait up." He held up a hand for Maggie to stop. He opened the barn door and stepped inside. The sound of a gun being cocked froze him in his tracks.

"That was too easy," Stanley said.

"Why, yes, it was." Maggie moved to stand behind Stanley and raised her rifle, bringing the butt down on the man's head.

Stanley crumbled to the ground.

"I thought you wanted to shoot him," Zach said, grabbing a bridle from the wall to use on the man's hands. His wife never failed to surprise with her gumption.

"I did." Her teeth flashed as she grinned. "But then I heard Mama's voice saying it wouldn't be proper for a lady to shoot a man, no matter how vile that man might be. So, I did the next best thing and gave him a powerful headache."

Zach laughed and secured Stanley with a piece of rope, then pulled Maggie close, caressing the darkening bruise on her face. "I'm sorry I didn't get there before he hurt you." He wanted to throttle the man who would harm a woman for petty vengeance.

"I'm fine." She rested her cheek against his chest.

"I'm going to shoot both of you." Stanley cursed and struggled to sit up.

"I don't think so." Zach squatted in front of him. "If you so much as look at my wife again, I'll do more than hit you over the head. Although, that was Maggie who knocked you out cold." He grinned.

The man spit into the dirt. "What are you going to do now?"

"Leave you here until morning. Then, I'll ride you to the sheriff's office and wash my hands of you. I'm awfully tired, though." Zach rubbed his hands down his face.

Despite the pain in his side, he scooped Maggie into his arms and strode toward the house. The minute he returned from dropping Stanley off at the sheriff's office, he intended to court Maggie as she deserved. They might have gotten hitched without the courting, but he was determined to make his wife love him if it took the rest of his life.

Thank You, God, for letting me find her.

Inside, Maggie sleepily ordered him to put her down and sit. "I need to clean and stitch your wound."

"It's fine."

"No, it isn't." She set a pan of water on the stove, then opened a cupboard and removed a bottle of whiskey and a small sewing kit. "You aren't the first man to be stitched up on this ranch. I learned how a long time ago."

"But you're exhausted."

"No more than you." She knelt in front of him and cut away the soiled petticoat bandage. She made a noise deep in her throat and offered him the whiskey.

"No thanks. I don't imbibe."

"Very well." She poured a healthy dose of the liquor directly into his wound.

He groaned and bit his knuckles. When she'd finished pouring, he whistled through his teeth, then glanced into her face. "Why are you smiling? Do you get pleasure from causing me pain?"

"A little." She kissed his cheek. "Sorry, but the sound you made reminded me of a tiny kitten."

"I growled."

"You *meowed*." She giggled and dropped a clean rag into the pan of water. "Ready? Would you like a stick or a piece of leather to bite down on?"

"No." He could stand anything she dished out. He hoped. Clenching his hands into fists, he took a deep breath and looked away as the needle pierced his skin.

His little wife had a definite mean streak.

Chapter 9

Maggie lay in bed the next morning, her body aching and her heart pounding. Today was the day Zach would return from dropping Stanley at the jail, and there was so much work to do in preparation.

She wanted the chores done so he could relax at the end of his journey, a nice supper on the table, and her looking clean and presentable. Zach deserved so much more after risking his life to save her, but it was the best she could do.

Smiling, she donned the faded brown dress she used for work and thought of her good news. She'd made her peace with God after coming so close to death. It's what Pa would have wanted, after all. He'd often told her that life on earth was nothing more than a breeze headed to a greater place. She'd see him again someday. So, she intended to spend her brief time on earth with the man she'd loved for as long as she could remember.

Hair braided and hanging down her back, she shoved her stocking feet into boots and hurried to the barn. "Good morning, Cricket. Ready to work?"

Her horse whinnied in response, nuzzling Maggie's pocket for a treat.

"I wouldn't dare visit without a sugar cube, sweetie." She held her hand out flat for the horse to retrieve the sugar, then led her from the stall. Moments later they were trotting across the pasture. A quick perimeter check of the fence line. See whether the hired help needed her assistance. . .her mind ticked off the day's chores.

A spot of color drew her close to a fallen tree. Lying across the bark was a bolt of emerald green fabric. The very same she'd admired at the mercantile. That silly man. Why hadn't he just given it to her? She slid from the horse and retrieved the fabric, noticing a matching silk ribbon.

She smiled and secured her treasures behind the saddle, then continued her ride. Back at the ranch, she put the fabric in the house, then returned to the barn. Each stall needed fresh hay, a job Zach usually took care of, but this was definitely something Maggie could do. It might take a little longer, but she'd get the job done.

She climbed into the hayloft and grabbed the pitchfork. As she tossed down hay, she thought of how it had felt for Zach to carry her to the house. Like she was the missing piece to his pie. She was determined he would fall in love with her. She'd be the best wife she could be until he couldn't resist her.

Humming "Amazing Grace," she tossed hay faster. Small pieces of straw fell in the folds of her skirt and in her hair. Yep, life was going to be—

Her foot slipped, her arms windmilled as she started to fall. She screamed and grabbed the wood that made up the floor of the loft. Her legs kicked the air. She glanced at the ground.

Too far to fall. She'd definitely break something. Thinking of Zach while in a high place was not the best idea. Why did she always fall when thinking about him?

She tried to pull herself up, but lacked the strength in her arms. "Now what? I'm in quite the predicament. How wonderful it will be for Zach to return home and find me a crumpled pile on the barn floor."

"Maggie!"

Her hands slipped at Zach's cry. "Don't do that. I'll fall."

He scrambled up the ladder to the loft. "Sweetheart, what in tarnation are you doing?" He gripped her wrists and pulled her to safety.

"I thought I'd hang here for a while. What do you think? I fell." *Thinking of you!*

"Why didn't you have Dan take care of the horses? I left him a list of instructions." He frowned.

"I wanted to surprise you." She brushed off what little hay was left on her skirt.

Zach plucked a straw from her hair. "You succeeded." The corner of his mouth lifted. "You're home early."

"I rode as fast as I could. A man likes to be home when he has a beautiful wife waiting for him."

Her face flushed. "Oh. Uh, thank you for the fabric."

"You found it." He tapped her nose. "I suspected you'd try and take over my chores."

She shrugged, returning his smile. "Are you hungry? Daisy made a fresh batch of biscuits and there's honey."

He slipped his arm around her waist. "I'm starving."

His eyes told her it wasn't food he was hungry for. Heavens! She wasn't sure her heart could handle him growing closer to her.

"Wait." He dashed away, returning with a handful of wildflowers. "I picked these on the way."

"They're beautiful. Thank you." She tilted her head. What was he up to? She gasped. Was he courting her?

The look in his eyes said he was. Well, two could play at that game. She'd court him so hard he wouldn't know which end was up. She slipped her arm through his and fairly skipped back to the house.

"Why don't you get cleaned up," she told him, "while I put these in water and get the biscuits and honey. . .honey." She winked and sashayed into the kitchen as his eyes widened in surprise.

She bit back a giggle and waltzed to the cupboard. She pulled down a jar and filled it with water from the inside pump.

"What's got you in a twirl?" Daisy glanced up from kneading bread dough.

"Zach is home."

"Ah, to be young and in love again." She sighed and stared out the window. "It's a marvelous feeling."

Maggie grinned. Yes, it was. Absolutely marvelous.

Zach washed in the basin and donned a clean shirt. It didn't take a genius to see Maggie was turning the tables on him and doing the courting. He chuckled. Who could out-court who? He slicked back his hair and strode to the dining table.

A cleaned up, very lovely Maggie sat at one end. Zach stared down at his regular dining place, then picked up his cup and plate to move to the chair next to hers.

"I never could understand why a man and his wife couldn't sit next to each other when they're home alone." He winked. He'd never grow tired of seeing her blush.

Daisy carried out a tray with coffee and biscuits. Her steps faltered a bit to see him out of his usual place at the table, but she continued as if everything was normal. With a sparkle in her eyes, she poured their coffee. "Good to see you home, safe and sound, Mr. Colton."

"It's good to be home." He put his hand over Maggie's.

Maggie cleared her throat and slipped her hand free, suddenly engrossed in placing her napkin just right in her lap.

"Daisy, I think I must have the most beautiful wife in the Ozark Mountains." He put two sugar cubes in his coffee. "Wouldn't you agree?"

"Very much so, sir." Daisy laughed and left them alone.

"Well. . ." Maggie toyed with her fork. "My husband is quite a handsome fellow. You should see him. Tall, strong, and fearless."

Zach took her hand. "Not fearless, darlin'. Not at all."

Her gaze locked on his.

"My fear is losing you. When Stanley took you, I thought my heart would stop. When I saw you hanging from the loft, I'm sure I gained some gray hair."

She smoothed his wheat-colored hair away from his face. "Not a single strand."

He took her hand and placed a kiss in the palm. He started to lean toward her when the sound of a wagon stopping in front of the house halted him from kissing her. He tossed down his napkin and stood. "I'll see who it is."

A short, portly man climbed from the wagon. With purposeful steps, he made his way to the front door.

Zach opened it before he could knock. "Mr. Mason. Please come in."

"I'm not here for fellowship, Mr. Colton. I'm here to offer my sincere apologies to you and Mrs. Colton on behalf of my no-good nephew." The man twisted his hat in his hands. "He overcharged you on the back pay for your mortgage, thinking he could pocket the difference. I've sent him back to New York, with his tail between his legs. The money he took has been deposited in your account to the sum of fifty dollars."

Zach turned and gathered Maggie into his arms, twirling her around. "How about that trip to Hot Springs?"

"Put me down. We have a guest." She playfully slapped his shoulder. "May I offer you a cup of coffee, Mr. Mason?"

"I would appreciate it, thank you."

Maggie took his hat and hung it on a hook, then led the way to the dining room. "Please, have a seat. I'll return with a cup for you."

Mr. Mason nodded and took the seat across from Zach. "I know I should have had my nephew arrested, but he is young and foolish. I hope he's learned his lesson, and I am glad that Miss Maggie chose you for her husband rather than that scoundrel."

"So am I." Zach leaned back in his chair. "I'd like to pay the ranch off, free and clear, Mr. Mason. Is there enough in our account?"

He nodded. "And some. The sale of your horses put you comfortably in the black. I only wish I had been at that auction."

"I can let you have first pick of the next batch." Zach watched as Maggie set a cup in front of the banker and poured it full of coffee.

Dan could handle things for a couple of days, allowing Zach and Maggie to have a true honeymoon. The roses in her cheeks, her shy glances, all told him she no longer looked at marriage with him to be merely a business arrangement. He knew for sure he didn't see things that way. Could it be possible she actually loved him enough to make their marriage more. . .traditional?

"Zach?" Her brows drew together. "Is something wrong?"

"No." He smiled. "Everything is perfect." He gave her hand a squeeze and explained his plans for paying off the mortgage.

Tears shimmered in her eyes. "That was Pa's dream. I can't wait to write Mama and tell her." Maggie ran her hand across his back as she resumed her seat. "Thank you, Zach."

Mr. Mason cleared his throat. "I feel I may have intruded on a tender moment between you two. Thank you for the coffee, but I must be going." He stood, took a sip, and marched to the door.

Maggie glanced at Zach and giggled. "How utterly improper we behaved."

"I'll see him out." He placed a kiss on her forehead. "Then, maybe you'd see fit to behave a little more *improperly*."

She clutched the neckline of her dress and blushed.

Zach walked the banker to his wagon and shook his hand. "Thank you for making the long drive out here. You could have sent a message."

"No, I needed to do this in person. My nephew stole from several of the fine people on this mountain. I wanted to assure you it won't happen again." He took his seat and gripped the reins. "Now, get back to your lovely wife and breakfast."

"Good day, Mr. Mason."

"Good day, Mr. Colton."

Zach could barely contain his excitement. His dream had become a reality. He was a ranch owner. Not a ranch he'd built himself from the ground up, but one he'd received when he'd married not the young girl he'd held a fondness for, but the beautiful woman he loved.

She stood on the porch, the sun shining on her dark hair, looking like an angel God had sent to reward Zach for every good thing he'd done in his life.

He bounded up the stairs and took Maggie in his arms.

Epilogue

Hot Springs, Arkansas

Maggie leaned over the railing of their balcony. "I've never seen so many people. I had hoped to visit the springs without a crowd."

"I doubt that's going to happen." Zach moved her hair and kissed her neck. "Maybe we can ride past the town and find a solitary spot."

She turned and put her arms around his neck. "Could we?"

He smiled. "Give me five minutes to put on a clean shirt."

When he went back in their room, Maggie surveyed the milling crowd below them. She wanted to shout to the heavens how much she loved her husband. Last night, their first night as true husband and wife had surpassed her dreams. God had truly blessed her.

"You would have liked Zach, Pa." She wiped away a tear. In her last letter to her mother, she'd thanked her for sending Zach after her the night she'd tried to run away. Who could have guessed a childish act of rebellion could have resulted in such a wonderful gift?

Zach's arms reached around her waist. "Ready?"

"Very."

Hand in hand, they made their way to the stables. Soon, they were riding through the crowd and headed out of town.

"Do you know where to go?"

"Nope. I'm going to follow the spring until it disappears. Underground somewhere. There has to be a pool not used by the tourists. Very few would want to venture far for their needs."

She rested her head against his strong back. "Good." Now they were together, she found she didn't want to share him. Of course, he'd be out of her sight when they returned home. There was work to do, after all. But that was another day. Today, he was all hers.

An odor wafted to her nose. "What is that smell? It's like sulfur."

"That's the spring." He patted her hands, which were folded in front of him. "I've heard that these smell less than some of the others in the country. Look, there's steam." He clicked his tongue, signaling for the horse to go faster.

They passed several log cabins, in which people in robes entered and exited. Some were so crippled they had to be carried into the bath house.

"Do you think they work? The springs?" she asked.

"I think they provide comfort rather than a cure."

Zach guided the horse into the forest surrounding the more touristy area. Soon, they came to a small bubbling pool. He helped Maggie down from her horse, then slid down and joined her.

"Oh, this will be wonderful. Hot water that I didn't have to pump and heat up." She unlaced her boots, removing them and her stockings. Seconds later, they were followed by her skirt and petticoat, leaving her in her new linen knickers. Her fingers fumbled with the buttons on her blouse. "Oh, why do women have to wear so much clothing?" She took note of how quickly Zach had shed everything but his long underwear.

"Let me help you." He laughed and helped her out of her blouse.

"Last one in is the rotten egg the spring received its smell from." She darted into the water. The hot water rid her body of the aches of the long horse ride from home.

She sank in up to her neck and closed her eyes. "This is heavenly."

"I'm glad you like it." Zach pulled her to a rock that provided a seat.

"Mama would be mortified to see men and women entering the bath houses in nothing but robes or wraps." She leaned back and closed her eyes. "Is it scandalous for us to be out here?"

"Very."

"Good." She smiled. "I don't ever want you to get bored with me."

"That could never happen, darlin'." His low voice warmed her more than the water.

She opened her eyes and turned her head just enough to look at him. "Does it hurt your wound?"

"No." He cupped her face. "We can stay as long as you like."

The water felt marvelous on his tight shoulders. The long ride to drop off Stanley, then north to Hot Springs, hadn't given the tension time to abate after Maggie's abduction. Now, with her sitting in his arms, he wouldn't move if the water was boiling.

When sleep threatened, they exited the spring and lay on the bank to dry off before donning their outer clothes. "What would you think about raising cattle?" Zach rolled to his side, supporting his head on his elbow. "We've plenty of land once it's cleared. Beef is always in demand."

Her eyes widened. "You really think we could?"

"I do. Soon, the Lazy S Ranch will be the best this side of the Mississippi. You wait and see."

Her face brightened. "We can hire more men. Improve the bunkhouse. Take cattle drives. Notice I said *we*." She grinned.

"Women do not go on cattle drives!" Zach flopped onto his back. "Forget I said anything."

"Women can do anything they set their mind to." Maggie got to her feet and stomped to her clothes. "I suppose you're going to use some excuse about how much you love me and couldn't bear it if I were to get hurt, *blah, blah, blah*."

"It's true."

"You can't always protect me."

"I can try." He grabbed the back of her shift and pulled her to him. "I do love you,

Maggie. You're my breath, my heart, my very blood. I can't help if I get a little overprotective. Try to understand."

She sighed and rested her forehead against this chest. "I do, truly. I feel the same way about you. Where's the trust in God that you tell me to believe in? When God decides to take me home, you won't be able to stop Him. No more than I could keep my father, or you could keep your mother." She raised her face. "All we can do is enjoy the time we have."

"When did you get so smart?" He tapped her nose.

"When I said I'd marry you." She smiled, sending his heart racing. "That was the smartest thing I've ever done. Thank you for the offer."

"I'd marry you all over again, darlin'." He lowered his head for a kiss. It wasn't until a cool breeze reminded him he was in his wet underclothes that he pulled his head up. "Let's head back and have supper."

"Men and their stomachs." She playfully slapped his shoulder then gathered up her clothes. "I hate that we have to go home tomorrow, but I am excited to plan on expanding the ranch."

"I'd like to talk about expanding our family."

She whirled around, eyes wide. "That isn't something one talks about in public!"

He glanced around. "There's no one here, and you sound like your mother."

"I do, don't I?" She laughed. "Stop trying to embarrass me, then. Some things are still better suited to be spoken of in the privacy of one's home."

He was pretty sure he heard her whisper she would love to have his baby. "I love you, Maggie Colton. I've loved you from the moment I met you five years ago. I wasn't ready to admit it then. When I saw you so sad and wounded in that shack, and how reluctant you were to accept my proposal, it cut me to my center. But, I couldn't let you go."

She stepped into his arms. "I may have been a reluctant bride, Zach, but I've been very glad I said yes. I've loved you for as long as I can remember. Now, kiss me."

He obeyed.

Cynthia Hickey grew up in a family of storytellers and moved around the country a lot as an army brat. Her desire is to write about real, but flawed characters in a wholesome way that her seven children and five grandchildren can all be proud of. She and her husband live in Arizona where Cynthia is a full-time writer.

Weeping Willow

by Marcia Gruver

Dedication

Racheal Reagan Jones, my apprentice editor, budding author, and cherished great-granddaughter. When I started this book, I had no idea your ancestors once lived in Port Royal. How cool is that?

Keep writing, honey! I love you.

Thou shalt love the Lord thy God with all thy heart, and with all thy soul, and with all thy mind. This is the first and great commandment. And the second is like unto it, Thou shalt love thy neighbour as thyself.
MATTHEW 22:37–39

Acknowledgments

My heartfelt thanks to:

My Agape Prayer Group Storm Sisters:

Allison, Brandee, Connie, Dee, Deseree, Emily, Ivie, Laura, Lindi, Jan, Judy, Marcie, Melinda, Myndee, Sandra, Stacy, Tiffany, and Zackie.

Bless you for going to the wall for me. Our anchor holds!

Chapter 1

Port Royal, Virginia
May 1858

The spring shower flashed and rumbled to a soggy end. The sun, darting between gray streaks of cloud, struggled against the gloom, eager to coax the cotton fields to life. Largemouth bass struck at dragonflies along the banks of the Rappahannock, and channel cats, immense dark shadows rising from the murky depths, skimmed the surface for food.

Willow's favorite swimming hole beckoned, but a dip so soon after the thaw would rattle her teeth. It wasn't too cold for a wade near the bank, to let the spongy mud squish through her toes, or to stand knee deep and skip rocks. Maybe wet a hook and bring one of those catfish home for supper.

It was a lovely day to be Willow Evangeline Bates, free at last of the smothering confines of a one-room schoolhouse. She had spent the last five hours of captivity drowsily peering out the window, bemoaning her fate.

Miss Penny had the best intentions, but the young schoolmarm's voice lulled Willow to blissful slumber, at least on the days when Julian Finney was absent. Julian's presence presented an entirely different dilemma. He made it hard for Willow, and every other female in class—Miss Penny no exception—to concentrate.

Was ever another boy so pleasingly knit together by the hand of God?

Julian's brows, skillfully drawn, swept away like graceful plumes from his whiskey-brown eyes, thick lashed and kind. His features were strong and even, his hair so black it shone. The determined set of his mouth couldn't conceal the graceful curve of his lips or the natural tilt at the corners. One fathomless dimple appeared when he smiled. Willow lived and breathed for his smiles.

A bright ray of light slanting through the trees signaled the storm cloud's final surrender. Willow crisscrossed the sun-dappled road, dodging the muck churned up by passing wagon wheels. At the fork, she left the road and trudged down a grassy slope, following the well-worn trail used mostly by schoolchildren and slaves from nearby plantations.

Reaching the swollen creek, she paused to scan her surroundings. With no one around to see her knickers, she lifted her skirts, took a running start, and sailed over wriggling pollywogs, darting water bugs, and schools of silver minnows.

Pleased with herself for clearing the creek with nary a splash, she picked her way over the rutted path to the lane leading to Fairhill, her family's sprawling plantation. The house passed to Papa from her grandparents. Willow never knew Grandpa Bates. He died twenty years before while felling a tree. Grammy grew too frail to survive another winter in the big, drafty house, so she up and ran off with Jesus.

Grammy's passing left a hollow in the depths of Willow's soul. Papa promised she would see her again in heaven, and while in no hurry to reunite, she'd give all she owned to see Grammy once more.

Willow slowed her pace, and her heart kicked up a notch. The sound of a plow parting new ground came from behind her on the path. Only, who would be plowing in the woods?

Spinning, she stared at the shadowy trail, her mind scrambling to identify the grating noise. It drew closer, just beyond the curve in the lane.

A black bear, fierce and wild, hauling a fresh kill in its teeth?

A runaway slave, desperate and dangerous, dragging his chains?

The former seemed unlikely. Bear sightings were scarce around Port Royal. The latter struck terror in her wildly beating heart.

Whatever the source of the nerve-shattering noise, no good could come of meeting it face-to-face. Dropping her knapsack, she lit out for the nearest sycamore.

Hugging the trunk, she pulled herself to a high branch, scrambling up the rough bark with her feet. Nerves tingling, barely breathing, she squatted on the sturdy limb and watched to see what frightful thing rounded the bend.

A high-pitched, off-key whistle split the air, a sour-note rendition of "Carry Me Back to Old Virginia."

Willow rolled her eyes. A bear would've been more tolerable.

Hiram Mayhew plodded into sight, dragging a big stick, the knotty end tilling a deep furrow through the damp black dirt. Hiram was an imp spawned to vex her. The skinny boy, with pumpkin-colored hair and freckles so dense they looked blasted on with a scattergun, made sport of tormenting her.

He stopped beneath her perch on the limb and stared at her knapsack, the one Grammy had sewn with bumpy, throbbing fingers. His low, menacing chuckle raised the hair on her arms.

"Willow Bates," he whispered, glancing around the clearing.

Inching forward, he stretched out a bare, muddy toe and nudged her sack, leaving a blob of gooey sludge behind. Apparently pleased by the mess, he stepped dead center of her bag and pressed an imprint of his foot with thick Virginia mud. Not satisfied, he swirled the foot in a wide circle, grinding in the muck.

The foolish boy had cast the die for his own demise.

"Raah!" she shrieked, sailing off the branch and landing beside him with a thud, snatching off his battered hat as she fell.

Hiram screamed, shrill like a frightened girl, and sat down hard on his behind, staring at her with full moon eyes. Mouth gaping, chest heaving, he dashed the tears off his cheek with a grimy forearm.

Doubled over, she laughed until she gasped for air.

Hiram scrambled to his feet. "You've gone and done it now." Dusting the seat of his pants, he glared. "I'd keep a watch over my shoulder, if I was you." He leaned in and sneered. "But you won't see it coming."

She lifted her chin. "It'll be worth it, however it comes."

Bending, she snatched up her ruined bag and turned to walk away. "The memory of you bouncing off your bottom will cheer me until my hair is gray."

"Wait!" he roared. His pounding feet caught up, and he spun her around. "You tell anyone about this, and you'll be sorry."

Jutting her bottom lip, she laid a finger on her chin. "Maybe Aunt Nelda. She enjoys a good laugh."

"Aunt Nelda!" His freckled ears blazed. "That's the same as telling the whole county."

Lifting the stick he'd been dragging, he held it in front of Willow to block her way. "Promise you won't tell, or I'll break your skinny legs."

"You'll do no such thing."

He drew back the stick and held it suspended overhead. "I will."

She quivered inside but mustered a fierce look. "Have you forgotten what Julian said? If he hears of you pestering me again, you'll catch it good."

Hiram lowered the stick, a crease forming between his copper brows. "Finney? I'm not afraid of that bowlegged leprechaun."

Willow balled her fists. "He's as tall and straight as a loblolly pine."

"And cute as a june bug?" Holding his middle, he bent over and roared with laughter.

She turned and jogged up the lane, partly to hide her burning cheeks.

"I'm not afraid of your cute little beau," Hiram called. Running to catch up, he thumped the middle of her back. "I'm not, you hear?"

Willow spun, her rage blazing hot. "You should be!" she shouted. "Don't think I won't tell him."

Hiram stuck out his fat, pink tongue. "Tell him whatever you please."

"You're a spiteful boy, and no one likes you."

He winced. "Grammy liked me. She always said I'm just high-strung."

Willow's eyes went to slits. "She was being polite. How could she look kindly on you after you nailed her cat's tail to the barn?"

Truthfully, Grammy had looked kindly on him, despite his misdeeds. Like her Savior, Grammy looked kindly on every living soul.

Fresh pain jabbed her, in the tender place where the heartache of Grammy's passing dwelled. "Why must you always mention my grandmother?" Turning aside, she wiped streaming eyes on her sleeve. "It's the cruelest thing you do."

"Let the girl be, Hiram."

Startled, Willow turned toward the deep, familiar voice.

Julian Finney rounded the bend, his lanky legs accounting for half his height. Tall and broad shouldered, he seemed more man than boy.

William Smyth, the reverend's son and Julian's constant shadow, dogged his heels.

"What's this, lass?" Julian tilted Willow's chin and wiped her tears. "Has he gone and made you cry again?"

Reaching Hiram in two strides, Julian gave him a shake. "Apologize to her."

Glancing at Julian for approval, William hooked his thumbs in his suspenders and said, "You heard him, Mayhew. Apologize to Willow."

Color rose from Hiram's collar. "She should apologize to me. You didn't see—"
Julian tightened his grip. "Do it now."

At fourteen, three years younger, and a head and shoulders shorter than Julian, Hiram wilted from his haughty stance and hung his head. "I'm sorry, Willow. I don't bring up your grandma to be mean."

She sniffed, not ready to surrender her pout. "Why, then?"

Hiram shrugged and wormed his grimy toes in the dirt. "I reckon I miss her too. Nobody ever treated me half so nice. I'm sorry she's gone."

Speechless, Willow swallowed a growing lump in her throat. Compassion toward Hiram was a brand-new sentiment, one she couldn't make peace with in a hurry.

Julian placed a reassuring hand on her shoulder. The set of his jaw, strong and blue-black with the shadow of fresh whiskers, caused her stomach to pitch and a pleasant chill crept up her spine. "Thank you, Julian."

Smiling, he smoothed her hair.

"We missed you today. Aren't you coming back to school?" She simply had to know.

He nodded. "Aye, tomorrow. First thing."

Her heart soared. Another dreary day like today would sap the life from her.

Nudging Hiram, Julian pointed toward town. "Get home, lad. But, heed my words . . .don't make this wee child cry again."

Willow's soaring heart lurched and plummeted to earth. Three years his junior didn't make her a child. On the contrary, recent musings about this boy in particular were hardly those of a youth.

Julian patted her head then tugged on William's sleeve. William fell into step behind him, and the two went their way, Julian whistling a tune she'd never heard before.

The haunting melody drifted back to her without a single sour note, but his parting words were a bitter pill.

A few yards out of Willow's hearing, William chuckled. "That little gal didn't care for you calling her a child."

Julian grinned. "You may be right."

William glanced over his shoulder. "Oh, I'm right. Steam poured from her ears." He elbowed Julian. "The madder she got, the prettier she looked."

Julian had to agree.

Pa claimed Willow Bates, with her pale blond hair and icy-blue eyes, was as fetching a lass as he'd seen on two continents. Julian couldn't judge the standard of girls outside Virginia, but young Willow was a rare beauty.

He glanced sideways at William. "She's a striking girl, for certain, but still just a child."

"Naw, Julian," William said. "She's nearly fifteen, same as me."

Julian laughed. "Like I said. . .a child."

William growled and leaped on his back from behind. Laughing, Julian pulled him over his shoulder and they scuffled until William said "uncle."

They reached the spot where the uneven trail split three ways. To the left, along an overgrown path, sat the small house Julian shared with his parents.

With a wave, William branched off to the right where he lived in a house much like Julian's, except his bulged at the seams with siblings.

Straight ahead, through a forest of tall red oak, loomed Fairhill, the Bates plantation. Smoke from the cookhouse that fed the swarming hive of workers rose over the treetops in a wispy spiral, and the cadence of a work song reached his ears.

Mr. Bates ran a thriving cotton business, with the help of the many slaves he held papers on. Julian's family didn't hold with slavery, and never would. Their stand wasn't popular in Virginia, so they held their tongues when they could, but Julian would never own another human life.

He swung past the lane leading to Fairhill, and the large estate came into view. The Bates land, stretching clear away to the banks of the river, made a magnificent display. The big white house, fronted by tall columns and well-kept grounds, shone like a stone set in crosshatched fields.

So much beauty, but the ugliness it represented churned the pit of his stomach.

His thoughts flashed to Willow, the offended spark in her eyes, the scowl on her delicate face. The girl had so much more to be angry about than being called a child. He hoped one day the blinders would fall from her eyes.

Hefting his satchel to the other shoulder, he gazed at the brilliant patchwork of light in the overhead branches and smiled. The warmth felt good after the cold, wet spring planting. He was glad to have it behind him and to be going back to school tomorrow.

Pa seemed troubled, even embarrassed, when Julian announced he would attend classes for the summer session. Most boys in Port Royal quit school by the age of sixteen. Some even younger.

Julian was the oldest in the class by far and had become more teacher than student, helping Miss Penny with the abecedarians who lined the front row.

He enjoyed teaching these little ones their alphabet, loved how their faces lit up when they realized they could string the peculiar letters together to make words.

Miss Penny urged him to consider teaching as a profession. Her praise pleased him, but Julian had other plans. He would remain in school, learning as much as possible, until he was old enough to apply to West Point. Nothing could sway him from his dream of graduating from military school. Not even Pa.

Aedan Finney had found an adversary in his adopted country. Instead of a fresh start, this new life had been quarrelsome and harsh with Pa. Unwilling to own slaves, and unable to afford help, keeping up with his few acres had near defeated him.

He spoke often of the old country, of Ireland's windswept coastlines and rolling hills. He scolded himself for leaving, saying God intended for man to lie down in green pastures, yet he'd left behind the greenest fields in all creation.

Unlike his pa, Julian held precious few memories of Ireland. They crossed the ocean when he was a boy of ten, leaving behind Galway, the harbor city where he was born. Julian took to Virginia like a hound to scraps. Though a slight brogue still lurked in his speech, he was a Virginian through and through.

God had led him to this land of promise, and he vowed never to leave it.

Chapter 2

April 13, 1861

You? Off to war? You're not even true blue Virginian, Finney. How does this skirmish concern a bog jumper like you?"

Willow's breath caught, and her gaze shifted to Julian. Once, Hiram's comment might have incurred rage and the challenge of a duel. Despite the difference in their ages, the two had made peace and even struck up a friendship. Over time, Hiram had taken William Smyth's place as Julian's shadow.

Hiram had matured over the last three years and ceased his constant annoyances. In truth, the boy had grown quiet and withdrawn, especially in her presence.

No longer head and shoulders shorter than Julian, Hiram had grown tall and sturdy, and miraculously, quite handsome. The brightness of his pumpkin hair had darkened to a pleasing auburn, striking against eyes the color of new moss.

Eyes that twinkled from across the room with friendly mischief.

"Tread lightly, young Mayhew," Julian teased. "You'd not appreciate my Irish ire. And who of us bleeds true native blood, save perhaps the American Indian?"

He lifted one of Hiram's locks. "I've never seen an Indian with hair this color, have you, Willow?"

She beamed at Hiram. "Nor one with freckles."

He blushed and ducked his head.

Julian raised his glass. "My blood is blue enough, and I'm proud to shed it for the fair state of Virginia, whether or not I share a passion for the cause."

Willow frowned. "You feel no sympathy for our troubles?"

He took a long swallow from his lemonade. "Not an ounce."

Hiram leaned in. "I'd keep those sentiments to yourself among this lot."

Julian surveyed the roomful of men gathered in Willow's front parlor, rowdily boasting and shouting words like *war* and *secession*.

He winked at Hiram. "I suppose you're right."

Three days before, the stench of war wound its way to Port Royal from Charleston, fouling the air with gloom. President Lincoln announced he was sending supply ships to Fort Sumter, and the Confederate government issued an ultimatum to evacuate the fort. Major Anderson's answer was no. Confederate General Pierre Beauregard answered his no with fifty cannons aimed at Fort Sumter. The Union agreed to leave, but war was declared.

Hiram lowered his voice. "If you disagree, then why enlist?"

Julian turned his back on the milling men. "I don't hold with Virginia's stand, but I stand with her. I won't take up arms against my friends and neighbors."

Willow cleared her throat. "Why aren't you loyal to our way of life, Julian?"

He furrowed his brow. "You mean the buying and selling of slaves?"

She flinched. "Of course not. I meant—"

"I know what you meant." He swept the room with scornful eyes.

Willow followed his gaze to her striking mother, idly taking a slice of orange cake without a glance at the girl extending the platter. Then to her father, seated regally in a high-backed chair while a staff of household slaves tended his guests. Framed in the window behind Papa's handsome head, the fields were dotted with men he owned, laboring over a harvest they shared no stock in.

Willow knew Julian's views on slavery. He'd stated them often enough. Seeing her life reflected in his burning eyes disturbed her more than she could say. Therefore, she said nothing.

"There's more at stake than Virginia's honor or state's rights," Julian said. "This feud is about greed, plain and simple. The trading in human lives for monetary gain."

He nodded at the agitated men. "If Lincoln succeeds in freeing the slaves, these sons of Virginia stand to lose their homes, their businesses, indeed, their whole way of life. They won't let that happen without a fight."

Flustered, Willow clutched his sleeve. "That's exactly the point. My father couldn't run Fairhill without help. Slavery is the only way he can produce and sell cotton, and cotton is America's leading export. The European economy depends on raw cotton. Fairhill is providing a service, both to our nation and abroad."

Julian moved to stand beside her, so close the sweet smell of hair pomade stirred her senses. "All quite true, but at what cost, little Willow?" He gazed down at her, his expression one of sadness. "Just because things have always been this way doesn't make it right."

He took her chin and gently turned her head. "Look there at Cletus."

She sought the slender man dressed in woolen britches and waistcoat. He stood across the room filling tall glasses with lemonade, his dark hands covered by white gloves. Cletus seemed a permanent fixture in the room. He'd been a house slave for as long as she could remember, faithfully tending her family.

His wife, Bethy, worked the kitchen. The plucky, cheerful woman cooked every meal the family shared under Fairhill's roof.

Willow glanced at Julian. "What of him?"

"I heard your father sold off that pretty little daughter of his. Annie, wasn't it?"

Father had indeed sold the graceful young girl, but only as a necessity. She had caused a stir among the males in the servants' quarters.

Frowning slightly, Willow nodded. "He did." Sensing what Julian might be alluding to, she cleared her throat and continued. "He sold Annie to the Clemson plantation, just as he promised Cletus, so she could remain close by."

Julian touched his chin and nodded. "That's very considerate. Now Cletus and Bethy can don their Sunday best and call on their daughter. They'll simply tap on the Clemsons' front door and be asked inside for tea. Perhaps they'll be invited to supper."

He made a sound of disgust in his throat. "Annie's as good as dead to them. They'll never set eyes on their daughter again."

Willow blinked up at him. "Father has taken first-rate care of Cletus and his family. I'm sure they appreciate it very much."

"The same care he'd take of any prized stock," Julian said.

An expression of pity softened his features. "Dear guileless girl. If you believe Cletus harbors anything but murderous rage toward your father"—he waved his arm around the room—"toward any of us here, then you deceive yourself."

Stunned, her gaze darted again to Cletus. He hovered about the long table, moving slowly and deliberately between their guests, humming softly. To imagine aught but kindness resided in the gentle, patient man's heart was unthinkable.

Murderous rage? Impossible.

Absently watching Cletus work, Julian sighed. "It's a wonder they don't slaughter you in your beds."

Willow's temper flared. "Cletus would never harm us, Julian. He loves this family." Her chin rose defiantly. "He *loves* us."

Julian patted her shoulder. "I covet your innocence, child. I truly do."

She glared at him through a red haze and stamped her foot. "I am not a child!"

The room stilled. A clatter of serving dishes and tinkle of glass were the last sounds to fade before silence filled the room.

Mama appeared at her side and clutched her elbow. Hard. "You've allowed yourself to become overtired, dear. Say good night to your friends, and I'll walk you upstairs."

Julian affected a bow. "I apologize, ma'am. I fear I've upset her."

Mama waved him off. "Take no more thought, dear boy. Please excuse us."

With a final heated scowl at Julian, Willow allowed herself to be led toward the stairs. *Led* was a generous term.

At the bottom landing, Mama gave her captive elbow a firm shake. "Why would you yowl like a cat in front of our guests?"

Her frown was fierce.

"I didn't mean—"

Another shake, and Willow decided to hush.

Verdie, Willow's maid and former nanny, fell into step behind them, and the three climbed the stairs. Near the top, Willow glanced behind her.

Verdie, her affection as constant as the spinning earth, graced her with a sweet smile. *Julian is wrong about our slaves. They love us.* The notion settled in her heart, and she dismissed his troubling words.

Inside Willow's bedroom, Mama nodded at Verdie. "I'll get her into bed tonight. Wait here, and I'll hand out her gown to be aired."

Nodding, Verdie backed out and closed the door.

The silent room gradually returned to life as Willow climbed the stairs in the custody of her mother. Julian watched her go, a mixture of sadness and delight in his heart. Sad that she seemed blind to the truth about her father's hapless human chattel. Delighted by her spirited fire and beauty.

She'd been molded by the dictates of polite society into a genteel Southern lady, but Julian missed the tree-climbing girl.

"She's really something, isn't she?"

Jarred out of his musings about Willow, Julian forced his attention to Hiram. The boy stared up the staircase, his eyes deep springs of longing.

Unfamiliar stirrings swelled Julian's chest, different from the childish protectiveness of a boy who thought himself a man. He couldn't put a name to it, but the emotion pushed up his throat like bile. He clenched his fists for fear he'd strike the yearning look right off Hiram's face.

A cluster of high-strung men crowded around them, hiding their fear of war with displays of braggadocio and exaggerated threats directed at the Union. They shouted questions at Julian, too fast for him to answer.

"What are they saying at West Point? Which side are they on?"

"I heard General Beauregard, who fired on Sumter, is a former West Point super-intendent. Is that right?"

"Will you enlist?"

"Of course he will, what are you thinking?"

"We'll crush those blackguards down in two days' time, won't we, Julian?"

Over the tops of their heads, Julian met Hiram's steady gaze. Without a doubt, the challenge mirrored there signaled a declaration of war of another sort. One from which Julian didn't intend to back down.

At some point along the stairwell, Mama had cast off her anger like a snake shedding its skin. Once inside Willow's room, she became a chameleon, her mood taking on the sunny brightness of the lemon-yellow quilt.

"Here, let me help you." Her gentle hands turned Willow and began unfastening her dress, chatting all the while about trivial matters that Willow barely heard in her preoccupied state.

Stripped to linen chemise and knickers, Willow held up her arms and shivered as Mama slid the cool fabric of her nightdress past her shoulders. Before the covers were barely turned, Willow scrambled on her knees to her pillows and wriggled beneath the heavy quilt.

Mama laughed, a soothing balm. Bending, she kissed Willow's cheek. "Good night, honey. I'll send Verdie along to stoke your fire." She drew up her shoulders. "There's a chill in this room."

Willow caught her wrist. "Can't we talk?"

"I have guests, dear."

"It won't take long."

Smoothing her skirts, Mama perched on the side of the bed. "Very well, what troubles you?"

Willow ducked her chin. "Why does Julian Finney consider me a child?"

Nodding sagely, Mama patted her clasped hands. "So that was the cause of all the commotion?"

She squeezed Willow's fingers. "My dear, Julian has been at university for two years now, socializing with his peers. It's only natural a girl your age would seem young to him."

"A girl my age?" Willow pushed to a seated position and crossed her arms. "I'll soon be eighteen. Why can't he see I'm a woman now?"

Mama fought to hide her amusement but failed. "Oh, honey. There's plenty of time to be a woman. Couldn't you remain my little girl a bit longer?"

Willow smiled despite herself. "I simply refuse."

Mama laughed. "You'll break your mother's heart."

Falling against her pillows, Willow gave in to bitter tears. "He's going to war, Mama. Heaven knows when he'll return." Her eyes widened. "He might be hurt, or. . ."

Drawing her close, Mama gently rocked her. "Hush, now. This little skirmish will be settled in no time, without a drop of spilled blood. Soon, everything will be back to normal. You'll see."

Willow sniffed. "And then he'll return to West Point."

Mama sat back and smoothed her hair. "He'll be done with school before you have a chance to miss him, and then he'll be home for good."

Willow wiped her eyes on her sleeve. "I miss him already."

Laughing, Mama rolled her eyes. "My goodness, Willow. The young can be so melodramatic." Standing, she crossed to the door. "Go to sleep, now, you hear? And, no more crying. You'll awaken with puffy eyes."

"Mama?"

She turned, her smile bright. "What now?"

"Cletus, Bethy, and Verdie. . .they're happy, aren't they? And the others?"

Crossing her arms, she leaned against the door frame. "What an odd question. Of course they're happy. They've been with this family since Grammy and Grandpa built the house."

She sighed. "I wonder at times what goes on inside your head. Hush, now, and let me rejoin my guests."

"All right, good night."

"Good night, honey."

"And Mama?"

"Yes?"

"Give Julian a pinch for me."

"I'll do no such thing!" she cried, her voice choked with laughter.

The door closed, and so did Willow's eyelids. She had just begun to doze when Verdie's thin, stooped form shuffled into the room. She headed for the fireplace in halting steps, burdened by an armload of firewood.

At the hearth, she bent at the waist, a moan escaping her lips. Quietly, piece by piece, she placed the stack of split oak in the storage bin. Without straightening, she shuffled forward and fed more wood to the fire, tossing a handful of kindling on top to help it catch.

Clutching her lower back, she rose, panting to catch her breath. Her eyes were closed, her lips gently moving. Did she curse her fate or whisper a desperate prayer?

How old was Verdie? She seemed twice Grammy's age when she passed. In fact, Verdie seemed eternal. As old as God.

How many nights had she hovered at Willow's bedside, giving comfort after a nightmare or nursing her through bouts of the croup, while Mama slept soundly down the hall? Yet, Verdie was expected to carry on in the daylight hours with little or no sleep.

She never complained. Then, how could she?

She stooped again, her trembling hand reaching for the woodpile.

Willow shot up in bed. "That's enough, Verdie."

Verdie cried out and whirled, her hands at her throat. "I'm real sorry, Missy Girl. I didn't go to wake you."

Regret stabbed Willow's heart. Why had she spoken so harshly?

"I wasn't asleep," she answered, in a much gentler tone. "But that's enough wood for now."

Confusion stole over Verdie's ancient face. "That much won't see you through the night. It's right cold in here."

She picked up another splintered piece from the pile. "I'll jus' finish laying this fire like Missy Bates say. Won't take me no time."

Willow slid out of bed and rounded the foot posts in bare feet. Taking the wood from Verdie's hand, she shooed her toward the door. "You'll have it so hot in here, a body can't breathe. Go on, now, like *I* said."

"But Missy Bates, she—"

"You leave my mama to me."

Her big eyes chock-full of uncertainty, Verdie backed out the way she came, closing the latch with a soft click.

Willow watched the door, waiting for her to return and insist on carrying out Mama's instructions. To do otherwise was unheard of in this house.

To cover for her, Willow stoked the fire herself then bounded back into bed, her toes numb, her body shivering. Lying there, recalling the strident tone she'd taken with Verdie and the resulting shock on her face, her stomach twisted in knots.

The bedroom door squealed open, and Mama crossed to the foot of her bed. "What's this Verdie tells me? Why wouldn't you allow her to lay your fire?"

Willow sat up, her heart pounding. "I wasn't cold."

"It's only mid-April. There's still a chill in the air, honey, especially in the early morning hours. I'll send her back up right away, before you come down with something."

She glanced at the fully laid grate and her back stiffened. Glaring at Willow, she shook her head. "I won't have you coddling them, dear. They have their tasks, and they do them well. You weren't helping Verdie."

"But, Mama, she—"

"No arguments. You have her in a fit of angst. Don't interfere again. Do you understand?"

Willow tucked her chin. "Yes, ma'am."

"I declare you're more like Grammy every day."

Willow's ears pricked. "Grammy coddled the slaves?"

"Heavens, yes. Especially Verdie." Her lips tightened. "I shouldn't tell you these things, but yes. She never settled with the idea of keeping slaves. She went along with your grandpa because, after all, what choice did she have? I swear, the woman treated them like family. Most upsetting to Grandpa."

"Why didn't you ever tell me this?"

She shrugged. "The subject never came up."

At the door, she pointed her finger. "Go to sleep this time."

"Yes, ma'am."

Sliding down on her pillows, Willow pulled the quilt over her chin. "Wait. . .Mama?"

"What now?"

"Is Julian still downstairs?"

She sighed, a puzzled look on her face. "I expect those men will be right there until dawn. They're terribly agitated, aren't they?"

Gripping the sides of her pillow, Willow groaned into the lumpy down. If not for her outburst, she'd still be downstairs too. With Julian.

Mama closed the door, leaving her to mourn her plight.

Slumber didn't come easy, but thoughts of Julian didn't keep her awake. The specter of Verdie's work-weary body and pained moans kept sleep at bay for most of the night.

Chapter 3

November 1861

Willow opened the front door to a blanket of freshly fallen snow. A foot or more had accumulated overnight while she slept. Somehow, she had made it through her morning routine without noticing the covering of white through a window or hearing it mentioned in the house. To find it waiting was a lovely surprise. She drew her wrap tighter and stepped out the door.

Someone had salted the porch and shoveled the path, but she picked her way carefully down the steps and along the cobblestones to the waiting sleigh Cletus had traded for the buggy.

The horses tossed their heads, blowing clouds of mist through their noses. Cletus sat hunched over the reins, staring over the treetops, deep in thought. Raising his head at the sound of her footsteps, he scrambled down on his side. "Wait, Miss Willow. Jus' wait right there, and I'll help you."

"Oh, you don't have to. . .please be careful."

He slogged around the back of the sleigh, clinging to whatever he could grasp, and worked his way along the icy ground to where she stood. "Let me give you a hand up. Them wet shoes on that step gon' be slick."

Once he had her settled, he picked his way back to his side and climbed aboard.

"You didn't have to go to that trouble, Cletus. I could've made it just fine."

His dark gaze lifted briefly to hers, and confusion furrowed his brow. It was a peculiar thing for her to say because the irony was, he did have to. He would always have to, and both of them knew it.

"Where we going this fine day, miss?" he asked, instead of the forbidden question shining in his eyes.

It was her turn to be confused. Cletus seemed so muddled lately. "To church, of course. The same place you take me every Sunday."

He grimaced and scratched his forehead beneath the brim of his hat. "The Lord's Day. It surely is." He shrugged. "Sometime, it get so busy inside my head, I forget what day it be."

They rode past the wrought-iron gates and turned onto the road. Willow tried several times to unburden her heart of the momentous news she had for Cletus, but she lost her nerve each time.

At last she spoke, her voice a feeble croak. "I saw Annie yesterday."

Cletus brightened and twisted on the seat. "Tell me, Miss Willow. Please, tell all you know."

After the things Julian had said in her parlor, Willow made every excuse to visit the Clemson plantation and bring home news of Annie's welfare. She felt the good deed was as much for Julian as for Annie's parents.

When giving her report, she focused on the good she saw and not the bad, telling them Annie was well, a hard worker, attentive to her mistress, and obedient to her master.

She avoided saying the girl lurked in shadows, walked in sadness, stood with stooped shoulders, and had bags beneath her eyes. She didn't dare tell that Annie's mistress was jealous and vindictive and often took a strap to her.

"Go on, please, Miss Willow? How's my Annie?"

Reluctant, Willow scooted forward and gripped the back of his seat. "She's. . .with child, Cletus. You're going to be a grandfather."

He drew in a sharp breath and closed his eyes. A smile lit his face, replaced at once by a grimace of pain. A single tear slid down his cheek. "Please don't tell my Bethy."

Forgetting himself, he clutched her hand. "Won't you promise not to, Miss Willow? She couldn't bear to hear it."

Willow gripped his fingers. "I won't tell."

He nodded and withdrew his hand. "Thank you, miss."

He swallowed several times before he could talk, his throat bobbing. "How soon you reckon?"

Willow pictured Annie as she'd seen her the day before. The girl had leaned against the dining table, molding her oversize apron to her belly, revealing the unmistakable swell.

Unfamiliar with the business of bearing children, she had no idea, and certainly couldn't inquire. She wasn't sure the Clemsons were even aware of Annie's condition.

She shook her head. "I can't say. I'm sorry."

Cletus worked his bottom lip with his teeth. "Don't you be sorry. I thank you for telling me. Otherwise, I might never have known." He gave her a trembling smile. "I'm sorely grateful for all you've done."

Once she might've related these words to Julian, as evidence of the man's appreciation and affection for her family. Now, she realized she didn't deserve his gratitude.

Ashamed, she had nothing fitting to say. Luckily, they were pulling in front of the church, so she fought back tears and busied herself with her cloak and gloves.

Hiram stood in front of the redbrick chapel, framed by the whitewashed doorposts. Waving, he hurried down the steps to greet her, a smile on his face and an umbrella tucked under his arm.

He held out his hand to help her down. "Good morning. You're nearly late." Opening the bulky umbrella, he held it over her head.

She laughed and pointed skyward. "It's not snowing."

Grinning, he lowered and closed the contraption.

"And"—she smirked—"nearly late is not the same as late."

He offered his arm. "Dawdling outside debating it will make us both late."

Laughing, she laid her hand in the crook of his arm and allowed him to walk her toward the church.

At the door, she glanced over her shoulder. Cletus still sat where they'd left him, staring straight ahead, his face a portrait of wonder and pain.

"Move on, boy!" A voice shouted from the yard. A disgruntled deacon glared at him, muttering under his breath. "Sitting up there woolgathering with all these wagons waiting to unload."

Cletus shot to life. Whipping the reins, he drove the horses forward and turned the sleigh toward home. He would return to fetch her in an hour. At least she hoped. He wasn't himself lately, even before she shared her news.

Guilt wriggled beneath the surface. Should she have kept quiet about Annie?

"Sure is a fine day," Hiram said, pulling her from her thoughts.

She laughed. "There's an overcast sky and a foot of snow on the ground."

He winked and tightened his grip on her arm. "Three fellows inside are saving you a seat. I'm the only one smart enough to wait for you outside. That makes it a right good day."

Willow laced her fingers to keep from scratching her head. Since Julian left, Hiram had changed. His behavior had run the gauntlet, from childhood tyrant to shy friend, and now to what could be mistaken as a contender for her affection. Surely, she imagined the last.

Hiram pulled open the heavy door and ushered Willow inside the chapel. Three sets of eyes, Sam Dillon's, Cleon Wilkie's, and William Smyth's, glared at him in unrepentant envy from the pews.

Reverend Smyth glared in unrepentant scorn from the pulpit.

"I told you we'd be late," Hiram whispered, tossing the umbrella in a corner and hanging her cloak on a peg.

After a stirring sermon on brotherly love, with a discourse on the merits of punctuality thrown in for good measure, the reverend dismissed the congregation. Clinging possessively to her arm, Hiram walked Willow outside.

Cletus wasn't in his customary place in the line of waiting rigs.

Hiram scanned the row of conveyances again. "Where's old Cletus?"

There were three constants in Willow's life: the grace of God, the direction the river flowed, and Cletus. Frowning, she peered down the road. "Perhaps the weather?"

Hiram nodded. "That must be it. I'm sure he'll be along."

Willow remembered the state of Cletus after he learned about Annie's condition, and her stomach lurched. Hopefully, bad weather was the cause of his delay, and not something dreadful.

She imagined him bursting through the Clemsons' front door, demanding to see Annie, and her heart cartwheeled in her chest.

"I can take you home," Hiram said at her elbow. "I have my sleigh."

He offered his arm, but Willow hung back. "I should wait. Papa will be so angry."

Hiram glanced overhead. "It's going to snow again. Let me get you home. We'll stop on the way and ask one of the field hands about Cletus. News travels faster than a telegraph in their quarters."

He led her to his sleigh and helped her aboard. She settled her skirts while he hurried around and climbed up beside her. "Are you warm enough? There's a blanket under the seat."

"I'm fine, thank you."

They jostled over the uneven ground, and Hiram turned the horses toward the road. Willow searched for any sign of Cletus. Only brilliant white fields and an empty road lay ahead.

She shivered. "I think I would like that quilt after all."

Hiram pulled it from under his legs and shook it out for her. "Do you hear any news from Julian?"

A slow ache spread in her chest. Julian had gone off to war seven months ago, on the first of May, two weeks after he stood in her parlor and announced his intention to enlist.

He returned to the house the day he left to say goodbye to her parents, though it was Willow he asked to write to him. She cherished the memory of his warm farewell hug and gentle kiss on the cheek.

"He used to write more often. Once Virginia joined the Confederacy, our stamps became worthless up North. The post office sent all his mail to the dead letter office."

Thinking of those undelivered letters, she groaned inside. Julian's precious words, lost forever.

Julian's behavior had changed as well. Each of his letters became increasingly more intimate, as if he had become a contender for her too. A prospect even harder to believe than Hiram's advances.

"I've received only a couple of letters since they started the Confederate Postal System. I hope to get another one any day."

Hiram ducked his head. "Will you write me too? When I go?"

Her eyes shifted his way. "Nonsense. They don't take boys your age."

"They do. The youngest serve as drummers, messengers, and orderlies, but some as young as fifteen are trained to fight."

Willow shuddered at the thought of Port Royal's youngest called to the battlefield.

"Besides," Hiram said, "I'm nearly eighteen."

It didn't seem possible, yet Willow herself had turned eighteen last month. She'd missed spending the day with Julian, so she hardly felt like celebrating.

"Will you?" Hiram asked.

"Pardon?" Focused on Julian, she'd lost track of the conversation.

"Write to me?" he persisted.

She touched his hand. "Of course."

Willow studied his familiar face, so serious, so eager, and her heart swelled. She couldn't imagine him with a gray cap on his head and carrying a musket. Only yesterday, they were children.

She giggled, her breath a vaporous cloud. "Remember how you used to tease me?"

He made a face. "I was an intolerable nuisance. How did you stand me?"

"Oh, I couldn't." She nudged him with her elbow. "I could hardly bear the sight of you."

Hiram sobered and looked away toward the icy pasture at his side. They rode in silence for so long, she feared her words had offended him.

"I hope you don't feel that way now," he said, stealing a peek at her.

Willow watched his somber profile. "Well, of course not. We've become great friends."

"Friends." He gave a shaky laugh and nodded. "Of course."

Willow felt guilty of some unintentional affront. Squirming inside, she tried to think what to say to bring back his playful mood. "Hiram, I—"

"Look there." Sitting taller on the seat, he pointed down the road.

Cletus sped toward them in the distance, the sled swaying and bouncing behind the horses.

Willow's breath caught. "He's going to tip over."

Hiram stood up and waved his arms, flagging Cletus to a stop.

Panic shone from the poor man's eyes. "I's dreadful sorry, Miss Willow. Truly I is."

She scowled. "You must never drive the sleigh so fast again, do you hear? You might've been killed."

He waved a trembling hand. "No sleigh ride gon' kill me, but your papa will."

"What kept you? I've been so worried."

He hung his head. "I'm real sorry, missy. Just getting slow, that's all."

By the look on his face, there was more to it, but she'd leave it for now.

Hiram jumped to the ground and helped her climb down on his side to avoid the deep snowdrifts.

She clutched his sleeve. "Papa mustn't know Cletus came so late."

He smiled sweetly. "I'll keep your secret. . .friend."

She searched his face for anger or sarcasm but found none. "Thank you," she whispered, taking his outstretched hand.

He helped her into her sleigh then backed away with a jaunty wave.

"Hiram," she called. "Won't you spend Christmas with us?"

Shock then pleasure flitted over his face. "Your folks won't mind?"

"They'd love to have you."

Beaming, he bowed at the waist. "I humbly accept your invitation."

Cletus pulled off and circled in the road, so sharply Willow thought they'd tip over. He nearly got a runner stuck in his haste, but he drove toward home at a much safer pace.

"That Mistuh Hiram growing up to be a fine boy."

Willow glanced over her shoulder. Hiram stood where they'd left him, shading his eyes against the glare. "Yes, he is. A real fine boy."

He'd been so nice, seemed so dejected, inviting him for Christmas seemed right in the moment. Giving in to her impulse may have been a mistake, however, considering his peculiar conduct. She certainly didn't want to encourage him.

Cletus began to hum in his deep baritone, one of the mournful tunes he often sang.

Willow once pointed out to Julian that the slaves were always singing, therefore, how could they be sad?

"Pay attention to the lyrics, girl," he'd said.

His answer burned in her chest as the words to Cletus's song echoed in her head.

Oh, Jesus, my Savior, on Thee I'll depend
When troubles are near me, You'll be my true friend
I'm troubled
I'm troubled
I'm troubled in mind
If Jesus don't help me
I surely will die

The humming stopped, leaving Willow singing unaccompanied in her head. Embarrassed, she swiped away her tears.

Cletus didn't seem to notice. "I reckon I'm gon' tell Bethy," he said, a firm set to his jaw. "She have a right to know, same as me."

"About the baby?"

He nodded.

"Won't it make her sad?"

"I suppose. But we ain't no strangers to sadness. We'll get through. We always do."

He grew quiet, lost in his thoughts.

Unwilling to intrude, Willow sat back and listened to the rhythmic crunch of the horses' hooves and the gentle swish of the runners.

Nearing the turnoff, Cletus cleared his throat. "Miss Willow, I owe you my thanks for your kindness to Bethy and me. I know you're risking trouble for it."

He looked over his shoulder. "I want you to know we're beholding to you."

Willow couldn't speak. She tried to express sorrow and regret with her eyes, but all she felt was shame.

Cletus tipped his hat then turned his attention to the horses.

They pulled in front of the house, where Papa stood scowling on the porch, his silver hair blown into a mane around his head. "What in thunder took so long?" he called, hurrying down the steps to meet them. "I was about to send out a search party."

Willow took his hand and stepped to the ground. "Entirely my fault. I dawdled after church talking to my friends. It won't happen again."

"It best not. Bethy stuffed a goose, and I'm rather looking forward to it. It's been warming so long, we're perilously close to having stuffed jerky instead."

"Yes, Papa," she said, stealing a glance at Cletus.

He gave her a discreet nod of gratitude. Clucking at the horses, he flicked the reins and drove the sleigh toward the barn.

Chapter 4

December 1861

C hristmas morning brought Willow two early-morning presents. First, another two feet of snow to adorn the world outside her bedroom window. Second, a letter from Julian delivered on her breakfast tray.

Tucked between her raisin muffin and hot cup of tea, the tattered envelope with "Soldier's Mail" scrawled in Julian's neat script was a gift she didn't expect.

Squealing, she held it aloft. "A letter today? The post office is closed for the holiday."

Verdie, her face wreathed in glee, clapped her hands. "It come yesterday. I held it back to give you for Christmas."

Too happy to scold her, and unwilling to wipe the snaggletooth grin from her face, Willow patted her hand. There were precious few ways for Verdie to offer gifts. She'd not take this one from her.

"I'm so pleased. Thank you."

Verdie's coffee-brown cheeks glowed. "You welcome, Missy Girl." She couldn't seem prouder of her offering if she'd written and posted the letter herself.

Wringing her hands, she pressed closer, peering at the envelope as Willow slit it open. Laughing, Willow shooed her toward the door. "Go on, now. Leave me in peace to read my letter."

The door closed. Willow held her breath and unfolded the single page.

52nd Virginia Volunteer Infantry Regiment
Pocahontas County, Virginia, December 15, 1861

My dearest Willow,

With pleasure, I take up pen and ink to greet you and answer your last letter. The aforementioned communication was met with unbridled anticipation and read until the creases are tattered. Some of the men get so few letters, they begged that I might share with them, but I steadfastly refused. I will selfishly keep you to myself. My company engaged in a fierce battle just two days past. Our forces, under the command of Colonel Edward Johnson, occupied the summit of Allegheny Mountain to defend the Staunton and Parkersburg Turnpike. The bluecoats attacked Johnson at sunrise. With the harsh winter wind bearing down, we fought undaunted until our artillery released a volley of round shot and canister, driving them back. Colonel Johnson led us straight through their middle, and we drove them down the mountain. Our company suffered a great loss of lives and many wounded, but we prevailed.

"Oh Julian," she whispered. He wrote so casually of lost and wounded men. What had this war done to him?

> *Those of us here speak often of home and hearth, and long for our loved ones. The subject of Christmas is on everyone's lips, and the hope that this madness might be finished by then, our fondest wish. The men of another company cut down a small tree and placed it in front of their tent, decorated with hardtack and pork. The sight of it elicits unspeakable melancholy.*

Willow tried to envision the tragic little tree. How could she possibly celebrate anything today? She sighed and returned to the letter.

> *The only thoughts of Christmas I care to entertain are those of you, surrounded by lavish food and loving family. How pleasant it would be to see you again, dear Willow. Even if you only scowl and stamp your foot at me. I close with great affection and fervent prayers.*
>
> *Yours faithfully, Julian*

Laying the cherished letter aside, she stared at the ceiling, concern for Julian an ache in her chest. She imagined him shivering in a canvas tent while she slept on a feather bed beneath a padded quilt.

The snow she considered a Christmas gift now seemed a hostile threat.

The door swung open and Mama swept in, uninvited. Her azure-blue dressing gown against her golden hair and fair complexion gave an impression of softness and serenity—two things Mama had never been.

"Good morning, my dear. Merry Christmas."

"Thank you, Mama. Merry Christmas to you."

She breezed about the room, picking up Willow's robe and hanging it on a peg, running her finger around the china bowl on her vanity, checking for cleanness, pulling Willow's slippers from under the bed, ready for her to slide onto her feet.

"Arise, daughter. Verdie will be in directly with hot water for your bath."

She caught Willow's big toe and gave it a playful shake. "Come, now. There's no time to lollygag about your room today. You have a gentleman caller coming to dinner."

Willow sat up straighter. "It's Hiram, Mama. Hardly a gentleman caller."

Pausing, she raised one brow. "He's a gentleman, and he's a caller. Don't sass your mama. "Besides"—she gave Willow a furtive wink—"I suspect Hiram believes he's just that. I've watched the way he looks at you."

Willow drew back. "Just how does he look at me?"

Her mama laughed, loud enough to flush a covey of quail. "Like a starving man at the last call to supper."

Effectively flushed herself, Willow swung her legs over and stood. "I won't entertain such nonsense today. I'm too happy." She held up the letter. "Look! News from Julian, at last."

Mama's eyes closed, and she breathed a sigh of relief. "That's wonderful, dear. I had begun to think—"

She drew Willow into an azure-blue hug. "Never you mind. I fear for him, is all. This war is a terrible thing for Virginia." She held Willow at arm's length. "Most of our boys will never come home. You know that, don't you?"

Cringing, Willow covered her ears. "Please, don't."

"I must, honey. We pray for the best but prepare for the worst."

Averting her eyes, Willow pressed Julian's letter to her chest. "I'll never abandon him to that fate, not even in my thoughts."

Mama brushed her cheek with gentle fingers. "You love him, don't you?"

"I've loved him all my life."

The billowing arms of Mama's dressing gown engulfed her again, and she leaned into the satiny comfort. "It's always best to marry for love," Mama said. "Sadly, it doesn't happen that often.

"Truthfully, I believe Hiram to be a more worthy match for you. He's from a good family with roots here in Port Royal. His father has holdings in Europe that this war won't diminish."

Staring over Willow's head, she frowned. "Young Julian is practically a pauper. What can he possibly offer you?"

Near tears, Willow opened her mouth to protest, but Mama held up a hand to shush her. "Don't fret. I won't interfere."

She gave a resolute nod. "In fact, I shall mention Julian's name to my prayer group. We'll petition him safely home."

"Bless you, Mama." An appeal to God from the Agape Prayers was tantamount to an ironclad guarantee.

Releasing Willow with a kiss to the top of her head, she continued her inspection of the room, her idle chatter about the day's festivities background noise for Willow's thoughts.

Willow strolled to the window and raised the blind higher, peering out at the fresh layers of snow. Cletus and Bethy ambled toward each other on the shoveled footpath. Cletus bound for the barn where Firefly, Papa's black stallion, would be stamping and snorting for his breakfast. Bethy was on her way to the kitchen for a rendezvous with her pots and pans.

It appeared to be a chance encounter, but they veered together as if drawn by unseen forces. Bethy lifted her face to his, and pain broke over it like splintered glass.

Forgetting to mind who might see, Cletus caught her head in his big hands and spoke something close to her ear.

She nodded several times and smiled.

Cletus wiped her tears with his thumbs, stepped aside, and allowed her to go her way. Glancing over his shoulder, he watched her, terrible sadness on his face.

Slaves weren't permitted to legally marry but were allowed to exchange the customary vows, if they wished. Cletus and Bethy had said those vows to each other many years ago, though the ceremony held no promise of "till death do us part." Something as simple as a master's whim could rip them apart forever.

Did they live with constant dread of the thing that finally happened, only not to them but their beloved child?

Willow whispered a prayer that it might never happen to these two so united by love.

Feeling guilty for intruding on their private moment, she left the window, but the touching scene would remain in her thoughts.

"I've laid out your best dress and shoes," Mama said. "I'll go see what's keeping Verdie."

At the door, her customary spot for sharing afterthoughts, she turned. "I want you to heed what I said about Hiram. I spoke in jest, but suppose the boy really does love you?"

Willow feigned a dubious look. No sense putting ideas in the woman's head.

Mama dismissed her with a wave. "You need to consider what I'm saying. Lord knows he's always dogged your steps."

"So he could stomp on my toes."

"Boys are at a loss when it comes to expressing their feelings. Instead, they make faces and tug braids. If you love Julian, so be it. Just don't break Hiram's heart. There's enough pain in Virginia these days."

She closed the door, and immediately Verdie opened it with a broad smile. Her eyes searched the breakfast tray until she spotted the envelope. "Was it a nice letter?"

Willow laughed and hugged her. "Very nice, indeed. Thank you again for your thoughtfulness."

Suddenly shy, Verdie lowered her lashes. "I wish I had more to give."

There was no doubt this woman loved her, and Willow loved her in return.

As her nanny, Verdie felt her most important job was getting Willow eligible for heaven. To that end, she prayed the salvation prayer with her at a young age and taught her Bible stories she recited from memory because she couldn't read.

Verdie nursed her, fed her, bathed her—all the things a mother does for her child. Their mutual love had grown naturally.

"Come on and get your bath," Verdie said. "I'm gon' pin up your white hair real nice today. When you slip on that pretty green dress, you gon' light up the whole house."

Once bathed and dressed, she let Verdie pull her to the standing mirror in the corner. As promised, her reflection seemed to glow.

Verdie, her fingers laced together beneath her chin, gazed in childlike wonder. "You so pretty, Missy Girl. Jus' like your porcelain doll."

Willow kept a lovely bisque doll in her room, fair complexioned with flaxen hair. It wore a princess gown and had a crown on its head.

A sudden thought pricked her heart. She had nothing else to offer Verdie for Christmas.

Smiling, she nodded at the porcelain doll. "Would you like to have her?"

Verdie followed Willow's gaze to the shelf and gasped.

"Go on, then," Willow said. "Take her. She's yours."

Lifting the doll from its place, Verdie held it reverently, her eyes brimming. "I never had anything so pretty in all my life."

Willow hugged her thin shoulders and wiped her tears. "Merry Christmas, dear Verdie." *I'm going to give you more pretty things. Just wait and see.*

Sniffing, Verdie urged her toward the door. "Get on with you, now. They waiting for you downstairs."

This year promised to be a Christmas like never before. The bony fingers of war had gripped Port Royal by the throat. The bleakness and desolation that began at Fort Sumter had spread over Virginia like a rash.

Mama made an effort, lining the hearth with handmade decorations and stringing up garlands she'd fashioned of ribbons and pine boughs. She had Cletus fell a fat Scotch pine for the front hall. Still, the presents tucked under the tree were lacking in all but good intentions, and all merriment and cheer had gone out of the day.

In the kitchen, pots sizzled and ovens blazed. The holiday meal Bethy had fretted over since dawn might want in substance but certainly not in imagination or flavor.

Willow entered the parlor, and Papa rose from his favorite chair. "Aren't you a pretty little thing this morning? Just the decoration this room needs."

He glanced at Mama over his shoulder. "Clara, will you look at Willow? Our little gal is all grown up."

Mama smiled from the settee. "Oh, Charles, you speak as if it happened overnight." She set her teacup on the table beside her. "The whole thing unfolded right under your nose."

The light from the fireplace shone in Papa's misty eyes. "Then I'll have to pay closer attention from now on."

A knock came at the front door.

"That will be Hiram," Mama said. She rose and walked to the embroidered bellpull in the corner to ring for Cletus. The familiar tapping of his heels echoed along the corridor as he passed the parlor on his way to the door.

"Come right in, suh," he said, his jolly voice carrying to the parlor. "Merry Christmas to you."

Seating herself, Willow pictured Hiram's shy smile and nod in return. His russet hair, mussed when he took off his hat, would be stuck up in front the way it had when he was a boy.

She and Mama shared a look across the room, her mother's earlier warning repeated in one lifted brow.

Willow answered with a small nod of her head. *I won't,* she vowed to herself. *I won't do anything to break Hiram's heart.*

"Right this way, suh," Cletus said. "They already in the parlor this morning."

The door swung open and Cletus stepped aside.

Julian crossed the threshold, a bundle of presents in one hand and one more tucked under his arm. His dimpled smile would melt the fallen snow.

Willow gasped and shot to her feet. Her eyes drank in every lanky inch of him until tears blurred him from sight. She'd only just read his words, written to her from some distant place. How impossible that he stood before her now.

Laughing, he limped across the room to shake her beaming father's hand.

Willow rubbed the tears from her eyes, only to burst into fresh sobs. Julian didn't have a gift beneath his arm as she'd thought at first sight. Instead, he held a crutch.

Julian's buoyant pleasure at seeing Willow again deflated and ran aground. On the journey, he'd imagined all the possible reactions she might have to his surprise. Crying wasn't among them.

Her mother gathered her close and patted her back. "Oh, honey, there now."

Julian's arms ached to hold and comfort her. Instead, he widened his eyes at her ma.

"She's happy to see you, Julian. She truly is. I believe the sight of your injury has upset her."

He waved the crutch at them. "This? Why, it's nothing at all." He took a few hobbling steps closer, straining to keep his balance. "See, I don't even need the old thing. Not really."

Willow darted to his side, wrapping her arm around his waist to steady him. "Don't be foolish, Julian. You look no braver teetering like a drunkard than you do leaning on a crutch."

She smiled up at him. "How is it you stand here before me? Only this morning you were miles away in a tent, writing me a letter."

He laughed. "I wrote that letter from a hospital bed. During the skirmish on Allegheny Mountain, I took a shot in the leg from a musket. God was gracious. The ball caused no permanent damage to the muscle nor shattered any bone, but the wound was deep enough to land me in the infirmary."

The shouting, moaning, bloody chaos of the field hospital flashed before his eyes, and he shuddered. "There were men there who needed my cot far more than I did. I asked permission to recover at home."

He slanted his head. "It didn't occur to me until I'd come halfway on the train that I no longer have a home in Port Royal."

His pa had written a few months ago. He and Ma packed their meager possessions and boarded a boat bound for Galway. Only the empty house and barren land remained. They intended to sell the place and urged Julian to join them in Ireland.

"Of course you have a home," Willow's pa said, patting his back. "You'll stay here with us. There are plenty of rooms in this big old house."

Julian shook his head. "Sir, I couldn't impose."

Mr. Bates gripped his shoulder. "Son, I insist."

"Merry Christmas?" a strained voice said from the door.

Hiram stood on the threshold, his brooding gaze locked on Willow's arm, tight around Julian's waist.

"I knocked," he finally said. "Cletus let me in."

Mrs. Bates closed her gaping mouth and smiled. "A very merry Christmas to you too. We've been expecting you, dear boy. Please come in."

She surged forward and took the presents Hiram held, laying them on a side table. "We've had the most wonderful surprise this morning, and it's quite thrown us off. Our very own Julian has come home on leave. I'm afraid he's been wounded, but he assures us it's not serious."

She glanced at Julian. "Isn't that right, dear?"

Julian held out his crutch again. "Fit as a fiddle."

Her laughter, much too loud, echoed in the rafters. Spreading her arms, she herded the group across the room. "Let's not stand about like cranes in a marsh. Sit down."

Julian watched Mrs. Bates with interest. Something had her feeling uneasy, and her nervous chatter gave her away.

He didn't miss the look she gave Willow, or the fact that her daughter withdrew from his side, offering her elbow instead as she helped him to the couch.

Before Hiram took a seat, he stood over Julian and offered his hand. "Welcome home. It's good to see you."

Julian searched his face for malice but found none. Only a hint of the former challenge lurking behind auburn lashes. "Thank you."

Hiram nodded and seated himself on Willow's other side.

"Well," Mrs. Bates said, her smile too bright. "Isn't this nice?"

As the peculiar day progressed, Julian felt *nice* wasn't a suitable word. The meal was certainly agreeable, and watching Willow open the gifts he'd chosen for her, especially pleasant.

However, they limped through the other festivities on their hostess's schedule under a pall of heavy strain.

Relief flooded Julian's exhausted mind when Hiram announced his departure.

"So soon?" Mrs. Bates fairly whined. "We haven't played any games yet."

Hiram stood and shook Mr. Bates's hand then nodded at his wife. "My apologies, ma'am. I really must take my leave."

His throat bobbed, and he cut his eyes to Willow. "I mostly came to wish you glad tidings, and. . .to tell you I'm leaving."

"Leaving?" Willow stood and walked beside him to the door. "Where are you going?"

Cletus appeared with Hiram's hat.

Hiram worried the brim, kneading it in his hands. "I'm going to enlist. I leave first thing tomorrow. I couldn't go without telling you goodbye."

Chapter 5

"You're walking much better today. There's hardly a limp at all."

Julian tightened his grip on Willow's arm and feigned an exaggerated hobble. "On the contrary, I'm much too feeble to be left on my own."

The admiration in his mischievous eyes warmed Willow to her toes. "You, sir, are an impossible fraud. You pretend to be frail only to have me pamper you."

He cocked his head at a jaunty angle. "I plead guilty."

His fingertips teased her forearm, and the hair stood up on her neck. "I willingly take on the roll of pretender, if I can keep you close by."

They were out for their morning stroll along the footpath they used as children. The air was cool, but sunlight reached them through the treetops, warming Willow's head through her hat.

The month of February arrived unseasonably warm, and most of the snow had melted. This shaded stretch of the well-traveled path still shone in spots with iced-over hollows. Willow carefully dodged them, fearing for Julian's wounded leg.

They reached the end of the trail and stepped onto the road leading to Port Royal. Willow urged him along the shoulder, avoiding the muddy ruts.

Julian chuckled and drew her to a halt. "You must stop being so protective, Willow. I'm not feeble."

"I don't want you to fall and reinjure yourself."

He caught her elbow and turned her around to face him. "My leg has healed, honey. I'm perfectly sound. The time has come for me to rejoin my regiment."

Willow glanced up sharply. "Oh Julian. So soon? I've tried not to think of you leaving."

He slid his gloved hand up her back and caressed her neck. "I've stayed longer than I should have. Any longer, and they'll think I've deserted."

He grinned. "Besides, I can't laze about being coddled with a war going on."

She stared at the icy ground, a chill settling around her heart. "Will this dreadful war never end?"

"Not until we get it fought, and that will take every able body."

He curled his finger beneath her chin and tipped up her head. "Nevertheless, it will end, little Willow. And I will come home to you."

Burying her face in the scratchy fabric of his coat, she inhaled the woodsy scent of him. "Do you promise?"

"I give you my word as a Southern gentleman."

She smiled to herself. "Spoken with an Irish brogue."

His heart, beating next to her ear, sped up. "Willow? Am I too bold to hope you'll wait for me?"

His words flooded past the cold dread of his leaving and warmed her with joy. "I should bat my lashes and ask for time to consider, but you'd see right through such posturing."

She tucked in her bottom lip. "The truth is, I would have waited though you never asked."

Julian groaned and pulled her closer, stealing her breath. She swayed against him, dizzy with emotion.

He lowered his head, and their lips met.

"I love you, Willow Evangeline Bates," he murmured against her mouth.

"And I you, Julian Patrick Finney."

His gentle kiss became deep and urgent. She responded with all the pent-up love she held inside.

Employing all the strength he could muster, Julian drew away from Willow and set her at arm's length. Thrilled by the passion and promise in her kiss, his longing would have to wait for the proper time.

He smiled at her then glanced overhead. "It looks like rain. We'd better get back."

She beamed up at him and nodded, happy tears shimmering on her lashes.

Hand in hand, they turned toward Fairhill, the only sound the crunch of melting ice beneath their feet.

Willow would be worth waiting for, and the memory of her soft embrace would get him through the rest of the war. Then he would return with all haste and make her his bride.

Chapter 6

Fairhill Plantation, Port Royal, Virginia
October 12, 1862

My dearest Julian,

Today marks my nineteenth birthday, and I must spend it without you in misery and grief. I will comfort myself with memories of last Christmas. The days since have passed in a desolate blur. How ironic that the war we thought would never begin seems destined to never end. The only bright spots in my days are yours and Hiram's letters. He's doing well and sends his regards.

I regret not having a good report to cheer you. Instead, this letter will serve to inform you of more of our many troubles, though our trials are naught compared to yours. I wrote to you about the occupation of Fredericksburg by Major General Irvin McDowell and his Union forces, and how they took that fair city from April last through August.

In mid-August, reports of Confederate activity in our area brought an expedition from that infantry downriver to Port Royal. They landed at several plantations along the way, but word had come to Port Royal of their arrival, so many of the homes were deserted.

The Union detachment wreaked much havoc in our town. They captured some of our citizens and destroyed the ferry used to smuggle recruits across river from Port Conway to Port Royal and on to Baltimore for training.

Father's promise to flee west to North Carolina, should they return, brought some comfort. However, not as much as I long to find in your arms.

Instead of wretchedness and gloom, I should write cheerful letters to raise your spirits. If only I were so duplicitous! But you know me well and would find me false. There isn't an ounce of cheer left in the whole state of Virginia, and I cannot pretend otherwise.

My need of you increases by the day, and I long for a single glimpse of your cherished face. My daily prayer is that God will rescue and shelter you and Hiram, as well as our beloved Port Royal.

I remain,
Your own loving and devoted Willow

Willow sealed the envelope and placed a gentle kiss on Julian's name scrawled on the front. How she missed him. He wrote often, letters filled with promises and plans for their future.

It wasn't enough. With a lonely sigh, she crossed the study to the double doors and pushed them open, stepping onto the porch.

Vivid fall colors rushed at her, a stirring portrait of the tragedy of war. Russet leaves, shriveled and battered, gave up the fight and fell, lifeless, to the ground. A line of blood-red maples, their brilliant hues strengthened by the sunrise, blazed across fields of snow-white cotton.

Willow trod respectfully over the carpet of dead leaves, resentful of the pristine cotton, its purity and innocence unsullied by pain and death. She squinted toward the maples in the distance, willing the scarlet splotches on the horizon to bleed into the fields, spoiling ambition and greed along with the crop.

Papa gave most of the slaves Sunday mornings off for their worship, so the grounds were deserted except for two giggling children playing chase around a tree. Across the yard, Cletus pulled open the barn door, a sack of feed on his shoulder for Firefly.

Evidently, the horse didn't know he had the morning off.

She lifted her hand to wave, but he didn't look up. His shoulders were stooped, his walk weary, as if he carried the weight of the world's problems instead of a single sack of feed.

Willow knew he bore the burden of another day without his daughter and grandson.

After her confinement, Annie had returned to her duties in the Clemson household sometime in the beginning of March. She seemed the same as before, only sadder and quieter, as if the birth of her son had doubled her earthly cares.

On several scouting expeditions to the Clemson house, Willow caught sight of the wee babe, swaddled and placed in a small cradle, near enough for Annie to pause her chores and nurse him. As he grew over the months since his birth, he moved from the cradle to a soft pallet in the corner where he babbled and cut his teeth on a yarn doll.

As far as Willow knew, little Samuel was the first of the Clemson slave babies to be kept inside the house. A beautiful boy, he had black hair and creamy skin with big eyes framed in dark lashes. Mr. Clemson doted on him.

Without fail, Willow sought out Cletus and Bethy after her visits and shared with them every detail. Bethy fairly danced with excitement, and Cletus broke out in joyful tears. Willow avoided real tears by keeping part of what she knew to herself.

The happy little boy had a smile for everyone but Mrs. Clemson. At the sight of her, he withdrew into his corner and pulled the covers under his chin. No doubt, the deep purple bruises on his chubby little legs were thanks to her hateful jabs and pinches.

All these things were on Willow's mind as she returned to the house to join her parents for her birthday breakfast.

Papa raised his coffee cup in greeting. "Here she is, at last. Happy birthday, my girl."

Mama offered a weak smile from her place at his side. Her customary seat at the big dining table was opposite Papa at the far end. When only the three of them dined, they huddled together, Papa at the head, the two women on each side of him.

Willow paused on the threshold, reluctant to enter. Her mind flashed to years before, when birthday gifts waited on her chair and the aromas of delicious offerings, varied and plentiful, wafted from the sideboard.

There would be little variety this morning. Bethy would have struggled to prepare a fitting meal with the meager provisions left in the pantry, but Willow was grateful for what they had.

A few days before, a rogue band of Federal soldiers rode up and pillaged Fairhill, stripping them of most of their goods. The grace of God and Papa's resourcefulness saved them from utter starvation.

Hearing of the raiding parties in town, Papa had buried what he could, leaving enough meat in the smokehouse and corn in the crib to avoid suspicion. Cletus shoveled piles of fertilizer over the disturbed ground, and the soldiers never looked twice at the spot.

"Come here, Willow," Mama said, reaching across the table to pour steaming tea into a cup. "I'm afraid there's no sugar, honey. I'll put a dollop of cream for you instead."

Papa rose and met her halfway with a warm hug. Tilting her chin, he solemnly studied her face. "We don't have anything special for you this year."

Smiling, he nodded at a single present next to her plate, wrapped in gaily colored scraps reminiscent of past celebrations. "Your mama knitted something pretty, though. I'm sure she wove love into every stitch."

He grimaced. "Anything else we wanted to give you will have to wait. But I hope you know we love you. You're the most precious blessing in our lives."

Her heart breaking, Willow gazed into her father's kind eyes. How could anyone capable of such love accept slavery as a way of life without questioning the inherent brutality? Grandpa Bates, against Grammy's wishes, handed down their legacy of shame, but Papa was without excuse.

It made no sense, but she had no right to judge. Not so long ago, she'd considered their way of life normal. Even necessary. Thankfully, Julian had loved her without condemnation, until her eyes were opened to the truth.

Slavery had been practiced since before the American Revolution, and not just in the South. Nearly every state or territory participated at some point. The inhuman practice had a firm grip on the country before she was born, and now men were dying to defend it. Only God's grace could fix the mess this nation had created for itself through iniquity and greed. Only by the cross of Christ would they find that grace.

Recalling the cotton fields, she now saw the pure white, bordered by crimson, as a picture of God's love. In the midst of suffering, sin, and death, God prepared a place of safety for them all, purchased by the sacrificial death of Jesus.

Love was the only safe place left, and the only hope for her family.

Ripples of determination braced her spine. She put flint in her eye and steel in her tone and forced the words from her mouth. "There's only one thing I want this year. I won't be satisfied with anything else."

Papa grunted and returned her gritty stare. "I've spoiled you, girl," he murmured.

She shook her head. "No, sir. You taught me to know my own mind and fight for what I want."

Grinning, he glanced over his shoulder. "She's got me there, Clara."

He propped his fists on his hips. "All right, then. Tell me what you want. If it's within my power to give, it's yours."

Willow shook inside with nerves but firmed her jaw and met his expectant gaze. "I want Annie back at Fairhill."

His grin faded, replaced by confusion. "Bethy's girl?"

She nodded. "And her infant son."

"Well for heaven's sake." His shrill voice made her cringe. "Why on earth would you want that?"

Willow opened her mouth, but no words came. She hadn't gotten that far in her thinking.

Mama spoke up in her stead. "Of course she wants Annie. It's a wonderful idea. Once this awful war is over, our girl will be getting married. She'll need help with her babies."

Papa frowned. "I thought we planned to give her Verdie."

"Verdie's too old. Willow needs a young girl to train up right."

Willow didn't deny her mama's assumption. She kept quiet and let them think what they liked.

"I don't believe Homer Clemson will part with them," Papa said. "He's unreasonably fond of that girl"—he shot Mama a weighty look over Willow's head—"and her offspring."

"Everything has a price, Charles. Isn't that what you always say?"

He winced. "Honey, things are not the same as they were. I'm not sure I could meet Homer's price."

"There must be something he wants."

Papa stared out the window, scratching his head. "I suppose I could offer him little Jewel. Homer's had his eye on her for some time."

"No!" Willow shouted, startling them both. Jewel was Verdie's great-granddaughter, a girl barely thirteen. "No slaves, Papa. Something else."

Mama sidled up to him, smoothing the lapels of his jacket. "Homer is downright covetous of Firefly. I believe he'd trade all he owned for that stallion."

Willow's heart soared. "He certainly would. He's been after you to sell him for years."

Stricken, Papa backed away, both hands in the air. "Now, you two stop right there."

Mama curled her fingers and rested them on her hips. "I thought you were a clever businessman, dear. Firefly has a handful of good years left, at best. Annie and her boy are far more valuable."

Papa shook a warning finger. "See here, woman. Don't think you can manipulate me into this."

"It's a fair deal. One Homer will accept. How else will our daughter have the staff to run her household? Julian will be no help in that department."

She glanced over her shoulder. "I'm sorry, Willow. The boy has peculiar ideas."

Papa pointed toward the barn. "You're forgetting what I paid for that horse."

"Too much," Mama said.

"He's prize stock, Clara."

"He's a gluttonous horse we can barely afford to feed."

She jutted her chin. "What will it be, Charles Bates? Are you going to give your daughter the only thing she truly wants for her birthday?"

He heaved a sigh and raised his hands in surrender. "I know when to wave the white flag. I'll go over there first thing tomorrow."

Reeling with excitement, Willow pressed her hands to her mouth. "Can't you go now?"

He gaped at her. "It's Sunday, girl. I can't disturb them today."

"Nonsense," Mama said. "Homer will be thrilled by your proposal. You'll actually be giving two people a present today."

Willow shot her a grateful smile. *More than two!* If Papa returned from the Clemsons' with Annie and Samuel in tow, it would be the greatest gift Cletus's family had ever received.

Chapter 7

Hours had passed since Papa rode out of the yard with Firefly tethered to the back of the wagon, the proud, beautiful horse prancing regally behind. Willow felt a twinge of guilt, remembering how much the horse meant to him.

Imagining the joy on Cletus's and Bethy's faces swiftly drove the guilt away.

Bethy passed the parlor several times, going about the duties she had to perform before Mama dismissed her for the day. Willow longed to fling herself in her path shouting, "Guess what, Bethy? Oh, guess what!"

The thought that Papa might not be successful on his quest stopped her. The disappointment would be too great.

Bethy appeared at the arched doorway, her head bowed, wringing her apron with both hands. "Missy Bates, I've cleared the supper table and washed up, swept the hall and mopped the kitchen." Her eyes lifted. "There be anything else?"

Mama glanced up briefly then waved her away. "No, that's all for today."

Willow cleared her throat. "The meal was wonderful, Bethy. You outdid yourself. Thank you."

Two sets of startled eyes swung her way.

Bethy nodded and backed out the door.

Mama shook her head and returned to her knitting. "Peculiar ideas," she whispered under her breath.

Willow rose and hurriedly followed Bethy down the back hall to the side door where Cletus would be waiting. He always came, when he could, to walk her to their quarters.

Seeing him there, Willow could hardly contain her excitement.

Cletus held the door for Bethy while she slipped into her coat, watching Willow with unguarded curiosity. "You need something, Miss Willow?"

Knuckles pressed to her lips, she beamed foolishly at them. "Nothing in particular."

Cletus glanced at Bethy, the two mirroring Willow's preposterous grin.

"You right sure?"

She nodded.

"Good evening to you, then," he said, backing out and closing the door.

"And a very pleasant evening to you both," Willow called, ready to burst.

"That girl been in the cooking sherry?" she heard Cletus ask from the porch.

"Ain't got none," Bethy said.

Their muffled giggles echoed from the yard.

Hurrying back the way she came, she rejoined Mama in the parlor, the woman's quiet patience maddening.

"What's taking Papa so long?" Willow asked, wringing her hands. "He's been gone all day."

"These things take time, honey. There will be haggling and blustering and a bottle of Irish scotch involved."

Willow sighed and walked to the window, leaning to peer across the dusky fields. "It'll be dark soon."

Mama chuckled. "Sit down, dear. You'll wear out the nap of the rug."

Willow frowned over her shoulder. "How can you remain so calm?"

A horse whinnied from outside. Holding her breath, Willow pressed her nose to the glass.

Papa's wagon pulled into the yard and rolled to a stop in front of the door. There was no sign of Firefly.

Climbing down, he spoke a few words to a bent figure huddled in the wagon bed. The figure stood on unsteady legs, drawing a ragged shawl tighter around a tiny moon-faced child.

Samuel!

Gripping the windowsill, Willow suppressed a victory shout. "Papa did it," she said, her voice strangely calm. "They're here."

Annie clung to her baby with one arm and climbed over the back rail to the ground. Swaying slightly, she stared toward the side yard where the slave cabins stood.

Papa barked something that set a fire under her. After reaching into the wagon for a small bundle that likely held her only possessions, she backed away from Papa a few steps then turned and lurched toward the cabins.

Willow gathered her skirts and ran. She tore down the hall to the side door where she'd stood with Cletus and Bethy. Pushing her way onto the porch, she gasped at the cool evening but didn't slow down. The yard was bathed in twilight as she hurried over the grounds to the slave quarters, Annie just ahead.

Blended voices drew her between the rickety cabins. Hidden in shadow, she peered around the wall, the warmth and crackle of a large fire beckoning.

Men, women, and children lounged in the backyard, some hunched over domino tables in the fading light, others huddled in groups on the porches, talking in quiet voices. The children played games they'd scratched in the bare dirt patches, their shouts and giggles a pleasant backdrop to the evening.

Someone pointed then shouted, and all activity stopped. The slaves, aware that Annie had slipped into their midst, began to rise and circle around her.

Annie, gesturing wildly with her free hand, began to explain in a quivering voice. Willow heard Firefly's name, followed by exclamations of disbelief all around.

A sob tore from Annie as Cletus and Bethy pushed through the crowd and enveloped her, so tightly Willow feared for little Samuel.

Cletus stepped back, the baby cradled in his arms. Shouting praise, he raised him to the sky, a flailing, squalling offering of gratitude.

From the depths of their bellies, a baritone groan arose from the group, part agony, part ecstasy, an ancient pain too vast to contain. Hands and faces rose to the sky; joyful tears slid freely down their cheeks. They linked arms and swayed under a blanket of emerging stars, tiny points of light shining down on their worship like a mighty cloud of witnesses.

Willow had never seen them like this, never imagined them having such depth of feeling. Such love for God. These people dancing in blissful worship around the fire were her brothers and sisters in Christ. One day they would all share heaven.

Her pounding heart shattered. Julian was right. About everything, and the realization ached in her chest.

What was she to do with the knowledge? These good people were captives of an unjust system, and change for them seemed hopeless.

She pressed her fist to her mouth and sobbed.

"Missy Girl!"

Willow shrieked and clutched her chest. She spun to find Verdie scowling down on her.

"What you doing out here? Your daddy gon' blister your legs, he catch you near the slave quarters."

"Nonsense." Willow sniffed and wiped her eyes. "I'm far too old for spanking."

"He'll skin you, then. Like a jackrabbit, he catch you out here."

"I want to see Cletus."

Fear sparked in Verdie's eyes. "He in some kind of trouble?"

Peering closer at Willow, she gasped. "Missy Girl, is you crying?" Unspoken questions flashed on her face. "What Cletus do?"

Willow's chin shot up. "Nothing. I need to speak to him, that's all. Now, please go fetch him."

Verdie scurried into the midst of her people and tugged on Cletus's sleeve. She spoke in his ear, and he jerked his head toward Willow's shadowy hiding place. Handing the baby to Bethy's waiting arms, he hurried along the back of the house, Verdie on his heels.

Turning the corner, he stared at Willow, kneading his eyes as if to clear them. "Miss Willow?" Panic drained the life from his face. "You know you can't be out here."

"I have something important to tell you."

"All right, then." Cletus licked his lips, his darting gaze searching the darkness behind her. "Go on and tell, but be quick about it."

Her heart swelled with all she intended to say, longed to say.

I did it for you because I'm sorry.

I did it to make amends for all you've suffered at our hands.

I did it because I love you.

"I wanted to tell you to enjoy your evening," was all she managed, and her voice shook more than her trembling body.

He frowned and tucked his chin. "Miss Willow, you done already—"

"And to tell you how happy I am for you and Bethy," she said, cutting him off. "And for Annie and Samuel."

Cletus tilted his head to the side. His mouth grew slack and he stared, disbelief, amazement, then gratitude transforming his face in the flickering light.

He reached a trembling hand and reverently touched her arm. "A fine good evening to you, Miss Willow," he said in a husky voice. Tears gathered in the creases of his face and ran along the edges of his cheeks.

His voice rose to a jubilant shout. "Good evening, happy birthday, and God bless your sweet soul!"

Willow darted forward and hugged him. "You're welcome," she choked.

Leaving him and Verdie wide-eyed with shock, she scurried back to the house before she froze.

One thing she'd learned this night. If any one of those mistreated people cared anything for her family, they were capable of more Christlike love than Willow would ever possess.

Chapter 8

Julian was missing.

His last letter arrived on April 15, four months ago to the day. Before now, a few weeks had been the longest span of time between letters. The wait for word had become Willow's obsession, and a trip to the post office a part of Cletus's daily routine.

He didn't seem to mind.

Some days, like today, he took the surrey, and Willow rode along with him. At the post office counter, she knew no letter awaited her, even before her turn came to be served. The clerk avoided her eyes as she moved forward in the queue, then tucked his chin and cleared his throat when she stepped up to the window.

"Nothing again today, Miss Bates," he said then lowered his eyes. "I'm sorry."

She gave him a trembling smile and hurried outside.

Halfway home, Cletus broke the gloomy silence. "Don't you worry, missy," he called over his shoulder. "I'm sure he jus' fine."

He shot her a feeble grin. "That boy quick and spry. No Yankee musket got the better of Mistuh Julian."

Willow's heart lurched. Hearing Julian's name mentioned in the same breath with a Yankee musket wasn't exactly a comfort.

"Something is wrong, Cletus. I feel it in my bones."

He turned on the seat. "You listen to old Cletus and not them lying bones. When they took Annie away, my heart grieved sore. But inside, I knew she wasn't lost."

He nodded. "I was right, too, thanks to you. Jus' like I's right about Mistuh Julian."

He studied her with a slight frown, seeming to search for words as he swayed back and forth on the seat. "Sometimes life be like this old rutted road, lots of rattles and bumps. But the Almighty don't ever take His eyes off His children, not even to sleep. He's watching out for you and Mistuh Julian, jus' like He watched out for my Annie. So don't you fret."

She met his eyes and drew comfort from the conviction burning there. "Thank you, Cletus. I'll try to remember."

They rode in silence again, though not the heavy quiet of dread. Willow sat back and rested her mind. God had used her, as unlikely as she was, to answer Cletus's prayers for his daughter. She would lean on God now and trust He heard her many petitions for Julian.

She settled deeper into the tufted seat, drowsy in the shade protecting her from the blistering August sun. For the first time in days, she felt at ease enough to drift off in peaceful sleep.

Startled awake, she sat upright. "Did you say something, Cletus?"

Cletus strained forward, one hand shading his eyes. "Look yonder, coming this way."

Willow leaned to see around him but saw only the horse's bobbing head. She stood in a crouch beneath the fringed top, holding the back of the seat to steady herself.

Past the shimmering heat waves, past the pits and ruts dug in the dirt after the spring rains, she made out the shape of a man waving his arms. A man in slouch hat and Confederate gray.

She gripped Cletus's shoulder so hard he flinched. "It's Julian! He's come home."

Cletus placed his calloused hand on hers and squeezed. "No, Miss Willow, look again. Mistuh Julian be all legs and shoulders." He squinted his eyes. "And he don't have ginger hair."

He glanced up at her, deep sorrow in his gaze. "That be Mistuh Hiram coming our way."

Sick with disappointment, Willow slumped in her seat. Patting tears from her cheeks with her hankie, she fought for control. Hiram mustn't think she wasn't happy to see him.

The surrey drew alongside him, and genuine joy warmed her heart. She'd missed him more than she realized.

They climbed down, and Willow enveloped him in a welcoming hug. "Cletus, look. It's our Hiram. I'm so happy to see you."

Hiram held on to her for a few beats longer than proper. When he released her, he held her at arm's length and feasted with his eyes. "Dear girl, I've missed you so."

A look crossed his face, one Willow hadn't seen in many years. A naughty boy caught in his transgressions. "I'm forgetting myself," he said. "It's a gift to see your face again, honey, but I've not come for my pleasure."

He ducked his head and swallowed. "I'm dreadful sorry to be the one—" He raised his head, and pain flashed in his eyes. "I wish I didn't have to tell you."

Alarm weakened her legs. "Hiram, please. What's wrong?"

"It's Julian."

Her hands rose instinctively to cover her ears.

Cletus placed a firm hand on her back. "Just say it, boy. Don't make her wait."

Hiram pressed his lips together and nodded. "Julian is missing. Presumed dead. I'm so sorry, honey."

She turned aside to escape his words, but the dusty road rushed up to meet her. Grasping hands and anxious voices were the last things she knew.

Willow awoke on the settee, the sting of smelling salts in her nose. Mama knelt at her side wiping her face with a cool rag. A tearful Verdie stood over them, wringing her hands.

In the corner, Hiram and Papa huddled, speaking in hushed voices. Willow made out "slaughter" and "mass grave." Moaning, she covered her ears and faced the back of the couch.

Mama pushed to her feet. "Charles! Kindly take that conversation outside."

"No." Struggling to sit up, Willow reached out to Hiram. "I need to hear. Come and tell me everything."

Hiram took Mama's place at her side, but he didn't go down on his knees. He maneuvered himself very carefully onto the settee with one leg awkwardly extended. Only then did Willow realize he'd been injured, and it brought tears to her eyes.

Hiram held tightly to her hand. In a soothing voice, shaky at first but growing stronger as the story unfolded, he told her of the Battle of Chancellorsville.

The skirmish began when the Union army attempted to flank General Robert E. Lee's Northern Virginia Army. General "Stonewall" Jackson's Rebels launched a surprise attack while the Yanks were settling down to supper. The bluecoats countered. In the resulting melee, locked into an overgrown area of wilderness, the men became confused and turned on their brothers-in-arms.

General Jackson, on a scouting mission with his staff, was set upon by his own men and badly injured. They removed his shattered arm, and he was transferred to a field hospital to recover. Days later, he died of pneumonia.

Hiram stared over her head with haunted eyes, as if the telling had transported him back to the battlefield.

She clutched his sleeve. "And Julian?"

"He hasn't been seen since that day."

"Did you see him go down?" Papa asked.

Hiram shook his head. "No, but I saw him just before the fighting broke out." He gently smoothed Willow's hair. "He talked of nothing but you and how much he missed you."

Choked by tears, she couldn't speak.

"I don't understand," Mama said. "If he was wounded or. . .worse, they would have notified us by now."

Papa shook his head. "Notified who? Julian has no family left in Port Royal. I suppose they might have notified his parents in Ireland."

Willow stilled, staring up at her father. "We must contact them at once."

He nodded and hurried for the door. "I'll go to my study and draft a letter to the post master in. . .what's the name of the town?"

"The city of Galway," Willow called to him. "In the province of Connacht."

Drained, she fell back against the cushions. Hiram's arms slid around her shoulders, and she sobbed against his chest. Over the days that followed, his arms never left her for long.

Days turned into weeks before they finally heard back from Ireland. Papa found them on the back porch, Hiram engrossed in telling an animated story intended to make her laugh, Willow pretending to listen.

Handing her the envelope, Papa sighed. "They don't have anything more to tell us. I'm sorry, honey."

She shook out the letter and unfolded the page, fighting tears as she read the angst-ridden words written in Mrs. Finney's hand. The army department had notified them of their son's disappearance. They had no further information. She closed with the promise to contact Willow if they heard anything else.

Willow walked into Papa's arms and wept bitter tears.

Hiram's injury proved serious enough to keep him home for good, so he spent every possible minute close to Willow. The only place she could escape him was her room.

Mama found her there one Sunday afternoon, lying across her bed with one arm shielding her eyes.

"Hiram is downstairs."

"I know," she murmured.

"The dear boy is trying to comfort you. Why won't you let him?"

Willow rolled away from the bright sunlight at her window. "Because he can't comfort me. No one can."

Mama sat down beside her. "He cares about you."

"Yes, and that's the worst of it. Hiram makes me feel better, no doubt. It would be easy to allow him to devote himself to me." She shook her head. "But it's wrong. I feel him drawing ever closer, and I cannot give him what he needs."

Mama patted her arm. "Of course, not now. Perhaps later, after you've grieved."

Willow bit her bottom lip and turned away. There would never be an "after" to her grief.

She'd known the two men all her life, but they were not interchangeable. Hiram could never take Julian's place in her broken heart.

Chapter 9

T he man loves you, Willow. He always has. Can't you try to love him just a little?"

"I love Hiram very much."

Mama slapped the arm of her wicker chair. "I'm not talking about amicable love. That will bring me no grandchildren."

"Mama, please..." Willow squared around in her chair, raising her shoulder to block out the unwelcome words.

She had slipped out of the house early hoping the lovely summer morning would bring a little peace, but the source of constant irritation had followed her to the back porch.

Sighing, Mama pressed her palms to her temples. "It's been two years, Willow. Julian—God rest him—is never coming back."

At Willow's stricken look, she softened. "I'm sorry, dear. Even Julian wouldn't want you to pine away like this. It's as if you died along with him."

Her words rang true. Some part of Willow had perished with Julian, but her love persisted. Though she knew not how or what still fed it, love for him consumed her.

Across the bright green lawn, young Samuel struggled, with stiff arms, to push the mower into the shed for his grandfather. Cletus, a proud grin on his face, allowed the sturdy three-year-old to tackle it on his own. Laughing, he hefted Samuel to his shoulders, and they disappeared around the side of the shed, prattling like chatterboxes.

The presidential proclamation and executive order issued by Abraham Lincoln two years ago had declared all slaves in the South to be free. Most of Papa's slaves had run off, headed north to the promised land. Some, including Cletus's family and Verdie, had stayed behind, serving the family as always.

Willow assumed their reluctance to leave was due to misplaced loyalty. When asked, Cletus said he and Bethy didn't know how to be free and were too old to learn, but he wished better things for Annie and Samuel. His words made her sad, and she vowed to one day help them all begin a new life.

With only half her calendar crossed off, momentous things had already happened in the year of 1865. Confederate strongholds at Petersburg and Richmond fell. General Lee surrendered to General Grant at Appomattox, and Grant sent out the order, "The war is over; the rebels are our countrymen again; and the best sign of rejoicing after the victory will be to abstain from all demonstrations in the field."

The Army of Northern Virginia agreed they would no longer bear arms against the United States government.

Last April, a man named Booth, an actor and Confederate sympathizer, stepped into President Lincoln's private box at Ford's Theatre in Washington, DC, and shot the quiet, dignified statesman in the head. Onlookers carried him to a boardinghouse across the street where he died the following morning.

The assassin fled to Caroline County. Booth crossed the Rappahannock and holed up at Richard Garret's farm, south of Port Royal, where his pursuers later took his life.

The end of the war had not officially been declared, but it was only a matter of time before the newly sworn president, Andrew Johnson, would tie up that loose end.

And still no news of Julian.

"Hiram is good to you," Mama droned, unaware of Willow's distracted thoughts. "That, you can't deny."

"I don't deny it."

Willow narrowed her eyes. "Where is all this coming from? Hiram told you, didn't he?"

The day before, Hiram had gone down on one knee in the garden, pleading for Willow to marry him. She had asked for more time.

Mama fanned a swarm of insects from her face. "Of course he told me. We want the same thing, Hiram and I. He's waited patiently, allowing you time to grieve." She sighed. "I do believe he'd wait forever."

Jutting her bottom lip, she blew a blast of air at persistent gnats darting around her nose. "I am not so inclined. I should have a houseful of grandchildren tugging on my skirts by now."

She gripped Willow's hand on the arm of her chair. "Won't you marry him, honey? It would make everyone so happy."

Willow sighed. *Everyone but me.*

She looked away. "I'm not ready."

Trying a new tactic, Mama loosened her eager grip and nonchalantly traced circles on the back of Willow's hand. "You're not getting any younger, dear. There's talk in town that you'll end up a spinster."

"Oh, Mama." Willow pushed out of her chair and leaned against the porch rail. "I'm barely twenty-one, though I feel one hundred. Do you think I care about such things, after all we've been through?"

Mama left her seat and came to stand beside her. "The war cost each of us dearly. Your father and I have lost everything. Including our dignity when those ruffian soldiers ransacked our home, pawing through our unmentionables, carrying off whatever wasn't nailed down."

Her voice deepened with unshed tears. "Now that it's over, we can give up, or we can try to rebuild. We have chosen to carry on, but we'll need help. Your marriage to Hiram could save us."

"Hiram's family money, you mean."

"Oh, honey," Mama said, tucking a curl behind Willow's ear, "it's about so much more than money. Would you deprive your father of his heirs? Me the comfort of grandchildren in my waning years?"

Willow suppressed a laugh. Her feisty Southern mama would never see waning years. She'd fight it harder than Virginia fought the Yanks.

Despite the absurd way her question was posed, her petition had merit. As the only child, Willow had certain obligations, whether she liked it or not.

She remembered Grammy's stories of how she and Grandfather Bates struggled to make Fairhill a thriving plantation, a legacy for their descendants. Willow determined in her heart to create a new legacy, one unspoiled by shame and the stench of slavery.

Unable to bear the joy her words would bring to Mama's face, Willow stared across Fairhill's endless fields. "Very well. I'll consider Hiram's proposal."

Mama drew Willow close for a one-armed hug, her other hand fishing for the hankie at her waistband. For once in her life, Clara Bates seemed unable to speak.

Cletus pulled the buggy away from the church and drove toward home. Hiram sat next to Willow on the upholstered seat wearing a broad smile, a welcome sight. He didn't smile often these days, due to chronic pain in his hip.

Specialists in New York determined that the pain would diminish but never leave him. On cold or rainy days, Hiram would forever be reminded of the war.

Willow grinned up at him. "What has you so merry?"

He shrugged and slipped his arm around her shoulders. "A fine sermon, the company of a lovely lady, and the promise of Bethy's Sunday roast waiting at home. All a man needs to be happy."

She smiled, noting how easily he called Fairhill home. In truth, he spent more time there than he did with his family. She had to admit he seemed to belong.

"Hiram?"

"Yes?" Distracted by something in the distance, he spared her a quick glance.

"How many children do you want?"

This got his full attention, and hope burned in his eyes. "Does your decision to marry me depend on my answer? If so, please throw me a hint."

She laughed. "Mama wants a houseful. My expectations are not so ambitious."

His eyes twinkled. "Are you trying to tell me something?" He waited, so still, he seemed to be holding his breath.

Willow steeled herself and surged ahead. "I'm saying I will marry you. If your offer still holds."

He sat quietly for several seconds. "I was wrong before. *Now* I have all a man needs to be happy."

Cletus, using all his powers of restraint, squirmed on the front seat. He turned his head to sneak a peek, his smile deepening the dimples on his cheeks.

Hiram pulled her close, burying his face in her hair. His whispered prayer of thanksgiving, breathed against her ear, nearly broke her heart.

Julian's cherished face rose up in her mind, and her bones ached with sadness.

Chapter 10

July 1865

Julian stood on the dock in Port Royal, shading his eyes from the afternoon sun, his heart a throbbing ache in his chest. The wretched state of the town after the Federal troops shelled and plundered made it almost unrecognizable, and bore witness to Willow's anxious letters.

The state of his own shelled and plundered body saddened him even more. Wincing, he clutched his stomach, the severe pain the aftermath of starvation and parasites. His collarbones stuck out, and his ribs were so lean he could strum them like guitar strings. His gait was that of an old man, slow and bent. His trousers were hitched tight at the waist to keep them up, and his hat felt too big on his head, shaved nearly bald to discourage lice.

Still, these light afflictions were nothing compared to the agony he suffered in prison camp.

They moved him to Rock Island Prison, twelve acres of dismal swampland where thousands of men would soon be crowded, in December of '63. Temperatures were below zero, rations few.

Julian survived a smallpox epidemic, malnutrition, and scurvy. Thousands were not so lucky, succumbing to famine or disease.

Yet, with all these things, he counted himself blessed. The grace of God and the hope of seeing Willow again kept him alive in captivity.

After Richmond fell and Davis, the Confederate president, fled, paroles and amnesty for Confederate soldiers began, and Julian was released. He'd gone to the home of a fellow prisoner, a minister, to mend and gain the strength and will to go forward.

Those few weeks spent communing with God and studying His Word saved Julian from the fate many other soldiers bore, landing in a soldiers' home or an asylum.

He was stronger now and ready to see Willow. Neither the devastation of Port Royal nor the state of his battered body could dampen his spirits for long. Soon, he'd see his love again. With her by his side, he could begin to heal his wounded soul.

First, he needed to put something in his aching belly.

He stepped off the dock and walked away from the river, headed for the center of town. The people of Port Royal were resilient and had worked hard to restore what the ravages of war had spoiled. Nevertheless, it would never be the same.

Would anything ever be?

A passing surrey pulled to a halt beside him, and a graying head swiveled his way. Wide eyes stared in shock. "Mistuh Julian? Is it really you?"

Julian's heart soared. "Cletus? Why, Cletus, how are you?"

"What do you think you're doing?" A woman's voice shrilled from the backseat. "Drive on."

"Missy Bates, look here, it's Mistuh Julian." Scampering off the seat, he clutched Julian's hand, pumping it like the crank on a well. "We thought you dead and gone, and here you stand in the flesh. It's a miracle."

His words stunned. Never once had Julian imagined that they believed him dead. He pictured Willow longing for him, praying for his release, not grieving his passing. The pain in his stomach flamed.

Mrs. Bates scooted to his side of the surrey. Hands folded in her lap, she looked him over, head to toe, before she spoke. "Hello, Julian. I must say this is quite a surprise."

Julian snatched the hat from his head. "Ma'am." He nodded, giving the top of his shorn head a self-conscious rub. "Yes, ma'am, I'm sure it must be a shock after all this time."

She chewed thoughtfully on her bottom lip then drew a determined breath. "I suppose you have plans to see my daughter."

Julian grinned and bobbed his head "I'm on my way to Fairhill straightaway." He spread his fingers over the ache in his middle. "I just need to eat something first."

Excitement rose in his chest, and he fought the tears he'd kept bottled inside. "How is Willow? I'm ever so anxious to see her."

Mrs. Bates snapped open the fan on her lap and waved the black satin in her face. "Willow is doing quite well, actually. She's very happy."

She lowered the fan so that just her eyes were visible. "She's about to be married, you see. Starting a new life and putting this unpleasant war behind her for good."

Breath escaped him, and he couldn't draw another. Port Royal shifted and spun. He clung to the surrey to anchor himself.

Mrs. Bates snapped the fan shut, her mouth a tight line. "Dear boy, I realize this must come as a shock. But I do hope you'll be happy for Willow and Hiram, after all they've been through."

"Wait. . .she's marrying Hiram?"

A steadying hand pressed against his back. Cletus.

The woman actually smiled. "Hiram came home wounded, you know. Willow nursed him back to health. The two were inseparable. What came next was to be expected."

Julian's mind flashed to his time as Willow's patient, to their long, companionable walks, Willow so anxious for him, so attentive. His withered stomach lurched. His head swam, and he fought a wave of sickness.

Mrs. Bates sighed dramatically. "Of course, she grieved for you. However, it's been years, and not a word. Naturally, we thought you were. . .well, gone. Willow moved on with her life. I'm sure you understand."

He nodded, his throat so tight he had to force the words. "Of course."

She beamed. "You always were a good boy. Now, if you will excuse us, we must press on."

Pulling a handwritten list from her bag, she waved it at him. "There's a great deal one must do to prepare for a wedding. Of course, dry goods are not as accessible as they once were. I'll probably have to order her dress from the catalogs."

Scowling at Cletus, she pointed at his empty seat. "Stop dawdling and come drive this contraption before we lose any more of this day."

Julian's grip on the buggy tightened. "I would like to say goodbye to her."

Her scowl deepened. Pulling a handkerchief from her bodice, she pressed it to her lips. "That would be most unkind of you, Julian. She's happy now. Do you really want to cast a cloud from the past on her future?"

Yes! he nearly shouted. Desperate, he pleaded with his eyes.

Her expression soured even more. Squaring her shoulders, she raised her chin and dismissed his request with a sniff. "I'll be happy to relay a message. Later, of course, once she's settled. Is there something you'd like for me to tell her?"

Backing away, he released his grip on the surrey because the strength in his hands failed him. "No." His lifeless voice sounded distant and hollow in his head. "There's nothing."

Beside him, Cletus made a strangled sound in his throat.

Julian glanced at him, and the poor man looked ill. Sweat beaded his forehead, and his eyes bulged. His frantic gaze darted between Julian and Mrs. Bates.

"Cletus!" she snapped, her face bright with anger. "I said to come here and drive."

With a last pleading look at Julian, he climbed aboard and flicked the reins at the horse.

Julian stood motionless in the street, watching them drive away. Forcing himself to move, he staggered like a drunkard to a nearby bench and eased down. His head throbbed, his heart ached, but the sensations were distant and dreamlike, as if his feverish mind refused to accept more pain.

The desolation of prison hadn't broken him because Willow was there, in his thoughts, his hopes, his dreams. He had believed the prayers he prayed and what he thought to be God's reassurances for the future. Now Willow was lost to him, and the absence of hope threatened to finish him.

He lost track of time, had no idea how long he sat on the hard wooden bench, shut off from the bustle of life around him, mourning his loss. Food was no longer necessary. He'd never hold it down.

Perhaps he should check into a hotel for the night.

Gritting his teeth, he pushed off the bench. He had nowhere else to go, but there was nothing for him in Port Royal. The steamer he arrived on would be finished off-loading. Soon it would be ready to take on more passengers and cargo. When it pulled from the dock, Julian would be on it.

He made his way back to the spot where he stood before so joyful and full of anticipation. The devastation of war he'd grieved over now seemed a fitting backdrop to his pain.

Turning, he took a last look at the town he loved before boarding the waiting vessel.

"Mistuh Julian!"

Julian jerked his head toward the sound of his name echoing across the docks.

Cletus hustled toward him, waving his hands. "Don't dare get on that boat."

The frantic man reached Julian and latched on, his momentum nearly taking them down. "You can't leave, suh. You'll be making a dreadful mistake."

Julian shook his head. "The mistake was coming here."

"No, suh."

"Willow belongs to Hiram now." Saying it aloud made him sick.

Cletus wagged his head. "No, suh. Now that you're here, she won't be marrying Mistuh Hiram."

"But if she loves him. . ."

"Ain't no truth to that. Mistuh Mayhew ain't the one she pining after."

Frowning, Julian searched his eyes.

"That's right." Cletus nodded. "And she gon' grieve the rest of her life if you leave."

He licked his lips and glanced over his shoulder. "I got to get back before Missy Bates finished in that store, or she'll strip off my hide. We'll be going home directly, and I'll send Miss Willow. You can ask her yourself what she wants."

He backed away, pointing at the boat moored to the dock. "Don't you get on board, you hear? I'll send her straightaway."

Julian held up his hand. "Wait just a minute. If Willow doesn't love Hiram, why is she marrying him?"

Cletus wrinkled his nose as if he smelled something foul. "Her mama is why. She saddled that girl every morning, rode her all day until she finally broke."

He tilted his head. "I never saw nobody hang on to hope the way that child has. She never once gave up, Mistuh Julian. I reckon she jus' finally gave in."

Julian's throat tightened. "Go get her. I'll be right here."

Chapter 11

A breeze kicked up, rippling the strawberry bush thicket at the edge of the yard. In two months' time, their autumn fruit would appear, seedpods filled with bright red seeds. Willow looked forward to the September display, assuming the deer didn't graze them down to shoots.

Annie crossed the yard, a few feet from the backyard gazebo where Willow sat knitting. The girl walked quickly and with purpose, likely on her way to tend her son.

Her steps faltered, and she lifted her eyes in Willow's direction, as if sensing her presence. Coming to a halt, she stared boldly at Willow for long seconds, expressionless. Lifting her chin, she placed one hand over her heart, and a glorious smile broke over her face.

Bringing her home to Fairhill had delivered Annie from unspeakable abuse and humiliation and had brought Samuel to a safe haven. Every ounce of gratitude she felt shone from her eyes.

Willow's chin began to quiver. She nodded at the lovely young girl, so much passing between them, she felt her heart would burst.

Then Annie was gone.

Willow stared at the place where she'd stood, basking in the affection still radiating from the spot, until a darting figure appeared in the corner of her eye.

She had known Cletus her entire life. In all those years, she'd never seen the genteel, dignified man in a hurry. Yet here he came, sprinting across the wide expanse of lawn to the gazebo.

Willow leaped up, her knitting falling in a puddle at her feet. Watching him come, she steeled herself.

Was it Papa, stricken with apoplexy?

Had the house caught fire?

Maybe the war had recommenced.

Mama?

Impossible. Nothing dared to afflict her.

Cletus sailed across the yard, arms pumping. He reached the gazebo and bent over, hands on his knees while he caught his breath.

Willow stared at the spectacle he made, speechless. "Cletus?" she managed to croak. "What's wrong?"

He raised his head, gasping like a landed trout. She hurried down the steps, caught him by the shoulders and sat him down.

He stared up at her with tortured eyes. "Missy," he wheezed. "I came as soon as I could. You got to hurry before he leaves."

"Who?" She gripped his shoulder, too hard because she already knew. She'd always known.

"Mistuh Julian."

"Where? Oh, hurry, Cletus. Where?"

"In town. Waiting by the docks."

Clutching her skirts, she ran.

A few feet away, she spun. "Why is he leaving?"

Cletus tucked his chin, eyes bright with smoldering anger. "Your mama told him he shouldn't ought to see you. On account of you marrying Mistuh Hiram."

Seething with rage, she sped toward the house, drawing up short at the back porch. Her mother leaned on the rail, glaring across the yard at Cletus.

Willow clenched her fists and stalked closer. "How could you?"

Mama steeled her jaw. "I did it for you."

Sickened by her words, Willow pointed behind her. "No harm will come to Cletus, do you hear? I may one day forgive you for this betrayal, but I'd never forgive you for that."

Lowering her lashes, Mama nodded.

Dashing around the side of the house, Willow collided with Hiram.

"Whoa!" he cried, steadying her. "Where are you off to in such a rush?"

Her heart plunged. She forced herself to look him in the eye. "Hiram. . ."

He touched her mouth. "I knew the minute I saw you. I haven't seen that look since Finney disappeared."

"He's alive," she whispered, unable to keep the wonder from her voice.

Hiram breathed a shaky laugh. "I won't say I wouldn't like to bait him for catfish and toss him in the river."

He stared over her head. "He's here?"

"In town," she said. "Waiting for me."

He lowered brimming eyes filled with pain. "I'm a foolish man, Willow Bates. I've sworn my life to making you happy. Now, the only way to accomplish that goal is to surrender you to Finney."

Groaning, he ground the heels of his hands into his eyes to stem the flow of tears. "I may as well see it through. Let me drive you to town."

Cletus hurried around the corner, anxious eyes darting to where Mama sat on the porch. "No, suh, Mistuh Hiram. No call for that. I'll take her."

Willow gripped Hiram's hands. "I'm so sorry."

His auburn lashes blinked back tears. "So am I." Drawing her hands to his mouth, he caressed them with his lips, longing in each tender kiss. "I'm glad he's alive, honey. Truly I am."

Turning her, he gave her a gentle push. "You best hurry."

Tears blinding her, she ran for the waiting buggy.

Cletus drove the horse toward town, talking wildly and waving his hands the whole way.

"There he stood," he said. "Big as life right on the streets of Port Royal. And all this time we reckoned him dead."

He glanced at her. "All except you. You never once believed it, did you, missy? You should've seen his face when she told him you about to marry Mistuh Hiram. I never seen a man turn so green."

Sick to her stomach, Willow shivered. "I crushed Hiram's dreams, Cletus. I broke his heart. I've never caused such anguish to a person."

Cletus remained quiet for so long, she wondered if he had heard.

"You done nothing wrong, child," he finally said. "Mistuh Hiram knew you couldn't give him your heart, else he wouldn't let you go so easy. You only agreed to marry him because he wanted it so bad, and to please your mama."

He turned to look at her. "Missy Bates never meant to hurt you."

Willow drew a frustrated breath and released it through her nose. "I know, but she nearly ruined my life."

"I reckon she thought she was saving it. She done what she thought was right, but it wasn't ever right. You belong with Mistuh Julian, and the Good Lord set things straight."

He grinned. "Just in the nick of time too."

She smiled through her tears.

"You go on and be happy, girl," Cletus said. "You spread so much of it around, you deserve your share."

He chuckled and nodded toward the docks. "And there stands your happiness, waiting for you just like he promised."

Willow scooted to the edge of her seat and searched the milling waterfront. Spotting him, her breath caught. Pale and gaunt, he stared toward the river, the fingers of one hand tucked into his pocket, the other wrapped around his suspenders.

Cletus pulled the buggy to a stop and helped her down.

She leaned to hug him and kiss him on the cheek. "Thank you."

Tears moistened his eyes. "I'd do most anything for you, missy."

Patting his arm, she took a deep breath and crossed the dock to stand behind Julian. She cleared her throat. "Hello, soldier."

Julian performed a clumsy but perfunctory about-face, his eyes bright with emotion. "Hello, little Willow."

Tilting his head, he smiled. "I thought I might never see you again."

She raised her chin. "I never thought that for a minute."

He moved closer but didn't touch her. "How I long to hold you. First, I need you to know something. I love you, but if you still want to marry Hiram, I'll understand."

Her heart stalled. Her smile faded. "Why would I want to do that?"

He placed his hand on his hollow chest, glancing down at his emaciated frame. "I'm not much to offer right now." He smirked. "If I was a horse, they'd shoot me."

She wondered if her eyes mirrored the pain shining in his. "Do you find me so shallow, Julian Finney? I've adored you since I first laid eyes on that skinny, lanky boy of the past."

She pointed a trembling finger at him. "You think these skin-deep afflictions matter to me? My love for you runs to the marrow of your bones."

Smiling through her tears, she walked into his arms.

Laughing, Julian drew her closer, his body even leaner than she had thought. She swallowed hard to force back bitter tears. "Don't fret, my love. It won't take Bethy long to fatten you up."

He nodded. "Aye, Bethy will have her chance. Then, we'll give my ma's cooking a crack."

He pressed his lips to her cheek. "I want to take you away, my love. Away from the pain and ugliness of war, to a place as beautiful as you are."

She tipped her head to study his face, her brows crowding together. "I thought you loved Port Royal."

"Port Royal is home." He kissed her nose. "But I'm hankering to see Ireland. And for Ireland to see you. First, we'll give your ma that wedding she's been planning."

Smiling, she nodded.

"When we come back to Virginia, I'll sell our land here and buy you a big house in town."

Remembering her obligation to Grammy, she stilled. "You understand that I'm meant to inherit Fairhill one day? Until then, I promised to help my parents rebuild."

He grew quiet, considering her words. "Without slaves, Fairhill will never return to her former glory, but I promise to work alongside your parents in whatever they decide to do with the place."

"So, we'll live there for now?"

After a pause, he nodded.

She gave him a stern look. "I'm afraid there's more required of you."

He held out his arms in surrender.

"There will need to be grandchildren underfoot. Perhaps a good many of them."

He laughed aloud. "I will sacrifice myself for the cause."

Remembering Cletus, she turned and smiled. Grinning, he glanced away, pretending he hadn't been watching.

"Wherever we live, Cletus and his family have a place with us. Verdie too."

Pain flashed in Julian's eyes. "Now, Willow. . .you know how I feel about that."

She touched his arm. "Not as slaves. Or servants. They're family, and I want to help them."

A proud smile rounded his cheeks. "That's my girl. They can stay at Fairhill for as long as they wish. Only, I may have a better idea. What about my parents' place? If we have no need of it, I'll deed it to Cletus. I'm sure he could make a go of it, and one day it will belong to that grandson you wrote me about."

"You would do that for them?" She wound her arms around his neck. "You're a wonderful man, Julian Finney."

He laughed and bent to kiss her, and a loud moan arose from the pit of his stomach.

His eyes widened in shock, and Willow threw back her head and laughed.

"Come with me," she said, pulling him toward the wagon. "I believe Bethy has a guinea hen in the oven."

"A roasted guinea?" He rolled his eyes. "Am I in heaven?"

Cletus accepted the hand Julian extended. "Welcome back, Mistuh Julian."

"Take us to Fairhill, Cletus," Willow said, hugging Julian around his narrow waist. "I'm afraid Bethy has her work cut out for her."

Cletus hurried around to the driver's seat. "We best get her started on a sweet potato pie. It'll take more than a scrawny old guinea to put some meat on those bones."

Julian handed Willow up on the surrey and climbed in behind her. "That sounds a lot better than hardtack and boiled pork." Hugging her close, he blinked away tears. "It's good to be home."

Willow leaned to kiss his cheek. "You were right all along. About everything."

He tapped her nose. "I've waited a long time to hear you say that." He slipped his arms around her. "My little Willow, no longer a child."

She gasped. "Oh, Julian, say it again. I've longed to hear you utter those words."

He laughed and kissed her. "My Willow."

Another kiss. "My lady."

He caressed her cheek, all his promises and plans for their future reflected in his eyes. "And soon to be my bride."

Marcia Gruver's southern roots lend touches of humor and threads of faith to her writing. Look for both in her Texas Fortunes and Backwoods Brides series. When she's not perched behind a keyboard, you'll find her clutching a game system controller or riding shotgun on long drives in the Texas Hill Country. Lifelong Texans, Marcia and her husband Lee have five children. Collectively, this motley crew has graced them with thirteen grandchildren and two great-grandchildren—so far.

His Anchor

by Carrie Fancett Pagels

Author's Notes

If you've read *My Heart Belongs on Mackinac Island: Maude's Mooring*, you'll recognize a number of characters in this novella. Sadie Duvall is Maude Welling's best friend. The prologue is one year prior to Maude's story, beginning in 1894, but then parallels Maude's story in the beginning chapters before moving into the month beyond, August 1895.

Some information related to *His Anchor*:

Mackinac Island is nestled in the Straits of Mackinac, where Lake Huron and Lake Michigan intersect. Some hydrologists consider it one lake: Lake Michigan–Huron or Lake Huron–Michigan. Limestone, beneath the water, contributes to the gorgeous turquoise- and sapphire–blue hues viewed there. It's a beautiful place between Michigan's Upper and Lower Peninsulas and is also populated by other islands. Even today, Mackinac Island allows no motor vehicles, save for emergency use except in the winters when residents use snowmobiles.

When the Grand Hotel was being constructed, workers had to pull the lumber over the icy Straits. I had the privilege of hearing the hotel's historian, Bob Tagatz, repeat a story he'd heard from one of the men's daughters. She'd recollected how distressed her father had been upon return from each haul. The men had to remain dead silent on the transport from the mainland to the island to listen in case they heard the ice begin to crack. And then they had to go back and get more!

What later became Newberry State Hospital was a brand-new asylum, built in the 1890s. The institution also housed a nursing school. Centered in the midst of the Upper Peninsula's booming lumber and mining industry, the town also became a center for treating psychiatric conditions. I grew up in Newberry, and my father, uncle, and other family members worked at the hospital. I lived only a few blocks away. The location is now a prison site.

Beeman gum was produced at the turn of the century. I grew up loving Beeman gum. It's hard to find today. Schlitz beer has been around since the late 1860s, and Stroh's Bohemian beer was the Blue Ribbon Winner at the Columbian Exposition in Chicago. I reference one of my favorite books, *Little Women*, by Louisa May Alcott, in *His Anchor*, and although I found information that the book, as we know it today, was published in two tomes, I wasn't able to determine the exact time frame when the merger into one novel happened. But, likely in 1895, my heroine's sister, Garnet, would have been reading one of the two Alcott volumes.

Fires happened on Mackinac Island, and across the country, due to the heavy use of wood for building, plus various other fire hazards. When my family and I were taking the ferry home from the island, after a book signing in the summer of 2017, we observed a fire. The danger is that a fire may jump to other wood structures as well. It was truly frightening. Firefighters from the island, and ferried in from Mackinaw City and from St. Ignace, battled the flames—and won. God bless them all!

I borrowed "Uncle" Bob, Robert Pietsch's first name, for my hero in this book and Maude's uncle in *My Heart Belongs on Mackinac Island: Maude's Mooring*. Bob passed away just before I received my edits. He was a loving uncle to my husband and children and will be remembered well.

Dedication

For Jacqueline Hyacinth Croteau Williams—
thanks, Jackie, for believing in my writing!

Acknowledgments

Father God, You know I couldn't do anything without You. Thank you to Jeff and Clark Pagels, who have been rooting for Sadie for some time and have accompanied me on my travels to the Straits of Mackinac. I would be lost without my amazing critique partner, Kathy Maher—simply the best! Thank you to Regina Fujitani, Beta Reader, for standing in the gap. With appreciation to author Gina Welborn who had the inspiration for this collection but then couldn't participate herself. Thank you to Dawn Lyndsey Bobay and Chuck Bobay, our "neighbors" in Mackinaw City, and for their friendship and encouragement and for the use of their names. Thank you to Cousin Laura Williams Kinney, and her husband, Tom Kinney, for permission to use their names. With appreciation to Mackinac Island Public Library Anne St. Onge for access to the historical resources room, and to Bob Tagatz, Grand Hotel historian, for his wonderful lectures at the Grand Hotel.

Prologue

Mackinac Island, Michigan
June 1894

All of Sadie Duvall's dreams crumpled into a rubbish heap as Robert Swaine's fist connected with Lt. Bernard Elliott's square jaw, and her beau crumpled onto the grassy knoll. "Stop!" The very word she'd been repeating to the handsome officer was now aimed at her best friend's young uncle.

Robert rubbed his fist, his face red, as he scowled first at Bernard and then at her. "Elliott deserves a sound thrashing."

Tears coursed down her face. Years had been invested in this moment—when an officer from the fort would ask her to be his wife and take her away from Mackinac Island. Away from the decaying French–Canadian cabin her family called *home*. Away from Pa's drunken tirades, and the sight of Ma working herself to death trying to support them.

The man who should have become her fiancé this night groaned as he rose to his feet and brushed at his navy woven-wool pants. With undisguised disgust in his eyes, Bernard pinned her there, beneath the lilac trees. "We're through, Sadie. Do you hear me?"

She sucked in a breath. A year of courtship ended by a man who'd been so dear to her—a man who should understand what she really needed. Which wasn't this outcome!

"Through? Good!" Robert narrowed his eyes, his fists yet clenched. "Be gone with you, then."

"No. . ." But Sadie's weak protest was greeted with Bernard's disdainful glance as he slapped his uniform hat back on his head and headed up the hill toward Fort Mackinac.

Robert took two steps closer and gently grasped her shoulders. "Did Elliott hurt you?"

"No." Not physically at least.

He frowned, his eyelids lowering almost closed. That was the same look he'd always given her when he'd not believed her. The same expression of consideration when she was fifteen, infatuated with him, and he'd had that awkward embarrassing discussion with her about his engagement to Miriam.

"Here, let me dry your face." Robert pulled a linen handkerchief from his breast pocket and gently patted her cheeks.

She stood there like a ninny, letting him treat her like the child he thought she was. If only he'd realized that she'd been a grown woman for years now. If only he'd realized that before Miriam had trampled his heart like a runaway horse.

If he'd not been so busy running his shipping interests, Robert wouldn't have had to physically correct Lt. Elliott's misconception that Sadie Duvall was his for the taking.

Thank God, he'd been watching the twosome from the dock, where'd he'd just moored his ship. A man leading a woman into a secluded part of the fort's gardens was up to no good. Why hadn't Sadie realized that?

"Let me walk you home." The anger, fear, and care he had for this young woman caused his voice to rumble.

"No. I'm all right." She brushed dirt from her dress.

The cad didn't even have the decency to bring a blanket with him.

"Do you realize what you've just done?" Her voice quivered in anger.

Saved her from being compromised? "From the tone of your voice, I suspect you don't understand, yourself."

"He was my last chance, Robert, and you've ruined it!"

Last chance? Elliott had been about to ruin her reputation. "I rescued you."

"Bernard wouldn't have hurt me." Sadie nibbled on her lower lip, her eyes averted to the ground.

Snorting, he jerked his thumb over his shoulder. "You told him to stop and he didn't—I heard that."

"He was supposed to propose to me tonight."

Robert grasped her arm, the cotton fabric soft beneath his fingers. "Did Elliott tell you he'd marry you?" He turned her to face the direction they'd need to travel to her home.

A street sweeper passed by, eyeing them.

"Well, no, but from everything he said. . ." Her cheeks suffused with color. "And we've been courting over a year."

"Courting?" He'd not seen her anywhere in public with the young man, a dashing golden-haired dandy several years Robert's junior.

"Yes." She looked up, eyes wide. "We had picnics every Sunday afternoon on my day off. We went fishing."

"Like we used to do?" Picnicking for years on the bluffs, by the Arch Rock, by Sugar Loaf, and laughing and telling stories, he, Maude, Greyson, and Sadie.

"He even came to church with me. . . ."

"When?" He had no reason to be jealous, but the green-eyed monster squeezed his heart.

"Once."

"Did he ever take you to the roller rink or to dinner at Astor's?"

"No."

Robert had. Many times to both. "Ever out to eat at *any* of the restaurants in town?" He'd sported Maude and Sadie around to every single establishment on the island. That was before tongues began to wag about him and the too-young island beauty. Before he'd courted Miriam Beckett and become engaged.

"You're just jealous that I can be happy and get married. You're angry with me because of what Miriam did!"

His fiancé had eloped with one of the officers from the fort only a fortnight before they were to have wed. He swallowed back bile. "I'd never have treated

Miriam like that jackal just attempted with you."

"Well, you're not him."

"And thank God for that!" He wanted to tell her what he knew about the officer from the fort, but he dared not. She'd never believe him anyway.

"Just go away, Robert. Leave me alone!" Sadie stifled a sob as she pulled free from him and ran.

———⊷⊷———

The flimsy pine door slammed behind Sadie as she entered what was little more than a log shack. The stale scent of bacon grease and wood smoke greeted her nostrils and she wrinkled her nose. She was supposed to escape this sour smell. She'd hoped to become an officer's wife—to live in a beautiful two-story home at Fort Mackinac, or at a fort far away from here. Where she'd serve guests from china and crystal. Where there would always be enough to eat, and where she'd awake on a chill winter's morning in a warm, cozy house.

"Sadie?" Ma's voice carried from the back where Sadie and her sisters slept, sharing an old rope bed that perpetually sagged.

"Yes, Ma?" She began to cry again, a hiccup starting. She dabbed at her eyes with Robert's handkerchief.

"Come here, love."

Luckily Pa was nowhere in sight. Likely down at the bar, drinking away his worries over being unable to hold a job.

In several strides, Sadie crossed the open family area, where the hearth was flanked by two wooden benches, covered in pillows. Between them set an overstuffed velvet chair that Robert had brought in during the winter for Ma's comfort, after her long day at Witmer's Steam Laundry. Sadie rounded the corner to a short hall, which lead to her and her sisters' room.

Ma cocked her head slightly, her lips pursed, and set down the undergarments she was folding when Sadie joined her.

"Where are the girls?"

"Maude and Greyson have them right now. They were taking a carriage ride and asked if the girls wished to come." She shrugged. "Saw no harm in it."

Sadie drew in a slow, fortifying breath. Maude, her friend, was all-but-engaged to the handsome son of her employer, Mrs. Luce. "No harm other than you're left to do their work."

"The quiet has been nice, though." Ma smiled gently, though sorrow, and some other emotion, disappointment, washed over her pretty face. She reached into her apron's deep pocket and pulled out a newspaper clipping.

"What's that about?"

"You read it." Ma's lips disappeared into a thin line.

More tears slipped down Sadie's face. Ma cut out obituaries and other special notices from the leftover papers at the laundry. This didn't bode well. And after the altercation with Bernard and Robert, she wasn't sure she could hold back the sobs that threatened.

She unfolded the newsprint. A beautiful young woman smiled back at her from the paper. With thick, wavy, dark hair, sparkling dark eyes, and an ivory complexion, Sadie tried to place who she was. "I don't know her, Ma."

"Keep reading." Ma sank down onto the bed and began to roll socks together.

Miss Antonia Gaston of Lansing, Michigan, is engaged to Lt. Bernard Elliott of Mackinac Island. A September wedding is planned at the bride's parish church in Lansing. The paper slipped from Sadie's hands. "Oh!"

No wonder. No wonder all the excuses why Bernard couldn't squire her around on her one day off each week. No wonder when Mr. Foley, the island photographer, was making images in the street in front of Astor's, Bernard hadn't wished to be seen. When she and Bernard had walked past, the handsome officer turned away from the camera, claiming it wouldn't sit well with his superiors if he were in a promotional picture for the restaurant.

Did Robert know of this engagement? She dabbed at her eyes.

Ma took her hand and gave it a gentle squeeze. "Is this what you were crying about, love?"

Her lips parted, but she couldn't respond. She nodded slowly. Robert saved her from humiliation, and her mother had shown her the truth of the matter. A chill went through her, and she rubbed her arms. Three years of redoing Maude Welling's hand-me-downs, fixing her hair on her day off, and attending any officers' mixer event that Sadie could—all to get off this godforsaken island, and for what?

"I'm sorry, love. I know you thought that young man was special, but me and your Pa never trusted him."

Nor had Robert. But Robert Swaine had no right to give his opinion. No right to keep caring about her and her family. No right to make her want more in life. *But he had.*

Chapter 1

June 1895

Sadie shaded her eyes and scanned the deep sapphire waters of Lake Huron, to no avail—Captain Swaine must have taken her words, uttered a year ago, to heart. When would she once again spy his ship coming into port? Her gut clenched. Although she could have taken a boat if she had the funds, it felt as though the Straits of Mackinac hemmed her in, their zig-zagging currents too strong for her to escape. And now she was truly stuck, without the strength to procure her way out because she alone must care for her sisters.

Jack Welling raced down the hillside toward her, dodging the cows who were making their way up the hill to the fields near the former fort. The federal government would no longer be managing the National Park but would transfer ownership to the state. Mackinac National Park was now being converted to Mackinac Island State Park. So much had changed. *Ma gone. Pa missing. Bea working*.

Slowing his pace, Jack hooted, and then stopped. He bent over and clutched his knees, panting. "Hi ya, Sadie!"

"How're you doing, Jack?"

As he looked up, a knowing expression creased his eyebrows. "Prob'ly the same as you and Bea and Garnet and Opal."

"Maybe so." At least the boy had a father and his older sister to care for him. And someone to pay the bills.

The boy straightened. "Sorry that carrottop fired you from Mrs. Luce's place."

Sadie flinched. "She didn't fire me—Greyson's wife said they didn't need my services any longer."

Jack shrugged. "Same thing."

No more wages, regardless. "And all this activity and building on the island, yet no one willing to hire me except for Mr. Foster." At the tavern.

"Maude's still lookin' around for a job for you."

"And we're grateful for Bea working at your inn."

"Yeah." He rolled his eyes.

"I hope she's behaving." They badly needed her position.

"Sure! Hey, guess what? Mr. Hardy, the owner of the sawmill in Mackinaw City, stayed with us—givin' folks estimates for buildin' more cottages on the bluffs—and I asked him about your dad." He scrunched up his face. "He ain't seen him. Good thing, since somebody got killed down there recently, and it weren't him."

"Yes, poor man. Thank God for small mercies it wasn't Pa."

"Huh? How can mercy be small?" Jack's face again scrunched up.

"You're right."

"I'm right a lot!" He grinned but a shadow quickly passed over his face. "Would ya please write my uncle Robert and tell him to get back over here—he'll listen to you."

"What do you. . ." She patted at his arm but hit air as he swooshed away and raced down the hill.

She pressed a hand to her chest, sure she felt her heart beating through her worn cotton blouse. Why did Jack think Robert would listen to her? Was she truly responsible for him not returning?

"Sadie, girl!" Mr. O'Reilly called out as he passed by in his dray. "Ye're lookin' lovely, lass!" He winked and pulled off his blue work cap, revealing a shock of thick, white hair.

If his idea of lovely was being dressed in a dowdy tavern maid's uniform, then lovely she was. "Top of the day to ye, Mr. O'Reilly!" She heard the man's laugh carry over the sound of his draft horse's heavy *clip clops* down the street.

A gust of lake breeze ruffled her skirt and apron. Sunlight flickered over the Straits of Mackinac as a ship headed toward the port. *Not Robert's ship*. Why did that realization bring so much sadness with it? Because once upon a time, she had imagined her future, only and ever, intertwined with his.

Robert's steamboat sliced through Lake Huron, its cerulean waves punctuated by foamy crests. What an inauspicious return to such a beautiful place, with him attired in lumberjack's clothing aboard his own ship and not at the helm. His face heated. Why was he slinking into his own hometown like he was some kind of criminal? If finally listening to his doctor was a crime, then so be it. His many months of a healthy regimen had brought a level of vitality back that had vanished years ago.

Would Sadie Duvall, along with his niece, Maude, recognize Robert despite his many changes? He rubbed his clean-shaven jaw.

A young woman and her mother, Mrs. Lyndsey and her daughter, if he remembered correctly, stood near the rail, the daughter pointing. "The water in the Straits of Mackinac is as blue as sapphires."

Sapphire—like Mother's ring. Now that Robert knew the truth about that fop, Greyson Luce, who'd jilted Maude, he'd be sure to winch it out of his claws, for he'd never actually placed it on her slender finger. And with Sadie's lieutenant married and a child on the way, Robert had his own plans for that sapphire family ring—for his niece's sweet young friend who'd grown into a beautiful young woman. The railing, cool in his hands, felt slick from the spray. Was he putting himself on a slippery path? Putting up with her father as father-in-law one day had deterred most island men from even considering courting her. Might have been what ended the romance with the officer.

"Even from miles out, you can see the outline of the Grand Hotel—so expansive." Mrs. Lyndsey pointed to the cliff.

"We're staying there the entire season." Young Miss Lyndsey, a pretty blond who reminded him of Sadie, blinked up at him.

"I hope your stay on the island is very restful."

"And I hope Mr. Bobay will be here as well." Mrs. Lyndsey's words were full of unexpressed emotion that simmered beneath her clipped comment.

"Charles Bobay?" The railroad magnate had also turned thirty recently and like Robert was unmarried. "I believe all the shareholders should be here soon." Robert wouldn't mention that he, too, would be attending the meetings at the Grand.

"That's exciting news." Mrs. Lyndsey smiled approvingly at her daughter, who blinked several times. The girl stared down at her crocheted gloves and began to tug at the fingers.

"We best be getting to our seats now." Mrs. Lyndsey maneuvered over the ship's deck as though she'd had previous experience at sea. Her daughter, however, clutched the rail, her gait unsteady.

A blast sounded from the ship's horn as they entered the harbor. He should have been up there steering this ship. Instead, he'd arrived incognito and wouldn't be staying at the Winds of Mackinac, but hiding out at Aunt Virgie's, or the Grand, where he had business to conduct. But it had been his brother-in-law Peter's terse letter that drew Robert home for the first time since his sister's funeral. That and the remembrance of a certain beautiful young woman whose chances she believed he'd spoiled.

Soon the ship docked, and Robert tugged his cap low on his brow. He'd meet with family and friends on his own terms.

Robert disembarked, weaving in and out of the crowd to avoid the passengers. He caught his reflection in a plate-glass window by the dockmaster's office. Did he look young enough for Sadie Duvall to consider him?

He made his way toward the boardwalk and the Danner Stables.

Little Billy Lloyd, a wharf assistant whom Robert had trained, came alongside him. "Hey, don't I know you, sir?"

"Maybe." Stifling a grin, Robert slipped a coin into the boy's pocket, just like he had every day when he was on the island's main wharf, and ruffled his mop of curly hair.

"Mr. Swaine!" Billy's green eyes glowed. He shook Robert's hand so soundly that a few passersby turned to look.

"Shh!" He leaned in. "Quiet, Billy, I'm not announcing my presence." Not yet.

The boy made a motion as though buttoning his lips together. "Shoulda known you by your eyes."

The boy had previously described Robert's eyes as *odd*. Like the Cadotte men before him. Green, blue, and light brown swirled in his eyes like stormy waters near the island. "The color is called hazel." As he'd told him many a time before.

"That's a girl's name, though. It ain't right."

Shaking his head, Robert glanced toward the street for a dray driven by his cousin Stanley.

Billy patted Robert's back. "Captain Swaine, where'd you leave the rest of you?"

He laughed and reached into his rucksack and pulled out some Beeman's gum. "I'm chewing this instead of eating your mother's good cooking." Mrs. Lloyd was the head cook at Astor's. Robert offered the boy a piece and he took it.

"See ya, Mr. Swaine."

"I mean it now—don't tell anyone you saw me, Billy." Robert dug into his pocket and pulled a five-dollar bill from his wallet. The boy's eyes widened as he passed it to him. That was two weeks' wages on the docks.

"I can't take this, sir."

Robert wrapped his hands around Billy's knuckles. "Worth every penny to me."

"Thanks, Mr. Swaine."

He headed off toward the street, ducking his head and avoiding dockworkers who unloaded early season arrivals' belongings. When he lifted his gaze, he spied a young woman, attired in old-fashioned work clothes, head bowed and obscured beneath a wide bonnet. Her arms were wrapped so tightly around her middle that she appeared about to be ill. When she raised her head, Robert caught Sadie Duvall's beautiful profile. Her gaze was directed at Leon Keane, who stood at the entrance to the mercantile, a smug expression on his narrow face.

Sadie's brow furrowed and she rolled her lips together. She appeared oblivious to Robert as she wiped tears from her cheeks, swiveled on her heel and away from the store.

Robert strode closer to her. Sadie glanced in his direction. She gave him a quick once-over, showing no recognition. Or did she? And want nothing to do with him? Did she still blame him for setting that officer in his place? Robert watched as she brushed at her ugly faded skirt, turned on her heel, and walked away. His gut clenched. She looked as pitiful as the girl in his niece's favorite childhood story—a stepdaughter, named Ella, who was covered with cinders from cleaning out the fireplace each day.

Someone tugged on his sleeve. "Hey, sorry to bother you." Billy ducked his chin. "Wondered if maybe you'd seen Frank Duvall in St. Ignace—Sadie's been asking everyone on the island who's come back from the mainland."

Unspoken were the words *whom she could trust*—Sadie would have only inquired of people who wouldn't judge her or denigrate her father even further. "No, I haven't."

"She's got it awful rough, Mr. Swaine."

He flinched. Mrs. Duvall had died near the time his sister had passed on—both of pneumonia. "How long has Frank been missing?"

"Quite a while—I think all winter, at least."

The man might be a ne'er-do-well, but he was Sadie's father, and now she had the entire responsibility for her sisters. And what had Robert done to help? He'd secreted himself away and focused his attention on healing his body from all the neglect it had suffered while he'd captained his boats and expanded his business holdings.

So Frank Duvall was gone. Missing. What should he do? This might present him with an opportunity to put himself in Sadie's good graces. But he couldn't have her knowing what help he could provide. What was that the pastor in St. Ignace had said? "He who knows the good he could do but withholds it. . ." Didn't he say that was a sin?

For the first time in months, he had a concrete plan for what to do with himself on the island. And he'd pursue his mission with passion.

Chapter 2

The scent of stale beer, much of it spilled onto and soaked into the tavern's wide-wood-planked floor, battled with the odor of working men and the sardines some of the Norwegians ate like candy. Sadie pushed back a lock of hair on her damp forehead and examined the oak clock in the corner. Only five more minutes until the few remaining men, a trio of lumberjacks whom she'd asked about her father, left. While none recognized his name or description, all three were interested in knowing more about her—a little too interested, gauging by their sideways glances at her.

Mr. Foster, the tavern owner, pushed up his rumpled shirtsleeves, repositioning the black garters that held them there. "Hey, Sadie!" He cast her a sly glance. "Want a closing time brew?"

"No, thank you." She needed to get out of the tavern before the odious man had thrown back a few too many Stroh's Bohemian beers. Blue Ribbon winner at the Columbian Exposition in Chicago or not, it caused the man to leer at her like he'd done every night for the past week. How different this horrid job was from her position caring for Mrs. Luce. But when the infirm woman's son, Greyson, had returned, married—having jilted her best friend Maude Welling—Sadie had been let go. Greyson's new wife didn't want Sadie there.

"Suit yerself then." He scowled and filled his mug to the top with the pilsner.

She exhaled a sharp breath and tugged at her now-filthy apron. Like every night since starting, she'd have to wash and hang that and her work dress before she went to sleep. Right after she checked on her sisters and made sure they were safely tucked into bed.

Henry Harrison, the piano player, banged the keyboard cover shut. "That's all there is, fellas!"

The brawniest of the men pointedly turned in Sadie's direction, and she averted her gaze. She should have never talked with them about her father. Apparently, they'd misinterpreted her questions as interest. Or they just saw her as fair game without a father to protect her. But she still had God. Didn't she?

And thank the Lord, she'd no longer have to listen to Henry repeatedly playing "Daisy Bell," and singing other songs with lyrics so bawdy she had to tune them out. A dull throb droned in her aching head.

Sadie dipped her washrag in the soapy bucket of water as the men slowly walked past her, the oak floor planks groaning beneath them. Without looking up, she wiped the shellacked table clean, then dried it with another towel. Too bad it didn't sop up the odor of the whiskey that had spilled there.

"Goodnight, Miss Duvall." The third man had paused at the door.

No, no, no. Now he knew her name. She'd been stupid. Sadie's knees began to shake. Staring down at the table, she called out, "Have a blessed evening, sir!"

He made no reply, but the other two men's laughter overrode the slam of the heavy front door shutting.

What if they waited in the old fort gardens, which she had to pass when she left? Sadie had a knife and a horn that Robert had given her several years earlier. Although he'd meant it as a souvenir of sorts, the thing made enough noise to at least startle someone. Now Robert was gone. He was the first man who'd stolen her heart, though he'd taken it unwittingly. He'd rescued her from the officer whom she'd dreamed would give her a better life but had lied. And how had she repaid Captain Swaine? By fussing at him and sending him away.

"Lock the door, Sadie."

She turned the brass bolt on the door. Outside, darkness had finally cloaked the island. She'd never worked an evening position before, other than the few times she'd had to stay over at the Luce residence. What a contrast this job was to the task of caring for frail Mrs. Luce. But Mr. Welling had refused to pay Sadie's wages anymore, which was only right since Greyson Luce was no longer engaged to his daughter. And neither Anna nor Greyson wanted Sadie there. Sadie had only a day to make other work arrangements. At least there hadn't been a scene—Anna, the new Mrs. Greyson Luce, was too cold, too reserved, too utterly disdainful to stoop to arguing with a servant. Not that Sadie had protested. It was Greyson's mother who'd raised her thready voice to her new daughter-in-law. Sadie had spent a good ten minutes soothing the older woman and assured the invalid that she'd see her at church. And that she'd find a job quickly. No one, though, would offer Sadie a position. The bar owner was the only one who would hire her.

"Can I pour you one, Henry?" Mr. Foster hoisted a large mug as he called to the pianist.

"Not tonight."

Oh no, that meant she'd be alone with her employer. *Deal with the wolves within, or the wolves outside?* Sadie tugged at her suddenly too-tight collar. *Lord, help me now.* But she couldn't go running off. She had to finish her job. She had to pay for her sisters and herself, so they could eat and have a roof over their heads. Footfalls headed toward her and she unlocked the door for the musician.

"Good night, Miss Duvall." Mr. Harrison tipped his bowler hat at her as he headed out the door. "I'll keep my ears open for any news about your father."

"Thank you." She relocked the door and then flipped over the Closed sign, the bottom sticky with something. Sadie cringed. Was this to be the rest of her life? A barmaid in a rundown island tavern?

"Don't forget those tables in the corner."

Sadie retrieved her leather bag from behind the piano and set it on a bar stool. Tonight she'd finally receive her wages to make all this misery worthwhile. She grabbed her cleaning items and moved on to the corner tables, her back aching. From the corner of her eye, Sadie caught a fleeting movement outside, in the shadows beyond the gaslight. Were the lumberjacks waiting for her? She shivered, and then quickly moved on to finish up her tables.

"Sadie, you almost done? Time to close up." The owner's words slurred slightly.

Time for her to get her first pay. She'd worked hard. By her accounting there'd be enough for rent, food, and a little treat for each girl. Her tips that week had kept them fed at a bare minimum. If she never ate another baked bean in her life, she'd be happy, and certainly no more bean sandwiches *ever*. Her heart began to hammer at the thought of the money about to be pressed into her palm. It would be worth it all. . . . They'd be fine. For one more week, they'd be okay. But she'd not let him touch her. If he thought her pay entitled him to anything more than her waiting on customers, then Mr. Foster had another thing coming.

After putting her cleaning supplies away and hanging up her apron, Sadie approached the counter, and the till. She picked up the tooled leather purse that Grandpa had made for her years earlier, and fingered the design of the pines pressed into the buttery soft deerskin. Mr. Foster was locking the cash register. She saw nothing in his beefy hands. She waited. At least he wasn't ogling her. In fact, he seemed to be avoiding eye contact.

"You can go on now." His gruff voice made her flinch.

Not without her hard-earned cash. "My pay, Mr. Foster?"

He blinked and his jaw shot up a notch, but he looked past her at a painting of the Tahquamenon Falls, centered on the far wall. "Well, now, missy, the way I see it—you've just worked off your pa's debt to me this week."

"What?" Bile rose in her throat. Her head throbbed; the droning noise in it ratcheted louder. She was being robbed. Suddenly light-headed, she placed her hand on the oak countertop.

Foster sniffed. "He stiffed me for a large tab he'd run up here before he left." He shrugged his shoulders but still wouldn't look at her.

"I didn't cause his bill—he did." Anger burned like fire in her chest, and she fisted her hands. "You owe me my week's wages."

"He's your pa—and now we're squared up. I'll start paying you next week." His tone wheedled.

Next week she and her sisters would be out in the street, starving.

"No!" Sweat trickled down her brow. She had to have that money now. She must pay their bills or they'd be given notice. Her sisters couldn't go without food. "You'll pay me, or I'll report it."

He laughed, a wicked, low chuckle that began in the middle of his dirty blue-striped shirt, his large belly jiggling the fabric. "And who'll you be telling?"

The sheriff who routinely put her father in the brink for the night? No. She fought back the tears overfilling her eyes, but she'd not let this bully see.

"Maybe there's another way for you to earn some money?"

Mouth agape in shock, Sadie whirled on her heel and strode to the door. She'd not come back to work here. The holes in each stockinged foot pressed against the thin leather of her shoe soles. She couldn't trust this evil man, and she'd not return.

Sadie unlocked and pushed the door hard, letting it slam behind her. She didn't care if the glass in it shattered to pieces—Mr. Foster had deceived her. *Oh, Lord, what am I to do? Oh, God, I've struggled so hard, so long.* Like a blur, the past year of working and caring for her sisters ran through her mind. Sadie wrapped her arms across her midsection, and rocked back and forth for a moment, trying to stem the tide of rising nausea inside her.

What about the lumberjacks? Were they hiding nearby? She dropped her arms from her waist, a cool chill of evening air washing over her. If only she had a cloak. If only she had something, someone to protect her. But even if her father were here, he'd be of no use. He'd never been the same since the winter he'd hauled wood over the ice covering the Straits of Mackinac for the Grand Hotel to be built. The men who'd transported the timber had to remain deadly quiet during their work, straining to listen for the sound of ice cracking—which could have meant instant death. Although the ice never had given way, thank God, something in Pa's very nature had snapped, changing his nature.

She was well and truly on her own. Not a buggy, not a single person on a bicycle rode past. Movement on the hard-packed road behind her hastened her forward.

"Stop!" A few steps ahead of her, a familiar man's voice warned right before she ran smack into his solid chest.

"Oh!" The light scent of cedar and spruce infused the soft wool of a familiar jacket. She took a step away as the man grasped her upper arms. Faint light from the stars and the sliver from the moon reflecting on the water provided only the barest illumination. The man's face was impossible to make out.

"Sadie, what are you doing out so late?" *Robert Swaine.*

The realization of who the baritone voice belonged to opened the floodgate of her tears. Such a good man. He'd saved her from Lieutenant Bernard Elliott, who'd had no intention of marrying her but every intention of stealing her virtue and ruining her reputation. Robert was the man she'd foolishly spent years pining over, who'd been so far out of her reach. An older, wealthy man, her time spent mooning over him had been wasted. But he'd been the one she could always count on, before Miriam crushed his heart.

"You're back!" Her control vanished, and she sobbed into his shoulder.

Comforting arms slid around her, settling like angels' wings on her back, strong but gentle. "Now, now—it can't be as bad as all that."

Oh, but it was. God knew it was. She shook with sobs.

Several sets of footsteps came in their direction.

"Gentlemen?" Robert's stern voice held a warning.

But something wasn't quite familiar about *this* Robert. Muscles bunched beneath his wool jacket. This was a sturdy man with no hint of pipe smoke on him, no faint wheeze in his steady breathing.

Sadie sniffed. She couldn't get out any words. This had to be Robert. She needed him. She leaned in against the man. How many years had she and Maude run to her handsome young uncle, so he could fix their little injuries? He'd been a rock for Sadie—an example of a stable and godly young man who contrasted with her father's poor behavior. Of course, she'd never been held in his arms like this before either.

"They're gone." His voice certainly sounded like Robert's, but this man was more compact and strongly built. Worry niggled against her comfort. He loosened his hold, but she remained leaning against him.

Waves lapped against the shore nearby. The wind rustled the lilac trees, wafting their sweet fragrance. Robert smelled nice—not like the men at the tavern. She carried the odor of smoke and stale beer on her. Maude's uncle would have scolded her had he caught her in this condition—would have asked what she'd been doing.

She'd failed to bring a lantern with her because she'd been so excited about getting her pay. Fresh tears welled up, and she began to hiccup.

"What happened? Did old Foster try something with you, Sadie?"

She stiffened and pulled away. "No. But he didn't pay me." A sob escaped her throat. Humiliation burned her. She couldn't tell Robert Swaine, a wealthy man, that she and her sisters were penniless. He'd think she was begging. Or worse.

"Well, Sadie girl, what does that matter? Why are you working for that worthless toad?"

She swallowed. "I. . .my father. . ."

Robert squeezed her hand. "Do you have any idea where he might be?"

"He was supposed to go find work at a mill on the mainland, or to a lumber camp in the Upper Peninsula."

"I saw him in St. Ignace quite some time ago. About a month after my sister, and your mother, succumbed."

"But not again?" She sniffed.

"No. I'm sorry. Now that I know, I'll start sending out word along the railroad."

"Oh." She'd forgotten he owned stock in Michigan railroads. She'd not been ashore on the mainland in years, and on a train only once in her life.

"And although that miscreant Foster didn't pay you, there are sufficient funds at the Island General Store to provide for you girls."

Girls? Her sisters might be girls, but Sadie was a young woman. Spine stiffening, she recalled the pain she'd experienced when she'd pined away for him, her best friend's uncle, who could never be a match for her. "My father. . .did he. . ."

"You didn't know?" But something in Robert's voice held tension. "I'm so sorry Mr. Keane didn't send word to you."

Not only had he never sent word, but when she'd asked for a line of credit, he'd refused her. Pride warred with gratitude. Robert had to have set something up for her and her sisters. "I'll inquire at the store soon, thank you."

The kind man wiped her face with his handkerchief, gently dabbing her tears away. She didn't want to feel like a child. Robert's presence stirred a longing in her for more. More than being his niece's friend. But all those feelings she'd had for him were just childish dreams—weren't they?

"Let me escort you home, my dear."

"Thank you, Robert." She sniffed. "We're staying at Mrs. Eleni's boardinghouse."

Grunting his disapproval but saying nothing, he looped her arm through his and walked her up the dark street toward the boardinghouse. As her arm brushed against his side, where she'd leaned in on so many occasions over the years, Sadie hesitated, then stopped. She'd never been in Robert's arms before, until this night, but many times she'd leaned on his shoulder, his arm wrapped around her on one side, and Maude on his other side. He told the most wonderful stories about ships and boats on the Great Lakes. And at Christmastime, Robert made the best Santa Claus. Had he been unwell? Because the Robert she knew required little padding for that role. He used to powder his hair and beard. When her face had pressed to his neck tonight, there was no beard.

"What is it?"

Ahead of them was the gaslight on the corner by her boardinghouse. A tiny, niggling worry pursued her.

"Where have you been, Robert?" He'd been gone too long.

He drew in a sharp breath. "Here and there."

He didn't say anything about being out on his ships. She'd heard he'd lost two. Should she press him for more? Sadie's palms began to perspire.

They moved closer to the gaslight. No beard, the man was clean shaven. And handsome—very handsome indeed. Sadie tried to catch her breath.

"Something wrong?"

Robert Swaine had sported a bushy beard as long as she'd known him. "So how long will you stay?" Sadie's mouth felt full of marbles.

He released her arm. "Forever, if that's what it takes."

The man her young heart had first pined for would never have said such a thing. His greatest desire was to be aboard ship, at the helm. "Captain Robert Swaine would sooner swallow his tongue than say those words."

"Some things, some people, are worth changing for."

Was she one of those people?

Chapter 3

Dawn light pierced the filmy curtains as Robert woke from a fitful night's sleep at the Grand Hotel—unable to shake Sadie's words from his head. The Captain Robert Swaine of years past wanted only to escape this island, out onto the Great Lakes. And with his bequests from his parents, he had. One by one, he'd acquired another ship and made investments in railroads. Lying here now, having lost his sister, two ships, his closest friend and fellow captain, and likely the goodwill of his brother-in-law, all he wanted was to make things right. Yet how did he do that?

He'd start by meeting with his brother-in-law, Peter Welling, and move on to telegraphing his mainland friends to check on Sadie's father. He got up from the bed and went to the door to retrieve his polished shoes. Zebadiah always did a fine job and started early, which meant Robert's broughams should have been returned by now. He grabbed the worn flannel robe that Aunt Virgie had made him when he'd earned his captain's license and put it on. After unlocking the door, he hesitated to open it. Hushed voices were followed by the rumbling of something falling and hitting the floor. What was that commotion in the hall?

Opening the door a crack, he peered out. Shoes were scattered across the floor. One of the maids had covered her mouth, staring at the mess, and then back at her empty cart. Quickly, she began scooping up the footwear and placing it back on the cart. Something about her looked very familiar. From farther down the hallway, another door opened. Attired in a silky-looking bedroom ensemble, Laura Williams strode toward the employee. "May I help you, miss?" Laura, his old friend, began pairing up the shoes and checking for room number tickets in each.

Robert closed the door and grinned. Leave it to her to show up here and take charge. And once she knew he was here, he'd likely have to add to his list of responsibilities. At least he could count on being entertained by Laura's stories of life as an actress.

A soft thunk sounded outside his door. Likely the shoes being placed there by the clumsy maid. He went to the armoire and laid out his clothes, then returned to the door and retrieved his buffed-to-a-shine shoes.

Two hours later, his now-dusty broughams took him to the Winds of Mackinac. He'd walked, instead of taking a carriage. Instead, he'd savored the fresh winds from the Straits stirring his blood and calling him to stay home, moving him to set his anchor here. With Sadie.

After mounting the steps to the broad covered porch, Robert opened the massive oak door. Bea Duvall rose from behind the inn's front desk when he entered. He'd heard from Cousin Stan, on his carriage ride home, the previous night, that Peter had hired Bea as a favor to Maude.

"What are you doing here, Captain Swaine?" The girl's brusque tone set his teeth on edge.

This place technically belonged to him and his niece, until his nephew also came of age, yet he had to answer *why* he was there? Because Peter Welling wasn't accepting how things stood. This had been Robert's home for many years. And now he had to explain himself to Sadie's sister? "I'm here to speak with Mr. Welling."

"He and Jack are eating."

Robert had had enough of being treated like a stranger. "I'll join them." He strode down the hall.

He stood in the doorway to the Winds of Mackinac's dining room.

His nephew, Jack, pushed back from the table. "Where's your beard, Uncle Robert?" He ran to him and they hugged. Robert rubbed his knuckles over the boy's tawny head. He'd shot up in the past year. Soon he may surpass his father in height.

Peter stood and cleared his throat. Not long ago, his brother-in-law welcomed him as a family member living under this very roof. Now Robert stood, awaiting an invitation to sit. Peter shot him an angry glance. "Jack, take your seat."

"Aw." But the boy complied.

"Come in and have a seat, too, Robert. After all, this is your home too." But Peter's voice implied otherwise.

Standing here now, it seemed he'd always been away on a ship, out on the Great Lakes. "Thank you. I believe this was my chair." Robert pulled out a well-used chair on the right side of the table, one that had a gash on the back. "There's my Indian flint mark."

"I found an arrowhead last week up at the arch." Jack grinned and shoved a buttered piece of toasted bread in his mouth.

"We'll talk about all your running around unattended later, young man." Peter glared at Jack.

Virgie had written Robert that Jack hadn't been given much supervision since his mother had died.

Robert settled into his chair. Hopefully Peter wouldn't ask about the Canary. "I won't stay long. I'll be up at the Grand, so no need to worry about me."

"I assure you, I won't." Peter's voice held a slew of frost but he'd not be deterred. "But since you look like you're not eating well, perhaps I should worry." He pointed to the hot pancakes covered in butter and maple syrup, a coddled egg, and two links of sausage. "There's more than enough for you."

Robert reached a plate of biscuits in the center of the table and grabbed two.

"How have you been, Peter?" Robert took a bite of his biscuit then set it back down. He tapped lightly on the table as he awaited his response.

Peter's ashen complexion, the new lines in his face, and the stoop in his shoulders told of his heavy burden. "Might sell this place."

This wasn't going to go well. And with Jack present, Robert had no intention of upsetting the boy. And the child had no need to know that what should have been his father's property, instead would be divided between his sister and himself when he came of age.

"Let's talk about this, Peter."

"In my office, then." Peter swiped at his mouth with his napkin, and then rose from his seat.

After giving Jack a smile and a wink, Robert followed Peter down the hall.

Stale cherry tobacco odor and the faint scent of brandy announced the inn's office as his brother-in-law's domain. But it wasn't his. Robert had to get Peter to realize that he didn't have the right to sell.

"Jack and I need to get away from here." Peter turned his back. "Away from the memories."

"She's gone too soon, Peter."

"Everywhere I turn, I see her."

"I know." Everywhere on the small island were reminders of Mother, Father, Grandmother, and now his beloved sister. At least out on the Great Lakes, he could escape the reminders. Or so he'd thought.

Robert laid the document from his attorney atop the teetering pile on what had been his sister's desk. "You should take a look at this information. At your convenience."

"And if I don't?" Peter arched one shaggy brow as though to challenge him.

Like the whipping currents in the Straits of Mackinac, Robert's temper flared. But like the good captain he was, he'd keep his eye on his destination. And coming here wasn't to push his beloved brother-in-law into another spell with his heart, if that indeed was what was causing his chest pain. Robert had his own fences to mend. Truth be told, if it was Sadie they were discussing, Robert would feel as Peter did. He'd want to protect her, to cherish her, and give her every comfort that he could. But would she accept his offerings? "Sticking your head in the sand won't make this debacle of my mother's go away. We have to move forward."

"And have my children take what I've worked so hard for?" Peter shoved a broad hand through his silver-streaked hair. "To put Maude in charge here?"

That was exactly one of Robert's goals.

───────────────◆───────────────

Someone banged on the Duvalls' door, rattling its rusting iron hinges until they might break, and then paused. It had to be their imperious landlady. Sadie locked eyes with Bea, who was dividing a long loaf of bread into five pieces. As the pounding resumed, Sadie flinched, but her younger sister simply scowled. Little Opal ducked under the table, and Garnet stood shaking, clutching the back of a narrow unvarnished chair.

"Your money tomorrow or you're out." Mrs. Eleni finally stopped abusing their door. "Do you hear me, Sadie?"

Cringing, Sadie hugged Opal to her chest.

Bea stomped across the narrow room and unlocked and flung open the door. "Sure my sister heard you, and so did everyone else in this place, Mrs. Eleni! Now let us eat in peace."

The elderly woman tugged her dark scarf closer around her head, her beetlelike eyebrows drawn together in her wrinkled face. She muttered something in Greek, probably an epithet, by the way she ground out each word. Then she turned on her squat-heeled black pumps and returned back downstairs, mumbling in her native language the whole way.

Bea exhaled loudly and closed the door with a thump.

Garnet popped up from beneath the wobbly table, nearly knocking it over. "Bea, I'm hungry, what did you bring us?"

"There's ham and cheese to go on the bread." Bea unwrapped the waxed paper from the meat.

"Yum!" Opal snatched a paper bag and opened it. "Cherries! I thought I smelled some."

Sadie waggled her finger at her youngest sister. "Go rinse them first."

"Ok."

A line formed between Bea's tawny eyebrows. "I can't keep doing this."

"I'll get another job soon." Sadie forced her lips into a half smile.

"Cook sent this."

"Bless the woman." She'd always been kind to Sadie when she'd visited at the Wellings' inn.

Bea cocked her head at her. "But Sadie—Captain Swaine told me there was money for us at the Island General Store. I saw him this morning. Papa must have left something there."

Sadie's lips parted, but she bit back her response. Their father hadn't left two dimes for them to rub together. So he certainly hadn't left funds at the store, despite Robert's implication.

"Why haven't you gone there?" Bea glared at her.

"I...didn't know." Not until last night when Robert mentioned it. "We've been there many a time, and the clerk hasn't said a word."

Bea shrugged. "And the captain said you know we could all stay upstairs above the store too." Her angry tone left no doubt that she was done providing anything extra for her sisters.

"You saw Robert Swaine, then?"

Bea's brow wrinkled as she divided the ham onto the pieces of cut bread. "Huh? What kind of dumb question is that? I just told you."

"No, I mean—didn't he seem different?" What she meant was—didn't he look even more handsome.

Bea blinked at her, her green eyes luminous. "Well, he's awful quiet. But he gave me candy like usual. And he's not staying at the inn, so something must be different like you say."

"I...see."

The girl's eyes softened. "I like him an awful lot. If only he wasn't so old."

"Bea!"

"Well, he's gotta be at least thirty. Maybe forty."

"Not forty—but too old for you." Sadie laughed. "Come on. Let's say the prayer and then eat." As they slipped into the chairs that Mr. Christy had made for them, her shoulders relaxed. At least their fellow church members had tried to help them the best they could. They sat at the narrow table, another of the Christys' gifts, and prayed over their meal. And she wouldn't ask the pastor for any further help. She had to hang on to what little pride she had left. When that was gone—what then?

Chapter 4

Robert turned the large brass key in the Island General Store's lock with a mix of both pleasure at having the means to open the building and discomfort, knowing that, rightfully, Peter Welling should be the one who had control of this structure. *Nothing I can do about it.* He relocked the door, went behind the walnut counter, and retrieved the inventory book. He opened it and scanned for the items he'd requested for the Duvall girls' upstairs apartment—*if* proud Sadie would give in and accept the space from him. But if Sadie knew the entire situation—of what his mother had done—he doubted she'd accept his offer.

The door swung open, jingling the bell that his mother had placed there many years ago, when he was a young boy. When Jacqueline Cadotte Swaine had finally given up hope that one of her sons, lost in the Civil War on the opposing side, would walk through the door, Robert had always known he was the *replacement* son, which made it all the easier to escape to the lakes, and all the harder when she died. But guilt was no one's friend.

Leon Keane's droopy-lidded eyes widened as he removed his straw hat and set it on the corner hat rack. "Good morning, Robert."

Robert tapped the inventory list. "Is all of this upstairs?"

Lips puckering, Leon nodded, strands of his thinning auburn hair bouncing against his wide brow. "All set up. Right as rain."

"Good. And, of course, Sadie has an open tab here—anything she wants."

"Yes, sir." Leon scratched his forehead. "It's just that Peter—"

Robert raised a hand. "Peter has no say in the matter."

A muscle in the man's lean cheek twitched, but he nodded.

"I'm going upstairs. Let me know if Sadie Duvall comes in, would you?" Now that he'd told Bea about the available funds at the store, perhaps she would. When the young lady asked the same thing her older sister had—whether their father had left it there for them, Robert once again hadn't answered. Was he lying by omission? *Father, forgive me.*

Robert went back outside and rounded the corner, to the side entrance, where a ladder hung from the side of the white-painted wooden structure, in the event of fires. The false front of the building seemed to be detaching. He'd send word to the best carpenter on the island to get it repaired. Now if only his fellow businessmen would repair their edifices as well. They all seemed to be distracted by the changeover of the National Park to a Michigan State Park, and too concerned with the legalities to focus on repairs.

He opened the door to the inside staircase and let himself in. He mounted the steps and headed to the upstairs apartment. His brother-in-law hadn't wanted to be bothered with renting out the space, and his sister, God rest her soul, kept only some extra furnishings that she liked to rotate in and out of the inn.

He unlocked the solid oak-paneled door at the top of the stairs and entered. The scent of oil soap, beeswax, and lemon tickled his nose. Mary Meeker had done her job quite thoroughly by the way the dusty, dank odor had been vanquished since he'd last stopped by. The first room was about eight paces by eight, more like a large closet, and a good place for Sadie to store Bea's things, since she was staying in the servants' quarters at the Winds of Mackinac Inn. In the main room, Keane had brought up a pastel, oval-shaped hooked rug that covered most of the floor. The narrow divan, an overstuffed chair, and a table should be comfortable for the Duvall girls. He went on to what he imagined would be Sadie's room, with lined Irish lace curtains at the windows, and a matelassé coverlet on the bed. A sturdy trunk and a bureau set where he'd instructed Keane to place them, as well as a substantial mirror over a small vanity table. This was a plain room but serviceable. The room for the other two sisters featured twin beds, side by side, with a small white wicker table between them. Hangers in the closet were empty. He smiled to himself. If it were up to him, he'd fill all the closets full to overflowing.

He removed his watch from his vest pocket and checked the time. Almost one. He'd go to the Grand for afternoon tea and speak with the lead housekeeper there. Knowing Maude and her ridiculous notions, no doubt his niece would follow through with her threat. He blew out a puff of air and returned downstairs.

Inside the mercantile, customers clustered, bent over a display of yard goods.

The bell on the door rang. "Good morning, Mr. Keane." Sadie's breathy voice made his heart lurch.

Robert moved toward the back, hoping to avoid her and her sister, but also to catch a glimpse of Sadie.

"Miss Duvall," the clerk called out, his voice strained. "I'm so very sorry I failed to send word to you earlier about your line of credit here."

Robert felt like slapping his forehead and that of the clerk's. No one but a dunce would have a line of credit for Frank Duvall.

"Credit?" Sadie's thin voice sounded ready to break.

"No, so sorry—I meant you had funds here credited to you that you can draw from."

"Oh, I see." From her pinched expression, Sadie no doubt saw all too well.

Robert puffed out a breath and averted his gaze.

With that, her youngest sister began heading toward the back of the store, where the books were, and directly toward Robert.

The little sandy-haired girl glanced at Robert briefly, then stood by a display of children's picture books.

He moved aside and pretended to be looking at a row of nautical books, while surreptitiously glancing at Sadie.

The child moved to his side and raised a book up to him. "Do you know what this cover says, mister?"

Treasure Island. He took the book in his hands, recalling days sprawled on the guest bed in Aunt Virgie's home, reading this book as a boy. "Ah, that is one of my favorites, but I'm not sure a young lady such as yourself would enjoy it."

"I'm Opal, and I'm not a young lady—my pa says I'm a whelp. But I don't know what that means."

What kind of father called his child a whelp? *Frank Duvall.* Robert inhaled slowly then exhaled. Unfortunately, there were a lot of Franks in the world.

"Opal?" Sadie moved toward them.

He fought the desire to run. He broke out in a full-blown sweat beneath his vest. It was as though he'd taken a good splash in a nor'easter.

"Robert?" Sadie's heart lurched. It really was him. Only thirty, premature gray had streaked his temples while threads wove through the rest of his dark, wavy hair, but they were few. Small lines clustered only around his large hazel eyes, which focused intently upon her. Too intently.

She pulled at her fingertips as though she had gloves on, which she didn't. Then Sadie hid her roughened hands behind her back.

"How are you doing this morning?" Twin dimples formed in his cheeks, complementing his square jaw and cleft chin. With all that dark beard removed, there was no doubt Robert Swaine was a handsome man. The same wealthy and attractive man that as a youthful girl she'd pined after.

Robert clasped her hands between his. "You look like you've seen a ghost." At the contact of his hands, warmth sped through her like spiced mulled cider on a cold winter's night.

Recollections flooded her mind—Robert roller skating with her and Maude, taking them for a ride in the carriage, hiking up to Arch Rock, his comical attempt to teach her to ride a bicycle. His visits home were always the happiest times she'd known. A tiny sob threatened to well up. She shouldn't be so needy. She didn't need to put her heart on the line.

Opal tugged on her elbow. "Sadie? That man wants to know when we're moving in upstairs."

Robert's cheeks flushed.

"What do you mean?" Sadie cocked her head at her sister.

"There are, indeed, living quarters upstairs available to you, should you wish to occupy them." Robert's lips twitched.

Her sister pulled again on her sleeve. "What's he sayin'?"

Dropping down on one knee, Robert looked Opal in the eye. "There are rooms upstairs where you and your sisters could live."

He looked up at Sadie. "If you wanted to."

"I do!" Opal clapped her hands and motioned for Robert to rise.

As he stood, he wiped at his knees. "Rather Spartan accommodations, I'm afraid, but I hope you'll be comfortable."

Nothing could be more Spartan that Miss Eleni's rooms. "I. . ." Pride grasped at her voice but hope shook it off. ". . .why that would be delightful." Maybe Papa had done something for them after all. And here, all this time, she'd thought he'd not given them a second thought. She'd give Leon Keane a piece of her mind when she was alone with him sometime.

Robert offered his arm and she took it, a frisson of excitement startling her. "Would you like to go look first?"

His gentle voice, and the way he treated her like a queen and not the tavern girl who'd just quit the job that put food on the table, made Sadie a bit giddy. "Certainly, thank you."

At the stairwell, he released her arm and Sadie suddenly felt sad. But she needed to lift her skirts to mount the steps. Robert gestured her forward. Her head swam. Less than a decade older than herself, Robert had been an object of her fascination for years—her notion of the ideal man with his attentiveness, his humor, and kindness. She almost tripped over her skirt hem, and Robert caught her elbow.

"Careful, Sadie girl—I can't have you falling."

No, she couldn't fall. But it certainly felt like she might.

Thank goodness they'd accepted the new quarters the previous day because they arrived home to an eviction notice. Sadie had known this moment was coming, but now, with Mrs. Eleni scanning the room, about to throw them out, the deep humiliation she'd *imagined* was replaced by gratitude. Because now, thank God, they'd have a place to stay. Her landlady marched through the apartment, like a colonel from the fort inspecting his troops. Sadie stiffened, wrapped her arm around Opal, and drew her little sister close to her. They'd worked so hard, Bea, too, to scrub and scour every surface of the rooms where they'd lived since losing their own residence after Ma died and Pa left to find work on the mainland. Soon most of the French–Canadian cabins on the island, such as they'd lived in, would disappear, while inns catering to resort guests would be built to replace them.

Jerry Meeker, one of the draymen that Robert had sent, emerged from the bedroom. He lumbered past them, Sadie's dilapidated trunk in his arms. His overall straps drooped from his shoulders like Papa's often did, and Sadie resisted the urge to pull them up for him.

"This it, Miss Duvall?"

She nodded, her cheeks burning. Those meager possessions already carried downstairs and this trunk were all they had to move to their new apartment over the store.

Opal clutched her rag doll to her chest, eyes wide, as Mrs. Eleni ran her finger over the mantel. Garnet crossed her arms across her skinny chest and glared.

The woman shrugged. "I guess the place looks all right, but with the many late payments you've made, I think I'm entitled to hold back the refund on your deposit."

Sadie had anticipated this response, had prayed about it, even had peace that God would work the situation out in her favor.

Someone cleared his throat, and Mrs. Eleni looked past Sadie and Opal to the doorway, her ruddy face turning a deeper shade of burgundy. "Mr. Swaine, how nice to see you." Her gruff voice left no doubt that she would prefer to not see him.

The tension in Sadie's body eased, even though her heartbeat also kicked up a notch. "Robert, thank you for coming by."

Mrs. Eleni glanced between the two of them, as Robert moved to her side, squeezed her hand, and released it. "Are you ready, ladies?"

Opal's features bunched into a frown as she hugged her doll even tighter.

Trying to keep her voice calm, Sadie spoke as gently as she could, "I believe so."

"Why are you keeping Sadie's money?" Garnet asked Mrs. Eleni.

Her wrinkled face collapsed into a sneer. "I'm not—you impertinent child."

A muscle in Robert's jaw twitched. "I don't believe she's impertinent—rather she's observant and heard what you said as I arrived. You can send the Duvall's deposit to them at the store."

He lifted his hat and gave her a brief bow, then turned them toward the door.

If Sadie never saw these rooms again, it would be too soon. They held the sourest of smells and the saddest of memories.

Robert lingered at the door, leaning in to speak with their landlady in a soft voice. "Mrs. Eleni, since when have you been so uncharitable?"

"It's the leases, Robbie. I'm so afraid." Was that a withheld sob in her voice?

"With the transition? Is this not your own boardinghouse?"

"No, it's a lease from the National Parks."

"Oh." He sighed. "I'm hearing the same from others."

"My lease renewed right before the Michigan Parks took it over, but they're saying they won't honor it—that I'll be charged double on the lease. What will I do? I'll have to leave the island. It's the only life I've known, Robbie."

So Mrs. Eleni was in a predicament not too far off from Sadie's own. Still, did she have to be so ornery to them? *Pride, too much pride, like your own.* That still, soft voice pinned Sadie to the stairs.

She couldn't hear the rest of Robert's and the landlady's whispers. Soon he joined her on the stairs.

Looking up into his hazel eyes, she smiled in gratitude. "Thank you, Robert," she whispered as they descended the steps.

Several hours later, the dray had been unloaded and their belongings unpacked. Garnet lay across her bed reading.

Opal sat atop her own new bed, patting her doll's head. "It's gonna be all right."

Sadie bent and pressed a kiss to her sister's head. "Yes, I'm beginning to think it might be."

"I like this place."

The delicate lavender paint on the walls and lacy curtains gave the room a feminine feel, while the bedding was cozy and substantial—wool Hudson Bay blankets were stacked in each closet for cool nights.

Garnet looked up from her copy of *Little Women*. "I think Mr. Swaine might have fixed this place up for us."

Sadie had thought the same thing when she'd entered what was to be her room.

She'd become so lightheaded that she'd had to sit atop the trunk at the end of the bed and Robert had held her elbow. The pink-tinged walls reminded her of sunsets over the west, over Lake Michigan, when she and Maude had watched with Robert and with Maude's parents. And the bedding and curtains were exactly like some she'd shown Maude, once, in a catalog. Had her friend told her uncle? Everything seemed brand new. And the scent of new paint indicated this apartment had only recently been made ready for them. Something didn't quite add up. She'd talk to the clerk on the morrow.

If Robert Swaine was the one sponsoring them. . . Her cheeks flamed. She could only imagine what the island wags would say. Sadie with no job. Robert home. A line of purchase credit at the grocery. . . . She needed to find a job. And quickly. If Maude could wander up to the Grand Hotel and be hired, perhaps she had a chance too.

Chapter 5

Sadie adjusted the lace-trimmed apron of her Grand Hotel parlor maid's uniform. How had two weeks passed so quickly? Between working at the Grand Hotel six days a week, looking after her sisters, and spending time with Robert and the girls on her free days, all had seemed a blur. Plus her best friend, Maude, had needed help with Mr. König, who, it turned out, was really Ben Steffan, the reporter. Sadie maneuvered her cart toward the ladies' parlor, where finally she'd been given purview. She pulled out her feather duster and began working on the cherry tables in the front corner.

"Mr. Swaine?" Laura Williams's voice dripped with cherry-cordial sweetness.

Ceasing her chore, Sadie strained to hear the beautiful brunette actress's conversation with Robert.

"Good to see you. Excellent performance last night."

Was that the sound of him kissing her hand? Sadie gritted her teeth.

"Thank you. You know I always love to see your face in a crowd—even without your beard—which I miss, by the way." She giggled in a suggestive manner that made Sadie fist her hands.

"Oh, Laura, come have afternoon tea with me, and let's talk."

He called the actress by her Christian name?

"Robert," Miss Williams's voice was hushed, and Sadie took two steps closer to the parlor to better hear, but the whispered words evaded her.

A deep laugh accompanied Robert's voice. "I've been helping a friend and keeping busy."

Sadie cringed. She pressed against the plastered wall. *A friend.* That's all she'd ever be. She waited, tears burning at the corners of her eyes.

Lavender sachet scent preceded Mrs. Fox. The housekeeping manager's boxy heels clicked on the marble floor as she entered the salon and eyed her.

Like a ninny, Sadie stared blankly before lowering her eyes and bobbing a curtsy.

"Sadie, please attend to your duties." The command was said with a softness Sadie hadn't noticed before.

"Yes, ma'am." She began dusting a bust of Mrs. Sophronia Evans, one of the shareholders for the Grand Hotel who'd recently passed away.

"Sadie?"

"Yes, ma'am?"

"Miss Lyndsey has requested you to serve as her lady's maid this week. Do you think you can help her?" Mrs. Fox clasped her hands at her waist. "They would compensate the hotel and you'd be given a temporary raise."

Enough to cover a trip to the mainland to look for permanent work and to find Pa? "Yes, ma'am. Thank you."

Two hours later, Sadie knocked on the Lyndseys' door. Dawn opened it, grabbed Sadie's hand, and pulled her into the room. "Oh goody! I'm so glad you came!"

Although they were about the same age, Dawn was the daughter of a Grand Rapids' textile manufacturer and had no doubt grown up in luxury.

"Mrs. Fox said you needed help."

"Unlike many of the young women of my set here at the hotel, I don't require five changes of clothing every day." Miss Lyndsey took two steps toward the wardrobe and pointed to a satin and lace inset gown of heavy ecru linen. "But I do need help, particularly for dinner attire."

Robert had told Sadie that Miss Lyndsey was expecting to spend time with Charles Bobay, a railroad magnate. But Sadie hadn't seen the two together, other than briefly in the hallways, and there, the young woman seemed struck dumb around the intriguing man. Granted, Bobay had a strong presence and was frequently surrounded by his railroad cronies. But although he could be intimidating, the staff loved the gregarious man.

"I'm to help you as you need, miss."

"I thought I'd be engaging in more activities, but. . ." The pretty blond's light eyes shimmered with unshed tears. "I fear I have no invitations."

"What of your friend, Mr. Bobay?" Sadie sucked in a short breath, shocked at herself. How had those words slipped past her lips? She was a servant. She waited for the well-deserved reprimand, staring down at the boot tips peeking out from beneath her dark skirt.

"My friend? I would like him to be so much more!" The young lady's voice held a tremor.

How well Sadie understood those sentiments. But Robert had mentioned that Mr. Bobay was considering returning to Detroit early, presumably due to the lack of Miss Lyndsey's interest. "Begging your pardon for my impertinence—"

"I don't stand on those silly rules. And you don't have to with me. And please call me Dawn."

"Yes, miss."

"Please call me Dawn, or I shall be upset."

"Yes, Dawn."

"Do you know Charles?"

"No." But seeing Dawn's disappointment, Sadie had to say something. "But I do know he came here specifically to spend time courting you—"

"What?" The young woman's shriek was a mix of joy and dismay.

"But he says you have shown no interest in him, and so he is returning to his business earlier than planned."

"No!" The shy woman Sadie had observed in the hallways seemed to have vanished.

The door opened and Mrs. Lyndsey, a striking woman with rich golden-brown hair entered, dark eyebrows raised high. She quickly shut the door behind her. "What's going on here?

"Sadie says Charles came here to court me, like you thought, Mama."

Removing a long pearl-tipped pin from her elaborately feathered hat, Mrs. Lyndsey sighed. "Then why isn't that happening? I've certainly given you enough time to be near him at all meals and on the porch in the evening."

"I think I can help." Sadie might not be able to do anything about Robert—*her friend*—but she could redirect the course of Miss Lyndsey and Mr. Bobay, before it was too late.

For the next two days, Robert kept Sadie informed of Charles Bobay's plans, and she in turn informed Miss Lyndsey and her mother. She stood by the tall armoire, one that Garrett Christy had designed just for this room, with roses artfully carved into the oak front. "This afternoon, Mr. Bobay is playing croquet with the investors. All of their wives will be there, and their children, as well. So you'll need. . ."

Sadie pulled out an ensemble appropriate to the activity and laid it on the bed.

"I did look right back into his eyes last night, just like you told me, and he gave me such a delicious smile."

Mrs. Lyndsey rolled her eyes. "A smile isn't delicious."

Stifling a laugh, Sadie pulled matching shoes from the bottom of the armoire.

"Aren't we presuming a lot if we just show up at the match?" Dawn twisted her linen handkerchief into a wrinkled mess.

Her mother sniffed. "It's open to the public, darling."

"Still. . ." Dawn exhaled a long sigh.

Someone knocked on the door, but before anyone could answer, a note was slid beneath it.

Dawn hurried to retrieve it, opened and read it—then squealed in delight. "You've done it, Sadie! Charles requested our presence at the match today."

Mrs. Lyndsey clapped her hands. "Praise God for answering your father's and my prayers."

Sadie had no mother anymore, and her father was nowhere to be found. She went to the armoire to retrieve some stockings.

"You have a heavenly Father."

She stilled, almost expecting to see someone else in the room with them.

Another knock on the door sounded as mother and daughter exchanged a quick embrace. Mrs. Lyndsey straightened her afternoon gown and strode across the carpet to the door.

Robert Swaine stood framed in the doorway. Sadie's heart lurched.

"I wondered if I could have a quick word with Miss Duvall?"

As she turned to face Sadie, the matron's eyes widened. "Captain Swaine wishes to speak with you."

Sadie curtsied, and eyes down, left the room. What was so urgent that he needed to converse with her now?

Outside in the hallway, hazel eyes locked on hers, and her knees weakened. "What is it?"

"Could you and the girls come up to the Canary tomorrow night?"

One of the other maids strode past them, arms stacked high with fresh towels.

"I have to work."

Robert grasped her shoulders, the warmth of his hands seeping through the coarse fabric.

He grinned down at her. "You don't have to work so hard, Sadie. I wish you'd let me help you."

Sadie pulled free from him. She couldn't keep relying on the help from her friends. She needed a permanent job when this seasonal position ended. She opened her mouth, but no words formed. She clamped her lips back together.

"I'm trying to free up your time tomorrow, if you'll allow it." His handsome face was so close, she could reach up and stroke his cheek if she dared. "I need assistance."

"What is this for?"

"I'll take you home later and tell you all about it." The warmth of his voice and of his breath on her cheek as he leaned in unnerved her. "But might I have permission to request Mrs. Fox give you early leave?"

She needed her earnings. But Robert had done so much for them. She nodded.

"Wonderful. I'll meet you in the lobby then?"

"No. Meet me behind the building." Mrs. Fox would have apoplexy if she viewed one of her girls leaving from the lobby with a hotel guest.

"All right." He cocked his head at her, his eyes lowering to half-mast, as if he might...

Sadie took a step away and reentered the Lyndseys' room.

Now, two hours later, Sadie stood outside in the back of the hotel, near her coworkers, palms damp, awaiting Robert's arrival. She needed a bath, her clothes required a good scrubbing, and her sisters' needs must be tended to. First, she'd hear Robert's request.

"Hey, Sadie!" Henry Meeker, one of the draymen unloading boxes behind the hotel, inclined his head toward the street. "Captain Swaine is down there looking for you."

"Thanks." Great, now all the workers knew. All eyes followed her as she lifted her skirt and hurried toward the hilly street. Granted, she'd spent years being escorted around the island by Robert. Now, though, it felt like she was doing something wrong. She was taking advantage of his generosity, for Mr. Keane had let it slip that Robert was funding both their apartment and their purchases at the store. Even now, when she'd tried to use her first paycheck for groceries, Mr. Keane had refused to take her money.

As she neared the carriage parked on the side of the street, Robert waved at her. After another dray loaded with crates turned into the back drive, she crossed the street, dodging horse droppings in the hard-packed dirt street to join him.

"There you are." Robert assisted her up into the one-horse carriage, a smaller gig than he normally drove. "Glad Mrs. Fox let you off early."

Truth be told, she was too. That bone weariness she battled every day kept threatening to overwhelm her. But here, now, with Robert, a surge of energy rushed through her.

When his hands lingered at her waist, Sadie held her breath. He was so close, his dark hair curling around his brow, his hazel eyes so serious. She could reach out and touch the cleft in his chin. She could lean her head down and kiss him and tell him how much he meant to her.

"Make way!" Someone whistled loudly behind them and the heavy sound of Belgian horses' hooves carried on the packed dirt as a drayman passed them in the street.

Robert set her in her seat, and Sadie felt his absence as he strode around to the other side, and then took his place. Loneliness, even in this busy summer place, lingered in the breech. This was an absence only Robert had ever fully filled. There had always been something about him that had made the world seem more promising, more filled with hope of good things to come.

"I need some help."

Two days later, bent over a utility cart at the Grand Hotel, Sadie couldn't stop smiling, recalling the beautiful family gathering she'd been part of. Dressed in an apricot ensemble borrowed from sweet Dawn, and with her sisters Opal, Garnet, and Bea attired in finery that Robert had somehow procured, the evening of her friend Maude's engagement had been magical. She'd never forget it. She and Robert had made the garden a fairyland for Maude and Ben and their special moment, by placing hundreds of candles, nestled in glass jars, in the garden. What a gift Maude had been given in having her dream come true...of the proposal she and Sadie had discussed when they were younger. A dream of a prince pledging his troth in a fairy garden—a fantasy Maude had, and Sadie had nurtured. What a delight to help make that dream come true. Now, though, Sadie had to get her head out of the clouds and back to work. She was still a maid, and she had chores, so she pushed her cart down toward the parlor.

"Sadie?" She looked up to find her supervisor casting her a questioning glance.

"Yes, ma'am?" Last night Mrs. Fox, who seemed quite attached to Mr. Welling, and she had sat at a long table together. They'd eaten from Cadotte family china and used Swaine family silver and drank from crystal glasses that Sadie had feared her sisters would destroy.

Mrs. Fox offered a gentle smile. "You've proven yourself, Miss Duvall, despite my misgivings."

What did she mean? Was she referring to her work or to her ability to step in as hostess alongside of Robert?

"Thank you, ma'am."

"You looked perfectly at home in the Cadotte cottage last night." Was that admiration or disdain Sadie heard in the woman's voice?

The *Canary*, as Robert and his family called the yellow home on the bluff, was more of a mansion than a cottage. "No, ma'am, I'm an islander and a family friend and have visited before, but I'd never presume to make myself at home there."

She arched an eyebrow at her. "Is that so?"

"Yes, ma'am." Sadie's cheeks heated and she stared down at her booted toes. "I hope people aren't making presumptions."

"Such as?" There was an edge in her voice.

"That Robert..." She couldn't say the words.

"People will talk, my dear. They always do." She adjusted the chatelaine dangling from her waist. "The question is what shall you say if tongues do wag?"

Sadie lifted her head. "I can't lose my job over this, ma'am."

"I understand." She sighed. "But do you care for him, my dear?"

Sadie sucked in a shallow breath. She dared not answer this question. "I best get back to work, ma'am." When another servant passed by, Sadie grasped the handles of her cart, her mop bucket slopping ammonia-scented water. Would she forever toil and clean the slops of folks who traveled far to view the Straits of Mackinac, where the waters of Lake Michigan and Lake Huron met and mingled and churned, where romances bloomed like the abundance of flowers that covered the town?

Laughter carried from inside a nearby room, its door left ajar. "Did you see how the captain looked at me over lunch?"

Was she speaking of Robert? Many ship and military captains stayed at the hotel.

"Why, he looked like he positively wanted to scoop you up with his teaspoon!" The woman's heavy Southern drawl, and the room, identified her as the Texas matron about whom the other maids were complaining.

"If it weren't for that maid, he'd be mine."

Maid? Sadie pushed against the wall.

"We've gotten rid of other maids, we'll send that blond packing too."

If only Sadie could take her cart, turn around, and run, but she couldn't.

The two women emerged from their room. The matron narrowed her eyes at Sadie and surveyed her head to toe. Just last night, Sadie had been bedecked in an apricot silk gown and beautiful jewelry, and had presided with Robert over a dinner for Maude and Ben. Now, she was back in uniform.

"You were eavesdropping, weren't you?"

"No. The door was open, ma'am."

Footfall from behind her announced Mrs. Fox, who must have lingered in the hall-way. "Mrs. Chandler and Miss Peacock, how do you do today?"

"Fine," Miss Peacock sniffed.

"But we'd be better if your staff didn't sneak up on people and listen in on private conversations."

Mrs. Fox cocked her head. "I walked by earlier and the door was open. So, I'm sure you said nothing you wouldn't want our staff to hear."

Both women assumed a sour expression.

The supervisor looked pointedly at Sadie. "And anything heard here is not repeated, am I right, Miss Duvall?"

Sadie bobbed a curtsy, and Mrs. Fox waved her to move on.

As she passed the other rooms, Sadie blinked back tears. She had to find something else. Before everything went awry.

Sadie scurried down the corridor to the main rooms near the porch. In a large alcove near the registration desk, she paused to watch Zeb, the shoeshine man, work. A ruddy-faced man was seated in the chair.

"'Yahsir." The black man polished the businessman's shoes, his long nose buried in a paper, yet he kept up a litany of comments.

"Yahsir," the bootblack repeated.

When the hotel guest left the shoeshine chair, he pressed some coins into the worker's hand.

"Thank you, sir."

As soon as the hotel guest rounded the corner, Zeb sighed. "Cheapskate!"

He rubbed the two coins together. "Won't barely cover the cost of my supplies."

"I know. I'm sorry."

"Sorry ain't gonna do me no good, Miss Duvall."

"For me, neither. I've got to find another job, Zeb, before one of these guests tries to get me run off."

He chuckled and she stiffened.

"I ain't laughin' at you, but at those society gals all jealous about your captain."

"He's not my captain." She'd like him to be.

"You tell him that then, miss." He jerked a thumb toward the concierge's desk, where Robert stood, his back to her, as he engaged in an animated conversation with the theater star, Laura Williams. The beautiful woman was about his age—and unmarried.

"He looks pretty taken with Miss Williams."

Zeb returned his supplies to their proper places and then wiped his hand on a cloth hanging from his waist. "Nah, she's not for him."

How Zeb knew this, she didn't dare inquire.

"Seems to me if you want a job away from the captain, you gonna have to get to the mainland, like you been talkin' about." The shoeshine man eyed her skeptically. "That man whose shoes I just shined done told me somethin' that might help you, miss."

"What's that?"

"They hirin' nurse trainees and all manner of young women to help at that hospital, over there in Newberry. Desperate, he said."

And wasn't she desperate too?

Chapter 6

With only several days of coaching Miss Lyndsey about displaying more attention to Mr. Charles Bobay, their romance was blossoming. Unfortunately, the same could be said of Robert and Miss Williams. The two were spotted everywhere together. Today, Robert had taken Opal and Garnet along with Miss Williams up to old Fort Holmes to hike and picnic. Not wanting to see them when they'd returned after work, Sadie had stayed late and fixed Miss Lyndsey's hair into a golden coif. The upswept style made her look like an angel and had earned Sadie a hug. Soon Mr. Bobay was sure to make his intentions clear. Was Robert doing the same with Miss Williams?

Sadie eyed the bicycles parked by the hotel as she walked down the hill. With only a word, she could request a bicycle, or two or three, and Robert would procure them. But that would be wrong to impose any further upon him. She walked on, under her own power—as she'd have to be if and when Robert finally married. Something was making her eyes water. Sadie bowed her head, the chill wind blustering smoke-scented breeze her way. She rounded the corner and glanced out into the furious blue straits, where whitecaps danced like sprites across the high waves.

The scent of smoke grew stronger as Sadie neared the Winds of Mackinac. Jack Welling rode down the side alley so fast that he looked like he'd fly from his bicycle. Sadie froze.

The boy slowed and then jumped from his Sterling, which had no brakes, and threw it into the grass. He ran to her and grabbed her arm. "Come on, Sadie! The Island General Store is on fire!"

"What?" *No, Lord, no!* The apartment had become a home. Their refuge. Were the girls there, inside? Had Robert left them and went off with the actress?

"Did you see my sisters?"

"No." He ran toward the inn, calling over his shoulder, "I gotta tell Dad and get some help."

Stan Danner drove past in a dray, water barrels strapped in back. "Make way!" he called to the carriage ahead of him in the street. "There's a fire! Make way!"

Sadie hurried past people clustered on the boardwalk. Her sisters. She had to get to them.

The fire crew carriage rolled by, with Greyson Luce clanging a bell as they went. Fear and determination were etched in his features. As upset with him as she'd been for throwing Maude over, Sadie was grateful for his assistance now.

All along the street, islander men vacated their workplaces and streamed into the street, many carrying buckets of sand. Sadie continued on, trying to catch her breath.

Arriving at the store, panting, Sadie rushed toward the side entry door and pushed past the crowd gathered near the fire wagons. She had to get to her sisters. She looked up at the side window. Opal's doll seemed to be waving down at her. Opal wouldn't have left her doll behind. Sadie choked back a sob and tried to open the door, but it was jammed.

The fire brigade volunteers had begun setting up to pump, and a queue of islanders passed buckets.

"Get back, Sadie!" Greyson yelled at her.

Robert pulled the carriage up beside the docks, secured the brakes, and handed Laura the reins. He patted the horses' heads to reassure the whinnying creatures, then ran off toward the store.

"That's Sadie up there!" Garnet stood, pointing, but Laura quickly got the child to sit, and wrapped her arm around her.

Sure enough, Sadie was climbing the ladder on the side of the store.

Lord, we need some help here. From shore, a water bucket brigade urgently worked. The fire carriages surrounded the building. The earlier breeze ceased, holding an eerie stillness. But thank God for that small mercy, for wind was fire's close friend.

Robert ran across the street, dodging manure. *Oh, God, don't let her die up there. I can't live without her.* He was almost to the building when a band of iron seemed to wrap around his upper arm.

"Stop! It's not safe." Greyson scowled at him, but Robert broke loose from his grip.

He pushed through the crowd until he got to the boardwalk, the smoke nearly overpowering him. He loved this woman, he needed her. Forever. He couldn't lose her now. Not like this. Not ever. "Sadie!"

Almost to the second floor, she looked down at him.

"I've got the girls. Come down!"

A powerful explosion split the air, and Sadie screamed. Fire rained down on him, scorching Robert's clothing, but he stepped in as Sadie hurtled toward him. He caught her in his arms and fell to one knee, wrapping his arms around her as gasps, coughs, and cries created a hellish cacophony of noise all around them.

Water poured down on them. First from the volunteer firemen blasting the wooden structure with their hoses, and then from above as the heavens broke loose. Sadie shivered, but he held her there, he in his sodden tweed jacket, and she in her maid's uniform.

"I love you, Sadie," he whispered. But he had to get her away from the building.

She pulled away, lips slightly parted, looking down at him with longing. He got up and wrapped his arm around her. He pulled her toward his carriage, which Laura was driving down the street. Opal and Garnet waved to her from the back.

"I thought they were in there." Sadie choked back a sob.

Robert took her hand, led her across to the harborside, and then continued up the boardwalk, following the carriage.

Thunder boomed overhead.

"I can't believe it." Robert tipped his head back to view an enormous black cloud, not uncommon in the Straits, moving quickly in their direction, yet without an accompanying wind.

Sadie, her face streaked with black soot, had never looked so lovely. Other than singed hair and clothing, she should be fine.

He could resist. He should. But Robert bent and covered her mouth with his, right there in the street, as the clouds opened up and poured down chill rain by the bucketsful. Nothing had felt more right than her in his arms, his lips covering hers.

If Robert loved her, and had kissed her so thoroughly right in front of everyone, then why did he still squire Laura Williams around the island while Sadie was working? She pushed a lock of blond hair from her brow then began dusting the piano in the ladies' parlor. Two matrons entered the salon and eyed her. She stiffened and quickly averted her eyes. Normally, guests took no notice of the servants. It was as though they were nonexistent. Although this was not open parlor hours, Sadie held her tongue. The two ladies, already dressed in evening attire, although it was hours too soon, took seats opposite one another at a round walnut tea table.

One of the waitstaff wheeled in a small tea cart piled with cookies, scones, and muffins, and with a teapot nestled in a cozy. When Sadie sent the young man a quick questioning glance, he simply raised his eyebrows in response.

"Thank you, young man." The older of the two women, with a pouf of silver hair framing her sharp features, nodded curtly.

"We'll pour our own, thank you." When the waiter left, the lady with auburn curls did indeed pour tea for the two.

Sadie continue to dust and shine the furniture as the two women chatted about the weather.

"And my, wasn't that something about the fire the other day?"

"The whole village might have burned."

The way fire leaped between wooden structures, indeed it could have. But the firemen and God put the inferno out quickly.

"And Laura Williams—abandoned in her carriage, while Captain Swaine dashed off to save some island girl." The woman tugged at her old-fashioned lace collar, secured with an amethyst broach.

"Shocking. I heard the silly creature was climbing into the inferno."

Of course, Sadie was trying to climb up. She wanted to rescue her sisters. She clenched and unclenched her fists.

The older woman sipped her tea, then set the cup down with a clink. "I should think Dr. DuBlanc should refer her to the asylum in Newberry."

"Indeed. But I hear there's a nursing shortage there."

"It's to be expected, with the sanitarium being so new. But at the least, I'd hope that young psychiatrist would offer his services before he begins his new position there."

How dare these ladies sit and judge her? Sadie's heartbeat kicked up, pumping heat to her face, as she spread lemon oil over the surface of a lamp table and rubbed it vigorously against the grain.

"Poor Laura. How humiliating to have her beau seen embracing another woman."

Her beau?

"Her beau?" The older woman repeated Sadie's own thoughts. "There's to be an announcement at the ball, after her last performance, and I believe he's to become her fiancé."

No. That couldn't be. Robert had tended to Sadie's burns, had made sure she and the girls were housed again. Had brought her and the girls up to the Canary to stay.

"Yet, he apparently keeps this other woman put up elsewhere."

"Scandalous."

"Once they're engaged, Laura will put a stop to that. Mark my words."

"A kept woman on this island?" The elder matron pulled a lorgnette from her handbag. "No doubt all these islanders know about it."

"She'll be drummed out of here."

"You'll see."

When the two pointedly glanced in her direction, Sadie turned and fled the room.

She was a third of the way down the hallway when a strongly built man backed out of a workroom. Garrett Christy pulled an elaborately carved console table into the hallway. Apples, deer, and pine trees covered its large rounded legs. He released the piece and looked up at her.

"Sadie, you're just the person I've wanted to see."

"Yes?"

His expressive features tugged and pulled. "I've got something to tell you."

Birdsong and a mourning dove's plaintive calls stirred Sadie from her slumber. She pushed aside the heavy bedcoverings on the tall bed, bringing alive the scent of dried lavender. She and Maude had slept in this bed on occasion when Mrs. Swaine had invited them up to her home. Light shown from alongside the curtains. *Oh no.* She was going to be late to work. Wrapping a robe around her, Sadie peeked into the halls. Robert's laugh carried up from downstairs. She padded downstairs, barefoot, as the grandfather clock softly chimed the hour. Six. My, that was terribly late. She strode toward the dining room.

"Sadie? Is that you?" Robert sat at the grand long dining table, smiling up at her as natural as could be, from behind a *Detroit Free Press* newspaper. In front of him lay a silver tray of pastries. Lemon poppy seed muffins, cinnamon rolls, and almond twists covered the tray, crowding one another out. He pushed back his chair, rose, and gestured to the chair beside him, as he pulled it out.

She raised a hand. "No, I can't sit. I have to get ready for work. I'm going to be terribly late."

Robert continued to hold the chair for her. A cool breeze gusted through the open window and rustled the lace dining room curtains. "Have no worry, I sent word to Mrs. Fox that you required some rest."

Her mouth went dry. "I need to work, Robert." She needed that paycheck. She needed to find another place for her sisters and her to live. But she sat in the proffered chair and allowed him to adjust it for her.

"Any word on Mr. Keane?" Dr. Cadotte, Robert's cousin, had attended the shop-keeper, who'd suffered burns and inhaled smoke.

"François says he'll be fine." Robert took his seat adjacent hers.

Although Mr. Keane's unattended pipe had caused the fire, which could have killed Sadie and her sisters had they been upstairs, she wished him no ill. "I'm glad to hear that. And we should pray for him and his family." How would he manage without employment? She understood that desperation all too well.

He poured more creamer into his coffee. "I've already asked my cousin to give him a position at the mercantile."

"No smoking allowed, I presume."

"Indeed." A smile tugged at Robert's lips. "I almost feel like I need to thank him, though, for bringing you here. You brighten the place by your presence."

And when Miss Williams found out, what then? "Is that so?"

"We need to get you settled in here for the long haul."

A rush of emotions surely shown on her face as she blinked in shock, clenched her teeth in anger, and sighed in frustration. For she and her sisters to officially take up residence here would make it look like she was Robert's kept woman, like those horrid women at the hotel had said. Her cheeks heated. She couldn't manage to make her protest, and reached for the silver tongs to choose an almond pastry that looked as twisted as her insides felt.

"We can't live here, Robert." She took a small bite of the flaky baked good.

"Why not?" Robert frowned and avoided looking at her. "You're Maude's friend, and I've known you for years."

So she was just his niece's friend and a charity case. That was all she was to him. She opened her napkin and shook it out before placing it on her lap. "But people will still talk."

Rosy circles bloomed on his high cheekbones. "Let them talk. I've nothing to hide."

"It wouldn't be your reputation that was tattered." She pushed the almond twist aside, her appetite fleeing.

Maybe the girls could stay, and she could go to the mainland and get a job. Find out if that man at the asylum might be Papa. With her not in residence at the Canary, then perhaps the rumors wouldn't go far. Sadie nibbled on her lower lip. "Could the girls stay here while I go to the mainland?"

"Certainly. I'd gladly accompany you to Newberry to see if that patient might be your father." He covered her hand with his, sending a thrill of warmth through her.

"Gretchen will watch the girls. And Aunt Virgie will be coming by too."

"That would help." Especially if she was hired on and had to save up money for a few months to bring the girls to the mainland.

He quirked a dark eyebrow at her, making her stomach do funny things. "I'd be glad to let Mrs. Fox know that I'll accompany you."

"Imagine how that would look. You and I going off on a ship, and then a train, together." No, she would do this on her own. She was going to Newberry. "What about Laura Williams? What would she think?"

Chapter 7

St. Ignace, Michigan

W hat are you whittling, Mr. Christy?" Sadie eyed the animal that was coming
to life in the craftsman's hands.

He laughed, stopped carving, and rubbed his thumb against his thickly
bearded jaw. "It hasn't told me yet."

Just like Robert failed to answer her question about Laura. His vague reference
that it wasn't his place to say, had lit the fire to send her on this journey with her fellow
church member and family friend.

Garrett Christy dug his knife tip into the wood to make eyes. "I need to carve the
mouth, and maybe then he'll talk."

"What?" She laughed. No wonder the Christy children were always teasing each
other. If only she knew how to make Robert spill the beans. He'd always held his secrets
close to his vest, much like Maude could do.

He bent his dark head over the piece of oak and continued to carve. "I think it
might be a lumberjack."

"Not a bear?" The scent of coal dust and light smoke filtered through the cabin as
the train rumbled on.

"Maybe a moose." He chuckled as he expertly dug out a chunk at the base of the
wood. "That would be his big feet."

"Only two feet?" She cocked her head to the side, the flickering light from the train
windows illuminating the long narrow form.

"He's my younger brother, who'll accompany you."

"I thought his name was Richard." That's what Rebecca Christy, Garrett's wife, had
said.

"Wait till you see him, and you decide which name best suits." He smiled and
continued to shave portions off until the wooden lumberjack's arms began to emerge.
"He'll have to take you to that place because he knows his way around there. I've got
a bushel and a peck of visiting to do at the lumber camp, while you two check out
whether the unidentified lumberjack might be your father."

How would it be, having a stranger accompany her? Maybe she should have allowed
Robert to bring her. "Your brother thinks that poor injured man is my pa?"

"Wasn't sure, but he wanted you to come." A shadow passed over his face. "My own pa
has had some narrow misses too. Don't know what I'd do if he'd ended up in such a place."

She'd never been to an asylum. Dr. DuBlanc made the modern treatments sound
promising, though. Water therapies and so on seemed to help some patients. Still, many

never returned home. Sadie chewed on her lip.

"Want some Beeman's?"

Sadie accepted the offered chewing gum. She'd spare her lip from further abuse. "Thanks."

Outside the windows, the forest began to thicken with massive pines, maples, and oaks, stealing away some of the fading sunlight. Garrett tucked his carving tools away, inside his leather satchel, and set it on the floor.

"I wish Richard had written you more information." The vibration from the rails caused her seat to shake slightly.

"He's a Christy. He doesn't say much."

Whereas Robert Swaine had always been a talker. He loved to spin a good tale. One of his traits that had caused her to fall in love with him when she was so young. Too young to marry. And then Miriam had caught his eye, and then crushed his spirit. Only now was he the old Robert she'd once known and loved. "I thought Rebecca said Richard's a big reader."

"He is, but he lets that librarian wife of his do the talking for both of them."

"I think Robert would do the talking for both of us if I let him." Yet he was remarkably closemouthed about Laura.

The conductor ambled through, rocking side to side, eyeing each of the passengers on either side of the rumbling train. He nodded at them, his wire-rimmed glasses so low on his nose that they looked like they'd slide off.

"You know the captain has your best interests at heart."

The hair on the back of her neck, tendrils that had slipped from her chignon, prickled. "Does he, now?"

The craftsman nodded. "I've known him a long time, and he's a good man."

If he was such an honorable man, then why was he flaunting another woman on his arm? "Do you know Laura Williams, the actress?"

"Of course. She's performed all over the Great Lakes. Even saw her in a hall in Cheboygan once, years ago." He rubbed his chin. "Captain Swaine brought her roses at the end."

"Oh."

He elbowed her gently. "Don't get so downcast. I think Miss Williams has been protected by him for years."

Like he tried to do for Sadie. "I see."

"I don't think you do." He smiled. "Let me tell you what an old lumberjack, Frenchie, told me about her. You know I don't like to repeat gossip, but this just might be the truth."

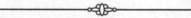

"I've never seen the like." Sadie stared in awe at the acres of redbrick buildings, all new, some rising two stories with pillars in front.

The federalist-style buildings were like those she'd seen in books, but having grown up in lumber camps and small villages, and then the island, she'd not actually seen such imposing structures. Her improved mood, at hearing that Miss Williams might not be a *miss* after all, caused almost everything to look better in the afternoon light.

"Pretty splendid, ain't it?" Richard Christy, a lumber camp boss, and at least a foot taller than herself, opened the wide, heavily embossed, engraved oak door to the Doctors' Offices building, a magnificent redbrick structure, standing two stories high and what looked like a hundred feet long. The entryway was so tall, the giant of a man didn't have to duck.

"It's amazing." Sadie stepped in to inhale the scent of lye soap and ammonia water as Richard held the door. Two giggling young women in starched white uniforms stood just inside the entryway and quieted when they craned to look up at the lumberjack.

"Smells clean, don't it?" Richard snapped his suspenders against his broad chest.

Sadie bit her lip, unsure of how to respond. This man lived in a lumber camp, not among the cleanest places in the world. "Um, yes, it does."

"Dr. Perry said to stop at the front desk."

Dark marble floors with a hint of pink threads gleamed as they crossed to a mahogany-finished desk. A dour-faced, red-haired woman, her head bent over what looked like a list, jabbed her finger at each line.

The two waited a minute before Richard cleared his throat and the receptionist looked up, irritation etched on her sharp features. "We're here for Dr. Perry."

"Do you have an appointment?" The snap in her voice and the narrowed eyes suggested she didn't think so.

"We sure do, ma'am. And may I say yours is the prettiest hair I've seen in these parts, save for my own sister's." The big man offered the woman what looked like a genuine smile.

"Thank you, young man."

Sadie glanced down the hall and spied a cherrywood door with a glass insert etched with Stephen Perry, M.D. She directed her attention back to the receptionist, whose cheeks now bloomed a flattering pink tone, bringing some life to her face. Sadie cleared her throat. "Should we go ahead to the office?"

"Let me announce you first, Miss. . .?"

Mrs. Robert Swaine. The name flashed through her mind so quickly that for a moment Sadie felt dizzy. She wasn't Robert's wife. Might never be. But if what Garrett had told her was true, there was still hope. "Miss Duvall."

With efficient steps, the woman stepped from behind the desk and down the hall to the office. She rapped at the door and then entered. When she emerged, she waved them forward, beaming up at Richard as they passed.

Richard held the door open for Sadie and she stepped inside the office, which smelled faintly of fresh paint. Inside, two leather chairs flanked a wide walnut desk, behind which sat a rather young-looking physician. With dark, wavy hair, matching dark eyes, and rosy cheeks, he looked more like a college boy than a department director.

The doctor stood and gestured to the chairs. "I believe you're here about our unknown patient?"

"Yes. We think he might be my father."

"Today, he's been asking for Opal and Garnet. We thought he meant jewels, but—"

"My sisters." Two of them. Tears pricked her eyes. "May I see him?"

Chapter 8

Miss Lyndsey and her mother each took one of Sadie's arms and pulled her into their spacious room. Dawn pulled the door closed and locked it. "What's happened, Miss Duvall?"

Sadie clasped her hands at her waist and kept her eyes focused on the pastel Aubusson rug on the floor.

Mrs. Lyndsey touched her shoulder. "Something is clearly not right. Didn't you find your father?"

"I did." Tears spilled over and Sadie wiped them away, her ammonia-scented fingers making them water even more. "But he's best left where he is."

Dawn handed her a linen handkerchief with embroidered edging. "I'm so sorry. Will he improve?"

Nodding, Sadie drew in a steadying breath. "It could take some time, but the doctors have hope."

Mrs. Lyndsey smiled. "So not only have you found your father—we've discovered that Captain Swaine is besotted with you."

Sadie blinked back her tears and looked into the kind woman's soft blue eyes. "Perhaps he's only doing me a favor." But he *had* said he loved her. The only other time he'd said that publicly to a woman, he'd announced his engagement the next day—crushing Sadie's too-young heart.

The pretty matron shook her coiffed, bronze curls. "No. I recognize that look. It's the way Charles B. looks at Dawn."

She turned to face her daughter. "Show Miss Duvall what Charles gave you after she'd encouraged you to show him a little interest in return."

The pretty girl blushed but she extended her left hand, displaying a rose-gold ring set with a large oval diamond.

"It's beautiful!" Sadie wanted to embrace the younger woman, but she restrained herself. Dawn, however, opened her arms and gave Sadie a hug.

"Thank you for helping me see that Charles really was interested in me."

"And you, my dear, need to open your big blue eyes and notice that Captain Swaine needs you as much as you need him." Mrs. Lyndsey sounded so much like Ma, that again, tears rose up.

Sadie sniffed. "Do you think so?"

Mother and daughter exchanged a long look and then bobbed their heads in agreement. "Mrs. Fox is going to help us get you ready for the ball tonight."

"What?" Sadie swiped at her maid's uniform.

"Your captain doesn't know you'll be there." Dawn almost squealed in delight.

"We plan to surprise him."

Sadie shook her head. "Captain Swaine is only going because Maude and her fiancé will be there. He promised them."

"No, he'll be there to witness Miss Williams making her announcement."

"Really?" Was it true? Had Mr. Christy's friend been correct? Would *Miss* Williams share what he said was the truth of her so-called spinsterhood?

"We're now your official lady's maids."

"I. . ." She'd already worked several hours. Needed a bath, needed her hair washed, needed to make sense of things too.

A knock on the door made her jump.

"Come in!" Mrs. Lyndsey crossed the room as the door opened.

Mrs. Fox entered, her arms stacked high with boxes. "For our belle of the ball tonight."

"The dress already arrived earlier." Miss Lyndsey stepped aside, revealing a blue silk moiré gown, laid out on the bed.

Sadie sucked in a breath.

"Captain Swaine was admiring the Worth gown in the shop downstairs." Mrs. Fox set the boxes down on a nearby table. "He said it matched his sweetheart's eye color perfectly. And since Miss Williams's eyes are a renowned lavender-gray, we knew he meant you, Sadie."

"I couldn't possibly accept it. He's already done too much."

"Oh, he didn't buy it." Miss Lyndsey exchanged a look with her mother.

"Robert wanted to order it, but he said he couldn't." Mrs. Fox opened the top box, which contained a glittering necklace, bracelet, and matching earrings. "Not until his beloved said she'd be his wife, which he wasn't sure would happen."

"But, who has sent all this?"

"According to the gift shop clerk, the purchaser *refused* to be identified." Mrs. Fox's stern voice cut off any more of Sadie's queries. "But it wasn't Robert Swaine."

"I'm grateful to whoever my benefactresses were." She looked at the Lyndseys, but they shrugged and gently shook their heads.

Ada Fox took Sadie's arm and led her to the full-length mirror and held the gown up beneath her chin. "A perfect match with your eyes, indeed."

A gentle rap on the door preceded Laura Williams's entrance into the room, accompanied by the soft scent of gardenias. "Hello, ladies! I'm here to help in any way I can. Heaven knows Robert has helped me and my husband, Tom, for years."

So it was true. Sadie could have clapped her hands in glee.

"He's to arrive soon. And when he hears my good news"—she gently patted her middle, which had a small swelling beneath the ivory lace of her gown—"Thomas Kinney will be positively over the moon."

"He may even race his wheelchair down the hallway, if I know him." Mrs. Fox's comment was met by a shocked reaction from Mrs. Kinney.

"You know my husband?"

"Yes, I attended him at a railroad investors' meeting in Detroit."

"He was without his private nurse?"

"Mrs. Fox!" Dawn Lyndsey rushed to Mrs. Fox's side. "Is that a new ring I see?" She yanked the housekeeping director's hand upward.

Blushing furiously, Ada Fox nodded. "I'm marrying my first love."

And Lord willing, Sadie would marry hers.

Robert poured himself punch into a sterling-silver cup etched with grapes, itching to be out of his new tuxedo. He already knew Laura's secret. And while his longtime friend, Laura's husband, had secured a promise from him years ago, Robert's assistance ended tonight. Beside him, his niece Maude and her fiancé Ben Steffan were whispering to one another.

"Do you really need me here?" Robert pulled his gold pocket watch from his vest. "This is a total waste of my time."

Ben gestured to the grand ballroom, filled with guests. "*Nein*, something good comes of everything we allow God to enter into."

Good thing Laura was finally going to settle down with her invalid husband and stop kowtowing to her agent's demands for both secrecy and so much travel. He slipped the watch back into its pocket. "I have too much on my mind to be up here tonight."

Maude, dressed in a deep rose gown, linked her arm through Robert's and patted his arm like he'd done to her so many times as a child. "When Ben and I marry, maybe there will be a double wedding."

"Your father and Mrs. Fox?" He narrowed his gaze at his niece. "They may have known each other a long time, but many years have passed since they've kept close company." The same could be said of he and Sadie. If he had his way they'd keep closer yet company for the rest of their lives.

Maude exchanged a meaningful glance with Ben as a waiter came by with a tray of canapés. Robert swiped several off the tray and Ben extended a china plate embossed with the hotel's gold lettering for him to set them upon.

"I didn't mean Father." Maude stared beyond Robert, at the entrance to the ballroom.

He heard a collective gasp. Ben grinned. Robert wasn't about to turn and gape at some young debutante dolled up and looking to snare a husband. Beauty went so far beyond good looks. Beyond clothing. Beyond wealth. In fact, when he next saw Sadie, he'd drop down on one knee, in front of all these patrons and propose to her even if she was still dressed in her maid's uniform.

"I'm leaving." He spoke to Ben, but he was still distracted by Mrs. Fox's earlier assertion that Sadie *had* to stay late at the Grand that night.

Sighing, Robert swiveled around to speak with his niece. But his breath stuck in his throat. Dressed in the gown that he'd said would match his beloved's eyes, Sadie stepped carefully over the highly glossed wooden ballroom floor and toward them. Mrs. Laura Williams Kinney flanked her on the left, Mrs. Fox on the right, and Miss Lyndsey and Mrs. Lyndsey followed them until Charles Bobay stepped out from the crowd to direct the Lyndseys to a table. Charles might be just as much in love with Miss Lyndsey as Robert was with Sadie.

Crystals glittered atop Sadie's hair, which had been coiled into swirls. A triple strand of large pearls hung from her neck and a pink rosebud was pinned to a lace scarf at her shoulder. He swallowed hard. Had Sadie been born into wealth, she'd have been married years ago—off to the highest bidder. Her gaze met his and didn't falter.

Laura signaled the bandleader to begin as she escorted Sadie forward and placed her gloved hand in Robert's. "I believe this first dance is for you."

When he was unable to move, looking down at Sadie, so beautiful, her hand fitting perfectly in his, Laura nudged him. "I'm afraid I've monopolized you far too long, Captain. And I have another dance partner."

Pushed by a porter, Thomas Kinney, veteran of the Indian wars, lacking the use of one hand and only partial use of his legs, was wheeled into the room. As the crowd gaped, Laura began to "dance" with her husband. Robert directed Sadie onto the floor.

"Do you know the power you have over me at this very moment?" He took her into his arms, and swept her into the waltz, a dance he, Maude, Sadie, and Greyson had all practiced years earlier.

"I know you'd give me anything I want." Her breathy voice stirred a longing in him so strong that he almost shook.

His heart thudded in his chest, pounding out her name. "I've already given you the best gift I have."

"Your heart?"

"You always were a good guesser." He pressed a kiss against her soft brow as they were joined by Maude and Ben on the ballroom floor.

Sadie laughed. "This isn't a guessing game."

Then let there be no doubt. He released her and took a step away before kneeling on one knee. "Marry me, or let me forever live in sorrow without you."

Covering her mouth with her hands, Sadie seemed to be laughing.

Maude playfully jabbed his shoulder. "You borrowed that line from our very first play."

"What can I say, it applies here equally well." He stood and took Sadie into his arms. "Say you'll be my anchor."

"I will."

ECPA-bestselling author **Carrie Fancett Pagels**, Ph.D. is the award-winning author of over a dozen Christian historical romances. Twenty-five years as a psychologist didn't "cure" her overactive imagination! A self-professed "history geek," she resides with her family in the Historic Triangle of Virginia but grew up as a "Yooper" in Michigan's Upper Peninsula. Carrie loves to read, bake, bead, and travel—but not all at the same time! You can connect with her at www.CarrieFancettPagels.com.

After the Ball

by Martha Rogers

Dedication

To my husband Rex, who supports me in every way
with my writing and is my *"First Love Forever."*

Delight thyself also in the LORD:
and he shall give thee the desires of thine heart.
PSALM 37:4

Chapter 1

C hase Edward Thornton, you must make a decision soon." Chase's mother pulled on her gloves and smoothed them over her fingers.

When his mother used his full name, she meant business, and there was no escape. Chase made no comment and let her go on with her ultimatum.

"The ball is coming up soon, and you need to choose an escort. This is something you can't put off until the last minute. With your father being honored, this will be one of the most important affairs of the season. All of the suitable girls will be taken if you don't ask one in the next few weeks."

Chase held up his hands. "Slow down, Mother. The ball isn't until August, and this is the first of June. I'm not going to invite anyone this early as I have no desire to rush into any relationship I have to nurture for nearly three months. Plenty of young women will still be available when the time comes."

He had no intention of asking any of the daughters of his father's wealthy friends, but he couldn't let his mother know that this early. What he did with his social life was his own business and would stay that way.

"You're twenty-seven years old and one of the most eligible bachelors in Dallas. You'll have your pick of the young ladies, and it's high time you picked one and settled down. Most young men your age have already. Even your sister has married and she's younger than you."

True, his sister and most of his friends were married, but he still had things he wanted to do before that happened in his life. Besides, he was still young and had plenty of time ahead before taking on the responsibility of a marriage.

His mother picked up her purse and hooked it over her arm. "I can see talking to you is like talking to a statue, but I do hope you're listening. Your father has great plans for you, and it's time you get on to satisfying them."

Oh, yes, his father's plans. Problem was, they had nothing to do with ranching. His father may have become a successful oil man and built up a company bringing in more money than he needed, but Chase had no desire to follow in his footsteps.

"I know that, but right now, I'm getting ready to go out to Grandpa's ranch for my summer visit. I'll be leaving shortly."

"Your grandfather's ranch is the last place you need to be. Your father made the wise decision to go into the oil business, and he expects you to take over one day."

"I'm sorry, Mother, but this is part of the agreement I have with Father. As long as I work for him, he'll give me the two months every summer to help Grandpa."

"I know, but I don't have to like it." She adjusted her hat so the plume on it fell to one side, away from her face. "I'm off to my luncheon now. Please remember what I said about asking someone to the ball." She leaned over and kissed his cheek. "Please drive safely, and we'll see you in August. Also, let us hear from you once in a while."

As soon as his mother left, Chase changed into denim pants and a light cotton shirt and exchanged his black dress shoes for brown leather boots. Summer in Texas was too hot for the suits his father required for the office, and he'd be sweating out on the ranch even in light cotton. He wished again he could keep a horse in the city, but it was much too dangerous in the streets filled with more motor cars each day.

He checked his suitcase one more time before leaving and heading down to the garage. He'd take the roadster since his mother didn't like riding in the open car. He loved the wind against his face as he drove, although it didn't quite measure up to a gallop across the fields on the back of Black Cloud.

As he breezed down the road to his grandfather's ranch, he looked forward to two months without his mother's constant nagging for him to find a girl and settle down, as if that was going to happen anytime soon. If anyone snagged him for a husband, it might be Susannah King.

Not quite up to his mother's standards, Susannah loved the same things he did on the ranch. They'd spent many an afternoon racing across the fields on their horses. She'd beat him about as often as he'd beaten her. He had to admit she was better at roping, but she'd had more experience than he had.

While he only spent summers on the ranch since his parents moved to Dallas when he was ten, she had lived there all her life. Her father was the foreman and ran the ranch for Grandpa. Because of that, she'd learned the same skills as the cowboys.

An hour later he drove through the gates of the Circle T Ranch. His heart swelled with anticipation of the months ahead in the wide-open spaces of the Texas countryside. The land rolled with low hills dotted with groves of trees. Small groups of cattle rested in the shade of oaks and elms on this lazy summer afternoon.

Summer on the calendar hadn't actually arrived, but that didn't mean anything in Texas. The bright sun in a cloudless sky was proof of that.

The ranch house and outbuildings came into view and joy filled his soul. Nowhere else on earth would he rather be than on this ranch with his grandparents. If things went the way he hoped, the Lord would see fit to keep him here permanently. He'd much rather live here herding cattle than figuring profits and losses in the oil business.

He honked as he drove into the drive up to the house. The front door flew open and his grandmother ran down the steps to meet him.

"I thought you'd never get here." She grabbed him in a bear hug and squeezed tight when he exited his car.

"Well, I'm here, and I'm hungry."

"As if that's something new." She released him and grabbed his arm. "You know I have apple pie waiting for you. Greta and I made a batch of cookies as well."

He walked with her up the steps and across the porch, all the while glancing over his shoulder for a glimpse of Susannah.

"She's in the house."

Heat rose up from his neck. Was he that obvious? Of course Granny knew everything about him and what he was thinking. She could read his mind quicker than anyone around.

Susannah stood in the middle of the parlor. Her blond hair hung loose on her shoulders with the sides caught up and secured with a blue bow that perfectly matched her eyes.

His voice caught in his throat. She was even more beautiful than the last time he'd seen her months ago. Her smile sent his heart to racing. He finally managed to speak. "Hello, Susannah."

Susannah's heart hadn't stopped pounding since Chase's car had driven up to the house. He was here again at last. "Hello, Chase."

"Well, now that's out of the way, I'll go fetch the pie. You two have a seat. I'll be back, but not too soon." She winked at Susannah and headed for the kitchen.

"Please sit. I know you've had a long drive from Dallas, so you must be tired." Susannah gestured toward the chair near the sofa where she sat down on the edge. She waited for him to do the same and clasped her hands in her lap.

He remained standing. "Why aren't you out with your father? You enjoy riding so much."

"I decided not to go today. They don't need me, and I. . .I wanted to be here when you arrived." She couldn't possibly have met him dressed in dirty trousers and boots with dust and grime from the range on her face. If she had, he'd never think of her as anything other than another hand on the ranch.

"I'm glad you stayed behind. I was hoping to see you soon as I could." He shuffled his boots across the carpet and rolled the brim of his hat in his hands before finally relaxing into a chair.

Chase grew more handsome every year. Susannah had fallen for him on one of his summer visits when he'd rescued her from being trampled in the corral. She'd fallen off the fence rail while watching her pa break a horse. She'd been only nine and he'd been twelve, but she'd lost her heart to him that day and hadn't been able to retrieve it since.

"How are things in Dallas? I'm surprised your father is willing to let you come out here for two months every year."

From what she'd read in the Dallas newspaper, he spent more time socializing than working. Every time she read an article or saw a picture, he was with a different woman.

"Booming as usual. Father almost said no to this trip, but he doesn't go back on his promises, and my coming here is one he made a long time ago. So, you're stuck with me for the next two months."

And that she didn't mind at all. Two months in the summer and occasional visits during the year didn't do much for her hopes of a relationship other than friendship with him, but a girl could always dream.

Mrs. Thornton returned with a tray laden with plates of warm apple pie and a pitcher of cream. She set them on the marble-topped table in front of the sofa.

"Now that the greetings are all out of the way, tell me how you father's getting along."

"He's doing quite well with his business, as you already know. I don't know if he told you, but he and Mother are planning a trip abroad. Mother's quite excited about it."

"What's this I hear about a big to-do honoring him for something or other? We received our invitation in the mail recently."

"It's an award from the city of Dallas for all the business he's brought with his leadership and influence in the oil industry."

Susannah picked up her fork. "You must be quite proud of him."

"Oh, I am, but I don't see why they have to go to the extent they have. They're planning a huge event with dinner and dancing at some posh place in August. Don't understand why they don't just give him the award at a ceremony at the courthouse and be done with. They're spending a lot of money."

Mrs. Thornton shook her head and grinned. "Honey, that's the way they do things in the city. You should know that by now."

"Well, it sounds terribly fussy to me." Susannah popped a bite of pie into her mouth and savored the rich cinnamon and sugar flavor of the apples. Things like this big award affair were another reason she was thankful not to live in Dallas. The ranch suited her just fine.

She set her plate on the table and leaned back to listen to Chase and his grandmother. She may as well forget any hopes of his ever being interested in her since she didn't want to live in Dallas and have to participate in the social events. Besides, his mother would probably voice great objections. She had never paid much attention to Susannah in all the times the family had visited the ranch.

All she could hope for was the friendship she and Chase had developed through the years. They may disagree about some things and have their arguments, but that was half the fun of being friends. One thing was certain. This was going to be a very short two months.

Chapter 2

Susannah groaned and pulled the pillow over her head to ward off the streams of dawn filtering through her window curtains. Then she remembered Chase had arrived home and threw back the sheet. She didn't want to waste one minute of the time he was here.

She finished her morning routine and stood before her wardrobe. Would Chase be joining her father and the other cowhands or would he stay around the house and help his grandmother? She grabbed a cotton shirtwaist and her split skirt. He'd be out on the range, of course. That's what he loved to do.

As much as she enjoyed the etiquette and cooking lessons Mrs. Thornton thought it important for a young woman to know, Susannah much preferred riding with her father and his men. They'd be rounding up calves and branding them soon, and she never missed the opportunity to participate.

She strolled across the yard to the main house as the sun rose higher in the eastern sky. She loved this time of morning when the world was just beginning to awaken. The cooler morning air would soon be warmed by the sun, and if the past few days were any indication, today would be hot.

Mrs. Thornton had insisted that Susannah come and dine with her and Mr. Thornton for meals since her mother's death. A bunkhouse and kitchen full of rowdy men was not the place for a young woman according to Chase's grandmother. Mama had always cooked breakfast for Susannah and her pa until her passing last year, so Susannah enjoyed the time with Mrs. Thornton. The dear woman had taken over the role of mothering, although Susannah was well past the age of needing someone to look out for her.

When she entered the house, Chase stepped down into the entryway. "Good morning, Susannah. Granny said you'd be up to have breakfast with us." He offered his arm. "Shall we go and see what's behind those delectable aromas coming from the kitchen?"

"Today is Thursday, and Mrs. Thornton always has fresh homemade cinnamon rolls for breakfast on Thursdays. Cinnamon and yeast are creating those aromas tempting you."

They entered the dining room where Mr. Thornton already sat with his newspaper. He glanced up at them. "Good morning, you two." He laid his paper aside. "One of these days we'll get news delivered out here that's not already several days old."

Mrs. Thornton backed through the door from the kitchen. She carried a platter of scrambled eggs and bacon as well as one filled with the cinnamon rolls. "Greta knew you were coming, Chase, so she made a larger batch this morning. She knows how you love them."

She placed the food on the table then tilted her head and pointed to her cheek. "Do you have a kiss for your granny this morning?"

Chase laughed and bent down from his height of well over six feet to kiss his petite grandmother's cheek. "You know I always do."

He pulled the chair out for his grandmother, and Susannah hurried to take her place so he wouldn't come all the way around to her side of the table to do the same for her.

After they were all seated, Mr. Thornton bowed his head and offered thanksgiving for the meal and the hands that prepared it. After he said amen, he spread his napkin across his lap. "Well, son, are you ready for a good two months of work?"

"Yes, sir, I'm looking forward to it. I don't like being closed up in an office five days a week with no chance to enjoy the outdoors. Dallas is getting too big with so many cars on the streets that it's getting to be a hazard to even take a walk."

Susannah served her plate with eggs and two slices of bacon as well as a cinnamon roll. She paid little attention to the words between Chase and his grandfather, but she did savor the sound of Chase's deep voice. She'd heard that voice in her sleep, in her dreams, in her musings for as long as she could remember.

When his father decided to move to Dallas to become the head of the oil business created by the discovery of a nice deposit of oil on a portion of the Thornton land, she had been devastated. He may be three years older than she, but they had been best of friends.

Now that they were older, her feelings for him ran much deeper, but she'd never let on to him how she longed for him to come back for more than two months every summer.

Although her parents insisted on her attending college, Susannah had seen no use for what she had learned. She wanted to be a rancher like her pa, and not a teacher as she had studied to be.

Mrs. Thornton's voice broke through Susannah's reverie. She looked up, startled. "Excuse me, what did you say?"

"I said you look dressed to go out on the range today. I had hoped you would go into Perryton with me for a little shopping. I plan to stop in and visit with my seamstress, and I thought we might find something for you as well."

"Ordinarily that would be lovely, but this is Chase's first day back, and I'd like to spend some time with my old friend." Shopping had never been Susannah's favorite activity, but she indulged Mrs. Thornton now and again because it brought the older woman so much pleasure. "Maybe we can do it later in the week."

"I'll hold you to that." Mrs. Thornton folded her napkin and laid it beside her plate. "If you'll excuse me, Greta and I have things to do."

Mr. Thornton stood and Chase jumped up. "I suppose it's time for us to get busy ourselves."

"Yes, it is," his grandfather said. "That sun will be hot enough later, so we must take advantage of the cooler mornings."

Susannah held back laughter. Almost mid-June in Texas meant heat whether it was morning or night. Still, getting morning chores completed before noon was always a good way to start.

Chase walked beside Susannah but directed his remarks to his grandfather. "Are you still shutting down all work between one and four in the afternoon?"

"I am. Our friends south of the border have the right idea for a rest on hot afternoons. A siesta never hurt anybody, far as I could tell."

Susannah enjoyed that time of rest as well. After a hearty noontime meal, she retired to her room and took the time to read. Her secret vice lay in the dime novels she bought in Perryton, but those were gradually being replaced with something called a "magazine" with western stories. She much preferred the smaller books and carefully guarded her hidden library. Mrs. Thornton was amused by the stash of books, but if her father knew, he'd throw them all out as trash. Someday, she might write one of her own.

Enough daydreaming. She had a handsome man by her side for the rest of the morning, and she wouldn't spend one more minute thinking about anything else.

Chase listened to his grandfather's talk about what they would accomplish that morning, but his eyes wanted to do nothing more than savor Susannah's beauty. She wore her long honey-colored hair in a braid down her back, and her hat hung over it, dangling by the chin strap holding it in place.

She strode with confidence into the stables where her horse waited to be saddled. Although it was still early, the yard was busy with activity as the men saddled up and readied for the day ahead.

Chase hurried after Susannah. Black Cloud's snickering and stomping hit his ears before he came near the animal. It'd been awhile since he'd ridden his favorite horse, and he looked forward to their time together.

Susannah saddled her own horse. "Black Cloud has really missed you since the last time you were here. He's acted different and seemed to sulk. Your grandpa had the doc come out and check on him, but he couldn't find anything wrong. I think it was just a case of loneliness and wanting you around."

"Yeah, I can understand that."

The same as Chase himself had been since the last time he'd come to visit. Somehow he had to get his father to see that ranch life was the one best for Chase and not checking numbers and barrels of oil. Besides, if he didn't come back to the ranch, he'd never be able to convince the girl beside him to spend the rest of her life with him.

As soon as Black Cloud sensed Chase's presence, his head started bobbing up and down, and his front hoof pawed the earth. Chase reached out to him. "Hey, boy, I've missed you. Let's get that saddle on and do some riding."

In a short time, Black Cloud stood ready. Susannah led her mare, Mariah, out of the stall. "Looks like we're all set. Let's go join the others."

He followed her out to the yard where his grandfather spoke to his men. They paid no attention to Susannah. Either they were so accustomed to her being with them that they didn't see her as the woman she'd become, or they shied away because of her father. Chase bit back a smile. He suspected a little of both played as factors in their attitude toward the prettiest cowgirl he knew.

Chapter 3

Susannah unsaddled her horse and brushed her down for the night after they returned from their afternoon rounding up strays. At least she didn't have to worry about being on the fence-mending team. Neither Pa nor Mr. Thornton wanted her doing that, and she was happy to go along with them.

"You know, you could let one of the hands do that." Chase leaned on the stall railing.

The brush popped from her hand. "Chase! The least you could do is give a girl a warning." She picked up the wayward brush and continued her chore. "I'd rather be doing this myself. We understand each other." She patted the mare's back. "Don't we, Mariah? You're the best." This one she'd raised from a foal, and she was a good ride.

"When is Grandpa planning to breed her?"

"Not until next year. He has plans for King's Glory to be the sire." She had all but begged her father to ask Mr. Thornton for the mating of the ranch's best sire to her favorite mare.

"Now that should be a good combination." He pushed back from the stall. "I'm heading on up to the house. See you at supper."

"Okay." She kept her head down until she was sure he was almost out of the barn before turning to stare after him. Why did he have to get better looking every time he came out to the ranch?

Later, when she looked in the mirror, she gasped. Chase would never see her as anything but a cowgirl looking like she did now. Her braid had come loose, and her hair resembled the bird's nest in the oak tree near the house. Smudges of dust and dirt from rounding up calves smeared her cheeks as well.

After washing her face and brushing out her hair, she donned a dark-blue skirt and cream-colored shirtwaist. Never one to go along with city fashion changes, she stuck to more simple garments that allowed her freedom of movement. With no one to help her with the stylish upswept hairdos, she left her hair loose on her shoulders with the sides pulled back and secured with a hair clip.

She pinched her cheeks to add a little color before making her way up the path to the main house, which sat on a rise across from the stables. With a sigh, she stopped at the front door before entering the house. How could she ever compete with the beautiful socialite women Chase saw in Dallas?

Then she grinned. Those women weren't here to spend the summer with him, but she was. No matter what else happened, she'd have the best summer ever by his side.

With new confidence, she stood taller and walked into the house.

"Hello, is anyone downstairs?" She closed the door behind her and glanced into the parlor.

Mrs. Thornton waved a hand in Susannah's direction. "Come in, my dear. Supper will be ready in a few minutes. We've been discussing the cattle drive."

Susannah's confidence soared higher. Here was a subject she could discuss with no problems at all. She had already helped her father figure the number of cows they would take to the Fort Worth stockyards next month.

"Pa says the number of cows ready for market is good, and should bring a favorable price. We've worked hard to get them ready."

"Grandpa has been telling me about how hard you've worked this past spring. He says you've learned to rope as well as any cowboy around these parts. You'll have to show me." Chase stood and grinned at her.

Heat rose in Susannah's face, and warmth spread throughout her body. "Maybe I will. I'm better than ever since I've had more time to improve."

"Ouch, we'll see about that. Of course, you'll give me a little extra time to improve my skills since I'm out of practice."

A smile lit Mrs. Thornton's face. "I'm going to check on dinner. Everything should be ready by now. Greta has been a wonderful help since I haven't been able to do as much as I once did."

"Let me do that and you stay here and visit with Chase. I'll be right back." Before Mrs. Thornton could object, Susannah hurried to the kitchen to help Greta, the wife of one of the older ranch hands, Jake. They'd been on the ranch almost as long as her pa.

She grabbed an apron off of a hook inside the pantry and tied it around her waist. "Hi, Greta," she called. "I'm here to help get all this wonderful food on the table."

"Bless you, child. My feet get tired this time of day." Greta swiped her arm across her forehead.

"Everything smells so good, and I can't wait to eat it. Is that fresh peach pie I smell?"

"Yes, and it's made from the first batch from the trees in the orchard."

Pa and Jake had helped Mr. Thornton plant six peach trees years ago, and now they enjoyed their fruit in the summer months.

Greta set the hot pie on a cooling rack. "Chase loves peaches, and I plan to make all of his favorite foods while he's here. If you'll take some time off from your riding and roping, Mrs. Thornton and I could teach you a lot about cooking and other things around the house."

"That would be nice, but I want to spend every minute I can with Chase, and riding with ranch hands is one way to do that."

"When he asks you to be his bride, you'll be sorry you didn't learn how." Greta handed Susannah a platter. "Take this meat out to the table, and I'll bring the green beans and the potatoes."

Susannah grasped the plate loaded with fried steak and pushed through the swinging door to the dining room. Greta meant well, but Chase asking her to marry him loomed as likely as an ice storm in July. He had his father's oil business in Dallas to run, and he didn't need a cowgirl by his side in the city.

———————◦◁▷◦———————

All through dinner, Chase admired Susannah's ability to engage in conversation with his grandparents. Her laughter and smile brought new love to his heart for her. She displayed none of the fake mannerisms of the socialite young women who tried to charm him with their wiles.

After his favorite dessert, his grandfather laid his napkin beside his plate. "Chase, I'd like you to join me in my office to discuss some business dealings."

Chase would much rather take a walk with Susannah, but pleasing his grandfather must come first. If he didn't demonstrate that the ranch was important to him, he would never be asked to join his grandfather's business.

"If you'll excuse me, Grandmother, Susannah." He smiled at Susannah. "Would you do me the honor of staying with Grandmother awhile so you and I may talk later?"

Pink rose in her cheeks, but she nodded her assent. With his spirits lifted, he pushed his chair under the table. "Good. This shouldn't take long."

He followed his grandfather to the office on the other side of the stairwell and foyer. Grandfather sat behind his desk and pulled open a drawer.

"I want you to see how the ranch is doing and get some idea of how we're running things." He laid a ledger book on his desk and beckoned to Chase.

Chase scooted a chair over to sit at the desk next to his grandfather. As his grandfather pointed out the numbers, Chase gulped down his comments. The profit/loss statement didn't look as good as he'd believed it to be. The ranch wasn't in trouble, but it wasn't making as much as in the past.

Grandfather closed the book. "So, you see, we're holding our own, but this next drive to market must be very good."

"Yes, sir, I do see, and I'll do everything I can to make sure it is."

"I know you will, son, and Frank King will be with you. I don't ride on these trips like I once did, but I trust him and you to make a good sale."

His grandfather was only in his late sixties, but a recurring heart problem had taken its toll on his health. Chase grew more determined than ever to see this drive through to a good profit.

"I also know you've said you want to stay here and help run this place. Are you absolutely sure it's what you want?" Grandpa Thornton peered at him with piercing dark-blue eyes, much like his own.

"I am. This is what I've wanted to do since I was old enough to walk and ride a horse. An office on the third floor of a building in the middle of a busy city isn't where I'm supposed to be. I've prayed about it a number of times, and I still come up with the same answer. I belong here."

"Hmm, and does a certain blond-haired little cowgirl have anything to do with it?"

Heat rose from Chase's neck and flooded his face. "I've loved Susannah almost all my life. I've dated socialites and debutantes, but none holds a candle to Susannah."

"What does your mother have to say about that?"

Chase breathed in deeply then expelled it. "She doesn't know about my feelings for

Susannah. She's continually telling me it's time to find a girl from those in her social circle and settle down."

"And that's not what you want to do."

"No, sir, it isn't. The only one I want to settle anywhere with would be Susannah."

"Then it's time you told her."

Chase slumped back in his chair. "Not as long as I live in Dallas. Susannah would never want to live in the city."

He sat up and leaned forward. "Deep down, I believe my father would like to be here as well. The oil rigs may have sent him on another path, but his heart is still here. Just as mine always will be."

"I appreciate that, son." His grandfather pushed back from his desk and stood. "We'll see how this summer goes and talk more before you go home." He grinned and raised his eyebrows. "Now, don't you think it's time to take that pretty little gal on an evening walk?"

Chase jumped up. "Yes, sir, I do. Thank you."

He hurried from the office in search of Susannah. He found her in the kitchen with Granny and Greta.

"Susannah, would you care to walk with me? We haven't had time to do much visiting since I got here."

She grinned at him. "I'd like that very much." She untied her apron and hung it on its pantry hook.

He took her hand in his and led her out the back door. Dusk was settling in and a few stars twinkled in the heavens. The heat of the day had cooled to a bearable temperature for a stroll around the grounds and to his grandmother's flower garden.

"I love this time of evening. All the animals are in for the night, and our chores are done for another day. It seems so restful and peaceful to me." Susannah lifted her face toward the sky and breathed in the evening air fragrant with Mrs. Thornton's roses.

Chase couldn't agree more, and walking by her side made it a special time. He squeezed her hand, but no words would come from his mouth. They had dried up worse than the creek down in the pasture in the heat of the summer.

What could he say to this girl about whom he dreamed constantly? She was everything he could ever want in a woman. She loved the ranch, horses, and riding. Somehow he had to convince his mother that Susannah was the one he needed by his side for the rest of his life and also convince Susannah that he loved her and wanted her as his wife.

Susannah squeezed his hand. "It'll be getting dark soon, so maybe we'd better go back closer to the house."

He didn't want the evening to end, but the sky had begun to darken. The light from the windows at the back of the house beckoned. He drew her closer to his side.

"This has been one of the nicest evenings I've had in a long time. The city is always so busy with crowds of people filling the streets and automobiles outnumbering the horses."

Susannah gave a sigh of contentment. "It is rather peaceful with only the breeze through the trees and the distant lowing of cattle."

They neared the front entrance again and stopped on the porch. Chase fought the love rising in his chest.

Susannah sighed again. "I'd best be getting back to my house. Pa will be looking for me to talk about tomorrow and his plans for our work."

On impulse, he leaned over and kissed her cheek. "Thank you for spending time with me. I'll. . .I'll see you in the morning."

She stepped back, her eyes wide with surprise—or was it fear? She said nothing, but turned and ran toward her home next to the bunkhouse.

Well, he had either messed up their whole summer, or he'd given her a hint as to his real feelings for her. Either way, the rest was in God's hands.

Chapter 4

Sleep eluded Susannah. Her heart beat faster with each remembrance of Chase's kiss. Even if it was on her cheek, it had been a kiss. Then her spirits fell at the thought he had kissed her solely out of friendship. She wanted it to mean so much more than she had a right to expect, but that didn't mean she had to stop dreaming.

When dawn finally broke through and colored the sky in hues of pink, she rose from her bed and prepared for the day. Pa had said he'd be mending fences in the south pasture today and didn't need her if she wanted to stay back at the ranch.

Maybe today would be a good time to do that. Seeing Chase this morning would be a little more difficult than usual because of last night. She lifted her fingers to touch the spot on her cheek where his kiss had landed.

She donned a dark-blue skirt and light-blue shirtwaist instead of the split skirt she'd been wearing the past few days. As she smoothed the skirt over her hips, she sighed with relief that fashion still allowed for a flare to the skirt and did not adhere strictly to the pencil-slim ones that were becoming the rage according to the seamstress in town.

She peered out her window to the stable yard below and waited until the men mounted up and headed out for the day. She'd have to hurry now to get to the kitchen before Greta put away the food from breakfast.

When she entered the dining room of the big house, Greta was clearing the table. "Is there anything left?"

Greta laughed. "I knew you'd be here soon enough. Berry muffins and bacon are warming on the stove."

Susannah hugged her. "Oh, thank you. I thought I smelled bacon when I walked in the door." Greta's muffins always tempted the appetite as well. "Is Mrs. Thornton around?"

"She went upstairs right after the men left. She'll be back down shortly." Greta waved her hand. "Now you go get yourself something to eat."

"I will." Susannah didn't have to be told twice to help herself to one of Greta's creations.

She poured a cup of coffee and placed a muffin and two slices of bacon on her plate. Instead of returning to the dining room, she plopped down at the kitchen table.

Mrs. Thornton breezed through the swinging door from the dining room. "Ah, there you are, Susannah. I'm going into town today to meet with my seamstress, and I'd like for you to go with me since you're not working with the men today." She grinned and wagged a finger at her. "Remember, you said you'd do that the next time I asked."

Susannah had forgotten, but she'd keep her promise. "I'd like that. Soon as I finish eating, I'll run out to the house and freshen up." Besides, anything would be better than a boring day of sitting around the ranch doing nothing, especially on a day as pretty as this one.

"Splendid. I'll have the buggy brought around and we'll leave in about half an hour. Will that give you time?"

"Yes, ma'am, that's plenty." Susannah gulped down the rest of her coffee and the last piece of her muffin.

Mrs. Thornton spoke with Greta about lunchtime, and Susannah placed her dishes on the counter. "I'll meet you out front, Mrs. Thornton. Thanks for the late breakfast, Greta."

Greta smiled and waved at her as Susannah pushed through the door and headed to her house. Within fifteen minutes, she hurried back outside and up to the hitching post where the buggy sat ready and waiting.

Jensen, the stable man, held the reins. "Good morning, Miss Susannah. I take it you're goin' into town with Miz Thornton. Wondered why I didn't see you ride out with the boys today."

Susannah smiled at him. "I decided to stay around here instead, and Mrs. Thornton invited me to go into town with her. How are you feeling today?" Jensen had been around the ranch as long as Susannah could remember. Once he had ridden with the crew, but age and an old leg injury had caught up with him, so now he managed all the horses and other stock in the stables and barn.

"Doin' well, and thanks for asking. You think you might ride later today?"

"That depends on how hot it gets."

"I'll have Mariah ready for you if you decide you want to." He flashed another smile as Mrs. Thornton appeared. "Mornin', Miz Thornton. Nice day for a drive into town."

"Thank you, Jensen. We'll be back around lunchtime, but Greta will have your meal ready whenever you want to go up if you don't want to wait for us."

"Thank you. Y'all have a nice day now." He helped Mrs. Thornton into the buggy and handed her the reins.

Of course, Mrs. Thornton would be driving. The lady still liked to be in control. Susannah stepped into the buggy and sat beside her.

The ride into town would take close to thirty minutes, and Mrs. Thornton wasted no time in getting to the point of her trip into the small town southwest of Dallas. "I'm in need of a few summer outfits, so I'm asking Daisy to make some skirts and shirtwaists. It's time for us to get you a more elegant gown than what you usually wear to church socials and the like."

Susannah gulped back her refusal. She'd said no to Mrs. Thornton so many times, maybe now would be a good time to take her up on her offer. "That would be nice, but I don't need anything really fancy."

"Of course not. That's not your style. But you do need something a little more up to date. With your coloring, you'll look pretty in about anything you choose."

The compliment sent a little heat to Susannah's cheeks. If only she could believe that. If what Mrs. Thornton said was true, Chase would be paying more attention to her as a woman and not as the girl he grew up with like a sister.

Mrs. Thornton's offer of a new outfit was more than kind. Although the new styles didn't look all that enticing to Susannah, perhaps Daisy would have some ideas. It'd be nice to have a finer dress for church and the socials planned for the summer months. Perhaps a new dress would catch Chase's eye. She shook her head and scolded herself. Why bother? He wouldn't be here long enough to notice her anyway.

When Chase returned to the ranch for the afternoon siesta time, a strange car sat in the yard. He furrowed his brow. Who would be driving out here this time of day? No one except his family knew he was out here, and the car didn't belong to them or any of his friends.

When he dismounted, a man jumped out of the car and hurried toward Chase. "I've been looking everywhere for you."

He recognized one of the reporters for the Dallas paper and gritted his teeth. "How did you find me?"

"It wasn't easy, but I have my sources. What I want to know is what you're doing out here instead of being in Dallas."

"I don't think that's any of your business, but if you must know, this is my grandfather's ranch. I spend a couple of months every summer helping him."

"I see. That's very thoughtful of you, but I imagine all the pretty, unattached ladies in Dallas are sad you're not there for the summer theater season and lawn parties."

"That doesn't concern me at all. Parties and socials don't appeal to me like they do others I know."

"That's interesting. It leads me to the other question I have for you." The reporter pushed his hat back on his head and crossed his arms over his chest. "Who are you planning to take to the awards gala for your father in August?"

Chase's eyebrows shot up. "And what business is that of yours?"

At that moment, a buggy carrying his grandmother and Susannah rolled into the yard. His grandmother waved and stopped the buggy at the hitching post.

The reporter glanced from Chase to Susannah and back, but he made no comment.

Granny and Susannah alit from the buggy, and Granny headed straight for him.

"And who is this visitor with us?" She extended her hand in greeting.

The newsman removed his hat and grasped her hand. "I'm Thad Cooper. It's a pleasure to meet you, Mrs. Thornton."

Granny didn't show any surprise that the reporter knew her name. "This young woman is Susannah King. She lives here on the ranch, and we've just come from town. We're going inside to have lunch. Would you care to join us?"

Chase opened his mouth to protest, but Mr. Cooper declined first. "Thank you, but I have to get back to Dallas."

"Very well, but if you change your mind, you're welcome. It was a pleasure to meet you." She turned to Susannah. "Come, let's take our purchases up to the house."

They walked away, but Granny stopped at the foot of the steps leading up to the porch. "You *are* planning to join us, aren't you, Chase?"

"Yes. I'll be right up as soon as I say goodbye to Mr. Cooper."

As soon as the women were out of earshot, Thad let out a long, low whistle. He grinned and punched Chase on the arm. "Looks like a lot more than cows are your interest, Thornton. Susannah King is one pretty little filly. She wouldn't by any chance be the one you're planning to take to the ball, would she?"

"And what if she were?"

Thad slapped his thigh and laughed. "It'd make some pretty good news, I'd say."

"Then I suggest you don't report it. I haven't asked her yet." Chase gulped. Until this moment, the thought of asking Susannah to the gala had not occurred to him.

"I see." Cooper hopped into his car and turned on the motor. "You're missing a good chance if you don't."

Chase didn't move from his spot as the car backed from the yard and turned onto the road leading to Perryton. What just happened? Had he told a reporter he'd be taking Susannah to the awards dinner?

He'd like nothing more than to ask Susannah, but what would his mother say? Was he ready to risk her certain displeasure? He'd rather have Susannah on his arm than any other women he could picture.

He gazed up toward the house where she had gone with his grandmother. The awards dinner might be just the thing to let her know how much he cared about her. And if she knew how much he cared, would she consider marrying him? He shook off the thought. He had no idea if she even cared enough about him to go to the dinner much less marry him, even if he did hope to stay on the ranch.

With that thought filling his heart, Chase led Black Cloud to his stall. As soon as he finished taking care of his horse and cleaned himself up a bit, he'd be up at the house joining Susannah and his grandparents for lunch. Now he had to figure out a way to ask her and pray she would say yes.

Chapter 5

Susannah checked the cinch strap on Mariah. Even though she trusted Jensen to do his job, she still liked to make sure all was well before she mounted. This morning the crew planned to round up strays and check on the calves that would be ready for branding next week. Yesterday had been fun in town, but today, she was ready to be back on the range.

Rounding them up caused no problems because she had a good horse to help, but branding was another thing. She still squirmed and flinched when the hot brand hit the flesh of the young cattle. It was one activity she didn't mind missing.

She mounted Mariah and joined the others as her father gave instructions for the day. He divided them into two groups. One would go west and south, the other would head north and east. Webster, the cook, would have the chuck wagon in one location and both teams would meet back there for the noon meal.

Her father also assigned two men to check the fences for any breaks or weak spots that may have shown up since the last check. With the assignments finished, Susannah found herself beside Chase on the team headed west and south.

She studied his profile while they rode. Last night, she had sensed he was on the verge of asking her something or telling her something important when Mr. Thornton mentioned Chase's father, but he'd hesitated then changed the subject.

Whatever it was must not have been important enough for him to say, since he'd left it unasked.

He turned toward her and grinned. "What? Did I leave egg on my face or something?"

Heat flushed her cheeks. She'd been caught looking at him instead of the trail. She shrugged. "Just wondering if you're missing any of the summer activities in Dallas. Your friend came to visit yesterday, and I figured he came to ask you to come back to Dallas with him."

A frown replaced the grin. "No, I don't miss anything in Dallas, and that man yesterday was not a friend."

The terse response whetted her curiosity, but Chase was not about to reveal anything he didn't want her to know. He never had and never would, so as much as she wanted to know who the man was, she wouldn't ask about him.

"I see. He seemed friendly enough, but he didn't stay long."

"He had business to take care of back in the city."

Other questions rose, but Chase's tone of voice cut them off. She'd better find something else to talk about in a hurry, or he might leave her behind.

"What do you like best about being here on the ranch? I love everything, but then I live here."

The grin reappeared. "I love everything about it as well. Your dad has a great crew, and Grandpa trusts him completely with everything on the ranch."

"I'm sorry Mr. Thornton isn't able to ride with us anymore. It's nice he has you to come every summer, even if it is for such a short time."

"If things go the way I hope, that will change. Since his heart attack and being told to take things easier for a while, Grandpa has been much more open with me about the ranch's finances, so I'm hoping that means he'll give me more responsibility to bring me back here more often."

Susannah's heart pounded at his response. She hadn't expected that answer at all. How she'd love for him to be around more often. Even if he showed no interest in her whatsoever, they'd still be friends and enjoy life on the ranch.

He slapped Black Cloud's reins. "I see a stray. Let's go get that little doggie." He took off for the brush.

She followed after him, and they sent the little calf scrambling back to the herd with his mother. They spent the remainder of the morning following the same procedure with other strays until Hank, one of the cowboys, held up his hand.

"Time to chow down. Chuck wagon's waiting for us. Let's go."

Susannah's stomach growled in anticipation. Whatever it was, Webster would make it taste like a gourmet meal.

When they arrived at the site, the other crew had already arrived and was sitting around with their food-laden plates.

Webster wiped his hands on his apron. " 'Bout time y'all showed up. These fellers wanted it all."

Chase and the others dismounted and headed for the chow line. Susannah followed, but stood back and waited until they had filled their plates before taking one herself. The first year she'd ridden with them, they'd tried to make her go first, but she had squelched that in a few weeks. They were the harder workers and deserved more food. She'd be happy with whatever was left, and she hadn't gone hungry yet.

After placing a piece of cornbread on her plate, she turned to find Chase waiting for her.

"Come on over here and eat with me."

She didn't need a second invitation to join him at a rock where he had set his plate. Once she sat down, he reached for her hand and held it as he said a quick blessing.

Her heart soared with love for this man who made no bones about his faith in private or public. She had no doubts whatsoever about his being a Christian.

He released her hand. "I love Webster's stew. His meat is always so tender."

Indeed it was, but she'd rather talk about anything besides food. "How will you manage to help your grandfather if you're in Dallas most of the year?"

"We're still working on that. If things go the way I hope, I'll be here for much longer than two months a year."

"But what about your work for your father? How is that going to be affected by your being away?"

"We still have some knots to untie to make it all work." He leaned back on an elbow and pushed his hat brim up. "I've seen what you do on the ranch when I'm here, but what do you do the rest of the year?"

"I spend some time with your grandmother. She's done so much for me since Mama's passing. I wish I hadn't been an only child, but I can't do anything about that." If not for Mrs. Thornton to talk to and to take her into town once in a while, the loneliness would have been more than Susannah could bear.

"I was glad you went into town with her. I'm not sure it's safe for her to go that distance alone."

"Oh, she never goes alone. If I can't go, Jensen takes her or your grandfather goes with her."

"Glad to hear that." He pointed at her plate. "You'd better finish that up in a hurry. We have a couple more hours of work before we head back to the house. Don't want you fainting from hunger out there." He grinned, picked up his plate, and stood.

He sauntered back to the wagon and dumped his plate and utensils into the dishpan Webster had ready.

Susannah made quick work of what she had left and scampered up to follow suit. If what he had told her came true, maybe she'd be seeing a lot more of him in the coming year. She dumped her dishes and headed for Mariah. Who was she kidding? More than likely if Chase moved to the ranch, he'd bring a wife with him, and that she had to consider. She grabbed Mariah's reins and swung up into the saddle. As much as she'd rather not think about it, the time had come to quit daydreaming of a future with Chase, and stay clear of him as much as possible.

After they returned to the ranch house, Chase brushed down Black Cloud and gave him a bag of oats. Something had gone wrong out there after lunch. Susannah hadn't come anywhere near him nor said a word to him upon their return.

Usually she took care of Mariah before going to her house, but today she'd handed the reins to Jensen and mumbled something about being tired. He'd see her at supper tonight, but he'd been hoping to talk more with her while they cared for their horses.

The idea about asking her to the awards gala danced about in his mind, but it wouldn't settle anywhere. Maybe he needed to talk with Granny. She'd give him advice as to what he should do since she probably knew both him and Susannah better than anyone else around the ranch did.

With that goal in mind, he loped up to the house and to his room to clean up and change clothes. Then he'd find his grandmother and talk with her.

Half an hour later, when he came downstairs, he found her sitting in the parlor, her crochet hook darting in and out of thread coming from the ball in her lap.

She glanced up when he entered the room. "You're not resting like the others?"

"No, ma'am, I wanted to talk with you. I need some advice, and you're the one to give it." He sat in a wingback chair across from her.

"What's on your mind? Could it have anything to do with Susannah?" She dropped the crochet project to her lap.

He flinched. She did know him better than anybody else. "Umm, yes, ma'am, it does."

"Son, I know you care for her. I can see it in your eyes when you look at her. I know of no one I'd rather see you with than our Susannah, but others may not feel that way."

"You're speaking of Mother and Father. I don't think Father would mind as much as Mother would. In fact, I know she wouldn't approve. She's expecting me to choose one of her friends' daughters. She's said it often enough."

"Do you think Susannah would leave here and go to Dallas with you?"

"I wouldn't ask her to. I'm hoping Grandpa will let me take over the running of the ranch. I have the business skills I need, and he's already shared the financial situation with me. Father knows where my heart is, and although he'd be initially disappointed, I don't think he'd stand in the way of my decision."

A grin spread across Grandma's face. "I was hoping that was your intention. James and I have discussed it a few times. It's not going to happen overnight, but I believe it will eventually. That should make things easier for Susannah."

"Yes, but how can I know she wants more from our relationship? We've been friends for so long, I'm afraid she can't think of us as anything but." Nothing in her attitude or behavior had shown otherwise in all his trips here.

"I think you might be surprised about what she really feels and thinks."

Her smile and soft words gave him a glimmer of hope for a future with Susannah. Now for the hard part. "That man you met isn't my friend. He's a reporter from Dallas. He tracked me down out here looking for some tidbit for his paper." Chase paused, and rubbed his hands together. "I sort of led him to believe I was taking Susannah to the awards dinner. I want to ask her, but do you think she'd go?"

"Now that's a question only she can answer. You need to ask her."

"Ask who what?" Grandpa sauntered into the room, his hair still slightly mussed from his afternoon nap.

Granny lifted her cheek for his kiss. "We were talking about Chase inviting Susannah to the dinner in August."

"That's the best thing I've heard all day—or all week for that matter. Taking a young lady as pretty as Susannah to the ball is sure to make some tongues wag in disbelief."

Especially his mother. She'd be unhappy, but he had to work up the courage to ask so Susannah would have time to do whatever it is that women have to do to get ready for a formal event.

He stood and leaned toward his grandmother. He kissed her cheek. "I'm going to do it. . .soon as I get the courage."

Both she and Grandpa clapped. "Good for you, but don't wait too long."

He didn't know how long that might be, but his heart soared with anticipation. He looked forward to suppertime and seeing Susannah again.

Chapter 6

Several weeks passed and every day Chase scanned the Dallas newspaper for any hint of what the reporter had learned. Pictures of his mother attending various teas and luncheons appeared on the society pages, but nothing about him. It was hard to believe, but he accepted it with great relief and gratitude toward Mr. Cooper.

Once again, he sought his grandmother in the parlor while Grandpa napped. After a hard morning of riding the fences and repairing broken sections, he should be resting as well, but he needed Grandmother's advice once again.

She glanced up from her reading when he entered the room. "I had a feeling you'd be down to talk with me today. You still haven't asked Susannah to the ball, have you?"

"No, I haven't, and I don't know how to do it." He sat with his arms on his thighs and his clasped hands hanging between his knees.

"I would say to ask her like you'd ask any other young woman to attend such an affair, but I don't think you see it that way."

"You're right. It's a whole lot easier with the women back home, because they expect to be asked, but Susannah has no clue what I want to do."

"The Independence Day celebration in town is coming up, and I think it'd be a perfect occasion to ask Susannah to attend with you. She cares a lot about you, and if you spend time with her away from the ranch, you might get the courage to ask her to the ball."

"That's an idea I hadn't thought of, but it's a good one. I'll do that tonight after supper." He sat back in the chair with a relieved sigh. Escorting Susannah would be a pleasure he could look forward to.

"You can't tarry too long to ask her to the ball. August is right around the corner, and she'll need time to prepare. I've already mentioned to my seamstress that we need a ball gown for her. Daisy is already making mine, and she has Susannah's measurements, so she can get started right away."

Trust his grandmother to be thinking ahead. Maybe if he'd had a sister, he'd be more up on such things with women. "If things go well with the festival in town, I can ask her then and pray she says yes."

"Oh, I don't think that will be problem." Granny picked up her book, her signal for him to find something else to do.

He kissed her cheek. "Thanks, Granny. It looks as though you have things under control."

"Humph, you do your part, and I'll take care of whatever else needs to be done." She waved her hand. "Now scoot, and get a little rest yourself before you have to go back out in the heat."

"Think I'll see if Greta left any dessert from lunch lying around. I could use a cool drink too." He grinned and sauntered into the kitchen.

Sure enough, Greta had left a pitcher of lemonade and a plate of his favorite cookies on the table. He poured a glass, grabbed several cookies, and strolled out to the back porch to sit and enjoy his snack in the shade. He savored the cinnamon and sugar in the crisp vanilla cookie and the coolness of the lemonade.

If Susannah agreed to go with him to the ball, perhaps then he could show her how much he cared for her, no, *loved* her. He wanted her to be a part of his future here on the ranch. The more he talked with his grandfather, the more Chase realized the ranch could well be his one day.

After he finished his break, he prepared to go back out with the crew. He didn't intend to slack off one bit. He had to show them how much the ranch meant to him and the care he would give it. A team of cowboys had to trust their boss to take care of not only the ranch and livestock, but also to provide decent wages for them. That's exactly what he planned to do if all went as he hoped.

Later that evening, after supper and time spent with Grandpa in his office, Chase went in search of Susannah and found her on the front veranda, rocking in the gathering dusk.

"Mind if I join you for a bit?"

She glanced up at him and smiled. "I'd like that."

He dropped into the rocker beside her. Never had he been so thankful for his grandparents' design of a porch that stretched across the front of the house in a wide expanse of wood and railings. This is where they had spent many an evening with him as a young boy, and now he could enjoy it with Susannah.

Crickets chirped in the dusk, lending a noisy, yet peaceful sound to the evening. The soft glow from the lamps in the parlor gave enough light to shine on Susannah's face. Complete contentment complemented her sun-tanned complexion and gave a golden glow to her hair.

They sat in silence for a good ten minutes. Even though he'd practiced what he wanted to say, Chase's tongue now became as dry as a bleached cow skull out on the prairie. Finally, he swallowed hard and forged ahead.

"You know the Independence Day Festival is next week."

"Yes, and I can't wait to enjoy the festivities. Pa says this year they've added a few more cowboy competitions."

"So I've heard, but what I'd like to know is if you'd do me the honor of attending the festival with me?"

When she stopped rocking and sat still without answering, his heart plummeted. She wasn't interested in spending her free time with him.

After another minute or so, she turned to face him. "If you're sure you want to take me, I'd be honored to go with you."

He let his breath out with a gush of air and grinned. "Of course I want you with me."

She stood and ran her hands along her skirt. "I think it's time to go inside before the nighttime pests start their hunt."

"Then let me walk with you to your house." He offered his arm, and she tucked her hand under it.

Together they meandered down the steps, across the yard, and past the stables to her home. At the door, he paused and held her hands in his.

"You've made me very happy this evening, and I look forward to going to the festival with you." He leaned forward and kissed her forehead.

She stepped back and pulled her hands from his. "Good night, Chase. I'll see you in the morning."

With that she slipped through the door and left him standing in the dark. Next time, he'd aim farther down and taste those beautiful lips of hers. A grin spread across his face and filled his heart with happiness. He stuffed his hands into his jeans pockets and strolled back up to the house. This had been one fine evening and he had another ahead. All was right with the world.

Susannah closed the door behind her and leaned against it for a moment before dashing up the stairs to her room and flopping on her bed. What had she done? Her resolve to stay away from Chase disappeared like the morning mist. He had asked her to the festival. It was something she'd dreamed about for years. Last year she thought he'd come close, but then he was needed back in Dallas for something to do with his father's business and the holiday.

There was no such hindrance this year, and now her heart beat wildly in anticipation. She already had an outfit picked out. It was one Mrs. Thornton had helped her with. A smile wrapped itself around her heart and spread across her face. It may end up being nothing more than this one time with him, but she'd take it, no matter what.

After changing into her nightgown, she sat on the edge of the bed. Chase had said he wanted to spend more time on the ranch in the future. If that was the case, maybe she needed to spend less time on her horse and more in the kitchen with Greta, or she might never attract his attention as more than a friend and riding companion.

Greta and Mrs. Thornton would both like that. They'd pleaded with her enough times about learning something more than riding and herding cattle. Maybe Greta would teach her how to make Chase's favorite peach pie.

She swung her legs up onto the bed and pulled them close to her chest. She rested her chin on her knees and envisioned serving a slice of pie to Chase and telling him she'd made it herself. That would get his attention.

Satisfaction with her plan washed through her and she shivered in delight. Pulling the sheet up over herself, she laid her head on the pillow and imagined the day when she could serve Chase a meal she herself had cooked. Tomorrow she'd approach Greta about teaching her the basics of cooking and taking care of the kitchen.

Chapter 7

The day of the festival arrived, and Susannah helped Greta pack a picnic supper basket. "Do you really think Chase is going to like what I've cooked for him?"

"Oh, he'll like it all right, no matter how it tastes, because you cooked it. You don't have to worry, though. You're a quick learner, and everything turned out delicious." Greta wrapped two cloth napkins around the tin of fried chicken.

"I hope so. If I'm going to get him to think of me as more than a cowgirl friend, I need all the help I can get."

Greta's laughter rang out in the kitchen, and she hugged Susannah. "Dear child, you don't need to worry about that. He's already in love with you, and if this fried chicken and peach pie don't help him along in declaring it, he's not as smart as I think he is."

Susannah returned the hug and placed the chicken in the basket. "I'm going to run to the house and clean up a little bit. He said we'd leave at two and it's almost that now."

"Go on then. I'll finish this up and put it on the table by the door."

After hanging her apron on the hook by the pantry, Susannah skedaddled back to her room to tidy up her hair and put on a fresh blouse. This was the closet Chase had ever come to showing anything other than friendship, and she needed to look her best.

Satisfied with her appearance, she picked up one of her mother's wide-brimmed straw hats. She may be out in the sun almost every other day, but a red nose would never do today.

When she headed up the walk toward the house, Chase was waiting on the front porch. "Right on time. I like that." He held up the basket and a quilt. "Looks like we're ready to ride."

He grinned and loped down the steps to meet her, offering his arm. "Your carriage awaits you, my lady." He led her to the buggy by the gate. "I figured my roadster might be a little much for Perryton, so we'll travel the old-fashioned way." He stowed the basket and quilt in the boot then helped Susannah climb up into the buggy.

She didn't care how they traveled as long as it was together, but she did prefer the buggy for today. She'd been in the roadster with Chase only once, and with the wind in her face and the noise, she'd found it hard to talk to him.

He climbed up beside her and winked. "I hope that's a peach pie in the basket. I smelled it baking this morning."

"It is, along with fried chicken."

Chase grinned and snapped the reins. She clasped her hands in her lap, suddenly at a loss for a topic of conversation. She wanted something different from the ranch and the work they did every day, but she didn't really want to hear about Dallas.

He broke the silence. "So, what have you been doing the past few days? You didn't ride with us out on the range."

Heat rose in Susannah's face, and she tilted her head so the brim might hide it. "I had some things to do with your grandmother."

"I see. You know she's really fond of you. She always wanted a daughter, but my father is now her only child, and her one granddaughter lives down in Houston with her husband."

"Since Ma's death, she's been like a mother to me, and I'm quite fond of her. She and Greta have taught me so much."

"Whatever those two ladies teach you is bound to be good. They'd work circles around my mother, but then Mother has others who do it for her at home so that she has time for all the charity and fund-raising activities she's involved in."

When they approached Perryton, the streets were already beginning to fill with people celebrating the holiday. Chase turned in at the church and hitched the buggy behind it. When he helped Susannah down, his hands lingered at her waist. "What would you like to do first?"

The pressure of his hands sent tremors of joy through her, and she couldn't think clearly. Where did she want to go?

Finally gathering her wits about her, she said, "Let's walk over to the contest tent. I want to see if Greta's peach preserves won a ribbon."

Chase released her waist and hooked her hand at his elbow. "If it didn't, something is the matter with the judges' taste buds."

They made their way through the crowd. Children chased each other across the streets, and vendors enticed people with their food that varied from hot sausages on a bun to ice cream made in wooden buckets and packed in ice and salt.

Flags flew from the poles at stores and the bank, and red, white, and blue banners hung high on wires across the streets. Signs announcing the rodeo competitions adorned posts and doors along the main street as did signs for the ball game between the Perryton Redbirds and the Prairie Rock Texans to be held at four o'clock in the new ball field at the park. After the game, when the sun went down, a fireworks show was planned.

"I've never seen so many things going on in this town before. Looks like I've been missing out on all the good times." Chase smiled at Susannah and held her hand firmly on his arm.

Susannah's heart threatened to burst open with Chase's closeness. She didn't blame the young women they met along the way for giving him second and even third looks. Let them be envious. He was her escort today, and she intended to enjoy every moment of it.

At the contest tent, tables had been set up to display the entries in various categories from quilting and embroidery to jams, jellies, preserves, and homemade pies. The judging had taken place early this morning so as to have the winners exhibited when the festival opened at noon.

"There's the area with the jams and jellies over there. I told Greta she should enter her peach cobbler, but she said it isn't as good cold, so she'd rather take her chances with the preserves and canned, spiced peaches." Susannah tugged on Chase's arm and led him in that direction.

"Oh, look." She squealed and clapped her hands. "Greta won the blue ribbon for her preserves."

Chase laughed and grabbed her hand again. "The judges are smart. Circle T peaches are the best. Greta's recipe was a guaranteed winner."

"And we get to have her preserves with our biscuits at breakfast." Susannah pointed to another table across the tent. "There are the quilts. I'd like to see them. Mama's won a ribbon two years ago."

After viewing several other exhibits, Chase walked her back to the street. "Would you go down to the livery corral with me? The owners enlarged it for the events they've lined up."

"Yes, that'll be fine. Did any of our boys enter the contests?"

"I didn't hear any of them mention it, but then, I'm not around them when they're talking and playing cards and such out at the bunkhouse."

A large crowd had gathered to watch the bareback riding, but Chase managed to work his way through it to get close enough so they could see the activity in the corral. A cowboy let out a yell, and seconds later a horse bucked its way from the gate.

Susannah's heart pounded. These horses were bucking harder and faster than the ones Pa and the boys rode back at the ranch. She gripped Chase's hand and prayed no one would be hurt, thankful Chase wasn't entered in any of the events.

Her blood chilled when the cowboy in the arena flew into the air and then down onto the hard-packed dirt. He landed on his backside and sat there a few minutes to catch his breath while several other cowboys handled getting the horse back into his stall. She shuddered and buried her face on Chase's shoulder. What if it had been him? She couldn't bear the idea of his being hurt.

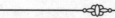

Chase held Susannah close as her body trembled. She shouldn't be frightened or surprised about a cowboy falling off a horse. Things like that happened all the time on the ranch when breaking horses. Must be some other reason.

"Would you rather go back and watch some of the other games? The baseball game should be starting soon."

She stepped back and blinked. "Oh, um, yes, I think I'd like that."

He guided her back up Main Street where the music from the band at the park filled the air with patriotic songs. Perryton had a lot more things going for it than he'd imagined. As they passed the bandstand on their way to the ball field, his determination to take over the ranch for Grandpa one day grew even stronger. This is where he wanted to put down roots and raise a family with Susannah.

She squeezed his arm. "I've only seen the Perryton Redbirds play one time, and they won that game. I hope they win today. I like baseball."

Chase grinned and led her to the grandstand. "I like it too. I follow the big guys from Chicago and New York in the papers."

After the game started, Chase sat back and enjoyed Susannah's excitement as she yelled for the hometown team. In the end, the Redbirds won by two runs. She plopped down beside him, clapping her hands.

"Oh, my, that was so much fun, and they won. I'm going to ask Pa to bring me into town for another game soon."

"I can do that if you like."

She grabbed him in a hug. "I'd love that. Thank you." Then she jerked back, her eyes open wide. "I'm sorry, I shouldn't have done that."

He took her hand to leave the stands. "Why not? You were happy and gave me a hug." And he'd be even happier if she happened to do it a few more times. "Let's go find that picnic basket. My stomach says it's time for fried chicken."

She nodded, but said nothing more as they walked back to the buggy. They found a place near other picnickers, and he spread the quilt.

They talked about everything from the cattle back at the ranch to the upcoming fireworks. He had to ask her soon to the ball, but he couldn't get the words out with all the other things going on around them. Maybe on the ride home after the fireworks would be a good time.

When the sun sank below the horizon, the band struck up their music again and the sky filled with red, white, and blue bursts of color. Susannah giggled and covered her ears.

When it ended, she sighed. "That was beautiful. I wanted it to go on forever."

"Fireworks never cease to amaze me. The town council did a bang-up job, and that's no joke."

Susannah's hearty laughter caused him to chuckle. He loved her laugh, her enthusiasm, her excitement. . .well, everything about her. He helped her with the basket then folded the quilt. They walked arm in arm back to the buggy where he lit the lanterns on either side to give them light on the road home.

Susannah sighed happily. "This has been the most wonderful day. Thank you for asking me to come with you."

He settled beside her in the buggy. "You did me the honor of allowing me to escort you." Now was the time to ask her the more important question, but the words wouldn't come.

She snuggled against him and laid her head on his shoulder. If only this could mean she cared about him as more than a friend she'd known almost all her life, he'd be as content as she looked at this moment.

When they reached the ranch, he stopped in front of her house and helped her down from the buggy. This time he wouldn't let her go until he asked her. He stared at her lips, resisting the temptation to claim them with his.

She gazed up at him with a question in her eyes. Now was the time or he'd never get the words out. "You know the awards dinner and ball for my father is coming soon. I want to know if you'd do me the honor of attending the ball with me."

Her gaze held his for a moment before a grin appeared. "I would be delighted to go with you. I was going with Pa, but I'd much rather have you as an escort."

He wanted to shout out his joy, but instead he did what he'd wanted to do all evening. Cupping her face in his hands, he bent to claim her lips. When her arms went around him and the kiss deepened, the fireworks going off in his heart and soul rivaled any that he'd seen tonight or ever before.

When he lifted his head, he caressed her cheeks with his thumbs, ready for a repeat. She blinked at him then pulled away.

"I. . .I have to go in. Thank you for. . .for. . .everything." Then she ran up to the door and disappeared inside.

He stood for moment staring at the closed door. Had he made a mistake in kissing her? She had responded and seemed to have returned his feelings, but if that was true, why had she run off?

She'd said she would go to the ball with him, and that reminder chased away his doubts. He'd take things a little more slowly in the days ahead, at least until he knew where things were going to stand with his grandfather before heading back to Dallas.

Chapter 8

For the next week, Susanna avoided Chase by going late to breakfast and lunch when he and the others had left. Her lips still tingled with the memory of his kiss, but the invitation to the ball tied her nerves into knots she hadn't been able to undo.

Friday morning, she again arrived at the main house after the men had ridden off for the day. Mrs. Thornton still sat at the table drinking coffee.

"You've been avoiding us all long enough. Get something to eat first, then I want you to sit down and tell me what's going on. Chase told me he'd invited you to the ball, and you said yes."

There was no sense in trying to avoid Mrs. Thornton this morning. Judging from her tone of voice, she would have something to say after she heard Susanna's explanation. After selecting a biscuit and fruit, she sat down next to the elderly woman.

"Yes, he did invite me, but now I'm scared, and not sure I want to go." She bit her lip and kneaded her hands in her lap.

Mrs. Thornton waited with her head tilted for Susanna to continue.

"Well, that's not quite true. It's not that I don't want to go, I guess. I'm not sure I'd fit in with all those society women in Dallas he's used to seeing. Besides, I don't have anything nice enough to wear."

"Horsefeathers, as my mother used to say. That's no excuse at all, especially when I've already asked my seamstress to make you a dress. All you have to do is pick the color and the pattern you want from her book, and she'll have it ready for the affair."

Susanna set her coffee cup down so hastily she sloshed coffee over the brim. "I can't let you do that."

"You can, and you will. You're going to be the prettiest girl at the ball."

Tears brimmed in Susanna's eyes. Even a new dress wouldn't be enough for her to measure up to the others there. But Mrs. Thornton's offer came purely from love, and Susannah couldn't reject her generosity.

Mrs. Thornton reached over and covered Susanna's hand with hers. "My dear child, you are like a granddaughter to me, and Chase asked you to accompany him because he cares so much about you."

She started to argue, but then touched her lips. He had kissed her, so he must care for her a little. Her thoughts jumbled and indecision ate at her stomach. She pushed her plate away, no longer hungry.

Mrs. Thornton stood. "Go and freshen up or do whatever you need to do, because we're going into town this morning and order that dress for you."

The stern but loving look from Mrs. Thornton forbade Susanna to disagree. "All right, I'll meet you in twenty minutes." It'd take that long to get her wits about her.

She hugged Mrs. Thornton. "Thank you for this generous gift. I hope Chase will like it."

"If he doesn't, I'll have a word or two to say to him. Now go on, we have things to do."

"Yes, ma'am, I'm going."

A little over an hour later, Susanna stopped the buggy in front of the dressmaker shop and jumped down to hitch the horse to the post. Mrs. Thornton lowered herself to the ground and dusted off her skirt.

"Now let's go in and see what you'd like to have for the ball."

When they entered, Daisy welcomed them with open arms. "At last. I've been wondering when you'd finally come in so we could start on that ball gown." She led them over to a table where she had stacked bolts of fabric.

Mrs. Thornton had said she'd spoken with Daisy, but it sounded like they'd done more than talk. An array of colors in various types of fabric lay wrapped around cardboard centers. Daisy pulled out a few.

"I think this blue would look beautiful with your blond hair and blue eyes. Of course, it would be better if you had a paler complexion, but I suppose we'll have to get along with our darker skin tones." She picked up another one. "Of course, peach or this pink would do just as well."

Susannah did like the blue best, but Daisy's remark about her suntanned skin reopened the threads of doubt that still lingered in her heart. She fingered the blue fabric and said, "I love this color, but will it be right for the ball?" She'd never been to one so had no idea what colors were appropriate for such a formal occasion.

"Believe me, dear, the women will wear whatever colors they desire, and most of them will wear what looks best on them."

Mrs. Thornton put another bolt beside the first one. "I think this will look lovely with it."

"Yes, it will. We'll use the silk for the underskirt with the silk chiffon over it." Daisy turned to Susannah. "Look through those books over there and find the style you'd like."

Susannah did as instructed and leafed through the pattern books. She stopped at a page of elegant ball gowns. "I like this one with the square neck and draped sleeves. I want a little fuller skirt and this does have one, but will I have to wear a corset?"

Daisy pursed her lips and ran her gaze over Susannah from head to toe. "You do have a tiny waist, but a corset is really necessary to get the proper shape for an Edwardian gown."

That part didn't appeal to Susannah at all, but she supposed she could bear it for one evening. "Then this is the dress I'd like."

With the decision made, Daisy began her measurements. For the next hour, she discussed the fabrics and how they would be layered and put together. She had lace trims and fabric flower designs from which to choose as well. When they concluded all the details, Daisy gave them a date for the first fitting in one week.

Mrs. Thornton stood. "Thank you, Daisy, for all your help. Now, Susannah and I have other errands to run."

"What about shoes to match the dress? I'm sure Mr. Binkley will have some nice styles from which to choose."

"I'm sure he will, but I have the perfect pair of shoes for Susannah. I'm pretty sure we wear nearly the same size." Mrs. Thornton headed for the door. "Come along, Susannah. I want to see about something else. You can try on the shoes when we get home."

Susannah followed her out to the street. That was the strangest visit with Daisy she'd ever had. After the fabrics and trim had been selected, Mrs. Thornton had dominated the conversation with her ideas and suggestions, something she'd never done before. Susannah could only hope and pray the final production would be worthy of a ball in Dallas.

Chase sought out his grandfather when he returned from the range for the afternoon. The end of his time on the ranch was drawing near, and he wanted to know his status for the future. When he entered the house, Grandpa called out to him from the office.

"Chase, come in here. We need to talk."

That was exactly what Chase had hoped to do. He had to convince Grandpa to give him a partnership on the ranch. His mother would be furious, but his father would understand. With both Grandpa and Dad arguing his case, his mother might be persuaded to accept the decision. As much as he loved and respected his mother, the time had come for her to realize he had to choose his own way in life.

When Chase sat down at the desk as he'd done before, Grandpa opened his ledger book once again. "I know how hard you've worked this summer, Chase. Jim King says you're as good as any of his boys who've been here awhile."

Chase rolled the brim of his hat in his hands. "I'm glad to hear that. He has a great bunch of men working with him."

"We also talked about your future here, and I'm ready to talk with your parents about your staying here permanently if that's what you really want." Grandpa sat back in his chair and steepled his fingers under his chin.

Relief flooded Chase and washed over his soul. He wouldn't have to argue after all. "I'm sure. It's what I love, and I'm good at it."

"Well, your father says you're good with the oil business as well." Grandpa grinned and leaned over to push a piece of paper toward Chase. "Read that and see what you think."

Chase took the paper and read it, excitement tying his nerves in a knot. By the time he reached the end, his hand shook as he laid the paper back on Grandpa's desk. "I never expected anything like this."

The contract named Chase as full partner in the Circle T Ranch with it becoming fully his upon the death of his grandfather. "This is much more than I expected."

"So, are you up to the task?"

"Yes, sir, I guarantee I am."

"All right then. After this awards thing for your father, I'll talk with him and your mother. If things work out as I hope, you'll be back here in time for fall roundup." He sat back and grinned. "Now you can do something about your future with Susannah. I can't think of anyone I'd rather have as a granddaughter than that pretty girl."

Chase wanted to shout with joy. "I intend to do just that. As soon as you talk to Father and Mother, I'm going to ask her to marry me."

Grandpa stood and extended his hand. "Welcome to the ranching business, Chase. I pray you won't regret your decision."

"I won't." The question now would be how his parents would take the news. He wanted to tell Susannah the good news, but he needed to wait until Grandpa told his mother and father first. If his mother objected, he'd have to stand up to her.

After his grandfather left the office, Chase remained to sit quietly and contemplate his future. He gazed at the books, ranch photos, and framed maps lining the walls of the office. All spoke of the history of a ranch begun in the early days of Texas history and carried on by Thornton men. Grandpa had been born here and raised his family here. His oldest son died in an accident on a trail ride, and his youngest chose oil over cows.

Now it had come to Chase to continue the line. With Susannah by his side, and her father's expert handling of the herds and men, the Circle T would be around another generation.

He leaned back in his chair and said, "Well, Lord, You've answered one prayer of mine, and I thank You, but it isn't going to mean much without Susannah. If You see fit to incline her heart in my direction, I'd be most grateful. She's the first girl I ever loved, and I sure pray You'll help make her the last one."

Chapter 9

Chase left in the middle of July with the promise to keep in touch with Susannah. Missing him cut a hole in her heart and created more doubts about accompanying Mr. and Mrs. Thornton to Dallas. But Chase had called twice and written three times to make sure she didn't back out on her promise to come with his grandparents.

She packed her bags with what she hoped would be adequate attire for the weekend. Mrs. Thornton had been a big help in selecting what would be appropriate for the different activities. Although she had asked, neither Chase nor his grandmother would tell her how his mother viewed Susannah's coming. Their reluctance to answer the question didn't bode well with Susannah, but a promise was a promise.

Mr. Thornton had bought a new Packard for the occasion, and it now sat in front of the main house waiting to be loaded up for the trip. It was a bright-red two-seat sedan with a black top. Susannah and Mrs. Thornton would ride in the back seat. Mr. Thornton and his driver would be in the front.

Susannah closed the lid on the suitcase and set it on the floor. Her dress for the ball hung on the wardrobe door. The silky, light chiffon overskirt billowed in the slight breeze blowing through the window. She fingered the lace that trimmed the neck and sleeves that was dyed blue to match the dress fabric. The same lace adorned the waist and would emphasize her tiny proportions.

The horn sounded an *ooga-ooga* blast in the air. She'd just finished covering her dress and had picked up her bag as her father appeared in the doorway.

"Here, let me get that for you. You take care of your dress." He reached for her valise and nodded toward the hanger.

"Pa, am I doing the right thing? What if Chase's mother is angry with him for asking me to be with him?"

Her father hugged her to his side. "Honey, it's what Chase wants that matters, not his mother. True, she probably didn't like it when he told her, but he hasn't changed his mind, so go and have a good time."

She kissed her father's cheek. "Thanks, Pa, I'll try." The horn sounded again. "I think that means we'd better hurry."

Her father laughed and hurried from the room. She gathered up the bag covering her dress and hooked a hat box over her wrist. Ready or not, she was going to a ball.

At the car, Mrs. Thornton handed her a coatlike garment. "I know it's warm, but a duster is essential to keep your clothes from getting dirty while riding. And you'll need the scarf to cover your hair."

Susannah donned both and climbed up to the back seat, which turned out to be somewhat softer than she first imagined. Mrs. Thornton joined her, and they said their goodbyes to everyone who had gathered to inspect the automobile.

She spent the hour drive to Dallas listening to Mrs. Thornton once again go over what to expect when they arrived. Susannah would have her own room at the hotel that also housed the ballroom where the event would be held. The Thorntons would be in a room close to hers. The dinner would begin promptly at six, and Chase would be at her door fifteen minutes before.

The closer they drove to the city, the faster the butterflies in her stomach fluttered, and the faster her heart beat. Would she ever make it through this night? She breathed a silent prayer for the calming peace only the Lord could give her.

When they arrived at the hotel, the doorman assisted Susannah and Mrs. Thornton from the car and a bellman took care of the luggage. Susannah gazed up at the seven-story structure and blew out her breath. All around her, the buildings on Main Street stood four to five floors high.

"Come along, Susannah. No time for gawking at things now. You can see more from the window in your room."

"Yes, ma'am." She followed Mrs. Thornton into the lobby and waited by the elevator while Mr. Thornton checked them into their rooms. She removed the duster and scarf and draped them over her arm, glad to be rid of the extra layer in this heat.

The elegant surroundings served only to enhance her anxiety. She had never seen such intricate carvings on posts and around the ceilings, or furniture in such rich hues of maroon and gold. The Thornton ranch home was beautiful, but nothing like what surrounded her in this hotel.

Mr. Thornton finished checking in and guided them into the elevator. When the car lurched upward, Susannah's heart lurched along with it. "Is this thing safe, Mr. Thornton?"

"Yes, my dear, it's quite safe, and will take us to the fifth floor in about a minute."

When the car stopped and opened onto the carpeted hallway of their floor, Susannah rushed through the doors. "Which way are our rooms?"

"Down this way, follow me."

Mr. Thornton led the way down the corridor to Susannah's room and handed her the key. "We'll be right next door in case you need anything."

Susannah inserted the key in the lock. "Thank you for everything. It will be nice to rest a bit before time to get ready for the dinner."

Mrs. Thornton looked tired also. "Yes, and don't forget, Chase's mother has arranged for two young ladies to come to our rooms and help us dress. They'll take care of our hair as well."

With that she turned toward her room. Susannah stepped aside to allow the bellboy to set her luggage in the room. "If you need anything, miss, please call the front desk and let us know. Mr. Thornton has taken care of everything else. Have a good stay." He bowed and exited, closing the door behind him.

Susannah explored her surroundings. This was certainly more than she expected. Her room had its own bathing facility with a washstand and a bathtub. Fluffy white towels filled a shelf to the left of the mirror above the washstand. A muted-green spread covered the bed with matching pillow shams at the headboard. The walls were painted ivory, as was the wood trim. Besides a bed, she had a comfortable chair and a table with a lamp beside it. A large wardrobe dominated one wall.

She sauntered over to the window and, just as Mrs. Thornton had said, she could see so much more from this height. At the sight of numerous multistoried buildings, she gasped and shook her head. The streets below teemed with activity as horse-drawn vehicles vied for space with motor cars. She'd never want to live in a place like this, with so many people and so much noise.

After staring out the window for a few minutes, Susannah decided to lie down and rest until time to dress for the evening. With her nerves all tangled in knots, sleep wouldn't come, but lying down beat pacing the floor in anxiety. Instead of the dinner, she switched her thoughts to Chase and the smile that had won her heart. Being with him tonight would make everything all right.

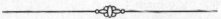

"Mother, I'm sorry you feel the way you do about Susannah, but you haven't given her a chance. She's the one I've chosen for tonight, and if things go the way I pray they will, she'll be the choice for the rest of my life." Chase reached for the doorknob.

His mother stood by the door with her arms across her chest. "I still don't understand why you're interested in her. I know she's a nice, sweet girl, but she can't hold a candle to the young women here in Dallas."

"She does in my eyes, and I'd appreciate your acceptance of her tonight."

"I've already said I'll be nice to her. I may not like it, but I still have manners and know how to behave." She pulled her shoulders back and glared at him.

"Thank you, Mother. I think you'll change your mind once you spend more time with Susannah." Her displeasure stirred up his own anger, but he kept it under control as he pulled the door open. "I'll see you at the dinner."

All during the drive to the hotel, he'd fought both anger and frustration. His mother still hadn't been told of his decision to move back to the ranch. His father had had his suspicions and had spoken with Grandpa. Then he'd given his blessing and assured Chase he and Grandpa would take care of his mother.

When he arrived at the hotel, he had the valet park his car, and went inside. Granny had called with Susannah's room number, so he headed for the elevator. He exited on her floor and strode toward her room. He lifted his hand to knock, but dropped it back to his side and offered up a prayer for a wonderful evening for the two of them.

Then he rapped on the door, and Susannah opened it right away. His heart did a double take at the vision before him. Dressed in blue that intensified the blue of her eyes, Susannah's beauty shown like the stars in a clear Texas sky at midnight. She would put those society girls to shame.

He swallowed hard and offered his hand. "You're beautiful."

Pink tinged her cheeks. "Thank you. The girl your mother sent over worked wonders with my hair. I must remember to thank her."

Chase smiled. "Yes, please do." It wouldn't hurt for Mother to know that Susannah appreciated the kindnesses shown to her instead of expecting such favors, as most of the young women in their circle did.

When they exited the elevator on the floor where the event was to be held, friends of his father and members of the oil baron's group mingled for cocktails in the foyer. That didn't interest Chase at all and it wouldn't Susannah either.

"Let's go on into the main room and find our dinner table." He held her hand in the crook of his elbow and led her inside. Threads of joy filled his heart, and he couldn't help the smile on his face as people turned to stare at the beauty walking beside him. Tongues would be wagging and questions asked as to who she was all evening long.

His parents greeted them at the table. Mother kept her promise and welcomed Susannah, but not in the warm way she greeted other guests around her. He chose the seat next to his father with Susannah on his right side. That way she wouldn't have to try to carry on a conversation with his mother.

He leaned close and squeezed Susannah's ice-cold hand. "Your dress is the prettiest one here, so relax and enjoy the dinner."

During the meal, he beamed with pride at the way Susannah handled the conversation with the woman next to her. Although her hands trembled in her lap when his mother asked her a few pointed questions, she smiled and answered in a way that sent his heart soaring high with love.

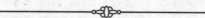

If only she could keep her hands from shaking so. Mrs. Thornton's careful scrutiny of every move and word turned her veins to ice water.

"Susannah, that's a lovely dress. Wherever did you find such beautiful material in Perryton?"

"Mrs. Thornton's dressmaker ordered it from a store here in Dallas. She's a truly gifted woman with the sewing machine."

"Yes, she is." Mrs. Thornton gave her quick smile before turning her attention to the woman beside her in dismissal of Susannah.

A lump lodged in Susannah's throat. Their conversation was low, but the way the women kept glancing Susannah's way, she was certain she was the topic of conversation.

Several times Susannah glanced at Chase as he talked with his father. She loved him so much, but this was not her element, and she'd never fit in with these people. Although this was an evening not to be forgotten, at the moment, she truly wished it was over.

Chapter 10

Later, after the awards and Mr. Thornton's speech, a combo of instruments took the stage, and the ball began. After the first dance with Chase, other young men claimed Susannah's hand for the next two. When the third one ended, she thanked her partner and scanned the room for Chase.

Their gazes locked across the room, and her love for him took her breath away. How would she be able to return to the ranch knowing it may be months before she'd see him again?

He hurried to her side. "See, I told you others would want to dance with you."

"It's one time I'm grateful Mama made me learn a few years ago when she was in good health. At least I didn't step on their toes."

"Let's not go back to the table. The terrace is quiet and away from the crowd." He led her to one of the tables on the flagstone terrace.

It was much quieter, although the music and conversations from inside carried out into the night air. Susannah settled into a wicker chair. The glow from lights in other buildings and the street dispelled any darkness and eased the discomfort hiding in her heart.

Before they had a chance to talk, Chase's grandfather appeared. "Here you are. I need you to come with me to speak with your father about our plans. We won't have time tomorrow before we have to leave to be back on the ranch."

Chase stood and glanced down at Susannah. "I'm sorry. This won't take long, and then I should have some good news. Will you be all right here for a few minutes?"

"Yes. It's nice and peaceful, and I can rest my feet. I won't go anywhere."

He squeezed her hand then disappeared back inside with his grandfather. She'd much rather go back to her room upstairs and get out of the corset and finery restricting her movements, but she'd stay until Chase returned.

She moved her chair out of the direct light into the shadows near a grouping of several ornamental trees set in decorative pots. After closing her eyes and relaxing as much as possible, contentment settled over her like a cooling breeze on a warm day. She could do this for Chase for a few more hours.

The voices of several women near the entrance to the terrace broke into her peace. One mentioned Chase, and she sat up straighter. Before she could speak to let them know she was there, they continued their conversation.

"Did you see the girl with Chase?"

"Yes. I've never seen her before. Who is she, and what in the world is she doing here with him instead of one of us?"

"Well, I found out who she is. She's the daughter of one of the cowboys out at his grandfather's ranch, and came to the city with Chase's grandparents."

"A cowboy's daughter? She's probably looking to get her hands on some of the Thornton money by latching on to Chase."

The other woman gasped and her voice squeaked. "That little tramp. What makes her think Chase would even consider such a thing, when he has nearly every single girl in our crowd ready to marry him?"

Susannah's blood turned to ice again, and tears welled in her eyes. She didn't belong here. The women continued to talk for another minute or two, but Susannah had heard enough. As soon as they went inside, she slipped back into the ballroom and made her way around the edge of the room to the main entrance. From there she ran to the elevator and rode it up to her floor.

Once in her room, she flung herself across the bed and let the tears pour forth her anguish. Her doubts and fears had borne fruit and had never tasted so sour. Her one night with Chase was over, and she'd never come back to Dallas. If only she didn't have to wait for Mr. and Mrs. Thornton to go back to the ranch. If only she could go right now.

She kicked off her shoes and curled up on the bed, hugging one of the pillows to her chest. Tonight had been the biggest mistake of her life.

Chase sat with his father and grandfather in one of the side rooms off the main ballroom. His mother paced in front of him, the anger in her eyes boring into his soul.

"Chase Edward Thornton, I can't believe you would do such a thing. First you bring that. . .that girl to the biggest event of the year, and now you say you want to quit your career with your father to pursue some dream of being a cowboy. It's ridiculous."

"I'm sorry, Mother, but my mind is made up, and my plans are set. Dad and Grandpa support me, so why can't you?" He clenched his hands between his legs to control the anger rising in his own heart.

"Why? You have to ask why? After all I've done to make sure only the best girls in Dallas were invited to our parties last spring, and after all your father has done to secure your future with the company, you have to ask why?"

Dad stood and took hold of her arms. "Helen, stop this now. Chase is an adult and able to make his own decisions about his future. He and his grandfather have come to an agreement, and although I will miss having him in the office, I want him to follow his heart and seek the life he wants for himself. Both he and I have prayed about it and feel this is best for him."

She cut her gaze to Chase. "Do your future plans include that Susannah girl?"

"If she will have me, I most definitely plan to ask her to share my future." Hurting his mother hurt his own heart, but he wouldn't let guilt keep him from the girl he wanted in his life forever.

His father held Mother against his chest and let her sob. Grandpa joined them. He patted her back.

"Helen, you'll see it's for the best. Chase will be happy, and Susannah is a wonderful young woman who knows all about the ranch and will be a great partner for him."

Grandpa raised his eyebrows and peered over at Chase. Chase glanced at his watch. Susannah! He'd left her alone much longer than he had intended. He sprang from his seat. "I have to go find Susannah. She probably thinks I've deserted her."

He stopped and kissed his mother's cheek. "It'll all work out. I love you, but I also love Susannah. Please accept that and wish us well."

She reached out and cupped his cheek before turning once more into her husband's embrace, and Chase darted out to the lobby and into the main ballroom. When he reached the terrace, Susannah was nowhere to be found. He ran back inside and scanned the crowd for some sight of her.

"Are you looking for Susannah?" His grandmother stepped to his side.

"Yes. Do you know where she went?"

"Yes, but first I have to tell you what happened." She pulled him over to the privacy of a corner.

His heart lurched, and his blood ran cold. "Tell me. Is she hurt or upset because I didn't come back?"

"Neither of those. I saw you leave with your father and grandpa, so I went looking for Susannah. Before I found her, I overheard two young women talking about you and her." She gripped his arm. "What they said wasn't pretty or nice. They inferred that Susannah only wanted your money. I confronted them and gave them a piece of my mind, but then Susannah ran past and out the door. I caught up just as the elevator doors closed, so I imagine she's up in her room."

Now his blood ran hot. "Who were— no, I don't care who they were. I've got to find her."

"Yes, you do, and you must stay at her door until she will talk with you, even though I imagine that's the last thing she wants to do right now." She swatted his arm. "Now go!"

He hugged her. "Thanks, Granny. She will have to listen to me."

On the elevator, he gave the operator the floor number and leaned against the wall. His fists clenched and unclenched. How could those women have been so cruel and hateful? But why should he be surprised? They acted no differently than his sister's friends when they didn't get their way or they didn't like someone.

By the time he reached Susannah's door, his nerves had calmed some, but he inhaled deeply then let it out in a rush of wind, his anger replaced by his deep love for Susannah. She had to listen to him. He had so much to tell her.

He rapped on the door, but there was no answer. After the third time, he pounded, and said, "Susannah, please open this door. We have to talk, and if you don't answer me, I'll stand here and shout through the door. Everyone on this floor will hear what I have to say." He wouldn't actually do that, but she didn't know it. Their entire future rested on her willingness to listen to him.

She wanted to tell him to go away, but Chase was stubborn, and most likely he would stand in the hall and shout at her. He might as well see her tear-washed makeup, rumpled hairdo, and wrinkled dress. He'd see she would never measure up to the society women of Dallas and send her back to the ranch.

When she finally opened the door, he stood poised to knock again. "Whatever you have to say, Chase Thornton, isn't going to make any difference. I don't belong here with your family and all of your friends. My place is back home with Pa, and the sooner I get there the better off I'll be."

"Will you at least listen to the news I was going to tell you earlier?"

How could she resist his plea with those blue eyes drawing her in like a moth to flame? She at least owed him that much. "All right, I'll listen, but I still say it won't make any difference. My mind is made up."

"Oh, but I think it will make a difference, and I hope it will change your mind as well." He stepped into the room, careful to leave the door slightly ajar.

She bit back a grin at his proprietary, but turned away from him to escape the pull of the face she loved. He'd already weakened her resolve, and if she gazed into his eyes now, every bit that was left might be drowned in their depths.

His hands touched her shoulders. "Please, look at me."

Tears welled in her eyes, and she turned toward him, keeping her head bent downward.

He cupped her face in his hands and lifted her head to meet eye to eye. "Granny told me what happened downstairs, and I'm so sorry. Those women are jealous of anything and anyone that gets in the way of their plans."

Heat rose in her face. Granny heard what those women said? This couldn't get any worse. What would his family think now?

He reached down and grasped her hands in his. "Susannah, what happened was awful, and I'm so sorry." He pulled her to him and wrapped his arms around her. "I love you, and I want to make sure nothing like that ever happens again."

Her heart jumped then pounded. He loved her. But even as he said the words she'd longed to hear, they could not change what was. They could never be together, because she would not leave the ranch. "I love you too, but it will never work. I can't live here in Dallas."

"And I don't expect you to. I don't want you to live here."

He didn't want her here, where he was, so what good was his love? She tried to push back, but his hold tightened.

"The good news I said I had to share is that I'm coming back to the ranch and becoming partners with Grandpa. I don't plan to leave there either."

Hope soared in her heart. Would he really give up everything with his father to rope and brand cattle the rest of his life? She tilted her head backward to see his face. The love shining there dissolved every last bit of her doubt.

"It's what I've wanted to do for more years than I can count. Grandpa needs me, and the ranch is the only place I want to be. But more importantly, you're there."

The love she'd held in check for so many years now filled her heart and overflowed to engulf her in a joy greater than any she'd ever experienced. "You're truly coming back for good?"

"Yes, and please say you'll marry me, help run the Circle T, and make it the best place on earth and me the happiest man."

How could she say no to that? She reached up and circled the back of his neck with her fingers. "I would like that very much."

He bent his head and captured her lips with his. A wave of emotion washed over her so deep that she could go under and never come back up. With that one kiss, all her doubts and fears about his ever loving her crumbled at her feet.

What those women had said earlier made no difference to her now. They may have thought she wasn't good enough for Dallas, but the truth was that she didn't have to be. Chase wanted her, and that's all that mattered.

He ended the kiss but held her close. "I can't wait to tell Granny and Grandpa. They'll be overjoyed. They've wanted you for their granddaughter for a long time."

She may have come to the city to attend a ball, but it was what happened after the ball that made all the difference. Then he bent his head toward hers to kiss her once again. As the kiss deepened, her heart filled with every dream she'd ever had of Chase.

When he ended it and stepped back, her heart longed for more.

He stroked her cheek with his fingers. "I've wanted to do this for so long, but I had to be sure my future would be at the ranch and not in Dallas."

She kept her fingers hooked behind his neck and grinned. "I've prayed for this for as long, but God is never too early or too late. He answers prayers at exactly the right time."

"And our time is now." He held her close to his chest.

His heart beat as rapidly as hers, and she closed her eyes to listen. Her future now held a promise even greater than she could ever have imagined.

Martha Rogers is a freelance writer and the author of the Winds Across the Prairie, Seasons of the Heart, and The Homeward Journey series as well as the novella, *Key to Her Heart* in *River Walk Christmas* and *Not on the Menu* in *Sugar and Grits*. She was named Writer of the Year at the Texas Christian Writers Conference in 2009 and is a member of ACFW. She writes the weekly Verse of the Week for the ACFW Loop. ACFW awarded her the Volunteer of the Year in 2014. Her first electronic series from Winged Publications, Love in the Bayou City of Texas, debuted in the spring of 2016. Martha is a frequent speaker for writing workshops and the Texas Christian Writers Conference. She is a retired teacher and lives in Houston with her husband, Rex. Their favorite pastime is spending time with their twelve grandchildren and four great-grandchildren. Visit her website at www.marthawrogers.com

Lighter Than Air

by Lorna Seilstad

Who are these that fly as a cloud. . .?
ISAIAH 60:8

Chapter 1

Rural St. Louis, Missouri
April 1900

Seven easels stood propped on the front lawn, and Ella Mason smiled at the apron-clad young ladies poised behind each one.

"Remember." She walked behind her students. "Art connects us to all of humanity and all of history. Man has expressed himself on cave walls, on paper, and on canvas since the beginning of time." She stopped to examine Annie's landscape and laid her hand on the girl's shoulder. "Well done, Annie. Anyone can paint a cloud. Only you can paint it the way you see it."

Annie stuck the end of her paintbrush in her mouth.

Without missing a beat in her lesson, Ella gently pushed the paintbrush away. "Art is not only about self-expression, it's also about self-discovery."

"Miss Mason! Look!" Opal jabbed a finger toward the western sky.

Ella spun and glanced upward. A dot in the sky moved closer. She lifted her hand to shield her eyes from the sun. The dot expanded to a yellow-and-blue-striped orb.

Isabelle discarded her paintbrush and climbed onto the rock wall for a better look. "Is it a hot-air balloon, Miss Mason?"

"Yes, I think it is."

Opal joined Isabelle on the wall. "Why is it falling?"

Ella studied the colorful object. It was descending—rather quickly—but was it actually falling? The lower half of the balloon seemed tucked up inside the top like a giant parachute. Her heart lurched. She'd only seen a hot-air balloon once, but she recalled that the entire thing had been inflated. Could this balloon be in some kind of trouble?

It had taken only seconds for the dot to come into their view. A man tossed a rope over the side of his basket with an anchor attached to the end. The anchor bounced along the field like a child's pull toy, but when it reached the grove, its teeth sank into a pin oak and held fast.

The balloon at the end of the tether fought for freedom, then seemed to give up and plummet from the sky.

Isabelle screamed, Opal shrieked, Annie gasped, and Ella bit her knuckles to keep from crying out.

Lord, save this man.

The aeronaut leaned over the side and tossed something out. Was he hoping to slow his descent by discarding the ballast? Still, the balloon fell.

The basket skimmed the top of the trees and the wilted balloon listed to the side. It caught and ripped. Branches gave way beneath the basket. It tipped and pitched the man to the ground.

Ella whirled. "Annie, fetch my doctoring basket. Opal, tell Miss Gatrell what has happened and ask her to send for the doctor. Isabelle, run for Mr. Ernest. We'll need the wagon. The rest of you, stay here. Understand?"

She hiked up her skirts and raced across the yard. The man lay motionless on the edge of the grove. What would she do if he were dead? As the principal of a girls' boarding and day school, Ella knew how to pull splinters and bandage cuts. She'd even become quite adept at diagnosing most minor ailments, but broken bones and internal damage were certainly beyond her scope of abilities.

Dropping to her knees beside the fallen aeronaut, she breathed a prayer, begging God to let the man be alive. He was lying facedown, so she placed her fingers against his throat and felt the drumming of a steady pulse.

"Sir? Sir? Can you hear me?"

Her questions received only a moan as an answer.

"Sir, I need to see where you are hurt. Can you roll over? I'll help you as best I can." She eased her arm under his chest and lifted. The man was little help, but she managed to flip him onto his back.

Her gaze swept his face and she gasped.

She knew this man.

Leave it to Titus Knott to crash into her life once again.

Moving hurt. Titus didn't want to open his eyes yet. Instead, he attempted to rectify his jumbled thoughts. Where was he?

The mattress beneath him told him he was in a bed. What hurt? First and foremost, his head. After that, it was hard to tell what ached more—his leg or his ribs. He cracked open one eye.

"Ah, there you are." A young lady hovered above him. "Stay awake. I'll get the doctor. He's speaking with our principal."

Principal? Good grief, was he in a school?

The doctor eased the door open. "Hello, young man, I'm Dr. Aldworth." He sat down in a chair beside the bed. "You've had quite an adventure."

"Where am I?" Titus's voice came out thick.

The doctor offered him a glass of water. "You're at Rosewood Meadow Girls' Boarding School, and I think you'll be visiting them for quite a while."

Titus attempted to push up on his elbow, but the doctor pressed him back in place. "Take it easy, son. You've got a concussion. You'll need to stay here in bed for at least a week."

"A week?" A woman's voice came from the doorway. Titus imagined it was the principal of the school, but the doctor blocked his view of the matron.

The doctor stood. "Ah, Miss Mason. Nice of you to join us. I was just about to find out who our patient is."

"His name is Mr. Titus Knott." She crossed her arms over her chest. "And he isn't staying a minute longer than absolutely necessary."

The doctor looked from the man in the bed to the young principal in the doorway. "You know one another?"

"We do." Titus locked gazes with the principal. No longer a girl, she'd grown even more beautiful since they'd last seen each other. Her Coca-Cola-colored hair was styled in a pompadour, and while her chestnut eyes held no warmth toward him, they remained as expressive as always. "Hello, Ella. Thought I'd drop in after—how long has it been?"

Her peach-tinted lips curled. "Six blessed, Titus-free years."

He winced. Her words stung almost as much as the ache in his head.

"Perhaps I should give my patient a complete examination now that he is awake, Miss Mason, and meet up with you in your office." The doctor grasped the door and closed it, forcing Ella to step back out of the rom.

The doctor lifted Titus's wrist to take his pulse. "I've never heard Miss Mason speak like that to anyone."

"We didn't part on the best of terms."

"Lover's spat?"

"A difference of the minds." Titus ground his teeth as the doctor probed his ribs. "Oh? How so?"

"She made up her mind that I wasn't the man she wanted."

Chapter 2

A knock on the door drew Ella's attention. "Come in."

Clementine King, the school's cook and housekeeper, carried a tray laden with a teapot, two cups, and two slices of sweetbread. The cinnamon scent filled Ella's office. "I thought we could share a little snack."

"Bless your heart, Clementine. You always know exactly what I need." Ella rose and took the tray from the older woman. She placed it on small, round table by the window and indicated Clementine should take one of the winged chairs. She sat down in the other and poured the tea. "Have you been in to meet our visitor?"

"The doctor wasn't finished with him, but I'll meet him soon enough." Clementine added a sugar lump to her cup and stirred it with a silver spoon. "I don't think it's proper for him to stay here, Miss Mason. Not with all these impressionable young ladies around."

"I understand." Ella forked a bite of her sweetbread. How many times had Clementine's sage advice helped Ella avoid a crisis? Yet, this time, there didn't seem many options. "Still, I don't see as we have a choice. If the doctor says Titus can't be moved and needs time to recover, then we'll have to give it to him."

"Titus?" Clementine narrowed her eyes. "Since when did you start calling a stranger by his given name?"

Ella's cheeks warmed. "He's not a stranger. I knew him before I attended teachers' college."

Clementine set down her cup and leaned closer as if searching for clues in Ella's face. "You two were sweet on one another?"

Ella forced a smile. "We were young."

"Young love is still love, Miss Mason." Clementine stood up. "And all the more reason the man shouldn't stay here. Soon as he's able, we'll move him in with Ernest and me at the caretaker's house, and I'll tend to him. That ought to keep the busybodies at bay."

Ella set her cup on the saucer with a chink. "Thank you, Clementine, but I don't think he'll be here that long. Titus—Mr. Knott—isn't the kind of man to stay in one place. He's a scientist, always on the verge of the next great discovery."

Clementine picked up the tray. "He might discover you all over again if you're not careful."

Ella rolled her eyes as her friend left the office with the tray in her hands. Despite Ella's advanced age of twenty-five, Clementine insisted that Ella would yet marry. Sure, there had been a few suitors, but as the principal of a girls' school, her freedom to court was greatly limited.

Since none of her suitors had truly captured her interest, Ella had never considered what would happen to her position at Rosewood if she were to marry. The chief benefactress and owner of the school was Charlotte Rosewood-Dasher, a wealthy widow with a desire to raise women's position in society. A suffragist, Mrs. Rosewood had instructed Ella to teach the girls in the school to be independent thinkers. "When we get the right to vote," she'd said, "I want them capable of making wise decisions." Mrs. Rosewood herself had interviewed and selected Ella to serve as principal, saying they were kindred spirits. She insisted the female students have every opportunity to develop their own unique abilities. To that end, she provided the best of everything. Besides traditional studies, the girls would be free to explore art, music, and drama in addition to learning to ride. She expected a strong emphasis on oratory and reasoning skills, because the young women who completed her school were to know how to be persuasive.

However, Ella doubted Mrs. Rosewood's forward thinking extended to a married teacher, and it would take a man with more than hot air to make her consider leaving the girls in this academy.

She glanced out the window. In the courtyard below, several girls played a game of croquet. The rest of the young ladies, thirty-five in all, were most likely studying, writing letters home, reading, or talking with their friends. The other two teachers at the school, Miss Harriet Young and Miss Glynes Gatrell, were probably grading papers or preparing lessons as she should be doing.

She moved to her desk and picked up her lesson plan for literature. Tomorrow the girls would still be giddy with excitement over the balloon crash, and she'd have to work hard to get them to concentrate on diagramming sentences.

Ella sighed. Once again, Titus Knott was making a mess of her orderly life.

Three days had passed since the accident and Titus had yet to see Ella. A doughy woman named Clementine brought him meals, and her husband, Ernest, came each morning to help him clean up for the day. He'd also brought him a cane, which allowed Titus enough assistance to make it to the water closet on his own.

Today, however, he planned to go farther. Three days was enough convalescing. The ache in his head had ebbed to a dull pounding and the light no longer tormented his eyes. His ribs bit when he took a deep breath, but his sprained ankle had gotten stronger. He wanted to see beyond these four walls—and he wanted to talk to Ella.

Titus sat on the edge of his narrow bed and took in the sparse room. Clementine had told him he was in the spare room on the main floor. The girls, she'd explained, were housed in the above two floors where he was not to even think of venturing. He took no offense at her warning since he knew she had the young women's safety at heart.

Besides the bed and a straight-back chair, there was an oak washstand with a serviceable white stoneware basin and ewer. His clothes hung from a cast-iron hook on the wall. His gaze drifted to the one adornment in the room, a painting.

The eighteen-by-twenty-inch framed landscape sported trees, a green valley, and a sky full of airy clouds. What was the speck in the sky? Had the painting been damaged? He leaned closer, glanced at the artist's signature, and blinked again.

Ella, his Ella, had painted a miniscule balloon in her painting. Had she thought of him as often as he'd thought of her, recalling the dream he'd often shared of becoming an aeronaut? Perhaps he still held a corner of her heart.

After dressing, he made his way to the door, which opened to a short hallway. He leaned heavily on his cane and started the trek to what he guessed to be the center of the house. Clementine had told him the Rosewood Meadow School was actually the former Rosewood residence. It had been remodeled for use as a school after Charlotte Rosewood had remarried, and since the benefactress had no children, she decided that she could call all the girls who came through these doors her own.

He paused to catch his breath. Who would have thought a short walk would be so taxing? Maybe he'd go only a little farther before returning to his room.

With his eyes fixed on the next set of doors, he limped forward. He staggered and fell against the wall with a thud. The doors swung open, and Ella appeared in the hallway. Her gaze landed on him.

She hurried to his side. "Titus, you are not supposed to be out of bed!"

When she wrapped her arm around his waist, he groaned. "Don't scold me like one of your pupils."

"Don't act irresponsibly and I won't." She helped him into the room she'd come from and to a tapestry-covered chair near a chessboard. Once he was seated, she poured a glass of water and handed it to him. "What are you doing up and about?"

"I wanted to speak to you."

"Me? Why?"

"You've not come to see me." He downed the cool water. "But your painting has a balloon."

"What are you talking about? Are you delirious?" She pressed the back of her hand to his forehead and shook her head. "It wouldn't be proper for me as an unmarried principal to enter the room of an unmarried acquaintance."

"Yet you can talk to me here?"

"This is the parlor, and anyone is free to come and go. I believe we'd be above reproach here."

He motioned with his cane to the chair beside him. "In that case, please sit down. I'd like to catch up."

"Titus, this isn't a social call."

"Then." He released a slow, tired breath. "Let me at least tell you how I ended up in your backyard." He fingered a chess piece. "Do you still play chess?"

She smiled. "Well enough to beat you." After settling in the chair across the board from him, she made sure each of her boxwood weighted chess pieces was perfectly centered on its own square. "You were saying—"

He aligned his ebony pieces. "I'm a professor now. In the fall, I will be teaching science at the new Millikan University in Decatur."

"Is that your first appointment?" She moved her pawn forward.

"No, but I took a year off to work on my experiments." He set his black pawn in front of hers. "I like James Millikan's philosophy. He wants the institution to embrace the practical side of learning."

Ella sighed and moved her knight behind and to the right of her pawn. "That figures. You've never understood the importance of the classics."

"He wants the practical to be taught alongside the literary and classical. Don't worry, your precious *Iliad* and *Odyssey* will still have a place on the shelves." His ebony knight took a matching position on the opposite side of the board.

She set her bishop near his knight. "And Shakespeare?"

"Ah yes. If I recall, you've always been particularly fond of *A Midsummer Night's Dream*." He moved his pawn to block her advances, then met her gaze. "I believe you once quoted it to me. 'The course of true love never did run smooth.'"

Two crimson flowers bloomed on Ella's cheeks. "And I believe your favorite quote was 'We are such stuff as dreams are made on' from *The Tempest*. You've always been a dreamer." She captured his knight.

"You'll be pleased to know I have a new favorite Bard quote. 'This above all: to thine own self be true.'"

" 'And it must follow,'" she continued in a serious hushed tone, " 'as the night the day. Thou canst not be false to any man.'"

He made another move, then looked up. "You can trust my words, Ella. I've changed."

"I highly doubt that." She laughed wryly, continuing her play. "Anyway, what difference is it to me? You'll be gone soon enough."

Her words stung. But why? Was it because she'd injured his pride? Shown a lack of trust in him? He drew in a breath. How could he convince her that his words were true and not full of hot air?

She captured his bishop. "Where were you headed, anyway?"

"I've been doing some experiments for the weather bureau. I plan to participate in a balloon race in a few weeks."

"That sounds dangerous."

"I'm an experienced aeronaut with more than three hundred ascensions. Before the other day, I'd never had an accident." He captured her castle. "Please tell me my balloon equipment is safe."

"It is. I had Ernest store it in the barn."

"Thank you. I'll need to repair the burner. Its failure caused my crash landing. I hope I can still make the balloon race. They are offering a two-thousand-dollar purse."

"Truly?" Her eyes widened. "So you will be leaving soon."

Did he detect a note of sadness in her voice? "Between my injuries and the repairs, I'm afraid you won't be able to get rid of me right away." He looked up from the game. "Check."

She studied the board, worrying her lip between her teeth. "Checkmate." She made her final move with a flourish and knocked over his king.

Titus laughed. "Your reasoning skills are wasted on literature. You should have been a scientist."

She pushed to her feet. "That would have certainly made you happy."

"Ella—"

With her shoulders held stiff, she walked to the doorway. "Are you sufficiently recovered to see yourself back to your room? If not, I'll call for Ernest."

"I'm fine." With some effort, he rose to his feet and leaned on his cane. "Thank you for the game, Ella."

"Miss Mason." She turned toward him. "I'd hate for the young ladies to get the wrong idea."

He nodded. "If that's what you'd like."

"It is."

Chapter 3

How could a staircase grow overnight?

Ella lifted her skirt and climbed the winding stairs, which seemed like they went on forever. She had to get to her private quarters before anyone witnessed her distress. Why did Titus have to land in her backyard?

Once she reached her room at the top of the stairs, she dropped onto the chair in front of her walnut dressing table. Red-rimmed eyes stared back at her from the rectangular mirror as tears coursed down her cheeks. She withdrew a handkerchief with a tatted lace edge from the top right dresser drawer and dabbed at her eyes.

Why had Titus's presence unnerved her so? She hadn't thought of him in years. Well, not often, at any rate. But now, simply being with him again ignited a host of memories that paraded through her thoughts like circus ponies, each one dressed with finery and feathers.

She moved to her washbasin, dampened a cloth, and washed her face with the cool water. Yes, they'd had some wonderful times together. Once, she'd sprained her ankle, and a stubbornly gallant Titus had insisted on carrying her all the way home. On another occasion, she recalled how he taught her how to ride a bicycle. He'd been so patient with her—and so proud when she'd mastered the conveyance. Yet, despite the good times, she'd known the truth about Titus, so she'd broken his heart and sent him away to the university. How was she to know her father would pass only a few months later?

No, she mustn't go there. She dried her face on a towel. She needed to gather herself. If one of the girls were to come to her door, what would they think of a crying principal?

A few warm memories did not change the facts, and they certainly did not change the man. Titus talked a good talk, but when he was needed most, he'd be gone. That's how it was. Titus called himself a man of science, but what Ella wanted—what she needed—was a man of faith.

With a lamp lit beside him on the nightstand, Titus opened the Bible that Ernest brought him from his retrieved belongings. He had to pack light in a balloon, so besides the Bible, his carpetbag contained only a couple of changes of clothes and a photograph he always kept close.

Guilt lay heavy in his chest. Ella made no appearance during the rest of the day, and now that the dinner hour was nearing, he knew she'd be busy. Seeing her had stirred up old feelings and old memories. He wasn't the man he once was. Gracious, he'd been but a boy back then. Pride had controlled most of his choices. He still fought the urge to put himself first, but he'd made a true attempt to change.

He opened his Bible to his favorite verse. "Therefore if any man be in Christ, he is a new creature: old things are passed away; behold, all things are become new."

Is that what he needed to do with Ella? Let the old things pass away? Let her see he was a new creature?

He closed his eyes and spoke the words in prayer. In the room above him, a girl screamed. Then, he heard a thump. A few seconds passed, then he heard another shriek.

"Fire! Fire! Fire!"

Chapter 4

Tossing the Bible on the bed, Titus grabbed his cane and wobbled from the room as fast as his injured leg would carry him. Upstairs, like a fish swimming against the tide, he fought his way through hysterical girls to get to the room the shrieks were coming from. Above the desk, flames rose, consuming a curtain panel. He grabbed the curtain and hurled it out the window to the stone porch below. Then he snatched the ewer from the washstand and doused the window frame. Steam hissed from the charred wood.

Ella rushed into the room, coughing at the smoke. "Where's the fire?"

Titus pointed out the window. "Looks like one of the girls removed the lamp's flue so she could heat her curling wand over it." He pointed to the green glass kerosene lamp with the offending instrument still in place. "When a breeze came up, I'm guessing the curtain blew in and caught fire."

A moan came from the far side of the room. Titus and Ella turned toward the sound. Ella hurried over and helped the young lady sit up. "Opal, whatever happened to you?"

She coughed, then rubbed the back of her head. "I—I think I fainted after I screamed."

"I did hear a thump downstairs." Titus chuckled as he poked at the wood, making sure all cinders had been extinguished.

Ella shot him a frown as she helped Opal stand. She led her toward the door. Opal paused. "Who is that man? He saved my life. I should thank him."

"I'll be sure to pass your thanks on to him, but first we need to get you to some fresh air." Ella smiled back at Titus. "Not only did he save you, but he quite possibly saved the school."

The smoke made Titus's throat scratchy, but Ella's words were a balm to his spirit. She now had a reason to speak to him. It was a chance for a new beginning, a chance to see he'd changed, and he didn't plan to let it go up in flames.

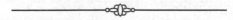

It was no use.

Ella released a long sigh. Clementine intended to get her way, and she was not a woman to be dissuaded. Ella leaned back in her chair and let Clementine continue her rant.

"I'm telling you. If that man can race up the stairs to the girls' rooms, he can sure walk across the lawn and stay in the guest room in the caretaker's house." Clementine propped her hands on her rounded hips. "Can you imagine what the mothers would say if they heard a man had been in your girls' rooms?"

"He was putting out a fire, Clementine. We owe him our thanks, not our condemnation."

Clementine huffed. "You can thank him any way you want. Throw him a party. Make him a cake. But that man needs to be out of this school before those mothers get wind of his presence. Some of them would pull their daughters without blinking an eye."

"But he'd be imposing on you and Ernest. You don't mind?"

"Not as much as losing even one of these girls."

Ella leaned forward and folded her hands on her desk. "All right. Please have Ernest help him relocate and be certain you explain the reason. I believe he'll understand." She tapped her fingers on the oak surface. "And I think I'll take your advice on the party as well."

Clementine's eyes widened. "You're throwing the man a party?"

"No, but we'll publicly thank him tomorrow night at dinner. Can you make a special meal?"

"I suppose I can change my menu plans." Clementine patted her salt-and-pepper bun. "Are you planning on inviting him, or do you want me to do that too?"

"I'll pen an invitation right now and drop it by his room before Ernest comes for him."

"Are you going to make a habit of this?"

"A habit of what?"

"Having the man to dinner."

"Perhaps." Ella withdrew a sheet of stationery from her desk drawer. "It's only charitable. He has to eat, and it's rude to make him do so alone."

Clementine placed her hand on the doorknob. "True, but you'd better be careful. Those mothers love gossip almost as much as their daughters."

After Clementine left, Ella picked up her pen and dipped it in the inkwell. Her pen poised over cream-colored stationery, she hesitated. Titus deserved to be thanked in a public way, but inviting him to regularly dine with her, the other teachers, and the girls, was extending an invitation beyond what was called for. Was she being charitable or reckless? She had always enjoyed Titus's company, but she needed to think with her head, not her heart. This was her school, and the parents trusted her with their daughters.

Perhaps she'd only offer an invitation to tonight's dinner. After learning of that outcome, she'd make a decision on any further dinner invitations.

She wrote the note, and with a decisive nod, sealed it.

It was a safe, reasonable decision—or was it? Perhaps Titus was already coloring her judgements. Nothing about allowing the balloonist to stay seemed safe or reasonable.

⁂

Stopping in front of a mirror in the hallway outside the school's dining room, Titus checked his bow tie. It hung lopsided with one loop larger than the other. He tugged one end to even it up, but instead the confounded thing came undone.

For heaven's sake. He could fly a balloon, but he couldn't tie a tie.

"Need some assistance?" Ella laid a hand on his arm and urged him to turn. She lifted her hands toward the droopy bows. "You never could master one of these. Didn't your father teach you?"

"I doubt he ever wore a tie."

"There." She placed her hand on his chest, and the intimate touch warmed him from the inside.

He covered her hand with his own. "Thank you."

Two girls tittered behind them. Ella, red-faced, jerked her hand away. "Ladies, shouldn't you be in the dining room?"

They both snapped to attention and sucked in their cheeks, a futile effort to gain control of their grins. "Yes, Miss Mason." They bobbed their heads, then scurried away.

"I'm sorry about that." Ella sighed and rubbed the bridge of her nose. "They see what they want to see."

"I don't know. I'm sure you've taught them to be excellent observers of the world around them." He offered her his arm. "Shall we?"

She gently pushed his arm downward. "I'm sorry, Titus. That wouldn't be appropriate. I must think of the example I'm setting. These girls are quite impressionable and they're my responsibility."

Disappointment poked him, but he needed to be patient. "I understand." Then, taking his cane in hand, he followed her into the dining room.

As soon as they entered, he saw Ella stiffen. Any connection they'd felt, although brief, had been squelched. How did she do that? How could she seem so warm and affectionate one moment and so stoic the next? She'd always been a stickler for rules, but this was much more than that. It was a deliberate attempt to keep him at arm's length.

He sighed and took in the surroundings. Elaborate molding encircled the enormous dining room. Apparently, a wall must have been removed to make the area large enough for all of the students to dine together. Three tables, each seating twelve people, were set up in a *U* shape. The young women stood as Ella entered and remained standing while she took her place at the head table. She gestured to an empty seat to her right, and Titus moved to his assigned position.

Her gaze swept the room. "Good evening, ladies."

"Good evening, Miss Mason," the singsong sopranos said in unison.

She turned to him. "Good evening, Professor Knott."

He held her gaze and replied slowly. "Good evening—Miss Mason."

The students snickered.

She scowled at them. "Tonight, I've asked Professor Knott here to publicly thank him for his heroics regarding yesterday's fire, and Mrs. King has prepared a seven-course dinner in his honor as well. I shudder to think what could have happened to our school if not for his quick thinking. Please join me in a round of applause in his honor."

After a moment, Titus dipped his head and the applause died down.

"Now, ladies, I'd like to remind you of the importance of etiquette. Etiquette comes, as you know, from the French word for 'ticket.' Good manners are your ticket to open doors, and poor manners will close them. A woman of influence cannot afford to let something as basic as table manners stand in the way of her making a difference in the world. Your table captain is present to aid you in the development of your manners. Please accept her admonitions." She paused. "Now, I believe Miss Elizabeth Jeffries is giving tonight's grace. Lizzy?"

After a girl with a long blond braid stepped to the center of the room and offered a prayer, all of the students looked to Ella. When she sat, they followed. Titus held her chair, then sat down himself. She shot him a glare as if he'd overstepped with the simple gesture. But she had just spoken about the importance of manners, and for a gentleman, seating a lady was at the top of the list.

She scooted her chair so that it was tilted away from him and spoke to the woman on her left, making her position clear. She could speak about him publicly, but she had no plans to speak with him privately at the table. Surely he could win her over. It had never been a problem when they were younger.

He leaned close, his breath blowing against a tendril of hair by her ear. "So, who's our table captain?"

"I am." She faced forward, spreading her crisp, linen napkin across her lap, and in the process elbowed his side, sending a message she wanted distance.

He grinned. This was going to be fun. Ella, Miss Manners Mason herself, was in charge, and if she thought she could shut him out, he'd make himself impossible to ignore.

Titus shook out his napkin with a snap. A few girls turned in his direction, but Ella overlooked his faux pas.

Ella introduced the parties at the table. They included the school's other two instructors. Miss Young, a tall woman with a long narrow face and a sharp nose, taught French, Latin, and history; and Miss Gatrell, a sweet-faced woman in her twenties whose smile took up too much of her face, taught the math and music courses. Besides the four adults at the table, several students sat with them. Miss Young explained that those who sat at the "teachers' table" alternated each week, then each girl introduced herself.

Titus glanced at the girls seated at the other tables. Until Ella began eating, no one moved. Fascinating. Did Ella enjoy this control? She'd always liked traditions, but wasn't this a bit much?

In front of him sat a plate with an assortment of olives, radishes, and celery. He picked up a piece of celery and the crunch echoed at the silent table. He repeated the gesture with the radishes, then popped the olives in his mouth like gumdrops.

The girls at the table glanced from him to Ella, but the principal didn't even flick a look in his direction.

"Each meal, the girls take turns serving," Miss Young explained as a student removed the empty relish plates. "It helps them understand both the roles and responsibilities of the staff and of the lady of the house."

Ella nodded to Clementine, and the rotund cook signaled her "staff" to serve the next course.

A bowl of beef consommé was placed in front of Titus. He picked up his spoon and dipped it into the steaming bowl. Lifting it to his lips, he blew on the spoon and then slurped its contents. He heard giggles to his left and his right, but still, Ella did not respond. What was it going to take to get a reaction from her? Even a glare would be better than this cool detachment.

Miss Gatrell blotted her lips with her napkin. "So, Professor Knott, how long have you been an aeronaut?"

"About five years. I was introduced to it in college, and now I've made over three hundred ascents."

One of the students leaned forward, resting her elbow on the table and holding her chin in her hand. "It must be so fascinating."

"Lillian." Ella straightened, placing her hands in her lap. The young lady's expression clouded and she quickly copied the action.

"There's nothing quite like it, Miss Lillian." He flashed her a grin in an attempt to soften the correction. "When you go up in a balloon, it doesn't feel as if you're rising. Instead, it feels as if the earth is falling away."

"Truly?"

Before he continued, he flicked a glance at Ella, who immediately looked away. The rest of the table, he noticed, hung on his words. Ah, he did like an audience. He drew in a deep breath. "But you can hear noises clearly for a long time. Then, at last, all the noises blur together. They create the most amazing symphony, unlike anything created in a concert hall."

"Oh my." Miss Gatrell smiled dreamily. "That reminds me, you must hear our girls' glee club. Angels, if I say so myself."

"It must be their capable director." Titus paused as a girl arrived and removed his empty bowl. Another brought a plate containing boiled whitefish. His hand hovered over the three forks to the left of his plate. If he selected the correct one, perhaps Ella would offer him a smile, but if he selected the wrong one, perhaps he could break through her stony exterior. After all, as table captain, wasn't it her job to correct his errors in etiquette?

He snapped up his dinner fork and the girls at the table gasped.

Lillian leaned forward. "Professor Knott, that's your dinner fork. Use this one." She held up the fork on the outside.

"Lillian." Ella's voice was kind, but firm. "One does not correct one's guests."

"Oh." The girl poked at her fish. "I apologize, Professor Knott."

"That's all right, Lillian." He turned toward Ella. "One shouldn't ignore them either."

Tension rippled through the air like a current of hot air, suffocating them all with silence.

At last, Miss Gatrell set down her fork. "Professor, what exactly do you teach?"

He sighed. "My field of study is meteorology, but I teach a variety of applied sciences."

"The weather? Hence the balloon for observation?" He nodded, and Miss Gatrell went on. "I was recently discussing with Miss Mason the need for our students to have a course in applied sciences. However, I fear our coursework already has the three of us stretched thin. Perhaps you could augment their education by offering a few classes to those who are interested."

Ella's head snapped up. "Professor Knott will be busy repairing his balloon and recuperating. We don't want to inconvenience him."

"Nonsense, it wouldn't be any inconvenience. I'd love to teach your young scholars." He placed his hand on Ella's arm. "After all, I believe you said how important it was for your girls to have every advantage if they're to become women of influence. In today's world, every lady ought to have a firm grasp of the sciences."

Miss Gatrell clapped her hands together. "Perfect. I was scheduled to begin a bridge club tomorrow afternoon but I will announce a change in plans if that works for you, Professor?"

He turned to Ella. "If Miss Mason agrees."

"It seems as if it's all arranged." She forced a smile. "Professor Knott and I can discuss the particulars after dinner."

If he hadn't been watching closely, he'd have missed the tremble of the fork in her hand. He was getting to her. Strong, sure of herself Ella Mason was watching her neat little world unravel.

Chapter 5

Ella marched outside to the school's north portico with Titus following behind. A cool breeze ruffled her dress, but did nothing to assuage the heat of anger building inside her.

She whirled toward Titus. "What did you think you were doing? I know full well that you are aware of the difference between a fish and a dinner fork. And slurping soup? How could you, Titus? You made me look like a fool."

"What? How?"

"These young ladies are my responsibility. They know we are acquainted, so anything you do reflects on me."

"I think you're exaggerating."

"Don't you understand what I'm teaching these girls?" Anger burned in her chest and her stomach cinched tight. "I want them to do the right thing at the right time for the right reason. I want to live in harmony with others, but I know there will be a time and a place for them to take a stand on something. When that time comes, it's my hope that they will have established themselves as ladies of influence."

"You're stuck in the past, Ella." He leaned on his cane. "Today's modern lady doesn't have to have impeccable manners or a profound knowledge of Latin for someone to listen to them. Come out of the dark ages you seem to love so dearly."

"Are you wearing petticoats under that suit?" She tugged on his pant leg. "You have no idea what a woman must do or not do in order to be taken seriously. This isn't a game. These young ladies will go into the real world and be expected to be knowledgeable in nearly every area—manners, art, music, mathematics, the classics. If they can show they are well educated, then perhaps others will listen to their opinions on all kinds of social matters."

She sank down on a bench and drew in a deep breath. She needed to get control of herself. Everything in life had come easily to Titus. He was smart, handsome, and charming. His parents, though not well off, had never discouraged a single one of his outlandish dreams.

Still, he was a man of science. Wouldn't he listen to reason?

First, she needed to stop lecturing him. She looked up at him. The man who'd been her first sweetheart stood before her. But beyond their tender kisses, he'd also been her friend.

She patted the empty place next to her. Once he was seated, she took his hand. "What we teach the girls here could change the world. I know you think I cling to traditions, but I'm equipping women who will be fighting for the right to vote, for the right to make their own choices, for the rights of the poor, and for the rights of children. I may not be a fighter, but I'm building an army of strong women who will be able to fight for anything they choose."

"You do make quite a general." He chuckled and traced the back of her hand with his thumb. "And I think you're quite a fighter."

"So you won't undermine my authority here?"

"I never meant to do that." He grew quiet for a moment. "I simply miss my friend. It's hard to be near you and feel a distance between us. It was never like that before, and to be honest, no one has ever enchanted me the way you do. Can we at least be friends again, Ella?"

A whiff of his sandalwood soap reached her nose, mixing with his words to create a spell around her heart. But pretty words had never been hard for Titus. Thank goodness, he'd have his balloon patched and repaired soon. What could it hurt to extend friendship for a few days?

She released his hand and pushed to her feet. "Friends, Titus. Nothing more."

Chapter 6

Ella walked to the chalkboard in front of her literature class. She often took the last part of the lesson to share a quote by her favorite educator, John Dewey. Her students would then discuss the quote at length.

She pointed to the words she'd written on the board before class and then blinked. The quote she'd selected had been replaced. She recognized the masculine writing as that of Titus.

"Apparently, today's quote by Dr. Dewey is 'Every great advance in science has issued from a new audacity of imagination.'" She read the words aloud with a smile. Did he never give up? "So, ladies, what do you think Dr. Dewey meant?"

Opal's hand shot up and Ella called on her. "I think he meant that imagination is important even to scientists."

"Very good, Opal." She glanced around the room. "Anyone else? Lizzy, you seem to be thinking. What's on your mind?"

The girl toyed with her braid. "I think the most important word in that quote is audacity."

Ella took a step closer. "Go on, Lizzy."

"I think he's saying that all scientific advancements came from thinking beyond the accepted. That someone had to think of the outlandish possibility first."

Applause came from the doorway. Ella turned to see Titus. She gave him a stern look, then motioned him inside. "Professor, would you like to comment on our discussion?"

"I have no need." He made a bow in front of Lizzy. "As this young woman has already brilliantly expounded on Dr. Dewey's point." The girls giggled and he waited until they quieted. "Ladies, Miss Mason has allowed me to offer you the opportunity to attend an optional science lecture today after your classes. We will be discussing the power of the audacious thinker. So, if you're of a mind to come, put on your outlandish thinking cap and meet us outside on the portico."

Chatter broke out among the girls. No doubt he'd charmed them all into attending his lecture, and by the end of the day, these girls would secure the rest of the students as well.

"Ladies." When no one responded to Ella, she scowled at Titus, then crossed her arms over her chest. "Ladies." She spoke louder. "Class is not over."

Titus shrugged and lifted his hands in a gesture of innocence.

She sighed and clapped her hands. Titus might see himself as an audacious thinker, but it was chaos that seemed to follow him wherever he went.

Brilliant, magnetic chaos.

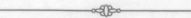

If he had to guess, Titus believed every girl in the school had turned out for his lecture. He'd set up his supplies in hopes of capturing both the students' interest and imaginations, including a Bunsen burner he found tucked in a closet. If he were honest with himself, he also had to admit a secret hope of winning Ella's approval. She loved her girls, and if he could win them, perhaps he could win her as well.

"Good afternoon, ladies." He glanced around the group and spotted Ella, Miss Young, and Miss Gatrell all watching from the side. "Thank you all for coming. While I love all science, meteorology is my favorite. Does anyone know what that is?"

Of course one of the girls thought he studied meteors, but another correctly identified the science of weather. "Today, I'd like us to make a cloud." Murmurs of excitement rippled through the crowd. "But I'll need some assistance. Who would like to help?"

Several hands shot in the air, and he selected a young lady he learned was named Georgia Bellows.

"All right, Miss Bellows. Do you know how clouds are made?"

"No, sir. I don't think so."

"Then you are in for a treat." He motioned her toward the table where he'd laid out the supplies. "Clouds, ladies, are formed when the invisible water vapor in the air condenses into visible water droplets or ice crystals. So basically, a cloud is a large collection of very tiny water droplets. The drops are so small and light that they can float in the air." He lit the flame beneath the Bunsen burner and set a water-filled beaker above it. "All air contains water, but near the ground it is usually in the form of an invisible gas called water vapor."

"Miss Bellows, would you please pick up that milk jar and set it over here?" After she complied, he went on. "I'd like you to pour about an inch of this boiling water into the jar and swirl it around."

Miss Bellows used the tongs attached to the beaker to pour the water into the milk jar, then swished the hot water around. "Is that sufficient?"

"Perfect." He pointed to the bottle's cap. "Now, I'd like you to place the milk jar's cap upside down on top of the jar." He paused and watched her complete the task. "When I tell you to, place a piece of ice from that bowl onto the lid for a few seconds. Then, here's the important part. On my signal, lift the lid. I'll blow this chalk dust into the jar and you can put the lid back in place. Understand?"

She nodded and he signaled her to begin. She reached for a piece of ice and set it in place. Just as he'd described, she lifted the lid, and he blew the chalk dust into the jar. Once she'd replaced the lid, *ooh*'s and *aah*'s came from the onlookers as a cloud formed in the milk jar.

"Time to release your cloud, Miss Bellows. Go ahead and lift the cap."

As soon as she did, the tiny cloud escaped and rose.

"Now, Miss Bellows, cloud maker extraordinaire, what do you think goes into making a cloud?"

She shrugged. "I don't know."

"Yes, you do. Let's put the pieces together." He pointed to the boiling water. "What about this? What kind of air do we need?"

"Warm, moist air?"

"Exactly!" He moved to the ice. "And what did this do to that air?"

She bit her lip, then smiled. "It cooled it."

"Yes!" He picked up a piece of chalk. "This is the tricky part. What happened when I blew the chalk dust into the jar?"

She cocked her head to the side. "That's when the cloud formed, right?"

He nodded. "It was. Clouds need a cloud condensation nuclei or very small particle that can float in the air to help the water vapor condense into clouds. Sometimes it is sea salt in the air, but it can also be dust, smoke, or volcanic ash. When billions of these droplets come together, they create a visible cloud." Bringing his hands together, he said, "Let's give Miss Bellows a round of applause."

When the clapping ended, he asked if the students had any questions. To his delight, they had many. Why are clouds white? Why do they turn gray? Why do clouds float? How do clouds move? And why are there different kinds of clouds?

He had the young ladies sit down before he began to answer their questions. He hadn't planned for his lecture to go on so long, but he saw something in them that made his heart sing. Many of these young ladies possessed a curiosity—even a hunger—for knowledge. Perhaps Ella, with all of her classics, hadn't stolen the joy of discovery from them after all.

He glanced in her direction and found her smile warm and approving. She mouthed the words "thank you" and his chest swelled. Beside her, an unfamiliar lady had joined them. Her pinched face seemed less than impressed with his lecture. Would she voice her displeasure to Ella? And if she did, would his efforts be dashed before they'd scarcely begun?

Chapter 7

Ella invited Opal's mother, Mrs. Docia Finnerty, to her office for lemonade, despite her desire to send the woman away. Mrs. Finnerty, a gossipy know-it-all, had a habit of showing up unannounced and uninvited, but Ella knew that an important part of her position as principal was listening to the concerns of her girls' parents.

"Just who was that man?" Mrs. Finnerty asked even before Ella could close the office door.

"His name is Professor Knott." Ella poured lemonade from a fat-bodied Limoges pitcher into a matching tumbler. The green and deep-purple grape design painted on both the pitcher and the tumblers matched the décor of her office perfectly, and the gold-rimmed accent was a detail often appreciated by the mothers with whom she spoke. Mrs. Finnerty, however, said nothing about the lavish tumbler. "Professor Knott's balloon crashed on the property the other day, and he's offered to provide some classes while he recovers from his injuries and makes repairs to his balloon."

"But he's a *man*."

"Yes, ma'am, he is."

"What if he isn't who he says he is? What if he's a con man or some kind of criminal?"

Ella had to fight back laughter. "Criminals don't generally fly around in balloons, Mrs. Finnerty. Besides, I know Professor Knott. We attended high school together. Professor Knott went on to the university while I attended Christian Female College."

"But this is a school for girls. Why would you let a man teach them? I did not enroll my Opal thinking some stranger was going to drop in and teach her about clouds."

The grating sound of Mrs. Finnerty's voice only added to the irritation of her comments. Ella drew in a calming breath. "Ma'am, I understand your concerns, but having a professor of Mr. Knott's quality instruct our young women, if even for a short time, is an opportunity I would hate for them to miss. In fact, I'd consider myself negligent if I let this chance pass by. Did you see how enthralled the girls were with his lecture? They were hanging on his every word."

"Of course they were." The mother frowned. "He was flattering that plain Miss Bellows left and right. Everyone knows she doesn't have half the intelligence of my Opal."

"*Both* girls have excelled academically." Ella took a cool drink from her glass. "I believe Professor Knott asked for volunteers and randomly selected Miss Bellows. Your Opal would have made a fine volunteer as well."

Mrs. Finnerty frowned, set her tumbler aside, and stood. "This drop-out-of-the-sky professor may have hoodwinked you, but I'm not so easily persuaded. I'll be keeping my eye on him, Miss Mason, and you'd do well to do the same. Remember, these girls are quite impressionable, and I'm sure other parents would agree. What would they think of you entertaining a man inside the school?"

"Entertaining?" Ella's eyes widened. "Professor Knott was injured and couldn't be moved. Now that he's better, he's moved in with Clementine and Ernest in the caretaker's house."

"But my Opal told me he'd been up in the girls' quarters."

"To put out a fire." Ella pushed to her feet, anger niggling its way to the surface. "Mrs. Finnerty, I take my position as principal very seriously." She kept her voice even and her demeanor calm. "I would do nothing to jeopardize these girls academically, emotionally, or morally, but please remember it is also my job to see that they receive the very best education I can offer, and right now, that education includes lectures by Professor Knott. He can teach them scientific matters we cannot. Please do not attempt to stir up problems where there are none."

"Well," Mrs. Finnerty huffed. "I never—"

Ella had overstepped, but she did she really care? Mrs. Finnerty had no right coming into her school and telling her who should and should not teach, and implying that her decisions had somehow put the students in danger. Still, she couldn't have a busybody like this mother telling tales to the other parents.

But before she could offer an apology, Mrs. Finnerty yanked open the door and marched from the room.

What had Ella done? Let her pride get in the way of prudence? She not only loved these girls and the school, but she was also proud of all that had been accomplished here.

And more than that, she'd been proud of Titus today too. Watching him awaken such a sense of awe and curiosity in her girls almost brought tears to her eyes. He was an outstanding educator. Why didn't Mrs. Finnerty see that? The woman seemed determined to see character flaws where there were none.

Ella almost laughed. Did Titus have character flaws? He certainly did, but Mrs. Finnerty didn't need to know what they were. He had always been the dreamer, the audacious thinker. His quest for knowledge outweighed everything, including love and making wise choices.

But even if Ella wasn't fully convinced of Titus's character, she had no doubt about his intelligence. She never had. Without a doubt, he'd always been the smartest man she'd ever met, and based on what she saw today, he could teach the girls a great deal in very little time.

So despite Mrs. Finnerty's threats, Ella would not deny the young ladies in her care access to Titus's great mind. Their education was more important than her position.

Besides, he'd be gone in less than a week, going wherever the wind blew.

Chapter 8

Living in the caretaker's home had its challenges. The stairs Titus could manage. The inhabitants, however, put him on edge. He sat at the kitchen table and looked over at Ernest, a man of few words. Very few.

For Titus, silence always begged to be filled with conversation, but since he didn't sense that would be welcomed, he kept his mouth shut until he felt as if he'd burst.

He swallowed the last drop of his coffee. "I was thinking I could take a look at my balloon this evening. Your wife said you put it in the barn. I appreciate your gathering and storing it for me."

"Couldn't leave it hanging in the trees, could I?" Ernest pushed back from the table and stood. He started for the door and stopped. "You coming?"

Titus jumped up, knocking his cane over in the process. "Yes, sir."

Ernest chuckled. "Well, come on."

The short distance between the house and the barn would have worn Titus out a couple of days ago, but today he managed without being out of breath. The pain in his ribs was now only a dull ache too. Standing in front of the students earlier today had reminded him of how much he enjoyed teaching and had filled him with a sense of purpose, even if it would last only a few days.

Inside the barn, he spotted four horses in stalls and a half-dozen milk cows. A tiger-striped cat sat preening on a stack of hay. Titus rubbed his chin. He'd not thought about it, but the school was on a significant plot of land that would have to be tended and possibly farmed. Did Ernest take care of all of it by himself? Titus's respect for the quiet man grew exponentially.

"Your balloon is over there." Ernest pointed to a corner of the barn.

The colorful blue and yellow silk balloon was stuffed inside the basket. The anchor, rope, and sacks of ballast lay beside it. Titus prayed that the burner was there too.

He ran his hand along the wicker basket, and its familiar texture made him itch for the air. He pushed the silk fabric aside and discovered the burner, and to his delight, the aneroid barometer. The oak-encased instrument, a graduation gift from his favorite professor, not only showed the barometric pressure, it could determine altitude. He tipped it over and smiled. It seemed to be in excellent condition.

Or was it? He tapped the glass lens, but the needle remained steadfast on the word "change" and it seemed to be heading toward the word "rainy." Had he been so distracted he'd not noticed the weather? Perhaps he'd hit his head harder than he thought.

With the barometer in hand, he walked outside and tipped his gaze upward. An ominous green-gray sky greeted him, and cumulonimbus clouds churned on the horizon. He sniffed the air. The west wind carried the smell of damp earth. He studied the birds. All seemed to be flying low. A small herd of cattle on the hillside clustered together. Not a good sign.

He glanced again at the barometer as dark nimbostratus clouds blew in. The tree branches swayed in the gusty breeze. The barometric pressure dropped farther and now read "stormy." Between the reading, the wind, the birds, and his gut instinct, he felt a storm coming on, and if this rapid decline in conditions was any indication, it was going to be a big one.

He hurried into the barn. "Ernest! What do you do with the girls when there's a bad storm?"

"Like a twister?"

"Yes. Exactly."

Ernest scratched his head. "Miss Mason and the others usually shuffle them off to the cellar. They don't like it much. They claim it's full of cobwebs. Why?"

"I think one is coming."

"You sure?"

He didn't waste any more time giving Ernest an answer. Instead, as fast as his injured ankle and cane could carry him, he made his way to the main building, rain now pelting his face.

In the front hall, he yanked the bell cord over and over until the girls came running. Clementine rounded the corner. "What in heaven's name are you doing?"

"Is there another fire?" Miss Birmingham asked.

"No, a bad storm." He raised his voice. "Ladies, we need to get to the cellar as soon as possible."

Grumbling and whining filled the hall. Their instructors tried to calm them.

They didn't have time to coddle the girls. "Ladies! Move, now!"

They grew silent and followed the teachers ushering them toward the stairs. He scanned the group. Where was Ella?

Ella didn't like the clouds forming in the sky. When she and Opal had ridden out, she'd not seen anything that signified rain, but now, she wasn't so sure.

"We'd better head back, Opal." She nudged her quarter horse to pick up its pace.

Opal did likewise. "Miss Mason, I want to apologize again for my mother's intrusion into school affairs."

"You don't need to apologize, Opal." Ella glanced at the young lady. When Opal had asked to speak with her privately, Ella had thought a ride a pleasant way to spend time together. Opal was one of her brightest students, and she certainly didn't need to carry any responsibility for her mother's actions. Still, Ella didn't want to encourage a rift between Opal and her mother. "Your mother is simply concerned about you. As your parent, that's her job. As your teacher, helping you grow academically is mine."

Opal skirted a dip in the path. "But I like Professor Knott. I don't want him to have to go. My mother says either he goes or I'll have to."

Ella sucked in her breath. She should never have crossed the woman. "I'm sure it won't come to that. Professor Knott won't be staying long."

"Did you and your mother ever disagree?"

Ella seldom shared her personal life, but Opal seemed to need the disclosure. "We never truly got along, Opal. My home life was chaotic."

"What do you mean?" The girl's voice rose over the wind.

"Every day was something new." Ella had to nearly shout to respond, but she wanted to keep Opal calm and figured their conversation was the best way to do so. "One year we had a big Christmas with a tree and a goose like in *A Christmas Carol*, and the next year, my mother forgot about Christmas completely."

"How horrible. You must have been devastated."

"I found solace where I always had. In my books." A wind gust tore Ella's hat from her head and sent it spiraling into the trees. "Enough talk. We need to get going. Opal, can you handle your horse at a gallop?"

"Yes, miss. I think so." Opal wiped raindrops from her cheek. "And if I can't, I'd better learn fast, right?"

"You'll do fine. Just follow my lead."

No sooner had she spoken the words, than a crack of lightning split the gray sky. Opal screamed. Ella's horse surged beneath her, bolting across the pasture.

"Miss Mason, hold on!"

Chapter 9

Contrary to everything she wanted to do, Ella forced herself to ease up on the reins. Her father had told her long ago that horses are flight animals. They run and lose their heads when they are afraid. "You," he said, "must keep your head."

With rain beating her face, Ella lifted the reins. To run at full speed, her horse would need his head down. If she could raise it, it would slow him. She grabbed a handful of mane at the crest of her horse's neck, just above the withers. Then, stepping down in her stirrups, she leaned back. She'd need the strength in the saddle to slow the horse. Holding only one rein in her right hand, Ella lifted her elbow and pulled back.

With his head turned, the horse was momentarily unbalanced. Would he slow and turn?

She kept her pressure firm. Finally, his mind seemed to reengage and he responded. He turned, trotting sideways, and then came to a stop at last. Ella stared into the distance from whence she'd come. Wind whipped the branches in unnatural directions. She raised her hand, trying to shield her eyes from the drenching rain. Where was Opal?

Movement to her left caught her attention and relief filled Ella's heart at the sight of Opal's horse. The girl reined her horse in. "Miss Mason, are you all right?"

"Yes." Ella's heart hammered against her ribs. With the storm raging around them, what was the best course? There was no place where they could take shelter, but riding back now could be equally as dangerous. And what if they'd gotten completely turned around? They could be heading away from the school rather than toward it.

"Opal, do you know which way the school is?" Ella shouted.

"Isn't it this way?" Opal pointed across the meadow. "Those are the trees I painted the other day."

"Perfect." Ella urged her horse into a trot. "And Opal, you're a genius."

No matter how often Titus peered into the storm, there was no sign of Ella and Opal. After a head count, he'd learned that the schoolgirl, too, was missing. When Clementine and Ernest came to take shelter in the cellar, Ernest told him that the two of them had gone for a ride. Ernest said Miss Mason often did that, taking one girl out for a little special time.

Titus wanted to go after them, but Clementine said it was foolish to do so. He had no idea where Ella and Opal had ridden, and his injured leg might make it impossible to ride.

"She can take care of herself," Clementine said. "She's done it for years without you, Professor."

So now, while everyone was tucked in the cellar, he remained on guard at the window, his chest squeezed so tight he could scarcely breathe.

A dark spot appeared in the distance. He stepped outside, wind and leaves pelting his face. Two horses neared. Were they riderless?

No. He released the breath he was holding. They reached the yard and stopped. Opal dismounted and raced for the house, but Ella took the reins of the girl's horse and headed toward the barn.

What was she doing?

A branch near the barn cracked and came down with a swoosh.

Opal raced up the steps and he pulled her inside. "Go down to the cellar with the others. The storm is getting worse."

"But Miss Mason—I can't leave her out there."

He gave the girl a gentle shove. "Go on. I'll take care of her. I promise."

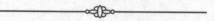

Both horses deserved a good rubdown, but Ella dared not take the time to do it. Once inside the barn, she heaved the barn door shut and bolted it. She unsaddled the tired beasts and put them in their stalls then tossed a wool blanket on each of them. Thankfully, Ernest had filled their feedbags with oats.

The wind howled through the hayloft and something pinged against the tin cupolas. Hail? She hurried to the side door and cracked it open. The wind grabbed it and swung it wide. She attempted to pull it shut, but it wouldn't come. The hail she'd heard suddenly stopped. She needed to get to the school and make sure her students had taken shelter.

Could she make a run for it now?

Chapter 10

Holding a blanket over his head, Titus opened the front door, prepared to bolt to the barn. Torrential rains fell, lightning zig-zagged across the sky, and trees bowed low in the violent wind gusts. An ominous roar filled the air. Then, he saw it. A rope tornado reaching from the sky toward the earth less than a mile away.

Lord, please, no.

He slammed the door shut again, a sickened feeling in his stomach. He'd never make it to the barn, not with a twister out there. Common sense told him to join the others in the cellar, but the meteorologist in him couldn't tear himself away. Instead of going down to the cellar, he ran up the stairs to the windows, thankful his injuries had healed enough to permit the strenuous movement. Here, no trees blocked his view. All his life he'd wanted to see a cyclone close, but looking at one forming so near both fascinated and terrified him.

The windows shook against the pull as the tornado approached. Glass shattered somewhere down the hall. The twister, while small, uprooted trees and spewed them out like weeds picked from a garden. Then, just as quickly as it had formed, the tornado rose back into the clouds.

Ella! Forgetting his cane, Titus limped down the stairs, thanking God that none of the school's buildings had received a direct hit. But had there been damage? Was Ella all right?

He paused at the cellar door only long enough to yell down the stairs. He told them the worst part of the storm had passed, but to wait ten minutes before they left the safety of the cellar.

Titus hobbled across the yard toward the barn, hating that the short distance was taking so long to traverse. Every beat of his heart pounded Ella's name, praying she'd taken cover in some part of the barn. At least he could see the structure was still standing. What would he do if he found her injured?

He unlatched the barn door and threw it wide. "Ella! Ella! Where are you?"

She stepped out of the tack room. He rushed to her and drew her against his chest. She trembled in his arms. After a few seconds, he took hold of her shoulders and urged her back far enough that he could see her face. "Are you hurt?"

"No. Wet, cold, and scared, but not hurt." She rubbed her arms. "What about the girls? Are they safe? The school?"

He shrugged out of his suit coat and draped it around her. "I had your students and staff take shelter when I saw the storm coming. Even Clementine and Ernest were in the cellar when the twister came, so everyone is fine, but I didn't take time to see if there was any damage to the school."

"It was a tornado then?" She paled, swaying slightly.

He took hold of her cold hands and drew in a deep breath. "You were out here alone—I've never been so scared in my life."

She gave him a weak smile. "You crashed a balloon last week. I think you've had more frightening experiences than what happened to me."

"No, Ella." His brow furled and his lips pressed in a thin line. "I was more afraid today. I couldn't bear to lose you again."

Silence stretched between them. Had he said too much? He ached to draw her into his arms, but it was too soon. She hadn't turned him away, but she was like a colt in need of a gentle hand. She didn't trust him. Why should she? He'd been so young and full of himself back then. Now, he needed to prove himself over and over before she could believe his words were true.

Ella shifted from foot to foot, biting her lower lip. "Shall we go see if there's any damage? I want to see my girls."

Unwilling to break the connection between them, he kept hold of her hand and led her to the barn door. He hoped she sensed the unsaid message he wanted her to hear. Whatever they found out there, they'd face it together.

Chapter 11

Glass littered the portico from a broken window on the second floor, and Ella skirted the pieces as she made her way to the front door with Titus right behind her. She flew up the stairs and hurried inside.

Shrill conversation came from the parlor and dining room. Whenever the girls were excited, their pitches seemed to elevate. She could hear no wailing and for that she was immensely grateful.

"Miss Mason!" Opal, the first to spot her, came running over. "Are you all right?"

"I'm fine." She removed Titus's suit coat and returned it to him. "Was anyone injured?"

Miss Young drew near. "Thanks to Professor Knott, everyone is safe."

"Ladies." Ella spoke loudly. "Please remain inside. Some windows have shattered, and I don't want anyone getting cut before we can clean up the mess. If your room is one that lost its window, please sleep in a friend's room. Right now, Professor Knott, Ernest, Clementine, and I are going out to survey the property. Return to your rooms and prepare for bed. I'm afraid there will be much brush to clear tomorrow." She paused and took in the tear-streaked faces of her students. "And be sure to say a prayer of thanksgiving for God's providence in this storm. We have truly been blessed today."

Miss Young and Miss Gatrell herded the young ladies, still atwitter after the evening's adventure, up the stairs.

Titus turned to Ella. "Do you want to get out of your wet things? We'll wait."

Clementine crossed her arms over her ample chest. "She most certainly does. We can't have her catching her death."

Ella started to protest, but could see from the set of Clementine's mouth that she needn't waste her breath. She hurried to her quarters, shed the damp clothes, and put on an Oxford-gray skirt and pale-pink shirtwaist. Since her riding boots were soaked through as well, she put on a pair of low-heeled shoes and did up the laces. She glanced in the mirror and decided the only hope for her hair, which now hung loose, was to secure it in a braid and put on a wide-brimmed straw boater.

Downstairs, Titus waited with Ernest and Clementine in the parlor.

He smiled when he saw her. "You look like you did in school."

She laughed. "That bad?"

"You look fine." Clementine waddled between them toward the door. "Let's go see what we have out there. Ernest, you coming, or you staying in here lollygagging?"

"I'm right behind you, dear." He took long strides and reached the door first. He held it open for her and Ella caught a rare twinkle in the man's eye. He truly loved his wife, warts and all. Would she ever have that kind of love?

Outside, a fresh rain scent greeted them. The storm had blown over and the sky was clear, with a gauzy orange-red sunset on the horizon. How odd that only half an hour before they were in the center of a tempest.

The number of broken branches and torn limbs took Ella's breath away. A few trees seemed stripped of all of their leaves.

"Oh, my stars!" Clementine pressed a hand to her chest.

Ella turned to follow her friend's line of sight. She sucked in a breath, then wrapped an arm around Clementine's shoulders. Although it seemed the school and barn had been spared damage for the most part, the caretaker's house had not. An uprooted tree had destroyed the front porch. Was there additional damage to the house that they couldn't see?

The foursome carefully crossed the leaf- and branch-littered yard. The fallen tree looked much larger lying on the ground than it ever had while standing. While it hadn't directly fallen on the house, the largest branches had taken out the porch and sliced open the upstairs bedroom.

Titus lifted his gaze to the damage. "Well, I'm certainly glad I wasn't sleeping in that room."

"That's your room?" Ella's face paled. "Obviously, you can't stay there until we get it repaired. None of you can sleep here until we fix the house."

Ernest picked up a limb. "Clementine and I can go in and out the back door, Miss Mason. We'll be fine, but the professor may have to go back to the school for a few days."

Clementine met Ella's gaze with a look of warning. She knew what Clementine was thinking. Having Titus back within the school's walls would only give Opal's mother more ammunition. But it couldn't be helped. What kind of example would she be to the girls if she turned out the man who'd saved them all not once, but twice?

Titus touched her elbow. "Ella, maybe it's time I found a place in town to stay."

"That might be a good solution, Miss Mason." Clementine moved to stand beside Ernest. "With Opal's mother on the warpath—"

"No." Ella squared her shoulders. This was her school. No parent was going to push her to do his or her bidding. "That won't be necessary. We have cleanup to do here, and we can use your assistance. Besides, you have a balloon to repair."

Even as she said them, the words stung. Once he'd made his repairs, Titus would be free to fly away. A dot on the horizon like she'd once painted in a landscape. A lifetime ago.

Last week, his departure couldn't have happened soon enough, but now she wasn't sure what she wanted except for this horrendous day to finally be over.

A carriage, driven at a high rate of speed, rumbled into the drive. Ella stopped her stick gathering and looked up.

The lady inside the carriage didn't wait to be helped down. Hands aflutter, she strutted across the lawn. "Opal? Opal, where are you?"

Opal hurried to her mother. Mrs. Finnerty drew her daughter into a smothering embrace. Finally, she released her. "I came as soon as I heard there'd been a storm out in this direction. Are you hurt?" She didn't wait for an answer. "And what on earth are you doing with that rake? I do not pay this school for you to do manual labor."

Ella had left her "troops" and followed Opal. She draped an arm around the girl's shoulder. "Today, we are all working together and learning about comradery. We had quite a scare, but everyone is fine. Tomorrow, classes will resume." She pointed to a table set with tall glasses of lemonade. "Would you care for a cool drink, Mrs. Finnerty?"

"Yes, Mother. Let's have a glass. You sit down and I'll bring you some lemonade." Opal scurried away.

Ella directed Mrs. Finnerty to the chairs they'd uprighted earlier that morning. A cool breeze ruffled Ella's hair and she patted it back in place. She sat down beside Opal's mother and sighed. She had more important things to do right now than hold Mrs. Finnerty's hand.

That wasn't fair. Of course any mother would be concerned after hearing the news. She made a mental note to have all the girls write letters home explaining the events and make sure their parents knew they were safe.

Opal returned with three glasses. She handed one to each of the ladies, then sat down with her own. "We were never in danger, Mother. Professor Knott saw the storm coming and sent us all to the cellar."

"Professor Knott?" Mrs. Finnerty whirled toward Ella. "He is still here?"

All compassion flitted from Ella's thoughts. She recalled what Opal had told her. That either Titus left or Opal would have to. The very idea made Ella fist her hands. "Yes, ma'am. I told you he was staying, and we are grateful he did. If it hadn't been for him, we would not have known to take shelter from the impending storm. He's been staying in the caretaker's house."

"That house?" She pointed to the damaged structure.

Ella nodded. "We'll have the tree cleared and repairs made straightaway."

Titus hobbled over and introduced himself. Ella stifled a laugh at the charm he seemed to be pouring on as thick as maple syrup on a stack of pancakes. He then dismissed himself to return to his work.

"I must say he's an affable fellow." Mrs. Finnerty sipped at her lemonade. "But I still don't think it's proper to have a man around here."

"There's always a man around here—Ernest. Remember?"

"But he's married to Clementine. Your professor is a handsome bachelor." She glanced around the storm site. "Are you certain that house is habitable?"

"It is," Opal piped up. "Except for the guest room upstairs."

Mrs. Finnerty narrowed her eyes at Ella. "Isn't that where you said the professor is staying?"

"He'll return to the house as soon as repairs are made."

"Return from where?" When Ella didn't answer, she abruptly stood. "Opal, gather your things. You're coming home."

Opal looked from Ella to her mother. "What's wrong? What did I say?"

"You did nothing wrong, Opal." Ella laid a hand on the girl's shoulder. "But you should do as your mother says."

"No." Opal spoke softly, but with more determination than Ella had ever heard from the young lady. "No, I'm not going."

"What did you say?" Her mother's pitch rose.

"With all due respect, Mother, I'm not leaving." Opal drew in a deep breath. "You placed me here to be educated and that is exactly what has taken place. I have learned how to speak my own mind, and more importantly, when I must do so. I believe this is such a time. Professor Knott has done nothing wrong and neither has Miss Mason. I am staying here."

Mrs. Finnerty pointed an accusing finger at Ella. "What have you done to my daughter?"

"Only encouraged her God-given mind to think." Ella wanted to rant, to release all her pent-up thoughts of Mrs. Finnerty's ignorance, but she held her tongue. "Mrs. Finnerty, I understand your concerns for Opal. Truly I do. But I can assure you that Professor Knot will be back in the caretaker's house in two days, and gone for good by next week."

"Are you giving me your word?"

"Yes, ma'am. I am."

Mrs. Finnerty sniffed. "Then, you can stay, Opal—for the week."

A little thrill of victory filled Ella's heart. Her student—Opal—had spoken up for herself. She'd put together a thoughtful and valid argument in a matter of seconds. If Opal could stand up to her mother in a respectful way, who knew where God would take this young woman and what battles He had for her to fight?

She glanced across the yard to see Titus working. Cane tossed aside now, he looked up from his sawing and smiled at Ella. He tugged off his leather gloves and wiped his brow with a handkerchief.

What had she just done? What had she promised Mrs. Finnerty? Titus would be gone in one week? What if he couldn't get his repairs done in that time?

And most of all, what if she didn't want him to go?

Chapter 12

Inside the barn, Titus made his way to his balloon, still ensconced in the corner. The last few days had been full. He'd work beside Ernest most of the day and then teach a lecture in the afternoon. The girls had been full of questions about the tornado, and he'd been delighted to see their fascination with weather. Now, with the tornado cleanup complete, he finally had time to begin repairs to his balloon.

With Ernest's help, he moved the basket and its contents outside. Together, they withdrew the envelope and spread it on the lawn. Then, without a word, Ernest departed for the barn.

Titus tugged on the balloon's edge, smoothing it out, looking for tears. Thankfully, his injuries seemed to have healed fairly well. His head no longer ached, and he could function despite the occasional pinch in his ribs. He also found that once he wrapped his ankle, he could manage a full day's work with only a slight limp.

He glanced toward the school expecting young ladies to begin trickling out. The envelope's cornflower-blue and lemon-yellow vertical stripes were certain to draw a crowd, but he spotted only Ella crossing the lawn. His heart skipped a beat at the sight of her.

"It's bigger on the ground than it looks in the sky." Ella stopped beside the balloon.

"She's about 50 feet tall and three times that around her girth when inflated. Sixty-thousand cubic feet of pongee silk." He moved toward the top to meet her. "And it can hold two passengers of medium weight. Want a ride?"

She ignored his question. "Does she have a name?"

"Every aeronaut names his balloon. Mine is named *Elinor*."

Her mouth formed an *O*, but no sound came out. She cleared her throat. "For someone special?"

"Yes." He paused, then turned to her. "You. I believe your favorite character in *Sense and Sensibility* was Elinor."

"You remember?"

"I remember everything about you."

Her cheeks bloomed like pink roses. She pointed to a strip on the right. "Is that a tear?"

He chuckled at her ability to change the topic. "Sort of. It's the vent and it's supposed to be there." Then his gaze landed on a different spot. Carefully easing down to the ground, he examined the spot and wiggled his fingers in the gaping hole. "This, however, should not be here."

She settled on the grass beside him. "Can you repair it?"

"Yes, but it's going to take longer than I expected."

Her smiled faded. "How long?"

"I'm not sure, why? Are you anxious to get rid of me?" He flashed her a teasing grin.

"No, that's not it." She bit her lower lip. "Oh, never mind. What can I do to help?"

He explained the repair process, which included triple-sewing the tear in the silk and covering the area with four coats of varnish. "If you could work on the sewing part, I can get started repairing the burner."

"Can we remove this net?" She tugged on the spiderweb of rope stretched over the balloon's surface. "And what is this stuff? It's the toughest rope I've ever seen."

"We'll push it back so you can have better access. The net is made of Anjou hemp, treated with rubber. It keeps the balloon in place and attaches the basket to the balloon."

"And those?" She pointed toward the basket.

"One is a load ring and one a basket ring. Neither was damaged." He pushed to his feet and retrieved a leather pouch fastened inside the basket. He held it out to Ella. "This is my repair kit. It contains a long needle and silk thread. I never leave home without it, and no one besides me has ever used it."

She accepted the pouch as if it were a treasure. "I will endeavor to do it the honor it deserves."

He chuckled, took her hand, and placed a kiss on the back. "You'll have to provide your own thimble, my lady, lest you prick one of your lovely fingers."

Her colored heightened again and she pulled her hand away. "I'd best fetch it promptly then."

She lifted her skirt and glided across the lawn. Titus finally tore his gaze away from her retreating form. Their short time together this afternoon filled him with optimism. Their friendship felt rekindled, but there was more. She wanted to help him.

Did he dare hope that deep down she wanted to be near him?

Ella knelt on the lawn with a paintbrush in her hand. She drew the brush along the length of the repaired silk. The strong odor of the varnish made her wrinkle her nose. For the last two days, she'd devoted her afternoons to sewing the delicate silk. At first, she'd told herself it was because she had to keep her promise to Mrs. Finnerty, but then she had to admit the truth to herself.

Being with Titus brought her a kind of happiness and joy that she hadn't realized she'd been missing. Easy conversations, deep discussions, and even the casual exchange of the day's happenings all seemed more significant when they shared them with one another. This man—this Titus—was and wasn't the same person she'd parted ways with six years ago.

Sure, he had the same adventurous, fun-loving, charming, confident spirit, but he also had a new humility she found endearing. Still, he'd said nothing of God. The Titus she'd grown up with thought he didn't need God.

She glanced from the silk balloon in front of her toward the school. Today was the day she'd promised Mrs. Finnerty that Titus would be gone. She could tell the woman that his balloon was not yet in order, and that was true, but she needed to ask Titus to move to a hotel in town. And she needed to do it this afternoon.

In truth, she didn't want him to go.

"What's on your mind, Miss Mason?" Titus walked behind her chair and brushed her shoulder with his hand. He walked to the burner he had set up on a board laid across a pair of sawhorses and picked up a screwdriver.

"I was thinking about how much you've changed."

"And if I know you, you're wondering why?" He set down his screwdriver and wiped his hands on a rag. "Could we take a walk?"

She looked at him. A walk alone was far different than working side by side on a project in a public place.

He extended his open hand toward her. "Ella, just once, break the rules."

Drawing in a deep, steadying breath, she let him help her to her feet. It was a walk between friends. There was nothing wrong with that, right?

They started down a path that circled the outer rim of the property. It wove its way between the trees, but Ella knew the entire path was in full view of the school. While this gave their walk a level of propriety, it also made her feel vulnerable.

"Ella, I'm sorry for the way I acted in high school. I was an arrogant boy back then. You did the right thing in sending me away." He rubbed the back of his neck. "It hurt, but I thought I was destined for scientific greatness. Sooner or later, I thought you'd realize what you missed out on when you heard about my amazing discoveries or inventions." He gave a wry laugh. "I was so full of myself. I thought I knew everything."

"Mostly, you did." She gave him a sideways glance and smiled. "You were the smartest person I'd ever met. You knew more than the teachers."

"But I didn't know more than you."

"Really?" She gave a little laugh. "Maybe you hit your head harder than we thought. If I remember right, you thought my mind was full of fantasies because of all the books I read. You said if I'd read a few scientific books, I might actually find something useful."

"Ella." He stopped on the path. "You knew my words were full of hot air. You knew I wasn't the man I needed to be. The man you needed me to be. The man God was calling me to be."

"God?" Her voice came out as barely more than a whisper. "That was the main reason I broke it off with you. You said you didn't believe in God."

"A prodigal can return."

Tears filled Ella's eyes. "I thought you'd changed, but I didn't know. I wanted it to be because of Jesus, but I was afraid to ask."

He thumbed away the tear making its way down her satiny cheek. "I've changed, Ella. I want to be the man you always thought I could be. I'm not asking you to let me into your heart. For now, I just want you to let me be in your life."

Her pulse quickened, and she unglued her eyes from him. He was asking so much and yet so little. She'd always taken the safe path, but Titus would never be the least bit safe to love. If she said yes even to this, he'd have a hold on her heart all over again.

Chapter 13

Walking back to the school in silence, Titus fought the urge to stop Ella and kiss her until she forgot about her school and her passion for teaching, and thought of nothing but him. But that wouldn't be fair, and he couldn't put her in that position. So, he kept a respectful distance at her side and waited for her to answer his request.

She stopped when they reached the edge of the portico. "I'm afraid, Titus."

"Of what?"

"Losing you and losing myself." She looked at the building. "And losing this place and these girls."

His throat tightened. "I understand."

"No, you don't." She turned to him. "Titus, you can't possibly know what it means to love two things and realize you can't have them both. You've always believed you could have anything you want. Fly in the clouds? You did it. Go to a university? You did that too." She wrapped her arms around her midsection. "You can have it all—a family, your dreams, your inventions—but I can't love you and keep my position here. Because I'm a woman, I can have only one."

"So, you choose Rosewood Meadow?"

She shook her head. "I don't know. I need time."

"Ella, I might be able to have it all, but I'm willing to give it all up for you."

The front door opened and a middle-aged woman marched down the stairs toward them with a suitcase and Opal in tow. "You ought to be ashamed of yourself! Carousing with this man in plain sight."

"I beg your pardon." Titus stepped between Ella and the distraught woman. "We have not been carousing. We simply went for a walk."

The woman, whom he guessed was Opal's mother, jabbed a finger in Titus's chest. "Why is he still here?"

Ella nudged Titus out of the way. "I can address this, Titus. Please."

Reluctantly, Titus stepped back. He glanced at Opal, her eyes red-rimmed. Had her mother made her cry? And why was she carrying a suitcase?

"The balloon belonging to Mr. Titus Knott is not yet repaired. I know I gave you my word that he'd be gone in a week, and I apologize. I considered asking him to secure lodging at a hotel in the city, but the more I considered it, I realized traveling to and from the city would take away the time he needs to complete his work and would deprive our students of his valuable science lessons."

"Don't you mean deprive yourself of his companionship?" Opal's mother bit out.

Ella stiffened her shoulders, her lips pressed in a thin line. "As long as I'm the principal here, I will make decisions that I feel are in the best interest of my girls."

"Then we'll just see how long you remain in that post." The woman tugged on Opal's arm, pulling her along behind. When she reached the carriage, she stopped and turned. "He shouldn't be here. I've spoken to a number of Rosewood Meadow mothers, and they all agree. I know that Mrs. Rosewood-Dasher has returned from her trip, and I can assure you that she'll hear about this immediately. By morning, we'll all know her opinion on this matter. If I were you, I'd send that professor packing."

Ella's face blanched, but she didn't flinch. "It is your choice to speak to Mrs. Rosewood-Dasher, just as it is mine to allow the professor to remain. Opal, you are always welcome to return."

They watched the carriage rumble down the drive and turn onto the road amid a chorus of crickets and cicadas.

"Ella."

"Don't." She lifted the hem of her skirt and dashed inside, leaving Titus alone in the waning daylight.

A rock settled in the pit of Titus's stomach. What had he done? Why hadn't he counted the cost of his presence? He could have left days ago, but he'd wanted to stay and be near Ella. His whole life he'd done as he pleased, but had his lackadaisical attitude ruined everything for her?

He glanced across the yard where the balloon still lay on the grass. He couldn't repair the damage he'd done to Ella's position, but if he worked all night, he could repair the balloon and leave before dawn.

Young ladies crowded into the entry hall, but they cleared a path when Ella approached. They pummeled her with a barrage of questions.

"Miss Mason, why did Opal's mother make her leave?"

"Miss Mason, why was Opal's mother yelling at you?"

"Miss Mason, will Opal come back?"

"Miss Mason, where's Professor Knott?"

Ella reached the staircase, climbed four stairs, and turned to face the clutch of girls. She cleared her throat, trying to keep the tears at bay. "Young ladies, Opal's mother decided she wanted her daughter to leave for a while. I do not know the particulars." Her voice cracked and she took a deep breath to steady it. "I hope each of you know how much you mean to me. What do I always tell you that I want most from you?"

Isabelle raised her hand. "To do the right thing at the right time for the right reason."

"Exactly." Ella scanned the faces of the young women before her, trying to memorize each one. Her heart stumbled and a tear escaped. Would Mrs. Rosewood-Dasher allow her a final address or time to make a smooth transition to a new principal? "Ladies, I've told you often that there will be a time and a place for you to take a stand on something. Tonight, I want you to know that it may come when you're least expecting it. It might even seem to drop out of the sky."

With that, she hurried up the stairs to her room. Miss Young and Miss Gatrell would see that the girls were settled and do it much better than she would tonight. She sat at her dressing table and dropped her head into her hands. Hot, angry tears began to flow.

Why had she let Titus stay? Why hadn't she put the needs of the girls first? That had always been her rule. Her safety was in traditions, rules, and constants. It was her job to keep all the pieces in place here just like she needed to do back home with her family. When her mother had her fits of melancholy and couldn't function, Ella had failed to save her family, and now, she'd failed this school family as well.

Titus might be brilliant, but he was a fool if he loved someone like her.

She lay on her bed staring at the ceiling and thinking about her students. Nothing thrilled her more than seeing them grow and learn. Nothing, that is, except for being with Titus. His face drifted into her thoughts. Not the man of today, but the impish boy of her youth. When her father had died, she'd almost written to ask him to return. She'd wanted him to be the answer to all her woes, but she knew he couldn't be. Titus wasn't ready to love anyone but himself back then.

But now?

Rolling onto her side, she bunched her feather pillow under her head. Titus had given his life to the Lord. He was a new creature. Was she allowing him to grow or was she keeping him away to protect herself? She asked God to help her figure out what to do. In the morning, she would have to make a decision. She could send Titus away and probably keep her position, or ask him to stay and say goodbye to Rosewood Meadows. He'd left the first time when she'd asked years ago, and she didn't hear from him for years. If she asked him to go this time, she was certain she would never see him again.

Her throat tightened as tears seeped onto the pillow. What would Jane Austen's Elinor do? Ella had always felt like the character was a kindred spirit. After all, it's tough being the sensible one, the one to shoot down the whimsical urges of others. Like Elinor, Ella had always been the one to hold up a cautionary hand and warn others to stop and think about their actions.

But Ella understood something else about Elinor. She might seem to be all business, but inside, she was as full of emotions as her sister, maybe even more so.

Ella was supposed to be teaching girls to be strong, to be ready to do the right thing. What kind of role model was she right now?

Sometime during the night, sleep finally claimed Ella. She awoke with a start when she heard noises outside. Hurrying to the window, she drew the curtains aside and squinted to see two figures on the lawn. Her breath caught. In the pre-dawn light, she saw the dark outline of a balloon.

Titus was leaving.

Chapter 14

With dawn a mere half hour away, Titus staked down his balloon's guy ropes. Once his balloon was inflated, he'd have to cut the lines himself. It wasn't the best way to do it, but he imagined he could pull it off.

He heard the screen door slam on the caretaker's house and looked up to see Ernest striding toward him.

"You leaving?" the man of few words asked.

"Trying to." Titus didn't feel like conversation either. His body had mostly mended, but his heart had been splintered.

"Thought you loved our Miss Mason."

"I do. That's why I've got to go." He lit the burner and pulled the cord to test it. A blast of hot air shot into the dawn sky and the scent of burning fuel filled the air. He then carefully tipped the basket on its side.

"Strange thing. Love." Ernest helped Titus attach the net to the basket. "What makes this thing float like a cloud?"

"The heated air is less dense than the air around it. The denser air pressure pushes in on the balloon and is displaced. Buoyancy is an upward force just like a boat floats in water." He double-checked the guy lines again, then began to fill the envelope with air. "It's actually pressure that makes the balloon rise."

"Pressure that makes this thing lighter than air? It reaches all those new heights because of pressure?" He held the upper ring of the envelope aloft while the air began to fill it.

Titus adjusted the burner and nodded. "Basically, that's it."

Ernest rubbed his chin. "Yep, strange thing. Love."

Titus scratched his temple. That was one of the oddest—and longest—conversations he'd had with Ernest. What did love have to do with the way a hot-air balloon takes to the sky?

He glanced at his gentle giant of an aircraft. Not yet aloft, it expanded on the grass like dough rising in a bowl. In a few minutes, it would be upright.

Cries of delight drew his attention toward the school. Young ladies filtered across the lawn in a steady stream, all mesmerized by the inflating blue and yellow balloon on the lawn. Someone had obviously spotted it and alerted the others.

The first to arrive was young Georgia Bellows, his assistant cloud maker. "Professor, are you going to take flight?"

He chuckled. "I certainly hope so."

"Are you going to leave?"

He whirled at the sound of the familiar voice to find Ella standing behind him. Her dark hair hung loose about her shoulders, and she'd donned a peach shirtwaist with her dark skirt. He gave the burner another blast of hot air. "It's for the best, don't you think?"

At that moment, the balloon rose to an upright position, and the crowd of young ladies cheered. Titus began to tie on sandbags of ballast. When he'd secured the last bag, he looked at Ella. She stepped forward, securing a scarf around her head.

He took a step back. "What are you doing?"

She smiled. "Going with you."

His heart thundered in his chest. "Up there?"

"Anywhere."

Dare he believe it? Her face was peaceful and her eyes held no doubt, only love. Joy surged through him, making him smile so wide his cheeks hurt.

Without another word, he scooped her up and lowered her inside the wicker basket. He hopped in as well. After a couple more blasts from the burner, he signaled to Ernest to release the guy ropes.

He snaked an arm around Ella's trembling waist and called out, "Miss Gatrell, get a preacher back here. There's going to be a wedding when we come down."

Chapter 15

Ella felt as if she were riding a cloud. Except for the occasional burst of hot air from the burner, they glided along in silence at the edge of the sunrise with the earth falling away. Her fears fell away too, replaced with awe.

The words he'd painted inside the basket warmed her in a special way. WHO ARE THESE THAT FLY AS A CLOUD...? ISAIAH 60:8.

She sighed. "Oh, Titus, I can't even describe this. It's breathtaking."

"I know." He clasped her hand in his. "Ella, are you sure about this? I mean about me? I know I told Miss Gatrell to fetch a preacher, but I don't want to pressure you."

She nuzzled into his side. "Pressure isn't a bad thing. Sometimes it makes you see something you've been missing or sets you free."

"Lighter than air."

"Pardon?"

"Something Ernest taught me." He squeezed her hand. "Go on."

"All my life I've taken the safe path, wanting to create assurance for myself. When things became tough, I relied on traditions. Last night, I realized safe doesn't make you lean on God. It makes you lean on yourself."

"So, we're more alike than you thought?" he teased.

"Apparently." She turned, lifting her face to his. "I'm passionate about teaching, but I love you. If I can't have both, I choose you, Titus. I choose you."

He tugged on the burner cord and sent a blast of air into the balloon. It lifted above the low clouds, lighter than air, taking them wherever the wind blew.

The earth rose toward them as the balloon began its descent. Ella gripped the edge of the basket.

"Is that Rosewood Meadows?"

With a grin, he nodded. "We were lucky."

Titus had explained the limited navigation control of a balloon. He also warned her that landing could be the roughest part of a balloon voyage, but she wasn't afraid.

As they descended into the open yard, Ernest ran to meet them. He grabbed hold of the basket and held on. Slowly, the envelope deflated and fell to the ground like a limp rag doll.

Titus climbed out of the basket and then lifted her out as well.

Clementine waddled over. She stood back and surveyed Ella. "You seem to look in one piece."

"Oh, Clementine, it was amazing."

The woman clucked her tongue. "Well, I've been told there's to be a wedding. Is that true?"

Titus squeezed Ella's hand. "Yes, ma'am."

Clementine stepped between them, pushing Titus aside. "Then off with you. We have work to do. This fine lady is not getting married looking like a scarecrow."

As they neared the school, a parade of carriages pulled into the drive. Ella sucked in her breath. Who were all these people?

The carriages stopped and she watched the passengers file out, recognizing Opal's mother, other parents, and Mrs. Rosewood-Dasher. Ella's pulse quickened. So much for her wedding day.

The parents parted for Mrs. Rosewood-Dasher, who looked like royalty in a fine gunmetal-gray day dress with ivory lace trimmings. Her matching hat was neither ostentatious nor understated. The mark of a true lady.

Ella admired Mrs. Rosewood-Dasher. The woman had put her trust in Ella, and Ella's heart tugged at the thought of letting her down.

"That's him." Opal's mother made her way to the front and pointed at Titus, who stood a few yards away.

Mrs. Rosewood-Dasher stepped toward Titus. She glanced at Ella. "Introductions, Miss Mason."

"Pardon me." Ella took her place beside the school's patron. "Mrs. Rosewood-Dasher, I'd like you to meet Professor Knott, my fiancé."

The older woman lifted her eyebrows. "When do you plan to wed?"

"Today." Ella moved to stand next to Titus. "I understand this tenders my resignation."

"And why would that be?" Mrs. Rosewood-Dasher spoke loud enough that the curious parents could overhear the conversation. "Would marriage make you less intelligent? Less able to instruct these young ladies?"

"No, ma'am."

"Is marriage not part of God's plan? Would it make you unable to manage a school?"

Ella straightened her shoulders. "No, ma'am, it would not."

"Then I see no reason you cannot remain in your post. From the onset of this school, we've had the goal of helping young ladies become women of influence, and you, my dear, are certainly a woman of influence." She took Ella's hand. "And I hear Professor Knott has been instructing our students in the area of science." She turned to Titus. "This may not be a fine university, sir, but I believe, if you agree, we could certainly offer you a teaching position here as well."

He dipped his head. "I would be honored."

"And you'll need a place to live." She tapped her finger against her lips. "I think we'll build your home over there. It would be close enough to the school to see to its needs, but far enough away to give you and your family privacy."

"Ma'am, you don't need to do that," Ella breathed.

"Nonsense." She waved a hand in the air. "Now, you said you were getting married today, and I believe I've interrupted the festivities. I'll be going."

"Please stay. I'd be honored." Tears stung Ella's eyes.

"It would be my pleasure, dear." She shooed Ella with her gloved hand. "Now, off with you to get ready. It's time for Titus Knott to get changed so he can tie this knot."

As Ella climbed the steps into the school, she heard her patron directing the parents to arrange chairs and collect flowers. They'd come to see her terminated, but instead, they would see the principal wed.

Chapter 16

Clementine walked into Ella's room with a frilly white dress in her hands. She laid the garment across the bed and spread it for Ella's viewing.

Ella rose from her dressing table and gasped. "Where did this come from?"

"Don't you recognize it?" Clementine smoothed one of the puffy gigot sleeves. "I took one of your old summer dresses and reworked it. I added a little lace and a bit of a train."

"But when?"

"I started making adjustments the day that professor landed in our yard. I saw the love between you two. Years might have separated you, but I figured that love might pull you back together. Just in case, I started on this." She fingered the lace on the bodice. "You'll make a lovely bride, Miss Mason."

"Clementine, thank you from the bottom of my heart, and for the hundredth time, please call me Ella."

Tears glistened in the woman's eyes and trickled over her rounded cheeks. "I don't think I could do that, but I'm truly happy for you." She kissed Ella's cheek.

Half an hour later, Ella descended the wide staircase where Ernest met her. "Professor Knott said you didn't have anyone to give you away. Will I do?"

She slipped her hand into the crook of his arm. "Absolutely."

Opal met Ella at the door with a bouquet of lilacs. Ella lifted the delicate blossoms to her nose and inhaled the blessed scent. She paused to thank God for all that had happened, then made her way down the makeshift aisle on the portico toward the man she loved.

How Clementine managed such a feast on short notice Ella would never know. With the wedding brunch completed, Titus tugged her outside, saying he wanted a moment alone with his bride.

He drew her into the garden and she marveled at how everything seemed brighter and more beautiful today.

He held her hands. "I love you, Mrs. Knott."

"Oh, my." She giggled. "I've been Miss Mason so long, I'll have to get used to that."

He reached into his pocket and told her to turn around. With her back to him, he set something about her neck.

Ella touched the necklace and felt the cool weight found only in pearls. "Titus, where—"

"These were my mother's. She told me to give them to a woman who loved all of me, including the adventurous, crazy inventor."

"And you think that's me?" she teased, turning back to face him.

"I'm certainly hoping so." He placed his hands on her waist and pulled her close. "There's one tradition we've missed, my love. And I know you're a stickler for traditions."

"And what tradition is that?"

"I haven't yet kissed the bride." He lifted his hand to cup the back of her head. "Did you know ancient Romans thought souls mingled in a kiss?" He stared into her eyes, then lowered his gaze to her lips. Ella's heart beat faster and faster, then at last, he closed the distance between them.

He tilted her head back and kissed her, softly at first, and then with a soaring intensity. She swirled in the dizzying, swaying world of his love, lighter than air itself.

Lorna Seilstad brings history back to life using a generous dash of humor. She is a Carol Award finalist and the author of the Lake Manawa Summers series and the Gregory Sisters series. When she isn't eating chocolate, she's teaches women's Bible classes and is a 4-H leader in her home state of Iowa. She and her husband have three children. Learn more about Lorna at www.lornaseilstad.com.

In Due Season

by Connie Stevens

Dedication

To Ralph and Helen Vogel
Thank you for the sweet gift of
your friendship.

Chapter 1

Papa's question shouldn't have surprised her, but Leah Brown's jaw muscles clenched involuntarily regardless of her attempt to school her features into a smile. She dipped her head and pretended to concentrate on stirring honey into her tea, swallowing the familiar bitterness prompted by his announcement.

Papa remarrying?

She swallowed a gulp of tepid tea. "Aren't you asking the wrong person?" She glanced at him over their breakfast table. "Mrs. Voth's opinion is the one that counts."

Her father's gray eyes crinkled into an adoring smile. "Daughter, your opinion is important too." He poked his last bite of eggs into his mouth. "I know how close you and your mother always were."

Leah's heart pinched. "I'll always miss Mama."

"I will too." Papa reached across the table and laid his hand over hers. "And I'll always be grateful for the way you cared for her during her infirm years." Moisture glistened in his eyes as he squeezed her hand. "Working with me in the apothecary and taking such good care of your mother, and the house. . .and me. You would've—"

She thrust both palms up. No, she'd not let him finish the sentence. Whether or not she would have made a good wife and mother was irrelevant, and she detested the words that only served to remind her that those titles were stolen from her the day the man she loved left her at the altar. "Caring for you and Mama has always been—"

Resentment nipped her and she pushed it away. The harsh feeling had nothing to do with her parents.

"—my privilege."

Papa's chin whiskers twitched as the corners of his mouth turned up. "But you didn't answer my question. How would you feel about me marrying Helen Voth?"

How could she mind? While she knew Papa had loved Mama, his loneliness since her death had manifested itself on his countenance. He couldn't hide his longing for the kind of companionship Leah couldn't provide, and Mrs. Voth was a pleasant woman. Perhaps the widow Voth could return the smile to Papa's face.

"Papa, I don't mind. I want you to be happy." *Happy.* Even as she spoke the word, a thread of envy spiraled through her, and she bit her lip. Now wasn't the time to give freedom to the tears of regret that often accompanied her when she extinguished her lamp at night. The time had come for her to put away the fairy tale of marriage. Everyone seemed to have their roles. Hers was the maiden lady, as some of the elderly women said. She drew in a breath as she rose and straightened her shoulders. "I like Mrs. Voth. She's a very nice lady." Picturing the two of them living out their September years together wasn't hard.

Papa stroked his beard. "Yes, she is." He took a sip of coffee and cleared his throat. "Harold stopped by the apothecary yesterday afternoon while you were out."

Momentary confusion made Leah pause with her teacup halfway to her lips. "Who?"

Papa's eyebrows pulled together. "Harold Stuart. The representative from Cunningham Pharmaceuticals. The fellow who invites you to accompany him to dinner almost every time he comes through town."

Yes, Harold. He wasn't a bad sort, but he didn't interest her in the least. Her sip of tea tasted bitter despite the honey, and she shrugged. "He must not know I'm the town spinster."

"Leah." Papa's brows dipped in a reproving frown. "You are a greatly beloved child of the King. Circumstances will never change that. To belittle yourself is to disparage God's creation." His tone softened. "And you are my beloved daughter as well."

She swallowed back the lump forming in her throat and pushed whispered words past her lips. "I know that, Papa."

He went on. "Harold Stuart is a fine man. What would it hurt to accept his invitation?"

Leah pressed her lips together for a space of a few heartbeats. "All he ever talks about is medicinal compounds and his knowledge of pharmaceuticals. Last week, he stood there and talked for twenty minutes about the benefits of paregoric." She didn't add that the man was probably close to fifty years old and slicked his thinning hair with so much pomade she was amazed his hat didn't slide right off his head. But she refused to entertain the real reason she couldn't stir an iota of interest in Harold Stuart.

She rose and scooped up their breakfast dishes. "I'd like to go into the shop a bit early today, Papa. I have some invoices to record before we open." A twinge of guilt stabbed her over the fib. She'd recorded those invoices two days ago, but seized them as an excuse to bring the conversation to an end. She deposited the dishes into the dishpan with a clatter—anything to drown out the taunting memory that poked its bony finger in her face more times than she could count.

Jilted. . .jilted. . .jilted.

"Leah?" Her father's voice pulled her back to the present.

"I'm sorry, Papa. I must have been woolgathering. What did you say?"

Her father's patient smile eased her angst. "We've discussed you taking over the apothecary one day—not that I'm ready to retire yet. But one day I will, and if you are interested, you will need to further your education. The School of Pharmacy at the University of Kansas relocated to Bailey Hall last year—not those dusty basement rooms in the old chemistry building anymore—and it's become one of the most progressive in the country." He tapped his finger on table. "There are several women in the pharmaceutical field now. You could apply for a scholarship and I could help make up the difference for your tuition."

Leah studied the lines around her father's eyes. Love swelled within her. She'd do anything to make him happy. If following in his footsteps was his dream, she'd consider the possibility. Besides, she might even gain a level of respect from Whitley's town folk if she became the pharmacist. Her single status cast a shadowed pall over her future, but if the community no longer looked on her with pity, she could hold her head up a little higher. Once again—she'd long ago lost count—she silently asked God to bury the image she carried in her head and heart of Gareth Shepherd, her beloved. The man who ran out on her the day before their wedding fifteen years ago.

Gareth Shepherd hammered the new pin into place on the wheel of the surrey his boss had taken in on trade, and shook it to test its strength. It didn't wiggle.

"How's it coming, Gareth?"

Gareth glanced up as Orsen Dansby, owner of Dansby Wainwrights Inc., entered the workshop. Orsen's wife trailed at his heels.

"Fine, sir. Another hour and I should have it ready to go." Genuine affection for the man tipped the corners of his mouth into a grin. After several years of drifting from place to place and job to job, Gareth thanked God for putting Orsen Dansby in his life. The man was more than an employer. He was the mentor who had shown Gareth what it truly meant to serve Jesus.

Harriet Dansby stepped over to the two-seater surrey on which Gareth was working. "Orsen, is this the carriage for St. Margaret's Hospital?"

Mr. Dansby winked at Gareth. "Yes, dear."

His wife circled the conveyance, examining the newly painted body and slightly worn seats, prattling about her charity work at the hospital.

Mr. Dansby rubbed his hand over his balding head. "Gareth, when you get finished here, I believe we can sell this surrey for thirty-five dollars."

His wife stopped short and shook her finger at her husband. "Orsen, you already promised you would donate this one to the hospital. This carriage will be a blessing to the patients at St. Margaret's. Since they opened the indigent ward, there's been a big increase in the number of patients arriving from all over Kansas and Missouri."

Gareth's boss grinned and patted his wife's hand. "Don't have apoplexy, my dear. I'm only teasing."

Gareth grinned and bent his head over his work, sliding the newly repaired wheel onto the axle, while Mrs. Dansby went on about some of the poor unfortunates at the hospital. Gareth only half listened.

"So many women who have no families." She tsked and shook her head. "There's one woman, Audelia Rose is her name—"

Gareth froze.

His boss's wife chuckled. "She says her husband always called her Dandy, short for Dandelion, because he said she 'weren't no rose.'" The woman laughed and continued chattering about the woman named Dandy, but the blood in Gareth's veins turned to ice.

Audelia Rose? Dandy? Short for Dandelion? The name and nickname were both far too familiar to be a coincidence. How many women in the state of Kansas bore such a name?

He'd wondered how he might feel if he ever found his mother—not that he'd been searching for her. Fifteen years of anger and resentment washed over him, and he clenched his teeth. His fingers gripped the wrench while bitterness contended with scripture's mandate to forgive.

Harriet Dansby gave her husband a peck on the cheek. "I'll see you at dinner. Don't work too late." She flittered out of the shop, waving over her shoulder as she left.

Gareth sucked in a shallow breath. So his mother was a patient at St. Margaret's Hospital. An unmistakable nudge poked him, but he tried to ignore it. Why should he go and see her? Dansby Wainwrights Inc. had enough work lined up to keep him busy for many weeks. He didn't have time to go all the way across town to visit the woman who ran away and destroyed his life fifteen years ago. Had it not been for her, he'd be married and likely would have a family by now. Reconciling with his mother wasn't his responsibility.

He yanked the wrench to tighten down the wheel hub, and it slipped from his grip, busting his knuckles against the spokes. He clamped his lips down on the expletive that rose to his tongue. His vocabulary had changed when he met Jesus, but sometimes. . .

"Gareth, when you get that one finished, take it on over to St. Margaret's." Mr. Dansby patted his shoulder.

His boss took the choice out of Gareth's hands. He blew out a sigh. "Yes, sir."

Mr. Dansby paused. "Everything all right?"

Gareth straightened and rubbed his bruised knuckles. He nodded. "Got some, uh, disturbing news, is all. Reckon I need to pray about it."

The older man's eyes bored into Gareth's. "That's always a good practice. Anything you want to talk about?"

Did he want to talk about it? Should he share the shame that had driven him from his home and all his plans and had dogged him for fifteen years? He knew his boss well enough to know the man wouldn't judge, but speaking the words thrust the reality of the past into today, and Gareth wasn't sure he wanted to revisit that painful time. Didn't his faith in Christ assure him his past was just that—in the past? Why should he dredge up those memories?

Mr. Dansby still stood in front of him, awaiting an answer.

Gareth placed both hands against the rim of the wheel and slumped, his head bowed. "That woman Mrs. Dansby was talking about—the one named Dandy."

A long silent space of time passed. His boss didn't press him. "My mother was Audelia Rose Shepherd, but my father—or rather my stepfather—always called her Dandy."

Chapter 2

A man from the hospital administrative offices shook Gareth's hand and introduced himself as Phineas Reynolds. "Mrs. Dansby told us you'd be bringing this surrey by today. It will certainly be a help. Please thank your boss for me."

"I will, sir." Gareth sent his gaze up all three stories of the brick wall, trying to imagine if his mother might be looking at him from one of the windows. After a long talk with his boss and mentor, he'd spent time in prayer and knew what he had to do. "Mr. Reynolds?"

The man looked up from his appreciative inspection of the surrey, and arched his brows in reply.

"Who do I talk to about inquiring after one of the patients here?"

Mr. Reynolds pointed. "Go around to the front door. There is an information desk. Someone there can direct you."

Gareth drew in a deep breath and blew it out. "Thanks." He dusted off his trousers and shirt, ran his fingers through his hair, and made his way to the hospital's front entrance.

"Excuse me."

An elderly nun sitting at the desk looked up. "Yes, young man?"

"I'm looking for Audelia Rose Shepherd."

The nun ran her finger down a lengthy list, her lips moving as she checked the names and room numbers. "I don't see—"

"Uh, she might be in the indigent ward." Gareth's mumble was barely audible, even to his own ears.

"I see." The lines in the nun's face deepened. "If that is the case, her name wouldn't be on my list. These are only paying patients in regular rooms." She sniffed and pointed over her shoulder. "Go all the way down that hall and turn left at the double doors. One of the nurses might be able to help you."

Gareth followed the nun's directions and entered a dingy hallway, where he encountered a haggard nurse. "Ma'am, I'm looking for Audelia Rose Shepherd. Is she here?"

The nurse gave a brusque nod and jutted her chin toward the door behind her. "In there. But you can't go in there."

Gareth halted his steps. "Why?"

" 'Cause all the patients in there have consumption."

"But she's my— I need to find her."

The nurse heaved a sigh. "Sonny, I done told you all them folks is diseased. You can't get near them."

"But you and the doctors go near them." The argument was a weak one, but it was all he had.

A derisive snort flapped the nurse's lips. "I don't go in there any more than I have to, and the doctor. . ." She blasted a short laugh. "He's supposed to come around once a week, but the last time he was here was near a month ago."

Gareth's fingers curled into fists, and he spun and stalked to the door.

"I warned you. If you go in there, pull your neckerchief up over your face and don't stay but a minute."

The rest of the nurse's admonishment was lost when the doors swung closed behind him. He scanned the room. An involuntary shudder ran through him and his stomach convulsed. More than two dozen cots were so crowded next to each other, there was barely room to step between them. Coughing, retching, and moaning collided in his ears and a putrid stench accosted his nostrils. Nausea rose in his throat. A fleeting prayer left his heart—*God, I hope she's not here.*

A pitiful collection of women with sunken eyes, pallid skin, and wispy, stringy hair filled the line of cots along each wall. When was the last time these people were bathed? Judging by the sound of their hacking coughs and labored breathing, they hadn't seen any medication recently either.

He walked slowly down the center aisle, casting searching glances along the rows of cots. He came to the end and turned to double back. She wasn't here, and he was glad of it. But if she'd already died, that meant she'd left this world before he could tell her—

"Gareth?"

The croaked, broken voice barely pushed his name out in a raspy whisper. He halted and sent his gaze back to look again.

A wasted, gaunt woman lay on a cot to his right. Years of wrong choices had ravaged her body, and her green eyes had lost their sparkle, but there was no doubt about her identity.

He stepped over to her bedside and forced a single word from his lips. "Mama?"

Moisture flooded her eyes, but when he reached out to her she stiffened and pulled the filthy, ragged blanket up over her mouth and nose. "Don't. Don't touch me."

Gareth glanced to and fro and spied a short-legged, rickety stool. He pulled it over beside his mother's bed. A dozen questions burned on his tongue, but he restrained them. What could he say? *How have you been?* The answer to that was plain to see. His mother saved him the trouble.

"I never expected to see you again." A barking cough broke off whatever else she might have said, and she pressed a rag to her mouth.

"Mama, I must ask you to forgive me."

Her brow dipped. "Me? Forgive you?"

Gareth nodded. "I hated you. I had no right. Those ugly feelings had a stranglehold on me for a long time. But I asked God to forgive me and He did. Now I'm asking you."

She merely stared at him a long moment. "I've wondered how you were and wished I could tell you why I left."

He couldn't deny wanting to hear her explanation, but even now, after he'd struggled all these years and thought he'd surrendered his resentment to God, the canker of bitterness still gnawed at him. "I know what Pa told me, but that's all I know."

She narrowed her eyes and pursed her cracked lips. "Let's just say your Pa wasn't the fine, upstanding man everyone thought him to be." She turned away and began to cough.

He stood. "Mama, I'll let you rest, but now that I've found you, I won't leave you alone."

The rag she held to her mouth came away with dark blood stains. "Why?"

Gareth leaned forward and planted his hands on his legs. "Because Jesus loves you, Mama, and so do I." He straightened and stepped sideways to the end of the cot. "I'll be back soon."

She snorted. "No, you won't."

Leah stood in front of the small cottage and tried to see it with different eyes. As a child, she and her friends used to pick bouquets of wildflowers for the elderly woman who had lived in it. *Granny Walker.* The memory of the sweet old lady's sugar cookies made Leah's mouth water. The cottonwood tree in the yard was much larger than she remembered, but the blue checked curtains at the window were the same, though faded.

Mr. Doyle, the bank manager, cleared his throat beside her. "It's been empty for several years and will require some work before it's habitable." He tipped his head as if he was measuring the width and depth of the little porch. "I can assure you, Miss Brown, that the house can be had at a very reasonable price."

Her childhood memories might've made the place all the more appealing were it not for the adjoining property. Against her will, her gaze drifted across the wide, rolling field and found another house in the distance, perched on a low bluff where she'd sat many Sunday afternoons with Gareth Shepherd. The porch swing was no longer there, but she could see it in her mind and hear the creak of the rusted chains on the Kansas breeze. The pain that sliced through her heart wasn't as sharp as it had been fifteen years ago. Now, a hollow ache echoed in her chest. Did she possess the starch in her spine to reside in the little cottage where a glance out the window would trigger such memories?

"I'll think about it, Mr. Doyle."

The banker twisted the end of his mustache. "Don't wait too long."

She bit her lip to keep from smirking. "It's been empty over five years, Mr. Doyle. I seriously doubt you will be inundated with buyers in the next two weeks."

Leah sent one last fleeting glance toward the Shepherd home. Perhaps if she planted a hedgerow along the western edge of the small yard, it might block the view of her former beau's house. Her face warmed and chagrin nipped her at the childish thought.

Grow up, Leah. You aren't eighteen anymore.

Besides, it wasn't truly the Shepherd home any longer since Mr. Shepherd passed away a month ago. The man had turned into a bitter recluse in the years following his wife's death—much like she'd sequestered herself behind the counter at the apothecary when Gareth disappeared. A reflection gave her pause. Did others view her the way she'd seen Mr. Shepherd?

Mr. Doyle bid her good day and took his leave, but Leah lingered and wrestled with her muddled thoughts. The idea of going back to school and completing her degree still played through her mind. She'd given the catalog from the University of Kansas a perusal when it arrived a few days ago, but was becoming a pharmacist what she really wanted? Papa would be thrilled if she did.

What a cruel trick the years had played on her. When she was eighteen years old, all she dreamed about was getting married and starting a family like her friends. She could barely call them friends anymore. Since they were all married and raising their families, she was rarely included in their circle, except for special events. Her label of town spinster repelled every eligible man for miles around. Most of the time her escort was Papa. Even then, her singleness made her conspicuous and uncomfortable. But her circumstances had narrowed her choices to two—go off to the university where she'd be the middle-aged woman in a sea of young folks, or stay in Whitley where she lived with the patronizing comments and snooty gossip whispered behind hands. Becoming a pharmacist wouldn't be her ticket out of Whitley, but it might garner her a level of respect. On the other hand, why should she pursue a goal not of her choosing? She didn't mind working at her father's apothecary, but it wasn't her dream.

She turned away from the cottage and made her way back toward the apothecary. Her life had been stagnant long enough. It was time to chart her own course. With Papa's upcoming wedding to Helen Voth, Leah couldn't bear to remain in the house where she'd grown up. The widow was a charming person and made her father happy, but how could Leah live under the same roof with the newlyweds?

As she walked, she cast her gaze heavenward. "Lord, please help me know what to do. I'm tired of people feeling sorry for me and treating me as if being single is some kind of disease. Give me Your peace. Help me to be content with the life You've given me."

Even as the prayer left her lips, a thread of discontentment over her life tightened another knot in its noose. She truly did wish for peace, but wondered if it would ever be hers.

Perhaps investing her savings in the little cottage was the next step in her life.

Gareth pushed the mop across the floor and tried to ignore the muffled coughs penetrating the walls of the indigent ward. At this time of night, most of the patients should be asleep, or so he'd thought. Working this second job meant he could pay for better care—palliative care, the doctor had called it—for his mother, and he was grateful. But he assumed the night shift would be quiet. He hadn't counted on listening to the suffering of those unfortunate ones whose bodies were ravaged by consumption. An involuntary shudder shook him. He'd asked God to give him an extra paycheck, but surely God had made a mistake.

Chapter 3

Leah blinked at her father's announcement as she cleared the table of the supper dishes. It wasn't unexpected, but she thought she'd have a little more time. A momentary sense of loss invaded her thoughts, followed by a twinge of envy. Both were ridiculous.

Papa patted Mrs. Voth's hand and grinned. "At our age, we can't afford to wait too long."

The widow gave his arm a playful swat. "Oh, Ralph." She stood and joined Leah at the sink. "We aren't planning a big ceremony. Just a small gathering after the Sunday morning worship service. I thought we should wait until October, but your father is very persuasive. So we agreed on August the eleventh."

"Hmph." Papa's grumble reached Leah's ears. "That's still almost three whole months."

Despite her tenuous emotions, Leah managed to smile at her father. "Papa, you've always told me good things are worth waiting for. Isn't marrying Mrs. Voth a good thing?"

"Not fair." Papa carried his coffee cup to the sink. "You're using my own words against me." He pecked Leah on the cheek.

Mrs. Voth picked up a dish towel and leaned closer to Leah. "I thought you were going to call me Helen."

Leah glanced at the two of them. She had to admit they were right for each other. But no newlyweds, young or older, needed a third person living with them. Now was as good a time as any to break the news to them.

She cleared her throat. "I have something to tell you."

Papa's eyes lit up. He likely thought she'd decided to go to the university. She hated to disappoint him.

Papa tucked Helen's hand into the crook of his arm and waited, anticipation arching his brow. "Well?"

"I. . .I spoke with Mr. Doyle today."

"Fred Doyle? From the bank?" Papa's countenance reflected his confusion.

"Yes." Leah shifted her gaze to Helen. "You know that little cottage with the green shutters at the far west end of Flint Street?"

Helen nodded. "You mean Granny Walker's old house?"

"That's the one." Leah returned her focus back to Papa. "I'm thinking about buying it. It needs work, but it's basically sound, and it would be a. . .good investment. . .for me."

Helen reached out her free hand to Leah. "Honey, you know you are most welcome to stay right here, in the house where you grew up. This is your home, dear."

A genuine growing fondness for Helen soothed the frayed edges of Leah's emotions. "I know. But it's best if I take this step."

Her father nailed her with a steely stare. "We need to talk about this—"

"Papa, I've thought about it and prayed about it. I'm thirty-four years old. It's time for me to put away childish things, as scripture says, and be responsible for myself."

Her father stroked his short beard. The creases between his eyebrows deepened. "Is this because Helen and I are getting married?"

"No, Papa." Guilt spiraled through her, but her response was at least partly true. While her father's upcoming wedding had indeed prompted her to take the first step toward independence, the restlessness of unfulfilled dreams drove her to make the decision. "It's simply time. I want nothing but happiness for both of you."

It's not going to happen for me, and I'm too old to believe in fairy tales.

Leah stepped out the door of the bank, her stomach in a knot. She'd done it. She'd withdrawn money from her savings and signed the papers. But the excitement she thought she'd feel over moving into her own home withered into resignation. She supposed she should think about how she was going to furnish the place.

Holding to a sedate pace, she made her way two blocks down the street past the apothecary. A quick glance through the window revealed Papa finishing up for the day and preparing to close. She continued on toward their home and resisted the temptation to stop by the dry goods store. After all, she had a trunk at home crammed with items she'd collected years ago. But moving into an abandoned cottage as an old maid was very different from the breathless excitement she'd enjoyed as a bride.

Except she never actually was a bride.

Memories of evenings with her mother stitching towels, sheets, and pillow slips eased into her mind. The linens still sat, unused, in her bedroom trunk. A familiar ache formed in her chest. She'd not opened that trunk in years, certain that doing so would unleash a fresh onslaught of pain.

Ridiculous. Refusing to use those items she'd collected in preparation for setting up her own household was foolish and impractical. And she couldn't afford to be impractical.

She arrived at their modest house and let herself in the back door. The mantle clock tick-tocked an admonition to begin supper preparations, but she'd made up her mind and wanted to act on it before Papa came home. In her room, she lifted the coverlet off the trunk and took a deep breath. The hinges, unaccustomed to motion, screeched a protest as she opened the lid.

Everything was exactly the way she'd left it fifteen years ago, with one difference: the musty smell from being hidden away. She picked up a small bundle tied with a blue satin ribbon—the kitchen towels Mama had hemmed before she'd gotten sick. The bow her mother had fashioned lay flattened into a sad, unrecognizable blob of blue satin. Beneath that she pulled out two rolls of muslin. As she unrolled the material, an ache formed a hard lump in her throat. Patiently embroidered in a swirled design of blue forget-me-nots and tendrils of ivy, two elegant initials flowed along the hemmed edge of the pair of pillowcases: *G & L.*

She'd believed she had no more tears left, but a single droplet slipped from her lashes down her cheek and dripped onto the yellowed muslin.

Gareth drained his coffee cup and pushed back his chair. "Thanks for a good breakfast, Mrs. Morrison."

His landlady gave him a short nod. "Welcome. Letter come for ya in the mornin' mail. Settin' on the table in the parlor."

"Thanks." He grabbed his hat, curiosity stirring his feet into motion. Who would be sending him a letter? His limited circle of friends were right here in Kansas City.

The envelope with his name emblazoned across the front sat propped against a chipped vase. Gareth picked it up and read the return address. Coffey County Magistrate's Office, Whitley, Kansas. Fingers of dread spiraled through him. He tore back the flap and extracted the missive. His eyes scanned quickly down the page.

Dear Mr. Shepherd,

We regret to inform you that your father, Mr. Randall Shepherd, passed away in April after what the doctor described as a short illness. The property he owned, a seventy-acre farm in Coffey County on the outskirts of Whitley, is now bequeathed to you as his only heir. A resident of nearby Osage County has expressed interest in purchasing the land if you are inclined to sell. There are several documents that will require your signature before the court. Before any transaction can be finalized, your identity must be confirmed. Please name at least one reputable person known to the court who can verify your relationship to Mr. Randall Shepherd and come at your earliest convenience.

Sincerely,
Averill Dalton, Court Clerk

A breath he didn't realize he was holding whooshed out on a wave of unexpected grief. His father—or rather, his stepfather—was gone. Had they kept in touch over the years, he might have known the man who had raised him was ill. Remorse warred with the memory of their bitter parting. Pa had made his feelings clear. The whiskey had loosened his tongue, or perhaps the rage over his wife's—Gareth's mother's—departure. Either way, Pa had spat out the hateful revelation that sent Gareth packing.

But the inheritance surprised him. Why would the man leave all his holdings to him after their estrangement?

If he didn't get moving, he'd be late. He shoved the letter into his pocket and strode out the door and down the sidewalk, covering the six blocks to Dansby Wainwright Shop in just a few minutes. His boss was pushing open the wide double doors as he arrived.

"Mornin', Gareth."

He mumbled a reply and headed toward the back of the shop where his tools were lined up with meticulous care. The message he'd read a few minutes earlier paraded through his mind.

"Somethin' eatin' at you, Gareth?"

He glanced up to see his boss standing behind him with his thumbs hooked in his suspenders. Mr. Dansby beetled his thick eyebrows, concern carved into the lines in his face. He leaned against the workbench, blocking Gareth's access to his tools. "Want to talk about it?" The man who had, in effect, become like a father to him waited.

Gareth dug the wadded up letter from his pocket, smoothed it as flat as possible, and handed it to Mr. Dansby, who scanned the missive.

"Your father has passed. I'm sorry, Gareth." Genuine sympathy threaded Mr. Dansby's tone.

Gareth lifted his shoulders. "I have some pretty tangled-up feelings about it. We didn't part on good terms after I found out he wasn't my real father."

"I see." Mr. Dansby rubbed his chin.

A sigh blew past Gareth's lips. "Haven't seen him for fifteen years." He gestured toward the letter his boss still held. "I'm not sure what to do about that."

Mr. Dansby studied the letter again. "According to this, the man claimed you. He gave you his name. He could've disinherited you, but he didn't. That should mean something." He handed the letter back to Gareth. "Seventy acres of land. That's not a small gift."

His boss had a point. The inheritance was worth some money—enough, perhaps, to pay for a private room and the best care for his mother. The irony confronted him, but Mr. Dansby had taught him not to question the way God worked.

Gareth nodded. "Appears I might need some time off to travel to Whitley."

Mr. Dansby laid his hand on Gareth's shoulder. "Take as much time as you need, son."

Gareth reined in the team in front of Whitley's one and only livery. He set the brake on the buckboard he'd borrowed from Mr. Dansby at the man's insistence—in case there was anything Gareth wished to bring back with him.

"Pfft. What would I bring back?" Years of pleasant memories had been crushed in the shadow of the final few days he'd spent here.

He'd debated all the way from Kansas City whether he should simply slip into town, take care of his business, and slip out again. But doing so without seeing Leah was the coward's way out. How many times in the past fifteen years had he started to put pen to paper, explaining why he'd left and begging her forgiveness, only to throw the missive into the stove? The weight of regret he'd carried since the day he walked out on her still hung about his neck. She was likely married with a family by now, but at the very least he owed her an apology.

A sweeping appraisal revealed a few changes in Whitley—a new dry goods store, a bigger hotel, the post office and telegraph now stood in a different location. But his gaze sought out Brown's Apothecary.

The small brick building hadn't changed. Still at the corner of Fourth Street and Main, the sign out front appeared as though it had been recently painted. The front window glinted in the sun, preventing him from seeing inside. If Mr. Brown was behind the counter, he could tell him where to find her.

He jumped down and brushed dust from his shirt and trousers before crossing the street to the apothecary. The little bell above the door announced his arrival, and a familiar voice—a female voice—stroked his ears.

"I'll be with you in a minute."

He sucked in a deep breath. *Leah.*

The sight of Gareth Shepherd standing at the counter when she turned around nearly caused her knees to buckle. The tin of sulfur in her hand clattered to the floor as she clapped her hands to her mouth. Her breath vacated her body.

Just when she'd determined her life would turn a corner, the sight of the man who had hurt her so deeply jerked her back into the mire of bitterness.

Chapter 4

Blindsided by a tangle of emotions and Gareth's unexpected presence, Leah braced herself on the edge of the counter to steady her trembling legs. The years had only enhanced his handsome features. His shoulders and build bespoke of a man accustomed to work, and she suspected he was a bit taller than she remembered. His hair had darkened to the shade of over-ripened wheat, but his eyes—those eyes that had lingered in her dreams—were still the color of a Kansas summer sky.

But now those eyes brimmed with remorse as he stared back at her. She groped for words, and apparently so did he, for neither of them spoke for an eternity.

Yanked between contempt and anguish, frustration and longing, she was hard put to handle them one at a time, much less in an avalanche. Part of her heart screamed to send him away. How dare he simply show up here unannounced, uninvited, and unwelcomed? The cold chill that had gripped her the moment she'd laid eyes on him now dissolved in a rush of heat.

He found his voice before she found hers.

"Hello, Leah."

Countless times, she'd imagined what she might say to Gareth Shepherd if she ever saw him again. Would she fling herself into his arms or throw something at him? She tried to pull in enough breath to speak, but the words barely croaked out. "What are you doing here?"

Gareth dropped his gaze and fumbled with the hat in his hands. "I came to take care of some business. My. . .family's farm. Papers to sign." He crushed the brim of his hat in his fist. "I had to see you." He looked up at her. "No, I needed to see you. I wanted to see you."

A faint whisper wound itself through the confusion tumbling in her mind and worked its way to the forefront. The tiny spark had burned in the depth of her heart for fifteen years, and now it fanned into a flame she couldn't quench. But at the same time, the pain and stigma she'd borne for so long grabbed control of her tongue.

"You think you can just stroll in here and demand to see me? You are the lowest, most selfish cad I've ever known." Once her voice found freedom, it crashed past the restraints she tried to employ. Each word screeched indignation. "How could you just disappear without a word, or even a goodbye?"

She couldn't have held back her resentful tone if she'd wanted to. And she didn't want to.

Her heart hammered against her ribs and she curled her fists. "Just get out!" No doubt people walking past the front door could hear her, but she didn't care. Her voice cracked with building volume. "Get out of here!"

Gareth stood there like a statue. Why didn't he move? Why didn't he say something? And why did his eyes fix on hers like they were reaching out for a lifeline?

"What in heaven's name is going on out here?" Papa pushed back the curtain that separated the counter area from the work area. "The whole town is going to hear—" He halted halfway to the counter. "Gareth Shepherd? It's you."

The statue finally opened his mouth. "Yes, sir. It's me."

Papa stepped over to Leah and slipped his arm around her shoulders. "I won't shriek at you like my daughter, but I'd be curious to know the answer to her question. How could you just disappear without a word? And on the eve of your wedding day?"

Gareth hung his head. "You both deserve some answers." He raised his head and met Leah's gaze. "I tried a hundred times to write to you. I just couldn't find the right words. But please believe me, I've regretted hurting you more than anything I've ever done. At the time, I felt there was no other choice."

The tumult rushing through Leah's insides made her quake. No choice? Was he run out of town at gunpoint? How could he not simply come to her, face-to-face, and break off their engagement if he'd changed his mind? Why couldn't he write a dozen words in a note to her?

Why did you leave me, Gareth? Why? The moisture clinging to her lashes fell and dripped down her face.

Gareth took a step closer. He pulled a handkerchief from his pocket and held it out to her. She caught her breath and stiffened. When she made no move to accept it, Papa took it and pressed it into her hand.

"Daughter, I've watched you grieve for fifteen years. Heaven knows I wanted to have a man-to-man talk with Gareth myself when he—well, when he left." He took a step back and crossed his arms. "It's your choice, honey, but I think you'll regret it if you send him away without listening to what he has to say. A heart that refuses to forgive is a hard and bitter heart. You don't want to live like that."

Papa's gentle wisdom defused her anger. She wiped her tears, but still clung to Gareth's handkerchief.

Gareth cleared his throat. "Thank you, Mr. Brown. Leah, can we talk? I'd like the chance to explain why I left. Please?"

After wondering why for so long, the prospect of finally learning his reasons now scared her silly. She cast a pleading look at her father, willing him to direct Gareth to leave, but he simply nodded.

Needles of panic poked her, and she gestured toward the door. "But people come in and out all day."

"Then let me take you for a ride out to the meadow where we used to walk." Gareth glanced over at Papa. "Mr. Brown?"

Leah could have sworn she saw Papa's lips twitch, and before he could reply, she placed her hands on her hips. "I'm not a young girl anymore. You don't need to ask my father's permission." She lifted her chin. "It's against my better judgment, but I'll go."

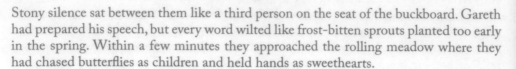

Stony silence sat between them like a third person on the seat of the buckboard. Gareth had prepared his speech, but every word wilted like frost-bitten sprouts planted too early in the spring. Within a few minutes they approached the rolling meadow where they had chased butterflies as children and held hands as sweethearts.

Gareth pulled the team to a stop in the shade of two towering cottonwoods. "Do you want to get out and walk?"

Leah turned her stiff, expressionless face to him. "No. Papa says I should listen to what you have to say. I'm waiting."

She wasn't making this easy, but he couldn't blame her. He deserved every bit of her wrath. He drew in a slow, deep breath and began.

"Two days before our wedding date, I saw my mother get into a buggy with a man I didn't recognize. She was carrying a carpetbag. I didn't know what to do, what to think. When my father came in from the fields that evening, I told him what I'd seen. He was quiet, but it was the kind of quiet you know comes right before a storm.

He got pretty drunk that night. In his rage, he bellowed that I wasn't really his son. My mother was already in the family way when she met him, but he married her and gave me his name when I was born."

Gareth rubbed his hands over his face. "I could only imagine how the news would spread like wildfire that my mother had run off with another man and I was illegitimately born. I couldn't subject you to that kind of scandal and censure—to that stigma. I know I hurt you when I left. But, Leah, marrying me would have caused you worse pain. I left to protect you."

She remained quiet, but Gareth suspected a cyclone was building inside her. Was she repelled by the circumstances of his birth? Or was she gathering steam to spew more anger at him? He tipped his head to try and catch a glimpse of her face. Only then did he realize she was trembling.

"Protect me. . .from what? The stigma?" She hissed the words through clenched teeth. "So you inflicted the stigma of spinsterhood on me instead. I've believed all these years that I wasn't good enough for you. I've put up with the snide remarks, the looks of pity, being excluded from social events because they were for couples. How many men do you think are willing to court a woman who is labeled the old maid of Whitley? Every morning when I look at myself in the mirror, I'm reminded that I wasn't worth your commitment."

Tears coursed down her cheeks, and Gareth longed to gather her into his arms and tell her she was wrong—leaving her was the hardest thing he'd ever done. But she didn't appear receptive of any offers of comfort yet. He waited, and let her rail at him.

A visible shudder waffled through her, and she fisted the tears away. "While every other woman in town is married and raising a family, I put on a mask every day so people won't see the pain I carry around. Only God knows how many tears have soaked my pillow at night."

Every word she choked out, every sob, was a hammer blow to his heart.

"You couldn't write a note? Not even a single sentence? Not even an 'I'm sorry'?"

She sniffed. "Maybe you weren't sorry, is that it? Your story is very different from the one your father told. How am I to decide who to believe?"

Gareth laced his fingers together to prevent them from reaching for her hands. "I don't know what my stepfather told you. The night he flew into a drunken rage, he told me to get out and never come back. My heart grieved, not only for you, but also for my family. The next morning—the day before we were to wed—I stood outside your house before dawn. I wanted to tell you why I had to leave, but I just couldn't. It was still too raw."

He climbed down from the buckboard seat and held out his hand. She sat still and stared at him, as if deciding whether or not she could trust him to help her down. After a long minute, she took his hand. The moment he cocooned her small hand within his large one, his pulse kicked up to a gallop. Standing by as her protector, her champion, was all he'd dreamed about for more than half his life. He wished for time to stand still. But once she stood safely on the ground beside him, he released her hand, sorry he felt obliged to do so.

He walked through the meadow grass, not knowing if she'd accompany him. When she did, hope swelled in his chest. Just ahead, clusters of daisies nodded their heads in the sun. He bent and picked several, remembering the daisy chains she used to make. Could they resurrect the good memories and find their way back to what they once had?

No, he doubted continuing as if there'd never been a moment of separation between them was possible. Too much time had passed. Attempting to turn back the calendar and return to their youth was a fantasy. He plucked a few more daisies and added them to his handful.

"Leah, I hope you will believe me when I tell you I've never forgotten you." He held out the bouquet. "Daisies were always your favorite. Do you remember?"

With hesitancy, she reached to take the peace offering from him. "Of course I remember. My bridal bouquet was going to be daisies."

Chapter 5

Leah stole a glance at Gareth sitting across the table from her. Why on earth did she think this was a good idea? When he had asked her out to dinner yesterday, she feared everyone in town would stare at them as they sat in the café. Word would spread soon enough that the man who'd jilted her was back in town. Her counteroffer, inviting him to the house for dinner, afforded them privacy from prying eyes. Thank goodness Papa was helping to carry the conversation.

"So, do you like working at the wainwright shop, Gareth?"

Gareth nodded. "Yes, sir. My boss, Mr. Dansby, has not only taught me a trade, he's been a good friend and a great example of a Christian." He forked up his last bit of apple pie. "This was a fine supper, Leah. Thank you."

She swallowed hard. "Would anyone like more coffee?" She began refilling cups without waiting for their answers. It gave her hands something to do.

Papa stirred a splash of cream into his cup. "I believe I'll sit out on the porch and enjoy the cool breeze. You young folks have things to talk about." He pushed back his chair and ambled, cup in hand, to the front door.

Young folks? Papa's eyesight must be failing.

She began gathering up the dishes, hoping the silly tremors in her fingers didn't cause her to drop any of them. Gareth picked up his plate and carried it to the kitchen.

"Can I help with the dishes?" One corner of his mouth lifted. "I was hoping we could talk some more."

A quiver danced through Leah's stomach. "I'd like that."

A twinkle glinted in the corner of his eye to accompany his cockeyed smile. "Help with the dishes or talking?"

A soft laugh soothed her jitters. "Both, I suppose." She poured hot water from the stove's reservoir into the dishpan and added some thin slices of soap.

His nearness stirred her in a way it never had before, when they actually were young folks. But caution niggled. Fifteen years ago, she thought she knew everything about him—his goals, his passions, how he'd react in any given situation, what made him happy. Now she wasn't so sure.

He wiped a plate and laid it on the worktable. "I found my mother."

Her hands paused in their task. "You did? Where?"

"Kansas City. She's in a hospital there." He picked up another plate and ran the towel over it. "I heard someone say her name and knew it had to be her. There aren't too many women whose given name is Audelia Rose, but go by the nickname Dandy." He related the events leading him to locate his mother.

"That's amazing you could find her after all these years." Leah bit her lip. Given the circumstances by which Gareth's mother had left Whitley, she didn't wish to embarrass him by asking nosy questions. "You said she's in a hospital?"

Gareth nodded. "She has consumption."

A chill shuddered through Leah. "Oh, Gareth, how awful."

A tiny scowl pulled his eyebrows together. "She's in a pretty bad way. I took a second job to try and earn enough money to get her better care. The doctor doesn't give her much hope, but I want her remaining days to be as comfortable as possible."

He set down the roasting pan he'd finished drying. "You may think she doesn't deserve any consideration, running off the way she did, but I want to tell her about Jesus."

The compassion in his voice made her heart turn over, and moisture collected in the corner of her eye. She whisked it away with her forearm. "What kind of second job did you get?"

A sheepish expression pulled at his handsome features. "I'm a night janitor at the hospital. The hospital administrator made a deal with me. They took Mama out of the indigent ward and put her in a semiprivate ward with only three other patients where she gets better care and medicine. Instead of paying me in cash, they are applying my wage to her bill." He blew out a breath. "I guess it's not much of a job, mopping floors, emptying slop jars."

"I disagree." She set the last cooking pot on the drain board. "You're doing a very noble thing, Gareth. Some may look down on a man who works as a janitor, but it's honest work and you're using it to demonstrate Christ's mercy and grace." She lowered her gaze and studied the suds in the dishpan. "I admire you."

He shrugged. "If I can sell my stepfather's house and land, I'll have enough money to pay for a private room and special nursing care." He reached for the dishpan. "Let me empty that for you."

He carried the dishwater to the back door and tossed it out. "So what about you? I'm surprised you aren't married, with a bunch of little ones. Certainly you've had a stampede of bachelors beating down your door, all wanting to court you."

His words froze her in place. If she moved, surely she'd break. By his tone, the statement was sincere, albeit naive. Did he really think she'd entertained a host of suitors? Had he not heard her when she'd unleashed her storm of anguish at him over having been labeled a spinster? Her throat tightened and she drew in a slow breath in an attempt to steady herself. He must have misunderstood her pause.

He swabbed out the dishpan with his towel. "I'm sorry. That was a stupid thing to say. You told me you took care of your mother all those years after she'd had a stroke. Her passing must have been very hard on you."

Leah shook her head, willing the bitterness in her heart to recede. He obviously didn't understand how being left at the altar branded her as unwanted, tarnished goods. Hurt and resentment collided with hesitant hope. How could she allow the feelings for him that she thought she buried years ago to resurrect when she desired to throw the nearest blunt object at him at the same time? If she truly wanted to nurture her anger and bitterness at him, why did she invite him to dinner?

She knew the answer. The moment Gareth stepped into the apothecary, every shred of emotion she'd tried to press away like a dried-up flower in a book bloomed to life, as fragrant as the first rose of summer. Truth be told, she'd never stopped loving him, regardless of the pain and shame he'd inflicted by walking out on her. Was she being foolish?

She poured two fresh cups of coffee and they sat across the table from each other. She took a sip, and then another before answering his question.

"No, I haven't married, and haven't had suitors knocking at my door. Well, if you don't include Harold Stuart."

He jerked his head up and plunked his coffee cup on the table. "Who's Harold Stuart?"

She gave a dismissive wave of her fingers. "A salesman with Cunningham Pharmaceuticals. He comes through here regularly."

"Hmmph." He leaned back in his chair, a scowl lining his forehead. "Leah, can you understand my reason for leaving? Can you believe me when I say I was trying to protect you?"

A deep sigh slipped past her lips. "What I heard—what the entire town believed—was that your mother left in a hurry because she'd gotten word her mother was ill back East. Your father said her stage was held up and she was killed."

Gareth shook his head. "That's not what happened. I suppose he didn't want people to know she'd lit out with another man." He turned his coffee cup around absently. "What did my stepfather say about me?"

She suddenly didn't want to tell him the story that everyone in town had heard and repeated. Maybe because for the first time, she questioned it herself. "He. . .he said you. . . that you got cold feet and went off in search of adventure." She couldn't keep the regret from threading her voice.

He emitted a groan that sounded as though it echoed all the way from his toes. "Leah, I'm so sorry. All I can do is tell you the truth and pray you'll believe me and forgive me for hurting you."

The sorrow, evident in his eyes, sagged his posture as he rose from his chair. "I'd best be going. Thank you again for supper." He halted, his hand on the back of the chair, as if wondering whether or not to say more. Apparently deciding against it, he plucked his hat from the hall tree. "Good night."

He stepped out the front door, and the thought occurred to her that perhaps he'd paused, waiting for her to say something. With a sigh, she retired to her room and readied herself for bed. As she pulled back the covers and sat on the edge of the bed, she prayed.

"Heavenly Father, I'm not sure what to do. It's so much to take in and digest. Should I believe him? I'm afraid to risk my heart again. Lord, I've waited so long and have given up ever being truly happy. Dare I hope?"

Leah went over the list of things she wanted done at the cottage with a local handy-man. "Scrape off all the old peeling paint and whitewash the clapboard. I'd also like the shutters painted. And could you please check the roof and see if any repairs are needed?"

"Yes, ma'am." Mr. Sanders rubbed his chin. "What about them floorboards on the porch? A few of 'em gonna need replaced."

Leah tapped her pencil on the apothecary counter. "Do whatever is necessary, Mr. Sanders, but let me know first."

Mr. Sanders nodded and tipped his hat to her as he left. Before the door closed completely, it opened again and Harold Stuart stepped in with a smile wide enough to show every one of his teeth.

"You're looking exceptionally lovely today, Miss Leah."

Leah gave him a polite smile. "Good afternoon, Mr. Stuart."

He sidled up to her. "I altered my regular itinerary just so I could stop by to see you. I wanted to show you an article in the new science journal I received. Since you and I share the same interest in science and pharmacy, I knew you'd enjoy discussing. . ."

Harold rambled on about his new science journal, and Leah half listened as she picked up her clipboard and inventoried a new shipment. She murmured a muted response from time to time so she wouldn't appear completely rude. For some reason she couldn't imagine, the salesman for Cunningham Pharmaceuticals had the mistaken impression that she was not only interested in science, but also in him.

". . .and I entertained thoughts of spending time with you the entire day yesterday. I hope you will do me the honor of accompanying me to lunch. I will be the envy of every man in town."

She cringed inwardly and hoped it didn't show on her face. "Mr. Stuart, I—"

"Now, now." He held up a bony finger. "I told you to call me Harold."

"Harold." The muscles in her jaw tensed. "I'm flattered by your invitation, but I really must decline. My father needs me here at the apothecary, and as you can see, we are quite busy." She held up the clipboard as evidence of the validity of her statement.

"Oh. Well, perhaps. . ." His Adam's apple shimmied like an aspen tree in a stiff wind. "Perhaps another time."

She didn't wish to hurt his feelings, but she hoped he'd lose interest. The only man with whom she wished to keep company was Gareth. She walked to the door with Harold to bid him good day.

Gareth stood at the window of the lawyer's office across the street from the apothecary and watched as some dude in a black cheviot suit, red bow tie, and a derby exited the shop. Leah followed, standing in the doorway. The dandy stopped on the sidewalk and turned, captured her hand, and bowed to place a kiss on her fingers. Gareth jammed his fists into his pockets and his stomach tightened. Even worse, when the fancy man climbed into his buggy and tipped his hat to her, she smiled.

Chapter 6

Gareth perched on the edge of his chair and drummed his fingers on the county clerk's desk. It seemed logical that everything should have been in order when they contacted him by letter. He suppressed a sigh.

The clerk shook his head. "I'm sorry, Mr. Shepherd, but the tax receipt document isn't on file. They were supposed to send it from the county seat in Burlington to confirm no liens exist on the property. We can't proceed without it." The man thumbed through the neatly stacked papers on the desk and held out his hands. "It's not here."

Gareth slumped against the back of the chair. "How soon do you think you can arrange to have all the documents in order? My employer is expecting me back by the first of next week."

The clerk pushed his spectacles up on his nose. "I'll wire the Burlington courthouse today, but it will take at least a couple of days for the document to arrive."

Gareth huffed. Even if he rode to Burlington himself, it would take him a full day each way. He pushed away from the chair and stood. "All right. I'll check back on Friday."

The mousey man flicked an invisible speck of dust from the desk. "Yes, sir. I know you don't want to waste time."

Spending a few extra days in Whitley—especially if that time was spent with Leah—wasn't exactly what Gareth would call wasting time. However, he didn't want to take advantage of Mr. Dansby's good nature. As soon as he could get a telegram sent to Kansas City, he'd stop by the apothecary to see if Leah might join him for a picnic lunch.

The telegrapher was an old schoolmate from years ago, and greeted Gareth with an air of curiosity. "Gareth Shepherd. Heard you were back in town. My condolences on the loss of your father."

"Hello, Micah." Gareth shook the man's hand. He didn't bother explaining that Randall Shepherd was his stepfather. "I need to send a wire."

Micah pulled the pencil from behind his ear. "To?"

"Orsen Dansby, Dansby Wainwrights Inc. Kansas City." Gareth rubbed his chin, considering how to word the telegram, calculating the cost per word. "Business taking longer than expected. Return delayed. Next week soonest."

Micah scribbled down the message. "I'll get this right out."

"Thanks, Micah." Gareth pulled a few coins from his pocket and slid them across the counter. "I'll come back later to see if there is a reply."

He turned and discovered Leah standing in the doorway. Warmth spilled through him at the sight of her. He smiled and stepped closer so Micah wouldn't overhear him asking her out for lunch. "I was just coming to see you."

But the expression on her face halted the invitation before the words formed on his tongue.

The paper in Leah's hand crumpled within her curled fist. They hadn't spoken of Gareth's plans or the length of his stay. Certainly she shouldn't be surprised that he wanted to return to Kansas City as soon as possible. After all, he had a job there. Two jobs, actually. Nevertheless, hearing it spoken from his lips sent shards of warning down her spine.

She searched Gareth's face. "Sounds like you're in a hurry to leave. To get. . .home."

The word came out on a croaked whisper and left a bitter taste in her mouth. In truth, Whitley was no longer Gareth's home, and the sudden wish that it was startled her.

Gareth's eyes skidded over to Micah and back to her. "Some of the paperwork needed for the sale of my stepfather's property has been delayed. I needed to let my boss know."

Realization emerged from the secret place in her soul where hope hid. She'd surreptitiously clung to a private desire that Gareth had come home to stay. She held her breath, waiting for him to say the words.

He didn't.

He rubbed one finger alongside his jaw. "The sooner the sale of the property is complete, the sooner I can arrange with St. Margaret's Hospital to have my mother moved to a private room with a special nurse."

Of course. She couldn't fault him. Gareth was doing what God would have him do for his mother. She'd have done the same for Mama, given similar circumstances. Her chest began to ache and she released her imprisoned breath. But giving her lungs freedom to breathe again didn't relieve the ache, and she didn't dare voice the question she longed to ask.

Are you coming back, Gareth?

Nothing on his countenance indicated he'd read the question in her eyes, nor did he seem inclined to continue discussing his plans. Perhaps he felt it was none of her business. Either way, she refused to be vulnerable again. One carefully placed brick at a time, she erected an invisible wall around herself. But how did she make it high enough, wide enough, and strong enough to create an impenetrable defense? Could her heart survive watching him walk out of her life a second time?

She acknowledged his comment with a short nod and tried to remember why she'd come here. Her gaze fell to the paper crushed in her hand. Oh, yes, Papa's telegram.

"If you'll excuse me, Papa needs this order sent right away." She stepped past him to the counter. He didn't bid her goodbye, nor did the door slap closed in its frame, so she assumed he still stood there.

She smoothed the wrinkled paper out and pushed it across the counter to Micah. "Can you send this to Cunningham Pharmaceuticals, please?"

Micah picked up the paper. "Sure thing, Leah. Put it on your father's account?"

She nodded, acutely aware of Gareth's presence behind her. "Yes, please."

Sure enough, when she turned, there he stood. He held the door open for her. She mumbled her thanks and accelerated her steps toward the apothecary. There was nothing left to say.

"Leah."

She slowed her steps but didn't stop. When he came alongside her, she regarded him with cool politeness.

"Leah, I wanted to ask if you would accompany me to lunch."

If she was ever to forget Gareth Shepherd, she might as well begin now. "I'm sorry, Gareth, I need to get back to the shop." She kept walking.

"Leah, wait." His hand on her elbow stopped her, but she didn't turn to face him. Looking at him would destroy any shred of starch she had left.

"Are you angry about something?" Uncertainty colored his tone.

She stiffened her spine. "What would I have to be angry about?" What indeed? He'd left her once and was preparing to do so again. The only difference was this time she was forewarned.

"You seem angry."

Do I? She pushed away the inclination to say something hurtful. "That would be pointless. After all, you and I no longer have an understanding. As soon as your business here is completed, you'll return to Kansas City."

Gareth stepped in front of her and she had no choice but to face him. "I asked you a question a few days ago, but you didn't answer me. I suppose you needed time to think about it. Can you—will you forgive me for hurting you?"

She could still hear her mother telling her that forgiveness was a choice. A lump took up residence in her throat, despite repeated attempts to swallow it. She tested the stoutness of her brick wall to make sure it was intact and reinforced before she spoke.

"It. . .it's been w–wonderful to see you again, Gareth, but—" Tightening in her throat cut off her words. She pulled in a deep breath and held her voice to just above a whisper. "I can't. I can't do this again."

She hurried down the sidewalk and ducked into the apothecary. Papa was studying a pharmaceutical journal. "Papa, since we aren't busy, I'm going home early."

He mumbled a distracted reply, and she slipped out. Walking down the alley instead of the street, she arrived at their bungalow without encountering anyone. A sigh shuddered from her spirit as she entered through the back door.

The daisies Gareth picked for her a few days ago wilted in a mason jar on the kitchen table. The daisies—like his promises—wouldn't last.

Gareth shuffled down the street. The image of Leah's face appeared in his mind and her words accosted his heart—*I can't do this again.* His shoulders sagged beneath the weight of sadness. Just ahead a man hailed him. He looked familiar. . .his hair was white and his step was slower, but—

"Reverend Lockridge?"

The pastor's kind eyes and smile hadn't changed. "Gareth Shepherd." He clasped Gareth's hand and pumped it. "I heard you were back."

Gareth nodded. "Yes, sir."

The old preacher cocked his head. "Good to see you, son. But you look like you've lost your last friend."

Gareth shrugged. He knew beyond any doubt his feelings for Leah were stronger than ever, but she was slamming the door and holding it shut. "You may be right. But then you always were perceptive."

Pastor Lockridge slid a friendly arm around Gareth's shoulders. "I'm a good listener, and I know a Friend who will never leave you."

Gareth had known the preacher since he was a boy. If he could confide in anyone, it would be this man. He nodded again.

They walked a half block to the church—the same church where he and Leah were supposed to have been married. Pastor Lockridge motioned toward the back pews. "Have a seat, son. I expect you're carrying a heavy burden. Have you seen Leah Brown since you've been here?"

"Yes, sir." A knot formed in his stomach at the mention of her name.

"Reckon she was a might surprised to see you." The preacher leaned back and crossed his arms. "Why don't you start from the beginning."

Gareth began tentatively, but when he saw no judgment in the old preacher's eyes, he poured it all out—what truly happened with his mother and stepfather all those years ago, why he left, his desire to protect Leah from censure and scandal, and how he'd recently found his mother. Pastor Lockridge was right—he was carrying a heavy load.

"I can't blame Leah for being defensive. I've regretted hurting her every day for the past fifteen years." He met the pastor's gaze. "My wish is to do whatever it takes to heal her broken heart. But like I told you, I've made a commitment to my mother and to the hospital."

The preacher nodded slowly. "You said your mother didn't expect you to return."

"But surely you see that I must." His tone was laced with urgency. "I believe God wants to use me to show her His love in a way she can see and understand."

Reverend Lockridge leaned forward, his forearms on his knees, asking pertinent questions and listening to Gareth pour out his heart. Finally, he laid his hand over Gareth's.

"You keep your word, son—to your mother, to Leah, and to God."

A flicker of encouragement flared to life, but was quickly doused. "I'm afraid it might be too late to keep my word to Leah."

The lines around the preacher's eyes deepened when he smiled. "God's promises don't always happen exactly when we want them. But that doesn't mean He's not faithful. It just means He wants us to trust Him. His promises happen in His time, not ours." He straightened. "There is a verse in Galatians that says, 'And let us not be weary in well doing: for in due season we shall reap, if we faint not.' Don't give up, son."

Gareth carefully weighed the pastor's advice. "No, sir, I won't. God never gave up on me. I just pray I can convince Leah to give me another chance."

Chapter 7

Gareth scrawled his signature on the bill of sale and handed it over to the county clerk. After an extra three days of waiting, all the details seemed to kick the procedure into a gallop.

"Is that everything?"

The clerk tapped the edges of the papers into a neat stack. "All except for this." He pulled a bank draft from the bottom of the stack and placed it in front of Gareth. The amount still made him blink. He never expected the seventy acres to bring that much—more than sufficient to give his mother every comfort for her remaining days.

"The buyer knows I'm taking a few personal things from the house, right? My mother will appreciate seeing them."

A tiny scowl furrowed the clerk's brow, as if the detail were beneath his notice. He waved his fingers. "Yes, yes."

Gareth thanked the clerk and tucked the bank draft into his pocket. A quick stop at the telegraph office to notify Mr. Dansby he'd be home by the end of the week, and he headed to the livery to retrieve the buckboard. The smaller items he planned to take back to his mother would fit into a few crates the livery man had given him.

He hitched the team and headed out to his family's farm that no longer belonged to him. The place looked desolate as he pulled up in front of the house, but he experienced no remorse over selling it. Despite the good memories from his childhood, the ugly memories from his last few days there overshadowed them. The ensuing years had dogged him with bitter images and hateful words, haunting his days and condemning his thoughts—until he'd met Orsen Dansby and the man had taken him under his wing.

He lifted the latch and pushed open the door. Odd, how his entry to the house where he'd grown up felt intrusive. His stepfather's accusations still rang in the canyons of his mind. He shook off the memory.

He collected the items he wanted to keep and packed the mementos he knew his mother treasured into the crates, and loaded them onto the buckboard, grateful for Mr. Dansby's insistence that he bring the conveyance. He dragged his mother's trunk from the bedroom, surprised his stepfather had kept it. He lashed the crates behind the seat so they wouldn't bounce around, and tied the trunk in place.

Gareth pulled off his hat and dragged his sleeve across his brow. He placed one hand on the corner post of the front porch, and bowed his head. "I know, God, what I have to do. You've spoken to my heart and ordered my steps to go and minister to my mother. This place holds bitter memories for her. For me too. But I pray You will break down her hardened heart so she will listen when I tell her how much You love her."

He turned and stared at the crates and his mother's trunk. The contents were nothing more than a few trinkets, an old china doll, a couple of housedresses, a hairbrush, a looking glass, the faded apron she always wore when she baked bread, a worn quilt. Nothing of great worth, but they were pieces of who his mother was. "Lord, help her to see she is loved."

With one last look at his childhood home, he climbed into the buckboard seat and turned the team in the direction of town. A short distance down the lane and beyond the fields, he approached a little cottage he recalled from when he was a boy.

He liked the sweet old lady who used to live there. She'd made cookies for the kids so they would come by and visit her. At first the place appeared abandoned. But when he drew closer, he noticed someone had scraped the clapboard siding and had begun whitewashing the front. The shutters had been removed and sported a fresh coat of green paint, and weeds were piled up in one corner of the yard, waiting to be burned. The sight of the work being done on the little cottage brightened his mood. Maybe the new owner of his old home would brighten it up in much the same way.

As the buckboard rolled back into Whitley, tempting aromas wafted to greet him from the café. Fried chicken, if he didn't miss his guess. His mouth watered and another memory triggered. A smile pulled at his lips as he remembered the day he and Leah had sneaked off from the gathering at the church Fourth of July picnic. Their favorite meadow, alive with wildflowers, had offered privacy so Gareth could gather his nerve. It was the day he'd asked her to marry him.

Forsaking caution, he steered the team past the apothecary, the dry goods store, and the livery, to the modest bungalow surrounded by a white picket fence, with blue hydrangeas in the front yard. He hopped down from the buckboard and stood for several long moments at the front gate. Three days ago, Leah had made clear her unwillingness to forgive him. Would she even open the door now so he could tell her goodbye?

Driven by Pastor Lockridge's encouragement and scripture's mandate to not grow weary in well doing, Gareth let himself in the gate and climbed the steps to the front porch. "God, You promised in due season You would bring about Your will if I don't give up. I trust You."

Before he could raise his hand to knock, the door opened and Leah stood in front of him. His breath left his lungs in a rush. Framed in the late afternoon sun, she was even more beautiful now than when she was eighteen.

A desire he'd kept restrained for well over a decade rattled its shackles in an effort to break free. He longed to scoop her into his arms and carry her off, find a preacher, and never be away from her for a single day ever again. But he was here, standing on her porch, to tell her just the opposite.

"Hello, Leah."

"Gareth." The breeze stirring the tree branches almost drowned out her whisper.

He rubbed the back of his neck. Looking into her deep hazel eyes made his throat ache, but he couldn't look away. *Let us not be weary in well doing: for in due season we shall reap, if we faint not.* "I came to tell you that all the papers have been signed and I have the bank draft for the sale of the property." He touched his shirt pocket.

Her shoulders lifted. "So that means you're leaving."

He nodded. "At first light." *Please understand, Leah.* "This money will take care of my mother's needs and make her as comfortable as possible."

She interlaced her fingers, clutching her hands at her waist. "Will you—" She pressed her lips together as if fearing the answer to her unasked question.

He waited.

"Will I. . .what?"

She caught her bottom lip between her teeth and looked past him toward the buckboard. "I see you're all loaded up."

He leaned to block her view behind him and make her look at him. "Leah, will I what?"

"Come back." He could barely hear her. "Will you come back?"

His stomach fell like a rock. Oh, how he wished he could assure her of his return. "I can't promise. I have no way of knowing. . ."

Tears glistened in her eyes and an invisible fist punched Gareth in the gut. Only a cad would put her through this twice. He caught hold of her hands. "Pray with me that my mother will come to know Jesus before it's too late. If I can, I'll try to come back, but—"

After Gareth's departure and a week of sleepless nights, Leah pulled the covers up to her chin and stared into the darkness of her room. How could she trust Gareth? He'd already walked out on her once. The only difference this time was that he'd come to say goodbye. He said he'd try to come back, but. . . She didn't hear much after that. From the looks of the crates and bundles and the trunk tied onto the buckboard, it appeared he didn't plan on returning any time soon.

"Oh, God, I want to believe him, but I don't think I can take any more pain. My common sense is telling me to guard my heart." She squeezed her eyes shut against the burning tears.

Stay busy. She needed distractions. Perhaps she'd been hasty in dismissing the idea of going to the university. What did she do with that catalog? Reading through it again might open a new door. Papa had said he'd help with expenses. She sighed against the darkness. If she went to the university, the campus would be filled with young people, and more than likely, young couples. Why put herself in a place where she'd be surrounded with reminders of her unfulfilled dreams? Besides, she'd already decided getting her degree wasn't what she wanted.

Papa and Helen's wedding was to take place in a little over a month. As much as she liked her father's bride-to-be, she was anxious to move out of the bungalow. Her new little house at the edge of town was almost ready. Mr. Sanders had told her two days ago he'd have everything finished in another week. She could stop by the dry goods store and purchase yard goods to make curtains. She imagined fresh blue gingham at the front window. But hanging curtains and arranging her possessions wouldn't keep her busy for long.

Unable to sleep, she rose and lit the lamp on her dresser. Occupying her hands was one thing, but her mind wasn't cooperating. When she closed her eyes, all she could picture was Gareth driving away, as if turning the page in a book.

She stood in the middle of the room, as aimless as dandelion down at the mercy of the wind. She covered her face with her hands, and Gareth's plea whispered to her soul. Not his plea to forgive him—his request that she pray for his mother.

She sank to her knees at the foot of her bed. "Oh, Lord, I've been so selfish. All I've thought about is how hurt I was, and likely will be again. But Gareth's mother is dying, and she needs You. How can I refuse Gareth's wish that I pray for her?"

She spent the next hour in a season of prayer in which she poured out her heart to God—for Gareth's well-being, for wisdom as he spoke to his mother about the Lord, and for Mrs. Shepherd to find peace with God before she died.

"Please hear my prayer, Lord." She wiped her tears and rose. Her gaze fell on the trunk in the corner. The lid creaked as she lifted it, and the flickering light from the oil lamp cast ghostly shadows on the contents.

She lifted each item out, dismissed the grief over the things she'd so carefully prepared for her married life, and determined to use them for her cottage. The linens, tablecloth and napkins, a teakettle and other sundry kitchen pots and utensils—each one destined to grace her new home. If God ordained her to live out her days alone, then He'd be her companion. This was her future.

At the bottom of the trunk she found the embroidered pillowcases. Pushing away encroaching resentment, she tossed them aside with the intention of throwing them into the burn barrel in the morning.

She refolded the table linens and quilts and layered the kitchen utensils with them to return them to the trunk. Perhaps now she could sleep. She reached to extinguish the lamp, but halted her hand. Her gaze was drawn back to the pillowcases. The ivy tendrils with blue forget-me-nots were lovely. Maybe she could snip out the stitched initials. She buried the pillowcases back in the bottom of the trunk and put out the light. She slipped between the cool sheets and closed her eyes, willing her tumbled thoughts to cease and her emotions to quiet. Her muscles relaxed and she grew drowsy. Just before she drifted off, the image of Gareth Shepherd's face caressed her subconscious and filled her dreams.

Chapter 8

Leah waved as her father urged the horses forward, taking the borrowed wagon back to the livery. She called out to him as he waved back. "Thank you, Papa. I'll see you tomorrow."

She entered the cottage that smelled of fresh whitewash and surveyed the crates, her trunk, and the hodgepodge of furniture. If she took her time, the task of finding a place for everything might stretch into a few days. After that. . .she'd find something to keep herself busy.

She rooted through the crates and pulled out the things she'd need for her first night in her new home—bed linens, a pillow, a towel, a single place setting of dishes. She opened her trunk and pulled out a doily her mother had made and arranged it on the back of her mother's chair—the one Papa had given her for Christmas when Leah was just a girl. She ran her hand over the tapestry upholstery and remembered her mother sitting by the fire with needlework in hand.

A soft sigh wafted through her lips. She couldn't truthfully say living alone was what she wanted. But this is what God had decreed for her, and Papa and Helen could start out their marriage without her underfoot.

She placed her clothes in the small wardrobe and dresser and then made up her bed. With a bit of pushing and shoving, she rearranged the few pieces of furniture in the tiny bedroom. She hadn't realized the single bedroom window faced west.

The sunset gilded the sky, and she propped her elbows on the windowsill to admire God's artistry. Gold, orange, and purple streaks enhanced the deepening twilight. Fireflies played tag with each other. Grass rippled in the wind across the field that separated her cottage from the Shepherd place. She pushed away the increasingly familiar pangs that stole through her chest every time she thought of Gareth. Now, it seemed she'd be afforded a view of his childhood home when she arose every morning and retired every night.

She changed into her nightclothes and stretched out on the bed, the crickets serenading her from the open window. A memory tickled her mind—the time she'd gotten so angry at Gareth for using crickets as bait when he went fishing. How could he stick a fishhook through a creature that sang so beautifully? He'd laughed and teased her about being sentimental about a bug. She drifted off to sleep with the image of Gareth's blue eyes and breath-robbing smile dancing through her dreams.

Leah forced a smile she didn't feel and greeted the two women who came into the apothecary. Edna Henson's reputation in Whitley as a gossip was superseded only by her ability to exaggerate. Her friend, Phoebe Crenshaw, peered over her spectacles at Leah.

"Oh, my dear, I was so sorry to hear the news." Mrs. Crenshaw patted Leah's hand. "How are you holding up? If you need a shoulder to cry on, dearie, you can count on me."

Leah clamped her teeth and counted silently to ten. Mrs. Crenshaw must have mistaken the pause as an invitation to pry.

"I don't figure you ever expected to see that Shepherd boy again, not after what he did all those years ago. Folks are saying he came back just to see how much money he could make by selling his father's farm." She clucked her tongue. "Why come back at all if he didn't plan to stay—that's what I'd like to know." She shook her head. "You poor thing."

Leah sucked in a breath and tried not to let her tone sound like a hiss. "Ladies, did you have need of a medicinal compound today?"

Mrs. Henson swept Leah up and down with an appraising look. "I need a box of Ayer's Cathartic Pills and a bottle of paregoric." She leaned forward. "You know, I tried those soda mint tablets your father suggested for my sour stomach, but they didn't work worth a hoot."

Leah bit her lip. If the woman would refrain from eating so much rich, fried food, her ailment might be alleviated. "As I recall, my father recommended you see Doctor Ward for your stomach." Before the woman could retort, Leah smiled. "I'll fetch those things for you right away, Mrs. Henson." She scurried into the workroom behind the curtain, but the woman's *tsk-tsk*ing followed her.

"No wonder she can't find a husband, as opinionated as she is."

"That Shepherd fellow had a lot of nerve showing up here again. She should have sent him packing. Such a pity."

Leah snatched a box of Ayer's pills from the shelf and tried to block out the busybodies' conversation. But Mrs. Henson didn't seem inclined to lower her voice.

"It's simply her destiny. Some women are doomed to be old maids their entire lives."

"Edna, you shouldn't say such a thing."

"Why not? It's true, isn't it?"

Leah could picture Mrs. Henson smirking.

"When the same man who jilted her years ago returns and jilts her again, I call that destiny."

Leah could take no more. She pushed the curtain aside and stepped back to the counter. "Well, I call it gossip." She plunked down the pill box and the paregoric. "That will be a dollar and eighty cents."

"Well, I never!" Mrs. Henson huffed. "I'll just take my business elsewhere." The woman turned on her heel and headed for the door.

"But, Edna..." Phoebe Crenshaw hurried after her. "This is the only apothecary in town."

As the two women exited, they nearly ran over Helen in the doorway. Papa's bride stepped out of their way and glanced over at Leah. Her expression confirmed that she'd heard at least part of the exchange. She crossed to the counter and caught Leah's hands in hers.

"Don't listen to those old biddies. They have nothing better to do than to stick their noses in everyone else's business." Helen gave her a quick hug. "I came to ask you to join your father and me on a picnic tomorrow afternoon after church."

"Thank you, Helen. That's very kind, but you must admit that part of what they said is true. Some women are destined to be single. I'm one of them."

"Oh, nonsense. When the right man comes along—"

Leah halted Helen's words with an uplifted hand. The right man had already come along. But time had sifted through her fingers like sand, and there was no going back to change the circumstances.

Leah had never before wished to stay home on a Sunday morning, but she dreaded having to face Mrs. Henson and Mrs. Crenshaw again—not to mention half the town who felt it their responsibility to offer her advice or inform her of all the reasons they believed she wasn't yet married. But skipping church would only give the gossips more fuel.

She slipped into the pew with Papa and Helen like everyone expected. But she'd already decided against accompanying them on the picnic. With their wedding only three weeks away, Leah was quite certain Helen and Papa didn't need her tagging along. Solitude felt more appropriate today anyway.

After the service, she pleaded a headache—which really was true—and left Papa and Helen to enjoy their afternoon without her. But instead of walking home, she turned in the opposite direction.

Clouds skittered across the sun, and a pair of mourning doves cooed a melancholy ballad as she walked. Before long, she reached the meadow where she and Gareth had stopped the day he had arrived back in Whitley, where she'd poured out all her pain and anger at him, and where he'd begged her forgiveness.

Guilt pricked. Whether consciously or unconsciously, she'd withheld her forgiveness. The question confronted her—did she think refusing to forgive would hurt Gareth as much as he'd hurt her? Resorting to retaliation wasn't who she wanted to be.

The clouds thickened and the sun went into hiding. Distant thunder growled. Leah made her way through the prairie grass to a patch of daisies, and fell to her knees.

"Oh, God, as often as I've tried to forget Gareth, it seems I'm unable to do so. I'm not strong enough. Please, God, take this terrible love for Gareth Shepherd away from me. It's too heavy for me, and I beg You to free me of it."

Raindrops began to fall, mingling with her tears. Was God weeping with her? Or was He shaking His head?

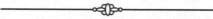

Gareth watched the nurse tuck crisp, fresh sheets around his mother. He pushed the window of the private room open, and fresh air wafted in.

He snagged the two extra pillows from the shelf. "Mama, let me prop you up so you can see the view out your window. There's a park with lots of trees, and a fountain, and children playing." He eased her forward and stacked the pillows behind her. He noted with satisfaction that the stomach-turning odor that had clung to her a few weeks ago was gone. She now smelled of rosewater, and her hair was clean and neatly braided to one side.

She leaned back against the pillows, the effort of sitting forward having taxed her. Her voice was weak. "I hear children laughing."

Gareth smiled and nodded, but the wrinkles on his mother's face deepened when she frowned at him. "I still don't know why you're doing this. I don't deserve your kindness."

Gareth slid a chair over to her bedside and pulled his Bible from his pocket. "I'd like to read to you the reason why I'm doing this."

He flipped a few pages. "This is what Jesus said. 'As the Father hath loved me, so have I loved you: continue ye in my love. If ye keep my commandments, ye shall abide in my love; even as I have kept my Father's commandments, and abide in his love. These things have I spoken unto you, that my joy might remain in you, and that your joy might be full.'"

Mama's sunken eyes glazed with confusion. "Why would God want me to have joy after the way I've lived—what I've done?"

She'd just thrown the door wide open. "Mama, do you love me?"

Moisture glinted in the corners of her lashes. "I know I didn't show it by running off the way I did, but I do love you."

"If it were in your power to do anything to make me happy, you would do it?"

Her nod was nearly imperceptible. "Yes, I would if I could."

Gareth laid the Bible across his lap and leaned forward. "Because I'm your child. Don't you see? God created us, we are His. He loves us so much He sent His Son to die in our place, to pay for our sins."

She shook her head. "That doesn't make sense. Why would God love people who have broken His commandments?"

Gareth set the Bible aside and took his mother's feeble hand. "If I did something terribly wrong, you would still love me, because I'm your son. Our fellowship might be broken, but if I asked you to forgive me, that connection could be restored."

He picked up the Bible and continued reading. Every time he glanced up, his mother was staring at him, as if trying to hold on to every word. Hope kindled in his heart. If he could just make her understand.

Please, Lord, let her hear with her heart.

"Son, do you believe that?" She lifted a shaking finger and pointed to the Bible.

"I do, Mama. Every word."

Gareth gave her time to contemplate what he'd read to her. Her eyelids fluttered closed, and Gareth assumed she'd fallen asleep. But as he rose quietly from his chair, she whispered, "I don't think God could ever forgive me."

He stood there and watched the tense lines in Mama's face relax as her breathing became less labored. He slipped out and leaned against the wall outside her room. Trusting God's forgiveness and mercy was easy for him. It was the forgiveness between people that created chasms of discouragement. "Oh, Lord, please help Leah find it in her heart to forgive me."

Chapter 9

The back door of the apothecary opened and Leah leaned back to peer around the curtain that hung between the front counter and back storage room. "Papa?"

"Yes, daughter, it's me." He wore a silly schoolboy grin when he pushed the curtain aside. "Helen and I got back yesterday. It was a short honeymoon, but we had a lovely time. Sunsets, late suppers, long walks."

Leah forced a smile. As much as she loved her father and stepmother, she wasn't in the mood to hear details about their honeymoon. "Sounds nice. I'll stop by your house later and say hello to Helen."

Papa peered over her shoulder at her clipboard. "And how are things at *your* house? Do you need anything?"

She squirmed inside but gave a nonchalant wave of her hand. "Not a thing. I'm just fine." She pretended to study the shelf containing assorted bottles of preparations. "Should I order more tincture of arnica?"

His brow dipped into a frown. "There are a dozen bottles back there in the storage room."

Heat crept up her neck. It wouldn't do to let Papa think she was distracted. "I suppose that's enough." *Enough?* They didn't normally sell more than one or two bottles of arnica per month.

She avoided looking back at Papa, afraid she'd see that look he always gave her when he could practically read her thoughts. "This order is about ready to send. Do you want to take it to the post office?"

Papa hung his hat on the rack behind her. "No, I've already been to the post office this morning. Harold Stuart should be coming by this week. Just give the order to him."

Harold. The memory of his last visit intruded into her mind. He wasn't a bad sort—not really. But she had nothing in common with him, and the recollection of his lips touching her fingers made her cringe. She had no desire to hurt his feelings, but likewise had no desire to keep company with him.

Papa slipped his apron over his head and wrapped the strings around his waist. "I left the mail in the back on the desk. There's a letter for you."

Even without looking at him, she had a feeling he was watching her, gauging her reaction. Her unwilling gaze traveled to his, and sure enough, he arched his eyebrows as if to ask what she was waiting for.

"Go ahead." He sent her a pointed look and relieved her of the clipboard. "I'll finish this up." He tipped his head toward the curtain-covered doorway.

Anticipation tangled with apprehension. A sliver of hope drew her to the back room. An envelope lying in the middle of the desk bore her name and *Whitley, Kansas* written in a masculine hand. A Kansas City return address confirmed her best hope and worst fear. The letter was from Gareth.

She stared at it. Nearly a month had elapsed since she'd watched him drive away. He'd not given her any indication that he intended to return—only that he wanted her to forgive him. While she longed to hear from him, a nagging voice in her head told her what was in the letter. He'd likely written it was nice to see her again and he wished her well, or something to that effect. If she wasn't worth his commitment years ago, why did she ever allow herself to hope it might be different now?

The unopened seal on the envelope taunted her and her fingers hesitated, poised and ready to tear it open.

Don't. He could have chosen to stay. He could have promised to return, but he didn't. If that had been his intention, he would have told you straight out. Why let him hurt you again?

This wasn't a decision she needed to make now. She pulled her reticule out of the bottom drawer of the desk and shoved the envelope inside. If she chose to read it, she'd do it in the privacy of her little house.

Over the course of the next week, Leah forced thoughts of Gareth to the shadows of her mind. She opened the apothecary early and stayed late every day, and urged Papa to go home to his bride once he'd gotten all the medicinal compounds prepared.

The western sun painted long, dark shadows by the time Leah hung the Closed sign on the front door and twisted the key. She pulled the shade down over the glass and pulled off her apron. She welcomed the weariness that seeped through her bones. It helped her fall asleep with minimal tossing and turning.

She locked the back door and set out down the alley and across town. The walk to the cottage was a little over a half mile, and she picked daisies and buttercups along the way. Perhaps they'd brighten her little place.

Dusk had fallen by the time she reached home. She lit one lamp but had no desire to build a fire in the stove. Another cold supper would suffice. She sat and nibbled on crackers, cheese, and a bit of sausage. New curtains adorned the window, and the colorful rag rug she'd just completed last night lay spread under the table and chairs. But despite the long hours at the apothecary and her efforts to create pretty things for her house, she could not staunch the flood of heartache that was her stubborn companion. She chided herself. She should be grateful and excited to dwell in a place of her own, but the emptiness within her echoed with loneliness.

Gareth's letter—still unopened—sat on the bedside table. Every evening she picked it up and memorized the curves and loops of his handwriting on the front of the envelope. But her imagination fueled the apprehension she'd felt the day it arrived. Now dread stayed her hand from opening it.

A knock on the door sent a jolt through her and she sucked in a breath. She jumped up and held her hands to her waist for a moment. She didn't normally have callers, especially in the evening.

Had Gareth returned? Her foolishness at refusing to read his letter shook a finger at her. What if he'd told her in the letter of his plans to return?

She smoothed her hair and brushed cracker crumbs off her skirt. Her heart galloped as she stepped to the door. But when the door swung open, disappointment wilted her. Harold Stuart stood on the porch with a bouquet of wildflowers in his hand.

He pulled off his derby. "Good evening, Leah. I hope you don't mind me calling unannounced, but I just arrived in town, and you were the first person I wanted to see."

The breath she'd been holding escaped in a rush. "G—good evening, Mr. Stuart."

He handed her the flowers and held up a finger. "Harold."

She worked to keep from sighing. "Harold. Thank you for the flowers, but I thought you understood that I'm not receiving gentleman callers."

He fidgeted with the brim of his hat. "I understood you were busy during the day, but you didn't say anything about the evenings." He indicated the front porch with a sweeping gesture of his hand. "Could we sit for a while?"

A few minutes. Sitting with him a few minutes wouldn't hurt. "All right." She stepped out and closed the door behind her. Grateful she had no porch swing, she sat in the single rocking chair. Harold's expression reflected displeasure at not being able to sit beside her. He chose to pace the length of the small porch as if groping for whatever he wanted to say. Finally, he stopped and faced her.

"Miss Brown—Leah, I hope you'll not find me presumptuous. I've attempted to communicate my feelings over the past several months, so it shouldn't come as a surprise that I wish to court you."

She swallowed hard, and spent the next hour being as persuasive as she could without being unkind. Eventually, Harold took his leave, but not before stating he looked forward to seeing her when he came through town again. After he left and she returned inside, she remembered the pharmaceutical order she was supposed to have given him.

"Drat!" A trip to the post office would be in order after all.

Leah tore the page bearing the month of August from the calendar. While she could have sworn time had stood still since Gareth's departure, the new month bore witness to the fact that he'd been gone almost six weeks. His letter still remained on her bedside table unopened. Papa had asked about it, but when she didn't answer, he thankfully hadn't pursued the topic. She couldn't give a logical reason why she feared opening the letter—only that she felt sure it said what she didn't want to read.

During the darkest hours last night, she'd realized she was tormenting herself by staring at the unbroken seal every day. She took the envelope with her to the washstand in the corner and tucked it behind the mirror. At least the sight of it would no longer mock her.

Gareth smoothed the hair back where Mama's tears had stuck loose tendrils to her cheek. "Do you have pain, Mama? I can have the nurse bring you more laudanum."

The lines across her brow deepened. "No. It makes me sleepy. I want to hear you read."

Conflicted emotions tugged at him. He gave joyous praise that she was listening as he read God's Word. But knowing she was in pain and refusing medication to ease it made his stomach hurt.

He turned to the Gospel of John. *Gracious God of heaven, open my mother's heart. Let her see Your love and mercy.*

He took a deep breath and began reading the account of the woman who was caught in the act of adultery. When he read to the point where the people demanded that the woman be stoned to death, he glanced up. A tear slipped down Mama's face, but she didn't turn away, so he kept reading.

"So Jesus told the people who were standing there, 'He that is without sin among you, let him first cast a stone at her.' Do you see what Jesus did?" He pointed to the page. "He showed every one of them who accused her that they were sinners themselves."

Mama's only reaction was a widening of her eyes.

"Listen to what Jesus said." Gareth found the place where he'd left off and continued reading how those who accused the woman all departed and left her standing there alone with Jesus. "I can imagine Jesus looking the woman straight in the eye when He asked her, 'Woman, where are those thine accusers? hath no man condemned thee?' I suppose the woman shook her head and told Him, 'No man, Lord.' Can't you picture the look in Jesus' eyes when He said, 'Neither do I condemn thee: go, and sin no more.'"

A soft gasp drew his focus to his mother's face. "Jesus didn't stone her?"

"No, Mama." His voice cracked. "He forgave her. The Bible says if we confess our sin, He is faithful and just to forgive us our sins."

A coughing spasm held her in its grip for several minutes, and the handkerchief she held to her mouth revealed streaks of blood. Gareth gave her a sip of water and a spoonful of codeine. He again offered the laudanum, but she shook her head and pointed to the Bible and rasped, "More."

He took his seat and picked up the Bible again. "When Jesus' friend died, He told the man's family, 'I am the resurrection, and the life: he that believeth in me, though he were dead, yet shall he live: and whosoever liveth and believeth in me shall never die. Believest thou this?'"

Mama crooked her fingers in a weak gesture for him to come close. Gareth leaned forward so his ear was near her lips.

"Read it again."

Chapter 10

The calendar might have declared the month to be September, but the summer heat wasn't ready to loosen its grip. Instead of her customary cup of tea on Sunday afternoon, Leah mixed a pitcher of lemonade. The water from the spring-fed well made the beverage refreshingly cool.

A warm breeze greeted her when she stepped out onto the porch, and set the curls that had escaped their pins to dancing against her cheek. The rocker creaked when she sat and sipped her lemonade.

The hymn the congregation had sung in church that morning lingered in her subconscious and she began to hum. *Thou, O Christ, art all I want; more than all in Thee I find.* She had to admit the words struck a chord within her. Ever since the day she'd hidden Gareth's letter behind the mirror, she'd been aware of the whisper of God moving in her heart, wooing her to make a choice. She'd chosen misery instead of joy, melancholia instead of gladness, and restlessness over contentment. Starting today, that had to change. Her worth was measured in God's love for her, and that made all the difference.

The loneliness that had dogged her for so long was still her companion, but the edges of its oppressiveness had softened. "Lord, I've been full of self-pity for so long, and You've been patiently waiting for me to remember You promised to never leave me or forsake me, to recognize You're always near."

God beckoned to her heart, and she set her glass on the porch beside the rocker and rose to join Him. She strolled through the meadow between her cottage and the Shepherd homestead, pausing occasionally to watch a butterfly or admire clusters of sunflowers and Queen Anne's lace. A cheery goldfinch balanced precariously on a thistle, pecking at the black seeds hidden deep within the center of the purple bloom. How long had it been since she'd spent more than a few minutes searching the scriptures for seeds to plant and nurture in her soul? God had given her so much, surrounded her with reminders of His presence. Even her singleness—once regarded as her stigma—now served to point her to the One who would never leave her. For the first time in more years than she cared to count, she didn't feel sorry for herself.

She opened her arms wide and turned in a slow circle, her face tilted toward heaven and her heart open to God's embrace. As she walked, she listened for God's music in the wind and rustling grass. Meadowlarks and cicadas chimed in to provide the harmony. "Thank You, Father, for the way You love me." The rays of the sun wrapped her in God's warm smile.

"Lord, once again I ask You to quench my feelings for Gareth. Take this love for him away from me. If it is Your will for me to remain single for the rest of my life, You will always be enough. Forgive my selfish pride and the way I wallowed in my own lament. You are all I need. I love You, Father."

She lingered in the meadow, letting God's faithfulness spill over her like soft rain on a drought-parched prairie. The contentment she'd been missing for so long filled her being, and she began to sing.

"Rock of ages, cleft for me, let me hide myself in Thee."

After a time of worship in the middle of the meadow wildflowers, Leah made her way back to the cottage with the weight of disconsolation lifted from her. Her glass of lemonade still sat beside the rocking chair on the porch, but there was something else. She squinted and shaded her eyes with one hand, straining to see across the space between her and the cottage. What was that on the rocker?

She drew nearer, and within a few yards of the porch, she halted. Flowers? There was a bunch of daisies on the seat of the rocker. She slowly stepped onto the porch and picked up the bouquet. The stems were wrapped and tied with long strands of prairie grass. Her gaze skittered down the road toward town. Had Harold stopped by again?

I hope not. Who else would have brought them? Papa? Not likely.

The sound of metal hitting the ground carried on the wind. She glanced back and forth. There wasn't a soul in sight. But the sound continued—metal scraping dirt. Still clutching the daisies, she moved hesitantly around the side of the cottage and paused at the back corner.

Her breath vacated her lungs and her heart hammered.

Gareth.

On his hands and knees, bent over whatever it was he was doing, he didn't appear to see her there. He set aside a trowel and reached for a bucket that contained a clump of daisies. He extracted the flowers from the bucket and gently nestled them into the hole he'd dug beside her back door.

She blinked and sucked in a short breath, but the air couldn't support speech. She gulped another breath. Her pounding pulse drowned out every other sound, and her knees trembled. "Wh–what are you. . . doing. . .?"

He jerked his head up, eyes wide, mouth agape. "Oh." He scrambled to his feet and dusted his hands together. "It's a. . .just a. . ." He gestured toward the daisies nodding in the breeze. "They're for you."

She curled her fingers a little tighter around the bouquet. "I meant, what are you doing *here*?" Her breath returned in spasmodic hiccups. "How did you know where I live now?"

He lifted his shoulders and sent her a charming smile. "I went by your house—that is, your pa's house—and he told me you'd bought this little place." He angled his chin toward the daisies he'd planted. "I thought it needed a little dressing up, and I knew there was nothing you like better than daisies." Was that a smile playing around the corners of his mouth?

She shook her head, fearing the motion might cause the apparition standing before her to disappear. He didn't. "I. . .I never expected to s–see you again."

341

Puzzlement etched furrows across his brow and he tilted his head. "You didn't get my letter?"

Guilt rose up from her belly and heated her face. "I did, but—" What would he think of her when she told him what she'd done? "I didn't open it."

Confusion rather than anger pulled a frown into his expression. He took two steps toward her. "You didn't open it? Why not?"

Oh, how foolish she'd been. She brought the daisies in her hands up to her chin. "I was afraid. . . . No, that's not right. I presumed it said you weren't coming back, that you'd be staying in Kansas City."

Once unleashed, the words fell from her lips. "When I saw the letter was from you, I couldn't bear to read those words—written down as if etched in stone. I thought if I didn't read the letter, I could pretend it said whatever I wanted it to say. After a while, I knew I was lying to myself, and it was too hard to look at the envelope sitting there, so I—"

He arched one eyebrow. "You what?"

She dropped her gaze and studied the flowers quivering in her hands. "I hid it—so I wouldn't have to look at it." She jerked her eyes back up to meet his. "I'm sorry, Gareth. I was so sure you'd written that you wouldn't be back, and I just couldn't make myself read those words."

He took another step, and another, until the distance between them closed. He reached out and captured her hand. Sorrow defined the lines around his eyes.

He gave her hand a squeeze, and his voice grew tender and husky. "Ah, my sweet Leah. I'm so sorry I gave you reason to distrust me. You'll never know how much I wish I could go back and change the past."

He thumbed a tear from her cheek.

"If you had opened the letter, you would have read that my mother apologized for her actions keeping you and me apart. A week before she died, she made me promise to go home to Whitley and to you. That's what she said. It was an easy promise to make and to keep."

He tugged gently on her hand and drew her closer. "You see, my heart was already telling me to do exactly that."

An unseen fist tightened around her chest. Half afraid to utter the words, she whispered, "I prayed for your mother. Did she. . ."

A tiny smile wobbled over his lips, accompanied by moisture glinting in his eyes. He lowered his head for a moment. When he raised it up again, he blinked and dragged the back of his hand across his eyes.

"Mama passed away quietly—gently—while I held her hand." His gaze locked onto hers. "Thank you for praying. Mama came to know the love and forgiveness of Christ a few days before He took her home."

Leah slipped her hand up and covered her lips with her fingers. "Oh, Gareth. I'm sorry for your loss. I'm sorry so many years went by with no contact with her. But I am oh, so grateful that God gave her a second chance, and He let you be the one to introduce her to Jesus."

An overwhelming realization seeped through her. Gareth forgave his mother after the choices she'd made turned his life upside down, and as a result his mother was able to see and know the forgiveness of God. Leah's breath caught and tears tracked down her face. How could she withhold the forgiveness for which Gareth had asked? God didn't refuse to forgive her, waiting until He decided whether or not she deserved it. She stared down at her feet.

Gareth placed two fingers under her chin and coaxed her to look at him. "God gave Mama another chance. Will you give me another chance? Forgive me, Leah."

She caught his fingers in hers. Despite the dirt from transplanting the daisies, she kissed his fingertips. "I forgive you, Gareth. I forgive you."

He wrapped his arms around her and twirled her around. When they both stopped laughing, he tenderly cupped her face in his hands and brushed a soft kiss across her lips. "I've never stopped loving you."

She slipped her arms around his neck and whispered against his shirt. "I've waited fifteen years to hear you say those words."

Connie Stevens lives with her husband of forty-plus years in north Georgia, within sight of her beloved mountains. She and her husband are both active in a variety of ministries at their church. A lifelong reader, Connie began creating stories by the time she was ten. Her office manager and writing muse is a cat, but she's never more than a phone call or email away from her critique partners. She enjoys gardening and quilting, but one of her favorite pastimes is browsing antique shops where story ideas often take root in her imagination. Connie has been a member of American Christian Fiction Writers since 2000.

Heartfelt Echoes

by Jennifer Uhlarik

Dedication

Good friends—the kind you can count on in your darkest moments, when life is crumbling all around you and all others have abandoned you—are hard to come by. I am blessed that God placed one such friend in my life more than fifteen years ago. She so patiently listened as I cried on her shoulder each night for hours. She pointed me back to God, reminding me of His goodness and love, even when it felt like He was working against me. Her love and support saw me through a really dark season until I finally broke through into the light again. I have been proud to try and repay the favor as she has walked some of her own difficult roads. Shannon, thank you for a friendship that, in my mind, rivals the friendship shared between David and Jonathan. I am blessed and humbled to call you my friend, and my life is richer for knowing you.

Chapter 1

Travis McCaffrey stared at the front door of the mansion before him. Victoria Gordon Sessums lived *here*? He extracted her letter from his inside coat pocket and reread her cryptic words.

Travis,
*   I am sorry to write you in this manner, but Millie needs you. We both do. Please come to Virginia City immediately. It is urgent.*

Sincerely,
Victoria Gordon Sessums

Despite the terrible memories Virginia City held, Travis had dropped everything to cross the Sierra Nevada and come to Millie and her mother's aid.

Yet he hadn't expected this.

Years ago, pretty Millie Gordon had told him that her mother was well off. He'd believed it easily. On the few occasions the woman had visited her daughter at the California School for the Deaf, Victoria's clothing, the fancy gifts she'd bought Millie, all oozed wealth. But this home was so large and refined it almost made his skin crawl. What could he, a livery-owner's son, do for a family living in such luxury?

He knocked firmly on the door and, while waiting, took in the picturesque views surrounding him. Situated a little way up the mountain, the mansion overlooked the valley where Virginia City lay, the craggy hill rising behind it. The lavish house was perfectly situated to enjoy both views. He scanned the town below. It had grown immensely in the twelve years he'd been gone.

A sudden whoosh of air alerted him the door opened. Travis turned to find a portly gentleman in dark pants and gray coat, waiting expectantly.

"Hello. I've come to speak with Victoria Sessums." After losing his hearing at eleven, Travis had learned lipreading while at the deaf school. That skill, coupled with his ability to speak clearly, allowed him to act like a hearing person when it suited. And right now, far from home with no friends, such skills suited his purposes very well.

The stout man shook his head. "I'm sorry. Mrs. Sessums is not receiving guests."

Travis concentrated on the man's lips. "Oh. Uh. . .she asked me to come."

"I'm sorry. The lady of the house is unavailable. Please return another time."

As the man shut the door, Travis braced a hand against it. "Please. I've traveled from San Francisco to see her. Could you at least tell her Travis McCaffrey's here?"

The gent's brows lifted. "McCaffrey—from San Francisco?"

"Yes, sir."

"She's expecting you." The man motioned Travis inside. "Wait here while I announce your arrival."

Travis stepped inside. Once the man disappeared up an impressive arching double staircase, Travis studied the nearby rooms. To the left, a parlor with grand fireplace and lavishly detailed furniture. To his right, a dining room with a long table and many chairs, two huge flower arrangements topping the surface. Directly ahead, an arched doorway led to other parts of the house, though the butler reappeared on the landing above, beckoning him upstairs before he could see more.

Complying, Travis went up the stairs and followed to the last door on the right side of the long hall.

"You may enter." The butler pushed the door open then disappeared down the hall.

Travis peered into the brightly lit bedroom decorated in rich golds and purples, everything of the latest fashion except for one old chest. The well-worn piece, positioned at the foot of the bed, stuck out in the opulent surroundings. His eye traveled from it to the bed itself. Propped up against a huge pile of pillows, Victoria Sessums smiled weakly at him. She waved him inside.

For an instant, he stared. What had happened? The woman was a mere shadow of the one he recalled from her infrequent visits to the deaf school. Her dark hair was pulled into a simple braid, a few stray curls framing her jaundiced face. Her features, once plump and healthy, were drawn and frail. He finally uprooted his feet and walked to the bed.

"Thank you for coming, Travis." She signed and spoke the words, then motioned to a richly upholstered wingback chair beside the bed. "Please, sit."

Aware he was staring, he took the offered chair. "Forgive me for being blunt, ma'am, but what happened?"

She shook her head and began to sign again. "I fell ill months after my husband, Walt, and I married."

At her stumbling gestures, Travis held up a hand to stop her. "If signing is too taxing, ma'am, I can read your lips almost as well as sign language."

A weak smile broke across her frail features. "Thank you. Signed conversations are difficult."

He nodded. "I understand. Please, continue."

"The doctor says I have gastric fever." Her features grew pinched, as if she were fighting not to cry. "He hasn't said so, but I fear I'm dying. I grow weaker each day. I don't know how much longer I can hang on."

Without thinking, he took her hand. "I'm truly sorry."

"Thank you." Victoria squeezed his fingers. She paused, eyes closing, whether due to weakness or emotion, he wasn't sure. After a moment, her chest heaved and she looked at him again. "Travis, I'm afraid for Millie if I die. I know your school works hard to teach its students skills to earn a living, but I want someone to look after my daughter. She shouldn't be on her own. Walt is a good man, but he and Millie haven't gotten along well. She wouldn't be happy staying here."

His thoughts reeled. "What are you asking, ma'am?"

"I know you two meant a lot to each other. She often wrote about you in her letters to me." The woman paused. "I want *you*—and your family—to make sure she's safe and happy."

A memory struck him—of standing in his father's livery when he was fifteen and Millie was fourteen. Of the kiss he'd stolen, and the deep blush that colored her cheeks. *Lord, I've dreamed of marrying her since that moment, but—*

Travis's gaze fell to the coverlet. "Long ago, I vowed to Millie that I'd do anything to help her." Swallowing, he lifted his gaze. "But we lost touch years ago. I don't know why. Her letters just stopped, despite my continuing to write."

Victoria's sunken eyes welled with tears. "She didn't stop writing because she quit caring, Travis. It's because of me—things I did. I—" Her words stalled, and settling a hand on her stomach, she gulped several deep breaths.

"Are you all right?" Travis leaned nearer.

Her distress passed quickly, and she turned a weak smile his way. "I'm sorry. You should know, I forced Millie to undergo a surgery meant to restore her hearing. Unfortunately, it didn't. The outcome. . .changed her."

He shook his head. "I don't understand. Changed her how?"

Again, Victoria gripped her belly, leaning forward with a wince. She gulped numerous deep breaths again before sinking back into the pillows. "Hand me the bell, please." She pried her fingers from his grip and waved at the bedside table.

There, Travis found a small crystal handbell and passed it to Victoria. She shook it vigorously, then let her arm fall limp. "I'm sorry. I'm not feeling well. I brought you here to ask you a great favor."

He leaned even closer. "How can I help?"

"Millie won't simply agree to go to San Francisco with you. Not yet. I was hoping you'd stay. Win her trust again."

Lord, I'd do anything to have Millie's friendship again. "How?"

"Her birthday is coming. I'd planned to buy her a saddle horse. I want you to break it for her." She took another gulping breath, concern etching her features. "You and your father still do that, right?"

He nodded. "I've taken over the horse breaking, ma'am." Since Travis graduated, he and his father had worked to build their livery into the largest in San Francisco. They'd made a name for themselves, in part because of the quality horses they offered for rent, trade, or purchase. But could his father do without him for weeks or months?

Despite her distress, she mustered a smile. "Then. . .please stay? I'll get you money to buy the best horse you can find, and train it. We've an excellent barn and corral that you're welcome to use. Just stay close and rekindle your friendship with Millie."

Motion from the doorway drew his attention, and the gent who'd answered the door and a woman in a maid's uniform hurried in.

Gripping her midsection, Victoria latched onto his hand, and Travis turned to her once more. Her eyes burned into his. "Please?"

The butler grabbed Travis's arm and pulled him up, Victoria losing hold of his hand in the process. "You must go now. Mrs. Sessums needs her privacy." He roughly guided Travis toward the door.

All thoughts of his father handling the livery without him fled as he turned to Victoria. "I'll do it."

Victoria nodded faintly, even as the apron-clad woman fetched a bowl and pushed it into her hands.

The butler shoved him into the hallway. "Please see yourself out."

"Wait!" The door closed, and for one dumbfounded moment, he stared. She'd promised to get him money to buy Millie's horse. How was he to start without it?

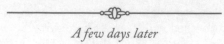

A few days later

Worry clouded Millie Gordon's thoughts as she perused the mercantile's offerings of patent medicines, tinctures, and salves. Momma had grown so weak she was rarely out of bed. Despite the wide gulf that had often separated them, Momma's illness frightened Millie. She was wasting away so quickly. For three months, the gastric fever had ravaged her. Nothing the doctor tried had helped. Millie had little hope the medicines in the apothecary case would do anything either, but she had to try.

Lord God, just when I thought I'd have a chance to get to know Momma—when she'd finally settled in one place—she had to marry Walt Sessums. . .and get sick.

Straightening, she scanned the mercantile for the owner, Abel Perkins. Seated behind the counter at a rolltop desk, he wrote in a book. She waved. When he didn't notice, Millie rapped her knuckles against the counter. Mr. Perkins looked her way, held up his index finger, then finished his scribbling. Finally, he approached, tying an apron around his waist as he came.

Millie almost smiled, though when only the left corner of her mouth twisted upward, she sobered. Instead, she waved. Mr. Perkins had always been kind to her, patient. He was one of the few in town who wasn't put off by Millie's scarred, drooping face or her inability to speak. In fact, he'd made some effort to learn how to sign with her, though his attempts were basic, at best.

"Can I help you, Millie?" The affable store owner signed slowly, laboring over each word.

Millie reached for the bag where she kept paper and pencil but quickly recalled leaving her bedroom without them. Instead, she pointed to two of the brown bottles in the apothecary case. Mr. Perkins opened the cabinet from behind and, crouching, peered at her.

He removed the correct bottles and set them on the counter. Millie read each label and handed her choice to him.

"Please put this on Walt Sessums' account." She signed the request.

He held up his hands. "Sign slowly, please."

She sighed. She was long removed from the safe cocoon of the deaf school where everyone spoke in sign fluently. She started again, belaboring the motions.

Mr. Perkins retrieved his ledger book and, turning to Walt's page, marked the purchase in pencil. Millie glimpsed the balance Walt owed, but before she could be sure of what she saw, the book snapped shut, keeping the secret hidden. Had it said *$30* or *$300*? If the latter—

Millie dismissed the thought. Walt's mercantile balance was none of her business. At least her mother's husband allowed her to purchase under his account.

"Thank you. Have a nice day." She signed slowly this time.

"And you, young lady." He waved goodbye.

Millie stepped from the mercantile, bottle in hand, and perused the busy street. People hurried along the boardwalk, the wooden planks vibrating with their footsteps. Wagons, buggies, and riders on horseback traversed the street.

Glimpsing two boys on the bench near the corner, her nerves tingled a caution. One flicked a glance her way before returning to his conversation. Dare she walk past them? They were just the sort, if not the very ones, who'd often picked on her for her scarred features and deafness. Apprehension growing, she scanned the street, finding Walt's surrey a half-block down on the far side of the street. The driver, Jack Embry, stood checking the team's harnesses and hadn't noticed her. She could wait until he did, but. . .

No. Since when had she become too fearful to cross the street? She'd done that and far more in San Francisco. Steeling herself, she turned and headed his way.

Millie weaved through the crowd. As she neared the bench, something hooked the toe of her boot, and she stumbled and fell forward, landing on her hands and knees. The medicine bottle broke, slicing her palm. The pungent liquid burned like fire as it touched the fresh wound. Millie cried out, and in an instant, the crowd stopped, backed up a step. Tears stinging her eyes, she pushed onto her knees—just as one of the boys withdrew his outstretched foot.

A strong hand wrapped about her upper arm, not altogether roughly. Walt's right-hand man, Tim Blevins, an unattractive man with a badly pockmarked face, hoisted her to her feet and turned her to face him. After a cursory glance, he brushed dirt from her dress as if she were an invalid unable to care for herself. Seeing the gash marring her palm, he wrapped a soiled bandanna around her hand.

His lips moved. The words, without someone to interpret them, were lost to her. She glared at the boys as the little imps fought to keep from smirking. When she caught the eye of the boy who'd tripped her, his mouth cracked wide in obvious laughter. Millie faced Blevins and signed her words.

"He tripped me. Purposely."

Blevins scowled in confusion.

Lord, why? Why does Walt insist I be escorted by these men if none of them can speak my language?

Her anger didn't stop her from continuing. "Because of him, I broke the bottle of medicine I bought for Momma."

Still confused, Blevins turned to the carriage driver, Embry, who'd also come to her aid.

As she tried to make them understand, a tall, broad-shouldered stranger pushed through the crowd and snatched the two ruffians from the bench by their collars and dragged them to Blevins. The boys fought to wiggle free, but he held them firmly.

351

Blevins and the stranger exchanged words and, after an instant, Blevins took charge of the boys, angling away from the crowd.

Millie looked at the new man as he pushed his hat back, revealing familiar brown eyes and a smile that she instantly recognized. Her heart seized—with happiness and fear all at once.

Travis McCaffrey—here?

His eyes flicked to the right side of her face, and his warm, wonderful smile melted—into shock. No, *horror*.

Just like Peter's had.

Sobbing, Millie clamped her bandaged hand over her drooping mouth and hurried to Walt's surrey.

The near-elation Travis had felt at seeing Millie Gordon's beautiful profile had set his belly to quivering. However, when she'd turned, revealing the deep scar on the right side of her head and the way her mouth sagged at one corner, he couldn't help the momentary shock. Was *that* what Victoria meant about the surgery changing her?

Millie bolted into the street, darting in front of a horse and rider who were forced to draw to a sudden halt. Travis lunged across the crowded boardwalk to follow, but the burly, prematurely white-haired fellow who'd stood next to Millie's rescuer clamped a firm hand around Travis's arm.

The man's lips moved. In such close proximity, Travis couldn't see clearly. He jerked free and stepped back. "You mind repeating that?"

"I said, my friend and I have this handled. Don't butt in."

"And just who are you?" Travis eyed the man.

Whitey's brows rose, and his lips quirked into an amused expression. "Reckon I should be asking you that question."

"I asked first."

The man's expression hardened. "Jack Embry. I work for Mr. Sessums—her mother's husband. And you are. . .?"

"Travis McCaffrey. Millie's friend." At least he hoped she would still call him that. Despite Victoria's assurances, perhaps he was assuming too much.

Embry looked over his shoulder, and Travis with him, as Millie scrambled into an expensive surrey across the street. When it didn't immediately pull away, Embry scanned the street and waved. The pockmarked man he'd handed the boys off to headed toward it.

A humorless smile parted Embry's mouth as he faced Travis. "Now's not a good time. We need to see to that cut on her hand, get her back home. You'll have to see Miss Millie another time."

Irritation clawed Travis's spine. "Rest assured, I'll do that."

Travis faced the spot where Millie had fallen. Several large pieces of a broken bottle lay at the edge of the boardwalk, one rimmed in her blood. He collected the largest pieces, unable to ignore the overpowering odor of alcohol—a stench he'd grown all too acquainted with years before—and tossed them into an empty crate in the alley.

Hurrying, Travis ducked into the mercantile.

A man approached the counter. "May I help you?"

Travis gulped at the familiar sight of Abel Perkins. He'd run a mercantile in Virginia City for many years—though during Travis's youth, the store had been a quarter this size. "A young woman just bought a bottle of patent medicine."

"Yes. What about it?" Mr. Perkins squinted at him.

"The bottle broke outside your store. I'd like to replace it for her."

"Of course." The man eyed him as he crouched behind the case. A moment later, he returned with a bottle and an expectant look.

He must've spoken the price while hidden behind the case. Travis fished in his pocket. "I'm sorry, how much did you say?"

"Fifty cents."

Travis emptied his pocket and counted his last coins into Mr. Perkins's waiting palm. After buying Millie's horse and the patent medicine with his own money, he *really* needed to get Victoria Sessums to repay him.

"I know you. Travis, right?" Mr. Perkins cocked his head. "Travis Alcott, son of—"

"No, sir." He hadn't been Travis Alcott in more than a decade, and he had no desire to be associated with that name now. "The name's McCaffrey, son of Finn and Hannah McCaffrey."

Perkins's eyes widened slightly. "Finn McCaffrey, the stagecoach driver?"

"Yes, sir. That's my pa, though he hasn't driven a coach in about twelve years. He runs a livery in San Francisco now."

The man smiled. "Your pa's a real good man. Please tell him Abel Perkins says hello."

"I will. Thank you for your help." Medicine in hand, he hurried outside, all too glad to leave that conversation behind.

While he'd been inside the store, the crowd had thinned and the sun had faded. Thankfully, the carriage hadn't moved. Millie's head bobbed in and out of view through the oval window at the back. His heart racing, Travis headed toward the surrey.

As he neared, the pockmarked man looked up from attending to Millie's hand. Travis tried to catch her eye, but she turned her back to him.

"You need something?" the man with the blemished face asked.

Travis nodded. "I'd like to give something to Millie."

Embry strode up from somewhere nearby. "I'll pass it along."

Flicking his gaze from the man's lips to Millie's petite form, Travis's heart stalled. Why was she under guard? "I'll give it to her myself, if you don't mind." He brushed past Embry, circling the surrey to approach from the direction Millie faced.

The pockmarked man slid from the surrey's front seat and settled a big hand on Travis's chest. "*She* minds."

Travis brushed his hand aside and stepped up to the carriage. "For you, Millie." He signed the words.

Equal parts panic and sadness filled her eyes as she lowered her uninjured hand from covering her scarred features to reach for the offering. She took it, placed it on the bench, and signed as well. "Thank you."

Pockmark motioned to Embry, drawing Travis's attention in the process. "Get her out of here—now!"

The carriage lurched as Embry climbed aboard, grabbed the reins, and urged the team into motion. Startled, Travis stepped back out of the way. Once it was well past, he started across the street.

Pockmark caught his arm and turned Travis to face him. "You don't hear pretty good. I said she didn't want to see you."

A sardonic laugh bubbled up from Travis's gut. "You don't know the half of it."

At the sight of an approaching wagon, Travis strode across the street, passing Abel Perkins as he swept up the broken glass. Travis stopped beside his big chestnut gelding and tightened the cinch on his saddle.

Pockmark approached again, and Travis turned. "You gonna answer me?"

Travis's nerves crackled. "Answer you what?"

The other man scowled. "I said, what do you want with Millie Gordon?"

"I showed you what I wanted. To give her that medicine. Is there something wrong with paying her that kindness?"

Pockmark glowered. "Next time, listen when I tell you to steer clear of her."

Indignation filled Travis's chest. "Exactly what is *your* business with Millie Gordon? Do you think you *own* her or something? Why are you holding her against her will?"

The blemished man jabbed a finger toward Travis's face. "You got a big mouth, mister."

"When I need to. I've also got a powerful curiosity, and I'll use both to get to the bottom of what's really going on."

Pockmark struck, his fist sinking deep into Travis's belly. Unprepared, Travis doubled over, gulping for air. Pockmark's knee connected with his face. Pain exploded through his skull. His surroundings grew hazy, the images dark and dreamlike. Blinking, he caught sight as another man appeared from down the boardwalk, his lower half draped in white. The new man raised something long—*a gun?*—and Pockmark disappeared.

Travis tried to speak, though before he could, the world faded around him.

Chapter 2

Bleary-eyed after a night filled with dreams of Travis McCaffrey and Peter Xavier, Millie sat while the butler's wife, Edith, brushed through her dark hair and pinned it in place. Perhaps Momma was used to being waited on hand and foot, but Millie wasn't. Not after ten years at school, learning to do for herself. Were it not for her injured hand, she'd have refused the help and arranged her own hair. Yet because her hand still ached, she appreciated the assistance. Her hair pinned up, Millie allowed Edith to assist her into her dress.

Prepared for the day, Millie retrieved the medicine Travis had bought and meandered toward Momma's quarters. She turned into the doorway, but seeing blond-haired Walt Sessums occupying the wingback chair beside Momma, Millie pulled back into the shadows before either saw her.

Walt smiled, pushing Momma's dark curls away from her pallid face. Eyes full of concern, he spoke in what looked to be a coaxing way. Propped against her pillows, Momma shook her head. He gripped her hand and spoke again. After a hesitation, Momma closed her eyes and nodded, spurring Walt to tip a water glass to her lips. She sipped, then took a longer drink. Settling back again, she smiled weakly at her husband.

Millie should be happy for Momma, yet the sight of Walt at her bedside stirred darker feelings. Jealousy. Anger. For ten years, Millie had longed for Momma to take an interest in her life. Maybe even settle somewhere near the deaf school so they could be together. Instead, Momma left her at the school, visiting only half the Christmases and three summers. During any other holiday times, Millie went to Finn and Hannah McCaffrey's home.

She'd loved those years at the school. There, she'd had friends and an outlet for her creative side. She'd learned not only reading and writing, but how to sew, garden, and ride a horse. She'd walked through the busy streets of San Francisco with little fear, having learned to navigate well in the hearing world near the school. And none of the townsfolk had picked on her, perhaps because the deaf students were a common sight traipsing between the school grounds and Finn McCaffrey's livery.

Despite those things, she'd ached for her mother to truly take an interest in the life she led. Instead, Momma traveled the country on the arm of one rich man after another, a new one every few months. After Millie graduated, Momma brought her along on her adventures, though such a life was foreign and uncomfortable to Millie, particularly with no one accompanying them who knew how to sign with her.

That is, until Peter stepped into her life.

Only after Millie's unsuccessful surgery—and Peter's rejection—did Momma put down roots. For reasons unbeknownst to Millie, she'd chosen Virginia City. They'd arrived the previous summer, and a long-overdue hope grew in Millie's heart. Perhaps she and Momma might finally get to know each other as she'd dreamed. But her hopes were dashed when Momma took a sudden interest in wealthy mine owner Walt Sessums. They'd married within months after Millie and her mother arrived in the bustling mining community. He'd treated Momma like royalty—except for once, the only time Millie had seen them argue. It had been late one night, soon after they'd married. Millie had awakened to the feel of slammed doors and heavy footsteps almost running through the hall connecting their bedrooms. She'd risen to see what the commotion was and found the two screaming at each other in the hall. They'd stopped when she appeared, Walt leaving to sleep elsewhere for the night. Momma never shared what they'd fought about, and it never happened again. Things had been tense for a few weeks afterward, though when Momma fell ill, Walt's whole demeanor changed. The sicker she became, the more attentive he grew.

Inside Momma's bedroom, Walt rose, leaned down, and kissed her pale cheek. They spoke a moment more before Walt strode from the room, likely on his way to the mine.

Millie waited for the telltale flash of sunlight to illuminate the foyer downstairs, signaling Walt had exited. Then she entered her mother's room. For once, her mother seemed comfortable, the ravaging illness not causing her immediate distress.

Millie took a seat in the chair Walt had vacated.

"Hello, my beautiful girl." Momma signed slowly, her smile deepening.

Millie frowned. "Momma, don't." She looked away as she scolded. "I am not beautiful." She hadn't been since the New York doctor—an acquaintance of Peter's father—had operated on her, promising miraculous results of hearing restored. Momma had pushed for the surgery, wanting to give her daughter the gift of sound. But Millie knew nothing other than the silence she'd been born into. She functioned fine without hearing and was against the surgery.

She should have stood her ground. If she had, her mouth would still work, rather than leaving her with a perpetually crooked smile and the deep scar near her right ear.

Momma's hands flashed, and Millie looked at her.

"You know I don't like such talk, Millicent. You *are* beautiful." She paused an instant, then signed again. "What happened to your hand?"

Sighing, Millie handed the bottle of patent medicine to her mother. "A boy tripped me in town, and I cut my hand."

Concern etched Momma's ashen features. "Did Blevins or Embry help you?"

Millie chafed at the irksome question. Walt insisted on having her driven in the carriage wherever she went, as if she were royalty. At least she hoped that was how he meant the overprotective kindness. It rather felt like he—they—thought her a helpless imbecile. But now was not the time to have that discussion. "Yes."

"Did Edith help you bandage it properly?"

Millie sighed. "I did it myself." She'd insisted on caring for her own needs, despite Edith trying to help.

Momma offered a weak smile. "Did you tell Walt's men about the boy?"

Her frustration must have shown, for Momma's countenance firmed. "What's wrong?"

Millie scowled. "Blevins and Embry don't understand. They won't learn the signs. I don't *need* their help. Not if they won't even *try* to speak to me. Why does Walt insist on their babysitting me everywhere I go?" She signed furiously, her annoyance peaking.

"Darling, Walt means well. He believes if you could learn to read lips and speak—like your friend Travis did—that people will be more open to you. They'll receive you better, and you'll be more successful."

At the mention of Travis, a knot formed in Millie's throat.

"Didn't you *try* to explain that you were tripped? What about the paper you carry? Couldn't you—"

"It's strange you'd mention Travis just now." Dare she tell Momma of his unexpected appearance?

Momma sank into the pillows, fatigue etching her features. "Why?"

"He was there yesterday when I was tripped."

A visible wave of relief swept over Momma. "Thank goodness. I feared he wouldn't return."

Millie's brow furrowed. "What do you mean?"

Momma's deathly pale cheeks flushed. "I asked him to come."

"Why would you do that?" Millie's hands trembled as she signed.

"Because you need someone to look after you once I die. Travis will."

The blunt words came like a mule kick to the gut. Millie rocked to her feet, signing furiously. "You are *not* going to die, Momma, so stop planning for your demise. Besides, I am twenty-three years old. I can take care of myself, despite Walt's ridiculous notions!" She headed for the door, but turned back before she exited. "You should *not* have asked Travis to come. In case you've forgotten, he didn't want me."

Travis roused and inhaled deep, his senses assaulted by a strange mixture of odors. Mustiness. Rotting wood. Stale sweat. *Whiskey.* At the oddly familiar mix of smells, his heart hammered, and he pried his eyes open, though the right was mildly swollen.

One glance at his surroundings caused his belly to clench, and a wave of pain swept him. How had he gotten *here*? He jerked into a sitting position, wholly unsure whether he could keep the contents of his stomach where they belonged. He gulped a couple of breaths, the stale air causing his gut to roil worse. Travis lunged up, flinging the door wide as he bolted from the cabin.

He stopped a few feet beyond the doorway and planted both hands on his knees, gulping huge breaths. *Not funny, Lord. This is the one place I told You I wasn't willing to go.*

The home he'd lived in from age nine to twelve. The place where some of his worst memories had occurred.

Yet here he was. Someone had played a mighty cruel joke. Was it the fella who hit him? Not likely. He wouldn't know Travis's connection to this place.

Travis's stomach settled, and he straightened, his head throbbing fiercely. His hand strayed to the knot above his eyebrow. It had likely blackened his eye.

The yard hadn't changed much. The old, mature trees were even bigger now. The small creek still flowed, though it looked low. Not uncommon for the time of year, if his memory served. Darker memories pounded the floodgate of his mind, though as quick as they came, he shoved them away.

His big chestnut watched him from the sturdy corral, alongside another horse. A bay gelding with a star and one white sock. Travis's mouth went dry. He approached the corral, and the bay met him at the fence. The familiar horse nudged his chest once, then nuzzled his hip pocket—the one he kept sugar chunks in to treat the horses he broke, a trick Finn McCaffrey—the man who would become his father—had taught him the day they'd met.

Dumbfounded, Travis rubbed the bay's neck. He'd broken the horse five years ago—one of the first he broke without his father's help. A livery worker had sold the horse one night after he and Pa had gone home. But how had it—?

The weight of someone's gaze laid heavy between his shoulder blades, and Travis spun toward the cabin. In the doorway stood the muscular man with dark hair and beard, deep-brown eyes, and familiar features that had haunted his nightmares. Rather than the scowl Travis had long tried to forget, the man wore an expression he couldn't quite describe. Sadness for certain, mingled with trepidation and perhaps. . .hope. His lips parted in a weak attempt at a smile.

Travis's spine stiffened. "How in blue blazes did I get here, Clyde? And where'd you get that horse?"

Clyde Alcott swallowed hard. "Forgive me the stupid question, but. . .you never talked. After losing your hearing, I mean. Did it come back or something?"

Travis loosed a sardonic laugh. "No, I'm still *quite* deaf. And it wasn't that I *couldn't* talk. It was that my *Pa* never much cared to hear what I had to say. If you recall, you used to smack me around for asking too many questions. But I guess that's too many drunken stupors ago for you to remember, isn't it?"

Clyde looked away an instant before he met Travis's eyes again. "Iffen you can't hear me, how do you know what I'm sayin'?"

Travis glared. "I read lips. As long as you look at me and speak normally, I've got a good chance of understanding you. Now. . .answer my questions. How'd I get here, and where'd you get this horse?"

Clyde hesitated. "Abel Perkins scared off the fella who hit you, then brought you out to me yesterday."

"Why?"

The elder man shrugged. "He recognized you straightaway as my son."

Travis spit into the grass at his feet. "I'm nothing of the kind. I'm the eldest son of Finn and Hannah McCaffrey. Maybe if you'd've been sober twelve years ago, you'd remember signing away all your rights and responsibilities to me."

Clyde mopped a shaking hand over his beard.

"What about the horse, Clyde? Who'd you steal him from?"

Clyde shook his head. "I didn't steal him. I bought him—from McCaffrey and Son's Livery in San Francisco about five years back. I got the bill of sale inside if you don't believe me."

A shiver gripped Travis. *Clyde* bought the bay? But that would mean he'd been at the liv—

Teeth clenched, Travis barged up to the older man, mind spinning. "I don't know what game you're playing, but you wanted nothing to do with me when I was a scared, grieving kid. Heck, you probably even blamed me for Ma's death. And quick as you could after I lost my hearing, you signed over all your rights. So don't you dare think that taking me in for a night squares us. It doesn't. Not even close. Now get out of my way so I can get my boots and get out of here. I have work to do." It was already far later than he'd intended to pick up Millie's horse and head to her place.

Pain etched Clyde's features, but he stepped aside.

Travis brushed past the man and, eyes adjusting to the dim interior, he searched the space near the bed. Where had Clyde stashed his boots? To Travis's right, Clyde plucked his boots and hat from near the back door.

Travis snatched the offered items from Clyde's hands and, donning his hat, marched outside, sitting to pull on the well-worn boots. As he tugged his pant legs over the boots, he found Clyde bridling the chestnut.

"I can saddle my own horse, thank you." He ducked between the corral bars.

Silent, Clyde stepped back, and Travis resumed the task. Within moments, he had the chestnut saddled and ready to ride. As he mounted, Clyde positioned himself near the corral's gate.

"I know you got little reason to trust me, but iffen you ever need anything, I hope you'll ask."

A knot tightened Travis's throat. "Fine. Open the gate. *Please. . .*"

The older man complied.

With a route of escape before him, Travis looked at Clyde. "That's the last thing I'll ever ask of you. And just like you said to me the day you gave me up, *good riddance.*"

Travis reined the chestnut through the opening and spurred him into a lope.

Good riddance, indeed.

Chapter 3

Millie looked up from her reading as Edith pushed her bedroom door open. The thin woman smiled and raised her hands to sign something.

"Your mother needs you."

Millie's happiness at the maid's signed comment was eclipsed by concern. Not more than an hour ago, Momma had slept peacefully. She laid aside the book. "Is she well?" Millie signed slowly.

Confusion marred Edith's features, and she entered to scribble something on the paper Millie kept for such purposes. When she showed it to Millie, it repeated her signed statement.

Millie scribbled her own thoughts, showed Edith the page, then signed the question again. "I understand. Is Momma well?"

The maid smiled and wrote something. *She's having a good day.*

Nodding, Millie donned her shoes, then scurried down the hall. Momma sat a little taller than usual, with a bit more color in her cheeks.

Lord, please let this mean she's recovering.

"Come in, my beautiful girl."

Millie ignored her mother's weak, sloppy motions—and the fact that she persisted in calling her *beautiful*—and instead, raced to the wingback chair.

"Edith says you're having a good day."

"Better than usual." Momma smiled.

"Maybe because Walt was gone overnight." Guilt struck her, but she always felt better when Walt's business kept him from home.

Momma's eyebrows arched upward. "Millicent."

"Forgive me. Walt is your husband. I should be more respectful."

"I'm glad you understand that." Momma paused, her stern expression giving way to another smile. "I have a surprise for you."

"You do?" How could Momma have orchestrated a surprise?

She nodded, continuing to sign. "For your birthday. It's in the barn."

Her birthday. She'd been so concerned with Momma's health, she'd forgotten about it. "What is it?"

"Go see."

Millie almost smiled, but the awkward drooping of her mouth kept her from it. She rose, kissed Momma's forehead, and trotted down the back staircase, through the kitchen, and out toward the barn.

Her eye went to the corral where a large chestnut horse and a smaller golden one with white mane and tail stood swishing flies. She walked past, entered the barn, and searched the stalls. Finding no one to ask, she turned from the barn again. When she faced the corral, Travis McCaffrey was leaning against the corral fence, smiling.

"Happy birthday."

Her stomach plunged to her feet.

Surely Momma didn't mean that *he* was her birthday gift!

Blast it all. He was hoping for at least a smile, but. . .*nothing*. Just that frightened, almost lost look he'd seen the day before.

Travis walked toward Millie. She darted a glance to either side, almost like a cornered animal searching for an escape. But he was no hunter, and she wasn't his prey. He grinned as he neared. "Hello, Millie. It's good to see you again."

She hesitated an instant, then straightened. "Thank you for the medicine."

He drew up short, disappointment shrouding his heart. "I—" His hands stalled. "I haven't seen you in five years, and all you have to say to me is *thank you for the medicine?*"

Her brown eyes welled with tears, her expression one of resignation, sadness, and fear. "What do you want me to say?"

Her mild hostility hurt as much as the previous day's gut punch. "I don't know. . . maybe 'Hello, Travis'? or 'It's nice to see you again after all these years'? How about, 'What happened to your eye?' Maybe those would be a good place to start. . . ."

She rolled her eyes heavenward, then pinned him with a glance. "Hello, Travis. Nice to see you again. Why are you here?"

Another verbal gut punch. *Lord, what have I done to upset Millie?* From the day he'd arrived at the deaf school, she'd been nothing but kind to him, full of fun and humor. They'd shared everything with each other for years, even after they'd graduated and she moved away. Right up until her letters stopped arriving.

"Your mother hired me to break a horse for you—for your birthday. That's her." He indicated the little mare in the corral.

Millie's expression softened, bordered on interested. She approached the corral, and he followed.

Her eyes widened. "You broke her?"

Travis shook his head. "Not yet. She's green broke. I'll be here a while, gentling her for you."

Millie's features paled. "So you're staying. . . ."

"For as long as it takes." She might've been able to ignore his letters, but she'd find it harder to ignore him in person.

Millie looked none too happy, though she said nothing. Travis retrieved a rope from one of the fence posts, slipped between the corral bars, and led the horse to her. Tying the mare to the fence rail, he rejoined Millie and fished a bit of sugar from his pocket.

He smiled. "Give her this."

"You still carry sugar in your pocket?" The right corner of her mouth twitched, though it never fully bloomed into a smile.

"Always."

She held the cube out to the mare who took it after investigation. Travis handed her a couple more, and she again fed them, one at a time, to the animal. When they were gone, the mare nudged Millie's hand, and she rubbed the horse's neck.

An old, familiar comfort settled over Travis. But with so many things to say, so many questions to ask, he sobered. He touched Millie's arm. "I'm so sorry—about your mother's illness. I was shocked when I saw her." The first time he'd seen Victoria a week ago, she looked worse than today. Yet even with today's seeming improvement, the woman was far from well.

Millie's chin trembled. "Thank you. It's been difficult."

For as long as Travis could recall, Millie had longed for her mother. He'd prayed for God to bind their hearts together for years. As much as he'd wished to propose and marry Millie after she finished her schooling, Travis understood that mother and daughter needed time together. He'd always expected he'd give them this time, and then Millie would return.

Only. . .she hadn't.

"Why didn't you write—tell me where you were and what was happening? I'd have come sooner."

Millie shook her head. "Please don't, Travis."

"Don't what? Talk to you? Care about you? I've missed you!" Desperately. He'd longed for the day they'd see each other again, but in his wildest imaginings, he hadn't expected *this* reception. Never dreamed she'd stop answering his letters and let him lose track of where she'd ended up.

"You made it very clear this is what you wanted." She signed quickly.

"I did? How?" If he knew what he'd done, he'd never make such a mistake again.

She heaved a big breath. "I should let you work. I have things to do too." Millie rubbed the mare's nose, then hurried toward the house.

Dumbfounded, Travis stared after her.

Lord, I don't understand. I've wanted to marry Millie Gordon for years. Why would she think I wanted things this way?

Scrubbing his neck, Travis finally loosed the mare and, coiling the rope, turned toward the barn.

He found Pockmark and Embry watching him, both wearing amused smiles.

"Quite a shiner you got there, friend."

Travis's belly knotted. "I'm not looking for trouble."

Pockmark's eyebrows arched. "Whether you're looking or not, you found it."

"Thought we told you to steer clear of Miss Millie," Embry added.

Both men closed in, and Travis backed up, the corral impeding his retreat. "I'm here at Mrs. Sessums' request. If you don't believe me, please talk to her."

"Well, now. That's a right good idea. Let's all go." Pockmark shoved him toward the house.

Chapter 4

One Week Later

Millie shook the crystal bell furiously and thrust the bowl into Momma's hands, then drew her mother's braid behind her shoulders. Laying the bell aside, she settled a reassuring hand on Momma's back. Even through her nightshirt, Momma's skin was cold, almost clammy.

Lord, how much more can she endure? I beg You, heal her.

Again, she shook the bell until the floor vibrated with footsteps. Lawrence rushed into the room and, as always, motioned for her to go. Millie edged toward the door, frustrated tears pooling in her eyes. Edith scurried in and, looping an arm around Millie's shoulders, coaxed her down the back stairs to the kitchen. There, she opened a canister, dumped a fine layer of flour on the counter, and wrote in the dust.

Wait outside, please. Once this passes, I'll fetch you.

A sob threatened to choke her, and Millie turned toward the door.

Lord, please help Momma!

Outside, she sat on the bottom step, elbows on her knees, and both hands clamped over her mouth. Motion flickered in the distance where Travis worked with her mare in the corral.

She'd avoided the barn—avoided *Travis*—since he'd arrived the week before. His appearance in town had been unexpected. Finding him *here* was downright disconcerting. Particularly since his presence at the barn meant she couldn't escape the house—and Walt's overbearing presence—as easily. Spending any time near Travis would only cause her own tender heart to betray her. Especially since she'd never stopped loving him.

Only Travis hadn't wanted her.

She cupped her face in her hands and tried to pray—for Momma and her own lingering hurt. When no words would come, she wrapped her arms around her legs, and laid her head on her knees.

Lord. . .?

Could He even hear her? For a long moment, she sat like that, but finally looked around.

She gasped when she found Travis just feet away, brown eyes full of concern.

"Hello, Millie. What's wrong?" He approached as he signed the question.

The weight of five boulders settled in her chest. "Momma is very sick."

Travis's expression creased with worry. "I'm sorry. She's worsening, isn't she?"

"Yes." Her limbs trembled at the admission.

"Remember when we would pray your mother would come visit—move close to the school?"

The memories washed over her. They'd started the practice on her thirteenth birthday when a courier delivered a package from Momma. Inside, she'd enclosed a letter that said she'd been detained, wouldn't make it for Millie's birthday after all, but she'd visit *soon*. It was the second time Momma had stood her up. Millie had sobbed so hard she'd been unable to attend classes. Travis's parents had brought her to their home for the night, had tried to comfort her. But only after Travis shared about his own father giving him up did she begin to calm. From the shared pain of their parents' selfishness, she and Travis had begun to pray together.

"I've never stopped praying that you two could settle things. If you'd like, I'll pray with you now."

The feeble wall she'd erected around her heart cracked, and Millie lunged into his arms. He held her while she convulsed with sobs, his strong arms cradling her. She sank into the familiar safety. *Lord, I've missed this man. It feels like no time has passed, yet so much has happened.* For long minutes, she cried into his shirt, resisting pulling away for fear she'd never feel his embrace again. Finally, when her tears abated, she drew back with an apologetic look.

"Sorry about your shirt."

He ran a hand over the wet spot and grinned. "I'll gladly wear a wet shirt if I can hold you again."

Oh, that he would—but. . .Millie drew back a step.

Travis squinted at her. "What's wrong?"

"I'm confused. You speak like a man who loves me."

His eyes widened. "I do love you! I've never stopped. Why would you doubt that?"

"Because. . ." How could she speak her mind without seeming forward? *Lord, help me. . . .*

"Why, Millie?"

"Because you sent me away. When I finished school, you told me to go with Momma, get to know her, build a life with her." Her hands flew. "I was miserable without you. Half of me was missing."

"I was giving you time to get to know each other. You always longed for more with her. What right did I have to stand in the way of that?"

"But I longed for a life with you too!"

Travis's brow furrowed. "Now I'm confused. If you wanted a life with me, why did you stop writing?"

Her hands shook as she signed. "Because you seemed so happy in your letters, like you were doing so well. Everything was good for you. Life was moving on, and you didn't need me at all."

"Is that what you think? That I was so happy, I never thought about you? No! I missed you every day, and when you stopped writing—when I didn't know how you were doing—I was frantic. My girl was missing, and I had no way to find her!"

"You say I'm *your girl*, but when did you ask me? I've waited for five years. I've hoped. And when your letters kept saying how good things were, with no mention that you missed me, it felt like you *didn't* miss me at all."

Flabbergasted, he stared. "I'm sorry, Millie. After all this time, I thought you knew. I intended to propose after you finished school. But your mother arrived, wanted you to travel with her. If I proposed then, you might not have gone. You might've resented me for keeping you from her. And I didn't write about how lonely I was for fear you'd end your time with her. But in every letter, I asked when you'd return to San Francisco. I've been waiting for you to come home so I *could* propose!"

Her thoughts spun. "Then you *do* love me?"

"Yes!" He signed feverishly, a frustrated smile crossing his face. "I love you, Millie Gordon, more than I ever imagined I could. And before any more time goes by. . ." He dropped to one knee. "Will you marry me?"

Lord, is this real, or am I dreaming? Her lungs could hardly draw breath. When she didn't immediately answer, Travis's eyebrows arched upward in fearful expectation. She raised quaking hands to sign. "Yes I will marry you." The left side of her mouth curled upward into a crooked smile before she realized.

"There!" Travis rocked back to his feet. "Finally. I have missed your smile."

She sobered quickly and shook her head. "Are you *sure* you want to marry me? My smile is broken and ugly. I hate it."

"It's beautiful."

Millie tried to protest, but Travis clasped her hands between his, then released them to sign. "Shh. Stop arguing. *You* are beautiful."

He cupped her chin and leaned in. Millie's heart pounded as his lips touched hers, gently, soft and seeking, then gradually deepening. She melted into him and was only vaguely aware when, with one arm, he hoisted her up, her toes dangling above the ground. With his other hand, he brushed her scarred cheek, her neck, and twined his fingers into her curls. He deepened the kiss until her heart threatened to pound out of her chest. After several long seconds, she twisted her face away, muscles like warm butter. He leaned his forehead against hers, his breath fanning her skin into gooseflesh.

Travis finally lowered her back to her feet, then grinned. "I'd be happy to do that again too."

She swatted his arm, another lopsided smile overtaking her mouth. "Not until we can see the preacher."

His mouth cracked, and his shoulders shook with laughter. When he sobered again, he motioned toward the barn. "How about we pray down there, out of the sun?" At her acknowledgment, he tucked her hand in the crook of his elbow and led her toward the building. Heart still struggling to believe the turn of events, Millie leaned into him, resting her head against his arm. It *felt* real.

It felt *good*.

When they stepped into the barn's interior, Walt stood to the left of the door, reaching for a box on a high shelf. At their entrance, he replaced the box and faced them.

Millie attempted to pull free of Travis's grasp, though he held her there. She cringed inwardly. *Lord, please don't let Walt steal the joy of this moment.*

Walt's brow furrowed, gaze lingering on their interlinked arms before he shifted his attention to Travis. "I'm sorry. Who are you and what do you want with Millie?"

Once Walt had spoken, Travis interpreted the words for her.

Millie tried to draw Walt's attention, but Travis spoke and signed an answer before she could intervene.

"My name is Travis McCaffrey. Millie and I are old friends from San Francisco. I've just asked her to marry me, and she's accepted."

"Have you now?" Walt's pale eyebrows rose in surprise, though a hint of—anger, perhaps?—brewed under the surface. "Isn't it customary to ask a woman's family for her hand before proposing?"

Travis nodded. "Yes, sir. Her mother granted me permission a few weeks ago."

"My gravely ill wife did that? Please. . .do tell how *that* came about!" Walt's anger bubbled just under the surface.

Travis must have seen it, for his answer was soothing. "I mean no disrespect, Mr. Sessums. As I said, Millie and I knew each other in San Francisco. I'd intended to marry her once she finished school, but things didn't work out then. So when Mrs. Sessums wrote and asked me to come, I came immediately."

Walt's expression was severe. When his lips moved again, Millie focused on Travis's translation. "And what do you do for a living? How will you support her?"

"My father and I run the largest livery in San Francisco, and I have a side business breaking and selling horses. I'm nowhere near this well-to-do, sir, but I can support Millie quite comfortably."

After an instant, Walt waved his hands, mimicking their language. "I see you signing to her. Are you deaf also?"

Travis tensed. "I am deaf, but I've learned to read lips."

"Well, then. You're proof of the very point I've said to Millie all along. She must adapt to the world, just as you have." He paused. "Just so *you* understand me. . .you're not to sign to her. You're delaying that process by speaking with your hands."

Travis's features hardened, though he restrained himself. "I lost my hearing at age eleven, sir. I'd learned to speak by then, so it was easier for me to learn to function in the hearing world. It took years to learn lipreading, even though I knew how to speak. It's an exhausting skill that requires much focus. Millie's extremely smart, but being born deaf, she'd find it more difficult to learn. You're handicapping her more by taking away the one language she *can* speak."

"This is my home, and I make the rules, son. If you don't like them, *leave*. But as long as she lives here, you're not to speak in gestures no one understands." Walt strode from the barn.

Travis stared, eventually turning to her. "Your mother married that man?"

"Yes." She gulped. "I avoid him. He won't allow the staff to sign with me, though Lawrence and Edith have learned a little."

He scrubbed a hand over his whiskered jaw. "Is he that hard on Victoria?"

"He seems attentive and caring toward her. They've only argued once that I recall."

"I don't like him. He doesn't care what's best for you."

She'd said the same to Momma for months. "Momma says Walt is trying to be helpful. He believes people will be more accepting if I learn to speak and read lips. But Peter had a deaf cousin who was subjected to this type of teaching, and she never could grasp it. He said that a man named Alexander Graham Bell is doing much in the deaf schools back East to change them from signing schools to oral schools."

Confusion masked Travis's face. "Who is Peter?"

Millie's heart stalled. *Oh, Lord. . .help me.* She clamped her eyes shut. "Peter was. . . my intended."

Lying atop his bedroll in the pitch-black barn loft, Travis's thoughts churned. Millie had so thoroughly set him aside, she'd gotten engaged to that Peter fella. By her account, a handsome, wealthy hearing man from Boston, sole heir to his father's fortune. She said he'd been kind and understanding when she'd been lonely, and the fact that he spoke in sign, thanks to having a deaf cousin, put her even more at ease.

All while he'd sat in San Francisco, naively thinking she'd return to him.

Mercy, but he'd been stupid.

Travis sat up, peeled the upper half of his bedroll off the hay and, reaching into the larger pile beside him, shoved an armful of the fresh bedding into place. Smoothing the bedroll down, he stretched out, though he sat up immediately when something jabbed between his shoulder blades. Patting the hay, he found a small burlap sack full of oddly shaped objects. Travis lit the lantern hanging on the post just feet away and unknotted the bag. Inside were three brown bottles, each with a small round neck and a palm-sized square body. Each one empty. Strange. He retied the top and laid it aside, extinguished the flame, and sprawled out, thoughts again stumbling over Millie's rich fiancé.

Father, You know I've wanted to marry this woman for years. I thought she wanted that too. But if she could forget me because my letters sounded too happy, did she ever really love me?

He closed his eyes, exhaustion pulling at his muscles, but sleep eluded him. After an hour of trying to sort his churning thoughts, he rose, relit the lantern, and climbed from the loft. Meandering to the first stall where a momma cat and her litter of kittens had taken up residence, he blew out the lantern, hung it on an exposed nail, then sat and pulled one of the nearly weaned kittens to his chest. It snuggled close, body vibrating with a contented purr. After several minutes, Travis closed his eyes.

When he next opened them, he lay sprawled in the hay next to a mound of kittens, bright light emanating from outside the stall. Was it morning? He quickly dismissed the thought. The light flickered like lamplight. Someone was here. Travis peered through the boards forming the stall wall. Walt Sessums and Pockmark— Blevins, he'd been told the man's name was—stood feet away, deep in conversation. A seemingly serious one. What would they be discussing at that time of night? After his earlier interchange with Sessums, he wanted to know, so he sat up and peered out. From that vantage point, he could see none of Sessums' face, but all of Blevins'.

"Ketteridge is expecting you to pay your debt to him in the next week. You better get this taken care of or you'll lose everything." Blevins hooked a thumb toward the barn door. "And stay away from the faro tables from now on!"

Back stiff, Sessums flung his hands wide.

"Don't get defensive. Just work faster."

Travis startled when one of the kittens clambered onto his lap. Scooping the squirming cat up, he focused on the men again.

Sessums shook his head vigorously.

"What's it been—three, four months? That's plenty long enough. No one's gonna question it. Just get her out of the way before. . ." Blevins turned away, gesturing toward the barn door again.

A chill swept him. Get *who* out of the way—and before *what*? Millie? Victoria? Both, maybe. Travis squinted, straining to catch more of the conversation, but the men had turned away. After more conversation, Blevins handed Sessums something, then lifted the lantern down. The pair walked toward the door where they paused while Sessums reached for the same box on the shelf that he'd accessed earlier that afternoon. Travis couldn't tell whether he took something out or put something in, but an instant later, Blevins pushed the barn door open and extinguished the lamp, plunging the space into darkness.

Their shadowy forms stepped into the moonlight and closed the door behind them. Travis dared not peek out to check whether they'd gone, for fear they might be outside talking. Eventually, he dared light his own lantern and emerge from the stall, heading toward the shelf and the box Sessums had accessed. Inside were three more bottles like the ones in the burlap sack, only these were filled with a white powder.

Chapter 5

As Millie sat in the wingback chair, Momma's eyes fluttered open, panic in her gaze. Upon seeing Millie, her body sagged and her eyes closed again.

"Thank God, it's you." Momma's signs were weak and choppy.

Millie settled a palm against Momma's forehead. Clammy skin. When the older woman opened her eyes again, Millie nodded. "Yes, Momma. It's me. Who'd you think it was?"

"Walt. He's bringing my breakfast." She shook her head. "I don't want to eat."

The pitiable comment turned Millie's stomach.

She brushed wisps of hair from Momma's face. "I won't let him force you."

Her throat knotted uncomfortably. *Lord, are we at this point already? I'm not ready. There are so many things I need to say to her. So many years we didn't have together. Please. . . I beg You, is there no miracle that can save Momma?*

As Millie tried to swallow her emotions, she rose to wet a cloth in the nearby basin then returned to sponge Momma's face.

"How is Travis—and your horse?" Momma could hardly lift her arms to ask.

Millie forced a lopsided smile to her lips. "He asked me to marry him yesterday."

Momma smiled at that. "And. . .?"

"I accepted, Momma." Surely giving Momma that small comfort wasn't wrong, despite her fear he'd almost certainly rescind the proposal due to Peter. Momma didn't need to know how hurt Travis had been, or that he'd walked away, shutting down all communication.

Momma tensed. "I hear Walt."

"Don't worry. I'll handle this." Millie hurried into the hall as Walt climbed the steps from the kitchen. He balanced Momma's tray on one arm and shook something into her bowl from a squat brown bottle. Paused on the top step, he stirred the bowl.

Millie approached, rapping her knuckles against the wall to draw his attention. He jerked his head up, eyes wide. When she beckoned him to follow her to her room, Walt's lips thinned with impatience. Thankfully, he followed, settling the tray on the vanity while she scribbled a message on the nearest paper.

Please don't make Momma eat. She isn't hungry.

She turned the paper to show him, then signed a single word. "Please!"

Walt scribbled an answer. *She needs her strength to get better.*

Millie shook her head, taking the pencil from his fingers. *Anything she eats makes her ill and weakens her more.*

Annoyance flashed across his face, and his lips formed one very understandable word. *No.* Tray in hand, he started down the hall.

No? Millie's heart pounding, she darted in front of him. Hands flying, she signed quickly. "Please, Walt. You're upsetting her! Just. . .leave her alone." Tears welled.

Setting the tray on a small bench lining the wall, he picked her up and moved her as if she were a mere rag doll. Then, retrieving the tray, he carried on.

Millie ducked in front of him again. "Stop!" Blocking his path, she reached for the tray. Her palms contacted the tray's corners, and in an instant, it tipped. Dishes flew. Watery gruel slopped down Walt's shirt and trousers. Utensils, bowls, and a small bud vase hit the floor.

For one horrifying instant, Walt stared, then dropped the tray. The back of his hand smashed Millie's cheekbone, causing lights and pain to explode through her skull. Disoriented, she collapsed, though she tried to sit up.

Walt pawed at her, pulled her up. Millie grabbed something from the floor—the bowl!—and swung, the vessel shattering against his head. He released her, and she fell, rolled away. Instinct took over, and she crawled, her hand again brushing something as she moved. She latched onto it just as Walt jerked her up and dumped her on the floor of her room. The door slammed, walls shaking with the force. Unsteady, she reached for the door. Locked.

Oh, Lord, help Momma!

Travis roused to sunlight flooding the barn. Morning. Despite his churning thoughts, both about Millie's former fiancé and her and Victoria's safety, he had finally managed to sleep a few hours. Unfortunately, now it was far later than he'd intended to rise. Pushing himself up, he tucked an empty bottle from the burlap sack into his bedroll, then donned his boots and hat. Empty canteen in hand, he headed outside to the rain barrel at the barn's corner. After he cleaned up, he'd find Millie so they could talk. He was still hurt by the fact she'd promised herself to another man, but he *did* love her and didn't want harm to come to her or her mother.

Perhaps after they talked, a ride to the sheriff's office might be in order. But what exactly would he say—that he'd eavesdropped on a secret, middle-of-the-night meeting in which he could lipread only parts of the conversation, giving him. . .a whole lot of nothing? That would get him nowhere fast.

He dropped the canteen and his hat and bent over the rim of the rain barrel, dunking his head, then mopped his face and ran his fingers through his dripping hair. As he brought a handful of water to his mouth to drink, something hit him between the shoulder blades. Startled, Travis spun to find Blevins a mere foot away, and ten feet behind him, Walt Sessums.

"Where'd you come from?" Blevins scowled.

Travis's skin prickled. "Uh. . ." Not good. Not at all. "Just woke up."

Blevins glanced at Sessums, then faced him again. "Where you been sleeping?"

Travis blinked away the water in his eyes, nerves flaring a warning. "The barn loft—where Mrs. Sessums told me to. . ." If he played dumb, maybe they'd believe he slept through their gathering.

"Well, now. That's a problem."

He furrowed his brows. "Why?"

Walt stormed up. "I'm done. This is *my* home. I don't like having men *I* didn't hire hanging around it. Take your things and get out."

Travis stared. "Yes, sir." He squatted to retrieve his hat and canteen from the ground. "Right after I talk to Millie." He attempted to skirt around Blevins.

The man caught Travis by the shirt. "You heard Mr. Sessums. Get lost. Now."

Actually, he hadn't, but. . . "You're gonna keep me from my bride-to-be?"

Blevins looked confused. "Bride-to—"

"She's not here," Walt interrupted. "A friend from town took her away for the day. I'll pass along a message where she can find you."

Travis's stomach lurched. From what he'd gathered, Millie had few, if any, friends in Virginia City. How could she, when Blevins and Embry escorted her everywhere? It was hard to believe she'd gone anywhere, given the fact Blevins was standing right in front of him.

"You mind telling me where she went? Maybe I can talk to her at her friend's place for a moment."

"I'm not sure." Walt turned to Blevins. "See that he leaves. Immediately." The man turned toward the huge house.

"Let's go." Blevins herded Travis toward the barn.

Stalling, Travis removed the stopper from the canteen and dunked it in the rain barrel. Air bubbled from its mouth.

Blevins gave him a shove, lips moving, though Travis didn't catch the words.

He looked up. "You're not gonna send me away without water, are you?"

"Hurry up."

Task completed, Travis corked the canteen and headed to the loft to gather his things. Blevins followed him up the ladder as Travis gathered bedroll and saddlebags. The man's eyes darted to the burlap sack, which Travis had left in plain view, then flicked a wary gaze Travis's way. Ignoring him, Travis scrambled down the ladder to saddle his chestnut and Millie's mare. Blevins shadowed him.

Within minutes, he led both horses from the barn, swung into the saddle, and started toward the house, Millie's mare trailing behind. He kept his mount to a slow walk, eyeing the mansion as he passed. Embry stood at the door, a bundle of wildflowers in one fist. As Travis neared, the door swung open and the maid looked out. When Embry watched him instead of turning to the door, the maid spoke.

"Can I help you, Jack?"

The fella turned only slightly and handed her the flowers, still eyeing Travis as he spoke. "These are for Mrs. Sessums. Tell her I hope she gets to feelin' better."

The maid received the flowers. "I'll see she gets them. Thank you." Then she looked directly at Travis and mouthed several words.

Get help. Millie's in danger.

Travis's belly knotted. What level of danger? Enough that he should risk confronting

371

Blevins and Embry to demand entry to the house? Or should he ride for town, get the sheriff, and return? He drew his horse to a stop and turned to Blevins, who was trailing him on foot.

Lord, I need some direction, and quick.

"What?" Blevins asked, charging at him. Embry also stepped nearer.

Travis slipped from his saddle to face the man. "Mr. Sessums said he'd pass my message to Millie. Tell her I'm not sure where I'll be, but I'll leave word with Abel Perkins at the mercantile."

"Right. I'll pass it along. Now git."

He flicked a glance from Blevins to Embry, and on to the maid. "If I don't hear from her by two o'clock this afternoon, I'll be back to find out why." And he'd bring help.

Chapter 6

Millie's right cheek ached, her eye nearly swollen shut where Walt had backhanded her. Yet that hardly mattered as she stared at the strange brown bottle she'd grabbed from the floor in her haste to escape. There were no labels, just a flaky yellowish residue on one side, probably the glue that previously held a label in place. Angling it toward the light, she found some sort of powder inside. Medicine? Doctor Tompkins hadn't offered them remedies when he'd seen Momma. He'd said there was little to do except make her comfortable. Was that what Walt had sprinkled into her food—something to ease Momma's suffering?

She removed the cork and sniffed. No scent. She shook a little onto the vanity. Nondescript white powder. Corking the bottle, she slipped it into her skirt pocket. Either this was medicine or something worse. With Momma's rapid decline— and Walt's insistent coaxing for her to eat and drink food *he* brought from the kitchen, despite the times she'd offered to feed Momma—

Millie clamped a hand over her mouth.

Lord, is he poisoning her?

She rushed to the door, jerking on the handle. Locked tight. She scurried to the window, jerked the pane upward, and leaned out. Blevins and Embry stood in the yard below, watching something in the distance. When she also looked, her stomach dropped.

Travis rode away, her mare trailing him. He'd left—without her? *Oh, God, please! I need him. Make him turn around.*

He rode like his horse's tail was burning. Leaving her for good, no doubt because she'd been engaged to Peter. *Father, please. . .make him understand I'd take all that back if I could!*

But he kept riding.

She was on her own.

Below, Blevins motioned for Embry to head to the barn, and once Embry left, Blevins stabbed a finger in Millie's direction, gesturing for her to close the window. Instead, she returned to staring after Travis, throat knotting painfully. How could she get out of this room and help Momma, particularly if Walt was poisoning her?

Angry gaze flicking to her window, Blevins disappeared into the house and, almost immediately, heavy footsteps pounded up the staircase. Her eyes widened when her door shook, then opened.

Both Walt and Blevins stepped inside, shutting the door behind them.

At the sight of Momma's husband, fury filled her chest. She stormed toward Walt. "Are you poisoning Momma?" She signed the question, hands flying.

He ignored her.

She hit his arm. "Answer me! Are you poisoning her?"

When he still paid her no mind, she marched around them, reached for the door, and opened it. Before she stepped out, someone grabbed her hair and jerked her backward, an arm circling her midsection. Pain seared her scalp. She clawed at the arm, tried to twist free, but her captor swung her to face the other man.

Walt bobbed into view.

He grabbed her face, fingers boring into her flesh. He spoke, his expression twisting into ugliness. Rearing back against Blevins' chest, Millie kneed Walt in the groin. He doubled over, but before she could kick him, Blevins threw her on the bed and flipped her onto her back.

Another backhanded blow landed against her damaged cheek and his hand clamped around her throat. Everything slipped into terrifying blackness.

Travis stopped in front of the mercantile and tied both his horse and Millie's mare at the hitching rail then retrieved the bottle from his bedroll. Before he slipped into the store, a horse at the next rail reached toward him. He turned toward the motion, noting Clyde's bay.

Travis rubbed the horse's neck, then, steeling himself, stepped inside. He couldn't avoid the man. Not when Millie was in danger.

Abel Perkins glanced his way as he reached for a can on a shelf behind the counter. Item in hand, the man turned and smiled. "Welcome back, Travis. Can I help you?"

Near the back corner where the men's hats were displayed, Clyde stiffened, glanced his direction, but faced the wall again.

Travis angled toward the storekeeper. "Do you know what this bottle is?" He held it out.

After a moment of study, Mr. Perkins walked to the apothecary case and picked out a bottle. "I reckon it's this." He handed Travis an identical bottle, except for the red label that graced its front.

Arsenic Trioxide.

Travis looked at the man. "What's it used for?"

Perkins shrugged. "Rat poison, mostly. Some use it to treat for bedbugs."

Rat poison. Bedbug killer. Both legitimate reasons to find several empty bottles at a house. Particularly in the barn. But hidden in a sack in the hay? "How long would a bottle that size last?"

"Depends on how big a rat issue you're having."

Travis leaned in, dropping his voice low. "Could this be used to poison someone, and if so, how fast would they die?"

Perkins's brows shot up. "Why are you asking such questions?"

Travis glanced back to be sure Clyde wasn't eavesdropping, then faced the store-keeper. "I've been working for Victoria Sessums, breaking a horse for Millie. I stumbled across a sack of these bottles, all empty, all missing their labels. I'm sure you know how sick Mrs. Sessums has been."

"You implying Walt Sessums is poisoning his wife?"

Travis scrubbed his neck nervously. "Mrs. Sessums told me to sleep in the barn. Late last night, Mr. Sessums and Blevins met there. Blevins said someone named Ketteridge is expecting payment of a debt in the next week, and if Mr. Sessums doesn't pay, he'll lose everything. In the same conversation, he told Sessums to *get her out of the way before. . .*"

"Before *what?*"

Travis shrugged. "I don't know. He turned, and I couldn't read his lips."

Mr. Perkins paled and strode down the counter to fetch his ledger book. As he returned, he nodded in Clyde's direction. "Clyde says Drew Ketteridge is a high-stakes gambler. He's seen Sessums and Ketteridge play in some of the same games."

Jaw clenched, Travis shot a look at the corner, though Clyde didn't try to inject himself into the conversation.

Mr. Perkins opened the ledger book and flipped to a page toward the back. *Sessums, Walt,* was scrawled across the top. Mr. Perkins skimmed the page once, then again. "He's got no such purchases."

Travis's shoulders fell. "None. . .?"

"No, but. . .this lends some credence to your story." Mr. Perkins showed Travis the balance owed—a total close to four hundred dollars. "He owes far more than any other customer. I've let him run up that bill, figuring he was good for it, given he owns one of the big mines around here." Befuddled, Perkins thought, then held up a finger. "Let me check something." He flipped to a page marked *Blevins, Tim.* Again, he skimmed the page, marking several lines with a check mark. As he reached the bottom, he showed Travis. Four lines, each noting *arsenic trioxide.*

Travis considered the dates. "He bought all those in the last three months, the same amount of time Victoria's been sick."

Mr. Perkins nodded, then flipped to another page. *Embry, Jack.* He marked three lines, one purchase a month for the last three months.

"Those men often buy supplies for their boss's place. In a three-month span, that seems like a little too much rat poison for one home, even one that large."

"I'd agree." Travis swallowed hard. "Can you point me to the sheriff's office?"

The storekeeper pointed toward the street, but the floor under Travis's feet vibrated. He turned as Clyde approached.

"You might think twice about going to the Virginia sheriff." Clyde shook his head. "At least if you're reporting Sessums."

Travis narrowed his eyes. "Why should I listen to you?" He made no attempt to hide the hard edge in his tone.

"I suspect Sessums is paying off the sheriff."

"Oh? And what makes you say that?"

Clyde shrugged. "I work at the mine. I've been in the saloon when he's been gambling. I've seen things. The sheriff overlooks things he oughtn't, and Sessums slips him money from time to time."

Travis couldn't help his scornful laugh. "You're holding a job now, Clyde? That's new."

Mr. Perkins jabbed him in the shoulder, and Travis turned. "Show a little respect, son. He's been working there nigh on twelve years."

Travis gritted his teeth. "Why're you sticking up for him?"

Perkins leveled an even gaze at him. "He's my friend."

"Do you know what kind of man your *friend* is. . .what he did to me?" He glared first at Perkins, then at Clyde. "He drank himself into a stupor every day after my ma died. Went to work drunk so often, he got fired. So he moved me here—away from everything that was familiar. He wouldn't get a job, so at the tender age of ten, I did. But when I got home that night and told him I was quitting school to work so we could eat, he tanned my hide. Made me quit. He'd've rather done without than let me work. And that wasn't the only time he hit me. He knocked me around whenever I'd try to talk to him. There were plenty of nights I went hungry because he'd spent all our money on whiskey. When I got sick and lost my hearing, he gave me up without a thought. Just signed custody over to some woman he'd never met." He shifted his attention back to Mr. Perkins. "So excuse me for feeling put out at hearing that as soon as I was gone, *then*. . .when he had no one to worry about but himself, *then* he got a job. Just like Clyde Alcott—always thinking of himself."

As Mr. Perkins started to answer, Clyde grabbed Travis's shirtfront, swept his legs out from under him, and dumped him on the floor. Travis latched onto Clyde's wrists, grappling to free himself, but Clyde dragged him over and pinned him against the face of the mercantile counter. Travis's hat tumbled to the floor.

"Yes! Yes, I did those things." Clyde's dark eyes clouded with grief. "All of 'em, and there's not a day I don't feel the shame of my actions. But you are going to shut up and listen for a minute."

Shock flooded Travis, and he quit struggling.

"Yes, I drank myself senseless, and I didn't take care of you—because I missed your mother so deeply, I wanted to die too. I knew I needed to stay here for you, and getting drunk was the only way I could dull the pain enough." He gulped, eyes darkening yet more. "Yes, I lost my job and moved you away from everything you knew—because I thought getting away from the haunting memories of your mother would help me sober up, care for you proper again. It didn't work, because every time I looked at you, I saw her. Every time you spoke, I heard her. Each time you touched me, I felt her." A lone tear streaked down his cheek. "And yes, I tanned your hide for quitting school—because I'd promised your ma that I wouldn't let you become an illiterate nobody like me. I promised her you'd get an education.

"I beat you—Oh, God, help me." Clyde's expression grew tortured. "And I will never forgive myself for those times." He pried one hand loose from Travis's shirt and cupped his cheek instead. "You were my son, and you deserved far better than that. I am sorry. From the depth of my being, *I'm sorry*."

Slack-jawed, Travis stared as Clyde pried his other hand loose and sat heavily. "And yes, I gave you up. Because I finally realized I was too broken and too drunk to be any good to you. So I signed over my rights and I sent you to that school. And I told you *good riddance* as you left because if I showed any weakness, any softness at all, I couldn't make myself send you away." Clyde swallowed hard, gulped a couple more breaths, then continued. "It nearly killed me, losing you too. I'd let you and your mother down. But that was when I started to pull my life together. I told myself I could get you back. I'd pick up the pieces and go after you. . .and I did. More than once. But by then, the McCaffreys had adopted you. You looked to be doing real good at that school. You were happy. I'd already messed up your life enough. It wasn't right to do it again. So I left you there."

Clyde hung his head, his body sagging like a man spent from hard labor. After a minute, he stood. "I'll come back tomorrow for my order, Abel." He shuffled toward the door.

Travis gaped after him, his throat knotted so tight he could barely breathe. His thoughts spun, shocked by the grief and hurt he'd seen in the man's eyes. A grief he'd been certain couldn't possibly exist in Clyde's stony heart.

But it was there, and it ran deep.

Abel Perkins appeared from behind the counter. "You should understand one more thing, Travis. For years, your father and I have been praying for you to come back. He even made a deal with God. If you'd come back even just once more, he'd give up whiskey for good. The evening after I hauled you out to him, I went by to check in. He made good on that promise, Travis. He was pouring out the whiskey when I rode up. Maybe it's been slow, but he's never quit trying to right his mistakes."

Travis glanced toward the street as Clyde rode out of view. Clyde had prayed for him—like he and Millie had prayed for Victoria?

A minute ticked by as his thoughts spun out of control. Never had he imagined the agony Clyde might've faced. Only his own.

God, I've been so selfish.

Finally, he pushed himself up and, grabbing his hat, stepped out onto the boardwalk. He scanned the street, finding Clyde riding away through the crowd.

Lord, help me. Please.

Travis strode to his horses, mounted, and followed. As he caught up, he pitched his voice loud. "Clyde!"

The man stiffened, drew up, and twisted in the saddle. His eyes grew wide with—was it hope?

Travis weaved through the crowd and rode up alongside him. "I've got a lot of things to chew on. A lot to think through. But I understand better now, and. . .you, um. . ." His heart pounded, and he struggled to look at his father. "You said I should ask—if I needed anything." He swallowed hard. "If that offer still stands, I could use some help. *Please.*"

The afternoon sun beat down on Travis's shoulders, and a strong westerly wind blew as he waited outside the Sessums mansion. After a moment, the door opened, and the butler, Lawrence, appeared.

"Is Millie here, please?" He looked past the man into the house.

"I'm sorry. She's unavailable."

The man's expression gave Travis pause. "What's that mean—unavailable?"

Lawrence cast a discreet glance at the upper floor, then faced him. "Blevins took her. I don't know where. Something bad is going on here. Mr. Sessums struck Miss Millie this morning, and Blevins carried her out, unconscious. He said he was taking her to the doctor, though I don't believe it. I fear for her, but I fear for Mrs. Sessums more."

Travis's heart stalled. Someone had laid a hand on his bride-to-be—and yet again, he didn't know where to find her. *Lord, why was I upset? Her past isn't important—only our future. But for us to have one, You gotta help me find her.* "You should be concerned. I think Mrs. Sessums is being poisoned. With arsenic."

Lawrence's eyes widened in horror, but other than to glance again over his shoulder, he didn't respond.

"Can you get her away from here?"

After a brief hesitation, Lawrence nodded. "I'll find a way."

Travis beckoned to Clyde, who stood back, holding the horses. As he approached, Lawrence stepped outside and shut the door.

Travis turned to Clyde. "I hope you don't mind me volunteering your place, but. . ." He shifted a glance to Lawrence. "Take her to Clyde's house—and don't let Sessums give her *anything* to eat or drink. We'll leave word with the doctor to come see her."

Clyde's cheeks reddened as he turned to Lawrence. "My place ain't much. Nothin' like here, just so you know."

After Clyde gave Lawrence directions, Travis shook the butler's hand. "Please protect her. She's to be my mother-in-law. . .*soon*."

A smile bloomed on Lawrence's lips, then faded. "Godspeed, son." He appeared truly concerned.

"Any ideas where he might've taken her?"

At Lawrence's negative answer, Clyde turned. "I got one. You can hide just about anything in a mine shaft."

Chapter 7

Head throbbing, Millie stared at the squalid little room. Her right eye had swollen completely closed, and her throat burned from when Blevins had choked her. She'd lost consciousness only to awaken in his arms as he guided his horse toward town. When she'd struggled, he'd drawn his pistol, tucked the barrel firmly under her chin, and made it quite clear she was to stop fighting.

Blevins had taken her into Virginia City, left his horse in a livery stable, then circled to the back door of the run-down little lodging house behind the stable. There, he'd forced her into the tiny basement room she now occupied. The only furnishings were a bed, two flimsy tables flanking the mattress, lamps topping each, and a rickety, ladder-backed chair. He'd locked her in the tiny quarters so many hours ago, she'd seen daylight fade and night fall through the one tiny window high on the wall. Sunrise couldn't be far off now. Yet, when she'd pounded on the door, tried to make any noise she could, no one heard her. And her attempts to reach the tiny window had proven futile, even standing on the chair.

Lord, I'm frightened. Blevins can't intend anything good.

As she prayed, something shook the door. Her heart rate jumped, and Millie scrambled from the saggy mattress into the corner, dragging the flimsy chair in front of her.

Seconds ticked by. Nothing. Had she imagined it, or—

The knob twisted, and the door shook again. Millie lifted the chair, the top rung of the chair's back braced against her belly and the legs pointed toward the door. The door swung open and Blevins peered in, a whiskey bottle in hand. The stench of liquor rolled like fog across the room.

Millie rushed him, chair in front of her like a lance. Despite her small stature, she drove it into his midsection, forcing him back. He slammed against the far hallway wall, and she ducked past, racing for the stairs. Immediately, he was on her. His arms circled her midsection and he wrestled her toward the room. At the doorway, she braced her feet on the jambs and shoved backward with all her might. The drunken man stumbled off balance. Again, he slammed into the wall, and both tumbled to the ground. Millie tried to flee, but Blevins caught her ankle, tripped her. She smacked the ground hard. By the time she found her bearings, he'd grabbed a handful of her hair, pulled her to her feet, and dragged her toward the room. He shoved her inside, and she toppled over the overturned chair, crumpling into a heap.

Lord, help. Please. Help me.

Blevins closed and locked the door. Pocketing the key, he turned on her, his movements slow and sloppy.

Still dazed, Millie pushed to her feet, pulling the chair upright. He stepped toward her and she backed up, dragging the chair in front of her. Her heart raced. He advanced again, and she retreated. He took a third step, but something skittered across their path. His whiskey bottle. His eyes tracked it momentarily before he bent to grab it. In that instant, Millie hoisted the chair and swung.

Wood and cane smashed across his head and shoulders, splintering. Blevins collapsed face-first onto the floor. Holding the remnant of the chair's back, Millie stared. When he didn't move, she dashed to the door, jerked on the knob. Finding it locked, she turned to fetch the key from his pocket.

To her horror, flames crawled up the wall and across the table from the overturned lamp, knocked sideways by a broken piece of the chair. Trembling, Millie dashed back to the unconscious man, dug in one hip pocket, then the other until she found the key. Eyes darting between the flames, the downed man, and the keyhole, Millie finally threaded the key into the lock. As she jerked the door open, flames leaped onto the ceiling and smoke filled the room.

Hesitating, Millie dashed back and shook Blevins. When he didn't rouse, she kicked him in the ribs. The man's eyes opened. His mouth cracked wide. Then she fled, racing down the hall, up the stairs, and out. She flew around the side of the building, and then stopped short. Flames had burned through the building's wall and were climbing toward the upper floors, helped by the strong wind. Circling past the burning section, she ran to the nearest windows and banged on one after the other, screaming as she went.

A bleary-eyed man opened a window and stuck his head out to yell at her. Millie motioned frantically until he turned. The fellow swept a glance back, hesitated, then disappeared.

Lord, let everyone get out. Please!

She turned to run, but strong arms caught her, held her tight, the stench of whiskey and smoke nearly overpowering her.

Bone-weary, Travis and Clyde exited the mine. Millie was nowhere within the tunnels, and they'd searched nearly without pause since the previous afternoon.

"I'm sorry." Clyde shook his head, his brown eyes full of concern. "I thought for sure she'd be here."

Pressing his eyes closed, Travis tipped his head back. "Lord, I need a sign. A miracle. Where should we look?"

He inhaled deep, the heavy scent of smoke on the wind.

Clyde touched his arm, drawing his gaze. "Maybe we should rest a few hours. We aren't at our best right now."

Travis shook his head. "She's in trouble. Maybe the dying kind. I can't just give up."

Turning away, Travis's chest constricted. Clyde clamped a reassuring hand on his shoulder, though Travis shrugged free.

Lord, please. Show me where to look. Travis stared at the horizon, forced himself to breathe, though the heavy scent of smoke permeated the air. Brow furrowed, he turned slowly until he found a strange red glow hanging over part of Virginia City.

"Clyde, something's burning."

The other man fixed his gaze on the same spot. Wordless, he glanced Travis's way, and they both hurried to mount up.

Neck and neck, they rode toward the red-orange blaze that was growing by the minute. Each new street they crossed, they peered into the darkness, searching for the source. Sparks and embers rode on the strong west wind, whipping and swirling over the city. Finally, as they crossed A Street, the blaze came into view. Flames engulfed a building as people rushed around it.

They tied their horses a few blocks from the fire and rushed toward the crowd. The Virginia City fire squad was hard at work, attempting to contain the blaze, though the neighboring two roofs had also caught fire.

Clyde approached a small circle of men who were talking and gesturing excitedly. Travis followed him.

"Who warned you?" Clyde asked a man, apparently injecting himself into the ongoing conversation.

"Dunno who she was, but I'd recognize her if I saw her. She had one real swollen eye, and her mouth hung down on one side."

Millie! Travis pressed in. "I need to find her. Where is she?"

The gent shook his head. "I don't know. I ducked back inside to warn everyone. Didn't see where she went."

Clyde suddenly swatted Travis's arm.

He turned as a woman spoke. ". . .saw that Blevins fella, the one what works for Sessums, haul her toward the livery."

Travis's heart hammered. The livery. He raced into the familiar territory and, finding the place buzzing with activity as people moved the horses to safety, he searched the barn. *Lord, let her be here. Please!*

He hurried up and down the rows, checking each stall. Blevins's mount waited nervously in one, still tied despite the stall door standing wide open. Neither Blevins nor Millie anywhere to be seen. Not on the ground level, anyway. He grabbed the nearest lantern and climbed to the loft, holding the light high. Travis peered into every shadowy corner. Nothing.

Something smacked the heel of his boot. Behind him, on the ladder, Clyde beckoned. "C'mon!"

Travis scrambled down, rehung the lantern, and followed him out the back side of the livery. There in the predawn glow, Blevins faced Millie, back to them. Millie, her right eye swollen terribly, flicked a glance at him, then signed. "Gun!"

"Blevins!"

At Travis's call, the man turned, movements unsteady, gun leveled in his direction. A burst of flame erupted from the pistol, bullet whipping past, fanning his cheek. Travis ducked then rushed him, tackling the man. Blevins went down, gun skittering from his grasp, and Travis reared onto his knees. He struck the man once, pulled back, and struck again. Blevins sagged and rolled onto his side. Travis reached for him, but someone latched onto his arm.

Clyde. And Millie just feet behind.

"The fire's spreading! Let's go." Clyde pointed. Flames danced along the barn roof's peak.

At the sight, Travis forgot Blevins. Rolling to his feet, he reached for Millie's hand. She took it, and they ran down the side of the barn to A Street. Flames had spread to several buildings, huge smoke billows flooding the dawn. They ran for the horses, and only when they'd reached them did Travis pause.

"Are you all right?" he signed to Millie.

"I'm fine." Her hands shook as she answered. "But I think Walt's poisoning Momma."

"I know. Lawrence said he'd get her to safety." He pulled Millie into his arms for an instant, held her tight, then released her. Shoved her toward Clyde. "Go with him. He'll take you to her."

"What. . .why?" Her hands flew with the questions. "Where are you going?"

Travis turned. "Clyde, get her to safety. Please. I'll be right behind you."

Before either Millie or Clyde could respond, Travis jerked his horse free and mounted. Charging back toward the livery, he guided the chestnut beside the barn, back to where he'd left Blevins. Only the man was gone. Travis circled once, dismounted, and ran into the mouth of the burning building. Smoke filled the interior as flames ate at the loft above.

"Blevins!" He raced to the row where Blevins's horse had stood. Through the smoke, a hazy figure tried to wrangle the terrified mount, saddle in one hand, the horse's reins in the other. The horse reared and lunged, angling toward him. Travis waved and yelled, driving the horse toward the nearest door. The big black gelding burst to freedom.

By the time he turned again, flames had spread down the nearby support beam, and the wood post buckled. The loft sagged.

"Blevins! Get out!"

The loft gave way, scattering burning hay and wood across the stalls beneath, burying Blevins. For one stunned instant, Travis stared. Then, fleeing, he caught up his terrified horse, swung into the saddle, and turned toward Clyde's.

Chapter 8

Millie sat rigid in front of the strange man Travis had left her with. He guided his horse out of town, well away from the fire. She repeatedly scanned behind them for signs of Travis. All she found was fire, smoke, and mayhem. Great fear gripped her heart.

Lord, keep Travis safe. And Momma. And the town.

After some time, the man turned onto a curving path, rounded a hill, and rode toward a dilapidated house. Beside the nearby barn stood Walt's surrey, and in the strangely sturdy corral, her little mare, the surrey team, and a bony old milk cow.

The cabin's rickety door opened, and Lawrence, dressed in only his suit pants and white shirt, sleeves rolled to his elbows, appeared. Millie grabbed the reins from the man and drew the big bay to a stop. She slid to the ground and ran to Lawrence, signing as she went.

"Where's Momma?"

The butler seemed to understand and waved her inside.

Millie found the main room, containing the kitchen, a table, and a lone, narrow, empty bed. She darted through the doorway off to the left. There, Momma slept in a second narrow bed while Edith and Dr. Tompkins kept watch.

At Millie's entry, Edith rose from her makeshift seat on the trunk in the corner and caught her in a crushing hug. They clung to each other, and when Edith finally pulled back, she inspected Millie's swollen eye.

Millie shrugged away from the attention. "How is Momma?"

Edith smiled and signed. "The doctor is helping her."

A lopsided grin overtook Millie's mouth. When she approached the bed, Dr. Tompkins rose from the chair beside Momma. He also attempted to look at her eye, but she brushed off the interest and sat on the edge of the mattress.

Momma's eyes fluttered open. A weak smile formed and quickly faltered. "What happened?"

"Walt hit me, Momma, but I'm fine. Don't worry." Perhaps when Momma was stronger, she'd tell her of her ordeal. "How are you?"

"The doctor says I'll get better now." She smiled, but her eyes closed quickly, and her hands rested against her chest.

Millie kissed Momma's cheek, then rose. Turning to the doctor, she wrote a question on the dirt floor. "Will Momma live?"

The doctor grinned, then scratched his own answer under hers. "Yes, now that I know what's ailing her."

Millie clamped a hand over her mouth to keep from sobbing at the answer. Edith drew her aside until she'd contained the emotion. Finally, she thanked the doctor, looked again at Momma as she rested, and went in search of the man who'd brought her here. She found him on the far side of the corral, rubbing down his horse.

"I'm sorry. . .who are you?" she signed as she neared. When confusion clouded the man's features, Millie bent and scratched her question into the dirt.

Face reddening, the man glanced at her written question, then shook his head rather sheepishly and spoke again.

Before her frustration had a chance to root, a faint smile bent the man's lips. He nodded toward a place behind her.

Millie turned to find Travis dismounting halfway across the yard. She hurried to him, and he pulled her into a huge hug. Her brave front crumbled, and she sobbed in his arms.

When she finally pulled back, she wiped her eyes and risked a look. "I didn't think I would see you again, the way you rode away yesterday."

Travis's brow furrowed. "Yesterday? Walt kicked me out, wouldn't let me speak to you. The maid warned me you were in trouble, so I was going for help."

"Then you weren't angry about Peter?"

He heaved a big breath. "I was angry, but when I nearly lost you a second time"—he pinned her with an intense gaze—"I realized Peter doesn't matter. Nothing matters except us and our future. If you'll still have me, I want to marry you. *Soon.* Before anything else happens."

A lopsided grin twisted her mouth. "Yes! I want to marry you. *Soon.*"

Grinning himself, Travis traced the curve of her cheek, then tipped her chin up and bent to claim her lips. She stood on tiptoes to meet him, her arms circling his neck. His hands settled at her shoulders, skimmed down her back to her waist as he pulled her nearer. But as they settled into the kiss, something smacked them both lightly in the side of the face. Separating from Travis, Millie found the strange man leading Travis's chestnut toward the corral, the mount's tail swishing as it passed. Travis laughed at the ill-timed fly-swatting.

"Travis, who is he?"

He sobered, an odd expression replacing his mirth. "I'll introduce you." He tugged her toward the man.

The fellow tied Travis's horse to the corral bars then turned to them.

"Millie, meet Clyde Alcott." He both signed and spoke the words. "My father."

Father. The word felt foreign when Travis used it in relation to Clyde—but strangely right too.

Confusion filled Millie's eyes. "Your father?" Then, understanding flared. "Alcott. Your—"

"My *first* father."

She shifted a crooked smile at Clyde. "Very nice to meet you. I'm Millie Gordon."

After Travis translated, Clyde smiled timidly. "Tell her I'm real pleased to make her acquaintance."

Travis shook his head. "If you expect to be a part of our lives, Clyde, I think you ought to learn how to tell her yourself."

Clyde's face paled. "Is. . .that. . .what you want?"

Travis nodded slowly. "Yeah."

A weight seemed to lift from Clyde's shoulders. "Thank you." A genuine smile—one Travis remembered from before grief and drunkenness had ravaged his father—crossed his face. "How do I say this to her?"

Travis signed slowly, and Clyde repeated. Once he finished, Millie stepped up and hugged him. Startled, Clyde stared back at Travis. "I like her."

He nodded. "I do too."

Clyde's gaze flicked to the path, and he suddenly stepped in front of Millie. "Take her inside. Now."

Travis turned to see Walt Sessums riding toward them. Travis caught Millie's arm and, holding her close so he blocked her from Walt's view, led her toward the little cabin. She peeked around him. Seeing Walt, Millie matched Travis step for step. Feet from the door, she ran ahead.

With her safely inside, Travis turned. "How'd you find us, Sessums?"

The man shrugged. "I've been searching for my wife since she went missing yesterday. When I saw you in town early this morning, I figured you'd lead me right to her." He glanced past Travis toward the corral and barn, then back. "I've come for what's mine. My surrey, my horses. . .and my wife."

"If she's here, she's not leaving."

"Is that so?" Sessums' expression remained stoic, though his eyes shifted from Clyde to Travis's and back to the little house. "Why?"

"You've been poisoning her."

Walt guffawed. "Poisoning her? She's my wife. I love her."

"Then why did I witness a middle-of-the-night meeting between you and Blevins when Blevins said the gambler, Drew Ketteridge, is expecting you to pay your debt to him? And why was Blevins suggesting you get your wife out of the way before you lose everything? You've been poisoning her with a bottle that looks like this." He produced the bottle from his back pocket. "Maybe trying to get at her money to pay off your debts?"

Sessums' jaw tightened. "You got a loud mouth and a runaway imagination, boy."

"Do I? Just to be sure, I checked with Abel Perkins to see what comes in such bottles. Arsenic. In his ledgers, he found where Blevins and Embry bought a bunch of it during Victoria's illness. You're a betting man. Want to wager that gastric fever symptoms closely match arsenic poisoning?"

Sessums eyed him, then Clyde, and urged his horse toward the corral, cutting between them. "You have no right to keep me from my wife. I'll take the carriage and team for now, but I'll be back—with the sheriff and warrants."

"Did I forget to mention?" Travis shifted as Sessums' horse neared. "I sent a telegram to the U.S. Marshals about what's going on." Clyde had suggested the telegram after warning Lawrence the day before. "They're surely on their way to investigate."

In a flash, Walt reached for his gun and swung toward Travis. From behind Sessums' horse, Clyde burst into view and leaped, tackled Travis, momentum carrying the older man over him into the dirt beyond. Travis's head smashed the ground, and stars danced before his eyes. Dazed, he flashed a look toward Sessums, his nerves sparking danger at the sight of his gun, still poised to fire. But the man slowly tipped face-first from his saddle with no attempt to catch himself.

The acrid smell of gunpowder, dirt—and blood—filled Travis's nostrils. From the left side of the house, Embry appeared on foot, his horse trailing behind him, a pistol in his hand. He rushed straight toward Sessums and, after tossing aside Walt's pistol and checking his pulse, turned toward Travis.

Embry holstered his gun as he bent beside Travis and flicked him a glance. "You hit?"

The question drew Travis from his stupor. No pain, except where his head had smacked the ground. "I don't think so. Where did you come from?" With Embry's help, he sat up slowly.

Embry steadied him. "I didn't know Walt Sessums was poisoning his wife until I caught Lawrence and Edith stealing her away from the house. Then I realized he'd roped me into that plot, having me buy the poison. Lawrence locked him in the outhouse, and I was gonna deal with him, but he got loose before I could take care of him. Been searching for him ever since."

Embry moved to Clyde's side and pressed his fingers to his neck. To Travis's horror, the back of Clyde's dark shirt glistened red in the morning sunlight.

Oh, Lord. . .Clyde's hit!

Embry tore Clyde's shirt, revealing a bullet hole under his left shoulder blade, blood leaking from it.

At the sight, Travis scrambled to Clyde's side. "Doc?" Travis hollered. "I need you out here!"

Lord, please. . .don't take Clyde.

Both Dr. Tompkins and Lawrence hurried out and, after assessing his injury, carried Clyde inside.

"How bad, Doc?" Travis's limbs trembled.

Producing shears from his bag, the doctor cut away Clyde's shirt and shook his head. Any answer he spoke was lost when he turned away.

Travis faced Embry. "What'd he say?"

Embry eyed him. "Is Alcott your pa?"

Travis nodded, almost numb.

"It ain't lookin' good. Doc wants you to wait in the next room, let him work."

Travis's heart stalled.

Embry herded him toward the doorway, Travis craning his neck to see until Embry shoved him into the other room. Millie met him there, took his hand, and guided him through what used to be his bedroom. Little had changed. Same bed, same quilt, same everything. Victoria Sessums occupied the bed, Edith the chair beside her, so Millie guided him to the one piece in the room that was different—the worn, wooden chest he'd seen at the foot of Victoria's bed both times he'd entered her room. Millie coaxed him to sit, and he complied, thoughts spinning.

Millie knelt, peering up at him. "Are you hurt?"

A long moment ticked by before he shook his head. "No." He was unscathed. . . because of Clyde.

Lord, please don't let him die on my account.

She slipped onto his lap and wrapped her arms around his neck. He buried his face in the crook of her neck, one long, stuttering breath escaping him.

Lord, please. I've been too angry, stubborn, and prideful to admit it, but Clyde's my pa, and I need him.

Epilogue

Ten days later

Seated in Victoria Gordon's opulent parlor, Travis watched Millie sign to her mother, seated on a matching settee across from Millie.

"There's a cute house for rent near Finn and Travis's livery. Once we return to San Francisco, we hope to get it. I'll live there until we're married—which will hopefully be only a few weeks from now." A beaming, if crooked smile appeared on his bride-to-be's face, a far more common sight since Victoria had improved—and, he hoped, since they'd become engaged.

Victoria grinned at her daughter, then turned to him. "You plan to rent a house?"

"At first." He spoke and signed. "I've saved plenty to build a nice home, but we want to be married soon. We'll take our time finding the right location."

"There *will* be room for me to visit, won't there?"

"Yes, ma'am. As often as your world travels allow."

"Oh, I won't be traveling like I once did." She shrugged. "I now have a mine to oversee."

Both he and Millie stared.

"What?" he finally asked. "You'll. . .be operating the mine?"

"I will. I paid Walt's debt to Mr. Ketteridge, so I own it free and clear."

Travis's belly clenched. "I mean no disrespect, but. . .do you know anything about running a mine, ma'am?"

Victoria laughed. "Very little, which is why I've promoted Jack Embry and your father. Both are loyal, hardworking, and knowledgeable men—with years of experience I can draw on, and both have agreed to teach me what I need to know. Once we have things running smoothly, I'll leave one of them in charge while I visit you in San Francisco."

Millie shifted a glance to him, then signed to her mother. "You are a woman of surprises, Momma."

Victoria prepared to answer, but stalled, mid-sign, and looked toward the entryway. "Travis, someone's knocking at the door, and Lawrence is busy elsewhere. Would you answer it?"

"Yes, ma'am." He went to the door, glancing back as Victoria watched him with an odd, almost expectant grin. His brow furrowed. "What?"

"Oh, nothing. . ." Victoria's grin deepened.

There most definitely *was something*.

Still distracted, he pushed the door open and spoke as he turned. "May I help y—"

388

Travis's mouth dropped open at the sight of his parents—Finn and Hannah McCaffrey—and siblings, Caleb, Janie, and Tessa. "Oh, my—" He launched himself at them, hugging each in turn. "What're you doing here? Didn't you get my telegram? I told you not to worry." After the fire had burned nearly all the business district and many Virginia City homes, he'd sent word to his family that they were all fine.

Ma kissed his cheek. "We got your telegram. And a day later, we got Victoria's, inviting us to come for your wedding."

"My wed—what?"

Ma entered the house, followed by Pa and his siblings. Dumbfounded, Travis brought up the rear. Millie turned then, face registering shock and joy, and flew from the settee to greet them. Ma and Pa caught her in a huge hug.

Travis turned a befuddled gaze on Victoria. "What did you do?"

She walked into the foyer. "I planned your wedding. I hope you don't mind."

He hurried toward the woman. "You did all this for us—while you were recuperating?"

"I told Lawrence and Edith what I wanted. They did the footwork." Her smile trickled away. "I did Millie a terrible disservice after she finished school. I thought she would enjoy seeing the world. She was far more tied to San Francisco—to you and your family—than I knew." She shrugged. "You've waited long enough. If you delay until Clyde and I could travel to San Francisco, it'll be another month, at least. So this may not be exactly what you hoped, but at least you'll be married."

He hugged her. "Thank you," he whispered. "If by the end of the day, she's Millie McCaffrey, it'll be perfect."

Victoria broke the hug and grinned, then nodded toward the arching staircase. With Lawrence's help, Clyde negotiated the last few steps from the upper room where he'd been convalescing. Just like Victoria, he also was thin, pale, and weak, but even Dr. Tompkins had said he was making wonderful progress for the severity of his wound.

Travis sidled up next to him and took over for the butler. "Are you up to meeting my adopted family?"

Fear flashed in Clyde's dark eyes, though he swallowed hard and stood a little taller. "I hate to imagine what they must think of me, but I reckon I owe 'em my thanks, at the least."

Travis smiled reassuringly. "They're good people, Clyde. You've got nothing to worry about."

Guiding him toward the knot of bodies in the center of the wide foyer, Travis touched Finn's arm. Both he and Hannah turned. "Ma. . .Pa. . .I want you to meet Clyde Alcott, my father. And Clyde. . .meet Finn and Hannah McCaffrey, my parents."

For an instant, tension filled the air before Finn extended his hand with a warm smile. "Clyde. It's a real pleasure to finally meet you."

Clyde took his offered hand, relief visibly washing over him. "Real good to meet you both too."

Victoria inched up beside Clyde and slid her hand into the crook of his elbow. Looking past him, she caught Travis's eye. "Your wedding clothes are upstairs in your rooms. You and Millie get changed and meet us out back so we can get you married."

She shifted her attention to Clyde, a demure smile flitting across her lips. "I'll make sure Clyde's well looked after while you're gone."

She didn't have to ask Travis twice. He fetched Millie and they hurried upstairs to their respective rooms and changed into the clothes Victoria had somehow commissioned without their knowledge. When Millie finally emerged from her room, an appealing shade of pink had crept into her cheeks. He drank in the sight of her, petite frame perfectly accented by the shimmering white fabric and lace.

"You're beautiful," he signed. So beautiful his lungs could hardly draw air.

The pink blush deepened as she stepped nearer. "You look very handsome yourself."

His hands settling at her waist, Travis pulled her into his arms and bent to kiss her, though before he could, she leveled one hand against his chest. "No. . ." She signed with the other, a teasing grin on her face.

"Why not?"

"After we're married, *then* you can kiss me."

He heaved a breath. "Then let's get married so I can kiss you whenever I want."

The deep pink of her cheeks flushed red, and Travis took her hand and led her down the back steps, through the kitchen, and outside. There, their family members had gathered, along with Lawrence, Edith, Embry, and the cook, as well as a preacher. Someone had erected a tall wooden cross in the yard and draped it with a garland of colorful flowers.

For an instant, they both drank in the sight before they descended the steps and walked, arm in arm, to meet the preacher at the foot of the cross. With Hannah translating the reverend's words into sign, they repeated their vows, and once they'd been pronounced husband and wife, Travis cupped Millie's face in his hands and ever so gently touched his lips to hers. She was finally his bride.

Millie twined her fingers into his lapels and pulled him nearer, seeking more. He gladly obliged, loosening the reins on the passion he'd long held in check. He kissed her with an intensity he'd only ever dreamed of. Shivers raced along his skin, starting at the crown of his head and rushing to his toes, despite the warm afternoon. His head nearly swam with the intoxicating sense of her nearness. As he slowly pulled back again, lessening the kiss until he broke it all together, Millie's pulse fluttered faster against his hand, and her cheeks flushed crimson.

The rest of the evening flew by, with a meal and conversation for hours before finally, everyone shooed them toward Millie's bedroom. When they stepped into the room, the oddly worn wooden trunk that had sat at the foot of Victoria's bed had been placed at the foot of Millie's, an envelope resting on its lid.

To Mr. and Mrs. Travis McCaffrey

"What's this?" Travis picked up the note and looked at his bride.

"I don't know. It's Momma's handwriting, though."

He sat on the trunk's lid and pulled Millie into his lap, his heart flip-flopping again at her nearness. With his arms around her, he unfolded the message.

Travis and Millie,

The one and only thing Walt and I ever fought about was money. Particularly, his expectation that I would hand over the Gordon family fortune to him to manage. I believe the moment I told him no was the moment he decided to poison me. It was also the moment I put the money where Walt wouldn't expect it to be—right under his nose.

Millie, I have always planned to leave you enough to lead a comfortable life, and I didn't want to risk Walt spending your inheritance.

Travis, thank you for loving my daughter so well. That love is truly beautiful. And thank you for coming to our aid. Both Millie and I have our lives back, thanks to you.

Victoria/Momma

Eyes wide, Millie twisted to look at him, and they both rose to open the chest. Inside, stacks of money lined the bottom of the chest at least a third of the way up—far more than he'd ever seen in one place.

After a long, stunned moment, Travis turned to his bride. "She doesn't expect us to keep this, does she? This is hers!"

Millie nodded slowly. "I think she does."

He puffed out a breath. "Millie, that's not us. You and I have never wanted to live an extravagant lifestyle."

"If you refuse it, you'll crush her. This is how she shows her love." She stepped nearer, a sultry look coming into her eyes. "And. . .who says we have to live extravagantly? We could save it for the children you're going to give me." She reached for him, slowly unbuttoning his shirt and planting a featherlight kiss on his bare chest.

His heart suddenly pounding, Travis let Victoria's letter slip, forgotten, from his fingers as he scooped up his bride and carried her to bed.

Author's Note

Thank you so much for reading *Heartfelt Echoes*. I hope you enjoyed Travis and Millie's story. They are two of many characters who stuck with me after finishing a previous story ...and demanded a story of their own. If you want to read more about Travis's earlier days and how he came to be with his adoptive family, please read *Mountain Echoes,* one of nine stories included in *The Courageous Brides Collection.* As always, thank you for allowing me to share the stories God has placed on my heart to tell.

Jennifer Uhlarik discovered the western genre as a preteen, when she swiped the only "horse" book she found on her older brother's bookshelf. A new love was born. Across the next ten years, she devoured Louis L'Amour westerns and fell in love with the genre. In college at the University of Tampa, she began penning her own story of the Old West. Armed with a BA in writing, she has won five writing competitions and was a finalist in two others. In addition to writing, she has held jobs as a private business owner, a schoolteacher, a marketing director, and her favorite—a full-time homemaker. Jennifer is active in American Christian Fiction Writers and is a lifetime member of the Florida Writers Association. She lives near Tampa, Florida, with her husband, teenage son, and four fur children.

Prescription for Love

by Erica Vetsch

Dedication

For my husband and best friend, Peter.

Go ye therefore, and teach all nations, baptizing them in the name of the Father, and of the Son, and of the Holy Ghost: teaching them to observe all things whatsoever I have commanded you: and, lo, I am with you always, even unto the end of the world. Amen.
MATTHEW 28:19-20

Dear Reader

Prescription for Love is a spin-off of a series I wrote several years ago. If you'd like to learn more about the Mackenzie family and how Phin and Michael came to be adopted, their story can be found in the *Colorado Dawn* collection from Barbour Publishing.

Chapter 1

New Orleans, Louisiana
June 1905

"Miss Morrison, until the mission board is satisfied that you have recovered fully from your illness, we will not send you back to Panama." Mr. Guillard tapped his papers into a neat pile and closed the file.

Her file.

Natalie pressed her lips together, trying not to let out in a rush all the things she wanted to say, knowing full well that Mr. Guillard was of a different generation, a man who had never been in favor of sending single women to the mission field and was always looking for either a reason for them to stay stateside or for young single male missionaries to marry them. She forced herself to speak moderately and respectfully.

"But I *am* very much better. I had almost recovered completely before I was called back to New Orleans." Natalie stacked her hands in her lap, consciously relaxing her muscles while maintaining her posture—though she could feel herself tiring. "I had thought to only spend a short while here before returning. Especially since there is a new team leaving in just two weeks. I planned to sail with them."

"While I can admire your zeal for your work, I cannot in good conscience allow you to return to the Panamanian jungles until you're more fit. You were laid quite low with fever for several weeks, and though you have been on the mend—if you'll pardon my saying so—you don't look particularly robust quite yet." He looked at her over the half-moon glasses perched on his bulbous nose. Mr. Guillard wasn't unkind, but he had a reputation for brooking no argument when he'd made up his mind. And evidently, he had the backing of the rest of the mission board on this at least.

Yet, how could she just accept his ruling? She needed to return to her work. Without it, who was she? Missions was her reason for being, what she was supposed to be doing, what her father would have expected of her. How could she be obedient to her calling if she couldn't even get to the people she was supposed to be serving?

"But, sir, what about my patients? The Ancon Hospital is short of nurses as it is. They need me." Her voice cracked.

"My dear, it is no shame to return home from the field when you've been ill. You were due for home leave soon anyway. The hospital will still be there when you are back to full strength. After all, as you said, we've a new team of four leaving for Panama City in two weeks aboard the *Caribbean Star*. Two doctors, an evangelist, and his wife who is also a nurse. They might all be new to the field, but they're good people."

Good people who knew nothing about what it was like to live and work in the tropical jungles of Central America. Natalie should be with them. She could help them transition to their new lives. After all, she had nearly five years of missionary service to her credit. To top it off, the evangelist's wife leaving with the group was a friend she had trained with, and Natalie had so looked forward to serving alongside Wanda in the hospital, teaching her the ropes of being a foreign missionary.

"For now"—Mr. Guillard opened another folder on his desk and scanned the top page—"the director of Marine Hospital is in search of a qualified nurse to assist one of their physicians in a new public health venture. While you are still not fully capable of returning to the rigors of hospital ward nursing, not even here in the States, much less in Panama"—he held up his hand to stay her protests—"your personal physician assures me that some light nursing is just what you need to keep your mind and hands busy while you regain your strength."

Natalie composed her expression, turning her head toward the office window that looked out on Rampart Street, where a motor car buzzed by in one direction and a dray pulled by a pair of shaggy draft horses clopping by in the other. Why did it feel as if everyone else was the motor car zooming past, while she was the slow, old wagon plodding in the wrong direction?

Mr. Guillard cleared his throat, and she returned her attention to him with a guilty start.

"As I was saying, the city board of health is concerned about some of our. . .shall we say. . .less prosperous residents not receiving proper health care and education." He studied the pages before him. "There is a doctor at Marine Hospital who has proposed a new approach. Because these people, mostly immigrant and ethnic families. . .Italians, Irish, Jewish. . .they congregate together and are not very open to outsiders. Especially the Sicilian Italians." His brows hitched toward one another over his nose. "This doctor has a plan to. . .well, perhaps I should let him tell you when you arrive. Provisions have been made for you to move into the nurses' quarters at the hospital."

Which meant the mission board would not be paying for her room at the boardinghouse any longer.

A knock sounded on the door, and Mr. Guillard's secretary poked his head in. "I apologize sir, but your ten o'clock has arrived."

"Of course." He removed his glasses and polished them on his handkerchief. "Miss Morrison, Avery here will give you the paperwork you need. Present yourself to the director of Marine Hospital, and he will take it from there."

"But, sir, if by some means I am able to satisfy the mission board that I am fit for travel in the next two weeks. . ." She left the question hanging as he rose and came to take her elbow, ushering her through the office door—not unkindly but definitely as if he was finished with the issue.

"I think that is highly unlikely. We will have another shipment of medical supplies going to Panama around Christmastime. Surely you can wait six months. Perhaps, in the meantime, you will find someone who will go with you." He raised his eyebrows and inclined his head toward his secretary. "Did I tell you Avery is preparing to go to the field by the end of the year? Perhaps the board will send him to Panama."

Mr. Guillard would never win a prize for subtlety. Avery Callan's eyes widened a touch, and he looked everywhere but at her face as a dull flush started up his neck.

Natalie took another calming breath. Mr. Guillard meant well, but he couldn't possibly know that Natalie had long ago been forced to close the door of her heart to anything romantic. She had taken up the stance of that greatest of missionaries, the apostle Paul, eschewing romance in favor of the work of the Gospel—even though it had broken her heart and caused her to hurt the one person she had loved above all others.

Mr. Guillard bustled past, heading up the wide staircase to the conference room on the second floor of the old mansion that now served as the mission's headquarters. Avery cleared his throat, handed her an envelope, and hurried back into his cubbyhole of an office without a word.

Natalie found herself on the top step outside, looking up Rampart Street. All the city smells swirled around her—smoke, cabbage, dirt, even a faint whiff of the river a few blocks away. The June afternoon was warm, though she was accustomed to hot weather. And some of the smells were similar to her beloved Panama, that hot, vegetation-and-mud smell she knew so well.

The envelope in her hand drew her attention. Mr. Guillard had already had it prepared before she even came to the appointment, so it wouldn't have mattered what she said to him in their meeting. His mind had been fully made up.

She had two weeks. Or she had six months. Either she would make great strides in regaining her strength and convincing the mission board to allow her to return to Panama, or she would have to wait six months.

Six wasted months.

He'd already wasted nearly six months, but such was the nature of pushing a new idea through government bureaucracy. Finally, he was finished with red tape and committee meetings.

Dr. Phineas Bartholomew Mackenzie swiped his black hair out of his eyes, reminding himself he was past due for a trip to the barber, and checked the inventory list one last time.

"This is it. They've approved everything I asked for. It's finally going to happen."

"That's astonishing." His friend and fellow doctor, Brian Trasker, leaned back in his chair and propped his feet up on Phin's desk. "How is it you get everything you want for that golden—excuse me—black chariot of yours, and I can't even get a brace of new bedpans for the surgical ward?" He laced his fingers over the front of his rumpled white coat and closed his eyes.

"Perhaps because I actually filled out the requisition forms and attended the meetings and pleaded my case, and finally practically kidnapped the hospital director and drove him through Little Palermo to show him how bad things were and where I thought we could help?" Phin grinned.

"Or, perhaps, it was because you were born with a silver spoon in your mouth, and the director didn't want to offend you or your parents who just happen to be friends of the president and the surgeon general, both of whom just happen to be his bosses?" Brian said it teasingly, not opening his eyes. He'd just come off a long overnight shift that had involved an emergency surgery and stitching up several stevedores who had gotten into a brawl sometime after three in the morning. His hilarious recounting of the drunks in the examining rooms had made Phin's sides hurt with laughing.

Phin sighed now. If Brian only knew. That silver spoon he'd supposedly been born with was a complete myth. He'd come into the world on a flatboat barge somewhere south of St. Louis, abandoned to the care of an uncle who was a petty thief, and eventually dropped into a St. Louis orphanage with many promises that the uncle would return to reclaim him.

Another in a long string of lies he'd been told.

Though the part about his parents—his adoptive parents—was true. They were well off, and they were friends of both President Roosevelt and the surgeon general. But that was neither here nor there. If Sam and Ellie's influence had come to bear on Phin's project, even obliquely, it hadn't been at Phin's behest.

Sam and Ellie.

Phin laid his pen on the blotter and picked up the silver-framed picture on the credenza behind him. His lips twitched as he took in the image of his thirteen-year-old self, stiff as if in full rigor, wearing a new suit and collar. He quickly looked past himself to the others in the photograph. His father, Sam, broad-shouldered, sandy-haired, blue eyed. His mother, Ellie, only six years older than himself that Christmas when she'd married Sam and took on two orphaned boys as her own.

Then there was his adopted brother, Tick. Michael, Phin corrected himself. Nobody called him Tick anymore. It was a nickname Phin had given the small boy back at the orphanage because he stuck so close to Phin all the time.

He'd been a little gupper at the time, frail, with a heart condition that stunted his growth and kept him from thriving.

Though with care and medication, he'd overcome the odds and grown into adulthood. Now he was a pastor.

A pastor who was finally moving to New Orleans to begin a new church plant and ministry. Phin and his brother would be reunited once more.

"You look moony. Homesick for the mountains?"

Phin glanced up at Brian who had cracked one eye open.

"No. I haven't lived in the mountains since I was a kid. I told you the family sold out all their silver mines before the market crashed. We moved back to St. Louis when I was fifteen. It's not the mountains I miss. It's the people."

"I've never met anyone who was so close to his family as you are. You talk about them as if you were all best friends." Brian yawned. "Makes me jealous. I've never been that way with my family. We all live right here in New Orleans, and we barely see one another."

"My family is all I can count on." *The only ones who have never left me on my own.*

"What about me?" Brian dropped his boots to the floor and stood, stretching and rubbing his stomach. "Are you saying you can't count on me?" He scrubbed his hands through his sandy hair and then smoothed it back.

Phin shook his head. "It's different. Family's just different. At least my family is."

"Well, let's go see this contraption of yours then I'm falling face-first into the closest bunk. And if a dockworker shows up wanting some needlework done, you're on your own. I sewed enough stitches to make a ball gown last night." He yawned again.

Phin slipped the inventory list into a desk drawer. "I need to stop by the dispensary and get a couple of things on the way."

When they finally arrived at the back courtyard of Marine Hospital, both Phin and Brian had their arms full of glass bottles. Phin's pockets bulged with medicine packets too. "You know you could've gotten an orderly to carry this stuff out here. That's what orderlies are for." Brian shifted his load.

"They're busy, and we were coming out anyway. Isn't she a beauty?" Phin strode up to the ambulance, which gleamed black and shiny in the afternoon sunshine. The high wheels were dark red, and MOBILE DOCTOR'S OFFICE had been painted on the sides of the vehicle in bright gold lettering. The words had been repeated in smaller letters in Italian, Gaelic, and Hebrew. The sides had screened windows on the upper halves to let in air and light, and he'd had some nifty shelving built in to hold all the supplies he would need.

"You'll look like a gypsy. All you need are some bells and some pots and pans dangling from the roof and you can masquerade as a tinker." Brian set his armload of quart bottles on the ground beside one of the rear wheels.

"Very funny. I think she looks great." Phin ran his hand over the glossy paint. "This way, I can go right into the neighborhoods and treat people who would never come to a hospital or doctor's office."

"You're a brave man. I wouldn't want to head into Little Palermo alone."

"I won't be alone."

"Besides your driver, I mean." Brian helped Phin unload his supplies, careful not to break the containers of alcohol, camphor, and disinfectant.

"Actually, it will be more than just my driver going along, though I don't know if that means more or less protection." Phin grinned. "I've got a nurse."

"A nurse?" Brian's jaw dropped. "Are you serious? I can barely get a nurse to assist in surgery, and you just snap your fingers and the boss approves one to drive around town with you? Who is it?"

"I don't know. I just heard that I had been assigned one."

"You have some sort of Midas touch when it comes to persuading people." Brian shook his head. "I'm trying hard not to be jealous right now. I tell you what, turn your attention to the surgical department next, will you? I could use a new sterilizer, new lighting, and at least three new nurses, preferably with surgical training."

Phin laughed. "I'll see what I can do."

"I can't wait to meet the woman who will have to spend every day touring the slums with you. Think she'll be young? And pretty?" Brian waggled his eyebrows. "Will New Orleans's most eligible bachelor finally be snared?"

Phin sobered. "Not me. I'm immune from matrimony."

"I've never understood how someone so close with his family wouldn't want to start one of his own. It's not like the society mamas of New Orleans haven't pushed enough debutantes your direction." Stepping back as Phin swung open the rear door of the wagon, Brian waited for him to climb in before handing up the medicines.

Phin didn't reply. He'd been down the romantic road once before, and that was enough to last him a lifetime. There was no way he would trust his heart to another female again, not after having it handed back to him by the only woman he would ever love.

He hadn't been enough for her.

So she'd abandoned him.

"I doubt the new nurse will be young or pretty. More like a forty-year-old, built like a molasses barrel, and smelling of cabbage and peppermints. Someone my great-aunt Tabitha would call 'a comfortable soul.'" Phin slotted bottles into the racks built especially for them. "And I won't care a bit. As long as she knows how to treat patients, follow medical orders, and possibly speak a bit of Italian, she'll be perfect."

"Really?"

A feminine voice.

Phin froze, his eyes locking with Brian's, who still filled the back door opening. Brian pulled a shocked, guilty face and slowly turned around.

"I can assure you that I do know how to treat patients, I can follow medical orders, and while I only know a smattering of Italian, I can speak a bit of French and am fluent in Spanish."

Brian sent him a "you're-in-so-much-trouble-now" look and stepped aside. Phin braced himself, edged out of the wagon, and leaped to the ground. The minute his feet hit the pavement, his heart jolted into a gallop.

This was his new nurse?

Chapter 2

Natalie's eyes met the doctor's, and her head spun as if she still had yellow fever. Phin.

Dr. Phineas Bartholomew Mackenzie.

Her mouth went dry, and her thoughts whirled as she scrambled to organize them. Those beautiful dark eyes. . .so dark they glittered. Black hair still falling over his forehead. Thin. . .too thin, she'd always thought, with angular shoulders and long limbs.

Clean-shaven as always, he still gave off the impression that he was bursting with intelligence and energy, his mind always two or three steps ahead of everyone else. Dressed impeccably, knife-edge creases on his pants, snowy laboratory coat, neatly knotted tie, always the best-clothed man in any room. Even his watch chain glittered in the sunlight, polished to a gleam.

He was the best-looking, smartest, quickest-minded man she had ever met.

Though he never thought of himself that way, as better than or smarter than others. Everything about him, remembered, dear, precious. . .and. . .forbidden.

Her mind jerked back to that night, on his family's yacht, in the Mississippi moonlight where he had proposed, getting down on one knee, offering her his heart, his love, and his future.

And she—who had been warring with herself for weeks that summer about what God wanted versus what she wanted—had been forced to refuse.

Something flashed for just a moment in his eyes just now. Was it pain, anger, or just surprise?

"Hello. . .Dr. Mackenzie. It's nice to see you again." She called him by his title out of a mixture of protocol and self-preservation. Holding out her hand, she waited to see what he would do.

His eyes flashed again, but his face gave away nothing of his feelings—he'd always been good at masking those, assuming a devil-may-care attitude and pretending that nobody could hurt him. Was that the truth in this case? After all, it was almost five years since she'd left. Perhaps for him, it had all faded into distant memory.

He grasped her hand for an instant, and his touch made her heart throb like a jungle drum. "Miss Morrison. What a surprise." He loosened his touch, and she resisted the urge to tuck her fingers into a fist and hold them behind her back.

She noted that he didn't say it was nice to see her.

The other man cleared his throat. "I take it you two know each other?"

"Brian," Phin's voice was as dry as mummy dust. "May I present Miss Morrison?"

His black brows rose. "It is still *Miss*, isn't it?"

"Yes." Her chin went up.

"Of course it is. Miss Morrison, this is Dr. Trasker." Phin edged aside his long coat and put his hands into his pockets. "I take it you're the nurse assigned to the Neighborhood Health Project?"

She shook Dr. Trasker's hand, the good doctor holding her clasp longer than Phin had, his eyes appraising first her and then Phin, clearly curious but thankfully not asking what their connection had been.

"I am, though. . ." She fingered the cameo pin on her collar. "Only for six months at the longest. That's when I return to Panama." He might as well know this was a temporary situation at best. Perhaps she should ask the director for a different position. . . before Phin took it upon himself to refuse her the job.

"Six months, huh?" He rocked on his well-shined toes. "I'm surprised you can bear to be away that long."

An orderly stuck his head out the back door, saving her a reply. "Excuse me, Dr. Trasker. You're needed in the surgery."

With a frown, Dr. Trasker shook his head. "This had better not be more dockworkers." He gave a low wave to Phin and a nod to Natalie. "Nice to meet you, Miss Morrison. I hope we'll have more time to talk in the future, and I wish you well with this new venture."

When the hospital door closed behind him, Natalie took a deep breath. "I'm sure the director can find another nurse for you."

He smoothed back his forelock. "Quitting so soon?"

She quelled a flinch. "Of course not. I assumed that our past. . .association. . .would lead you to choose another nurse. Not to mention, I will only be able to stay six months at the longest. This position isn't permanent for me. Another nurse makes better sense for you."

He considered her comments for a moment and then shrugged. "That's not necessary. We're both professionals, and anything that happened between us is long in the past. Water past the levee, for sure. You might as well be useful for the short time you're here." He looked her over, his gaze sharpening. "You look. . .different. Have you been unwell?"

His powers of observation as a physician were all too keen. "I am quite well, thank you." She straightened her shoulders and made an attempt to look bright. He didn't need to know what had brought her back stateside. "I'm ready to tackle a little light nursing before returning to the mission field."

"Light nursing?" The corner of his mouth quirked up in a familiar way. "Didn't the director tell you what you would be doing?"

"He said I would be accompanying a doctor on house calls." Just about the lightest nursing there was.

For a moment, a small chuckle escaped Phin's lips, and she expected him to laugh, but he suppressed any lightheartedness. Disappointment wriggled through her chest. She had always loved his laugh, the way his eyes sparkled, the way his teeth flashed. That laugh had stalked her dreams at times, waking her up with such a sense of longing and loss that she'd sometimes cried herself back to sleep.

"I suppose that's true. Here." He stepped back. "Take a look inside and tell me what you think, and I'll explain."

She mounted the small iron steps into the wagon, ducking and taking a seat on the bench. Racks of medicines and shelves of instruments covered the end wall behind where the driver would sit, and a mattress covered a narrow bed along one side for transporting patients. Everything gleamed, fresh and new.

"It's a mobile doctor's office. There are more supplies under the bench too." Phin stood in the doorway. "Everything I might need, medical and surgical, though we'll only do surgery in the field if it's too dangerous to transport the patient back here to the hospital."

She ran her hand along the leather seat. No cloth here, easier to disinfect patent leather. "It looks wonderful, but I don't understand. Why don't the patients just come to you? Or have their local physician treat them?"

Phin pulled himself all the way up and into the wagon, taking a seat opposite her on the bed. "Most of the people we're going to see would never come to a hospital, and most don't have a physician at all. The part of town that used to be the French Quarter is almost entirely populated by Sicilian Italians with no money, very little English, and a big distrust of anyone in authority. Most of the men will be leaving the city to work on the plantations and farms in the outstate area, leaving behind their wives and children. The tenements are packed to the gills now, with most families only renting a single room. We're talking sometimes eight to ten people all living together in maybe a hundred or a hundred and twenty square feet of space. The poverty will shock you."

Natalie shook her head. "I doubt that. Panama is not a wealthy country by any means. The native Panamanians have similar fears of modern medicine and hospitals, though we're slowly making inroads. While the current building of the canal has brought some money into the country, for the most part, it remains as isolated and backward as ever. If anything, the influx of engineers, builders, and the military has made them distrust Americans even more." She clasped her hands in her lap. "We've discovered that if we start with the children, we can befriend and win the trust of the family. It's only then that we can share the Gospel and expect to have it received. It's no good going into an area of extreme poverty and need and telling the people that God loves them and they need a Savior but do nothing to meet their physical needs at the same time."

He sat back and stared somewhere over her shoulder, and she realized she had climbed up on her hobby horse and ridden like she was chasing down the leader at the Crescent City Derby. And he clearly wanted to hear nothing about it.

"Tell me more about what you're hoping to accomplish."

His attention came back to her, and he smoothed his trouser legs, aligning the creases. "The first thing I would like to accomplish is to get medical help to where it is needed. There are sick and dying immigrants in Little Palermo, and I know I can help them, if they'll just let me. The second will be to educate these folks out of some of their suspicions. In Sicily, where most of them are from, there is a rumor—and I have no idea if it's true or not—that if you become ill, the authorities will hasten your demise by having a doctor or nurse poison you, thus relieving society of the burden of caring for you. If we do manage to get a Sicilian to the hospital, they refuse to take any water or food. Forget trying to get medicine into them." He shook his head. "And third, I want to educate these folks on the necessity of basic hygiene and cleanliness, and the dangers of open cisterns as breeding grounds for mosquitoes. With Dr. Walter Reed's findings, it's of paramount importance that we minimize the places that mosquitoes can flourish."

Phin's face was animated, his eyes alight, and he drew a poker chip from his lab coat pocket, walking the small circle of wood up and down the backs of his knuckles.

Natalie smiled. "You still have that?" She gestured to the chip, once red, but now without much paint left. "Still practicing?"

He glanced down as if he hadn't even been aware of what he was doing, and shrugged, slipping the chip back into his pocket. "You never know when you might need to pick a pocket. At least keeping my fingers nimble has paid off well during surgeries." Putting his hands on his knees, he levered himself up, crouching slightly inside the ambulance and heading toward the door.

When she followed him, he helped her down, but he didn't meet her eyes, and he let go of her elbow the instant her shoe touched the ground.

"Are you sure you don't mind? My working here the next six months?" Somehow, the moment she'd seen Phin, all thoughts of trying to convince the mission board she was strong enough to return in just two weeks had flown right out of her head.

"It's fine. I'd like you to familiarize yourself with the contents of the wagon and where everything is kept, and if I've missed anything you think we might need. I'd like to leave here each morning at eight." He studied her again. "Are you sure you're up to this? The days might be long, depending upon what we find."

Another orderly trotted down the back stairs. "Dr. Mackenzie, you have a visitor. I showed him to your office."

Phin's brows rose. "A colleague?"

The orderly frowned. "He said to tell you 'Tick' had arrived?" The young man shook his head. "I'm sorry, sir. I know that can't be right, but that's what it sounded like."

Phin was already on his way to the door, the tails on his lab coat billowing out behind him in his haste. "Thank you, Barker. I'll see you in the morning, Miss Morrison."

The screen door slammed behind him, and he was gone.

Natalie glanced at the orderly, who seemed as bemused as she felt. He nodded and hurried away.

She drew her first deep breath since she'd looked once more into Phin's dark eyes. Six months as his nurse. He had shown no emotion beyond mild surprise at seeing her. Perhaps they could make this work. They were professionals, after all, and adults. They had a common goal of helping people through medicine.

Natalie only hoped her heart would cooperate with her head. It had nearly wrecked her completely to leave Phin the first time. She didn't know if she would have the strength to do it again. She would have to guard her feelings closely and remember her promise to her father. She belonged on the mission field.

Nothing had changed in five years.

Phin bounded up the stairs to his third-floor office, trying to outrun the feelings that had come swamping back when he'd looked into Natalie's eyes.

It had been all he could do to appear unaffected.

He hurried down the hallway, sidestepping a nurse carrying a stack of clean linens and a janitor slowly mopping the linoleum tiles. Pushing open his office door, he said, "It's about time, Tick."

His adopted brother, Michael, rose from his chair to his full height, more than three inches taller than Phin. His shoulders were so broad, and yet so thin, Phin had the impression that Michael's black suit coat hung on a hanger instead of on his lean frame.

Though Phin held out his hand, Michael ignored it and enveloped him in a hug. "Hey, big brother. It's been far too long."

Phin returned the hug briefly. He slapped his brother on the shoulder. "It's good to see you again. I can't believe you're finally here."

Michael resumed his seat, folding his long frame into the chair. "Mother and Dad send their regards. They're hoping to visit New Orleans in the late summer or fall."

Rounding his desk, Phin took his seat, leaned back, and propped his feet up on the blotter. "Though I would love to see them, maybe they would prefer to wait until the fall when it isn't so beastly hot. You know how the heat bothers Mother."

Michael nodded. "I know, but you also know how she is about her cubs. She is worried that you're working too hard down here, and she's determined to come and check on you. In fact, you should know, she expects me to send her a full report as soon as possible, though she won't trust half of it until she can see for herself that you're not wasting away down here."

He closed his eyes for a moment, remembering his adoptive mother with fondness. She might be little, but when it came to her "cubs" she could go full-blown grizzly in their defense. He also knew much of her concern about how he was faring was a result of how badly he'd taken the breakup of his romance with Natalie five years ago. When he looked back on it now, he realized how hard he'd fallen. Weight loss, insomnia, throwing himself into work to avoid the pain, avoiding friends and family who had known how much he had been in love. . .picking up the pieces and feeling back to his old self. . .not that he would ever really feel like his old self. . .had taken time.

"What shall I tell her?" Michael asked, propping his ankle on the opposite knee.

Phin shrugged, shaking his head. "Like you said, nothing you tell her will be believed until she confirms it with her own eyes, so tell her I'm fine, hale and hearty, and that I am working on a new medical venture." He dropped his feet to the floor. "It's quitting time for the day, though. Let's go have some dinner and catch up."

"Great." Michael rose. "Let's swing by my new church, and then over dinner you can tell me about your new plans."

They took a streetcar, and when they alit, Phin slipped his watch off its chain and put it into his pocket. He took his wallet from his inside coat pocket and put it with his watch, covering both with his hand. "You might want to mind your valuables. This part of town is rife with pickpockets," he cautioned Michael.

He laughed. "Anyone who stole my wallet would be mighty disappointed. I've got about four dollars on me at the moment."

Phin shook his head. Michael had little regard for money beyond what it could do to help someone else. Still, if he had four dollars in his wallet, he shouldn't be careless enough to let them be stolen.

They walked several blocks toward the waterfront before they reached the church. When they had climbed the cracked marble steps, Michael pushed open the carved wooden doors. The door stuck, and Phin bumped into Michael's back. "Sorry, Tick."

Inside, a musty, dusty smell hit Phin. The windows were boarded over, allowing only streaks of light to filter inside. Cobwebs hung from the pendant lights, and sheets covered the pulpit and communion table like cerements.

"What do you think?" Michael strode down the aisle, stepping over leaf litter and what appeared to be a mouse nest and turned to face Phin, arms spread wide.

Phin rubbed his forehead. "Are you sure about this? Your church in St. Louis was so successful. So big and nice."

Michael's expression grew sober. "Was it? Successful, I mean? There were a lot of people attending, I'll give you that, but the more people who came, the further I felt from them. It became harder and harder to really connect with my parishioners, to really pastor them and for us to share accountability. I feared the church was becoming more of a social gathering than a place of worship. When I tried to voice my concerns to the elder board. . ." He sighed. "Let's just say, it didn't go over too well. Maybe I didn't explain it well. It just seemed like we were getting too far away from the mission of the church, which was to preach the Gospel and disciple believers."

He mounted the three steps up to the dais and pulled the sheet off the pulpit. A cloud of dust enveloped him, and he waved it away. "Here, I feel needed. I feel like I can make a difference. There are so many here in New Orleans who need the Gospel. They need to know someone cares about them, about their physical and spiritual needs. The groups we're targeting in particular are those who work the docks, and those who come in on the cargo ships. There are a core group of believers here in New Orleans who are prepared to volunteer, to pray, to give, and to help me and my team get this mission off the ground." A shaft of light fell across his face, and his eyes glowed with passion for his cause. "Tomorrow, the cleanup on this abandoned church and the warehouse next door begins, and by the end of the month, we hope to have a soup kitchen and dormitory ready, and worship and prayer services happening. We've got a strategy in place to canvass the docks regularly, to meet the ships as they come in, and to get the word out to New Orleans residents so they can help. The more we get the word out, the more we can accomplish together."

Phin held up his hands, laughing. "Okay, okay. I've caught your vision. I'll help all I can."

Michael looked smug. "I knew you would. In fact, I'm counting on it. I have no connections here in New Orleans beyond the small group who called me to pastor this endeavor. You've lived here for years and must know plenty of people who can assist us. In fact, I'd like to visit some of the churches in the city to share our mission. Maybe you can put me in touch with someone who can help me set those meetings up?"

Over dinner they caught up on family doings. "Mother and Dad have been traveling a lot. They were in Boston, Philadelphia, and D.C. this past winter. They've been meeting with board members from state orphanages and private orphanages and with senators and congressmen about the plight of orphans in America." Michael leaned forward, knife and fork in his hands. "They've done so much for the orphanage where you and I grew up, using Aunt Tabitha's legacy." He smiled. "It wouldn't surprise me at all if they didn't find themselves in New Orleans with plans to open an orphanage here someday, since it seems you and I will be living here for a while."

"What about David and Karen and their kids?" Phin buttered a roll, remembering his aunt and uncle and their brood of six. "Their youngest is how old now?"

"Ten. And she's the image of her mother."

"And how is Celeste? It's hard to believe she's married and a mother in her own right now." Their cousin, once an orphan like themselves, had wed two years previously—the last time Phin had been home to St. Louis—and had produced a beautiful baby daughter the past winter.

"She misses you. They all do. You should plan a trip home soon. Our grandparents aren't getting any younger, and our cousins are growing up quickly."

"I know. I write often, and I do enjoy it when Mother and Dad come to New Orleans. As soon as I get this new venture off the ground, maybe I can make a trip home. Maybe even for Christmas." Christmas was the most important holiday for his family, a day to celebrate the Savior's birth, and also to celebrate the birth of their family. It was on Christmas Day nearly twenty years ago that Sam Mackenzie had proposed to Eldora Carter and decided to adopt Phin and Tick—Michael—in the bargain. And David and Karen had decided to adopt Celeste that day as well. After being unwanted, shunted from place to place, and enduring great hardship and peril, they had all become a family on Christmas Day.

"Tell me about this new thing you're working on with the hospital," Michael said.

So Phin did. With as much enthusiasm as Michael had shown for his new church and mission, Phin outlined the situation in Little Palermo, the needs of the immigrants there, and how he hoped to help them with his traveling doctor's office. "There's so much we can do in the way of public health education too. Most of this spring, the hospital director has been trying to educate the city council on the dangers of stagnate water as mosquito breeding grounds, and the need for a quarantine system for ships coming into New Orleans from Central America. There have been reports of yellow fever in those areas, and if it comes here, we're ill-equipped to deal with it."

Michael nodded. "Bureaucracy is hard to pierce sometimes."

"Hopefully we can teach people at a more grassroots level and bypass the bureaucracy."

"I don't know how you can make much progress all by yourself."

"I have to start somewhere. And I won't be all by myself." He broached the subject he'd been trying to ignore all evening. "And I would appreciate it if this didn't make it into any reports home to Mother and the family about it, at least not just yet. . . ."

Michael put his cutlery down on the tablecloth and wiped his mouth with his napkin. "What is it?"

"The hospital has given me a nurse who will accompany me and assist me on my rounds."

"That's good. It sounds like more work already than one man can do."

"The thing is, the nurse I've been assigned is. . .Natalie." The word came out raspy, as if from long disuse. . .which was true. He hadn't said her first name in more than five years.

His brother sat back, brows raised. "I didn't know she was back in the States."

"I didn't either, until this afternoon. She's home for six months and then she'll return to Panama. In the meantime, she's been assigned to the hospital and to me."

"How do you feel about that?"

Phin knew he could never fool Michael, but he decided to try. "It's fine. All that happened a long time ago. We're not the same people we were then. And she's a good nurse."

"I see." Michael said the words slowly, and Phin knew he did see, more than Phin would like. He decided to change the subject.

"I'll pay for dinner." Phin set a few dollars on the table and waited.

"Nonsense. I'll pay my share at least." Michael patted his pocket, frowned, and searched his person. "Where's my wallet?"

With a grin, Phin removed Michael's battered leather wallet from his own pocket. "I still have the touch. I lifted this off you not half a minute after I warned you against pickpockets."

Michael took back his property with a sheepish grin. "Some things never change, do they?"

Phin hoped his brother didn't discover the money he'd placed in the wallet for a good while. Michael could be sticky about that sort of thing.

Chapter 3

The next morning, Natalie climbed into the hospital wagon and took her seat across from Phin. He held a sheaf of papers, and a frown built across his brow as he read them.

"Bad news?"

"Not good. The army reports out of Central America. They thought they had the yellow fever outbreak under control in Panama, but it's come back again. And there are reports of it spreading to Cuba and Belize. Things we knew. But there have been two suspicious deaths down near the waterfront that the director suspects are yellow fever." He tapped the pages together on his knee. "The city officials seem to think the ship quarantine and cleansing measures they have put into place will be enough, but scrubbing won't stop yellow fever. It's a mosquito-borne illness. Unless we control the mosquito population, if the Fever comes here, it will spread." He fisted his hand and tapped it gently against the edge of the bunk where he sat. "Why is it so hard to believe that mosquitoes transmit the sickness?"

Natalie said nothing, but her muscles clenched. Yellow fever had come back to Panama? What of her friends there? What of the team that was going to leave in a few days' time?

"What can we do?"

He shook his head. "Be on the lookout for people with symptoms. Try to educate people about the dangers of unscreened windows, standing water, and not getting to a doctor if they feel ill. Beyond that, there isn't much we can do. One thing in our favor, it's been many years since there was an outbreak in New Orleans, but conversely, it's been many years since there was an outbreak in New Orleans. People grow complacent. And they're slow to receive new ideas about disease. Dr. Walter Reed proved that the mosquito is the vector for yellow fever, but some persist in thinking that it's a miasma or that it only happens to new arrivals in the city who aren't used to the area. The hospital director wants us to be on the lookout for anything suspicious, and we're to gather information and report to him if we see anything that concerns us."

The wagon pulled to a stop, and they climbed down and stood in the sultry summer air amid squalor such as Natalie hadn't seen in weeks. So, this was Little Palermo in the old French Quarter of New Orleans.

Filthy water stood in pools in the gutters, and lines of laundry hung between the buildings. A famished-looking dog gnawed on a shard of bone, and from a crate beside a door, a pair of miserable chickens flapped and squawked.

411

The stench of mud, garbage, smoke, and unwashed humanity hung in the air, and Natalie pasted on her most serene expression, trying to ignore the assault to her senses. She'd learned early in her missionary career not to show any distaste or disdain for the living conditions of others. Compassion? Yes. Condescension? Never.

Phin jumped down from the front seat, lithe and handsome, his dark eyes sparkling with interest and adventure. After what had to be months of preparation and planning, he was putting into practice his dream to revolutionize medical care for immigrants. It was that zest for life and for helping people that had first drawn Natalie to him, and even now, she felt the familiar pull. But she couldn't. She wouldn't. She wasn't staying. Her life and work were a long way from New Orleans. Her calling was to the mission field.

Their driver, one Luca Todisco, sat with his shoulders hunched for a moment before wrapping the reins around the brake handle and easing to the ground. He was a giant of a man with fists like hams and a beard so thick and long that Natalie couldn't tell if he wore a necktie. He spoke English well but with such a thick Italian accent, Natalie had to concentrate when listening to him.

"What do we do first? Do you have patients to see, or are we making a first foray?" Natalie smoothed the white apron she wore over a serviceable slate-blue dress. The hem was several inches above the ground, and she wore sturdy boots. A white kerchief covered her hair. Exactly the same attire she wore in the hospital in Panama. The outfit made her look both official and nonthreatening. At least that was her theory.

Phin reached into the wagon and took out his black medical bag. "We have no patients in advance. We're on a fact-finding mission today, assessing the situation. If we see someone in need of medical attention, we'll certainly try to help. But it would be unrealistic for us to be expected to be welcomed with open arms right away. We're going to have to build some trust. That's where Luca comes in, right Luca?"

"*Sì, dottore.*" The big man grinned, his large, white teeth a glaring contrast to his swarthy face. "And I provide-a safety, yes?"

"Right." Phin squared his shoulders and walked to the front door of a three-story brick building. He eased the door open with a creak and a scrape, and Natalie followed him into an open courtyard. A woman with a black shawl over her head stirred a huge kettle in the center of the open space, black smoke pouring from beneath the pot. She looked up, eyes wide, dropped the wooden paddle, and backed away, her hands clasped at her throat. She felt behind her for a doorknob, and disappeared into a room with a slam.

"Dottore, perhaps-a you let-a me go first, yes?" Luca eased past Natalie, putting his big hands on her shoulders and gently moving her out of the way. When he reached the center of the courtyard, he tilted his head back and bellowed, "*Attenzione! Un dottore è venuto a visitare! Venite fuori!*"

No doors opened, and several eased closed, though Natalie saw no one. No, wait. A pair of dark eyes peeped around a corner. . .small, bright eyes and a sweet little face. She smiled and wiggled her fingers at the child, a girl of about three, maybe? The youngster wore a smudged, white smock dress and no shoes and was in need of a comb or brush, but she was beautiful.

Natalie nudged Phin and inclined her head toward the child.

Luca scratched his head, turned and spoke toward the balconies surrounding the courtyard. *"Qualcuno qui è malato?"*

"What is he saying?" Natalie asked.

Luca answered. "I said that a doctor had come-a to visit and for the people to come out, and I asked if anyone was-a sick."

Phin inclined his head, watching the little girl, who had stuck one finger into the corner of her mouth and fisted her other hand into her dress, twisting it up to reveal her knees. "Maybe you should ask if anyone wants candy?"

"Hmph. You might-a be-a trampled," Luca said. *"Qualcuno vuole qualche caramella?"*

Natalie put her hand over her mouth to stifle the giggles. Children tumbled out of everywhere, behind boxes, through windows, down the stairs, through doorways.

Luca motioned them to come close, a torrent of Italian words flowing from him, accompanied by wide smiles.

Phin eyed them with a grin, and Natalie's heart lurched at his handsome features. He reached into his bag and pulled out a peppermint ball. With several quick moves of his hands, he made it disappear and reappear, to the gasps and giggles of his crowd. How often had he entertained children in the hospital with his slight-of-hand tricks? How often had he entertained her?

"Tell them they can each have a piece of candy if their mamas say it is all right," Phin said. His gaze moved from child to child. There must've been about twenty of them altogether. Natalie assessed them as well, looking for signs of any medical need.

Though quite a few would benefit from a bath, and there were the usual cuts and scrapes that went along with being a child, she could see no one in obvious distress.

Mothers were called, young and old, timidly venturing into the courtyard, encouraged by Luca. Phin greeted them, showed them his medical bag, and through Luca, spoke about the mobile doctor's unit, inquiring as to any illnesses in the building, any injuries.

While the women listened politely, Natalie knew they were skeptical. They offered no information, instead behaving as if Phin was a policeman or health inspector, someone to be deferred to but not invited in. They were facing an uphill battle here.

A commotion sounded near the doorway to the street, and a pair of children broke from the pack to run toward the man standing there.

"Papà! Papà!" The children threw themselves into the lean man's arms as he squatted to receive them. His duffel fell to the floor as he embraced them. Behind him, another man leaned against the door frame.

Phin handed the sack of candy to Luca. "Here, make sure each child gets one." He picked up his bag and went to the doorway, and Natalie followed. Skirting the happy family reunion, Phin came to a stop beside the other man.

"Sir, I am a doctor. How are you feeling?"

Even across the courtyard, Phin had spied something about the man that caught his attention. Up close, Natalie noted the man's flushed skin and the bright glitter to his eyes that often denoted fever.

The man scowled and straightened. "Go away. I am-a not sick. I am-a tired." He hitched his seabag over his shoulder with a wince and brushed past. As he crossed a shaft of sunlight, Natalie stepped back. As she looked into the man's eyes, her senses went on alert.

She stepped close to whisper to Phin. "That man is jaundiced, feverish, and probably achy." She had reason to remember all those symptoms, since they were the early signs of the illness that had laid her low for so many weeks.

Of course, they could also be the early signs of other illnesses, and it wasn't reasonable to feel a rush of anxiety, but uneasiness fluttered across her skin.

Phin nodded, motioned for her to follow and went after the man, mounting the stairs to the second floor. The man ducked into the first doorway and closed the door. Phin knocked.

No answer.

He knocked again. The door opened a crack, and a woman's lined face peered out. "No. Go away." She closed the door with a bang.

"Ma'am, please. I am a doctor. Dottore. *Per favore.*"

The door remained stubbornly closed.

Phin's hands fisted, and he shook his head. "Stubborn man."

"What are we going to do?" Natalie asked.

"Let's start with the man downstairs. Get some information. Fever and ache are symptoms of lots of things, and I didn't see the man's eyes in the gloom of the entryway. You're sure they were yellowed?"

Her chin came up. "I believe I have enough medical and tropical nursing experience to recognize jaundice when I see it." Not to mention having both cared for and been a yellow fever victim.

"Of course you do. But everything must be verified." He was on his way down the stairs again. "Luca, I need you to translate."

Luca gave out the last piece of candy and motioned for the sailor with the two children to come to them.

"Ask him what ship he works on and where it came from and if anyone on the boat has been ill."

Luca spoke rapidly, gesturing with every phrase. The man's arms tightened around his children, and a wary look invaded his dark eyes as he glanced from Phin to Luca and back again. Luca grew stern as the man refused to answer his questions, repeatedly shaking his head and hugging his children.

Finally, Luca pointed to Phin and made some statement that sounded threatening to Natalie's ears. The sailor shot them a fearful glance and began to speak.

"He says-a he works on a boat that-a come from-a Belize. The boat-a carry bananas, and the *capitano*, he no wanna wait for the quarantine, so he slip past into the bayou at night. This man, he say that-a two of the crew were sick, but they are feeling-a better now."

Natalie crossed her arms, gripping her elbows. Phin nodded. "Ask him about their symptoms."

"What is 'symptoms'?" Luca's brow furrowed.

"Ask him how they felt. Did they hurt? Did they have a fever?"

Understanding dawned. "Symptoms, yes."

Again the rapid-fire speech back and forth.

Finally the sailor shrugged.

"He says-a he does not-a know. Just-a sick."

"Thank him for us. *Grazie.*" Phin took Natalie's elbow. "We need to leave. We need to find that ship and the sailors who crewed it."

Phin climbed into the back of the wagon with Natalie as Luca took his seat. Opening the communication window at the front, he told Luca, "Let's get down to the docks and see if we can get a line on where they might unload a shipment of bananas without using the stevedores at the waterfront."

The wagon lurched, and Natalie grabbed the edge of her seat. "It could be something else besides yellow fever. We didn't ask if the man drank a lot of alcohol, which can cause jaundice. Or if he had any other symptoms. And the two suspicious deaths that were reported haven't been confirmed yet." Even as she said the words, she was totting up what they did know. Yellow fever wasn't often mistaken for something else. There were confirmed reports in Central America. It was summer, yellow fever season. A sick man had come from Belize and bypassed the riverfront quarantine procedures. She was sure he was jaundiced. And the way he had winced when he shouldered his rucksack meant he was in some pain, possibly joint pain. And his eyes had been fever-bright.

Then there was the fact that the man they had questioned had said the men had felt bad on the journey but were on the mend now.

That sounded like yellow fever.

A few days of being really ill, followed by a few where the patient appeared to recover, only to become seriously ill once more. But maybe they were just reacting to the hospital bulletin Phin had received that morning. Perhaps it wasn't anything but a bit of a cold or hepatitis or too much alcohol.

Gripping her elbows again, she suppressed a shiver.

It was too soon to panic.

Phin took out his notebook and tried to jot notes as the wagon rocked and clattered on its way to the wharf. He had learned long ago that he needed to write things down to get clarity and be able to remember details later for writing up reports.

Hopefully, they were on a hiding to nowhere, and the men would simply have fallen ill to an ordinary malady. Perhaps the man they saw did have cirrhosis of the liver or hepatitis. He would go to the harbor, see if he could track down someone from the ship, and be reassured.

Natalie held on to the bench as the wagon jolted over the railroad tracks and headed down to the water's edge. She looked so prim and efficient in her nurse's garb, her glossy hair covered with that white kerchief. The observations she had made about the sailor had been dead-on. She was a good nurse. He remembered the first time he saw her, a nursing student with wide eyes and an eager, wholesome quality. Even then, she'd had an instinctive ability to soothe a worried patient and to hone in on symptoms.

And she had been able to make him laugh. She was sweet and idealistic, passionate, and she had a positive outlook that had complemented his more cynical side. She had been a perfect fit for him.

Until she wasn't.

Bitter regret clamped onto his chest. He couldn't allow himself any hope that anything would end differently than it had before. He had misread her completely once, thinking that she loved him enough to stay. He wouldn't make that same mistake.

Tracking down the doctor aboard the banana boat proved frustrating. Luca used his considerable contacts and not a little bribe money. When they finally found the ship's medical officer, he was three beers into his shore leave. And he wasn't really a doctor, just a sort of corpsman.

There was no need for a translator, as the man was an American.

"A couple of the men came down with a bit of a bug. A bit of a fever, a few aches. Nothing to be concerned about. They stayed in their bunks for a few days. Then they both said they felt better." He made small circles with his glass on the tabletop in the riverfront hotel that catered to arriving seamen. "And I don't know where the captain is, and I wouldn't rat him out anyway. So he bypassed those snoops down at the docks. They forever hold a man up so he can't unload and get paid. And they don't do no good, nohow. Poking and prodding everywhere, gassing the place with poison."

Phin had insisted Natalie remain outside with Luca and the wagon, so he took notes himself. "What about jaundice?"

The man squinted. "What?"

"The men who were sick, did their skin or eyes look yellow to you? Did they have any tenderness to their liver?" Phin pointed to his upper right abdomen.

Shrugging, the man drained his glass. "They never said so. Look, the captain calls me the medical officer, but I ain't. Most of the time, I work in the kitchen. I can sew up cuts and wrap up sprains and the like if I have to. I don't know one sickness from another." He shrugged again, raising his glass and catching the eye of the bartender.

Phin asked a few more questions about the number of crewmembers and where the ship had been, but the sailor either didn't know much or was pretending not to know.

Emerging into the sunshine, Phin tapped his notebook against his leg. He needed to find that second sailor and see if he would submit to an examination. And he needed to check out the other crew members. If his suspicions were confirmed, he would need to inform the director at the hospital, the city health officials, and if necessary, national health officials.

"How do you find a crew full of sailors that the harbormaster doesn't know exists in a city equipped to hide them?"

"You should be careful talking to yourself out on the street. People might think you're touched in the head."

Phin whirled and grinned. "Hey, Tick."

At the nickname, his brother slanted him an aggrieved glance. "No one will take me seriously as a minister if you insist on calling me Tick."

"Sorry. Old habits. What are you doing here?"

"Working. I've come to canvass the area for a few likely souls to fill our mission and first church service. And to put up these bills." Michael lifted a sheaf of posters announcing the opening of the Sailor's Mission. "There's a bunch of volunteers busy cleaning out the buildings, and you wouldn't believe the aromas already spilling from the old kitchen. The Mission hired a woman named Centralia, and she's cooking gumbo that's making me hungry just thinking of it. Once word gets out about her cooking, we'll have more sailors and seamen than we know what to do with. And she's doing it on a pretty meager budget too." Michael scratched his head. "I don't know how, but I'm just going to thank God for His blessings."

"That's great." Phin scanned the river, dotted with ships from all over the world. A sting touched his hand, and he slapped a mosquito.

Michael swatted as one buzzed by his face. "I have a reason to be here, but what's yours? I thought you would be out with your mobile office seeing patients."

Phin motioned for Michael to walk with him. "I am. Sort of. I'm trying to track down a ship that bypassed quarantine measures." He pointed to a steamship drawn up to a dock along the riverfront. A quarantine flag hung from the bow, and a pair of men were shooting a stream of hot water at the deck. "There's a report that some of them are sick."

Michael tugged on his bottom lip. "You know that cook I mentioned? Centralia? She gave me a tip on where to find some men who were new to the city and might need the sort of help we provide at the Sailor's Mission. A fellow brought her a crate of bananas this morning, offered it to her for cheap. Said it was off a ship that hadn't been forced to pay the harbor fees. He told her he was staying at a boardinghouse on Dauphine, and if she wanted more produce, to let him know. I swung by the boardinghouse this morning and invited them to the Mission."

Phin halted. "That sounds promising. Can you take me to them?"

"Sure. It's only a few blocks from here."

Phin resumed walking. The medical wagon stood just ahead, with Natalie and Luca beside it in the shade.

Michael caught sight of them and strode forward, forging ahead of Phin.

"Natalie, how great to see you again." He didn't wait for permission, enveloping her in a big hug. "It's been far too long."

A stab of jealousy hit Phin, and he stuck his notebook into his coat and jammed his hands into his pants' pockets. Michael had always been affectionate, but seeing him hugging Natalie made Phin's own arms feel empty.

"Michael, or should I say Pastor Mackenzie? I had no idea you were in New Orleans." Natalie emerged from his embrace and righted her kerchief. "What a pleasant surprise." The smile she beamed at him would shame the sun, and again Phin fought down his feelings. Michael and Natalie had only met a couple of times to his recollection, but there had been an instant friendly bond between the woman he had loved and his brother.

"Michael, can you take us to the boardinghouse? I'd like to check them over as soon as possible." Phin pulled out his watch. This day was turning out nothing like he'd planned.

Natalie came to his side. "What did the doctor say?"

"Nothing useful. He's basically a glorified cook. Let's get moving." He held her elbow as he helped her into the back of the wagon. "We can talk on the way. Michael, this is Luca."

"Nice to meet you, Luca. You want to head to Dauphine between St. Peter and Toulouse." Michael followed Natalie into the wagon, and Phin jumped aboard, closing the door.

The only place to sit was next to Natalie. Michael had commandeered the pallet on the bench. Phin's shoulder bumped Natalie's as the wagon started, and he quickly righted himself.

But space was tight in the conveyance, and his leg brushed hers and their elbows touched. Awareness at each point of contact shot through him, ending at his heart, increasing its pace and making his breathing unsteady. He forced himself to concentrate on the task at hand.

"So, what is this about?" Michael asked, his expression open and curious.

"Just a feeling, but I want to look into it. There were some sailors who were ill, and the symptoms might be nothing, but they might be very troubling We received notice this morning that tropical fever outbreaks had occurred where this ship supposedly came from, and there were a couple of suspicious deaths reported this morning in the city that are awaiting autopsy to confirm cause of death."

"Tropical fever? Like malaria?"

Phin shook his head. "Worse. This might be yellow fever."

The look on Michael's face confirmed Phin's feelings. Yellow fever was the most feared epidemic in America. It came suddenly, struck in what appeared to be a random manner, and killed ruthlessly. The worst outbreaks in U.S. history had killed thousands. They now had a better understanding of how the sickness spread, but until they could convince citizens and leaders alike, the danger of widespread infection would persist.

When they reached the boardinghouse, Michael insisted on going inside with them. "I've met the men, down at the docks. I can introduce you."

Phin shook his head. "This isn't a social visit."

"Nevertheless, it might help to have at least a marginally familiar face."

Natalie followed along. "What if we find men who are ill?"

"Then we'll transport them to the hospital as quickly as possible."

"What if they won't go?"

She voiced Phin's fears. If the men were Italian immigrants, they would be resistant to going to the hospital. They would probably resist letting him examine them at all.

"Michael, now might be a good time for you to start praying." Phin opened the boardinghouse door.

"Start? I've been praying all the way from the riverfront."

Chapter 4

Natalie knew the moment she saw the man, listless, yellow, and holding his abdomen, that they were in trouble. Her eyes met Phin's across the sickbed, and he nodded.

"Luca, tell him he must go to the hospital." Phin bent and examined the man's eyes and palpated his abdomen, which elicited a groan.

"Signore, devi andare in ospedale."

"No." Fear ringed the man's jaundiced eyes. He rolled to his side, moaning. A trickle of blood came from his nose, and Natalie reached for the towel on the washstand. The man flinched and reared back, putting his hands up before his face to ward her off.

Natalie looked at Phin. How were they going to treat this man if he shied away from every contact?

"It's the same old fears and superstitions from Sicily." Phin scowled at the ceiling. "Luca, tell him we mean him no harm. Tell him we're here to help him."

Luca spoke again, rapidly, urgently.

Natalie knelt beside the patient, putting her hand on his forehead, following his movement when he tried to shrug her away. His skin was paper dry and hot, and his eyes bloodshot. "Shhh." Gently, she used the towel to wipe the blood from his upper lip. "Lord, please help me know how to help this man," she whispered.

The patient's eyes never left her face, but his shoulders relaxed a bit. *"Tu pregi?"* he whispered.

She raised her eyes to Luca, who said, "He asks if you praying?"

Nodding, she clasped the patient's hand. He gripped her fingers, eyes locking with hers. She bowed her head and whispered, asking God to help them help this man, to take away his fear, to give them wisdom. As she did, the man relaxed, his grasp becoming less frantic, his breathing steadying.

"Stay with him while we talk in the hall." Phin touched her shoulder, the way he had countless times when he'd left her with a patient. He and Luca and Michael went into the hall, closing the door behind them, and she loosened her fingers to check the patient's pulse.

While most fevers caused a patient's heart rate to increase, yellow fever slowed the pulse down. This man's pulse was very slow.

She had read the medical reports of Dr. Reed and Dr. Finlay, heard of the death of Dr. Lazear in the brave battle to identify the source and vector of yellow fever. She'd sat through many educational seminars taught by military and visiting doctors to the Panamanian jungle. She knew firsthand the dangers, and she assessed them in this case.

The windows were unscreened and wide open. On the street below, the gutters had stagnated water pooling in the cracks. Every house had an open cistern for collecting rainwater, since there were no freshwater wells in this part of the city. Mosquito breeding grounds abounded, and there was nothing to keep them from biting this yellow fever victim and carrying the poison to the next person they attacked.

She took the man's hand between her own, bowed her head, and prayed. For him, for his family, wherever they were, and for protection for the people of New Orleans.

Phin returned alone and began packing a few of the man's belongings into his bag. "Michael and Luca are canvassing the building to see if they can get more information about this man. Whether he has family in the city and such. And to find more of his shipmates. For now, let's do a thorough examination, take some notes, and see about transporting him to the hospital."

Natalie wet a cloth and bathed the man's face and chest. He had his eyes closed, and he lay still, as if moving hurt too much to contemplate.

Michael returned first. "That man, Luca. . .when you don't need his services anymore, I could sure use him at the Mission. He's talking to the first officer of the banana boat now."

"What did he find out?"

"There were eighteen men aboard the ship, the *Mendoza*. Only two were sick when they reached New Orleans, but since then, this man fell ill. His name is Mario Favaro."

At the sound of his name, the patient opened his eyes a slit and nodded. "Sì, signor. Mario," he whispered.

Phin concluded his examination, pulling the sheet up to the patient's armpits. Natalie finished writing down her notes in Phin's notebook.

"And does he have family?" Phin asked.

"From what Luca gathered, the man left Sicily rather rapidly a year ago when he found himself on the wrong side of the authorities there. He came to this country alone, found work aboard the *Mendoza*, and has been with the ship ever since."

"We need to persuade him to go to the hospital. He's very ill, and with no one to care for him here. . ." Phin folded his stethoscope and tucked it into his bag. "Natalie, read back his information, please."

Again a sense of familiarity swept over her. Phin always asked for a summation of an examination before he was finished. "Pulse 52, respiration 12. Temperature 102. Patient exhibits jaundice, back pain, liver tenderness. No vomiting as yet, but bleeding from nose. Signs of dehydration. Symptoms point to Bronze John." She used one of the common names for yellow fever, hoping that the patient wouldn't recognize it and panic.

Phin listened as he shook the mercury back down in the thermometer and handed it to Natalie, who wiped it with alcohol before returning it to the case inside his medical bag.

It took some time and much persuasion and assurances both from Michael and Natalie via Luca's translating, but Mario finally assented to a trip to the hospital. Luca eschewed assistance, gathering the sailor up in his arms and carrying him out into the street as if he were a child.

As they rattled over the cobbles toward the hospital, Phin outline his plan.

"We'll have to isolate him. Mosquito netting around his bed, screens on the windows, and mosquito bars hanging everywhere."

Natalie jotted his notes, though she knew the treatment by heart.

"We'll start him on quinine and cool cloths to reduce his fever, and encourage him to drink. Keep the ward quiet and dark."

He was businesslike and professional, but as he spoke, he smoothed back Mario's hair and folded a towel to place over the man's eyes to block out the light. Yellow fever caused atrocious headaches, and the darkness would soothe the man. He patted the man's shoulder. Natalie was warmed by his tenderness. Most people saw Phin as a sharp mind, quick of thought, quick of action, but she knew the softer side of him, the part that truly cared about his patients and their comfort and well-being.

Michael had joined Luca up front, and he stood by in the hospital courtyard when orderlies came out of the building with a litter to carry the man inside.

Phin placed his hand on Natalie's arm when she went to follow them. "This may be the first of many cases, you know. Or it could be as simple as a couple of men, and no one else will get sick. I don't want to be alarmist, but I have to notify people and I have to return to the tenement where that sick man from this morning wouldn't let us in. Can you take care of things here? Hopefully, this will turn out to be a mini-outbreak, and it will be over soon."

Michael stepped up. "I'll go with you to the tenement."

"We have to stop by the hospital director's office first. Then we'll go back to Little Palermo. The director can contact city officials. Hopefully, we won't need the sheriff and public health to help us persuade this other man to let us check him out and if necessary, bring him here."

When they reached the doors of Marine Hospital, the director met them, his face tense. "I'm glad you're back. I sent men out looking for you over an hour ago."

"But, sir, I've brought—" Phin began.

"There's no time for that now. Listen." The director put his hand on Phin's shoulder. "There are three already, and I expect more. I've put Dr. Trasker in charge of the ward, but I want you to relieve him. Take Miss Morrison with you."

"But, sir—" Phin tried again.

"We're going to need supplies, and we're going to need to get the city health officials on board."

"Sir!" Phin grabbed the man's arm. "Yellow fever. Aboard a ship called the *Mendoza*. They bypassed the quarantine, and they've got sickness aboard. I've brought a patient in with me, and there is at least one more, possibly two. Whatever is going on here will have to take a back seat to this."

The director paused. "Dr. Mackenzie, what do you think I'm talking about? There are three cases on the second floor now, and more will be coming in, I fear. The two suspicious deaths are confirmed as yellow fever. I've called in the city health already."

Natalie's throat constricted. It was worse than they feared.

"Three more? And I've brought in one just starting the toxic phase." Phin glanced at Natalie. "And there is another that should be checked out and possibly brought in."

The director took a deep breath. "I'm putting you in charge of the ward here. Follow the protocols we agreed on. Procure the supplies you need, and I will deal with the city health officials and formulate a plan of attack. Write down the location of the other possible cases, and we'll track them down."

"Will you quarantine the entire crew of the *Mendoza*? And if so, where?" Michael asked.

The director looked at him as if just realizing he was there. "That will depend upon what the city and state health officials decide. Now, we have work to do. Dr. Mackenzie, Miss Morrison, the second-floor west wing. Liaise with Dr. Trasker." He nodded and left at a smart clip.

Phin started down the tiled hallway toward the staircase and then paused, his hand on the wooden rail.

"What is it?" Natalie asked, almost bumping into him when he halted.

He inverted his lips, pressing them hard together as he rubbed his hand against the back of his neck as he looked from her to his brother. "This city isn't going to be a safe place, not with yellow fever. Not for either of you."

"Nor for you," Michael pointed out.

"I can't leave. I'll be needed here. But you two should go. I want you two to get out now before this turns into an epidemic."

"I can't leave people in need. And if this is an epidemic, there will be plenty of need." Michael crossed his arms and frowned. "I can help."

Natalie's spine straightened, her temper heating that he would think she would run away either. "I'm not leaving either. As a nurse, I'll be needed. Anyway. . ."

Phin's gaze sharpened on her face, his dark eyes intent. "Anyway?"

She should come clean. Allay his fears in this respect. "Anyway, I'm now immune to yellow fever. I contracted the illness while in Panama. It's the reason I was invalided home early."

His hand dropped from the rail and took her arm. "You've had yellow fever? When were you going to tell me? I thought you looked as if you had been ill, but I never dreamed." He studied her face, and she knew he was looking at her eyes for traces of lingering jaundice.

"I am fine. The illness had run its course before I ever left Panama. The mission board thought I needed some time to recuperate and sent me home to do so. I can't believe you think I would leave."

Something flashed in his eyes, and his face hardened. "You've left before."

She flinched, and a sinking feeling hit her chest. "That was different, and you know it. Now, let's get upstairs and see these new patients." She marched ahead of him, rolling up her sleeves. "We have work to do."

Phin dried his hands on the towel Natalie handed him, looking through the mosquito netting at the young man in the hospital bed, trying to keep the frustration out of his voice. He knew patient care at the hospital was important, but he felt trapped here. He should be in Little Palermo with Luca and the mobile unit. However, the director had insisted he remain in charge of this ward. Phin promised himself he would try again, as soon as the director returned.

"Keep an eye on the fever. If it goes up, and it probably will by evening, increase the dose of quinine as per the instructions in his chart."

Natalie nodded.

He didn't know what he would've done without her the past two weeks. She had practical experience in nursing fever patients, and she'd put that expertise to use, organizing the ward, creating schedules and supply lists, and training the handful of nurses assigned to the yellow fever ward.

Most were from Marine Hospital, but one had been sent by Michael. A black woman of considerable age who had nursed fever victims in Jacksonville, Florida, more than fifteen years before. A woman who, like Natalie, had survived the fever and was now immune. She had proven to be a stalwart.

Mary Sade—she was never called Mary, always Mary Sade—limped toward him, her arms full of clean sheets, favoring her left hip, which she said she'd hurt in a fall as a young woman. Phin suspected a poorly healed fracture was to blame, but he admired her grit in not letting that slow her down much.

"Doctah, that man in the last bed, he says he's feeling bettah, and he wants to leave. I told him to stay put until you said he could go, and if he didn't I would leg-rope him like a wanderin' hog, but you bettah go talk to him."

Phin smothered a smile at her homespun outlook, the first smile he had felt like raising for what seemed like a long time. Then he sobered. The pain and frenzy of the acute phases of yellow fever often required him to order restraints for his patients. He hoped that wouldn't be the case for Mr. O'Hara ever. "I'll speak with him." Weariness pulled at his limbs. Cases were beginning to surface more frequently, which made sense. Dr. Reed had proven that the incubation period in an *Aedes aegypti*, the mosquito that carried yellow fever, was about two weeks.

He started up the row of beds with Natalie at his elbow, where she'd been every time he needed her.

Natalie sighed and smoothed a stray strand of hair off her cheek, tucking it under the kerchief she insisted upon wearing in the wards. She made a notation in a chart as they walked. Dark smudges hung under her eyes. No one had gotten much sleep lately. Their exchanges had been purely professional after his jab about her leaving had hit home on that first day they had worked together. Why had he said that when he'd promised himself he wouldn't bring it up ever again?

She closed the file folder and crossed her arms over it, hugging it to her chest. "It's always the same with fever victims, isn't it? The initial symptoms abate, and they are sure they are getting well. And most do, but the ones who don't. . .they have no idea what is coming."

The question that Phin had been wanting to ask her fell off his tongue before he could stop it. "Did you enter the acute phase?" He wanted to yank the question back, since he'd vowed not to ask about her time in Panama. She had shut that part of her life off from him, and he wanted it to stay that way. But it was too late. He'd asked.

She shook her head, and his muscles eased. "I never progressed that far, thankfully." Bleakness crossed her face. "We lost almost all who did."

"What was the mortality rate?" He kept his tone clinical.

"About one hundred cases that we know of were infected, and of those, twenty-six entered the toxic stage. Of those, nine died."

"Was it mostly foreigners affected?"

"A real mixture. Canal workers, government officials, natives, and one missionary caught the sickness." She gave a rueful chuckle. "We'd best see about Mr. O'Hara before

423

Mary Sade loses her patience."

Mr. O'Hara spotted them and began to sit up, but Phin motioned him back. "Not so quickly."

"But I'm feeling foin now. Woke up ready to take on the world." He gently thumped his narrow chest. "No fever, and the body's in good nick now."

Phin parted the mosquito netting and bent over the patient. "That's good, and I'm glad you're feeling better, but I'm going to have to insist you remain here with us for a few more days, just to make sure."

"A few days?" His red eyebrows went up. "What about me family? They fled north, and I need to go to them."

Phin thumbed up the man's eyelid. Still some lingering jaundice but nowhere near as bad as it had been even twenty-four hours ago. He felt the man's forehead. Little or no fever. "How's your appetite?"

"I could eat a stove lid, I'm that peckish." He rubbed his belly. "That's a good sign, right?"

"A very good sign, but I'm going to have to ask you to trust me. We're under strict orders not to release any patient until he's been symptom free for at least six days. If you continue to improve"—Phin bent his best "doctor look" on O'Hara—"and not give your nurses too much trouble, then you'll be free to go with our blessing in a week or so. Until then"—he turned to Natalie—"a bit of arrowroot gruel for Mr. O'Hara."

"Yes, Doctor." Natalie removed the clipboard chart from the foot of the bed and made a notation.

"Arrowroot?" O'Hara pressed back against the pillows, his freckles standing out like scattered gold dust. "Here I am wasting away, and you want to give me gruel? I need some meat. Beef and potatoes. Or failing that, some good old salted oatmeal."

Phin gave him a stern look, and Natalie shook her head, her lips in a straight line.

"Now, Mr. O'Hara." Natalie had parted the mosquito netting on the far side of the bed and now bent over the patient, straightening the covers and putting the man's hands and arms beneath the blanket. "You'll do exactly as the doctor says. Your system has been under attack the last few days, and it is going to take time to regain your strength. Take it from someone who knows. And stay under those blankets. You've had a raging fever, and we don't want you to get chilled." She gave him a quick smile.

O'Hara beamed up at her, and when she put her hand against his brow, he shot Phin a mischievous look. "If a pretty colleen like you were to sit beside me and hold my hand, I'd be sure to get better."

Phin found his neck stiffening, and a reprimand formed on the tip of his tongue. But before he could voice it, Natalie had removed her hand from the man's face and bent a stern look on him. "Mind your cheeky ways, Mr. O'Hara, or it will be Mary Sade attending you, and you're already nearing the end of your rope with her. She's liable to give you the rough side of her tongue."

Someone cleared his throat, and Phin turned. The director, suit rumpled and hair disheveled, stood at the foot of the bed, partially obscured by the netting. "Doctor, could I see you outside?"

"Nurse?" Phin inclined his head, and Natalie followed him out, adjusting the protection around the bed—protection not for the patient, but for the rest of the city.

The director leaned against the windowsill at the far end of the hallway, his shoulders stooped. "It's officially an epidemic now. The incubation period for the first cases is over, and more and more new cases are being reported. City officials are putting their plans into action, but we're behind this thing, and it's going to gain momentum before it slows."

"What is the action plan?" Phin asked.

"First, Dr. Kohnke, the director of the City Board of Health, has been in communication with national health officials, requesting help. President Roosevelt has been contacted, and he's promised aid. Second, we're going to implement the measures Dr. Reed took in Havana. Every cistern will be treated with kerosene and covered with a screen. Areas with standing water will be treated. Any new case of yellow fever will be reported, and a fumigation team will be on-site within the hour, spraying down the house and setting up a screened isolation room for the patient. Saturdays and Sundays, the citywide fumigation teams will be out spraying for mosquitoes. Acute cases will be brought to the hospitals." He ran his fingers through his hair and then dragged them down his face. He had aged what seemed a decade in the past two weeks.

"How are the other wards coping with the new cases?" Phin asked. Originally, his had been the only yellow fever ward at Marine Hospital, but as of this morning, there were now three.

"As well as can be expected. Fourteen new acute cases brought in today. We'll no longer be accepting cases until they reach the acute phase, otherwise we'll be overrun." The director held up his hands when Phin opened his mouth. "I know. But that's how it has to be. Local physicians are being allocated territories to oversee all over the city. We have to act as a team, and we have to trust our teammates. Your job is here in the hospital for now."

"My job is out there." He pointed over the director's shoulder through the window. "It's the whole reason we created the mobile doctor's office. I should be on the front lines, diagnosing new cases, educating the public, getting into Little Palermo and other immigrant enclaves where they need the most help." Phin jammed his hands into his pockets. He knew his work here in the hospital was important, but any physician could give nurses the basic orders for palliative fever care. He needed to be out in the city.

Natalie put her hand on his arm, but he shrugged it off. He didn't need placating or calming. He needed to do the work he had been called to do.

The director took his leave, and Phin sagged against the windowsill. "I feel so hampered here. So closed in. I need to be out there, to see what's going on, to help all those people in need. I know there are dozens, maybe scores of people in Little Palermo who are falling ill, but they're either not reporting in or they're being overlooked."

"You can't do everything. Sometimes you have to trust others to do what you can't. You are needed here. You are making a difference. Are the people in your ward any less deserving of your help? Any less in need of medical care?" Natalie crossed her arms and tilted her head.

Her words brought him up short. She was right. He could do good here, and he would have to trust the local physicians, public health officers, and citizens.

God, help us. Help me. This is going to get worse before it gets better.

He pushed himself off the sill, squared his shoulders, and went back to the sick ward.

Chapter 5

Natalie stripped the hospital bed, wadding the blood and sweat-soaked sheets in on themselves and stuffing them into the basket at her side. Her eyes smarted, both from sorrow and lack of sleep.

Mr. O'Hara had put up a valiant fight. But in the end, the fever had prevailed.

Mary Sade hitched by, stooping to pick up the basket. "Honey, you need to get you some rest. I put a glass of milk and a couple cookies on a tray in the first exam room. You get yourself in there and eat those up before one of the orderlies finds it."

Milk and cookies.

"I need to make up this bed. There will be a new patient in need of it soon."

"I kin do that. You run along. I tole the doctor to take him a few minutes too. You both been workin too hard. This ain't no sprint. We been at this a month, and we got a ways to go yet."

A month since the first cases. A month of tense nursing, waiting for the second wave, and now seeing new patients daily. Every bed in Marine Hospital was full, as were the beds in every other hospital in the city. The mayor had even opened the administration building of the Touro Infirmary, which had been slated for destruction this summer, as a charity ward, to house the sick. Marine Hospital was only admitting those in the toxic stage, so Natalie and Mary Sade and the rest of the nurses were hard pressed.

Natalie slipped into the quiet exam room. As Mary Sade had promised, a tray sat on the desk. But it had two glasses of milk and four cookies on the plate. She sank into the chair and looked at the food, too tired to eat. Twelve-hour shifts six days a week, and an eight-hour shift on the seventh, for four weeks now.

A bead of sweat trickled down her temple, and she picked up a sheaf of papers from the desk to fan herself. The July sun beat against the drawn shade, trying to get in. The air was sultry, making even breathing an effort.

She leaned her head back against the chair and closed her eyes. Outside, yardmen clanged their tools and talked, one man giving orders. They were lighting the sulfur fires again to discourage mosquitoes. A rueful chuckle escaped her lips. They had become so commonplace, those stinking fires, that she hardly smelled them anymore. Her clothes reeked of sulfur, smoke, carbolic, and chlorine.

When the doorknob creaked, she opened her eyes, though her lids were heavy. Phin put his hand on the frosted glass panel and opened the door wider.

She sat up straighter and found her hands checking her hair and kerchief, before she remonstrated herself for caring how she looked. She eyed him, taking in the rumpled white coat, the wrinkled trousers, the scuffed shoes. That, if nothing else, told her of the hard hours he'd put in. Under normal circumstances, Phin took great pains with his dress, preferring to be well turned out at all times.

His dark hair hung over his forehead, and weariness clouded his normally bright eyes. "Did Mary Sade shoo you in here too?" he asked.

"Yes. I don't know where she gets the energy. She works just as long and hard as I do, but she still finds the vigor to boss me around."

"Not just you." He leaned against the examination table and reached for a cookie. "Aren't you having any?"

"I was trying to work up the energy."

His gaze sharpened and he straightened, but she waved him back. "I'm fine. Just tired. I'm the one person you don't have to worry about getting the fever, remember? I've already had it."

He sagged back. "I remember, but humor me and eat a cookie and drink your milk."

She picked up the glass. "I will, but only because I don't want Mary Sade to be disappointed." She took a sip, glad that the milk was still fairly cold. She couldn't abide warm milk. "What do you hear from the outside world?" With all her work, and with boarding on the top floor of this very building, Natalie hadn't ventured off the hospital grounds since the crisis began.

Phin finished his cookie and washed it down with his drink. "Nearly one hundred deaths have been reported, with more than a thousand cases of yellow fever. Who knows how many more unreported cases? Luca came by this morning for a moment. He's been working with Michael and city officials, trying to break down barriers in Little Palermo. That seems to be the part of the city hardest hit. They were heading out again today."

"Those poor people. So scared, so isolated by language and culture." She bit into a shortbread cookie, surprised at how good it tasted.

"Luca says the streets are bare. Shops are closed, the riverfront is a ghost town. According to the newspaper he brought with him, surrounding towns are enforcing a 'shotgun quarantine.' People trying to flee New Orleans are being met at train stations with shotgun-toting vigilantes who force them to stay aboard and move on or come back to the city."

"Can they do that?"

"They *are* doing it." Phin shrugged. "They're afraid. They don't want yellow fever in their town any more than New Orleans wanted it."

Mary Sade knocked on the door. "Dr. Mackenzie, they's some folk here to see you." Her eyes swept the plate, and a motherly, chiding gleam entered her expression. "You eat all that up, you hear? I don't make special trays for folks only to have them not finish 'em up."

They reached for the last two cookies with a guilty start and then grinned sheepishly. "Where are these visitors? And who are these visitors?" Phin asked.

"The same fellow who came by for you this morning, and he has a big yella-haired man with him. I tolt them to wait out in the hall. They don't need to be traipsin' through the ward upsetting those poor souls in there." Mary Sade lurched away, her grizzled white hair poking out from its pins and her calico apron flapping.

"I used to think I was in charge of the ward." Phin pushed himself up and smoothed his hands down his coat front, frowning as if just realizing his rumpled state. "I look like I've been dragged through a knothole backward."

"You look like you've spent hours bending over bedsides, treating patients." Natalie drained her glass and, in a total disregard of manners, wiped her lips with the hem of her apron. "Mary Sade was right. A little milk and cookies was just what I needed."

"Good. Natalie, you come too. You could use a few minutes more away from the ward." He offered his arm, and she rose and took it, conscious of him. They walked out into the hall, their footsteps echoing on the tiled floor.

Michael and Luca waited by the stairwell.

"Ah, *bella signorina*, so good-a to see you. You are a-working too hard. This terrible fever. It is too much." Luca advanced on her, taking her hands and squeezing them. He shook his big head, his beard brushing his chest. "So much-a sadness, yes? And always, we are-a finding you new people to look-a after, yes?"

Natalie squeezed back, though she wondered, with his huge hands, if he even felt the pressure. His dark eyes looked like burning coals, deep set and weary.

She turned to Michael. "How are you faring?"

He shrugged. "It's tough out there. Hardware stores are sold out of screening and mosquito netting. There isn't a mosquito bar to be had. Between the sulfur fires and the fumigation, I don't know if I will ever breathe freely again." Putting his hands against his lower back, he stretched and winced. "I've spent so much time bending over fever victims' beds, praying for them, trying to bring some comfort, my back will never be the same."

"I can sympathize." Natalie nodded.

He turned to Phin. "Mother and Dad are very worried, as you can imagine. They've sent several telegrams to me. How about you?"

Phin nodded, patting his white coat pocket. "Three telegrams and a letter."

"You might want to think about answering them. The message I got this morning is that they haven't heard from you in two weeks." Michael bent a knowing look on Phin. "They telephoned me this morning. I had to wait by the phone for an hour for the call to come through at the exchange. I assured them that you were fit the last time I saw you and that I would be coming out to the hospital today to check on you." He glanced at the crack of sunlight seeping around the window blind in the stairwell and stepped to one side, wincing at the bright light.

A low moan came from the ward, followed by a retching sound. Natalie turned to go assist the patient, but Mary Sade crossed the open doorway, basin in hand, comforting words already flowing from her lips. Natalie relaxed, sure that the sick man was in capable hands.

Michael grimaced. "Seen and heard too much of that lately." His hand went to his stomach. "I've never seen anything like it. I don't wonder that people fear yellow fever."

Phin put his hands into his pockets and leaned against the wall with a yawn. "Other than to come check on me, what brings you to the hospital?"

"Luca, actually. He found a patient for you, in a back alley down in Little Palermo. He's on his way up as soon as the orderlies can bring him. The nurses downstairs said he would need to be washed and clothed in hospital garb before they would let him on the ward."

"Standard admitting procedures. Can you tell me anything about him?"

"Sì, dottore." Luca's shoulders stooped, and he shook his big head. "He is old-a man. Nobody to care for-a him. He come from-a Sicily only a few months ago, and he very scared. Scared of-a dottores and the *polizia*. He get sick, he-a hide. He no look for help."

Natalie and Phin shared a look. It was the same old story. She drew her handkerchief out of her apron pocket and dabbed her temples. What they needed was a good old-fashioned rainstorm to blow through and cool off the city and bring some relief from this oppressive heat.

She glanced at Michael, whose fair coloring was ruddy with the high temperature, but curiously, he wasn't sweating like the rest of them. He rolled his shoulders and winced again. A slight warning bell rang in the back of her head.

"Michael, do you have a headache?"

He was rubbing his temple absently, and when he looked at her, his pupils were dilated.

"Yes, but it's nothing. Not enough sleep, I daresay."

Her hand went out to touch his forehead, and her heart dropped as her fingers met his skin. "You're feverish."

Phin tensed, coming forward to feel his brother's brow, to look into his eyes. "How long?"

"It's nothing, I tell you. A little headache. And I'm not feverish. It's hot outside." Michael brushed his brother's hand away. "You have plenty else to worry about."

"Come with me." Phin took Michael's arm. "Into the exam room. Luca, head down to the kitchen and tell them Dr. Mackenzie said they were to feed you. Ask for some ice cream. I know they've got some hidden away down there."

"Grazie, dottore, but what about Signore Michael?"

"We'll see to him. Come back up in half an hour or so."

Luca patted Michael on the shoulder. "You do what-a your brother says, yes?" His eyes were sober, though he tried to grin. "I will be back to see if you are being a good-a man."

Michael fussed. "Really, Phin. There's nothing wrong with me."

Natalie put her hand on Michael's other arm. "Please. It won't take long, and we'd rather be sure." The intensity on Phin's face, the fear in his eyes that she could tell he was trying to quell pulled at her. He loved his brother, a love forged in impossibly trying circumstances when they were both orphans so many years ago.

Michael sighed and tried another tack. "But what about the old man we brought in? Shouldn't you take care of him first?"

"Trust me, we'll put Mary Sade in charge of him, and he'll be as comfortable as we can make him in no time." She guided Michael toward the ward and the examination room just inside the door.

"Fine, but you'll see. I don't have the fever. I just have a bit of a headache. It will go away after I get some sleep." He protested all the way to the exam room where Natalie removed the glasses and tray from the counter and spread a clean sheet on the examination table.

"Sit up there." She pointed. "Remove your jacket."

Phin went to the sink on the wall and began to scrub his hands, his head bent.

Michael shrugged out of his suit coat. "You're awfully bossy, you know that?" The chiding irritation in his voice was new, and Natalie wondered if it meant he was in more pain than he was letting on. "And here Phin always said you were such a sweet, kind girl."

Natalie paused, her heart lurching. A sweet, kind girl. She drew a clean towel from the supply cupboard and handed it to Phin, not meeting his eyes. Did he still think that? Of course he didn't. He had been hurt and angry when she wouldn't marry him. Though they had worked together well this past month, he had kept everything on a professional level. No one would guess he had loved her enough once to propose.

When Phin concluded his examination, Natalie looked up from the notes she had been taking, summing up the symptoms the same way she knew Phin had. Fever, headache, backache, loss of appetite, fatigue. The early stages of the illness.

"That's it," Phin said, looping his stethoscope around his neck. "I've got a bed and a mosquito net with your name on it."

"But the hospital is only for acute cases." Michael stood and wavered a bit. Natalie reached out to steady him.

"The hospital is for people in need, and you need someone to care for you." Phin scrubbed his hands at the sink again. "I want you where I can keep an eye on you, and that means right here on my ward. Natalie, get him settled, and I'll check on the new patient Luca brought in."

Within the half hour, Natalie had Michael and their new patient, Aldo, in beds side by side in the ward.

Aldo, wizened, yellowed, and feeble, watched her with panicked, fever-bright eyes. When she tried to get him to drink some water, he refused, clamping his lips tight and shaking his head.

"But, sir, you must drink." His fever was soaring, and he was showing signs of dehydration.

"Here." Michael said. "Give it to me, and let him see me."

She parted the mosquito netting and gave him the glass. He took a long swallow, holding the water up so Aldo could see he had drunk about half. "He's afraid it's poisoned. He's afraid that since he's old and ill, you might try to get rid of him."

This time, the old man let her help him, and she cupped the back of his head, holding the glass to his lips. He drank a few sips and lay back, whispering, "Grazie."

Within a few seconds, he'd brought the water back up, accompanied by the dreaded "coffee grounds" emesis that indicated internal bleeding. Natalie helped him, holding the basin, wiping his mouth, mopping his face. He shivered, his body wracked with chills from the fever, and his eyes fluttered closed. He sank into unconsciousness.

Michael's eyes were wide, and he bit his bottom lip. Her heart went out to him, and she reached under the mosquito netting to hold his hand. "We're going to take the best care of you. And remember, most cases don't develop this far. Aldo here has several things working against him. He is elderly, and he went for far too long without any medical help or care. You are young and otherwise you've been in excellent shape, and you've gotten medical help right at the outset. We're going to support you through this, watch against dehydration or soaring fever, and keep you as comfortable as we can. You're going to be fine."

Michael squeezed her hand. "Thank you, Natalie. I apologize for insinuating earlier that you aren't a sweet, kind girl. Don't worry about me. God is still sovereign, and He is still good. Nothing will happen to me that He hasn't ordained."

She adjusted the netting over his bed, knowing he spoke the truth but having to remind herself of it constantly.

"Oh, there's one thing. I didn't think to mention it during Phin's exam because he's well aware of it already. I was born with a heart condition. I take digitalis every day. My pills. . ." He looked about uncertainly. "They were in my coat pocket."

A heart condition? Natalie swallowed and forced a smile. Fevers taxed the heart greatly. "We'll see that you get your medications. You need to rest now. I'll be back soon."

She gathered the tray and supplies she had used. When she reached the equipment closet, she found Phin, hands braced on the counter, head hanging.

Not knowing what to do but knowing she couldn't leave him, Natalie set the tray down gently and put her hand on his shoulder. "Phin?"

Without a word, he turned and put his arms around her, gathering her close and resting his chin on her head.

She said nothing, placing her arms loosely around his waist, offering him the comfort he seemed to need, trying hard not to savor the feel of being in his embrace.

"What will I do if God takes Michael away too?"

Phin sat beside Michael's bed. Around him, the rustle of sheets, the quiet, occasional moans, and from somewhere down the row of beds, soft snoring filled the air.

Mary Sade roamed from bed to bed, her lantern swinging gently in her hand. Two orderlies dozed on chairs, one at either end of the ward. The Regulator clock on the wall ticked softly.

Phin leaned forward, his elbows on his knees, fingers clasped. How many times had he tried to pray in the last hour, only to feel as if his mind and heart had hit a brick wall? Words wouldn't come.

On the surface, he had functioned, written orders, treated patients, met with the hospital director, and even showed a city councilman through the ward, outlining their methods and treatments. But underneath, he felt as if he walked on a rickety, swinging bridge over a vast abyss. If he looked down, the bridge would crumble and he would fall.

Michael had followed all the classic progressions of yellow fever over the past week. Soaring temperature, especially in the evening. Yellowing skin. No appetite. Joint pain. Headaches.

And then he had rallied, raring to get out of bed.

And through it all, Phin had held himself tight on the inside. Strict control, not looking inwardly at the thing that frightened him the most.

Michael stirred, moving his head from side to side on the pillow. After two good days where his symptoms had lessened, they had come roaring back this morning and worse than before.

To complicate matters, his heart was playing up. Phin had adjusted the digitalis so many times over the past week, he had created a chart of dosages and results and tacked it to the wall over Michael's bed.

And he'd telegraphed several colleagues around the country for advice. Dr. Charlie Mayo up in Rochester had been the most helpful, consulting his fellow clinic doctors and sending a detailed telegram in response as to possible treatment avenues.

Light flashed outside, quickly followed by a boom of thunder. Phin started, his head coming up. As if the lightning had torn a hole in the clouds, rain began to fall. The orderlies stirred and hurried around the ward closing windows as quietly as they could.

Mary Sade lumbered by, a pail in one hand, her lantern in the other. "Thank You, Jesus. Now maybe we kin get some relief from dis awful heat." Her dark skin glistened in the lamplight. "It's been hot enough to wilt a fence post."

"Phin, are you still here?" Michael whispered, his lips tight. "You should be asleep."

He forced a slight smile. "So should you. How are you feeling?"

"Lousy." His voice rasped, and Phin parted the mosquito netting to offer him some ice chips. Phin had found that the ice, though it melted quickly in this heat, was better on his patients' stomachs than gulping water.

"Thanks. What time is it?"

"Nearly two in the morning. Let me listen to your heart." Phin reached for his stethoscope.

"How's Aldo?" Michael tried to peer through the netting to the next bed, but he let his head drop, screwing his eyes shut. "I feel as if a thousand bees are stinging the inside of my skull. Is that normal?"

Phin chuckled, trying to concentrate on Michael's heart rhythms but not wanting to miss an opportunity to tease his brother and hopefully cheer him a bit. "There's nothing normal about your skull. I've told you that before."

"Bully." Michael shot back.

"Brat." Phin grinned at their old banter.

Michael sobered. "Seriously though. I feel rotten. How's my ticker?"

"Surprisingly well, all things considered. The combination of medicines Dr. Mayo suggested seems to be helping. And all the cool baths to keep your fever down."

His brother squirmed and scowled, and if he wasn't so jaundiced, Phin suspected he would see Michael blushing. "I don't know which is worse, being given a sponge bath by Natalie or by Mary Sade. My dignity has suffered a severe blow."

Not having the heart to tell him that a sponge bath from a nurse would be the least of the indignities visited upon his brother in the coming days, Phin drew the sheet up. "You should rest."

"I don't want to rest. I want to talk."

"You need to conserve your strength."

"No, there are some things I need to say, just in case. . ."

"Stop that kind of talk. You're going to be fine. It won't be fun for the next few days, and it will take you awhile to regain your strength, but you're going to come through this." Phin realized he'd fisted his hands on his thighs, and he made a conscious effort to relax. But his heart was pounding hard against his ribs, and a rivulet of sweat trickled down his spine. Thunder boomed again, rattling the windows, and he felt the concussion in his chest.

"Listen to me. I am no fool." Michael closed his eyes for a moment. "I have seen what this disease can do. I am ready to meet Jesus if that's called for. I'm not afraid. But I don't want to leave you without telling you. . ." A tremor went through him, and he took several deep breaths.

"Don't, Michael. You're taxing yourself."

His blue eyes, ringed with yellow from the jaundice and bloodshot from the attacking sickness, held Phin's.

"It's about Natalie." He swallowed. "I know you still love her. You always have. And she loves you."

"Stop." Phin put up his hand. He knew how he felt about Natalie. How he would always feel. But that's where it ended. She was amazing. Wonderful. Everything he wanted in a wife. But she didn't love him. Not enough to marry him.

And turning to her for comfort when he was scared had been a foolish thing to do, because it had caused to rear up all those feelings, so strong they nearly buckled his knees. Holding her in his arms, he had been spun right back to the moments before she had refused to marry him, those moments when everything had been possible and exciting and perfect. . . .

She hadn't said a word about that embrace since. Her manner toward him hadn't changed. She was professional, helpful, and so dedicated to their patients that he had been forced to order her off the ward and to bed, or else she would still be here.

"I've watched her," Michael continued. "When she thinks no one is looking. She follows you with her eyes wherever you are. She is always finding ways to make your job easier, coaxing a smile out of you, encouraging you. When she watches you, she has such a wistful, almost aching look of longing on her face, as if she would like nothing more than to run right into your arms."

"You're being fanciful. It's the fever talking."

"No, it's not. Phin, I know you. Maybe better than anyone else in the whole world. I know the things that scare you, because we come from the same place. You're so scared of being alone, of those you love leaving you. Like your uncle did, dropping you in the orphanage and never looking back. Like Natalie did when she chose a missionary life over being your wife. You hold tight to the ones you love, but if you suspect they're going to leave you, you pretend you don't care. Like you did when you came to care for Mother and Dad, but you were afraid they wouldn't love you, wouldn't adopt you and make us a family. You were terrible, breaking every rule you could, acting out, abandoning them before they had a chance to abandon you."

His words were barely a whisper now, and Phin knew what the effort to talk so much was costing him.

And he knew the truth of his brother's words. He did fear being abandoned by those he loved. And he tended to push away first so he wouldn't be hurt.

"Stop pushing Natalie away."

"Pushing her away? She's the one who left me, remember?"

"I know that, but since she's come back, have you talked to her? Really talked to her about what happened, why she made the choice she did, and whether she might have changed her mind about things now?" He moved under the sheet, as if everything hurt and he couldn't find a comfortable position.

Phin hadn't talked to Natalie. Not about anything personal.

And he didn't want to. Once you'd been hurt, why would you reopen the wound?

His physician's brain said, *To drain out infection. To clear out whatever might be festering in there.*

But his heart said, *That way is dangerous. If you peek under that bandage, it's going to hurt. And you don't want to be hurt like that ever again.*

"Rest, Michael."

"Did you send the telegram?" His eyelids fluttered closed.

"I did. They're praying. All of them."

A fleeting smile touched his lips.

Phin turned away, a hard lump in his throat. The next few days would determine Michael's future. The acute phase was just ramping up.

God, how can You do this to me? I can't lose him. For the first time in a long time. . . since Natalie had turned down his proposal, Phin felt a niggle of doubt as to the goodness of God.

And a swelling of doubt that he could find a way to go on if God chose to take Michael home.

Chapter 6

A knock broke through Natalie's slumber, and she sat up, trying to focus. What time was it? Thunder rumbled, and she groaned. It had rained during the night—it was still raining—and she hadn't closed the window. The knock sounded again, and she reached for her robe, draped across the end of the bed. As she stood, she slipped in the puddle of rainwater on the linoleum floor. She skidded across the room and into the door, saving herself from a nasty fall by grabbing the doorknob and the edge of her dresser.

Thoroughly awake now, she wrenched the door open. "What?"

Avery Callan, secretary to Mr. Guillard, the mission board chairman stood in the hallway, his hand poised to knock again, water dripping from his raincoat and glistening on his face. At the sight of her in her nightclothes and robe, he blinked and stared hard at the doorjamb beside her.

"My. . .my. . .apologies for coming to your room like this. The porter downstairs didn't tell me this was your lodging, he just said you could be found in room 443. I can wait downstairs until you are. . .um. . .properly attired." Red suffused his cheeks.

She was covered from her throat to her ankles, but her hair lay in tumbled strands around her face and shoulders, escaped from the hasty braid she'd fashioned before falling into bed last night. And her feet were bare.

"What's happened? Why are you here?" *What time was it?* "I can't meet with you downstairs. I have to go on duty. . ." She glanced at the clock on the dresser. ". . .in about twenty minutes. We're working twelve-hour shifts until this crisis is over, and I am due to go on at the top of the hour." And she still needed to do a quick washup, dress, and bolt some breakfast. How had Michael fared last night? Had Phin gotten any sleep? Her mind raced with all she needed to do, even as her body told her she hadn't rested long enough.

Avery cleared his throat as he dug inside his raincoat and drew out a damp envelope. "The director wished me to deliver this letter. There was a special meeting at the Mission last night and things have developed. Mr. Guillard asks you to come by the office at your earliest convenience."

"Why? What's happened?" She looked at the envelope, her name written in a neat, even hand on the front. "I can't leave the hospital. I'm needed here."

"Just read the letter. It will explain things. I have to go. It isn't seemly for me to be in a women's dormitory." Avery sketched a quick bow and hurried down the hallway, a trail of rainwater in his wake.

"Miss Morrison, I'm glad you're awake." Mrs. Bondurant, the hospital matron called to her from the end of the dormitory hall. "Dr. Mackenzie needs you on the ward right now. Two more nurses have contracted the fever, and we're shorthanded."

"Yes, Matron. I'll be right there." Natalie closed her door, tossed the envelope onto her dresser, and threw a towel onto the floor, scrubbing with her feet to soak up most of the rainwater. Reaching the window, she closed it, peering out through the rain at the sodden hospital grounds. Two more nurses sick? She drew a clean uniform out of the wardrobe and laid it on the bed.

The Mission director was going to have to wait. Once dressed, with her hair arranged neatly under her kerchief, she stuffed the director's letter into her pocket and headed to the ward.

When she arrived two floors down, every bed was full, and sometime in the night, three more cots had been squeezed in.

Rain continued to pound the windows on the south side of the building, but the orderlies were opening the windows on the north a few inches, because the air in the ward was stifling and thick with the scent of sickness.

Phin stood with Mary Sade at the far end of the ward, and when he looked up, he waved Natalie over.

"Say good night, Mary Sade." His voice was firm. "It's time for you to get some rest now."

"But my patients." The old woman swayed with fatigue, and both Phin and Natalie reached out to steady her.

"I've just had a good long sleep," Natalie said. "I'll see to the patients."

Mary Sade shook her grizzled head. "I ain't that tired."

"Doctor's orders." Phin motioned her down the ward, and she huffed and shuffled away.

Natalie went with her to the door. "I'll take good care of things. You don't have to worry."

"It ain't that." Mary Sade shook her head. "It's that I don't want to take the time. My house is clear over t'other side of the river. By the time I get there, I'll hardly have time to sleep before I got to get back."

"Ah, I see." Natalie tapped her lips, thinking. "I tell you what, why don't you just use my room here? It's right upstairs, so no time wasted."

"I can't sleep here." Her dark eyes widened. "What would the matron say? She don't much like me nohow."

"I'll square it with her. Dr. Mackenzie will order it if necessary. You know the matron will do anything for Dr. Mackenzie." Mrs. Bondurant held physicians in high regard, their word was law, and she seemed to admire Phin especially.

Mary Sade finally agreed, after Natalie called Phin over and he ordered her upstairs. She grumbled, but she went.

"You should be asleep too. Did you stay here all night?" Natalie asked.

"Let's walk the ward." Phin's face was haggard as he evaded her question. "I'll catch you up on everyone's progress."

There was encouraging news for some who seemed to be recovering from the worst of the illness. Phin gave orders for these handful to be started on a light diet and encouraged to drink plenty of fluids.

"If I was certain they weren't still vulnerable to passing along the disease, some of them could be released to return home. But we haven't done enough studies to be sure when that time of contagion is past, so here they stay until every vestige of the jaundice has subsided and they are showing signs of regaining their strength."

Others had maintained throughout the night. Yellowed, sunken into the pillows, given pain medications to help, holding their own but not improving. The old man, Aldo, was in this group. He lay with his eyes closed, his skin parchment dry, his thin chest barely moving as he took slow breaths.

Then there were the ones who had worsened overnight. Michael fell into this group. Jaundiced to an alarming degree, he groaned in his sleep, his lips in a grimace. His eyelids fluttered, and he arched his back. A trickle of blood leaked from his nose, and Natalie parted the netting to wipe his face.

Phin gripped the end of the bed, leaning over, his head falling. "He only wakens to vomit or from the pain. His skin is so yellow it's practically orange. His fever is dangerously high, and not even the sponge baths are working. I can't order an ice bath because the shock to his heart might kill him."

The anguish in his voice crushed Natalie's chest. She smoothed back Michael's blond hair, alarmed at the heat coming from his skin. The next twenty-four to thirty-six hours would be crucial, if the disease took its normal course.

She stroked Michael's cheek once and emerged from the mosquito netting. "Phin— Dr. Mackenzie—" Mercy, she'd forgotten they were on the ward, where a nurse calling a doctor by his first name was forbidden. "You need to sleep. You've been awake for more than a day. You won't do Michael or any of your patients much good if you collapse. And if you contract the disease . . ." Her throat thickened at the thought of it. "You'll be more vulnerable to the worst of it if you're run down."

"I can't leave him." Phin shook his head. "I won't leave him. He's my brother."

Natalie heard both the conviction and exhaustion in his voice. He could be so stubborn at times. A woman hurried by with a pitcher of water and a towel over her arm. Her husband lay in a bed about halfway down the ward, and was one of the few who had family to help look after him. Natalie had thanked God for these family helpers many times over the last month as they lessened her load quite a bit.

"Then you should do what other family members do. Roll out a pallet beside his bed and go to sleep. I'll wake you if there's any change."

He raised his head and squinted, as if his eyes were too tired to focus without an effort. "Sleep on the ward?"

She crossed her arms. "I'd prefer it if you went home and slept in your own bed, but I can understand you not wanting to go. You and Mary Sade are two of a kind. It would be easier on the nurses and orderlies if you'd at least sleep on the couch in your office, but a pallet on the floor will work just as well. If anything comes up, I'll consult with Dr. Trasker on the ward across the hall, and when it's time, I'll wake you."

He was asleep within moments of hitting the pallet. Natalie worked her way down the ward, taking temperatures, recording heart rates, and seeing that all Phin's orders were carried out. In addition, she held buckets for those who were still in the vomiting stage, changed bed linens, and encouraged patients to try to drink.

All the while, she battled with how to reduce Michael's temperature without resorting to an ice bath.

The work was hard, heavy, and at times disheartening. Seeing so much suffering tore at her heart and brought back her own memories of fighting the illness herself. She tried to remember all the things that helped. . .her caregivers speaking in low voices, careful not to blunder into the bed or move her too quickly, squeezing a few drops from a washcloth onto her tongue when her stomach wouldn't tolerate her taking even sips of water.

The rain finally eased off, and she requested the orderlies to open the north windows wider. The south ones remained closed and shaded as the day heated up. Ceiling fans were turned on to move the air, which had cooled with the rain but now steamed as the humidity rose.

Mary Sade appeared in the doorway in the mid-afternoon.

"It's too soon. You should still be asleep."

"Child, when you get to be my age, it don't matter how tired you are, you don't sleep for too long before your old bones are telling you to get out of the bed." She spied Phin, still sleeping beside Michael's bed. "That po' man is 'bout out of his mind with worry. I never seen a man who cared so deep for those he loves." She patted Natalie's hand. "It's a blessed woman who is loved by a man like that. I knows, cuz my husband was that kind of man."

She headed to the linen cart, and Natalie turned away. She had been loved like that once. And she had been blessed. But what could she have done? She was a missionary. She had been called. And Phin's life and calling were here.

In a few months, she would be back in Panama, and she would have to forget him all over again. But in the meantime, she decided she would treasure his friendship, cherish the time they could be together, and help and support him any way she could, both as a nurse and as a friend. All her life, she would have these months to cherish.

Thoughts of Panama reminded her of the Mission director's letter. Since she had a few moments, she drew it out, slipping into the hallway to read it.

Her eyes scanned the page, and her hands began to tremble. The mission board was satisfied that she was healthy enough to return to the field, and there was a ship departing from Mobile, Alabama, bound for Panama in one month's time.

A month? Just four weeks?

How could she leave New Orleans in the middle of the crisis? Yellow fever epidemics lasted for months. . .until colder weather drove away the mosquitoes.

And yet, she'd begged the Mission board to get her back to the field as quickly as possible.

But what about her patients here?

What about Michael Mackenzie? How could she leave not knowing if he would survive?

And what about. . .Phin? There was so much that had been left unsaid between them. When she had refused his marriage proposal, he had left her there in the park where he had asked her to be his wife, and she hadn't spoken to him since. The letter she had written him aboard the ship to Panama had never been mailed. She refused to leave again without speaking to him, but how could she bring up anything from their past when the present was so urgent and unsettled?

She slowly folded the director's letter and returned it to her pocket. He requested her presence at the office as soon as possible to discuss the details.

Her heart and mind were torn.

Her father's words, spoken in a rasp from his deathbed, rang in her ears. *"You will have to go for me, Natalie. You'll have to be the missionary I never got to be. Your place is in Panama."*

But something else in her heart whispered, *Your place is here.*

Which one was she to believe?

Phin woke slowly, his brain hazy, his shoulder and hip sore from sleeping on the floor. He kept his eyes closed, listening. The rain had stopped. A bed frame creaked. Metal touched glass. Sheets rustled.

He forced his eyelids to part. From his vantage point, he could see all the way to the far wall under all the cots. He would have to commend the janitorial staff. Not a trace of dust to be seen. Disjointed thoughts from his cotton-wool brain.

Forcing himself to sit up, he grimaced. He'd slept in worse conditions than this through most of his youth, but he wasn't a kid anymore. He creaked worse than an old barn door. He scrubbed his hands down his face, feeling the stubble rasping against his palms.

Remembering why he'd slept on the floor, he scrambled up and ducked under the mosquito netting of Michael's bed.

Mary Sade sat on the far side of the bed, sponging Michael's face and neck, her lips moving in what Phin knew were prayers for his brother.

"How is he?" The color of Michael's skin alarmed him but not as much as the tight, gasping breaths and the grimace contorting his brother's face. Touching his skin, Phin winced. He was burning up. The fever must be putting his heart under tremendous strain.

"Oh, he fightin' hard. I never seen a man fight so hard. Doctah Traskers thinks it won't be long now until we know, one way or t'other." Her gnarled hands wrung out another cloth.

"Mary Sade, I have the socks. Should we give it a try?" Natalie appeared at the foot of the bed, and paused. "Oh, you're awake."

"How long has he been like this? Why didn't you wake me?" Anger fueled by fear ripped through him.

"Don't yell." Brian Traskers hurried up. "I told them to let you sleep. I've been here covering for you. You've slept most of the day."

"Shall we go ahead, Dr. Traskers?" Natalie asked.

"Yes. It can't do him any harm, and it might help."

"What are you doing?" Phin asked. "And why wasn't I consulted on a change in Michael's care? He's my brother." He spoke loudly, and Aldo, in the next bed, groaned, throwing his arm up to cover his eyes.

Brian took Phin's elbow and steered him away from the bed. "We will consult in private so we don't disturb the ward."

When they reached the privacy of the exam room, Phin crossed his arms, his eyes gritty, irritated at being pulled away from Michael's bedside. "Well?"

"Phin, relax. We're all running on high stress and little sleep." Brian pinched the bridge of his nose. "Michael's holding his own. We're doing what we can to reduce the fever."

"What was Na—Miss Morrison doing with those socks?" Phin demanded.

"It's Mary Sade's idea. Something she says she's tried before. Since we can't use ice on Michael because of his heart, and sponging him is only getting us so far."

"Putting socks on him isn't going to cool him off."

"Listen. The procedure is to put warm cloths on his feet to increase the blood flow, then put socks soaked in ice water on him to cool that blood quickly, repeating often. I have no idea if it will work, and we'll continue with the sponge baths and medications, but I figure it can't hurt. Look, it might be an old wives' remedy, but some of those are born out of some truth." Brian tilted his head, giving Phin a long, compassionate look. "It's hard when it's family. For now, why don't you let me be his doctor and you be his brother?"

Phin forced himself to calm down. It wasn't easy. Seeing Michael in such distress sent panic waves crashing through him. *Please, God, don't let him die.* He closed his eyes, taking a deep breath.

"All right. I'm sorry. It's just. . ."

"I know." Brian punched his arm. "You care. That's natural. But we care too. And not just about Michael. About you too."

They returned to the ward.

"Mary Sade," Brian said. "Phin's going to sit with Michael and take over for you."

Phin pulled a chair up to Michael's bedside. Mary Sade handed over the wet cloth with a smile. "You be letting me know when you need more water or anything else, you hear? I'm gonna help Miss Natalie."

He nodded and bathed Michael's hot face.

Natalie lifted Michael's legs, and Mary Sade put an oilcloth underneath them. Applying the warm cloths, they worked together until Michael's yellowed legs turned a dull red.

"Now, get them cold wet socks on him." Mary Sade took one from the bowl of ice water, and without bothering to wring it out, slipped it on one of Michael's feet. He grunted, his brow furrowing, and he sucked in a deep breath.

Phin patted his shoulder while Natalie was quick with the other stocking. Mary Sade then picked up a hand fan and swished it over Michael's legs and feet.

Aldo groaned from the next bed, and Natalie went to his side, helping him sit up enough to drink a few sips of water. Phin studied her as she cared for the little Italian.

She'd lost some weight over the past month, and she hadn't been too robust even then, though now he knew why. But she hadn't murmured a word of complaint over the long hours, the heartbreaking work, or the changes in her plans.

She had been everything he remembered about her and more. And his heart longed for her more intensely than it ever had.

Five years ago, he had vowed to put her out of his mind and heart. He had refused to even say her name aloud. He had gone on with his life, deliberately not thinking of her, throwing himself into work and his family and ignoring the giant hole in his heart.

And all for naught. Because his love hadn't diminished. He hadn't been able to eradicate his feelings for her.

Now, God had brought her back into his life when he needed her most. Needed her nursing skills, yes, but needed her presence, her hopeful outlook, her rock-steady faith.

But not just those things. He had need of her as a man needs the woman he loves. For comfort and solace, for life and love and a future built with each other.

Bathing Michael's face, he questioned his courage. Michael said she still loved him. Did he dare believe it was true? Did he dare to offer her his heart one more time and hope that she would accept it, accept him?

Did he have the right to, if her calling truly lay in a foreign land?

What was right?

What was going to cause either of them the least hurt?

Could he live with the pain if she turned him down again?

Could he live with the regret if he never asked?

Hours later, Phin half dozed in his chair. Darkness had fallen again, the ward was quiet. Mary Sade's shoes swished on the floor, and Natalie's voice drifted through his mind as she spoke to a patient down the way.

Michael stirred, and Phin jolted awake.

"Some doctor you are, sleeping on the job." Michael's voice was raspy and dry, but having him lucid and talking sounded like sweet music to Phin.

"You're awake." Phin parted the gauzy curtain and touched his skin. It was cool and dry, with a bit of elasticity and a sheen of sweat. Bending quickly, he put his ear to Michael's chest. His heart beat, slowly and regularly. Phin straightened, his lips parting in a smile.

"I knew you'd make a good doctor. You can tell awake from asleep." Michael cleared his throat. "Can I have some water?"

As Phin turned, Natalie pulled aside the mosquito netting across the bed. She held a glass. Phin helped Michael raise up enough to drink. "How are you feeling?" he asked, when Michael's head lay on the pillow once more.

"Like I fell down a mine shaft?"

"I can understand that. You've been very sick."

Natalie wiped Michael's face and dried it with a clean towel. "Do you have any pain? Are you hungry?"

He grimaced. "Some, but not as much as before. And yes, I am. But mostly I'm thirsty."

Mary Sade spoke from the end of the bed. "I sure am glad to see you doin' better, Preacher. These two been 'bout beside themselves with worry over you. God been answering their prayers all right."

Brian plucked the chart from the hook at the foot of the bed and drew a pencil out of the breast pocket of his white coat. "I'm prescribing some broth and crackers for you, Michael, as well as some tea. If that stays put, we'll think about some more adventurous foods later."

Phin looked at Natalie, and she smiled at him, a full-force, full-of-joy smile that he hadn't seen on her face in more than five years. It hit him like a punch to the heart. How could he let her go out of his life again? If the chance to tell her how he felt ever came, would he be brave enough to take it?

Natalie gave instructions to the nurses coming on shift for the night before scooting a chair beneath the mosquito netting tent surrounding Michael's bed and sinking down onto it. She was so tired, but it was a good kind of tired, knowing she had done good work, and that today, on the men's yellow fever ward, they had lost no patients and there had been several, like Michael, who had made marked improvements.

"You're looking better all the time." She checked his pulse. "You're going to be yellow and tired for quite a while, but I'd say you're definitely on the mend."

"I gather the outcome was in doubt there for a while?"

"You were very sick." Releasing his wrist, she clasped her hands in her lap. "Phin was very worried. We all were."

"Where is Phin?"

"At a meeting of hospital, city, and federal health officials to assess how effective the efforts at mosquito control are. He'll be back later, though I hope he at least takes the time to eat and get some sleep."

"You should too."

"That is my next move. As soon as I drum up the energy."

"Before you go, can we talk?"

She sat up straighter. "Are you hurting?"

"No, no, not like that, though I will admit. . .I am hurting, for you and Phin."

"For us? Why?"

"Because I'm not blind. You're in love, and you're miserable." His eyes sought hers, full of compassion. "Tell me what's going on. Maybe I can help. At the very least, I'm a good listener."

Her lips trembled at his kindness and the weight on her heart. "I am in love. I have been since just about the first time I met Phin. But I shouldn't be. I have to return to Panama."

"But why?"

"It's my calling. I promised my father on his deathbed that I would fulfill the call to be a missionary. His dream was to take the Gospel to the people of Panama, but because of his ill health, he never got the chance. So I need to go in his stead. He said that when I was born, he dedicated my life to the Lord and the people of Panama, knowing he would never be able to go himself. He had contracted diphtheria, the same illness that took my mother right after my birth. He was partially paralyzed and never walked again."

"And he commissioned you as an infant to go in his place?"

She nodded. "Not just as an infant. We spoke of it many times. It was just always understood. I didn't mind. Not at all. I wanted to go. Until I met Phin. Like I said, I fell in love with him before I knew it, and then he proposed, and it caught me off guard."

"Natalie, have you ever considered that you were carrying a burden that wasn't yours? Perhaps it wasn't right of your father to ask you to fulfill his dreams. If God had truly called your father to be a missionary in Panama, He would have made a way for him to get there."

"But," Natalie protested, "I know God called me to be a missionary. He said to go to the 'uttermost parts of the earth.'"

"He also said to go to Jerusalem, Judea, and Samaria. He was telling the disciples that they were to spread the Gospel wherever they were. We're all missionaries, and you don't have to cross an ocean to qualify. You've been around New Orleans. A mission field opens up around every corner. Sicilians, Irish, English, German, good old-fashioned Americans. While I admire your passion for the people of Panama, it would be wrong to think those were the only people you were called to serve. What I do know is that any decision you make about Phin shouldn't be motivated by an unfair burden placed on you by either your father's last wishes or taking one phrase of one verse out of context." His voice was kind, brotherly. "I'm not saying you shouldn't be a missionary to Panama. Perhaps you should. But only after careful consideration and understanding what Jesus truly meant in the Great Commission."

Natalie considered his words. On the one hand, she knew he was correct, that Christians were to spread the Gospel wherever they were...but on the other, she had always thought that being a missionary meant leaving your country to head to a foreign land. Could she fulfill both the Great Commission and honor her father's wishes if she stayed in America? Or was she merely trying to justify staying so she could be with Phin?

Not that Phin had asked her to stay. Not this time.

If he did, what would she say?

Chapter 7

Phin headed up the hospital steps, buoyed by the council meeting news. Their efforts were working. Fewer than two hundred deaths so far. And while that was still a shocking number, if their estimates held, they were on track for fewer than five hundred. Almost a tenth of the number who had died in the last major yellow fever outbreak in New Orleans.

And Michael was on the road to recovery. Phin had had called his parents in St. Louis before his meeting.

"Praise the Lord!"

His mother had broken down, crying when he told her the news, dropping the phone. His father had picked up the receiver. "I take it you have good news, son?"

"I do. He's turned the corner. His fever has broken, and the pain is subsiding. It's early days yet, but he's going to make it."

Phin heard his father swallow hard and suck in a deep breath. "That's the best news possible. And what about you?"

"I'm fine. Better now that Tick's on the mend. I can't tie up this line long, but I wanted to let you know the good news."

"Wait, son, before you go. Your mother and I will be coming to New Orleans."

"You can't. The danger isn't over."

"Nevertheless, we've been praying about it, and we feel we should come. Michael will need some care, and your mother is concerned about the children. There are bound to be many orphans as a result of the fevers, and she's determined. . .and I am too. . .that we should be there to care for as many as possible."

Phin leaned against the wall, closing his eyes and holding the receiver to his ear. It was just like his parents to think of orphaned children at a time like this.

"I understand. But please, at least wait until fall. There's a travel ban in place anyway, that you can't break, but I will let you know the minute it lifts. Give my love to Mother and the grands and everyone there. Michael will write or call as soon as he can."

His parents, starting an orphanage in New Orleans. Having them here would be wonderful. Michael with his ministry to sailors and stevedores, his parents ministering to the city's orphans, and himself, with his mobile doctor's office, ministering to those who called New Orleans's poorest neighborhoods home.

Bounding up the stairs, he went first to the Women's Yellow Fever Ward across the hall from his own. "Brian, can you cover for me for a half hour or so? I'm on duty now, but there's something I need to do."

"Sure. Anything wrong?" Brian looked up from his notes.

"Nothing to worry about. And thanks." Phin headed for his own ward.

Michael was propped up, half sitting, and Mary Sade was helping him eat some broth. Phin stopped at the foot of the bed. "Have you seen Miss Morrison?"

"She went to the pharmacy. She be back soon." Mary Sade eyed him. "You need her?"

In so many ways.

His expectation must've shown on his face, because Michael mirrored Mary Sade's expression. "Should I say a prayer or two?"

"That would be appreciated."

Mary Sade sniffed. " 'Bout time."

Natalie appeared in the ward doorway, a packet in her hand. She gave it to one of the orderlies, and Phin started her way, taking her hand and leading her out of the ward.

"What is it?" She asked, trotting alongside to keep up.

"We're going for a walk."

"A walk? It's almost dark."

"You used to like walking with me in the dark." He laced his fingers with hers, glancing down at her. She wore a look of confusion and fluster. Good, she'd confused and flustered him plenty.

Once outside, he took the gravel path leading around the hospital to the parklike grounds in the rear. In the courtyard, parked for the night, his mobile doctor's office stood in a row of ambulances. The wagon had been pressed into service over the past few weeks and had lost some of its luster, but he didn't mind. Hopefully it would see many more years of service as he treated his patients in New Orleans.

When they reached the little flower garden at the center of the park, Phin stopped. The sun had slipped beneath the horizon, but its soft afterglow lit Natalie's face.

He took both her hands in his. His mouth was dry and his pulse hammering. "Now that I've got you here, I don't know how to start."

Her eyes caught the fading sunlight, wide and amber. "Phin, please, may I go first?"

A shaft of pain hit him. "No, not if you're going to tell me you're going back to Panama. I need to have my say first. Natalie Mae Morrison, I love you. I loved you five years ago, I loved you the entire time you were away, and I love you now, more than ever. I cannot bear to have you go out of my life without telling you how I feel. I know with certainty that my work is here in New Orleans, and I want to share that work with you. I want to share my life with you. I know you may say no, but there it is. I love you. I want you to stay. I want you to be my wife."

Now that the words were out there, he held his breath, half wishing he hadn't spoken. If she refused him, if her convictions remained the same, how would he go on?

The wait, while only a couple of seconds, stretched out interminably.

Then her hands came up, cupping his cheeks. "Phin," she blinked hard. "Phin, I am so sorry I hurt you. I love you so much. I don't ever want to hurt you again."

His hands came up to cover hers. What did this mean?

"Did you know your brother is a very wise man? He showed me the error of some of my thinking." She shook her head. "It's too much to go into now, but suffice it to say,

I don't regret my time in Panama, but that time has passed. My place is here now. With you." She pressed her trembling lips together for a moment, and his eyes zeroed in on the movement. "I love you, Phin Mackenzie."

She had barely gotten the words out before he had crushed her to his chest in a tight embrace. He kissed her, fiercely, with all the longing of five interminable years, with all the hope of the years to come.

When he was almost dizzy with the need to breathe, he tucked her head under his chin, kept her wrapped in his arms, and closed his eyes.

"Are you absolutely sure?" He had to know. They were in the midst of trying times, emotional times, and he didn't want her to have regrets.

Her arms tightened around his waist, her hands pressing into his back. "I am sure. I've thought and prayed and considered, and all the time, the only peace I could find was when I thought of staying here with you."

Phin didn't know how long they stood that way, holding one another, but he savored every minute.

The clatter of hooves drew his attention. One of the hospital ambulances turned into the courtyard. Another case.

Natalie stirred. "We should go."

Phin couldn't resist one more kiss. "To tide me over." He laced his fingers with hers for a moment. "I love you, Natalie."

"I love you too, Phin. Let's get to work in our mission field."

Erica Vetsch can't get enough of history, whether it's reading, writing, or visiting historical sites. She's currently writing another historical romance and plotting which history museum to conquer next! You can find her online at www.ericavetsch.com and on her Facebook Page www.facebook.com/EricaVetschAuthor/ where she spends WAY too much time!

JOIN US ONLINE!

Christian Fiction for Women

Christian Fiction for Women is your online home for the latest in Christian fiction.

Check us out online for:

- Giveaways
- Recipes
- Info about Upcoming Releases
- Book Trailers
- News and More!

Find Christian Fiction for Women at Your Favorite Social Media Site:

 Search "Christian Fiction for Women"

 @fictionforwomen
